D1547861

KONSTANTIN SIMONOV

THE LIVING AND THE DEAD

A Novel

PROGRESS PUBLISHERS
MOSCOW

Translated from the Russian by *Alex Miller*
Designed by *A. Vasin*

К. Симонов

Живые и мертвые

на английском языке

Printed in the Union of Soviet Socialist Republics

70302-772
С ————— 798-74
014(01)-75

THE FULFILMENT OF DUTY

FOREWORD

"War must be fought in war-like manner." The formula is Lenin's. Succinct, to the point, far-reaching in its implications, it covers all the elements of the dramatic human activity known as war. During the four years of bitter fighting, war drove from our lives everything that opposed it and obstructed the victory over fascism. War must obviously be written about in a professional manner. This is best illustrated by considering two extremes. No one wants war in our country, and this means that a flabby pacifism and Remarquesque sermons are absurd and ridiculous as far as we are concerned, since they are the products of frightened and immature minds. Such pacifism is the stick with which the blind man taps the road as he tries to make his way home during an earthquake. On the other hand, the aggressive "position of strength", with its "supermen" like the American pulp fiction heroes, is inconceivable in Soviet literature other than as an object of merciless denunciation.

To us, war is an active love for the homeland, a willingness to take up arms in its defence, and loyalty to the behests of internationalism. Without the Leninist teaching about war and the army in the contemporary world, it is impossible fully to understand the motive forces behind an armed conflict, the nature of the embattled armies, and the social make-up of the men in soldiers' and officers' uniforms. One sometimes reads talented works which have been weakened by their implicit thesis that war remains unchanged through the ages, as do the emotions it arouses.

The affirmation of these "eternal categories" is unhistorical and means lumping together religious, cabinet, dynastic, civil, just, and unjust wars. The hired mercenary, the cowed recruit or the citizen-soldier—can the feelings of the representatives of different epochs and social systems be equalised?

The creative understanding of man at war is one of the most complex literary tasks.

If he does not have a thorough grasp of military processes, big and small, the writer is left at the mercy of haphazard or false conceptions. The business of war demands more professionalism than any other, because the price to be paid for dilettantism is very high indeed.

I have been re-reading three novels by Konstantin Simonov: *The Living and the Dead*, *Not Born to Be Soldiers*, and *The Last Summer*. They have already been published in the Soviet Union as a trilogy, and a work to which the writer has given fifteen years of labour is now available to the Soviet reading public.

The Living and the Dead describes the first and, for the Soviet people, most tragic period of the Second World War. After it was published, Konstantin Simonov wrote that the basis of the novel was his "personal memories as a man who saw this war from beginning to end. I am thinking of writing about everything I saw, right up to the fall of Berlin, but I must begin from the beginning, even if that beginning brings back painful memories." It is this first novel that is now being offered to the English-speaking reader; but since the full trilogy has been published in the USSR, I shall be discussing it as a whole.

It begins with the first days of the war, and in the concluding chapters his characters are approaching the frontiers of East Prussia. "The liberation of Russia is nearly over. Europe next," says General Boiko.

The strategy planned by Hitler's General Staff envisaged smashing the Soviet Union in a single operation. "Operation Barbarossa" only covered action up to the Dnieper and the Western Dvina. This was to be followed by the pursuit of our completely shattered armies. And so, when we speak today of our own miscalculations in the initial period of the war, we should think a little more often of that initial, but decisive, miscalculation on the enemy's part. Soviet military long-term strategy, on the other hand, was prepared for a prolonged and difficult struggle.

There has been much controversy in Soviet criticism about the "higher truth" and the "truth of the trenches". And it was held by some that although the "higher truth" is more objective and correct, the truth of the trenches is nevertheless more human. But the controversy is purely academic. There are no two truths in war. Our soldiers could see the sky of the motherland from their slit trenches, and in those trenches they lived for her ideals. Only a person totally lacking in vision could possibly think otherwise. For our victory was not a divine miracle, it was the inevitable victory of a new social system. If the writer of talent understands and accepts Lenin's concept of a just war and grasps it in all its far-reaching implications, if he sees man at war not as an isolated, but as a social individual, then the truth of his writings will be integral and complete. Otherwise, the reader will be offered talented or ungifted but either way incoherent and sometimes distorted accounts of episodes in the war without the total and truthful expression of its essence. And it is works like these that give the critics an opportunity to divide the truth into "higher truth" and the "truth of the trenches".

In *The Living and the Dead*, as in the whole of his trilogy, Simonov endeavours to give a comprehensive picture of the last war. The narrative is chronological, and so we can clearly trace the evolution of what was to make the Soviet military doctrine so ultimately successful and superior. In the changing sequence of bloody battles, retreats, meetings and partings, the characters cannot yet make sense of events and sometimes they cannot even understand themselves. But the people carry on with the job whatever their personal feelings. Bitter experience helps them to make their decisions. There is much to give them cause for alarm and distress. But the predominant feeling is one of faith in victory. The meeting between Colonel Serpilin and a group of artillerymen colours the whole first part of *The Living and the Dead*. We are given a vivid picture of five blackened, gaunt faces, five dirty tunics lashed by tree branches, five German submachine-guns captured in battle, and a gun, the division's last gun, dragged all the way from the frontier near Brest, a distance of over four hundred kilometres, by the soldiers with their bare hands. No, Messrs nazis, you're not going to have it all your own way!

Who is it that gives us such a vivid picture of this handful of gunners and their leader, Sergeant-Major Shestakov, in the cap with its peak torn in half? Who is convinced that the enemy won't have it all their own way? Serpilin or the author? The narrative is objective in form, but Simonov's lyrical hero is present almost everywhere, now identified with one or another of the characters in the novel, now withdrawing a little way in order to study the man or the event more carefully.

We enter the densely populated world of the novel with its many levels of action. We hear Serpilin's imperious falsetto; we see his thin back, his long, bony face; we see Shmakov, the little grey-haired battalion commissar; we see tankmen in black helmets jumping out on to the road with an ugly look on their faces to stop the lorry in which the hero, Sintsov, is riding to the rear, and we watch as their commander, Captain Ivanov, authoritatively puts a stop to the panic and restores order in the woods near the front. We are profoundly moved by the beautifully written scene of the tragic death of General Kozyrev, once a pilot and now a general, and those who were in the fighting at that time, in 1941, will be able to understand his feelings: "He was in no way terrified at the thought of his impending death; he was merely saddened at the thought that he would never know how everything was going to turn out in the future."

The principal theme of the trilogy, the fulfilment of duty, draws the various social, philosophical, and historical threads into a single knot. This knot is pulled tight in *The Living and the Dead.*

What artist does not endeavour to penetrate into that holy of holies, the private world of the character, and to link a man's most intimate movements of thought and heart with his actions? With Simonov's characters, a sense of duty prevails over all else. He knows that half-hearted obedience is not enough in war. A good soldier, whatever his rank, puts the whole of himself into soldiering. The conditions of human existence in war are such that the individual personality is very often insignificant compared with the job which has to be done. That is the attitude adopted by most of the characters in the epic. The author's language and that of his characters is appropriate to the austere simplicity of their reflections. Simonov's language is level, somewhat dry, and sometimes even excessively laconic.

Simonov's most impressive characters are those in whom thought, feeling and behaviour are completely subordinated to the fulfilment of duty as a dominant passion and an ideal. Such is Serpilin, a truly unforgettable character of exceptional integrity.

A special feature of Simonov's talent is that he is perhaps more successful with characters based on real-life prototypes than with his purely fictional images. The discipline of creative journalism and a partiality for the diary as a literary form have stood him in good stead here. And, in this sense, Serpilin is not the only example. There is a brief glimpse in *The Living and the Dead* of a bald tank officer near Borisov, and the picture sticks in the memory. The sophisticated Lvov is described with subtlety and sureness, and the portrait of Batyuk is drawn in convincing detail. In all these cases, and in a number of others as well, we know the names of the real-life originals: some have been named by the author, others we can guess for ourselves.

Simonov knew many army people and knew them well. He "transferred" some of them into the novel, much as trees are transplanted with the soil still clinging to their roots. Such people organically grew into the trilogy. The author's own favourite character is the man who is outwardly severe and inwardly kind-hearted. Simonov is always ready to play on the contrast between austere manners and natural generosity of heart. The revelation of hitherto concealed warmth of heart in people outwardly forbidding is a recurrent (perhaps too frequent) motif in characters to whom the author himself feels drawn. "The more feeling he put into what he was saying, the more gloomy and unfriendly was his manner of saying it." This refers to Malinin, a stalwart fighting officer: "The regimental commander is pleased too, but he's not in the habit of showing it."

Many of the people in the novel have this trait of character. Is such uniformity intentional? The author most likely wanted to say that the Army and war are not conducive to noisy and wasteful displays of emotion, but demand above all action and then more action. He is right, of course, in the main, although the artistic embodiment of this idea could be varied more, since restraint, to say nothing of gloominess, certainly does not always mask a kind heart.

Be that as it may, Simonov's favourite characters value a man for his ability to get on with the job in hand without wasting words. Sintsov thinks of regimental commander Ilyin: "With a man like Ilyin, personal relations depend on how good you are at your job. Cope with the job, and the ice is broken. Fail to cope, and words won't help you at all." This yardstick is used by the author directly or indirectly on nearly all those who fight and act in his trilogy. Zakharov, a member of the Army Military Council, reflects on his new commanding officer: "What's good about Boiko is that he lives only for his job. No one can please him except by doing the job properly, and nothing outside that can bias him for or against a man—only the job."

I think I've found the reason for this uniformity. The general and unavoidable circumstances into which the people are thrown by war inevitably develop certain kindred features. War itself grinds character, reshapes it, polishes it, demands that one trait be replaced by another irrespective of personal wishes. Man goes to war and himself becomes part of war. The demand made of him is total. But even these rigorous conditions of life do not, of course, standardise human nature in all its variety. And if the sparing use of colour may be self-imposed, it sometimes revenges itself on the author too.

Once, in the notes to his novel *The Peasants*, Balzac observed: "A battle should not be described as in the dry accounts of the military histories, which for three thousand years have merely harped about the left and the right flanks or about the penetrated centre, but are silent about the soldier, his heroism, and his sufferings." From the very beginning, Soviet literature broke this silence with Fadeyev's *The Rout* and Serafimovich's *The Iron Flood*.... In Simonov's trilogy we see the fighting life of the troops, the responsible work of the staff, the day-to-day activity of the political workers, the life of the rear units—everything that goes to form the military organisation of socialism. We see not just battle scenes, but the people, their sufferings, their heroism. In Simonov, war reeks of petrol, oil and high explosive. It fires a machine-gun and falls in the snow, gets up again under fire on its elbows and on its knees and, with a hoarse "Hurrah!" or with a curse, or with a whispered "Mother", stambles through snow-drifts, walks, runs forward, leaving behind the dark blobs of sheepskin jackets, greatcoats and groundsheets on the blackened, trampled snow or on the scorched grass.

We see how the enormous machine of an army is fed with everything that it must digest in the short time remaining before an operation. We see the way in which dozens of different orders are issued, to bring in their train a variety of human actions and experiences. The author knows a great deal about war; he loves the army and the people in it with a deep and long-standing love that dates back, in my opinion, to Khalkhin-Gol, where he received his baptism of fire, and perhaps even earlier, to Ryazan, where he lived as a small boy on the premises of an infantry training school in the family of a Red Army officer. But the knowledge and experience gained directly from the war years were not enough for him to create the trilogy. Simonov believes in attention to detail. As I read through all three novels again, I can easily imagine what an enormous amount of work must have gone into writing this epic of the Patriotic War.

Every war is part of a whole known as "politics". Lenin said: "War of itself does not change the direction in which politics has been developing up to the outbreak of war, but only *accelerates* this development." In agreement with the general implications of this thought and proceeding from many years of experience as a "philosopher-practitioner" on the battle-field, General Kuzmich of the trilogy observes in his down-to-earth way: "War is accelerated life." The correspondence between war and politics, their dialectical interconnection, and the subordination of the first factor to the second are conveyed by the whole structure of the trilogy in time, space, and movement; and, moreover, by the genuine respect with which Simonov delineates the characters of the commissars—the political leaders, the Party's envoys among the troops—Zakharov, Malinin, and others. The author has been particularly successful with Fyodor Levashov, who has graduated from the trilogy to a separate story and has given his name to the title.

There is a war in progress, and the trilogy moves with it. So much has happened since we opened its first page. Here is Tanya, the little doctor, riding down the roads of the great German rout outside Stalingrad: "Today, everything she had seen was divided into 'ours' and 'theirs'. 'Ours' was alive, 'theirs' was dead: dead wire, dead trenches, dead men in the snow, and dead, abandoned guns and lorries." A formidable enemy, a cruel war, and our triumph was justified.... A year passes, and Serpilin is full of this feeling. After leaving Tanya and Sintsov at the roadside, he stands on the river bank with his hands behind his back, reflecting on the course of the operation, and he suddenly realises that he is happy: military matters are going so well.

Serpilin is killed before he can finish the operation; the last good news he hears is that our troops are fighting on the outskirts of Minsk. The author has given Serpilin an easy death—sudden and, for that reason, essentially beautiful, when a man has no time to feel horror at the thought of his own end. And through this—whether intentionally or not, I don't know—the stage which the war has reached is made very clear. Things have changed very much since General Kozyrev died so tragically in *The Living and the Dead*. Serpilin is killed instantly in *The Last Summer*, but he seems to depart slowly and even majestically, and he isn't really going out of the lives of those he leaves behind. What a big part he has played in the destinies of the people round him! The tempo of the novel in this chapter seems to slow down to a funeral march. All the echoes of Serpilin's going have been sensitively recorded, and this shows an awareness of our moral need to say good-bye to him unhurriedly, with deep reflection. The life of Serpilin, who has come to stay in our literature, has been brought to a worthy and dignified close.

In the last part of the trilogy, much space is given to two characters—Ilyin and Boiko. "You only just missed a lovely battle," Ilyin says to Sintsov knowing that Sintsov will understand what he means by the adjective.

"Lovely" means that the defeat of the enemy, the supreme aim of every battle, has been achieved; "lovely" means that the enemy's losses have been much greater than our own; "lovely" means that the job has been done as was planned and the right decisions were made as the situation changed.

Oh, Ilyin, you born soldier! It can now be affirmed that without Ilyin, junior lieutenant, at first chief of staff of the battalion and then, by the time of the Byelorussian operation, a regimental commander; without Boiko, the calm and methodical Boiko who is appointed Army Commander, the trilogy would not have the design which is only now finally revealed to us.

We can speak of them both in the words of the man whose opinion they valued so much: "There they are, young regimental commanders," thought Serpilin, looking with pleasure at Ilyin, whom he had recognised as a born soldier as far back as the summer of 1942.... "I hope he comes through in one piece. Very promising."

We are aware of Ilyin and Sintsov at various stages of the war. Sintsov with his misadventures belongs to Forty-One, Ilyin and his self-confidence as a victor to Forty-Four.

And now a word about Boiko. Remembering his age, Serpilin thinks at the moment "not about himself, or about Boiko, but about something far more important and nothing to do with age and youth, nothing to do with himself and the other man, but to do with war, the army, and the times in which we live and will continue living".

It is in this reflection that Serpilin comes to full inner maturity. He has already had occasion to think about his age and compare his own advancing years with the youth of capable commanders. "There were times," writes Simonov, "when he would think about this with envy, but now it was with a different feeling—with relief, perhaps, that here were people like Boiko at the age of thirty-five." Serpilin is far-seeing. He is a true son of his time and a pupil of history. He is motivated by the vital interests of society. He finds the source of his own happiness in his awareness of what he has in common with the people's cause. He is a real man, and so are his friends. Boiko and Ilyin are not killed: they reach Berlin.

Although what happens to them lies beyond the scope of the trilogy, we have no doubt that this is the outcome. They are alive to this day. Many commanders of our time will be able to recognise their own youth in these characters. They are still serving in the Army, having adapted to its new technology and new art of warfare. And we are sure of this because, although the novel is not completed in the chronological sense, it has been carried to its logical conclusion.

After the death of Serpilin and everything connected with it in the final part of the trilogy, there can only be a quantitative development. The world of the characters, their connections, the whole flood of events has been banked in. But Ilyin and Boiko, as if representing all the people in the trilogy, go further. They carry on to fulfil their duty, to fight under their country's standard in a professional manner.

That is how Konstantin Simonov wrote his trilogy—in a professional manner. He wrote it at a time when, like millions of people all over the world, he had become a soldier of peace.

And so, dear reader, you have before you Book One of the trilogy *The Living and the Dead*.

But just a few words more. The fact of the matter is that Konstantin Simonov and I are old, very old friends. During the Second World War, I was head of the literature and art department of the central Army newspaper *Red Star* in Moscow.

Life passes quickly. Not a very original observation. But every one of us on this Earth is fated to discover things for the first time. Only yesterday, I thought Konstantin Simonov a young man. Only the day before yesterday, we were wandering together round the ruins of Berlin. The day before that, we were flying to the front together. Once I met him in the editorial offices, and he said enviously:

"Have you flown across the front line? Some people have all the luck! Well, so what's happening out there in Bryansk forests?"

I replied:

"Never satisfied, are you! The assault on the Rybachi, then to Sevastopol in a submarine.... Whenever the sparks have been flying, you've been there. And now you're hankering for more!"

I remember every word distinctly. After all, it doesn't seem long ago since Simonov and I met. There were battles raging over the russet barkhans at Khalkhin-Gol.

Surely that was all only yesterday, or the day before? But, as it turns out, over three decades have passed since then. Is he really nearly sixty? I don't believe it! Hasn't there been some kind of mix-up in the machinery of time? So much has been written in recent years about the various principles of measuring it. For earthlings it flows much faster than for interplanetary travellers. Is this fair? Hasn't Einstein been up to something here? Certainly, time has been flying recently....

No, everything's in order. It's just that our generation is getting older and is surprised at this. Well, it is natural to grow older and be surprised at it. But in this naturalness there is still a strangeness that each must discover for himself.

Do you know how difficult and important it is for a writer to find his theme? Simonov didn't look for his. It found him. War. And before becoming his theme, it became his life. It is senseless and inhuman to love war. Who can become reconciled to grief? But one can love the conquest of grief. War is grief. The army is its conqueror: it is the sword of the country that wants peace. We give it our love. Simonov loves the Soviet Army. He knows it from top to bottom. He is himself a tiny part of it. He was in the war from the first day to the last. He is still in it. He is still in Berlin, editing his 1945 diaries.

His childhood was spent with an infantry battalion commanded by his strict stepfather, a participant in the Civil War, a born soldier. Simonov now spends hours at work in the military archives. He has shouldered a heavy burden. The years pass. His pen has produced an epic about the war. A panorama of battles that have long since died down. His characters come into our houses without knocking. They leave the pages of the book to live among us.

Simonov was courageous and tough in the war. He was courageous and tough in his work as a writer. Happy the poet whose lyrics, such as *Wait for Me*, have been memorised by millions, whose plays, such as *Russian People*, have been such hits. And the war correspondent has every right to feel proud of the notes written in dim dug-outs if they have become classic war reports like *June-December 1941*. And no critic need feel ashamed of an article like the one published on 14th April 1951 and entitled *On Goodwill*. All this, and much else besides, has been written by the same author.

Is Simonov himself happy? I don't know. Many claim that the true artist does not know true happiness. While he is writing, he falls prey to doubts, uncertainty, sometimes despair. When his work sees the light of day, he is already thinking about another one, better, more perfect, the one he has yet to write. Konstantin Fedin referred to the writer's work as convict labour. But it is, after all, voluntary. Does that mean that it is enjoyable? Of course. But it's hard, too. One thing I know: if Simonov has always written with comparative ease, his life has been a difficult one.

Decades have passed. His hair has turned white. There is a heavy shadow under his eyes, the mischievous twinkle is beginning to fade (or am I only imagining this?). When you are nearly sixty, you are approaching a deadline, however optimistically the after-dinner speakers may express themselves at formal birthday celebrations. Yet Simonov has much to look forward to. He need envy no one's energy. He has big plans. His talent has not been exhausted by time, but has matured. What matters most now? Why, good health, of course! And so I say:

"Greetings, old comrade! Greetings to you from the pages of your own book!"

Alexander Krivitsky

THE LIVING AND THE DEAD

2-825

CHAPTER ONE

The first day of the war caught the Sintsovs unawares, as it did millions of other families. Everyone had long been expecting war, yet at the last moment it came like a bolt from the blue. Apparently, it is impossible to be fully prepared for such a tremendous catastrophe.

It was on the hot tiny square outside the railway station in Simferopol that Sintsov and Masha learned of the outbreak of war. They had just alighted from the train and were standing near an ancient open "Lincoln", waiting for other passengers so that they could share the car fare to the military rest centre at Gurzuf.

As they were asking the driver whether there were any fruit and tomatoes available at the market, the radio spoke up in a hoarse voice and told the entire square that war had broken out, and life was immediately divided into two separate parts: that which had been a minute ago, before the war, and that which was now.

Sintsov and Masha took their suitcases to the nearest bench. Masha sat down, buried her face in her hands and, without moving, sat there as if stunned, while Sintsov, without even asking her agreement, went to the military commandant's office to arrange for return travel warrants from Simferopol to Grodno, where he had been serving for the last eighteen months as editorial secretary to an Army newspaper.

In addition to the general disaster of war, the family were faced with a personal misfortune of their own, and Political Instructor* Sintsov was enough of a soldier to realise the full extent of that misfortune: he and his wife were a thousand miles away from the war, here in Simferopol; but their one-year-old daughter had been left behind in Grodno close to the war, and no power on earth could get them back to her in less than four days.

When Sintsov went to see the commandant, five or six servicemen had already hurried in ahead of him. As he stood waiting in the queue, he tried to imagine what was happening at Grodno. "Too near the frontier—much too near; and the bombing—that's the main worry—the bombings.... True, the children can be evacuated immediately...." He clutched at this thought, hoping to calm Masha with it.

When he returned to tell her that everything had been arranged—they would leave on the return journey at midnight—she raised her head and looked at him as if he were a total stranger.

"What's been arranged?" she demanded.

"I got the tickets," said Sintsov.

"Good," said Masha without emotion, and again she buried her face in her hands.

She could not forgive herself for leaving her daughter behind. She had been talked into it by her mother, who had come to Grodno specially to enable Sintsov and Masha to go on holiday together. Sintsov also had reasoned with Masha, and had even been offended when, on the day of their departure, she had looked straight up at him and had asked: "Do we really have to go?" If she had not let them talk her round, she would be in Grodno now. It was not the thought of being there, but the thought of not being there that frightened her. She felt so intensely quilty about her child

* *Political instructor*—second-in-command of a platoon (company, battalion, etc.), and also responsible for political education. Apart from usual badges of rank, wore a red star on the left sleeve.—*Ed.*

back in Grodno that she hardly gave her husband a thought.

With her characteristic straightforwardness, she told him as much.

"Why bother about me?" said Sintsov, not in the least offended. "Everything's going to be all right."

Masha couldn't bear it when he talked like that, trying to comfort her when he could offer her no real reassurance.

"Give over!" she said. "What's going to be all right? What do you know about it?"

Her lips were actually trembling with fury.

"I had no right to leave! Don't you understand? I had no right to leave!" she repeated, hitting her knee with her clenched fist until it hurt. "It was a criminal thing to do!"

When they boarded the train, she fell silent and stopped reproaching herself, answering all Sintsov's questions mechanically, like a puppet. In fact Masha behaved mechanically all the way to Moscow, drinking tea, staring silently out of the window, then lying down in her upper berth and staying there for hours with her face turned to the wall.

Everybody round them could only talk of one thing—the war; but Masha didn't seem to hear even this. She was undergoing some kind of serious inner crisis to which she could admit no one, not even Sintsov.

As soon as the train stopped at Serpukhov, near Moscow, she spoke to her husband for the first time.

"Let's get out and stretch our legs."

They got out of the carriage and Masha took his arm.

"You know, I've just realised why I hardly thought about you at first. We'll find Tanya, send her off with mother, and I'll stay with you in the army."

"Have you already made up your mind, then?" asked Sintsov.

"Yes."

"And suppose you have to change it?"

She shook her head silently.

Trying to keep as calm as possible, he told her that the two problems—how to find Tanya, and whether or not she should join the army—should be kept separate.

"I refuse to keep them separate," interrupted Masha.

But he stubbornly went on to explain that it would be more sensible if he returned to his duties in Grodno while she stayed in Moscow. If they had evacuated the civilians from Grodno (and this was quite likely), then Masha's mother, with Tanya, would naturally try to get to her own flat in

Moscow. And the most sensible thing for Masha to do, if she didn't want to miss them, was to wait for them there.

"They might well have arrived from Grodno while we were on the way from Simferopol!"

Masha looked distrustfully at Sintsov and never spoke another word until they arrived in Moscow.

They proceeded to her mother's old flat on the Usachevka, where they had recently spent two carefree days on the way to Simferopol.

No one had arrived from Grodno. Sintsov had been counting on a telegram, but no telegram had been delivered either.

"I'm going straight to the railway station to organise my travel warrant," said Sintsov. "I may get the evening train. Try ringing; perhaps you'll get through."

He took a notebook out of his tunic pocket, tore off a page, and wrote down for her the telephone numbers of the editorial offices at Grodno.

"Wait, don't be in such a hurry, sit down a moment," she said, detaining him. "I know you don't want me to come along. But how can I do it anyway?"

Sintsov began explaining that she mustn't. He added a new argument to his previous ones: even if they let her go as far as Grodno now and accepted her for the army there—which he doubted—didn't she realise she was going to make things twice as hard for him?

Masha listened to him, turning steadily paler.

"And don't you realise," she shouted suddenly, "don't you realise that I'm a human being too? That I want to be where you are? Why d'you never think about anybody but yourself?..."

"What d'you mean 'anybody but myself'?" asked Sintsov, bewildered.

She didn't answer him and, for the first time, began sobbing bitterly. After her weeping fit was over, she sniffed angrily and, propping a tear-swollen cheek on one hand, said in a matter-of-fact tone of voice that he should go and organise the travel warrants, otherwise he would be too late.

"And one for me too. Promise?"

Infuriated by her stubbornness, he finally stopped humouring her and told her bluntly that they would not allow any civilians, much less women, on board the train bound for Grodno, that the Grodno area had already been mentioned in the news bulletin, and that it was time to look things soberly in the face.

"All right," said Masha. "If they won't allow it, then that's all there is to it. But at least you'll try! I'll trust you to. You will try, won't you?"

"Yes," he said gloomily.

That "yes" meant a great deal. He never lied to her. If they wrote her out a ticket for Grodno, he would take her with him.

An hour later, he rang her up with relief from the railway station to tell her that he had got a place on a train leaving for Minsk at eleven o'clock that evening—there was no direct train to Grodno—and that the commandant had told him that only servicemen were allowed to travel in that direction.

Masha made no reply.

"Why don't you say something?" he shouted into the mouthpiece.

"What can I say? I've been trying to get through to Grodno. They told me it's cut off for the time being."

"You could be putting my things into one suitcase in the meantime," he said.

"All right, I will," she answered.

"I'm just going to try and get through to the Political Directorate," he said. "They may have moved the editorial offices somewhere else. I'll try and find out. I'll be back in a couple of hours or so. Don't get depressed."

"I'm not depressed," said Masha, still in the same toneless voice, and she hung up first.

As Masha sorted out her own and her husband's things, one thought obsessed her: how could she have left her daughter behind in Grodno? She had not lied to Sintsov; she really couldn't separate her thoughts about her daughter from those about herself. She must find Tanya and send her back to Moscow, and she must stay with him there, on active service.

How was she to get there? What could she do about it? Then, at the last minute, just as she was closing Sintsov's suitcase, she remembered that she had a piece of paper somewhere with the service telephone number of a Colonel Polynin, one of her brother's comrades who had served with him at Khalkhin-Gol*. When she had stopped off in Moscow on the way to Simferopol, this Polynin had unexpectedly phoned to say that he had flown in from Chita, had seen Masha's brother there, and had promised to deliver a personal message to his mother.

* *Khalkhin-Gol*—a locality in Mongolia which was the scene of an attempted Japanese invasion in 1939.—*Ed.*

Masha had told him that Tatyana Stepanovna was in Grodno, and she had taken his service telephone number so that her mother could ring him at the Chief Aviation Inspectorate when she returned to Moscow. Only where was it, that telephone number? She hunted feverishly for it for some time before she finally found it and rang up.

"Colonel Polynin here!" said an angry voice over the phone.

"How d'you do! I'm Artemyev's sister. I must see you," said Masha.

But Polynin evidently didn't realise straightaway who she was and what she wanted. Then he finally cottoned on and, after a long and unfriendly pause, said that it would be all right provided it didn't take long. She could come in an hour's time and he would meet her at the entrance.

Masha herself didn't really know what this Polynin could do to help her.

Exactly an hour later, she was at the entrance to a big military building. She thought she remembered what Polynin looked like, but there was no sign of him among the people bustling round her. Suddenly, the door opened and a very young sergeant came up to her.

"You want Colonel Polynin?" he asked, and then apologetically explained that the Comrade Colonel had been summoned to the People's Commissariat, had left ten minutes ago, and had left a message that she should wait for him, preferably in the little garden on the other side of the tram-lines. When the colonel returned, someone would come to fetch her.

"But when will he be back?" asked Masha, remembering that Sintsov should be home soon.

The sergeant merely shrugged his shoulders.

Masha waited two hours, and just after she had decided not to wait any longer, had run across the tram-lines, and was about to jump on the next tram, a staff car drove up and Polynin himself got out. Masha recognised him, although his handsome face had changed considerably and now looked careworn and older.

She had the impression that every second was vital to him.

"I hope you don't mind," he said, "but let's talk here. I've got people waiting to see me inside.... What's the trouble?"

Masha explained as briefly as she could what the trouble was and what she wanted. They were standing side by side at the tram stop, and were being jostled continually by the people swarming round them.

"Well, now," said Polynin when she had finished, "I think your husband's right. They're doing everything they can to evacuate the families from that area. That includes air force families on our roster. If I hear anything from them, I'll phone you at once. Secondly, your husband's right about it not being the time for you to go there!"

"Even so, please, please do what you can to help!" said Masha stubbornly.

Polynin angrily folded his arms across his chest.

"Listen, do you realise what you're asking? It's absolute chaos at Grodno, don't you understand that?"

"No."

"Well if you don't, listen to those who do! It's absolute chaos out there!... I'm sorry to be so rude, but if Pavel was here he'd put it even more strongly. He'd give you a good brotherly talking too...."

He pulled himself up short, realising that in trying to talk her out of her foolishness he had blurted out too much about the absolute chaos at Grodno. She had a mother and a daughter there, after all.

"Mind you, the situation will sort itself out, of course," he added awkwardly. "And if the front is going to be near there, the families will naturally be evacuated. And I shall certainly ring you if I hear of the slightest thing. Fair enough?" He was in a great hurry and could no longer hide the fact.

When Sintsov returned home and found Masha away, he was at a loss what to do. She might at least have left a note! Her voice had sounded strange over the telephone; but surely she couldn't quarrel with him on the day of their parting!

They had told him nothing at the Political Directorate that he didn't know already: there was fighting in the Grodno area, and he would be told tomorrow in Minsk whether or not the editorial offices of his army newspaper had been moved elsewhere.

Until now, his own nagging anxiety for his daughter's safety coupled with Masha's state of utter distraction had taken Sintsov's mind off himself. But he now suddenly began to fear for himself: there was a war on, and he, and noone else, was going away that day to what might be his own death.

No sooner had the idea occurred to him, than he heard the intermittent ringing tone of a trunk call. He dashed across the room and snatched up the receiver from its cradle, but it was Chita calling, not Grodno.

"Who's that? Mother?" It was Artemyev's voice coming from somewhere incredibly far away through the buzzing of many voices on the line.

"No, it's me, Sintsov."

"But I thought you were already in action."

"I'm leaving today."

"Where's your family? Where's Mother?"

Sintsov put him in the picture.

"It's certainly no picnic for you out there!" said Artemyev's voice, hoarse and barely audible at the end of the six-thousand-kilometre line. "At least don't let. Masha go there. And I've landed up in the Transbaikalia. Can't do a thing about it!"

"I'm cutting you off, I'm cutting you off! Your time's up!" said the operator, drumming away in the earpiece like a woodpecker.

Before Sintsov had time to answer, the line went dead. The voices and the buzzing stopped, and there was silence.

Masha came in without speaking, her head bowed. Sintsov refrained from asking her where she had been and waited for her to tell him herself. He glanced at the clock on the wall. He had only an hour left.

She intercepted his glance and, sensing his reproach, looked him straight in the face.

"Don't be cross! I went for some advice about whether I mightn't be able to come with you after all."

"And what advice did they give you?"

"They said I couldn't for the time being."

"Oh, Masha, Masha!" was all that Sintsov could say.

She made no reply, trying to take herself in hand and quell the unwanted tremor in her voice. She finally succeeded and, in the last hour before parting, had she made a better job of pretending, or had Sintsov not known her so well, he might have thought her almost calm and even cheerful on the way to the station.

But when they arrived at the terminus, her husband's face looked ill and sad in the hospital-ward light of the blue dim-out bulbs. She remembered what Polynin had said: "It's absolute chaos round Grodno just now!" She shuddered at the recollection and impulsively pressed closer to Sintsov's greatcoat.

"What's the matter? Are you crying?" asked Sintsov, not used to her being in tears.

But she wasn't crying. She was just feeling frightened, and she had snuggled close to her husband as wives do when they weep.

Since nobody had yet become accustomed to the idea of war or to the blackout, the station was in confusion and turmoil that night.

For some time, Sintsov was unable to find out when his train was leaving for Minsk. At first they told him that it had already departed, then that it wouldn't be leaving until the small hours, and immediately afterwards someone shouted that the train for Minsk was leaving in five minutes' time.

For some reason, only ticket-holders were being allowed on to the platform; there was a sudden crush in the doorway, and Masha and Sintsov were so hemmed in on all sides that they didn't even get the chance of a final embrace. Pulling Masha towards him with one hand—he was holding his suitcase in the other—Sintsov at the last moment pressed her face so hard against the buckles of his crossed shoulder straps that they hurt her and, hastily tearing himself away, disappeared through the station door.

Masha ran round the station and came out by the railings, twice the height of a man, that divided the station yard and the platform. She had no hope of seeing Sintsov again; she just wanted to watch his train pull out from the platform.

She stood for half an hour at the railing, and still the train hadn't moved off. Suddenly she spotted Sintsov in the darkness, going from carriage to carriage. He was evidently trying to find a place.

"Vanya!" shouted Masha, but he didn't hear or turn his head.

"Vanya!" she shouted even louder, clutching hold of the iron railings.

He heard her, turned in astonishment, stood for a few seconds staring foolishly in all directions, and only when she shouted for the third time did he realise where she was and run up to the railings.

"You haven't left yet? When's your train actually leaving? Have you got a long wait?"

"I don't know," he said. "They keep saying it'll be any moment now."

He put down his suitcase and stretched out his hands. Masha put hers through the railings. He kissed them and then took them in his own big, warm hands, and held them, and stood there without letting them go.

Half an hour passed, and the train was still standing at the platform.

"Perhaps you could find yourself a place, dump your things, and come back?" suggested Masha as an afterthought.

"Why bother!" Sintsov shook his head recklessly, still not letting go of her hands. "I'll jump onto the footboard!"

Not only were they heedless of the people around them, they would have even considered it strange to think about them, so wrapped up were they in one another and the inevitable separation. So they either looked silently at one another, or tried to soften the parting with the usual words customary in a peacetime which had ceased to exist three days ago.

"I'm sure they'll be all right."

"Please God!"

"I might even meet them at a station on the way—me going, and them coming!"

"That would be wonderful!"

"I'll write to you as soon as I arrive."

"You won't have time for me. Just send a telegram."

"No, I'll definitely write. Expect to hear from me...."

"I certainly shall!"

"And you'll write to me too, won't you?"

"Of course!"

Even up to the very last moment, after four days of this war for which Sintsov was leaving, neither of them realised the full implications. They still couldn't imagine that everything, absolutely everything that they had just been discussing, would disappear from their lives for a long time, perhaps forever—letters, telegrams, meetings....

"We're off! All passengers aboard!" shouted a voice behind Sintsov.

Sintsov squeezed Masha's hands for the last time, snatched up his suitcase, wound his kitbag strap round his wrist, and jumped up on to the footboard at a run, since the train was already crawling slowly past.

Someone else jumped on to the footboard immediately after him, then someone else, and Masha finally lost sight of him. She thought she saw his hand in the distance waving a peaked cap, then she fancied it was someone else's, and then she couldn't see anything any more. Other carriages began gliding past, other people were shouting, and she was left standing alone, with her face pressed up against the railings, hastily buttoning up the raincoat over her chest, which suddenly felt cold.

The train, which for some reason had been made up solely out of suburban-line carriages, dragged its way across the Moscow and Smolensk regions in a journey interrupted by a series of nerve-racking halts. Most of the passengers in Sintsov's carriage and in the rest of the train were commanders on leave from the Special Western Military District who had been urgently recalled to their units.

It was only now, as they found themselves travelling towards Minsk in those suburban-line carriages, that they became aware of one another and were duly astonished. Each had gone on leave individually, not realising what a vast number of them—all supposed to take command in action of companies, battalions and regiments—had been absent since the first day of the war from units which were probably already engaged in the fighting.

Neither Sintsov nor the others were able to understand how this could have happened when the premonition of war had been in the air since April. From time to time, discussions of the subject flared up in the carriage, died down, and then flared up again. Men who were in no way to blame were suffering from guilt feelings and became jittery whenever the train stopped for any length of time.

As they passed through Vyazma, Sintsov regretted not having sent his father a telegram before leaving, but then decided it was just as well. The train had taken so long to reach Vyazma that his father might have been kept hanging about at the station and then not have met him anyway. There was no timetable, although there hadn't been any air-raid alerts throughout the first day's travelling. Only at night, when the train was standing in Orsha, did the steam locomotives begin whistling all round them and the window-panes start rattling. The Germans were bombing Orsha goods yard.

Even then, hearing the noise of bombing for the first time, Sintsov didn't realise that their suburban train was heading straight for the scene of action. "Well, what of it?" he thought. "Nothing surprising about the Germans night-bombing the railways leading up to the front." Sitting opposite him was an artillery captain returning to his unit at Domachevo on the frontier, and they both agreed that the Germans were probably flying from Warsaw or Königsberg.

If they had been told that this was the second night that the Germans had raided Orsha from our own military airfield at Grodno—the very Grodno to which Sintsov was going in order to rejoin the editorial offices of his Army newspaper—they would simply have refused to believe it.

But the night passed, and they were compelled to believe far worse. In the morning, the train dragged on as far as Borisov, and the station commandant, wincing as if from toothache, announced that the train would not be proceeding any further: the lines between Borisov and Minsk had been bombed and were now cut off by German tanks.

It was dusty and stifling in Borisov. German aircraft were circling over the city, and troops and vehicles were on the move, some arriving, some leaving. The dead were lying on stretchers just outside the hospital on the cobbled road.

A senior lieutenant was standing outside the commandant's office and roaring: "Get the guns dug in!" This was the town commandant himself, and Sintsov, who had not taken any small-arms with him on leave, asked to be issued with a pistol. But the commandant didn't have one; he had cleaned out the arsenal an hour ago and there was nothing left to issue.

Sintsov and his travelling companion, the artillery captain, stopped the first lorry that came their way. The driver was determinedly scouring the town in search of his warehouse manager, who had vanished and was nowhere to be found. Sintsov and the captain boarded the lorry and went in search of the garrison CO. The captain, who had given up any hope of finding his regiment at the frontier, wanted to obtain a posting to a local artillery unit, Sintsov hoped to find out where the Political Directorate of the Front was stationed: if it was no longer possible to get to Grodno, then at least they could send him to some other Army or Division newspaper. Both officers were ready and willing to go anywhere and do anything rather than be left hanging between the devil and the deep blue sea on this thrice-accursed leave. They were told that the garrison commander was at a military garrison town somewhere outside Borisov. On the outskirts, a German fighter flew overhead, raking them with its machine-guns. There were no casualties, but splinters flew from the side of the lorry. When he had recovered from the fright which had sent him diving face down on to the floor, reeking of petrol, an astonished Sintsov pulled out a nearly two-inch-long splinter which had gone through his tunic into his forearm.

It then transpired that the lorry was running out of petrol, and so, before trying to find the garrison commander, they drove along the Minsk motorway to a fuel depot.

There, they came upon a strange scene. A lieutenant, the officer in charge of the depot, and a sergeant-major were holding up at pistol-point a major in the uniform of the Engineer Corps. The lieutenant was shouting that he would shoot the major sooner than let him blow up the fuel tanks. The major, an elderly man with a medal on his chest, was standing with his hands up, quivering with indignation and explaining that he had come not to blow up the depot, but to ascertain the possibility of doing so. When the pistols were finally lowered, the major, with tears of vexation in his eyes, began shouting that it was a disgrace to hold up a senior commander at pistol-point. Sintsov never found out how the scene ended. The lieutenant, listening gloomily as the major reprimanded him, mumbled something to the effect that the garrison commander was at the barracks of a tank training school not far off in the forest, and so Sintsov went there in the lorry.

All the doors of the tank training school had been flung wide open and there wasn't a vehicle to be seen, except for two small tanks and their crews on the parade ground. They had been left there pending further orders, but no orders had arrived for the last twenty-four hours. No one had the slightest idea of what was happening. Some said that the school had been evacuated, others that it had gone into action. Rumour had it that the Borisov garrison commander was somewhere on the Minsk motorway, only on the other side of the town.

Sintsov and the artillery captain returned to Borisov. The commandant's staff were loading up preparatory to departure. The commandant, his voice now quite hoarse, whispered that orders had come in from Marshal Timoshenko to pull out of Borisov, withdraw beyond the Berezina, and hold out there against the Germans to the last man.

The artillery captain was suspicious and said that the commandant had let himself be taken in by a false rumour. But the commandant's staff were loading up, and they would hardly have been doing so without official orders. Sintsov and the captain again drove out of town in their lorry. The road was full of men and machines raising clouds of dust, only this time they were not moving in different directions, but eastwards away from Borisov.

An enormously tall man, bareheaded and revolver in hand, was standing on a narrow dyke in the thick of a traffic jam. He was beside himself with rage, stopping men and machines and shouting in a broken voice that he, Political Instructor Zotov, had to stop the army here, and that he was going to stop it, too, and would shoot every man who attempted to retreat. But the troops and vehicles surged on past the political instructor. He would let some of them through only to stop the ones behind, thrusting his revolver into his belt, grabbing someone by the tunic, then letting go, then pulling out his revolver again and turning round to seize hold of someone else furiously, but futilely....

Sintsov and the captain stopped their lorry in some trees near the bank on the other side of the dyke. The wood was swarming with troops. Sintsov was informed that there were some commanders nearby forming units. And, in fact, several colonels were in charge on the outskirts of the wood. On three lorries with their sides down, lists of personnel were being drawn up and companies were being formed and sent out in opposite directions along the Berezina under the command of officers appointed on the spot. Other lorries were piled with rifles which were being issued to all without small-arms. Sintsov also had his name put down and was handed a rifle with bayonet fixed but no sling, so that he had to carry it at the trail all the time.

One of the colonels in charge, a bald tank officer with the Order of Lenin on his chest, who had travelled from Moscow in Sintsov's railway carriage, glanced at his leave pass and identity card and waved his hand in exasperation, as if asking what on earth was the good of a newspaper at a time like this; but he then ordered Sintsov not to go far away: a job would be found for him, as an educated man. The colonel expressed it as strangely as that—"an educated man". Exactly what he meant by this phrase Sintsov was not to find out until the next day. Bringing his foot down smartly, he saluted, went away, and sat down by his lorry about a hundred paces from the colonel.

An hour later, the artillery captain came running up to the lorry, heaved out his kitbag and, happily shouting to Sintsov that he had been given command of two guns to be going on with, hurried off at a run. Sintsov never saw him again.

The forest was swarming with troops as before, and no matter how many were sent off in charge of an officer in various directions, there was no sign of them ever being drained off.

Another hour passed, and the first enemy fighter planes appeared. The Germans had spotted the concentration of troops in that sparse pine forest, and successive waves of aircraft now began strafing it. Every half hour, Sintsov threw himself down on the ground, pressing his head up against the trunk of a slender pine whose meagre crown swayed high in the air above him. At each attack, the whole forest opened fire. The men took aim standing, on their knees, lying on the ground, with rifles, machine-guns, and revolvers.

But the fighters kept on coming, and they were all German.

"Where are ours?" wondered Sintsov bitterly, and the men all round him were inwardly or openly asking the same question.

At last, towards evening, three of our I-16s with red stars on their wings flew over the trees.

Hundreds of men jumped up, shouted, joyfully waved their hands. A minute later, the three fighters returned, their machine-guns blazing.

An elderly supply officer who was standing next to Sintsov and using his forage cap as an eyeshade in order to get a better view of the Russian planes in the sunlight, suddenly pitched over, killed outright. A Red Armyman nearby was hit: seated on the ground, he kept bending over and straightening up again, his hands pressed to his stomach. But even now the men thought that it was all a mistake; and only when the fighters returned for the third time, sweeping over almost at tree-top level, did they open fire. The planes were flying so low that one of them was brought down by machine-gun fire. It broke up in the trees, the debris flying in all directions, and fell only a hundred metres away from Sintsov. The body of the pilot in German uniform was trapped in the wreckage of the cockpit. Although the whole forest was overjoyed for the first few minutes—"Got one at last!"—the inevitable realisation that the Germans had managed to capture our planes had a depressing effect on all.

At last, the long-awaited darkness fell. The lorry driver shared his biscuits in comradely fashion with Sintsov and pulled out from under his seat a bottle of warm, sweet lemonade that he had bought in Borisov. Both of them wanted another drink. The river was less than half a kilometre off, but neither Sintsov nor the driver had the energy to make the effort after all the horror they had been through that day. The driver lay down in his cab with his feet protruding, and Sintsov lowered himself to the ground, propped his kitbag up against a wheel, pillowed his head on it, and, in spite of his horror and bewilderment, thought determinedly: no, it couldn't be possible. What he had seen here couldn't be happening everywhere else!

With this thought he fell asleep, but was woken up again by the sound of a shot in his ear. Someone sitting on the ground two paces away was firing his revolver into the sky. Bombs were bursting in the forest, and there was a red glow in the distance. All over the forest, vehicles were roaring into movement, colliding in the darkness with one another and with the trees.

Sintsov's driver was also anxious to get away, but Sintsov acted like a soldier for the first time in twenty-four hours. He ordered the driver to stop panicking. Only after an hour, when everything was quiet—men and machines had disappeared—did he take his seat next to the driver. They then began looking for a road out of the forest.

As they drove out into the open, Sintsov noticed in front a small group of men silhouetted against the red glow of the fires ahead. He stopped the lorry and went up to them, rifle in hand. Two servicemen standing on the verge of the highway had detained a civilian and were ordering him to produce his papers.

"I haven't got any! None at all!"

"Why not?" insisted one of the servicemen. "Show us your papers!"

"Show them to you?" shouted the man in civvies, his voice trembling with rage. "What d'you want with papers? Who d'you take me for—Hitler? Why don't you try and catch Hitler instead? Not that you'd ever get him!"

The serviceman who had demanded the documents reached for his pistol.

"Go on, then, shoot, if you've got the nerve!" yelled the civilian in a desperate challenge.

This man was hardly a saboteur or German spy; more likely he had been called up for the army and had been driven to desperation trying to find his mobilisation point. But what he had shouted about Hitler would never do in front of men who had been driven frantic by their own bitter experiences....

Sintsov understood all this later, but he didn't have the chance to at the time: a dazzling white flare suddenly blazed up overhead. Sintsov threw himself down and heard a bomb explode when he was already on the ground. He waited for a moment before picking himself up again. All he could see twenty paces away was three mangled bodies. As if to imprint the scene on his memory for the rest of his life, the flare blazed for a few more seconds, sputtered briefly across the night sky, and vanished somewhere below without a trace, like a spark quenched in ink.

When Sintsov returned to the lorry, he found the driver under the engine with only his legs showing. They climbed back into their seats again and headed east for a few more kilometres—first along the highway, then along a forest road. Sintsov stopped two officers coming the other way and learned that there had been orders to abandon the forest where they had been yesterday and to move to a new line seven kilometres further back.

The lorry was proceeding without lights, and Sintsov got out of the cab and walked on in front to prevent it from running into the trees. If anyone had asked him what he needed the lorry for and why he was bothering with it, he would not have given a rational answer; he would have just said that was the way things had turned out. The driver, who had lost his unit, had become used to Sintsov and didn't want to leave him, while Sintsov, who had not reached his unit yet, was glad that, thanks to the lorry, he had the company of at least one living person.

It was only at daybreak, after parking the lorry in a forest where there were vehicles standing under nearly every tree and men were digging ditches and trenches that Sintsov finally found the garrison commander. It was a cool grey morning. On a forest path in front of Sintsov there stood a comparatively young man with a three-day stubble on his chin, a forage cap squashed down over his eyes, a tunic with pips on his collar-tabs, an army greatcoat slung over his shoulders and, for some reason, a spade in his hands. Sintsov was told that this was the Borisov garrison commander.

Sintsov went up to him and formally requested the Comrade Brigade Commissar to tell him whether he, Political Instructor Sintsov, could be used in his capacity as army newspaperman, and, if not, what were his instructions. The brigade commissar looked absently at his documents, then at Sintsov himself, and said with glum indifference:

"Can't you see what's happening? What newspaper d'you mean? How can there be a newspaper here at a time like this?"

His tone of voice made Sintsov feel quite guilty.

"You'll have to go to HQ, or rather the Political

Directorate of the Front. You'll be told there where to report," said the brigade commissar after a short pause.

"Where is HQ—and the Political Directorate?" asked Sintsov hopefully.

But the brigade commissar merely shrugged his shoulders and started talking to some other men nearby.

Sintsov went away and was still wondering what to do next, when he bumped into his acquaintance, the colonel of the tank corps.

"I've been looking for you! Where the hell have you been?" snapped the colonel. "See over there?" He pointed to a group of men sitting on the trunks of two felled pines. "We're holding a field court martial. You were a newspaper secretary, so you can help us keep the minutes!"

Sitting on the fallen pines were a black-haired Army lawyer, a fair-haired political instructor with Air Force tabs, a major of the NKVD troops with maroon tabs, and four Red Armymen under their command. All seven were having a rest; there were shovels lying at their feet, and two half-dug air-raid trenches yawned nearby. Sintsov introduced himself.

"Got a notepad?" asked the Army lawyer.

"Yes," said Sintsov.

"Good," said the lawyer. "We'll finish these trenches and then we'll get down to business."

The digging took another hour. Sintsov sat down on the ground, his legs dangling into the trench. Fatigue and hunger had made him sleepy, and he dozed off without realising it.

At first, he dreamed of his father's orchard in Vyazma, and of Masha walking there in military uniform with an army lawyer's tabs; then he dreamed of the flat on the Usachevka; a man came in with a face like Hitler's and asked, in the voice of the civilian killed the day before by the bomb, whether he could have anything to eat. Sintsov began feeling for the revolver at his side, meaning to shoot him; but the gun wasn't there....

He woke up when someone shoved him into the trench and then himself jumped down. The trenches had been dug not a moment too soon. Aircraft were flying high over the pines and plastering the forest with bombs.

Sintsov got through the whole of that day in a daze brought on by fatigue, hunger, and three sleepless days and nights. He would crawl into the trench until the raid was over, sometimes falling asleep as he waited; then he would climb out again and sit in the sun, dangling his legs down into the trench and dozing off again; or, when the arrested men were brought up and the army lawyer, the senior political organiser and the major were interrogating them, he would make a transcript of the proceedings, resting the notepad on his knee and forming the letters with some difficulty.

"Cut it short—just the gist!" the lawyer kept telling him.

The gist was that nearly all the arrested men were neither saboteurs, spies, or deserters; they had simply been proceeding from one point to another, looking for someone or something that they couldn't find because everything was in a state of upheaval and nothing was in its former place any more. Caught in the firing or in air raids, and having heard scare stories about German raids and tanks, some of them, fearing capture, had buried their documents and had sometimes even torn them up.

After interrogation, they were usually dismissed. Some were told approximately where they should go; others were told nothing, because those in charge didn't know themselves. Many of those who had been dismissed didn't want to leave, because they were scared of being picked up again somewhere else under suspicion of desertion.

All this was punctuated with bombing and machine-gun attacks, during which the accused and their interrogators jammed the trenches to overflowing with their tightly packed bodies.

Two particularly suspicious characters had been picked up. They were in uniform but had no documents, and since they were unable to give convincing answers about who they were, where they had come from, and where they were going, they were pronounced deserters and sentenced to be shot. The firing squad who marched the prisoners to the outskirts of the forest in order to execute them, described afterwords how one of them wept and asked them to wait, assuring them that he could explain everything; the other also told them to wait at first, but at the last moment, when the weapons were already trained on him, suddenly shouted: "Heil Hitler!"

One of those arrested that day proved to be insane—a very tall young Red Armyman with the arms and legs of a giant and a tiny, close-cropped head on the long neck of a child. The bombing had been too much for him, and he imagined that he had been taken prisoner by nazis wearing Red Army uniform. He had rushed out on to the road, his arms flailing, and had started screaming at the German planes as they flew overhead:

"Smash 'em, smash 'em!"

Everything was topsy-turvy in his crazed mind: he thought the men round him were German, and that the German aircraft were ours. With some difficulty, they restrained him and brought him in.

"What have you changed uniforms for, you fascists! I know who you are anyway! What have you changed uniforms for!"

All attempts to calm him down and explain that he was among his own people were of no avail: the harder they tried to convince him, the more wildly did the light of madness glitter in his eyes.

Suddenly, he looked round, darted to one side, snatched up Sintsov's rifle, which was standing propped up against a tree, and in three enormous bounds tore out on to the road.

"Run for it!" he shouted in a thin, whining, crazed voice, so that everyone in the vicinity heard that inhuman howl. "Get out! We're surrounded by fascists! Get out!" And he hopped about on the roadway, brandishing the rifle and alternately bending over and straightening up again.

Someone saw him dancing about on the road and screaming in panic and. without giving it a second thought, shot at him with a revolver several times in succession, but missed. Then someone else fired and also missed.

Sintsov realised that the lunatic was bound to be killed. There could be no alternative, now that he had started screaming in that terrifying and panicky way. Determined to save him and without any thought for himself, Sintsov dashed over to the Red Armyman. But as soon as the latter saw Sintsov coming for him, he whirled round and, levelling his rifle in both hands, rushed towards him. Sintsov distinctly saw the eyeballs rolled up in their sockets in a mad frenzy of hatred, and he jumped to one side so that the bayonet stabbed the empty air. He then seized the stock of the rifle with one hand and the barrel with the other. No one was shooting now for fear of hitting Sintsov. He and the deranged soldier fought frenziedly for several seconds, each trying to wrest the rifle away from the other. During the struggle, Sintsov gradually shifted his grip until he was holding the stock with both hands and the soldier was hanging on to the muzzle. In a final effort, Sintsov jerked the rifle towards himself with all his might.

It took him a moment or two to realise what had happened. The soldier had released his grip, bringing up his hands as if to clutch his head, but before they had even touched his face he had fallen prone on the roadway.

Only after he had fallen did Sintsov realise that he, and no one else, had fired the shot he had heard a moment ago. In the act of wrenching the rifle away, he had released the safety catch, and the man he had killed was now lying at his feet.

Even before he threw his rifle aside and squatted down beside him, Sintsov realised that the man was dead. He was lying face-down, the close-cropped and childlike head twisted awkwardly to one side and the blood running down his neck on to the dusty road. The bullet had gone straight through his Adam's apple.

"He nearly started a panic, the scum!" It was a tall captain with a fiery red stubble on his chin who had come up and was standing over the dead man, revolver in hand. He had been the first to start shooting. "Panic-monger! Scum!" repeated the captain. "Died like a dog—and serve him right!"

But although his voice was harsh and self-assured, his eyes were the guilty eyes of a dog. He seemed, with the violence of his language, to be trying to convince himself and the onlookers that he had done right to fire at the madman.

Sintsov was badly shaken. The first thing he had done in action had been to kill one of his own side! He had wanted to save him, and had shot him dead!... What could be more appallingly futile than that?

Even by the end of the day, he wasn't clear about the situation. First they said that Minsk was still in our hands; then, on the contrary, that the Germans had already taken Borisov. As evening drew near, the word got round that the German tanks had been stopped somewhere about seven kilometres away. True, heavy gunfire could be heard in front, and it was neither advancing nor receding. All this disjointed information came to Sintsov as if through a haze, what with the air raids, his troubled thoughts about the man he had shot, and further interrogations.

At sundown, a soldier came up to Sintsov and said that the colonel wanted to see him.

The tank corps colonel who, as the most energetic officer there, had taken charge of all the rest, was standing on the fringe of the forest by a tent camouflaged with branches. As Sintsov arrived, two signalmen were laying a field telephone cable up to the tent. Beside the colonel stood a battalion commissar in the uniform of a frontier guard.

"You were asking about the Political Directorate of the Front," said the colonel without preamble as Sintsov halted in front of him. "He knows where it is." And he indicated the battalion commissar. "Somewhere near Mogilev. He's going that way. He can take you with him."

The other officer nodded without speaking.

"I won't be a moment, I'll just get my things!" said Sintsov. "Can you hang on for three minutes?"

The other nodded again and glanced at his watch.

"I'll be quick!" said Sintsov, and he went off at the double to fetch his suitcase from the back of the lorry.

But the lorry was no longer there. After walking round for a minute or so, as if the vanished lorry might conceivably start up out of the ground, Sintsov remembered that he was being waited for, gave it up as a bad job, and ran back.

The frontier guard officer was standing by the tent, shifting impatiently from one foot to the other.

"Where are your things, then?" he asked.

"They were in the lorry, but it's cleared off. I've no idea where..." said Sintsov. "I'll go like this."

He was thankful that when dusk had fallen an hour ago, he had taken his greatcoat out of the lorry and thrown it over his shoulders.

"Yes," said the other, and he slapped his field bag, which was anything but full. "All my things are in here too. Haven't even got a greatcoat. It was burnt in the lorry."

He could have told Sintsov that he had lost everything: his house had been burned down and his family wiped out; but he only mentioned the burnt greatcoat and added:

"Let's get going!"

They walked two kilometres along the forest road until they came to an intersection with the Minsk motorway. All this time, Sintsov had assumed that they would stop at one of the vehicles hidden under the trees and drive off in it. He had not really taken any notice of what the battalion commissar had said about his greatcoat being destroyed by fire in the lorry. When they came out on to the Minsk motorway, along which there was fairly frequent traffic, and when the battalion commissar said: "We'll try and get a lift to Orsha"—only then did Sintsov realise that his companion had no transport and that they would have to try and hitch a passing lorry.

"You go on about two hundred paces and I'll stand here," said the other. "If I don't stop one, you have a try."

After he had walked the necessary distance ahead, Sintsov clearly saw the battalion commissar make several attempts to stop passing vehicles. He tried holding up his hand himself, but the traffic just roared by. At last, he saw the other stop a lorry, open the door, and speak to someone sitting inside.

Sintsov was about to dash back to the lorry. Just then, there was the roar of an aircraft diving to the attack. Sintsov automatically flung himself down, aware of the stifling reek of warm asphalt in his nostrils. He lay there for several seconds and when he turned his head and looked, there was no sign of the lorry on the road or of the battalion commissar. The bomb had scored a direct hit on the vehicle, there was a crater smoking in the asphalt, pieces of twisted iron were lying all over the place, and a loose wheel was trundling down the road towards Sintsov. It rolled on a few more paces, as if it wanted to come right up to his feet, started wobbling, and fell over with a sound of metal grating on asphalt.

And Sintsov was left standing alone on the Minsk motorway with the traffic going past him and with such despair in his heart that only extreme exhaustion prevented him from screaming or bursting into tears.

While it was still light, Sintsov walked on a few more kilometres and then, like thousands of others, spent that night in a ditch by the roadside, his forage cap under his head and his greatcoat collar pulled up over his face. He slept like a log for several hours, unconscious of the traffic roaring by on the road or of the thunder of night bombing, and he only awoke because someone had bent back his greatcoat collar and was touching his face.

"No, this one's alive," said a voice.

Sintsov opened his eyes and sat up. In front of him stood two boys of about sixteen. They were wearing clean, short artillery school greatcoats, with gilt crossed cannon on the black collar-tabs. Evidently, like Sintsov, they had gone without food for some time. Their childlike faces were drawn and their eyes were full of misery. They looked like fledgeling jackdaws that had fallen out of their nests on to the road.

"What is it, boys?" asked Sintsov, getting to his feet. "Where are you off to?"

The boys replied that they had been to Smolensk to rehearse for the summer sports parade and were on their way back to school in Borisov.

"Where's your school, then?" asked Sintsov. "In the town?"

They said that it was beyond, sixteen kilometres towards Minsk.

"As far as I know, the Germans are there now," said Sintsov. "I was in Borisov yesterday."

The boys stared at him incredulously, and then one of them looked away. Sintsov followed his glance and saw several motionless bodies on the verge some two hundred metres off and, in the middle of the road, a crater which was at that moment being steered round by a lorry on its way east. When he had fallen asleep the evening before, there had been no bodies lying there—which meant that a bomb had landed quite close by during the night, people had been killed, and he hadn't even woken up.

"We thought you'd been killed too," said one of the boys. "Where should we go now?"

"We're going back to our school anyway," said the other. "The Germans can't possibly be there."

Sintsov just couldn't convince them otherwise. They didn't believe him.

He then gave them a detailed description of the turning on the left immediately after the fifth verst-stone from where they were standing. They should turn off the main road at that point and follow the forest lane until they were stopped by sentries. Then they would be told whether they could continue further, or whether they should stay with the troops there....

After saying all this in a firm tone of voice which the two boys took as an order, Sintsov felt in his greatcoat pocket for a tin of food given to him the day before by the army lawyer, and insisted on them having a snack with him before they left. The tin proved to contain anchovies, which they ate without bread or water.

The boys went away. After saying good-bye to them, Sintsov stood for a long time watching the two slender figures receding into the distance.

Then he brushed down his coat and cap and set off east along the Minsk highway towards Orsha.

So many people in those days walked along that road, turning off into the forest, taking cover in roadside ditches from the air-raids, getting up again, and trudging along further on tired feet! There were a great many Jewish refugees from Stolbtsy, Baranovichi, Molodechno, and other little towns and hamlets in West Byelorussia. It was the eighth day of the war, and they were already this side of Borisov, which meant they had started out very early, in the first hours of the war....Thousands of people were travelling on every conceivable kind of cart, drozhki and wagon: bearded old men with sidewhiskers and bowler hats dating back to the last century; emaciated, prematurely aged Jewish women; children—every cart carried from six to ten dusty, swarthy children with darting, frightened eyes. But there were even more people walking alongside the wagons.

Among the ragged old men, women and children, Sintsov often saw young women who looked particularly out of place on that road. They were wearing fashionable coats which looked pathetic and dirty after several days on the road, and their heads were crowned with fashionable hair-do's that had slipped over to one side and were powdered with dust. Sintsov had first seen these hair styles during the campaign in West Byelorussia, and they now seemed particularly incongruous and pathetic. The women were clutching bundles of all shapes and sizes in dirt-blackened fingers that trembled with fatigue and hunger.

All were heading east; but coming in the opposite direction along either side of the road were young boys in civvies carrying plywood cases, imitation leather handgrips, and kitbags slung over their shoulders. They had been called up and were in a hurry to get to their designated mobilisation points, not wishing to be taken for deserters. They were going to their deaths, to meet the Germans. They were kept going by faith and a sense of duty. They didn't know where the Germans actually were, and they didn't believe that the enemy could turn up under their noses before they had even had time to put on uniform and pick up their rifles.... This was one of the grimmest tragedies of those days—the tragedy of men who died under air attack on the road or were taken prisoner before they had even reached their mobilisation points.

And yet peaceful woods and groves lay along either side of the highway. One simple scene was to impress itself on Sintsov's memory that day and stay with him for the rest of his life. Towards evening, he noticed a small village. It lay on top of a low hill. The darkling green orchards were bathed in the red light of the setting sun, the smoke was curling up from the cottage chimneys and, silhouetted against the sunset sky, on the crest of the hill, some small boys were driving the horses out to pasture for the night. The village cemetery came quite close to the highway. The village itself was tiny, but the cemetery was a big one; the whole hillside was covered with broken, lurching, rain- and snow-scoured crosses. This tiny village with its big cemetery, and the incongruity of the two together, shook Sintsov to the core of his being. A piercing, agonising feeling of love for his native land, which was already being trampled on by German jackboots somewhere back there and which tomorrow could meet with the same fate here too—this feeling wrung his heart. What Sintsov had seen during the last two days had told him that the Germans could indeed come here too, and yet he still couldn't imagine this land as belonging to the Germans. So many ancestors—grandfathers, great-grandfathers, and great-great-grandfathers—had lain down under those crosses one after another over the centuries, that this soil was theirs a thousand feet deep. It could not, and had no right to, fall into alien hands.

Never subsequently was Sintsov to know such paralysing terror. What was going to happen next? If it had begun like this, what was going to become of everything he loved, everything amid which he had grown up and for which he had lived? What was going to become of his country, his people, and the army which he had always considered invincible, and the communism which these nazis, already between Minsk and Borisov on the seventh day of the war, had sworn to annihilate?

He was no coward, but, like millions of other people, he had not been ready for what had happened. Most of his life, like the lives of all the rest, had been spent in deprivation, trials, and struggle; and so, as was to become clear later, the terrible weight of the first days of the war could not break their spirit. But in those first days the burden seemed intolerable to many, although they subsequently lived through it.

A year and a half ago, when Sintsov had been offered extended service instead of demobilisation, he had not been pleased, but he had consented on a matter of principle: his division was stationed on the River Bug, there were nazis on the other side, there was a premonition of war in the air, and he considered that, under the circumstances, Communists should not refuse to serve in the army.

And now, when what he had stayed in the army for had actually happened and the war with fascism had begun, he had found himself away from his unit, in the wrong place, wandering about like a lost soul, futilely pushing his documents under people's noses, looking for his editorial office which was goodness knows where by this time, and even, as a result of trying to find it, trudging back from the front like a deserter.

In spite of the battalion commissar's death, he was determined to get to Mogilev now he had been told that the Political Directorate of the Front was stationed there. But if this was a false rumour, he was equally determined not to look any further and to ask for a posting as political instructor to the first available rifle unit.

That morning, as on the evening before, he kept trying to hitch a ride; but again not a single vehicle stopped. In the end, he gave up in despair, stopped bothering to look round at the traffic, and spent the rest of the day trudging doggedly along the highway, wrapped up in his own gloomy thoughts, or not even thinking about anything in particular and merely picking up and putting down his leaden feet.

No doubt he would have finally made it to Orsha on foot, had not a lorry pulled up beside him when it was already evening.

"Where are you heading for, Political Instructor?" asked the colonel in the cab.

"Orsha!" said Sintsov gloomily.

"Why are you walking it?"

"I tried hitching a ride and got fed up," said Sintsov in the same gloomy tone of voice. "They won't take me, the scum!"

"Yes, plenty of scum about," said the colonel, "though less than you might expect under the circumstances. Let's see your papers!"

Sintsov unconcernedly held out his documents to the colonel, who gave them a cursory glance and returned them immediately.

"Get in the back. I'll take you there."

An hour's frantic driving took them into Orsha. The lorry wasn't the colonel's; he had only borrowed it, promising to take it no farther than Orsha. Like Sintsov, he was trying to reach Mogilev and hoped to make the rest of the journey by train. Sintsov and the colonel went to see the city commandant. The offices were in a school basement. There were some tables with a number of telephones, and a major—the city commandant—sitting behind them, stupefied by continual shouting.

"Will there be a train to Mogilev?" asked the colonel.

As the latter made his enquiry, the commandant slammed one telephone down and was in the act of rushing to answer another; but the colonel laid a firm hand on his shoulder, stopped him in his tracks, and forced the commandant to turn and look him in the face.

"Answer my question: will there be a train to Mogilev, and when?"

"Just a moment, Comrade Colonel!" said the commandant hoarsely. "There should be one...." And he hurried to the telephone to which he had been summoned. The longer he listened, the more furious he looked. Finally, he swore blackly and slammed down the receiver. "No train, Comrade Colonel! What d'you know about that! They've just informed us. Ammunition train bombed on the approaches to Mogilev. Both tracks destroyed. There'll be no train to Mogilev!"

"All right, to hell with it," said the colonel calmly to Sintsov. "They don't know a thing about it. All that carry-on about planes and blowing things up is just so much hot air. We could probably get through alright. Let's go to the station. We'll get some sense out of them there."

But getting some sense out of them at the station proved not so simple. The lights were out, and the military commandant and the station-master said in a confidential whisper that they didn't know anything yet. Finally, the colonel buttonholed a railwayman who told them in a whisper, as if it were a great secret, that a goods train for Mogilev was being assembled on the tracks beyond the water pump.

"Come on!" said the colonel.

Sintsov could see that this elderly and experienced man, who had seen a few things in his time, was also feeling lonely and in need of human sympathy. He told Sintsov how he had flown into Moscow from the Volga Military District, had been appointed chief-of-staff of a corps, had ended up in Borisov looking for his corps, had nearly been captured by the Germans, had spent a whole day commanding a company which had lost its CO, and had finally learned that his corps was nowhere in the vicinity but had gone to the Osipovichi-Bobruisk region, and so he was heading there via Mogilev.

"Of course, I could have stayed in command of the company," he said angrily, "but we can't take things into our own hands! Goodness knows, we've been at war for eight days and it's time to get organised! Once I've been appointed corps chief-of-staff, I have to report to my place of service, not just lie in the line with a rifle. When I handed the company over to a lieutenant, one blockhead had the nerve to accuse me of cowardice!"

"What did you do?" asked Sintsov.

"Me? I clouted him one on the kisser to teach him a lesson, and then left."

The colonel went bright red at the recollection, and his face, already intimidating enough with its bristling moustaches, looked positively ferocious.

They spent some time wandering about the tracks in search

of the train and, as almost invariably happens when someone turns up who is self-confident and knows exactly what he wants, another ten men or so tagged on, also trying to get to Mogilev for various reasons.

While they were looking for the train, German bombers staged a raid on the station. One after another, the steam locomotives began bellowing on the battered station tracks.

There were several dozen engines at Orsha junction, and, as they bellowed, they drew closer to one another, discharging clouds of white steam. It was an alarming noise and monstrously sad—far more terrifying than the thunder of the exploding bombs, to which Sintsov had become accustomed by now. It was as if the engines were protesting to someone: to the sky or to the world at large—protesting and asking for help; but the sky went on showering the black earth with bombs that exploded among the houses, railway tracks, and human beings lying on the tracks—deafened, embittered, miserable, and outraged to the core by everything happening around them.

When the alert had sounded, all who had made their way to the water pump and had been unable to find any train there, sat down for a rest on some heaps of slag by the tracks. No one wanted to talk, but it was impossible to keep quiet; each had too much on his mind. The conversation ran like water dripping from a not fully turned off tap.

"Whoever would've thought it?" came sadly out of the darkness from someone whose features Sintsov had not yet managed to distinguish in the darkness.

"But they did do a lot of thinking," rejoined the colonel after a pause. "Only when it came to the crunch—what a shambles!"

"It's fantastic the way everything's so disorganised," said the thin, astonished tenor voice of someone also invisible in the dark. "Simply fantastic!"

"My engineer battalion was stationed in Byelostok," said a deep bass. "But where it's got to now...."

"Whistle for it!" said someone in a cold, ugly voice.

All were silent for several minutes.

"They study the August catastrophe* in the academies, analyse it to bits, call Samsonov a nit, and now *they're* in the shit," said the cold and jaundiced voice that had answered

* *The August catastrophe*—a reference to the disastrous military operation on the Eastern Front in 1916 under command of General Samsonov during the First World War.—*Ed.*

the engineer. "Just a piece of cake—amble over into enemy territory, hardly any bloodshed... three cheers, etcetera, etcetera," he continued.

"We'll be on enemy territory yet, you mark my words, you over there—I can't tell your rank in the dark," retorted the colonel angrily. "Still, facts are facts. It's shambles, a terrible shambles.... And the thing is, there's nobody but us to clean it up!"

This sparked off a whole chorus of answering comments. Someone observed that the Russians take a long time harnessing the horses, but after that they move fast. The proverb was not sympathetically received.

"It's not 1812. We'd better look lively with that harness. Otherwise we'll be harnessing up all the way to Smolensk!"

Someone even suggested that the saying must be a German one. The men argued amongst themselves, but their voices all trembled with the same bitterness and sense of outrage. It wasn't the only-too-obvious chaos that was getting them down but, even worse, the fact that there was fighting in progress somewhere, their units were in action, yet they hadn't yet been able to rejoin them and there was no telling how they were going to do so.

"I nearly got shot as a saboteur yesterday," said someone. "They stuck a revolver in my face, just as if I was a horse. I helped to take Perekop,* and these bastards—they were only kids—stuck a revolver in my face."

"Hey, you, August Catastrophe!" called the colonel, as if remembering something, to the man with the cold voice that he had taken such a dislike to. "Are you coming with us to Mogilev too? Are you looking for your unit?"

But no one answered. The man who had been asked either didn't want to reply or had left. The others could be heard turning towards one another in the dark.

"Seems to have gone," said the deep voice of the engineer at last. "He was sitting here, by me."

"Of course, you get panic-mongers too," said the colonel after a pause, either in answer to the engineer or reacting to his own thoughts. "Some people need a gun in their faces. Only it does happen that the wrong man gets picked on.... Let's be on our feet!" He stood up first. "Goodness knows, maybe there's another water pump somewhere! Let's go and find out!"

* A reference to one of the final operations in the Crimea during the Civil War.—*Ed.*

They didn't find another water pump, but an hour later they met a pointsman who indicated some carriages standing on the line and confidently said that they were to be shunted on to the Mogilev train.

Exhausted by their fruitless search, all went to the carriages. Two brand-new little staff buses were standing on flats between the goods wagons.

"Let's get in the buses," said the colonel, and he was the first to climb up on to the flat and try the handle of a bus door. It was unlocked. "If they move off, we'll get a ride. If not, we'll at least be able to sleep till morning."

Sintsov also got into the bus, sat on the brand-new oilcloth seat, and felt it with his hands, as if in the last few days he had begun to doubt the existence of anything new and clean, leaned his head against the cold window-pane, and fell asleep.

In the morning, not yet fully awake, he couldn't at first understand where he was. He was riding in a bus. Some unfamiliar servicemen were asleep on the other seats near him. A green, warm, sunlit forest was flying past on either side. He thought he was travelling along a highroad. Only on recalling the events of the previous night did he realise that the bus was stationary on the flat and it was the train that was moving. The pointsman had not misinformed them: they were approaching Mogilev.

The military commandant at Mogilev took Sintsov's papers and read them through several times in succession with swollen, bloodshot eyes. He must have been very tired, because the first time he looked through them, he just stared at them and could make no sense of them at all; the second time, he could only distinguish separate words; and it was only the third time through that he began to grasp their meaning. He told Sintsov that the Political Directorate of the Front was about thirteen kilometres outside Mogilev.

"Go across that bridge you see through the window, turn left on to the Orsha road. Carry on for thirteen kilometres, and you'll see the Directorate in the forest...."

Sintsov was in luck. He managed to stop a pick-up on the bridge. There was a signals lieutenant sitting in the cab with the driver, and the back of the pick-up was piled high with grenades on which Sintsov made himself as comfortable as he could. The lieutenant took him as far as a dense forest, into the interior of which ran several newly-worn roads, and put him down on the outskirts.

Sintsov headed into the depths of the forest. The weather

had deteriorated and it was drizzling with rain. Dug-outs and slit trenches were being excavated everywhere on the slopes of the wooded hills, and four-barrel anti-aircraft machine-guns had been mounted in several places. The HQ and the Political Directorate of the Front had apparently just started digging in. Sintsov came across a divisional commissar standing in the roadway and talking to several political instructors. He was a gaunt figure in a yellow, rain-darkened leather coat. He had a good-natured, handsome face and straw coloured moustaches. He looked like Chapayev.*

Sintsov went to him. The commissar held Sintsov's leave-pass under the rain for several seconds. A drop of rain had made a lilac smudge of the Moscow office signature.

"I'm sorry to say I don't know where your newspaper office is just now," said the divisional commander, folding the pass in half. "I must admit I don't even know where the Political Department of your Third Army is either. Or, in fact, the whole...." He seemed about to say the whole Third Army, but refrained and merely smiled mirthlessly. "You'll have to serve here, with us...." And he handed Sintsov's papers not to Sintsov himself, but to a fat, red-faced battalion commissar nearby whose features seemed familiar.

"Here's a political instructor for you," he said. "Will Turmachev be away for long?"

The battalion commissar confirmed that he would and, asking permission to leave, took Sintsov away with him.

"So you're going to be with us," he said half an hour later to Sintsov, who was sitting beside him in a car hidden under some fir-trees.

They were both drinking tea in turns from a thermos on the floor of the car, and the battalion commissar had a handful of vanilla-flavoured biscuits in a newspaper on his lap.

"The wife packed them for me in Moscow," said the battalion commissar. "I told her not to be silly: 'What are you lumbering me with all that stuff for? I'm on army rations!' But I'm glad of them now...."

The biscuits were from Moscow, and so was the battalion commissar, the editor of a Front newspaper. The year previously, Sintsov had been sent to Moscow for a short course of journalism, and the battalion commissar had been a lecturer there. He was the first man Sintsov had met in the last five days whom he knew even slightly. Most important of all, there was at last no need to wander about, produce his

* Military hero of the Civil War.— *Ed.*

papers all the time, and listen to answers consisting of "I don't know" and "nobody knows". He had finally ended up in a unit, needn't look for anything else, could stay here, take orders, and do what he had set out to do when he went on active service.

Under the weight of all these accumulated feelings, Sintsov signed deeply.

"What's the matter with you?" inquired the battalion commissar.

"I'm sick of wandering about all over the place," said Sintsov.

"It's tough going all round," said the battalion commissar. "Turmachev was wounded by saboteurs yesterday. You didn't know him, did you?"

"No."

"He once worked on your *Military Banner*. He was driving a newspaper truck one night to the Political Directorate here. Someone signalled to him with a flashlamp to pull up. They wanted to check his documents. He produced them, and they shot him in the side with a revolver! And vanished. Who? Why? They got the paper out today," said the battalion commissar, apparently changing the subject, but still, in fact, telling Sintsov how tough things were. "But no one knows where to take it! The mail isn't coming through yet. In the meantime, we don't know which units are where. This morning I assigned all the men to lorries and sent them off by various routes to leave a slack of newspapers with every unit they happened to find. Very tough going," he concluded, and then he told Sintsov to go to Mogilev, look in at the printers, and help them get the edition out. "There's three of them there altogether—a secretary, a typist, and a head printer."

"Is there any copy?" asked Sintsov.

"Make do with what there is," said the battalion commissar. "I'll be there later. Anyway, what copy?" He shrugged his shoulders. "Maybe they'll bring some in by evening. They'll distribute the newspapers and bring in the copy. Why, have you got some yourself?" And he looked up at Sintsov.

But Sintsov merely glanced at him without saying anything. "What copy could I have?" he thought. "Oh, I've got some copy all right. I've seen more these last few days than in the whole of my life. But can they print all that along with the radio bulletin transcript that the editor's got on his knees under the biscuits? The bulletin tells of big battles on the frontier, and yet three days ago I couldn't get from

Borisov to Minsk. What am I to believe—the news bulletin, or what I saw with my own eyes? Or maybe they're both true: maybe there really are heavy but successful defensive battles in progress at the frontier, and I just happened to turn up in the sector of a German breakthrough and I've been frightened out of my wits and can't imagine that very different things have been happening elsewhere."

But even if both were true, the newspaper could not afford to reflect this. The radio bulletin printed on its pages claimed to be the truth, the whole truth, and nothing but the truth. That's how it was, and that's how it had to be.

"I haven't any copy," said Sintsov after a long silence, looking the editor straight in the eye. They understood one another.

It was already dark as Sintsov returned to Mogilev in the truck in which Turmachev, whom he had never met, had been wounded the night before. It was the same driver, too. Throughout the whole of the trip he kept talking about the incident, and every time they were stopped at a checkpoint, Sintsov, as he held out his papers in his left hand, kept his right hand firmly closed round the butt of the revolver which the editor had thoughtfully obtained for him in the Political Directorate.

Another issue of the Front newspaper was somehow or other set up and printed overnight in the old Mogilev printing works. Half of it was taken up with the Informburo's two latest bulletins, printed in large letters so as to fill as much space as possible. The rest of the copy was somehow collected towards midnight from the correspondents who had distributed yesterday's edition. It consisted entirely of brief reports of courage and heroism, and had been taken down verbatim from soldiers who had either been fighting a rearguard action for the last week or who had just broken out of encirclement. Initially under the pen of the correspondents, and then under the red pencil of Sintsov, who was interpolating notes to tally with the bulletins, these reports gradually lost everything that could have given some idea of where the fighting was currently in progress. Alongside bulletins which spoke of continued frontier battles, the reports even acquired a reassuring tone. Men were fighting, displaying courage, killing fascists.

Even from the terse accounts of the correspondents returning to the editorial office during the night, Sintsov established that what he had seen on the Minsk highway was not happening there alone. The Germans had broken through in many places. The situation, at least on the Western Front, was serious and uncertain, and it was not for a front-line newspaper to divulge it. He realised this and wielded his red pencil without hesitation. There was something else he couldn't understand. How had all this come about in the first place? It was beyond him, and he was tormented by the question: was it possible that, in spite of everything, we would not turn the position round in the next few days? Everything he had witnessed himself seemed to say: no, we would not! But inwardly he couldn't reconcile himself to this idea: his heart believed otherwise. And although he was right to believe his own eyes, the faith in his heart was stronger than all the visible evidence. He would never have survived those initial days without the faith with which he had been drawn almost unawares, like millions of other service personnel and civilians, into a war that was to last four years.

It was already nearly morning when, before letting the edition go to press, Sintsov dully read it through line by line, and only then did he spread out his greatcoat and lie down to sleep on the cold stone print-shop floor. The ancient little presses roared and strained, and the floor trembled perceptibly under his head. As he fell asleep, Sintsov thought about his daughter, and with helpless lucidity realised that, now that he was with another paper and on another sector of the front, it was completely beyond his power to get any news of her at all. At least, not until the situation had radically altered.

CHAPTER TWO

In the morning, four newspaper lorries drove out of the gates of the printing works. Each carried two correspondents and ten stacks of the newly printed edition. The method of distribution was to be the same as yesterday. The papers were to be taken by various routes, given out to anyone who happened to come along, and copy for the next edition was to be collected on the way.

Sintsov had slept on the print-shop floor for only three hours, and even then in two spells, because he was woken up by the arrival of the editor when it was nearly morning. He woke up in a complete stupor, tightened his belt, went out into the yard, sat in the cab of the lorry, and didn't really come to until they were driving out on to the Bobruisk highway. Aircraft were roaring in the sky, and there was a dog-fight raging over Mogilev. The Germans were dive-bombing the bridge over the Dnieper, and the seven or eight fighters covering them were tangling high in the sky with three snub-nosed Soviet fighters from Mogilev airfield.

Sintsov had heard that these fighters had acquitted themselves splendidly against their German, Italian and Japanese opponents in Spain and Mongolia. On this occasion, too, one Messerschmidt burst into flames and went down, and another headed out towards the horizon, leaving a trail of smoke. But immediately afterwards, two of our fighters began cartwheeling earthwards. Only the third and last remained airborne.

Sintsov stopped the lorry, got out, and stood for a minute or so, watching our fighter weaving in and out among the Germans. Then they all disappeared behind the clouds and the bombers continued roaring down on the bridge, which they seemed unable to hit.

"Well, shall we get going?" said Sintsov to his companion, a junior political instructor named Lyusin, who was sitting in the back on a bundle of newspapers.

This Lyusin was tall, active, ruddy-faced and handsome, with a bright lock of hair protruding from under his dashing, brand-new peaked cap. In his close-fitting uniform, with the well-tightened straps and the brand-new carbine he carried slung over his shoulder, he looked the most military of all the military men whom Sintsov had met during the last few days, and Sintsov was glad that he was lucky in his travelling companion.

"As you think fit, Comrade Political Instructor!" replied Lyusin, half rising and bringing his hand smartly up to the peak of his cap. During the night, when they had been getting the newspaper out together, Sintsov had already noticed Lyusin's eagerness, rare among military newspapermen, to follow army procedure to the letter.

"Perhaps I could sit in the back too," said Sintsov.

But Lyusin politely protested.

"I wouldn't advise that, Comrade Political Instructor! The senior in command is supposed to travel in the cab, otherwise it could be awkward. They might stop the lorry...." And he again applied his fingers to the peak of his dark blue cap.

Sintsov sat in the cab and the lorry moved off. The vehicle and its driver were the same as on yesterday's trip to Mogilev from Front HQ. He had, to tell the truth, wanted to move into the back, afraid that the driver would again start entertaining him with stories about saboteurs. But the driver sat frowning behind the wheel and never said a word. Either he hadn't had enough sleep or he didn't like this trip towards Bobruisk.

Sintsov, on the contrary, was in high spirits. The editor had told him during the night that our troops on the far side of the Berezina, on the approaches to Bobruisk, had given the Germans a trouncing the day before, and Sintsov was hoping to be there today.

Like many others who were not cowards by nature and who had lived through the first days of the war in the confusion and panic on the roads in the front-line zone, Sintsov was now particularly anxious to go on ahead to where the fighting was in progress.

True, the editor had not been able to explain precisely which units had trounced the Germans or exactly where this had happened, but Sintsov, in his inexperience, was not particularly worried. He had brought a map with him over which the editor had vaguely waved his finger round Bobruisk, and during the journey he sat studying it and estimating how much time it would take them to get there at their present rate of thirty kilometres an hour. He made it approximately three hours. Immediately after Mogilev, there had been fields and copses. The dense green was in many places criss-crossed by earthworks—some wide, some narrow. They were digging anti-tank ditches and trenches on either side of the road. Only occasionally could the army tunics of the engineers in charge of operations be glimpsed among the shirts and headscarves.

Then the lorry drove into a dense forest. And everything round them immediately became deserted and quiet. The lorry drove on and on through the forest, and they didn't meet a thing coming the other way—neither people nor vehicles. Sintsov wasn't seriously alarmed at first, but later he began to think it strange. The Front HQ was at Mogilev, the Germans had been engaged beyond Bobruisk, and he would have expected there to be headquarters and troops between these two points, which meant that there should be traffic on the road.

But here they were, halfway towards their destination, and then another ten kilometres, and yet another ten, and the road was as deserted as ever. At last, Sintsov's lorry nearly ran into a staff car travelling along the forest road. Sintsov opened the cab door and waved. The car stopped. There was an infantry captain at the wheel. He introduced himself as adjutant to the commanding officer of a rifle corps. Sintsov offered to go with him and distribute the newspapers among the corps units—all the stacks of newsprint were still lying untouched in the back of the lorry. But the adjutant hastily replied that he had been away from his corps, which had been transferred somewhere else in the meantime. He was now trying to trace it himself, so there would be no point in Sintsov travelling with him; it would be better to give him a few stacks of papers to take in the car and he would distribute them as soon as he found his corps. Lyusin got two stacks out of the lorry, the captain threw them on to the back seat, and the car accelerated and disappeared among the trees, while the lorry headed on towards Bobruisk.

Messerschmidts passed over several times. The forest came right up to the road, and the planes shot out from behind the tree-tops so fast that only once did Sintsov have time to jump out of the lorry. But the Germans didn't strafe them; evidently they had more important business in hand.

According to the map, it was just another ten kilometres to the Berezina. If there was fighting beyond Bobruisk, on the far side of the river, then on this side there should at least be rear units of some kind or second echelons. Sintsov kept turning his head to right and left, peering intently into the depths of the forest.

The baffling desertedness of the road began to get on his nerves.

Suddenly, the driver slammed on the brakes.

A Red Armyman was standing without a rifle but with two grenades in his belt on the side of the road at the point of intersection with a narrow lane that stretched far away towards the horizon.

Sintsov asked him what unit he belonged to and whether there was a commander in the vicinity.

The Red Armyman said that he had arrived from Mogilev in a lorry the day before with a detail of twenty men under the command of a lieutenant and had been left there on duty with orders to stop all individuals coming from the west and to direct them left along the lane to the forest lodge, where the lieutenant was forming a unit.

After turther questioning, it emerged that he had been standing there since the previous evening. They had been issued in Mogilev with one rifle to every two men: "Odd numbers—one pace forward—march!" There had been two of them standing there at first, but his partner had disappeared by morning. In the meantime, he had directed sixty individual soldiers to the lodge. He had evidently been forgotten. No one had relieved him, and he had not eaten since the day before.

Sintsov gave him half of the biscuits he had crammed into his kitbag and told the driver to carry on.

After another kilometre, the lorry was stopped by two militiamen in gray capes who jumped out of the trees.

"Comrade Commander," said one of them. "What are your orders?"

"What are my orders?" echoed Sintsov in astonishment. "You've got your own superiors!"

"No, we haven't," said the militiaman. "We were sent yesterday into the forest to catch parachutists if any jumped; but what parachutists could we expect to find now that the Germans are already across the Berezina?"

"Who told you that?"

"Soldiers. There goes the artillery now.... Can't you hear it, then?"

"It's not possible!" said Sintsov, although when he listened intently he thought he could hear the rumble of guns somewhere ahead. "Panic-mongering!" he said abruptly, trying to reassure himself, but in a tone of voice in which there was more stubbornness than conviction.

"Comrade Commander," said the militiaman, and his face was pale and thoroughly determined, "you're probably going to join your unit. Take us with you and sign us up as privates. What else can we do—wait until the fascists string us up on a tree? Or should we get rid of our uniforms?"

Sintsov said that he was indeed trying to find a unit, and if the militiamen wanted to come along, they could get into the back.

"Which way are you going?" asked the militiaman.

"That way." Sintsov pointed vaguely ahead. He no longer knew himself where he would be heading or for how long.

The militiaman who had been talking to Sintsov put his foot on one of the wheels. The other tugged at his cape from behind and whispered something. He evidently didn't want to go towards Bobruisk.

"—off, then!" snarled the first militiaman, contemptuously wrenched himself free, kicked his comrade in the chest, and scrambled into the back.

The lorry moved off. The second militiaman stood in bewilderment as it went past him and then, with a gesture of despair, ran after it, grabbed hold of the tailboard, and jumped clear over into the back. He was even more terrified of being left alone than of going further ahead.

Six enormous four-engined TB-3 night bombers flew over the forest with a slow, deep roar. They seemed to be crawling rather than flying across the sky. There was no fighter escort. Sintsov thought uneasily of the Messerschmidts that had just been snooping about over the road, and he felt sick with apprehension. But the bombers disappeared from sight unmolested, and in a few moments heavy bombs were heard exploding ahead.

According to a signpost that flashed by, it was only four more kilometres to the Berezina. Sintsov was now convinced that they would meet our own units at any moment, and that it was impossible that there should not be anyone else this side of the Berezina. Suddenly, several men dashed out of the woods, waving frantically. The driver glanced inquiringly at Sintsov, but the latter said nothing, and the lorry continued on its way. The men, who had meanwhile rushed on to the roadway, were shouting something with their hands cupped to their mouths.

"Stop!" ordered Sintsov.

A sergeant engineer ran up and breathlessly asked Sintsov where they were going.

"Bobruisk."

The sergeant wiped the streaming sweat from his face and, his Adam's apple bobbing up and down convulsively as he gulped down the saliva, said that the Germans had already crossed over to this side of the Berezina.

"What Germans?"

"Tanks...."

"Where?"

"About seven hundred metres from here. We've just been up against them!" The sergeant pointed ahead. "There was a detail of us moving up to lay a mine strip. They opened fire on us from a tank and killed ten men with one round. There's only..." he looked distractedly at the seven Red Armymen with him—"all told seven of us left.... Even if we'd had HE or grenades with us, what's the use of them against a tank?" The sergeant banged his rifle butt down on the ground in frustration.

Sintsov was still hesitating, unable to believe that the Germans were really so near; but the lorry's engine stalled, and they immediately heard the sound of intensive machine-gun fire to the left of the road, quite close, and unmistakeably this side of the Berezina.

"Comrade Political Instructor!" It was the first word from Lyusin throughout the whole journey. "Request permission to make a suggestion. Perhaps we could turn back until the situation's clarified?"

The expression on his usually ruddy but now pale face betrayed fear — which, however, did not stop him addressing Sintsov strictly according to form.

"Let's turn round," said Sintsov, also going white in the face.

It hadn't so far occurred to him that another half kilometre or so and they could fall straight into the Germans' hands. The driver turned the lorry round with a snarling of gears and Sintsov glimpsed the distracted faces of the soldiers he had left standing on the road.

"Stop!" roared Sintsov, ashamed of his own weakness, and he gripped the driver's shoulder with such force that the latter cried out with pain.

"Get in the back!" shouted Sintsov to the Red Armymen, leaning out of the cab as the driver willingly pulled up. "Come along with me!"

In spite of a year and a half of service with a military newspaper, it was the first time in his life that he had given orders by right as a man who had more pips on his tabs than any of the others. The Red Armymen jumped into the back one after the other, only the last one getting into difficulties. As his comrades heaved him bodily over, Sintsov realised that he was wounded: one foot was unshod and his trouser-leg was covered in blood.

Sintsov jumped down from the cab and gave instructions for the wounded man to be put in his own place instead. Realising that his orders were being obeyed, he continued giving them. The wounded Red Armyman was transferred to the cab and Sintsov climbed into the back. The driver, spurred on by the machine-gun fire, which was now growing louder to the left and right of the road, drove hard back towards Mogilev.

"Planes!" shouted one of the Red Armymen in fright.

"Ours," said another.

Sintsov looked up. The three bombers were returning directly over the road at a comparatively low altitude. The bombing that Sintsov had heard must have been their work. They were now returning unscathed and were slowly gaining height; but the keen premonition of disaster which had overwhelmed Sintsov when he had seen them on the way over, was still with him.

And, indeed, a tiny Messerschmidt dived down as fast as a hornet from behind the scattered clouds, gaining on the bombers with terrifying speed.

All the men in the lorry silently clutched the sides of the vehicle and, forgetting themselves, their recent fright, and everything else, stared up into the sky in horrified suspense. The Messerschmidt cut across the tail of the rear bomber, which had fallen behind the other two, and the TB-3 went up in smoke like a piece of paper kindled in a stove. For several seconds it continued on its way, losing height and belching more and more smoke; then it stalled and, leaving a black trail in its wake, fell into the forest.

The Messerschmidt flashed in the sun like a fine splinter of steel, soared upwards, wheeled round and, with a whine, came in on the tail of the next bomber. There was a brief crackle of machine-gun fire. The Messerschmidt soared up again, and the second bomber trailed over the forest for another half minute, rolled steadily over on one wing, turned upside down, and crashed into the forest after the first one.

The Messerschmidt screamed up and over in a loop, then came slantwise down on the tail of the third and last of the bombers. And the same thing happened all over again. A scarcely audible crackle of machine guns in the distance, the thin scream of the Messerschmidt pulling out of its dive, the long black plume spreading over the forest, and the distant rumble of an explosion.

"There's another three!" shouted the sergeant in horror, before he had recovered from what he had just seen.

He was standing up in the back of the lorry and waving his arms crazily, as if trying to save from disaster a second trio of bombers which had just appeared over the forest on the way back from their mission.

Numb with horror, Sintsov looked upwards, both hands gripping his belt. One of the militiamen was sitting next to him, his hands clasped as if in prayer and his fingers so tightly interlocked that they had gone white; he was willing the pilots to see that terrible steel hornet weaving about in the sky.

The same prayer was on everyone's lips, but the pilots either didn't notice, or noticed but could do nothing about it. The Messerschmidt came to meet the bombers, then zoomed up into the clouds and vanished. Sintsov had a fleeting hope that the German had run out of ammunition.

"Look, another one!" said a militiaman, grabbing Sintsov's arm and shaking it with all his might. "Look, another one!"

And Sintsov watched as two Messerschmidts this time dived out of the clouds and together, almost side by side, overtook the slow-flying trio with incredible speed and shot past the rear bomber. The TB-3 began to give off a trail of smoke, and the fighters, soaring gaily aloft as if overjoyed at having met one another, crossed paths in the air, changed places, and again flew over the bombers with a dry rattle of machine-gun fire. The bomber burst into flames from nose to tail and went down, disintegrating while still in mid-air.

The fighters went after the others. The two heavy aircraft were struggling to gain height, still trailing doggedly over the forest and leaving behind them the lorry-load of men, all silently huddled together in common misery.

What were they thinking now, what could they hope for, those fliers in the two slow-moving night bombers? What else could they do but trail on and on over the forest at that desperately slow speed, with only one hope—that the enemy might suddenly overreach himself, miscalculate, and come under the fire of the rear gunners?

"Why don't they bale out?" wondered Sintsov. Then the thought flashed through his mind: "Or haven't they got any parachutes?"

The rattle of machine guns was heard this time before the Messerschmidts were within range of the bomber, which was trying to beat them off. And then, suddenly, one of the Messerschmidts came up level with the bomber, almost grazing it, and without pulling out of its dive, vanished behind the wall of trees. It all happened so suddenly that the men on the lorry didn't at first realise that the German had been shot down. Then it dawned on them, and they yelled with joy, but stopped short; the second Messerschmidt had made another pass over the bomber and had set it on fire. This time, as if in answer to Sintsov's thoughts, several bundles tumbled out of the bomber. One fell like a stone; but parachutes blossomed out over the other four.

His partner lost, the German began circling round the parachutists, his machine guns sputtering vindictively. He was shooting the bomber crew up as they descended—the men on the lorry could hear his short bursts of fire. The German was saving ammunition, and the parachutists were coming down over the forest so slowly, that if the men on the lorry had been in a state to glance at one another, they would have seen their hands all making the same gesture: down, down, come down!

The Messerschmidt, still circling round the parachutists, saw them down as far as the forest, flew low over the tree-tops, as if on the look-out for something beneath, and then vanished.

The sixth and last bomber melted away on the horizon. The sky was empty, as if those enormous, slow, helpless aircraft had never been. No aircraft, no men sitting in them, no machine guns stuttering, no Messerschmidts—nothing; just a totally empty sky and a few black columns of smoke beginning to mushroom outwards here and there over the forest.

Sintsov stood in the back of the lorry as it raced along the road and wept with fury, licking the salty tears as they trickled on to his lips and unaware that all the others were weeping with him.

"Stop, stop!" The first to pull himself together, he started banging the roof of the cab with his fist.

"What is it?" demanded the driver, sticking his head out.

"We've got to look for them!" said Sintsov. "We've got to look for them! They could still be alive, those chaps that baled out...."

"If we're going to look for them, we'll have to drive on a bit, Comrade Commander; they drifted further on," said one of the militiamen, his face swollen with weeping, like that of a child.

They drove on for another kilometre, stopped, and got out of the lorry. All of them remembered about the Germans having crossed the Berezina, and yet they forgot them too. When Sintsov ordered them to break up and start searching for the airmen on both sides of the road, no one tried to argue.

Sintsov, the two militiamen, and the sergeant spent some considerable time scouring the woods to the right of the roadway and shouting and calling, but they were unable to find either parachutes or aircrew. Yet the men had come down somewhere here in the forest, and they must be found at all costs, otherwise they would fall into German hands. Only after two hours of stubborn and fruitless searching did Sintsov come out on to the road again.

Lyusin and the rest were already standing by the lorry. Lyusin's face was scratched, his tunic torn, and his pockets stuffed so full that one of the buttons had come off. He was holding a pistol.

"Both shot stone dead," said Lyusin dismally, and he wiped his hand across his scratched face.

"What happened to you?"

"I climbed a pine-tree. One poor devil was hanging upside down from the top, dead. He was hit on the way down, straight in the chest...."

"And the other?"

"The other one too."

"The nazis are playing cat-and-mouse with us!" said one of the Red Armymen with hatred in his voice.

"I got their documents," said Lyusin, reaching for the pocket with the missing button. "D'you want them?"

"Hang on to them."

"At least take the pistol, then." Lyusin held out the little Browning to Sintsov.

Sintsov glanced at the gun and thrust it into his pocket.

"Didn't you find any, Comrade Political Instructor?" asked Lyusin.

"No," said Sintsov.

"I've got a feeling that the ones who came down on the right drifted further on," said Lyusin. "We should drive on another four hundred metres or so, get out, and comb the forest in line abreast."

But they didn't have to search the woods after all. When the lorry pulled up after doing another four hundred metres, a small, stockily-built pilot in a tunic, with his flying helmet pushed down and almost covering his eyes, came towards them out of the trees. Bent almost double under the weight of his burden, he was carrying a second flier in overalls. The wounded man's arms were round his comrade's neck and his feet were trailing along the ground.

"Take him," said the pilot curtly.

Lyusin and the Red Armymen jumped down, took the wounded man from his shoulders, and put him down on the grass at the roadside. He had been shot in both legs. He lay on the grass, breathing heavily and alternately opening and shutting his eyes. While Lyusin expertly slit open his overalls and boots with a penknife, and bound up the wounded man with an emergency dressing, the little, stockily-built pilot took off his helmet, wiped off the sweat streaming down his face, and flexed his shoulders to ease the numbness left by the burden.

"Did you see it?" he asked gloomily at last, after he had finished wiping off the sweat and had pulled on his helmet again so far down, that it was as if he didn't want to look at anyone and didn't want anyone to see his eyes.

"Right overhead..." said Sintsov.

"You saw them making target practice of our fliers..." began the airman. His voice was trembling with bitterness, but he controlled himself and, without saying anything further, pulled his helmet even lower down over his eyes.

Sintsov was silent. He couldn't think of anything to say.

"Anyway, we bombed the crossing, destroyed the bridge and the tanks on it, and carried out our mission," said the pilot. "But if only we'd just had one fighter for cover!"

"We found your two comrades, but they're dead," said Sintsov.

"We're not alive any more either," said the pilot. "Did you get their weapons and documents?" he added in the changed tone of a man who had decided to take himself in hand and was fully capable of doing so.

"We did," said Sintsov.

"The best blind-flying and night navigator in the regiment," said the pilot, turning to the wounded man who was being bound up by Lyusin. "My navigator! We were the best aircrew in the regiment, and they went and threw us to the dogs!" he shouted, his voice again choked by a sob; and then, just as suddenly as before, he pulled himself together and asked in a matter-of-fact voice: "Shall we go, then?"

The wounded navigator was put in the back up against the cab where he would be jolted less, and his legs were propped up with bundles of newspapers. The pilot sat with his navigator. Then all the rest took their places. The lorry moved off, and almost immediately braked sharply.

It was at the crossroads where Sintsov had recently shared his biscuits with the sentry. The Red Armyman, still standing there, had seen the lorry coming back and had jumped into the middle of the road, brandishing the grenade as if intending to throw it under the lorry.

"Comrade Political Instructor," he asked in a voice that made Sintsov's blood run cold, "Comrade Political Instructor, what is this? I haven't been relieved for forty-eight hours.... Aren't I going to get further orders?"

If he firmly replied that there would be no further orders and that he would surely be relieved, Sintsov knew the man would stay at his post. But who could swear that they really would come and relieve him?

"I am relieving you of your post," said Sintsov, trying to remember the formula used by a senior in rank under such circumstances, but which had, as luck would have it, had slipped clean out of his mind. "I am relieving you of your post. You can make your report later!" he repeated, unable to remember any more and fearing that if his order was incorrectly phrased, the Red Armyman might disobey him, stay at his post, and be killed. "Get in and come with me!"

The Red Armyman sighed with relief, clipped his grenade on to his belt, and climbed into the back of the lorry.

No sooner had the lorry moved off than three more TB-3s appeared in the sky on their way to Bobruisk. This time they had one fighter for escort. It kept soaring high into the sky, then coming down and hurtling over them, in order to match its speed to that of the bombers, which were only half as fast.

"At least those three have got cover," said the pilot of the shot-down bomber to Sintsov, and the feeling of relief in his voice was quite detached from his own personal predicament. But before Sintsov could answer, two Messerschmidts dived down out of the clouds and headed straight for the bombers. Our fighter turned round to meet them, soared directly up at them, rolled over on one wing and, skimming past one of the Messerschmidts, set it on fire.

"He's got him, he's got him!" shouted the pilot.

The people sitting in the lorry were gripped by a vengeful joy. Even the driver, one hand still on the steering wheel, got right out of his cab. The Messerschmidt was coming down in flames. The pilot baled out, and his parachute opened high in the sky.

"Now he'll get the other one," shouted the pilot. "Just you see!" Without realising it, he was shaking Sintsov all the time by the arm.

The Russian fighter went into a steep climb, but the second German suddenly appeared above him. Again there was the stutter of machine guns. The Messerschmidt shot upwards, but our fighter went into a dive, leaving a trail of smoke behind him. A small black bundle detached itself and, almost too quickly for the eye to follow, began to fall down and down, and it was only just over tops of the pine-trees, when all seemed lost, that the parachute finally opened. The Messerschmidt calmly turned round and headed towards Bobruisk in pursuit of the bombers.

Tears streaming down his cheeks, the pilot had jumped to his feet in the back of the lorry, swearing horribly and brandishing his arms. Sintsov had already seen this five times and turned away in order not to see any more. He heard the stutter of machine guns again in the distance, and the pilot despairingly say "done for" through his clenched teeth, then cover his face with his hands and throw himself down on the floor-boards.

Sintsov had the lorry stopped. The German parachute was still swaying high overhead. Our pilot had already landed and it looked as though he wasn't far away—about two kilometres towards Bobruisk.

"Go into the woods and get that nazi!" said Sintsov to Lyusin. "Take the men with you."

"D'you want him brought back alive?" said Lyusin in a matter-of-fact tone of voice.

"See what happens."

Sintsov didn't care whether the German was taken dead or alive. All he wanted was for him not to meet the other Germans when they arrived.

Both wounded men—the navigator and the Red Armyman sitting in the cab—were lifted out of the lorry, put down under a tree, and left in charge of the Red Armyman with the grenades whom Sintsov had relieved of duty. "Whatever happens, he won't abandon the wounded," thought Sintsov.

Lyusin, the sergeant, and the rest of the Red Armymen went into the woods after the German. Sintsov took the pilot and the two militiamen and headed back in the lorry.

Once again they drove towards Bobruisk, keeping a sharp look-out on both sides and hoping to spot the parachute from the lorry. They believed it had come down quite near the road.

Meanwhile, the pilot they were looking for was, in fact, lying a hundred paces away from the road in a small forest glade. Not wanting to be shot up in mid-air by the Germans, he had coolly delayed pulling the ripcord, but had miscalculated the timing and acted a second too late. The parachute had opened almost at ground level, and the pilot had broken both legs and hit his spine on a tree-stump. He was now lying near that stump, knowing that it was all up with him. His body below the belt was numb and paralysed, and he could not even crawl. He lay on his side, staring upwards and coughing blood. The Messerschmidt that had shot him down had gone off in pursuit of the second flight of defenceless bombers, and one trail of smoke was already visible in the sky.

The man lying on the ground had never been particularly afraid of death. During his short life he had often thought without a qualm how he might one day be shot down or roasted alive, just as he had shot down others and roasted them alive. However, in spite of the innate fearlessness that was the envy of his comrades, he was now almost frantic with terror.

His mission had been to give cover to the bombers, but one of them had burst into flames before his eyes, the other two had headed off towards the horizon, and there was no way in which he could help them any more. He believed that he was lying on territory occupied by the Germans, and he imagined bitterly how the nazis would stand and gloat over him lying dead at their feet—he who had been featured in the newspapers dozens of time ever since Spain in '37! He had been proud of it to this day, and had even boasted of it from time to time. But now he would be glad if nothing had ever been written about him and if, when they arrived, the Germans found the body of a senior lieutenant unknown to them who had shot down his first Fokker over Madrid four years ago, and not the body of Lieutenant-General Kozyrev. He realised with rage and despair that he couldn't pull off his tunic with its general's insignia and the Hero's Star, and even if he could muster the strength to tear up his documents, the Germans would still recognise him and describe at length how they had made short work of Kozyrev, one of the Soviet Union's leading air aces.

For the first time in his life, he cursed the day and the hour, of which he had always been so proud, when Stalin himself had sent for him after Khalkhin-Gol, had promoted him straight from colonel to lieutenant-general, and had appointed him commander of the fighter planes for a whole military district.

Now, face to face with death, he had no one to lie to. He had been incapable of commanding anyone, apart from himself and his squadron, and he had become nominally a general while still actually remaining a senior lieutenant. This had been proved from the very first day of the war in the most appalling fashion, and not only in his own case. Lightning promotions like his had been the reward for irreproachable bravery and medals won at bloody cost; but, however it may have been with the others, he hadn't possessed—and his general's stars had not brought with them—the ability to command thousands of men and hundreds of aircraft.

Half-dead, shattered in body, lying on the ground and too weak to move, he became aware, for the first time in the last few hectic years, of the full tragedy of what had happened to him and the full extent of his involuntary guilt as a man who had rapidly climbed the difficult ladder of army promotion without once looking back. He recalled how casual he had been about a war which could break out at any moment, and what a bad commander he had been when it had finally started. He recalled his airfields, where half the aircraft had been unserviceable. He remembered his planes burnt out on the ground, and his pilots desperately taking off under the bombs and being killed before they could gain height. He recollected his own contradictory orders which, crushed and stunned, he had given during those first days, tearing about in a fighter plane, risking his life every hour, and yet managing to save virtually nothing.

He remembered today's tragic R/T call from one of the TB-3s which had gone to bomb the river crossing and which had been shot down in flames, and which it had been wrong and criminal to send out in the daytime without fighter support, but which had nevertheless volunteered and had taken off because the crossing had to be bombed at all costs and there were no more fighters left to give cover.

He had landed at Mogilev airfield after shooting down a Messerschmidt on the way, and he had heard in his earphones the familiar voice of Major Ishchenko, an old comrade from way back in the days of the Yelets Flying School: "Mission accomplished. Returning to base. Four of us shot down in flames. They're just about to get me! We die for the motherland! Goodbye! Give our thanks to Kozyrev for covering us so well!" He had clutched his head in his hands and had sat there for a whole minute without moving, fighting the impulse to draw his pistol and shoot himself there and then in the operations duty officer's room. Then he had asked if any more TB-3s were going on a bombing raid. He had been told that the bridge had been destroyed, but there had been an order to destroy the jetty and the floating equipment as well; there wasn't a single squadron of day bombers available, and so yet another trio of TB-3s was already airborne.

Without saying a word to anyone, he had dashed out of the duty room, boarded a fighter, and taken off. When he had dived out of the clouds and seen the bombers flying along beneath him unscathed, it had been one of his few happy moments in the last few days. A moment later, he had been engaged in battle with the Messerschmidts, and it had ended with him being shot down anyway.

Since the very first day of the war, when nearly all the new MIG fighters recently delivered to the military district had been destroyed by fire on their own airfields, he had taken his place in an old I-16, proving by personal example that one could fight Messerschmidts even in them. It could be done, but it was difficult, especially owing to the slower speed of the I-16s.

He knew that he would not surrender, and only hesitated about when to shoot himself: whether to try and kill some of the Germans first if they approached, or shoot himself now to avoid losing consciousness and coming round to find himself a prisoner.

He was in no way terrified at the thought of his impending death; he was merely saddened at the thought that he would never know how everything was going to turn out in the future. Yes, the war had caught them napping. Yes, they hadn't had time to re-arm. Yes, he and many others had lost their heads and given the wrong orders. But that the Germans would go on beating them as they had been doing in the first days—this terrible thought outraged his whole being as a soldier and his faith in his army, in his comrades and, finally, in himself, though he had added another two nazis to the twenty-nine he had shot down in Spain and Mongolia. If he hadn't been shot down today, he would have shown them a thing or two! And they had it coming to them! This passionate faith lived on in his shattered body, but with it, like an inseparable shadow, hovered the black thought: "But I shall never live to see it." If the priests weren't lying about a life beyond the grave, he would see the victory from there; but whether from heaven or hell—what did that matter?

His wife, who, as is typical of the petty-minded, exaggerated her importance in his life, would never have believed that he wouldn't think of her or remember her in the hour of his death. But he had forgotten her, and not because he didn't love her—he was still in love with her—but simply because his mind was on other things: the bitterness of defeat, the joy of victory, and the thought that, having drained the one cup dry, he would never be able to set his lips to another. And this was so great a grief that it left no room for the other grief, small and unfrightening at that moment, that he would never again set eyes on her beautiful and deceitful face.

They say that a man remembers his whole life just before death. It may be so; but all he remembered before his own death was the war. They say that a man thinks of many things all at once just before he dies. It may be so; but before his own death he could only think of one thing—the war. And when suddenly, half-conscious, he heard voices and saw with bloodshot eyes three figures coming towards him, at this moment, too, he remembered nothing but the war; and he thought of nothing except that the fascists were coming and he must fire at them first and then shoot himself. The pistol was lying on the grass near his hand. He fumbled for the butt and crooked his index finger round the trigger. He raised his hand with an effort and then, squeezing the trigger several times in succession, shot at the grey figures that loomed up in front of him as if floating in a blood-red mist. He counted five shots and, afraid of using up the last, put the revolver to his head and shot himself in the temple.

The two militiamen and Sintsov stopped over his body. Before them, covered in blood, lay a man in a flying helmet and with a general's stars on his pale-blue collar-tabs. It had all happened so suddenly that they hadn't had the time to collect themselves. They had emerged from the dense undergrowth into a glade, had seen the pilot lying on the grass, had shouted and started running, and he had begun shooting at them without paying any attention to their shouts of "Friends!" Then, when they had almost reached him, he had put the revolver to his temple, twitched, and lain still.

The elder of the two militiamen went down on his knees, unbuttoned the tunic pocket, and took out the dead man's papers. Shaken, Sintsov stood over him in silence, pressing his hand to the flesh wound in his side — just stood there, not yet conscious of any pain, but only of a numbness and of the blood seeping through his tunic. Three days ago, he had shot a man he had been trying to save, and now another man, whom he had also wanted to save, had nearly killed him, had then shot himself, and was lying at his feet just like the mad Red Armyman on the road. Had he perhaps taken them for Germans because of the grey waterproof police capes? But surely he had heard them shouting "Friends! Friends!"?

With his hand still pressed to his blood-soaked side, Sintsov kneeled down and took everything that the militiaman had removed from the dead man's breast pocket. On top lay a snapshot of a beautiful woman with a round face and a full, smiling mouth. Sintsov was convinced he had seen the woman somewhere before, but couldn't remember when or where. Under the photograph lay documents, a Party card, a military awards book, and identification papers made out in the name of Lieutenant-General Kozyrev.

"Kozyrev, Kozyrev..." repeated Sintsov, still trying to pick up the lost thread. Then he suddenly remembered — not just the woman he had known since his schooldays as Nadya, but the bloody face of the pilot whom he knew from the newspapers.

Sintsov was still kneeling before Kozyrev's body when the bomber pilot and the driver came running up, attracted by the sound of shooting. The pilot recognised Kozyrev instantly. He sat down on the grass next to Sintsov, silently looked over and just as silently returned the documents and, more astonished than shattered, made only one single comment:

"Yes, that's the way it goes...." Then he looked at Sintsov, who was still kneeling on the ground, his hand pressed to his soaking tunic. "What's the matter with you?"

"He got me.... Probably thought we were Germans," said Sintsov with a nod towards the dead man.

"Take off your tunic and I'll bandage you up," said the pilot.

But Sintsov, recovering from his shock and remembering the Germans, said that he could be bandaged later on, in the lorry, but they must now take the general's body to it. The two militiamen clumsily thrust their hands under Kozyrev's body, half lifted him up by the shoulders, the pilot and the driver took hold of him under the knees, and Sintsov brought up in the rear of the procession, stumbling, his hand still pressed to his wounded side, and conscious of increasing pain.

"You'll have to be bandaged up," repeated the pilot after Kozyrev had been laid in the back of the lorry and the lorry had moved off.

He hurriedly drew off his own tunic, then his undervest, and, ignoring Sintsov's protestations, gripped the bottom hem with his short, stubby fingers and tore it up into several strips.

"The bullet went through and out again. It'll heal," said the pilot in a knowledgeable tone of voice, pulling up Sintsov's tunic and bandaging him with the strips of torn linen. "You'll get there alive. Let me pull your tunic down again." He tugged at Sintsov's tunic and belted it up again tightly below the wound. Sintsov groaned, but bit his tongue.

"The devil alone knows why he shot you..." said the pilot apologetically, glancing at Sintsov, then at Kozyrev, and then back at Sintsov again.

A few minutes later, they arrived at the spot where they had left the wounded.

The navigator had lost consciousness, and the Red Armyman with the leg wound was lying on his back, breathing spasmodically. The soldier with the grenades was sitting beside them.

"Where are the others?" demanded Sintsov.

"They went that way," answered the Red Armyman, pointing towards Mogilev. "The wind carried the parachute quite a way. They've probably caught him. I heard shots."

They took on the two wounded and the Red Armyman, and went on.

The pilot insisted that Sintsov should sit in the cab this time.

"You look ghastly!" he said with concern. Sintsov did as he was told.

The artillery boomed louder in their rear from time to time, and occasional gusts of wind brought the sound of machine-gun fire. After two kilometres, they stopped. There was still no sign of Lyusin or the Red Armymen.

Sintsov fought down the impulse to drive on just a little further, listened again to the sound of firing as it wafted up from behind, and said that they would have to wait where they were until those of their comrades who had gone to look for the German came out of the forest.

They could still hear firing behind them. Sintsov felt inquiring looks being turned his way, but since he had decided to wait fifteen minutes more, he just sat and waited. It is at moments like this that the commander is born in a man, and this is what was happening to Sintsov, although it was the last thing on his mind.

"Just give them one more shout," he said, when the minute hand had reached the appointed division.

The older of the two militiamen, who had cupped his hands to his mouth goodness knows how many times already, hailed the forest in a ringing voice; but the forest was silent as ever.

"Let's go on a bit further," said Sintsov.

But they didn't get far. After only half a kilometre, a lieutenant in tank corps uniform came out on to the road and signalled them to stop. He had an ugly look on his face and a German sub-machine gun slung across his chest. Behind him, two more tank crewmen got up out of the roadside ditch with rifles at the ready.

"Stop! Who are you?" The lieutenant wrenched open the cab door.

Sintsov replied that he was from the editorial office of a Front newspaper and was at present looking for his men, who had gone to bring in a German pilot.

"And who are these men? How many of them?"

Sintsov told him that there were seven: a junior political instructor, a sergeant, and five privates. And for some reason, though he couldn't think why, he began to feel guilty.

"We've only just this moment picked them up, and they've been telling us how you helped them to desert!" sneered the lieutenant. "Now then, get this lorry off the road and we'll go to our captain. Then we'll sort out who's ours, who's yours, and who you are!"

These words infuriated Sintsov, but his growing sense of unacknowledged guilt prevented him from flaring up. Instead of him, it was the pilot who blew up, leaning over the side of the lorry.

"Hey!" he roared at the lieutenant. "Come here, you! I'm a major and that's an order! Come and take a look at this!"

The lieutenant said nothing. Almost quivering with fury, he went up to the side of the lorry and looked in. If what he saw there didn't entirely convince him, at least it mollified him.

"Carry on for a hundred metres and you'll see a side-road into the forest. Turn off there!" he said to Sintsov glumly, as if emphasising that he was acting within his rights. "I'm under orders not to let anyone through.... Portnyagin!' he called one of his tankmen. "Stand on the footboard, see them to the captain! Hold it!" He stopped the lorry again just as it moved off. "You men get out! You can stay here!"

Both militiamen and the Red Armyman with the grenades jumped down. The tone of the order brooked no shilly-shallying.

"Get going!" the lieutenant waved, not so much to Sintsov, as to the tankman standing on the footboard.

As the lorry turned off into the forest, its weight snapping the branches which had been piled in the ditch, Sintsov noticed two 37-mm guns hidden in the undergrowth with their muzzles trained on the road. Near the guns, two soldiers were sitting with their legs apart, a pile of grenades and a roll of telephone cable beside them. They were tying the grenades up in clusters.

Weaving in and out among the trees, the lorry emerged into a small glade full of soldiers. There was a lorry with ammunition boxes and a pile of rifles in the back. Next to it stood an armoured car camouflaged with sprays of fir.

A sergeant-major of the tanks was drilling about forty Red Armymen with rifles, making them fall in, march at the double, and about turn. Among them Sintsov glimpsed the familiar faces of the soldiers who had ridden with him in the lorry.

Near the armoured car, his elbows resting on a field telephone box, sat a helmeted captain of the tanks corps, monotonously repeating into the mouthpiece:

"Yes. Yes. Yes...."

There was another tankman, also helmeted, sitting beside him. Behind the two of them, shifting from one foot to the other, stood Lyusin.

"When *are* they going to bring up communications, I'd like to know?" demanded the captain, putting down the handset and rising to his feet.

He had been perfectly well aware of the lorry driving up and of Sintsov and the pilot getting out; but he asked the question as if he hadn't seen anyone at all, and only then did he fix his attention on the new arrivals.

"I'm the rear assistant to the commander of the Seventeenth Tank Brigade, who are you?" he demanded abruptly, all in one breath.

Although he had introduced himself as rear assistant, there was nothing of the rear about his appearance. The dirty, torn overalls on his well-built frame were burnt through on one side, his left hand was swathed to the fingers in a blood-caked bandage, he was carrying a German submachine identical to the lieutenant's slung across his chest, he hadn't shaved for some time, his face was black with fatigue, and his eyes were blazing with hostility.

"I...." The pilot was the first to begin, but it was only too obvious from his appearance who he was.

"No problems with you, Comrade Major," said the captain, interrupting him with a gesture. "From the shot-down bomber?"

The pilot nodded gloomily.

"But you there, produce your documents!" said the Captain, stepping towards Sintsov.

"I was just telling you..." began Lyusin, who was standing behind the captain.

"You shut up!" flung the captain over his shoulder, without turning round. "Speak when you're spoken to! Your documents!" he repeated even more rudely to Sintsov.

"You show me your documents first!" shouted Sintsov, flaring up at the captain's blatant hostility.

"I am in command of my own unit and am under no obligation to produce my documents for anyone," said the captain with unexpected gentleness in contrast to Sintsov.

Sintsov pulled out his identity papers and leave pass, only at this point remembering that he hadn't had time to obtain new documents at the editorial offices. Feeling unsure of himself, he began explaining the circumstances, but this only added to his uncertainty.

"Hm!" said the captain, handing Sintsov back his papers. "These don't make much sense! But supposing it's all as you say. What d'you mean by dragging people with you back into rear from the front line, and who gave you the right to do so?"

Ever since the lieutenant had said something of the sort to him on the road, Sintsov had been bursting to explain as soon as possible that the whole thing was a misunderstanding. He began telling how the soldiers had rushed out on to the road to meet the lorry, how he had taken them along with him to save them, and how he had then picked up another Red Armyman.

But he found to his astonishment that the captain did not see it as a misunderstanding in the least. On the contrary, he regarded it as deliberate.

"Fear has big eyes! Ten men knocked out by a tank shell—and in the woods, too? Rubbish! They fell down in fright, and instead of getting his men together, the senior in command abandoned half of them and did a bunk down the road. And you swallowed it! You'll collect a whole Army to go into the rear if you carry on like that—some are scared, and the others are looking for their units behind the lines.... They should be looking for their unit in front where the enemy is!" The captain swore and said more calmly, waving towards the sergeant-major drilling the soldiers: "That'll get them into shape again. Then we'll take them into action! But to take every panic-monger into Mogilev—as if there weren't enough of them there already! Here's where we need the men. The brigade commander has ordered me to scratch together three hundred reinforcements out of the troops wandering about in the woods, and get them together. I will, you can rest assured of that! I'm taking your junior political instructor—and you too!" he added on an unexpectedly challenging note.

"He's been hit in the side," said the pilot gloomily as always, with a nod at Sintsov. "He should get to hospital as soon as possible."

"Wounded?" echoed the captain, and it was clear from the distrust in his eyes that he had half a mind to make Sintsov undress and show the wound.

"He doesn't believe it," thought Sintsov, and he froze at the insult.

But the captain had now noticed the dark stain on Sintsov's tunic.

"Report to your political instructor," he said, turning to Lyusin, "and explain why you refuse to stay here and go into action. Or have you been wounded and hiding it from me too?"

"I'm not wounded!" yelled Lyusin in an unexpectedly shrill voice, his handsome face contorted in a snarl. "I'm not refusing anything! I'm ready for anything! But my editor ordered me to come out and then report back again, and I can't take things into my own hands without orders from my senior commander!"

"Well, what orders are you going to give him?" asked the captain of Sintsov. "The situation's serious. I haven't got a single political worker for the whole of the group. We only got out of encirclement yesterday, and today they jumped on me to plug someone else's gap. While I'm mustering a force here, the brigade's fighting it out to the last man over there on the Berezina!"

"Well, of course, you should stay, Comrade Lyusin, if you don't mind," said Sintsov simply. "I would too, if I...." He raised his eyes and looked at Lyusin, and only when he intercepted the latter's glare did he realise that Lyusin didn't want to stay behind at all and had been waiting for Sintsov to say something quite different.

"Well, that's that," said the captain. He turned grimly and looked Lyusin straight in the face. "Go to the sergeant-major and take command of the group with him."

"You can just report to my editor how you took the law into your own hands," shouted Lyusin in a thin voice straight in Sintsov's face, but he didn't get the chance to finish, because the captain forcefully spun him round with his bandaged hand and gave him a shove.

"He'll report, don't worry! Go and carry out your orders. Any disobedience, and it'll cost you your life."

Lyusin went off, his broad shoulders slumped, no longer the elegant and dashing soldier he had seemed that morning. Sintsov, feeling uncontrollably weak, lowered himself to the ground.

The captain watched Sintsov in astonishment, then remembered that the political instructor was wounded. He was about to say something, when the telephone emitted a faint peep. He snatched up the handset.

"Yes, Comrade Lieutenant-Colonel! I've sent one group along the old route. I've just formed the second. Where to?

I'll make a note of that now." He pulled out of the breast pocket of his overalls a map folded into four, looked for a point on it, and dented it with his thumbnail. "That's right, they've been set up behind cover." Sintsov realised that he was talking about the guns near the road. "And we've strung some grenades together in case. We won't let them through!"

The captain stopped speaking for a whole minute, listening to something with a happy expression on his face.

"Understood, Comrade Lieutenant-Colonel," he said at last. "Fully understood. But here we've just...." He wanted to say something, but was evidently interrupted at the other end. "All right, I'll finish!" he said in embarrassment. "I haven't any more to say either."

He put the handset down on the box, stood up, and looked at the pilot as if he was in a position to say something cheering to this man whose plane had just been shot down in flames and who had seen all his comrades shot down. And, indeed, he told the pilot the only thing that could cheer him up in the circumstances.

"The lieutenant-colonel says they're hardly likely to break through along the road today. The Germans only managed to get some of their tanks across the river. You stopped the rest on the far side of the Berezina. The bridge has been blown to smithereens; there's not a trace left."

"The bridge may have been blown to bits, but so have our aircraft. That's nothing to be proud of!" retorted the pilot; but it was clear from the look on his face that he was pleased about that bridge nevertheless.

"They certainly made a bonfire of you! We just about chewed our fingernails off," said the captain. He wanted to console the pilot. "The German came down here. I wanted him taken alive, but there wasn't much hope of getting the men to do that after what they'd seen!"

"Where is he, then?" asked Sintsov, struggling to his feet.

"Here, beyond those fir-trees. Only better not look at him," said the captain with a wave of his hand. "Looks as if he'd been under a tank...." Then, with a glance at Sintsov, who was pale from loss of blood, he added: "You can go, seeing you're wounded. I'm not detaining you."

"We've got another two wounded in the back of the lorry," said Sintsov, as if still trying to justify driving back to the rear, "and one dead." He wanted to say that the dead man was a general, but refrained. What was the point? "Let's go," he said to the pilot.

"I think perhaps I'll stay here," said the latter determinedly. He had been thinking about it all through the conversation, had made up his mind, and had no intention of changing it. "Will you give me a rifle?" he asked the captain.

"No, I won't." The captain shook his head. "I won't, my dear pilot! What d'you want to come to me for, and what'll we gain out of it? You get up there." He jabbed his bandaged hand at the sky. "We've backed out all the way from Slutsk, and we've been through hell because you boys aren't in the air enough. Go on, get airborne, for goodness sake, that's all we want of you! We'll cope with the rest ourselves!"

Sintsov stopped by the lorry, waiting for the outcome of all this.

But the captain's words were wasted on the pilot. He would certainly not have stayed if there had been any hope of getting another aircraft; but he had no such hope and had decided to fight on the ground.

"If he won't give me a rifle, I'll get one myself," he said, indicating the captain; and Sintsov realised that the irresistible force had met the immovable object. "Off you go; only see you get my navigator to hospital alright."

The captain said nothing. When Sintsov climbed into the cab, they were standing in silence side by side—the big, tall captain and the stocky little pilot, both stubborn, in an ugly mood, infuriated by their disasters, and ready to fight again.

"What's your name, Comrade Captain?" asked Sintsov from the cab, remembering his newspaper for the first time.

"My name? Want to file a complaint against me, or something? Half Russia depends on my name. Ivanov. Write that down. Or can you memorise it?"

As the lorry drove out of the woods on to the road, Sintsov again saw the Red Armyman he had relieved of his post. He was sitting with two other soldiers and, like them, was tying grenades together with telephone cable in clusters of two or three. He was chatting to his neighbours and smiling. He seemed happy enough. He had something useful to do, and he wasn't on his own.

It took two hours to reach Mogilev. The sound of artillery fire came up from behind at first, and then things became quiet. Ten kilometres away from the city, Sintsov saw horse-drawn guns deploying to their positions on both sides and an infantry column moving up the road. He was riding as if through a dense mist. He thought he was sleepy, whereas in actual fact he lost consciousness from time to time owing to loss of blood and then came to again.

Two fighter planes were weaving about high in the sky over the outskirts of Mogilev. Since the AA was silent, they were presumably ours. Looking harder, Sintsov identified them as MIGs. He had already seen these aircraft that spring in Grodno. They were said to be much faster than the Messerschmidts.

"No, things aren't so bad after all," thought Sintsov confidently through his fatigue and pain, himself not fully aware that his confidence stemmed not so much from the sight of the troops taking up their positions in front of Mogilev, or from the spectacle of the MIGs weaving over the city, as from his recollections of the tankmen who had stopped the lorry, and of the lieutenant who took after his captain, and of the captain who no doubt took after his lieutenant-colonel.

When the lorry stopped outside the hospital, Sintsov mustered his strength in one last effort. He held on to the side and waited while they removed from the back the unconscious navigator, the Red Armyman, who was groaning through his clenched teeth, and the dead general. Then he ordered the driver to take the lorry to the editorial offices and report that he had stayed behind in the hospital.

The driver hooked up the tailboard. Sintsov glanced at the bloodstained bundles of newsprint, remembering that hardly any of them had been distributed, and was left alone on the cobbled road.

He went into the reception hall, still on his own. He took the general's documents out of his pocket and put them on the table, fumbled for his own identity card, found it, held it out to the nurse, and, while waiting for her to take it, half-swung round in an odd sort of way and collapsed unconscious on the floor.

CHAPTER THREE

Two weeks after Sintsov had been wounded and when he was already taking two daily walks round the hospital gardens, orders came through to evacuate the hospital to Dorogobuzh. A rumour immediately got round among the patients that the Germans had crossed the Dnieper at Shklov and were closing in on Mogilev from the north.

Sintsov's wound had been "a lucky one", to quote the doctor who performed the operation. The bullet had just grazed the ribs.

Sintsov felt almost fully recovered, and so he went to see the hospital commissar about his discharge. The prospect of evacuation frightened him. He didn't want to have to look for his editorial office again.

"I've got the feeling they've already left," said the hospital commissar doubtfully.

But Sintsov firmly pointed out that this was impossible. If they had left, they would have taken him with them. The editor had promised.

Up to his ears in evacuating the wounded, the commissar did not press his point any further. After all, if the man wanted his discharge, let him have it!

Towards midday, after collecting his documents and his uniform, Sintsov walked out of the hospital gates.

Mogilev was half deserted and there was an atmosphere of tension. Barricades had appeared on the streets, and machine-guns had been positioned in the sandbagged corner-windows of the buildings.

The sentry standing in front of the Mogilev printing works, where Sintsov had counted on finding the editorial staff, was not in the mood for conversation. The doors and the iron courtyard gates were locked. There was no sound of machinery from inside—in fact it was utterly quiet. The whole place was dead.

An hour later, the Mogilev military commandant—the one whom Sintsov had called on two weeks previously and who was now even more dazed with lack of sleep—confirmed that the staff of the Front newspaper had left two days ago. "And they couldn't even inform me," thought Sintsov in dismay.

"Where have they gone?"

The commandant shrugged his shoulders and said that they hadn't reported their itinerary. Front HQ had been transferred to the Smolensk region, and the editorial staff had followed them.

"There was no point in getting yourself discharged prematurely. You'd have been evacuated with the hospital to Dorogobuzh, and you could have looked for what you needed from there in the normal manner."

Sintsov was depressed at the unlovely prospect of further wanderings.

"Listen, what units are stationed in the Mogilev region?"

"What do you want to know for?"

Sintsov replied that he wanted to get to HQ of the nearest division, stay with it awhile, and collect some copy for the newspaper so that he wouldn't have to arrive at the editorial office empty-handed.

The commandant reluctantly unfolded a map and indicated a small wood on the far side of the Dnieper about six kilometres from the Mogilev bridge. According to him, 176 Division HQ was stationed there.

After he had crossed the bridge over the Dnieper and walked three kilometres along the Mogilev-Orsha highway, Sintsov heard artillery fire to his rear on the other side of the river. He stood on the road for several minutes, listening to the alarming thunder of the guns, and then continued on his way, still worrying about what had been on his mind ever since he left the commandant's office in Mogilev. What was going to happen next?

Front HQ had been at Minsk, then at Mogilev, and now it had moved to Smolensk. In other words, a hundred and fifty kilometres nearer Moscow....

No matter how hard he tried to make himself think calmly, no matter what arguments he produced, there was no getting away from the geographical facts.

Two weeks in hospital had taught Sintsov a great deal. The rumours and talk had been such that one moment you were up in the air, and the next moment your hopes were completely dashed. If he had believed all the bad news, he would have gone crazy long ago. But if he had only accepted the good news, he would have finally had to pinch himself to bring himself down to earth again. That will do! After all, why am I in hospital? Why am I in Mogilev? Why are things like this and not otherwise?

At first, Sintsov thought that the truth about the war lay somewhere in between. Then he realised that this was not the truth either. Different people were telling good and bad stories. Whether or not they deserved to be taken seriously depended not on what they said, but on the way they said it.

All in the hospital had come into contact with the war somehow or other, otherwise they would not have ended up there. But amongst them there were many who knew only one thing—that the Germans brought death. What they did not know was that the Germans themselves were mortal.

The most credibility was to be given to those who knew both these facts and were convinced from their own experience that the Germans too were mortal. Whatever they said, good or bad, always seemed to imply this; and that was the real truth about the war.

The captain of the tank corps who had given Sintsov a dressing-down in the forest outside Bobruisk had been one such person.

It wasn't a matter of one man's cowardice and another's bravery. It was simply that the captain had been seeing the war that day in a different way from Sintsov. The captain had known perfectly well that the Germans were mortal and that if they were killed, they stopped moving. He had subordinated all his actions to this thought and, of course, the truth was on his side. Sintsov had wanted to take the men out of the danger zone. The captain had wanted to save the situation by throwing those same men into battle.

And, of course, if the Germans had not broken through to Mogilev at the time, it was because the remnants of the brigade in which the captain was serving, and all those who had made their way to the brigade that day rifle in hand had known—or, if they hadn't, had realised in action—that the Germans were mortal. Killing Germans and dying themselves, they had won twenty-four hours' grace. Towards evening, a fresh rifle division had deployed behind them.

Sintsov had been told this by the editor, who had come to visit him on his second day in hospital.

The editor, who had heard all about the journey to Bobruisk from the driver, complimented Sintsov, was alarmed for Lyusin, and cursed the captain for taking things into his own hands. His fat, good-natured cheeks wobbled with fury, and the beetroot-coloured veins actually bulged on them.

Sintsov did not share the editor's feelings. He knew that he had done many foolish things that day, but at least his behaviour had not been prompted by cowardice. Moreover, like all who find themselves laid up in hospital, he had been thinking about his wound and was unable to rid his mind of the bitter thought that the pilot might never have shot himself had it not been for those confounded grey policemen's capes that looked so much like German uniforms. He hadn't given it a thought at the time, but you have to have your wits about you in war. And, quite clearly, all the time.

Nor could he share the editor's fury about the incident with Lyusin. Junior Political Instructor Lyusin had gone out to distribute the newspaper and had ended up in action. Well, so what? It might not have happened, but it had. The only thing that troubled Sintsov was the memory of Lyusin's shrill voice and the sudden snarl on his face. Lyusin hadn't wanted to stay behind, and the captain had said: "Any disobedience, and it'll cost you your life."

He tried to explain his thoughts to the editor, but all he got by way of a reply was:

"What's this, then? Am I to send you all out to the units? Lyusin today, you tomorrow, someone else the day after?"

This protest was, in general, justified; but when Sintsov recalled that particular forest, that particular moment, and that particular captain, it suddenly didn't seem justified any more.

The editor and he talked for a whole hour, but still seemed unable to arrive at an understanding.

A few hours later, something happened which drove everything else clean out of Sintsov's mind for a long time to come.

He heard Stalin's speech over the radio.

There was a loudspeaker hanging up in the corridor near the duty nurse's table. The volume was turned up full and all the ward doors were opened wide.

Stalin spoke slowly and thickly, with a marked Georgian accent. At one point, in the middle of the speech, a tumbler clinked as he drank some water. His voice was low-pitched and not particularly loud. It might have seemed quite calm, had it not been for the laboured, tired breathing, and the water which he began sipping as he spoke.

But although he was agitated, his diction remained steady, and the rather thick voice flowed on, neither rising nor falling, and without exclamation marks.

In the discrepancy between the level voice and the tragedy of the situation, there was strength. This did not surprise anyone: it was expected of Stalin.

He was loved in many ways: with devotion and with reservations, with admiration and with apprehension. Sometimes he was not loved at all. But no one doubted his courage and his iron will. And at this moment, these two qualities seemed the most essential in a man who was the leader of a country at war.

Stalin did not call the situation tragic: it would have been hard to imagine that word on his lips; but what he was talking about—mobilisation of civilian reserves, occupied territory, partisan warfare—meant an end to all illusions. We had retreated almost everywhere, and we had retreated a long way. The truth was bitter, but it had been spoken at last, and people now at least knew where they stood.

That Stalin should have been speaking about the unsuccessful commencement of that tremendous and terrible war without any particular change of vocabulary—as if he were discussing grave difficulties which must be overcome as soon as possible—this, too, suggested strength, not weakness.

So, at least, Sintsov was thinking as he lay that night on his bed and, as his dying neighbour groaned nearby, recalled again and again all the details of Stalin's speech and the heart-rending appeal, "My friends!", which the entire hospital repeated throughout the whole of the following day.

One usually asks oneself this kind of question in boyhood; but Sintsov asked it for the first time at the age of thirty, as he lay that night on his hospital cot: "Would I give my life for Stalin if they came up to me just like that and said—'Die, so that he might live'? Yes, I would. And today more than ever before."

"My friends..." whispered Sintsov, repeating Stalin's words; and he suddenly realised that, in everything great, even tremendous, which Stalin had done and which he could remember, he had long missed those words spoken for the first time today: "Brothers and sisters! My friends!"—or rather, he had missed the emotion that lay behind those words.

Could only a tragedy like war call forth those words and that emotion?

A hurtful and bitter thought! Sintsov immediately dismissed it from his mind in fright as petty and unworthy, although it was neither. He was unused to it, that was all.

But the main thing that remained in his mind after Stalin's speech was a tense expectation that things would change for the better. And this expectation apparently began to be justified sooner than might have been thought—in the very first week.

The names of sectors which were the scene of bitter fighting began to recur in the bulletins every day. This inspired greater confidence, because the Bobruisk sector was prominent among the others. The Germans had indeed been marking time there for several days. The hospital had first-hand information of this.

But then an atmosphere of alarm spread round the wards. At first, there was a rumour that the Germans, instead of breaking through to Mogilev, had swung round from Bobruisk on to Rogachev and Zhlobin and had taken them. Then the editor suddenly dropped in for a moment to see Sintsov, asked after his health, said that if the newspaper had to be moved he would take Sintsov with him, and left with the haste of a man anxious to avoid answering any questions. Finally, the day after evacuation orders came in, the hospital started talking about the Germans having crossed the Dnieper at Shklov.

And so Sintsov was now walking along the side of a road parallel to the Dnieper, heading north towards that same Shklov, and wondering if there was any truth in the morning's rumours.

If, unfortunately, they were true, then it was understandable that the newspaper should have moved out of Mogilev, which was on the other side of the Dnieper. What Sintsov failed to understand was why they couldn't have found ten minutes to pick him up at the hospital as promised.

Even now, three days after their departure, Mogilev did not give the impression of a city about to surrender. What was all the hurry, then? His hurt feelings only strengthened Sintsov's determination not to return to the newspaper without some good copy.

The weakness consequent upon his wound was already beginning to make itself felt during the long hike. After six kilometres, at the point where the commandant had told him that the divisional HQ was located, he could see nothing in the forest but wheel-tracks, pits in the clayey soil, and branches of hastily removed camouflage. If HQ had indeed been here, then it must have left at least twenty-four hours ago, judging by those limp branches. When Sintsov returned to the road, three lorries tore past towing anti-tank guns, then an ammunition convoy, and then one more lorry with a gun in tow. Sintsov raised his hand hesitantly, but not one of the vehicles stopped.

Then a little staff car raced past. Sintsov had already given up hope of its stopping when it pulled up after another hundred metres. Sintsov ran up to it, panting for breath.

"What is it, Comrade Political Instructor?" asked the officer sitting next to the driver. He was a small, thickset battalion commissar with a red face and grey eyebrows. He was wearing a pair of heavy, double-lensed spectacles.

Sintsov explained that he was looking for 176 Division HQ. Before answering, the battalion commissar, with a far from encouraging look on his face, asked him to produce his documents.

"He's not going to take me," thought Sintsov. But the battalion commissar's face cleared after he had read the hospital certificate.

"I have to report to the 176th myself," he said returning the form, "but not till tomorrow. Right now I'm on my way to the 301st. That's as far as I can take you."

This suited Sintsov down to the ground. He thanked the battalion commissar and got into the truck. They drove on for a kilometre in silence; then the battalion commissar stopped the car and changed to the back seat.

"More sociable this way," he explained when they were moving again. "At least we can chat. I can't talk to you with my head screwed round all the time." And he smiled gently and offered Sintsov his hand. "Shmakov."

Shmakov proved talkative indeed. As he fired one question after another, he cocked his round white head sideways in a comical, bird-like manner and peered attentively and good-naturedly through his spectacles at Sintsov as if to say: "Come on! Come on! Anything interesting to tell me?" But when he was talking himself, he kept removing his spectacles, wiping them, replacing them, looking intently into the light, finding a speck of dust, wiping the lenses again, and then once more staring into the light. Without the thick lenses in front of them, his eyes were unhealthily bloodshot and the lids were puffy and swollen.

"I keep trying to find out why my eyesight's so bad," he smiled, intercepting Sintsov's look. "It's been pretty rotten for a long time now, and this last year it's been dead rotten."

Sintsov answered his questions reluctantly, without going into details: he had been at the front from the sixth day of the war, had been in various places, and had been accidentally wounded near Bobruisk. Shmakov must have realised that his companion was inwardly disturbed; he cocked his head inquiringly several times, stopped questioning Sintsov and began talking about himself: he had been called up to the army a week ago, had arrived at the front the day before as a lecturer for the Central Political Directorate of the Red Army and this was his first tour of the units.

"And just what lectures are you proposing to give here at the front?" inquired Sintsov. He tried to imagine himself taking an interest in a lecture at such a time.

"Generally speaking, my speciality is economics," said Shmakov, not noticing, or not wanting to notice, the irony in Sintsov's question. "But I lecture on various subjects: 'War and the International Situation', 'Germany's Military and Economic Potential', and, of course, on more general topics."

"Have you had a military training?" asked Sintsov.

"Well, now..." Shmakov wiped his spectacles again and peered intently through them into the light as if gazing somewhere into the distant past. "Like many Communists of my generation, I was a political worker during the Civil War. But strictly speaking, that's experience rather than education."

"Yes, experience," thought Sintsov bitterly. "And a fat lot of good it seems to be doing us now. The Germans aren't Whites, and Hitler's no Denikin...." And he angrily remembered a novel about the impending war, according to which the whole of fascist Germany started going to pieces as soon as our Air Force struck its first blow. That author should have been on the Bobruisk highway two weeks ago!

All these thoughts passed through Sintsov's mind in a flash, but he said nothing and merely sighed.

"Did you have a rough time of it?" asked Shmakov. He had noticed that sigh.

"It's not just me!" said Sintsov with feeling. "The whole business has been so heart-breaking sometimes...." And, sensing that he could trust the little grey-haired man sitting beside him, he waved his hand in a gesture of despair.

"Never mind," said Shmakov, and he even touched Sintsov's sleeve as if to reassure him. "We're holding them back just now; we'll stop them eventually, and then we'll turn the tables on them. Things have been worse before: Yudenich at Petrograd; Denikin taking Orel and marching on Tula.... But it was alright—we smashed them in the end."

"Denikin didn't have tanks and planes," burst out Sintsov.

"True, or, to be more precise, almost true," agreed Shmakov, again not noticing, or appearing not to notice, Sintsov's mood. "But there's a lot of things we didn't have then that we have now. We didn't have five-year plans, and we didn't have four million communists...."

"Why the pep-talk?" wondered Sintsov. Inwardly, he wanted to be reassured; but he was resisting the temptation to take at face value anything likely to give him that reassurance.

"Of course," said Shmakov, after a pause, "we did boast a lot before the war and we exaggerated some aspects, including our military preparedness—that's perfectly clear now. But it doesn't mean we should fly to the other extreme and underrate our potential strength because of the first failures. It's enormous, and it hasn't been allowed for by us, let alone the Germans. I can say this in all confidence, because I know something about this problem."

"But why underrate?" said Sintsov. "D'you think any of us wants to underrate? It's just that I've seen a lot lately—as much as I can take, and somehow I don't feel like singing 'All's well, my beautiful Marquise....' That song's out of touch with the times, as they say."

"It's not a Bolshevik song, to put it frankly," laughed Shmakov. "And we're Bolsheviks, so it's time to have done with all that."

"Have you been away from Moscow long?" asked Sintsov, with Masha in mind.

"Three days."

"Have they bombed it yet?"

"No."

"Is that the truth?"

"I'm not in the habit of saying anything but the truth," replied Shmakov in an imperceptibly changed voice, and he looked Sintsov straight in the face through his spectacles.

"Why aren't they bombing it? What's your opinion?"

"Because they haven't the resources for everything. They've thrown all their planes into action at the front, and they haven't enough to spare for Moscow."

"Really?"

"Really. We mustn't get the idea that the Germans' resources are inexhaustible. Some have already flown to that extreme, and they've been wrong! The next stage could be panic, and we have no cause to panic. Panic's not in our nature—though there's a black sheep in every family," concluded Shmakov with the same firm note in his mild voice.

And although everything that Shmakov had just said seemed very much like an indirect reprimand, Sintsov looked at him gratefully. His words had a ring of conviction that was a long way from ignorance about the true state of affairs. "Perhaps he talks like that because he was a political worker back in the Civil War, when Denikin was advancing on Tula..." thought Sintsov.

"Does that mean it's quiet in Moscow?" he said aloud.

"What can I say?" Shmakov shrugged his shoulders. "The scum's floating to the surface. But on the whole," he summed up after a moment's thought, "things are normal." And, as if inwardly making sure that he had given Sintsov a fair answer, he again fell thoughtful and then repeated, "Yes, normal!"

He had hardly finished speaking, when several lorries came tearing up towards them at a frantic speed. A hatless, dishevelled soldier was leaning halfway out of the cab of the last vehicle and yelling at the top of his voice:

"Tanks back there! Tanks!"

The driver, looking frightened, turned inquiringly to Shmakov without stopping the car.

"Carry on," said Shmakov calmly, "it's just another kilometre to divisional HQ. Some sort of panic on. There can't be any tanks...."

Sintsov remained silent. His common sense was outweighed by his reluctance to seem more cautious than this man on his way to the front for the first time.

"There can't be any tanks," repeated Shmakov half a kilometre further on. "They told me our troops are holding firm the whole length of the Dnieper, so how can there be German tanks this side?"

Sintsov kept silent. "How can there be German tanks?" he thought. "The devil only knows the answer to that!"

"Divisional HQ ought to be on the right, just here," said Shmakov, short-sightedly bringing up to his eyes a clipboard with a map thrust under the celluloid. He had the unshakeable conviction, typical of a man on his way to the front for the first time, that everything would be as marked on the map. "We'll stop and have a look. There'll be a sign of sorts somewhere."

But before he could tell the driver to stop, the latter braked of his own accord. Shells had started bursting one after another on the roadway directly in front of them. The road, which until then had been almost deserted, was suddenly swarming with vehicles: some were coming towards them, while others, which had been overtaking them from behind, started hastily turning round. Without waiting for orders, the driver of the car also began turning, but when another shell exploded with a roar, he suddenly dived out into the ditch.

Sintsov was in the act of opening the door to jump out and fetch the driver back, but Shmakov found an easier solution. "Stay in your seat," he said, calmly detaining Sintsov by the shoulder, and then he hurriedly sat behind the steering wheel, turned the car round, and parked it on the verge. He was only just in time. Another few seconds and they would have been smashed to bits in the stampede of oncoming lorries.

"Now let's get out," said Shmakov, and he went up to the ditch where the driver was cowering and called him by name. "Comrade Solodilov!"

The driver stood up, blinking with fright.

"Get in and take your place behind the wheel," said Shmakov.

The driver sullenly went back to the car; but Shmakov, instead of taking his seat, stood by the car, shifting from one foot to the other in an odd sort of way and peering at the shell-bursts ahead.

Sintsov experienced the familiar feeling of having lost his way.

"Listen, Comrade Battalion Commissar," he said, overcoming his reluctance to be the first to say that they would have to return. "Let's go back a couple of kilometres or so. I saw some anti-tank guns on the roadside. We could find one of the commanders and check whether it's possible to get to the Three Hundred and First."

As he said this, he was afraid that Shmakov, who had proved himself a stubborn man for all his apparent mildness, would not agree, and they would have to drive ahead into the unknown. But Shmakov listened to what he had to say, looked at the smoke hovering over the road in front, and climbed back into the car.

"I haven't even got a revolver, you understand. They wouldn't issue me with one," he said, as if justifying his consent to go back.

"A lot of help a revolver would be to you!" thought Sintsov, forgetting how nervous he had been himself in the first few days when he was unarmed.

"So you abandoned your officers and ran for it," said Shmakov, resting his elbow on the back of the front seat and looking sideways at the driver.

"Court martial me if I'm guilty," answered the other thickly, without turning his head.

"What's the point of a court martial? You should be ashamed of yourself, that's all," said Shmakov. "Are you a Komsomol?"

"Yes," replied the driver in the same thick voice.

"Then you should be even more ashamed," said Shmakov. "I'd die of shame if I ever heard of my son behaving the way you did just now."

"Where is your son, then?" asked the driver softly; and Sintsov realised that if Shmakov had to reply that his son was somewhere in the rear, then everything he had said so far would be just so much hot air to the driver.

"My son was a flier, an air-gunner," said Shmakov. "He was killed a week ago. Why?"

"Nothing," said the driver almost inaudibly.

"Stop!" shouted Sintsov, who had been keeping his eyes on the road.

They pulled up by an anti-tank gun which had been positioned in the ditch and which had looked from a distance like a clump of bushes that had somehow crawled out of the forest on to the highway. A bareheaded colonel with close-cropped grey hair was sitting beside the gun and drinking tea out of a thermos flask.

"Shove that car of yours two hundred metres further on," he said instead of greeting them when Shmakov and Sintsov alighted, "and then we'll talk!"

Shmakov ordered the driver to carry on and, jerking his head towards the north, told the colonel that the Germans were shelling the road about four kilometres back.

"I dare say," said the colonel, standing up and screwing the top on to his flask.

On hearing this calm and, as it seemed to Sintsov, mocking reply, Shmakov asked if the Comrade Colonel knew the whereabouts of any divisional HQ, it didn't matter which.

"Any divisional HQ, it doesn't matter which?" repeated the colonel in the same mocking tone. He put on his cap, then buttoned up the canvas thermos cover and slung it over his shoulder. "If it doesn't matter which, let's go to ours."

"Which is yours?" asked Shmakov.

"And who might you be?"

Shmakov produced his identity papers. The colonel glanced at them briefly and said that he was in command of 176 Division Artillery, had been checking the anti-tank defences there, and was now returning to HQ.

"How can I get to the Three Hundred and First?" asked Shmakov immediately.

The colonel shrugged his shoulders and said that 301st HQ was some eight kilometres to the north; but if the Germans were shelling the road, then there would hardly be any sense in going there until the situation had been clarified. And again there was a hint of calm mockery in that "hardly".

"But I was told that Three Hundred and One HQ was nearer, about four kilometres from here," said the factually-minded Shmakov.

Again the colonel shrugged his shoulders.

"When were you told this, and where?"

"Yesterday, at the Army Political Department."

"I wouldn't put too much faith in what they told you yesterday, Comrade Battalion Commissar. Ignore the time factor, and you'll spend the rest of your days as a prisoner-of-war. And there's no point in white-haired fellows like you and me getting themselves captured. Are you a lecturer too?" And the colonel half turned to Sintsov.

"No, I'm from the Front newspaper."

"Ah... " said the colonel non-committally, and he strode up to the car on his long, stork-like legs in their spurred, patent-leather boots.

Sintsov, Shmakov and the colonel's companion—a captain in charge of a battalion—had some difficulty in keeping up with him.

"Tell my groom," said the colonel, taking his seat in front and turning to the captain, "to bring my horse to HQ."

"What's the situation in your division?" asked Shmakov after they had moved off.

"Situation?" The colonel turned and mockingly raised his eyebrows. "The Lord Almighty and the divisional commander alone are in a position to know the situation and no one else. I can only judge from my own artillery angle."

"Well, how does it look from there?"

"We have the guns, we finally got the shells yesterday, and that means we're going to put up a fight. Yesterday we knocked out a company of Germans trying to cross the river. We sank six pontoons. But, of course, that's not a battle."

"As I was leaving Mogilev, I heard an artillery battle on the outskirts to the south."

"Well," said the colonel, "that means Serpilin's started already. They spotted a tank concentration yesterday from the observation post. But I can't give you the details—I've been here since morning. Anyway, we'll all be going into action soon, that's clear."

Sintsov liked the calmly ironic professionalism of this man who had not received any shells until the day before, had probably been worrying, but had ceased to do so now and was talking about the impending battles like a host standing in front of a table which is all laid and ready for the guests.

Divisional HQ was not in the place indicated on the map by the commandant at Mogilev, but a kilometre nearer, in a sparse pine wood.

In the middle of the wood under a big pine, a colonel was sitting on a folding stool at a folding table. A heavily built man, he was sweating profusely in the heat. There were two medals pinned to his tunic, which was unbuttoned over the hairy chest. This was the divisional commander.

On learning that Sintsov was from the Front newspaper, the colonel sighed deeply for some reason and said that correspondents weren't his concern; Sintsov could wait there for the commissar or go to the political department.

"It's none of my business, I've learnt my lesson!" shouted the colonel angrily. "Yes, I've learnt my lesson!" And his face took on an expression of fury, as if Sintsov had somehow offended him.

Sintsov moved away and glanced at his watch. It was after six, so he decided to wait for the commissar.

"I'm off to the political department," said Shmakov, coming up to him. "How about you?"

"I'll wait here," replied Sintsov, and he shook Shmakov's hand, fully convinced that he would never see him again.

"Perhaps you'd like a bite to eat?" It was the grey-haired artillery colonel who had been in the staff car with them and who happened to be passing. "My battery's beyond the woods. The gunners'll give you something to eat. Tell them it's my orders."

"No, thanks," said Sintsov, and he slapped his kitbag. "I've got all I need here."

And, indeed, he had a can of meat and a hunk of bread, both issued to him on his discharge from hospital.

"So you went to our commander and he sent you packing?" And the colonel, his eyebrows raised mockingly, nodded towards the divisional commander, who was creating quite an uproar at his folding table.

"Sort of."

"Don't take offence—try and put yourself in his position. When we were at the Finnish front, a correspondent arrived and rattled him in some way or other. He's quick to get his own back. He had him under arrest for ten days. It was the worst thing that could have happened. The correspondent turned out to be an author, and a famous one, too. He tried explaining it to our CO when he was being put under arrest, but His Nibs didn't take a blind lot of notice—he doesn't go in for improving books. I advise you to wait for the commissar. And one more piece of advice..."

But Sintsov was never to find out what the ironical artillery chief was about to tell him. A heavy shell burst in the forest, then a whole series, and everybody—Sintsov, the artillery chief, and the divisional commander—dived down into the yellow, sandy slit trenches between the pines. The Germans were not shelling HQ, but the battery beyond the forest where the colonel had invited Sintsov for a snack. This became clear from an exchange between the humorously inclined artillery colonel, who had gone down into the same trench as Sintsov, and the fat divisional commander sitting in the other trench about twenty metres away.

"A fine place you found for your battery!" yelled the fat colonel, bobbing up out of his trench after a shell-burst.

"Permission to report!" shouted the artillery chief in reply, also bobbing up out of his trench, and saluting. "I already reported that when you moved the command post here!..."

There was another shell-burst, and both colonels ducked down in their trenches.

"There was no need to report to me!" yelled the divisional CO, bobbing up out of his trench again, his face purple. "You should have moved the battery without reporting as soon as I transferred the command post...."

"Permission to report," shouted the artillery chief, saluting again, "that I reported to you and you ordered me not to move it, because...."

Another whistle, another shell-burst, both ducked down again and then stood up in their trenches.

"I'm not asking for the why's and wherefore's," roared the divisional commander, "I'm just giving you an order!"

The next time he ducked down in his trench with the artillery commander, Sintsov grinned despite the seriousness of the situation. The artillery colonel noticed him smiling and winked like a ten-year-old.

The bombardment stopped as suddenly as it had started. There were only a few slightly wounded in the whole forest.

"I order you to transfer your battery immediately!" shouted the fat colonel, clambering out of his slit trench with an effort and brushing the sand off his podgy knees.

"Yes, Sir!"

But the divisional commander wasn't looking at the artillery chief any more and was shouting to someone for transport. He was going to see Serpilin.

A minute later found him yelling into the telephone: "Serpilin, Serpilin! Zaichikov here!... How are you there, Serpilin? I'm coming over to you right away. Keep your shirt on!"

Apparently, good news was coming over the telephone.

"Skin 'em, Serpilin! Skin 'em alive, the way we skinned the Whites.... I'm coming over right away!" bellowed the colonel happily, as if for the benefit of the entire forest.

No sooner had the divisional commander driven off than some small-calibre guns opened fire, and then a report came in by telephone that the Germans had broken out on to the highway some three kilometres from HQ.

The artillery colonel got into a lorry and drove out on to the highway, heading for his battery.

Sintsov was going to dash up to him, but faltered at the last moment and stayed where he was. And although he managed to convince himself that he had wanted to go but had been too late, he knew at the bottom of his heart that he had funked it. A minute later, by which time he had pulled himself together, he really had made up his mind to go; but by now there was no one to take him.

He went a little nearer the operations duty officer's table and leaned back against a tall pine.

The news over the telephone became more and more alarming every minute. The tanks were two kilometres away, then one and a half, then one.... The operations duty officer and a major ordered the grenades to be issued and bottles of petrol to be made ready.

The petrol bottles were prepared, but it turned out that hardly anybody had matches. For several minutes, the tanks quite forgotten, all hunted through their pockets for boxes of matches and then shared out the contents. There was a roar of engines from the highway, then a violent burst of artillery fire. Everything suddenly went quiet. The operations duty officer wiped the sweat from his forehead, put down the handset on the table with a bang that rang out like a gunshot in the silence, and said that everything was alright. The intruding tanks had been wiped out by the artillery.

Five minutes later, a pick-up came weaving in and out among the trees, and out of the cab jumped the last man Sintsov would have expected to meet there. It was an old colleague of his from way back in the days of the Communist Institute of Journalists, the well-known Moscow press photographer Mishka Weinstein, now in uniform, but in every other respect exactly the same as before the war—fat, jolly, noisy, with two Leicas dangling on his chest.

"Hullo, Mishka!" said Sintsov, overjoyed, taking in both hands the massive fist of his old friend, whom nobody had ever addressed by any name other than "Mishka".

"Hullo, hullo!" answered Mishka with a grin, wiping with his free hand the sweat that was streaming from his round, frying-pan-like face. "When did you pop in here?"

"Pop" had been his favourite word ever since institute days.

"And where did *you* pop in from?" asked Sintsov, staring hard at Mishka and also smiling involuntarily.

"Well, you see, I was driving along the road and I saw them firing at some German tanks, so I popped up and photographed them. They smashed three tanks to pieces, only they were a long way apart. Still, never mind—stick them together, chop out the greenery, and there's a panorama shot for you—just the job!" And Mishka gave a thumbs-up sign.

"What have you come here for?" asked Sintsov.

7-825

"They told me I'd find divisional HQ here. I decided to call and ask if I might pop along somewhere else."

"They've just reported twenty tanks knocked out over the Dnieper near Mogilev," said the operations duty officer.

"Now that would be a real panorama! Shall we get in the pick-up and go?" And Mishka turned to Sintsov.

"Well...."

"You won't find Serpilin's command post without an escort," said the operations duty officer, breaking into the conversation once again.

"I'll find anything," said Mishka. "Only it's a bit dark for taking shots." He looked up at the already greying sky, pulled a face and, finally realising that it was no use trying to beat nature, calmed down and let his pick-up go to refuel. "Listen," he said, sitting down on the ground beside Sintsov, "you haven't got any eats with you, have you? I haven't had a bite since morning, Pioneer's word of honour!"

Sintsov unbuttoned his kitbag without saying anything and took out the bread and a can of meat. He knew that while Mishka was hungry it was useless asking him any questions, and he very much wanted to hear the news from Moscow.

Mishka produced a knife, opened the can in one circular movement, and began devouring the meat hungrily, spearing the chunks on the end of his knife and following up with generous mouthfuls of bread. Only after demolishing three quarters of the can did he turn to Sintsov and ask, with his mouth still full:

"Have you eaten?"

"No," said Sintsov.

"Here," said Mishka regretfully, and he offered Sintsov the can and the remains of the loaf. "That's me all over—forgetting about my friends," he added, still chewing. "Most embarrassing."

Sintsov took the knife and the jar from Mishka and smiled.

"Well, how's things in Moscow?" he asked, when Mishka had finished eating the last piece of meat, which he hadn't been able to resist spearing with his knife even as he was passing the can to Sintsov.

"Call me a liar, but I haven't seen anything of Moscow," said Mishka. "I've only popped back from the front twice for a couple of hours, handed in the photos, and been off back again. By the way," he recalled cheerfully, "Kovrigin of *The Star* was killed near Minsk. He was a good chap. Pity!"

He really did feel sorry for Kovrigin, but he was so pleased at having photographed the tanks that he was talking about everything in the same happy tone of voice, and he began telling Sintsov about his trips to the front.

Sintsov interrupted him to ask how he felt about the general situation after all these visits.

But Mishka was not in the least concerned with the general situation. He could see with his own eyes that we were getting the wrong end of things, to use his own expression; but he hadn't the slightest doubt that we would beat the nazis.

He didn't want to discuss serious topics, and he was frankly overjoyed when he saw his pick-up come back after refuelling.

"Did you get some grub?" he asked the driver.

The driver took a hunk of black bread out of the pick up. Mishka broke off half and started eating again. Sintsov went to introduce himself to the commissar who had just returned from the forward positions.

The commissar was a solidly built, long-nosed Ukrainian with heavy, drooping moustaches that gave him the appearance of a commanding officer rather than a political worker. Frowning, but patient, he listened to what Sintsov had to say and replied that he didn't know where the Front Political Directorate was at that particular moment. The Front had moved, but Army HQ was near Chausy, and Sintsov would probably be able to find out from them where the Front Political Department was located.

Sintsov explained that before leaving for the Army, he wanted to cross the Dnieper with the press photographer and visit the regiment which had just knocked out a lot of German tanks.

The commissar reacted to this proposition with the same frowning patience and said he had just returned from that particular regiment, but it would be better to make the journey after nightfall. They might not be able to get through in the daytime. If they were going to travel by night, they would have to take an escort with them.

"That's all right, we're already seasoned front-liners, we'll make it on our own, Comrade Regimental Commissar," said Mishka jauntily, waddling up to the officer with his mouth still full of bread.

"Seasoned or not," snapped the other, "you're not going without an escort! My political instructor will leave with you as soon as he's eaten. Are you only going to take photographs, or are you going to write as well!"

"Both," said Mishka.

"If you're going to write," said the other in the same morose voice, turning to Sintsov and ignoring Mishka altogether, "don't disclose the dispositions of the units. The Germans know too much as it is. They've got us taped, the bastards!..." The swear-word came as a shock, and Sintsov guessed why the man was so gloomy. Although he had returned from the regiment after a successful engagement, his jubilation was marred by something in the division's general predicament, and perhaps in that of the Army too.

"Comrade Regimental Commissar, the commander of the partisan detachment has just arrived," reported a young political instructor, coming up to the commissar.

"Good. Now you have something to eat straightaway and go back to Serpilin with these two in their pick-up." The commissar nodded towards Sintsov and Mishka, turned to a handsome, fair-haired boy in a leather jacket with a Mauser and grenades at his belt who had just dismounted from his horse, and went off with him into the interior of the forest.

An hour later, the pick-up rattled over the timbers of the bridge across the Dnieper and drove into Mogilev. Opposite the hospital where Sintsov had been a patient that morning, some lorries were parked at the kerb, and towards them wound a long line of stretchers bearing the seriously wounded. At the next crossroads, anti-aircraft gun crews in capes were dozing at their guns.

Everything in the town seemed to be proceeding quietly. Their documents were quietly checked, and they were quietly shown the way. Sintsov was delighted by the order he sensed everywhere. As they drove across the bridge and through the town, they were stopped by three night patrols in succession.

Finally, on the very outskirts of Mogilev, the political instructor stopped the pick-up outside a single-storey building.

"I'm just going to check that Serpilin hasn't moved somewhere else," said the political instructor and, showing his papers to the sentry, he disappeared through the gates.

Voices were heard behind the closely-curtained windows. A minute later, the political instructor came out again.

"That's the divisional operational group, and the divisional commander is in there now," he said quietly to Sintsov; and

Sintsov remembered the fat colonel shouting over the telephone: "I'm coming, I'm coming to you, Serpilin!"

"Where is Serpilin?" asked Sintsov. He had heard the name so often from so many different people that day that he felt he almost knew the man personally.

"Where he was before," said the political instructor.

They drove past the last houses on the outskirts, turned off onto a cobbled road, went under a railway bridge, and again ran into some patrolmen who came out of the bushes. This time there were no less than four of them.

"That's organisation for you!" said Mishka.

"Where there are troops, there's organisation," responded the political instructor.

The patrolmen checked their documents and ordered them to park the pick-up in the bushes. Two of them stayed with the vehicle, and the other two told them that they would be escorted to their destination. One went in front, and the second, rifle in hand, brought up in the rear. Sintsov realised that they were under guard and not just being escorted. Stumbling in the dark, they went down into a communications trench, walked along it for some time, then turned off into a full-sized trench and finally stopped in front of a dug-out door. The first patrolman disappeared into the dug-out and emerged a minute later with a very tall man — so tall, that his voice seemed to be coming from somewhere above them in the darkness.

"Who are you?" he demanded.

Mishka replied briskly that they were correspondents.

"What correspondents?" said the man. "What correspondents could be here at midnight? Who could be coming to see me at midnight?"

At the words "to see me", Sintsov knew that this was Serpilin himself.

"I'm going to make all three of you lie down on the ground, and you'll stay there till morning until I've checked your identities! Who sent you here?"

Sintsov said they had been sent by the deputy divisional commander.

"Well, I'm going to make you lie down on the ground until tomorrow," reiterated the other stubbornly, "and in the morning I'm going to inform him that he will kindly not send strangers to my regimental positions during the night."

The political instructor, who had not been expecting this turn of events and had been intimidated into silence at first, finally found his voice:

"Comrade Brigade Commander, it's me, Mironov, from the division political department. You know me, don't you...."

"Yes, I know you," said the brigade commander, "and that's the only reason I'm not going to make you lie there till morning! Judge for yourselves, comrade correspondents," he continued in a quite different tone of voice, with the suggestion of a smile in the dark. "You know the way things have turned out—we've got to be strict whether we like it or not. All you keep hearing round here is 'paratroopers, paratroopers!' But I don't want to hear a whisper about paratroopers in my regiment. As far as I'm concerned, they don't exist. If security is handled properly, there can't be any paratroopers. Go into the dug-out. They'll check your documents there in the light, and I'll be at your service. Mironov, you stay here."

Sintsov and Mishka went into the dug-out and emerged again a minute later. The brigade commander, in a good mood now, shook their hands in the dark and, cupping a lighted cigarette in the palm of his hand, began telling them about the battle which had only ended three hours ago and in which he and his regiment had wiped out thirty-nine German tanks. He was full of reminiscences about this engagement and talked about it with growing animation in a thin falsetto, so young-sounding that Sintsov wouldn't have given this tall officer more than thirty years on the evidence of his voice alone. Sintsov listened and was puzzled. What was this man with the young voice doing in the long-since obsolete rank of brigade commander, and why, with such a rank, was he only in command of a regiment?

"They keep on about tanks," said Serpilin, "but we've been knocking those tanks out and we're going to keep on knocking them out. Why? You'll see in the morning, at daybreak. I've got twenty kilometres of trenches dug in my regiment. It's a fact—no fooling! You'll be able to see for yourselves tomorrow. If they try it on again, so will we. That's one of them standing there, if you please!" And he pointed to a small black hump visible not far away. "Stopped a hundred metres short of my command post, and he's staying there like a good little boy, exactly where he was told to. Why? Because a soldier in a trench needn't flatten his ears back like a frightened rabbit."

Chain-smoking incessantly, he spent the next hour telling Sintsov and Mishka how hard it was to maintain the fighting spirit of the regiment when hundreds and even thousands of men who had broken out of encirclement had been streaming every day down the road across which the regiment had taken up its positions.

"Yes, there's plenty of panic-mongers there," said Mishka off-handedly.

The brigade commander was needled by the hint of arrogance in the voice of this man who had never known what it was to risk his neck in action.

"Yes, there's more than a few panic-mongers," he said. "But people are only human after all. It's terrifying enough for them in battle; but when they can't put up a fight, it's twice as bad! How does it all begin? A man's walking along a road behind the lines, and suddenly a tank comes straight at him! He runs the other way, and there's another tank heading for him! He flattens himself on the ground, and now he's being strafed from the air! Call them panic-mongers if you like. But we've got to look things soberly in the face. Nine out of ten aren't panicky by nature. Give them a breather, get them organised, then put them into normal battle conditions, and they'll prove their worth. Mind you, the way they are—wobbly at the knees and their eyes popping out of their heads—they aren't much use. You look at them, and you think—if only they'd all crossed the lines sooner. If only these were the last! But no, they still keep on coming. Mind you, it's a good thing. They'll still be able to fight. But it's awkward for us. Never mind, we haven't let them ruin our morale," concluded Serpilin at last. "Today's battle proved that. I'm pleased with my men, I must admit! Ever since morning, I was as jittery as a bride on her wedding-day. I haven't been in action for twenty years. The first battle's no joke! But I'm alright now, and I've got faith in my regiment. So I'm happy. Very happy!" he repeated, almost challengingly. "Anyway, that's enough waffling. It's stuffy in the dug-out and there isn't much room anyway. Have you got your greatcoats with you?"

"Yes."

"Then go to sleep here, up on top. If you hear machine-gun fire, don't take any notice. Just the Germans trying to shake us up a bit. But if the artillery opens up, kindly take cover in the trenches! Please excuse me, I'm going to do the rounds of the posts." He saluted in the dark and, accompanied by several other men who had silently joined him, he went off down the trench.

"We'll get no grub out of that one," said Mishka, half-accusingly, half-approvingly, after he and Sintsov had wrapped themselves up in their greatcoats and lain down on the ground.

For a long time Sintsov gazed in silence at the clouded sky in which there was not a single star to be seen. He dozed off, and then only a few minutes later, as it seemed to him, he heard the vicious rattle of machine-gun fire. Still half-asleep, he could hear it dying down and then growing louder—at one moment it seemed to be coming from where it had started, and the next moment it was somewhere else.

"Listen, Mishka!" He suddenly woke up with the impression that they were completely surrounded by firing and dug his snoring companion in the ribs.

"What is it?" asked the other sleepily.

"Listen, there's something funny about this. That shooting started in front, at our feet, and now it's somewhere behind us, at our heads. What does it mean?"

"Lie the other way round," joked Mishka, only half awake; and he started snoring again.

CHAPTER FOUR

When Sintsov woke up, the sky overhead was a deep, deep blue, the sun was shining, and there was only the distant, almost inaudible rumble of artillery to remind him of the war. After lying there for several minutes, alternately shutting his eyes tight and opening them again, Sintsov jumped to his feet. Mishka was sitting beside him, reloading one of his Leicas.

"What a day, just look at it!" said Sintsov joyfully.

The brigade commander came out of his dug-out, stooping low in the doorway. In the light of day, he turned out to be nothing like the young man Sintsov had imagined the previous night. Serpilin looked at least fifty. He was bareheaded, with a few yellow, greying strands of hair combed across in an unavailing effort to cover the big bald patch on his head. He had an ugly, long, equine face, deeply lined, and two rows of steel teeth in his mouth.

"Did you have a good rest?" he asked, smoothing with one hand the already flat hair on his head; and he smiled a broad, steel-toothed smile that suddenly made his ugly face seem good-natured and younger.

"Yes, thank you," replied Sintsov.

"I'd like some shots of the tanks as soon as possible," said Mishka impatiently. "They need tanks for the newspaper like they need bread!"

"Captain Plotnikov will be free in a moment. He's a battalion commander. You can go with him to his unit. He knocked out more tanks than anyone else yesterday. Any more questions for me? I'm going to be rather busy later on."

"Tell us, Comrade Brigade Commander," said Mishka briskly, "how come we never saw a single AA gun when we were driving across the bridge last night?"

"What do we want with that bridge?" demanded Serpilin in a voice which Sintsov was to remember for the rest of his life.

"I just thought," said Misha with a shrug of the shoulders, "supposing we have to go that way?" And he pointed towards the Dnieper.

"We won't have to," said Serpilin. "Our men haven't been digging trenches just to abandon them as soon as the enemy asks them to. It's an old story, even though they tend to forget it: they dig and dig, and then...." He waved his hand. "But we've dug in and we're not going to quit. As for the others, we're not concerned with them!" There was a note of bitterness in the last sentence. It was untrue, and he didn't really mean it; but it had been provoked by a feeling of which he was not ashamed. Serpilin knew what neither Sintsov nor Mishka did—that the Germans had already forced the Dnieper to the right and left of Mogilev, and if in the next few hours he didn't receive orders to retreat, then he and his regiment were doomed to fight in encirclement. At present, however, he neither expected nor wanted the order to retreat. He was inspired by the pride of a soldier who refused to believe that someone next to him was fighting badly and was retreating or fleeing. This was what he meant when he said that he was not concerned with the others. He had been digging in for ten days and nights, and had done the job properly. His regiment had fought well the day before, and must fight well in future. He believed this and considered that if it were the same with the others, then the war would be won. He was ready to die for this, and he preferred to die rather than retreat.

"What do you think, Comrade Brigade Commander?" asked Sintsov. "Will there be action today, or will it be quiet?" Something of Serpilin's suppressed uneasiness had communicated itself to him, and a dark surmise was stirring at the bottom of his mind.

"Quiet, I'm afraid," said Serpilin after a moment's thought. "And I'm afraid they'll try and break through at a weaker point. I've always had a fairly high opinion of the Germans' tactics—they're not bad tacticians," he added with a note of defiance which was completely lost on Sintsov. He then smiled grimly and tensely over some private recollection, but kept it to himself. "You haven't shaved, Captain Plotnikov," he observed, shaking hands with an officer who had just joined him.

The captain was certainly in need of shave. His eyes were red and tired, but he looked equally ready to do anything he was asked, or to go to sleep on the spot if allowed to.

"Sorry, Comrade Brigade Commander. I've had ten days and nights digging trenches, then the battle, and then the trenches to patch up again."

"I know all about that," said Serpilin, "but you ought to shave just the same. This cameraman's going to photograph you as the best battalion commander, and you haven't even shaved! Take the correspondents with you, see they get some shots of the tanks, and bring them back this evening." Serpilin nodded curtly and went into the dug-out.

Captain Plotnikov watched him go, ran his hand over his stubble, and said simply:

"Let's go!"

He went in front, with Sintsov and Mishka following on behind. The battalion commander really did look as though he hadn't been out of the trenches for ten days and nights. His cap was crumpled—he must have been sleeping in it—his boots hadn't been cleaned, and there were traces of hastily brushed-off mud on his tunic and trousers.

Serpilin had not been exaggerating when he had said that his regiment was well dug in. There were full-size trenches leading all the way to the battalion, and they were linked by so many communications trenches, main and reserve, that even heavy artillery fire would have been hard put to break down the organisation of the regiment. The command posts consisted of dug-outs protected by several layers of roofing, and machine-guns had been mounted on round earth platforms.

"Just the way the Japs dug in," said Mishka approvingly.
"What?" asked Plotnikov, turning round.
"Like the Japs on Khalkhin-Gol," said Mishka. "Until you'd winkled every single one out, it was no go!"
"Were you at Khalkhin-Gol, then?" asked Plotnikov without the slightest interest.
"I was."
"We were in action for the first time yesterday," said Plotnikov, and he continued on his way.
The battalion's front line skirted a grove of young oak-trees. In front lay a rye field, and then, the beginning of a dense pine forest, in which the Germans were positioned. A railway track ran out of the forest and, parallel and quite close to the railway, a highway. Both ran through the battalion positions and led to the regiment's rear. In front of the trenches, in the rye field, could be seen the smaller trenches of a battle outpost linked to the front line by communications trenches. In front of the trenches, in the rye, stood the German tanks knocked out in yesterday's battle.
"What about the rest of the tanks?" asked Mishka eagerly of the captain. "They told me fourteen were knocked out in front of your positions. I can see nine. Where are the other five?"
"There's five more behind the battle outpost, but in a gully. You can't see them from here."
"All right, I'll pop over there later," said Mishka. "But now let's go to the ones in the rye."
"Can't you snap them from here?" asked Plotnikov.
"Why? Isn't it quiet now?"
"Quiet?" echoed Plotnikov doubtfully, and he called a company commander, a fair-haired lieutenant of about twenty.
"Go down with them, Khoryshev," said Plotnikov, nodding towards Mishka. "They want to photograph the tanks. Take five men from the battle outpost, let them crawl up to the tanks, take cover there just in case, and then bring these two back."
He sounded listless and tired. He wanted to get shut of this garrulous correspondent as soon as possible and snatch at least some sleep.
"Will you be staying with me?" he asked, turning to Sintsov.
"No, I'm going too," said the latter. He wanted to feel those knocked out German tanks with his own hands.

"Very well, off you go," agreed Plotnikov in the same listless voice. "I'll stay here and get some shut-eye." His attitude to what they might think of him suggested the double indifference of a very brave and very tired man.

The tanks were further off than they seemed. The three men had to crawl quite a distance to reach them. But there were no German sub-machine gunners in the rye, and not a single shot was fired from the forest.

Mishka first photographed the tanks lying down or squatting on his haunches. Then, emboldened, he stood up. He wanted to take all nine machines, but couldn't get them into the viewfinder. Seven fitted nicely, but the other were out of frame. Mishka's face betrayed a frustrated but passionate desire to drag those other two tanks bodily up to the others.

While Mishka was photographing, Sintsov wandered round the tanks. Standing there motionless and dead in the rye, they didn't seem as big and terrible as he had expected. They were dirty, with low round turrets like giant bottle-tops. Several dead Germans lay nearby. There was a nauseating smell. Sintsov felt slightly sick.

After he had finished, Mishka took an escort and went off to the neighbouring company to photograph the rest of the tanks, while Sintsov returned to the company command post with Lieutenant Khoryshev. A tiny dug-out had been let into the foot of the railway embankment not far from the patrolman's box.

"Let's sit by the box," said Khoryshev to Sintsov in a less formal tone of voice. "I've got some grub and water there. The old patrolman's still living in it."

"Why?" asked Sintsov.

"Goodness knows, but he is, and he's not a bit scared! My men did a little job for him. They dug him a slit trench, and not one shell hit the box all through the battle—can you beat that?"

They went over to the hut. The patrolman was sitting on the embankment near the slit trench with his trousers rolled up to his knees and was sunning his bony, old man's legs with the veins bulging under the skin. His boots stood beside him and his foot-wrappers were drying in the sun. His eyes shut tight, he was slowly wiggling his bare toes.

"They gave him a German lieutenant's uniform yesterday," said Khoryshev with a smile, sitting down on the embankment beside him, "and he put it on straightaway—just tore off the epaulettes."

And, sure enough, the old man was wearing a dark-green uniform over his black satin blouse. On hearing Khoryshev, he half turned, sleepily opened one eye and, touching the sleeve of the uniform, said approvingly:

"Not bad material at all."

"Isn't it too warm for you?"

"Steam never broke any bones."

"Why haven't you gone to Mogilev?" asked Sintsov.

"What's the point?" said the old man indifferently. "You say you won't be pulling out," he continued, turning to Khoryshev.

"We won't," answered Khoryshev.

"Well then, I'll stick it out with you. I'm on duty."

"We're keeping Dad in food," said Khoryshev.

"There's that, too," rejoined the old man, again languidly half-opening an eye in which there was a twinkle of amusement. "They're good lads; but the Germans really laid it on yesterday—not half they didn't!"

"Did you have heavy losses?" asked Sintsov.

Khoryshev, blinking in the sunlight, pushed his cap down over his eyes and said that there had been appreciable losses in the company: up to thirty killed and wounded.

"Let's take our boots off as well," he said. "All that walking gives you sore feet."

He pulled off his boots, laid out his foot-wrappers on the sleepers, and then, like the old man, began wiggling his numb toes with obvious pleasure.

"Tarpaulin boots," he said, "from the military college. They hadn't got anything else. The boys took some boots off a German, an officer he was, and gave them to me—but they didn't fit. Too tight in the instep, and the uppers were too stiff. They probably treat them with something."

"Same as in tsarist times," commented the patrolman. "Ordinary officers' boots with a lining."

Sintsov likewise took off his boots. Khoryshev went inside the hut in his bare feet and returned with a pan of water, some bread, and three dried salt fish.

"Don't step on the rails, they're hot!" said the old man, and he looked dubiously at the fish. "Make you thirsty, they will!"

However, when Khoryshev didn't answer and offered him one of the fish instead, the old man took it without demur and started skinning it.

While all three of them were sitting and eating side by side, Sintsov stole an occasional glance at Khoryshev. He found it strange that this quite young, lively and practical soldier should have been in action against the Germans only yesterday, and yet today should be talking about the battle as if it were all in the day's work and there was nothing to be afraid of even if it happened again.

They sat there for another half hour, and then three scouts came up, each wheeling two German bicycles. They had been abandoned on the road early that morning by a German reconnaissance party which had come out of the forest. We had opened fire, two Germans had been killed, and the rest had fled into the forest. Khoryshev had given orders for the bicycles to be collected, and the scouts had brought them in.

"Leave three in the company, and hand over three to the battalion," instructed Khoryshev.

One of the scouts scowled.

"Hand them over, I said—hand them over!" repeated Khoryshev. "Or else Plotnikov'll blow up and collar the lot!"

The scouts went off. A minute later, a Messerschmidt began circling over the rye field, now soaring up into the sky, now diving down repeatedly the same spot.

"They're shooting up your mate," said Khoryshev calmly. "That's just where the tanks are."

The Messerschmidt circled over the field for about ten more minutes and then flew off. Sintsov was beginning to feel worried, but Mishka's portly figure appeared on the skyline. He came up, flopped down on the embankment, saw the unfinished fish in Sintsov's hands, said, "let's have that," and hungrily buried his teeth in it. Khoryshev went into the hut and fetched some more fish.

"Was that you being strafed just now?" asked Sintsov.

"It was," said Mishka, and burst out laughing. "I went down flat on my belly and wriggled under a tank. So there he was, buzzing about like a mosquito, but he couldn't do a thing."

"Did you photograph all of them?" asked Sintsov.

"Yes. We can go now."

Mishka finished off Sintsov's fish, then ate two more with equal despatch and drank up the pan of water. Sintsov put his boots on, said goodbye to the patrolman, and all three of them—himself, Mishka, and Khoryshev—returned to Plotnikov at the battalion.

Plotnikov was sitting in a dug-out at the telephone, monotonously chanting into the mouthpiece:

"Yes, I understand. Yes, I understand. I'll see to it." He replaced the handset and stood up behind his table.

"Well, did you get some sleep?" asked Sintsov.

"I did," said Plotnikov. "For what good *that* much did?"

"I'll photograph you now," said Mishka.

They went outside, and Mishka looked Plotnikov over with unconcealed dissatisfaction, noting the unshaven chin, the crumpled cap, the stained uniform, and the automatic pistol dangling over his stomach.

"That's no use," said Mishka.

He liked formal shots, and Plotnikov didn't look right for the part.

"Tighten your belt," instructed Mishka. "Why aren't you wearing a cross-strap? Have you got a cross-strap?"

"It's in the dug-out," said Plotnikov.

"Get it, then, so that you're in full uniform."

Plotnikov reluctantly went back into the dug-out, returned with his cross-strap, threw it over his shoulder, and hooked it on to his belt.

"Fasten your collar," demanded the remorseless Mishka.

Plotnikov fumbled at it and said irritably:

"The hook's come off."

Mishka sighed:

"Have you got a helmet?"

"No, I haven't."

"How come you haven't got a helmet?"

"Khoryshev, get one of the men to lend me his helmet," said Plotnikov. He was fed up and wasn't attempting to hide it.

Khoryshev brought a helmet, and Plotnikov put it on in place of his cap, Mishka straightened the automatic, adjusted the focus for the last time, and photographed Plotnikov, who didn't look any better for the helmet, the automatic, and, in general, all the changes in his external appearance insisted on by Mishka.

Then Mishka hurriedly snapped Khoryshev who, not expecting to be asked, hastily borrowed the captain's automatic and helmet, put them on, and, tense and unblinking, drew himself up to his full height in front of the camera.

"I'll send you a sergeant straightaway and he'll escort you to the regimental command post," said Plotnikov. "The brigade commander's phoned and ordered us to dig some slit trenches under the German tanks during the night and lay an ambush. I'm going to get on with it. It's nearly evening." He shrugged his broad shoulders wearily, turned his back on them, and went off towards the trench.

"Well now, did Plotnikov feed you, or didn't it occur to him?" asked Serpilin, when Sintsov and Mishka rejoined him.

"They did sort of..." began Mishka vaguely, but Serpilin took his answer as final and, without letting him say any more, asked:

"So you've done your job and can go now, can you?"

"Yes," said Mishka. "I've got to be in Moscow by tomorrow and hand in the material for the issue. But I'd like a photograph of you too."

"What d'you want one of me for?" said Serpilin. "Get going. Time's precious."

Something in his voice caught Sintsov's attention. Serpilin seemed to want to be rid of them as soon as possible. The gunfire, which had been coming from north and south all day, had shifted, as evening approached, far towards the east, behind them.

"Please allow me to photograph you anyway, Comrade Brigade Commander," insisted Mishka.

"Take the three of us, then—the commissar, the chief of staff, and myself, so that I can have a keepsake of my regimental comrades," said Serpilin. "Will you really do the prints?"

"Yes," lied Mishka, who had never sent out any prints in his life. "I'll do them and send them to you."

"Don't send them here," said Serpilin, again in the tone of voice that Sintsov had noticed earlier. "Send them to our wives. We'll give you their addresses." He summoned an orderly and told him to call the commissar and the chief of staff.

"Where are your wives?" asked Mishka.

"Theirs are at an army town in Ryazan. Mine's in Moscow. Have you a notepad on you?"

Mishka pulled a grubby jotter out of his map-case. Serpilin turned over a few pages, found a blank one, and wrote in big, firm letters: *"Valentina Yegorovna Serpilina, Flat 4, 16 Pirogovskaya Street."*

Pirogovskaya Street.... It was quite near the Usachevka and the Artemyevs' poky little flat, from which Masha had set out with Sintsov when she was seeing him off to Grodno.

"Grodno, Grodno..." he thought for the hundredth time during the last few days; and once again there was that sick feeling in the pit of his stomach, and once again he wondered helplessly what had happened to his little daughter.

The commissar and the regimental chief of staff arrived a minute later.

"He's offered to take our photos," said Serpilin, "and he's promised to send them to our wives."

And for the third time during the last few minutes, Sintsov sensed an unspoken something in his voice, a kind of sad and solemn finality.

Serpilin stood in the middle, with the commissar on his left, and on his right the chief of staff, a handsome young man with brown hair and sorrowful black eyes.

"You stand with them," said Mishka, turning to Sintsov, "only not right up close. Then I can cut you and make a separate print for your wife." He didn't want to reload the camera, and the film was nearly used up.

Sintsov took his place beside the others. Mishka clicked the shutter, picked up his notepad, and was going to write down the other addresses, when Sintsov, who wanted to make sure that the photographs really were delivered to these three officers' wives, advised them each to write a brief note home. Comrade Weinstein would send the messages along with the photographs. Sintsov knew that for all his dislike of printing photo graphs, Mishka would not for anything in the world lose a message from the front.

"What do we want to write for?" Serpilin was going to refuse, but then he noticed the sorrowful young eyes of his chief of staff and agreed: "Very well, we'll write. Two words each. We don't want to hold you up. You've got to get going."

"He's a menace!" said Mishka, when all had gone to write their letters. "Got to get going! Got to get going!" That means he's not aiming to give us any supper. I don't need telling I've got to get going; but at least I'd snatch a few minutes for supper. Not with him, though. He's throwing us out on our ear, the mean old so-and-so!"

"You don't understand what it's all about!" Suddenly it became absolutely clear to Sintsov what those photographs and letters meant. And an unexpected but firm decision—the outcome of all he had been through in the last three weeks—began to take shape in his mind.

"Wait for me here. I'll be right back," he said, and he opened the door to Serpilin's dug-out. "May I come in, Comrade Brigade Commander?"

"Come in."

Serpilin was sitting at a table and scrawling something on a sheet torn out of a field book.

"What is it?" he asked, breaking off; and he indicated a stool near the talbe. "Take a seat."

Sintsov sat down. Something in his expression must have caught Serpilin's eye.

"What's happened?"

"I'm not leaving with my comrade," said Sintsov. "With your permission, I'd like to stay with your regiment pending."

"Pending what?" demanded Serpilin quickly.

"I'd rather not leave your regiment," said Sintsov, evading a direct answer.

"Why?"

"It seems to me you've no intention of retreating. I want to stay with you." And Sintsov looked Serpilin straight in the eye.

"True, we've no intention of retreating," said Serpilin. "But we aren't the only pebble on the beach. You've seen how things are with us. Off you go and have a look at the others. There aren't enough correspondents, and there's plenty of units. Off you go, off you go," he concluded with uncharacteristic and forced cheerfulness. "I can't let you stay, there's nothing for you to do here." And he returned to his letter.

"Comrade Brigade Commander," said Sintsov in a voice that made Serpilin stare hard at him again. "I'm sick of running around like a rabbit, and I'm sick of not knowing what to write. It's the fourth week of the war, and I haven't put pen to paper yet. I don't know, maybe I've just been plain unlucky; but today, at last, I've been with a regiment where they've actually knocked out thirty-nine German tanks, and at last I've seen them with my own eyes. If a battle starts here tomorrow, I'll be able to see that with my own eyes too, and I'll be able to write something about it. I work on a Front newspaper. You have a front here; so where else should I be, if not with you?"

"Now look here, Comrade ... I've forgotten. You told me your name yesterday...."

"Sintsov."

"Look here, Comrade Sintsov," and Serpilin's face was grave. "I quite understand your eagerness to see some action, but there are occasions when only those on a unit's complement have to stay, and there's no necessity for outsiders to fight and die with it as well. If we just had fighting ahead of us, I'd let you stay. But it clearly won't just be fighting, it'll be fighting in encirclement. I guessed that much this morning, and I'm certain of it now. Did you hear the artillery?"

"I heard it," said Sintsov.

"You didn't listen properly," said Serpilin. "The Germans are on both sides of us now, and they're well beyond the Dnieper. I haven't been told officially yet, but I can hear with my own two ears. You might run into complications en route even if you leave right this minute. So off you go. Let me finish writing my letter. I haven't much time, and neither have you."

"Comrade Brigade Commander!" said Sintsov. "Comrade Brigade Commander!" he reiterated stubbornly, raising his voice in order to compel Serpilin's attention, the latter having already reached for his pencil.

"Well?" Serpilin looked up from his writing with evident annoyance.

"I'm a Communist, a political instructor by rank, and I request you to let me stay here. Whatever happens to you will happen to me. If we survive, I'll write it all up just as it was. But I won't be a nuisance. If I have to, I'll die no worse than the rest."

"Comrade Sintsov, mind you don't regret this afterwards!" said Serpilin, slowly looking him up and down, but in a much friendlier voice.

"I won't regret it," said Sintsov, convinced at that moment that he really wouldn't regret it, and realising that the matter was settled and there was nothing more to discuss.

"Tell your comrade that I'll be finished with this in a minute, so he can be getting ready," said Serpilin as Sintsov was on the way out.

"They've stocked us up with some grub for the road," said Mishka gaily, slapping his kitbag, which was almost near to bursting. "The brigade commander didn't tell us anything, but gave the instructions just the same."

"Listen, Mishka, I'm not going with you. I'm staying here for a few days," said Sintsov, without going into details.

"What d'you mean you're staying? How long for? What's the matter with you? Not enough copy?"

"No."

"Well, you can come back for more. You've got enough to be going on with in the meantime!"

"No, Misha, I'm staying!" repeated Sintsov stubbornly.

"Listen, that's stupid!" shouted Mishka, going red in the face and beginning to lose his temper. "You know I can't stay with you. Nobody's going to deliver the photos to the paper for me!"

"That's right," said Sintsov, "so you go!"

"And then it'll look as though I've left you here on your own!"

"Don't be a fool!" said Sintsov. "Get going and leave it at that!"

"Very well," said Mishka, who had just had an idea that could get him out of this unpleasant situation. "I'll pop into Moscow, hand in the photos, and come back to you, here. In three days at the most. But don't go anywhere else! Wait here, where you are! Word of honour?"

"Word of honour!" said Sintsov, responding to Mishka's warm handshake.

Mishka had instantly cheered up at this salutary brainwave.

"Listen," he said as an afterthought. "Write me a hundred lines now, so that I'll have some copy about how they knocked out those tanks. I'll see that it goes in with my panorama shot. You'll be published in *Izvestia,* and that won't do you any harm, will it?"

Sintsov remembered apprehensively what Serpilin had said about time being precious, and couldn't make up his mind whether or not to hold Mishka up any longer.

At that moment, Serpilin came out of the dug-out with an unsealed envelope.

"Here," he said to Mishka. "I've written it. Put the photograph in afterwards and seal it then. Are you ready and on your way?"

"Immediately. He's just—" Mishka nodded towards Sintsov—"going to write me some copy, and I'll be off."

Sintsov asked Serpilin's permission to go into the dug-out and write a couple of pages for the newspaper. It was already beginning to get dark outside.

"In you go," said Serpilin. "I'm leaving anyway. Did the others give you their letters?"

"Yes," said Mishka, slapping his food-stuffed kitbag.

"Have a good journey." Serpilin shook his hand and went off, not saying goodbye to Sintsov, who was now one of them.

Mishka, who would have been bored waiting on his own, went into the dug-out with Sintsov. Sintsov sat down to write. Mishka unbuttoned his kitbag, took out a piece of bread and sausage, and began champing away with an air of great concentration.

Sintsov wrote quickly and furiously under the pressure of time. Unaware that this was not just the first, but the last front-line article he was ever to write in his life, he described the knocked-out German tanks, the dead Germans lying in the rye, Serpilin, Plotnikov and Khoryshev, and, repeatedly, the most important thing of all—that it was possible, as it turned out, to set fire to oncoming German tanks without having to turn tail and run.

He wrote in haste, and all the implications of his recent decision kept running through his mind. As he wrote, it occurred to him that if he hadn't made this decision earlier and informed Serpilin about it, he might lose courage at this stage and leave. He felt ashamed of his weak-mindedness, not realising that different temperaments are strong in different ways, and their strength sometimes consists in not backing out of a personal decision even when they have become frightened of the consequences.

He wrote the whole article in twenty minutes by his watch, and followed it up with a few lines to Masha on the same page. They were affectionate, but they gave no hint of what was going on in his mind.

"Here, you are," he said, folding the pages in four. "When it's been typed out, give the rough draft to Masha. She may still be in Moscow. This is her telephone number. But don't tear off my personal note to her—give her the lot, rough draft and all. I've already written to her twice from the hospital, but I can rely on you more than on the post."

"I should hope so!" boasted Mishka and, with a sigh, he thrust the unconsumed sausage into his kitbag, took Sintsov's manuscript, and, as a token of special solicitude, put it separately in his tunic pocket.

They left the dug-out together. Mishka didn't like dwelling on his own or other people's decisions for any length of time. Even so, his insensitive but well-meaning heart was troubled by a vague premonition. He didn't like the idea of leaving while Sintsov stayed behind. He didn't like it at all.

"Look after yourself," he said, shaking Sintsov by the hand. "I'll pop in and see you. Promise!" And his square silhouette melted into the darkness.

Sitting on the edge of the trench and staring up into the starry sky, Sintsov thought how tomorrow evening Mishka would race into Moscow in his little pick-up, how he would develop and print his own photos, and how he would rush them, still wet, to the editor's desk. Only then, Sintsov knew, would he telephone Masha. It would be night, and Masha would lift the receiver, if she was in Moscow, and Mishka would tell her that he had seen her husband alive and well only twenty-four hours ago....

As for himself, in twenty-four hours'time.... He didn't know what would be happening to him then and he didn't even want to think about it now. One thing he did know: today's lull couldn't last forever; it would end tonight or in the morning, and then the fighting would begin. And he no more knew what would become of him in that battle than all the other men in Serpilin's regiment who were sitting here beside him in the trenches and—a kilometre or two further on—in dug-outs and communications trenches, and, even further off, in the slit trenches already dug, no doubt, by the hard-working Plotnikov in the rye field.

Neither Sintsov, nor Mishka—who had already sped across the Dnieper bridge and in his turn was wondering about Sintsov—knew what was to become of them in twenty-four hours' time.

Mishka, troubled by the thought that he had left his comrade at the front and was himself on the way back to Moscow, didn't know that in twenty-four hours Sintsov would be neither dead, nor wounded, nor scratched, but alive and well, only mortally tired and fast asleep on the bottom of that same trench.

And Sintsov, envying Mishka who would be in Moscow talking to Masha in twenty-four hours, didn't know that Mishka would not, in fact, be in Moscow or talking to Masha, because he would have been mortally wounded near Chausy that morning by a machine-gun burst from a German motor-cycle. This burst would hit his big, strong body in several places and Mishka, summoning up his last strength, would crawl into the bushes at the roadside and, bleeding profusely, would expose the film of the German tanks, of the tired Plotnikov, whom he had forced to don helmet and automatic, of Khoryshev, who had stood so gallantly to attention, and of Serpilin, Sintsov, and the sorrowful chief of staff. Then, driven by a last subconscious impulse, he would tear up with his fat and weakening hands the letters given him by these officers for their wives. At first, the scraps of torn paper would scatter over the ground near Mishka's bleeding, dying body; then they would lift off the ground and, tumbling over and over in the wind, would be swept along the dusty highway under the wheels of the German lorries and the caterpillar tracks of the German tanks crawling along on their way east.

CHAPTER FIVE

Fyodor Fyodorovich Serpilin was a man with one of those careers which will break before it will bend. His service records contained many entries, but he had spent his life concerned essentially with one thing: to serve the Revolution as a soldier in the best way possible. He had served in the First World War, had served in the Civil War, had served in command of regiments and divisions, had served as a student and then as an instructor in military academies, and had continued to serve even when an unkind fate had sent him to Kolyma.

He had been born into the family of a village doctor, his father being Russian and his mother a Tatar from Kasimov who had run away from home and been baptised so as to marry his father. Serpilin senior was still serving as a doctor in Tuma, on a narrow-gauge railway running through dense forest. There Serpilin spent his childhood, and it was from there that, as an eighteen-year-old boy, he followed in his father's footsteps and went to study at a medical school in Ryazan. While there, he became involved with a revolutionary circle, found himself under police observation, and would probably have ended up in exile, had not the First World War given him an army haircut.

In the winter of 1917, Medical Assistant Serpilin took part in the first fraternisations with the Germans at the front; then in the autumn, as an elected battalion commander, he fought the Germans advancing on Red Petrograd. When the Red Army was organised, he continued serving with the infantry—it suited his temperament—and finished the Civil War in command of a regiment at Perekop.

Those of his fellow officers who knew about his past treated it as a joke, calling him "the medical assistant" behind his back. That phase of his life was so much a part of his remote past, that it should have been dead and buried long ago; but he used on occasion to joke about his old profession himself. As far as Serpilin could remember, he spent most of his time after the Civil War studying. After taking a refresher course, he again took command of a regiment, then studied at a military academy, graduated, then, retraining for the tanks, served in the first mechanised units and, returning to the infantry once more and commanding a division for two years, obtained an appointment to the Chair of Tactics in the very Frunze Academy where he had graduated five years previously. But even there he went on with his studies, swotting up German in his spare time as the most likely enemy language.

When he was suddenly arrested in 1937, this knowledge of German was held against him, strange as it may seem, and so were the German military manuals found in his flat when it was being searched.

The immediate reason for his arrest proved to be the warnings, not at all fashionable at that time, which he had been giving in his lectures about the strong points of the tactical views held by Hitler's newly reinstated Wehrmacht.

He had been thinking about this yesterday when he had bitterly complimented the Germans on their tactics, smiling grimly at memories which Sintsov could not have hoped to divine.

After his arrest, which came as a terrible shock to him, he was accused of everything under the sun in addition to the original and, in his opinion, fatuous charge of disseminating propaganda about the superiority of the fascist army. His statements were twice sent for by Yezhov, and for all of six months, three investigators took turns at urging him to sign a confession to crimes he had never committed.

They finally gave him ten years, virtually without trial. Six months later, already in confinement, he beat the living daylights out of a fellow serviceman of Civil War times, a Trotskyite who mistakenly thought he could take Serpilin into his confidence and who began airing his views that the Party had degenerated and the Revolution had been betrayed.

To Serpilin, prison was mainly a useless waste of time. Remembering those four lost years now, in wartime, he would grind his teeth with fury. But not once throughout those four years did he blame the Soviet system for the way he had been treated. He considered it a monstrous misunderstanding, a mistake, a foolish blunder. As far as he was concerned, Communism had been, and still was, a sacred and unbesmirched cause. When he was released as suddenly as he had been imprisoned, he came out aged and physically worn; but his soul remained unravaged by the scars of old age and loss of faith.

He returned to Moscow on the first day of the war with only one aim in mind—to get to the front as soon as possible. His old comrades had been persistently trying for years to obtain his release, and they helped him on this occasion too. He went to the front without even waiting for reinstatement in the Party. He handed in his papers to the Party Commission and left to take over a regiment. He was even ready to command a platoon, just so long as he could get back without any shilly-shallying to his job, which was fighting once again, not just army service. He wanted to prove his capabilities as soon as possible. They had already returned him his arms and his rank, promised to reinstate him in the Party, and sent him off to fight the nazis. What more could he ask? But he wanted to show by his own personal example that many others who were still in the plight that he had been in, had been victims of the same absurdity as himself. Yes, absurdity.

This feeling mounted inside him with every day at the front. The Germans were strong—there were no two ways about it. There had been initial blunders, and now things were not getting any better.

The question arises: why had it been thought necessary, when war was in the air, to deprive the army of men like Serpilin? They weren't of course, the only pebbles on the beach. The army would win the war without them in any case. But why without them? What was the point?

He was thinking about this today, before dawn, lying on a truss of hay brought him by an orderly. The first successful battle had filled him with faith—not that his regiment was going to work miracles, although he would have liked to believe that too—but that things in general were not as grim as they had at first seemed.

The Army had, of course, been fighting better and had been inflicting heavier losses on the Germans than might have been imagined from seeing the men who had broken out of encirclement and were drifting through his positions. No doubt it was fighting in hundreds of places, much as his own regiment had fought its first battle here; and if, notwithstanding, the Germans were still moving forward, surrounding us and hemming us in, at least they weren't finding it easy and it was costing them dear. The sheer vastness of the theatre of operations and the throwing of our reserves into battle, plus more equipment, which was bound to reach them at the front in the normal quantities sooner or later—all this would finally stop the Germans on a line somewhere. The only question was, where was that line going to be?

Serpilin was not at all pleased about yesterday's lull. He realised that the Germans were not leaving him alone because they had lost any hope of smashing his regiment, but because they were, unfortunately, skilfully redeploying their forces. The results of this redeployment had already begun to make themselves felt. The enemy had broken through on both sides of Mogilev. That had been clear from the sound of artillery fire receding towards the east. Only an idiot could have failed to realise that. And here he was, stuck with his regiment, doing nothing and waiting for his own turn to come.

The last order to reach the division before communications with the Army were lost had been to hold tight on to the position. Well, for men who were ready to sell their lives dearly and who knew how to do so, this was not a bad order, especially if it was not to be followed by an order to retreat before it was too late. But what had happened to the neighbouring divisions? And how long were they going to continue—these endless breakthroughs and encirclements he was sick and tired of hearing about?

Thinking about what lay ahead, Serpilin feared more than anything else a belated order to withdraw. Anyway, if a battle started in the morning, there could be no withdrawal.

And there was going to be a battle alright. The division was covering Mogilev, there were roads converging at this point, there was a bridge across the Dnieper—and you don't leave that kind of knot in your rear without making some attempt to unravel it.

"What does he think he's doing here? Will probably get himself killed," thought Serpilin sympathetically with a glance at Sintsov, who was fast asleep beside him on the grass. "Still young, like my chief of staff. Young wife too, probably...." And Serpilin's thoughts went out to his own wife in Moscow, in the flat that went with his job at the academy. When they had arrested him, they had at least left her own room: someone had evidently had a conscience. "She's aged!" thought Serpilin tenderly. "Her hair's quite grey. She's worn herself out writing out applications for permission to visit me, and sending parcels, and doing the rounds of my colleagues and the chiefs. And she was so beautiful once. And so many hot-heads and fools in the different garrisons couldn't understand why she ever married her lanky freak and why she wasn't even unfaithful to him."

From the west came a distinct, reverberating boom: the Germans had sent over several shells at once.

"Plotnikov's getting it," noted Serpilin calmly. "So it's started."

Sintsov jumped up and, still half-asleep, began fumbling round for his forage cap.

"So you're still with us?" said Serpilin, casually brushing the hay off his uniform. "It's too late for regrets now...."

Sintsov didn't say anything.

"Well, let's go and do the rounds of my battalions. You wanted to see a battle. Now you're going to."

The battle, which began that morning on the sector held by Serpilin's regiment, lasted three days and nights without respite. By noon on the first day, the Germans had failed to push forward anywhere, despite a heavy barrage which they kept up without sparing their ammunition, and despite several attacks by tanks carrying assault troops. Another twenty burnt-out wrecks of tanks and gun-carriers stood before the regimental lines. There were said to be five hundred Germans dead in the rye field, which number Serpilin, who was wary of exaggeration, reduced to three hundred in his report to the division. The regiment lost even more men owing to the barrage and the tanks, and also because German sub-machine gunners mowed down an entire company as it fled the trenches. In half of the companies, commanders or political instructors were killed, and so was Plotnikov, who never did get the chance of enough sleep, and the regimental commissar, who was blown to pieces when a mortar bomb scored a direct hit on an observation post.

In the afternoon, Colonel Zaichikov, the divisional commander, finally got through to Serpilin, the last of his three regimental COs. He had been on the far side of the Dnieper since morning and, realising that he was surrounded, had turned the regiment in the second echelon there to face east with its rear to the river. Then, crossing the Dnieper, he had spent half the day with the regiment that was covering the outskirts of Mogilev. The German artillery shelling had been particularly heavy there, but the attacks had been weaker than those against Serpilin. The Germans must have wanted to avoid street fighting in the town, preferring to wipe out Serpilin first and then skirt round Mogilev, emerging at the Dnieper bridge. This, at any rate, was what Serpilin was told by Colonel Zaichikov, who arrived at the command post streaming with sweat, his hot hand thrust under his tunic and pressing against his weak heart, which was beginning to feel the strain after a day out on the forward positions. A heavily-built man with pouches under his eyes, he stood beside Serpilin, convulsively gasping for breath.

"Our Glushchenko's had it," said Zaichikov regretfully of his commissar, still gasping for breath. "It was senseless the way he got killed. A stray shell near the bridge."

"Whoever got killed sensibly?" responded Serpilin. "As I reported to you, my commissar's been killed, so I'm in mourning too."

"I know," said Zaichikov. "I've brought you a replacement."

He turned to the officer who had arrived with him, a small, red-faced battalion commissar with grey eyebrows and wearing double-lensed spectacles. Serpilin hadn't seen him in the division at all until now.

"A lecturer from none other than the Central Political Directorate", said Zaichikov, still fighting for breath. "Come to give us lectures; and you can see the sort of lectures we're getting here...."

"Shmakov," said the battalion commissar, saluting.

"Comrade Shmakov has personally expressed the desire to join your regiment. He fully understands the position. The order has gone out to the division," said Zaichikov, "so let me congratulate you on your new regimental commissar."

Serpilin looked quizzically at Zaichikov.

"Yes, exactly. Regimental commissar," repeated the latter. "The last thing that the late Glushchenko received from the Army Political Department before communications were broken off was an order about the restoration of the institute of military commissars. He wanted to visit the regiments personally with the news, but he never got the chance, poor fellow...."

"Well, it's a good thing," said Serpilin after a pause. "I've been used to it ever since the Civil War. A commander and a commissar. And it does underline the seriousness of the position...."

"For your information, Comrade Regimental Commander," said Shmakov, "in my time I was Commissar of the Forty-Second Rifle Division for about a year when we were fighting Denikin. True, after the Civil War I was immediately called up for Party work, and I've only been back in uniform for a week."

"It's hardly a month since he put on army uniform," said Zaichikov, nodding towards Serpilin. "He commanded a division too, once, and I cut my teeth under him after military academy; so you're both big cheeses here," he joked. But the joke fell flat. He couldn't get the dead Glushchenko out of his mind. "Have you many people left under your command, eh?" he said, pulling himself together and still trying to make light of things.

Serpilin reported his losses.

"Everybody's had heavy losses," said Zaichikov. "Very heavy losses!" he repeated; and he thought of Glushchenko again.

The brief respite ended, and the Germans renewed the attack before Serpilin could get the opportunity for a proper talk with Shmakov. As soon as the attack began, the new commissar took an escort and went to visit the battalions.

"Begin with the third, on the left flank," advised Serpilin. "It's nearer". And he added to himself: "And quieter."

That the commissar hadn't stayed behind hovering about the command post was much to Serpilin's liking, and this was all the more reason for looking after him as well as possible.

While this attack, the sixth that day, was in progress, Zaichikov stayed with the regiment and never left Serpilin's side. His presence did not embarrass Serpilin, the more so since the divisional commander merely gave two or three orders, and only ones which Serpilin himself had just been about to give himself. This showed that they were of the same mind about what was happening on the battlefield.

The divisional commander, in his turn, had not been overjoyed when Serpilin had taken over the regiment two weeks ago and he had found himself senior commander to an officer who was his senior in rank. In battle, however, he promptly forgot all about it. Although they didn't really know each other too well, their prewar acquaintance was important to both of them in the grave new situation and was conducive to comradely frankness.

As soon as the sixth attack had been beaten off with less difficulty than the preceding ones—the Germans were apparently beginning to run out of steam—the divisional commander hurried off to the neighbouring regiment.

"I'm not worried about you, Fyodor Fyodorovich," he told Serpilin bluntly as he took leave of him. "Naturally, I'm glad they gave you a regiment under me, though in all conscience I must say we should be commanding adjacent divisions. Then at least we'd feel easy in our minds about the flanks. But we're in action, and we haven't got any flanks! Only yesterday morning, I was at least in touch with my neighbour on the left. Now there's no sign of him!"

"Never mind," said Serpilin. "What we have, we have here. We'll command what fate has sent us. If we survive, we'll live to become generals. If we die, we'll go to our graves as colonels and brigade commanders."

"It's the nazis we should dig the graves for—and as many as possible," replied Zaichikov. "And we can do without the last rites. Their planes don't seem to be out today for some reason," he added, glancing up at the sky as he took his leave of Serpilin.

Talk of the devil and you hear his wings. Within less than half an hour, the Germans delivered a powerful air strike on the junction between Serpilin and the adjacent regiment. Forty aircraft dive-bombing in succession carved out a slice of terrain all the way down to the river. The horizon to the north was blotted out by a dense pall of smoke.

An hour later, when the bombing was over, Zaichikov was back at Serpilin's command post. But it wasn't the man Serpilin had seen an hour ago—winded, tired, but still strong and capable of keeping the situation completely under control. He was brought in on a stretcher, drained of all his strength and seriously wounded in the stomach by a bomb splinter. The surgeon, who had rushed over from the first-aid post, worked on him for a long time with the nurse, removing the splinter while the colonel groaned with pain.

When he was hit, the divisional commander had insisted on being brought to Serpilin's command post and not to the first-aid station.

The doctor, cursing inwardly, had been forced to obey. He was a young man, and he was nervous because Colonel Zaichikov was feared like the devil in his division, and was still scared of him even now that the formidable Zaichikov lay helpless before him.

After the German bombers had blasted the junction between the two regiments and had churned up the terrain all the way down to the Dnieper, the German tanks attacked the same place under cover of the smoke which had still not dispersed after the bombing, cut the two regiments off from one another, broke through to the bridge over the Dnieper, and were able to capture it before it could be blown up. The sub-machine gunners also broke through, riding in on the tanks. There were not many of them—a company all told—but the air-raid and the tank attack had been so unexpected and violent, and the submachine gun fire rattling in the darkness had seemed so intensive, that neither Serpilin nor the regimental commander cut off from him could bring themselves, in that first hour of disaster, to attack the still thin line of Germans who had broken through to the Dnieper.

They didn't risk it that evening owing to lack of experience and an exaggerated idea of the enemy's numerical strength. In the morning it was too late.

When Zaichikov was brought to the regimental command post, Serpilin was away. He had gone to his badly hit right-flank battalion to take charge of preparations for the morning battle.

The divisional commander had asked to be brought straight to Serpilin's command post because he suspected that the wound was fatal and he wanted to be in time to hand over the command of the division to Serpilin. When the doctor, as he cleaned the wound, was preparing to give him an injection, Zaichikov objected, fearing to lose consciousness even for a minute. He thought he might go off into the unknown without having had time to hand over the division to Serpilin.

Serpilin was with the battalion when he learned that Zaichikov had been gravely wounded. He gave only the most essential orders and hurried off to the regimental first-aid station, expecting to find the colonel there. But he wasn't; neither was the doctor, who had been summoned to the command post for some reason.

He found the doctor standing at the entrance to the dug-out, his blood-stained overalls buttoned over his tunic.

"Comrade Brigade Commander," whispered the doctor. "It's not my fault. I wanted to treat the wound in the best possible conditions, as I'm supposed to. But the divisional commander ordered...."

"So you were ordered, were you?" said Serpilin with a gesture of irritation. "There are times when we don't give orders to the doctors: they give the orders to us. Well? Will he be alive?"

"Everything possible's been done, but the wound's serious, and the conditions for treatment...."

"No use whining about it! Can you do any more now?"

"Nothing for the time being," replied the doctor.

"Off you go, then. There's a queue of wounded waiting for you at the first-aid station; they're lying all over the floor," said Serpilin, and he entered the dug-out.

Zaichikov was lying on a cot. His eyes wide open and his lips twitching, he was trying not to groan outloud.

Serpilin drew up a stool and sat on it, his bony knees pressed painfully up against the cot.

"I think I've fought my last battle," said the divisional commander, and a tear rolled out of his eye and trickled down his cheek. He wiped it away and let his arm fall back on to the sheet alongside his body. "Cover me with a coat. I feel cold."

Serpilin took his own greatcoat off its nail and laid it over the sheet covering the divisional commander.

"What are the Germans up to out there?" asked Zaichikov.

There was no point in hiding the truth from him, and in any case Serpilin didn't consider himself entitled to do so. Although wounded, Zaichikov was still divisional commander. Serpilin reported that the Germans had cut him off from his neighbouring regiment, had reached the Dnieper, and had in all probability taken the bridge. Zaichikov lay silent for several moments, taking in this information and collecting his thoughts. He had some difficulty in doing so, for they were running in several directions at once. If the Germans had taken the bridge, it meant that they had cut off all three regiments from one another at a single blow. He thought of Colonel Yushkevich, his chief of staff, who was now left in charge on the far side of the Dnieper.

"Everything's suddenly gone to pot," he said aloud.

"What?" Serpilin couldn't hear him properly.

"Nothing. Just thinking," replied Zaichikov in a whisper.

In his opinion, Yushkevich was a good chief of staff, but his lot was now far from enviable. After the loss of the bridge he had found himself caught between two fires and pinned down on a narrow strip of beach with the Germans in his rear. If he realised that he must try to break through to the east that night, he might save something at least; but should he fail to realise it, then he was done for!

Major Loshkarev, the commander of the regiment now cut off on the outskirts of Mogilev, was brave almost to desperation, but he was still very green as a regimental commander. Zaichikov was sure that he wouldn't lose his nerve, but it was difficult to say how Loshkarev would cope with a regiment on his own. Zaichikov even regretted that he had been wounded here, while with Serpilin, instead of with Loshkarev. He would be of more use over there, even though flat on his back, as he was now.

Then he thought self-pityingly about his wound and his wife and daughters. It had been girls every time, and when the last one had arrived, his wife had even wept because it hadn't been a boy.

"Difficult, when there are five daughters." He was thinking about his family as if he were no longer alive.

"Listen, Serpilin," he said, having finally collected his thoughts. "Be ready to take over the division. Write out the order."

"When I have to take over, I'll be ready," said Serpilin. "But let the order wait awhile! No one takes over a division when the commander's alive. You stay where you are and you'll be on your feet again. You're tough." And Serpilin gently touched him on the shoulder.

Zaichikov looked at him out of the corner of his eye and said nothing. After all, what was there to say? In Serpilin's place he would have given the same answer.

"Be ready just the same," he said finally, and he closed his eyes. There was some consolation for him in being at Serpilin's command post and not at the first-aid station, where he would have felt like just another wounded man amongst all the other cases. But here he was still the divisional commander. He lay for several minutes with his eyes closed, and when he opened them, he saw behind Serpilin the lanky instructor from the newspaper who had approached him in the forest not so long ago. He was wearing a filthy, mud-stained tunic and carrying a German submachine gun slung over his shoulder.

Sintsov had spent almost the whole day at Serpilin's side, first in one battalion, then in another. He had personally witnessed the tank breakthrough into Plotnikov's battalion positions. One tank had lumbered on to the railway embankment, had knocked the patrolman hut right over, and had kept up continuous gunfire only fifty metres away from Sintsov; the shells had been whistling directly over his head. Then Plotnikov had come out of the trench and thrown a cluster of grenades under the tank. The tank had caught fire, but Plotnikov had been killed a second later by a machine-gun burst from another tank.

Sintsov had then seen one of the companies take flight. The German sub-machine gunners had begun mowing it down; but Serpilin had taken command of a group of soldiers nearby and beaten off the sub-machine gunners with rifle fire and grenades, himself using a rifle from time to time. The old patrolman had been shooting away not far from Sintsov; but later, when Sintsov looked round again, he was already lying dead at the bottom of the trench with his German uniform open on his grey, bloody chest. Sintsov had also been using a rifle and had killed — he had seen it himself — a German who seemed to jump up out of the ground only ten paces away.

"Well, you've got your German too," Serpilin had said to Sintsov after the attack had been beaten off; he had apparently missed nothing of what had been happening round him. Then he had given instructions for the dead German's sub-machine gun to be given to Sintsov with two long spare magazines in a canvas sack. "Take them! They're yours by right!"

But all this had happened a long time ago, in the afternoon; and that evening, when it was already dark, Sintsov had gone with Serpilin to where the Germans had broken through after the bombing. He had lost Serpilin there, searched for him for a long time, fearing that he had been killed, and had been overjoyed, on returning to the command post, to discover that Serpilin was safe and sound.

And so it was a smiling Sintsov who entered the dug-out. He took in the whole scene at a glance: Serpilin, sitting with bowed shoulders on a stool; the divisional commander lying on Serpilin's bed with his eyes closed. The colonel's face was so white that Sintsov at first thought he was dead, until the latter opened his eyes and looked long and silently at Sintsov.

Sintsov also stood in silence, not knowing what to say or do under the circumstances. Serpilin sensed someone behind him and turned round.

"Well now, Political Instructor—had enough fighting? Not going to complain you've got nothing to write about, are you?"

Sintsov remembered his kitbag with the notebook still in it. He hadn't touched it once that day. He was hungry, but he wanted to sleep even more than to eat.

"Request permission to go, Comrade Brigade Commander," he said instead of answering Serpilin's question. He was feeling mortally tired—not in his arms or legs or even all over his body, but somewhere deep down inside. It was the result of all the dangers he had been through one after another in the course of the day.

"Why, d'you want some sleep?" asked Serpilin, with an understanding look. "You can go. You're free."

"I'll lie down near the dug-out," said Sintsov, ashamed that he should want some sleep when Serpilin, who must be much more tired than himself, was still very much awake.

Serpilin nodded without turning round.

"What's he doing here?" asked Zaichikov quietly, but Serpilin, at a loss for an answer, merely shrugged his shoulders.

As soon as Sintsov had gone out, Shmakov came into the dug-out. He was also carrying a German sub-machine gun. As he entered, he took it off, stood it in the corner and, wearily massaging his neck, went up to the bed. They had already told him that Zaichikov had been wounded and was with Serpilin. This was neither the time nor the occasion for asking questions. He stood there and said nothing.

"Did you get many sub-machine guns?" asked Zaichikov with a glance at him.

"Twenty," said Shmakov.

"They can lay on pretty intensive sub-machine gun fire," said Zaichikov. "It became obvious during the Finnish campaign that we needed to arm ourselves with them in quantity. But the authorities just dithered around. And they dithered right up to the beginning of the war. We're lucky to have ten sub-machine guns to a regiment, and they've got hundreds!" There was a note of exasperation in his weak, hoarse voice.

Shmakov began explaining what had been happening in the left-flank battalion. Serpilin and the divisional commander listened to him: Serpilin with attention, Zaichikov half-and-half, wincing every few seconds at the stabbing pains in his stomach.

"Guess I'm going to have a baby," he said at last, smiling with an effort.

"I'll move to your dug-out, Comrade Shmakov," said Serpilin. "We're going to set up a first-aid post for the divisional commander right here."

At first, when he had arrived, he had wanted to insist on the divisional commander being taken to the first-aid post; but then he thought better of it. When all was said and done, they were surrounded, and there was no knowing where the regiment's rear was, or where its forward positions might be. Let him stay here; there'd be no talking him out of it, and Serpilin didn't like beating his head against a brick wall.

"I don't need any first-aid post," said Zaichikov. "It'll look as though I drove you out of your own dug-out!"

"Oh yes, you do," said Serpilin decisively. "You needn't argue with me—I once had some experience as a medical assistant in the past."

Zaichikov smiled in spite of himself. He remembered Serpilin being nicknamed "the medical assistant" even as far back as his probationary period in the division back in nineteen thirty-three.

"Try and get some shut-eye if you can, Nikolai Petrovich," said Serpilin, rising. "The commissar and I will go and sum up the day's action, and then we'll come back to you for orders."

"As if you need any orders from me now!" thought Zaichikov without malice, following Serpilin with his eyes as the latter went out. "You're no Loshkarev. If things were otherwise, you'd be in command of a division yourself, or even of a corps, and you'd be giving me the orders.... If only we were in communication." He suddenly remembered that communications with the Army had been cut off and smiled bitterly.

Shmakov had entered his dug-out first and was now sitting on the bed of the commissar who had been killed that morning, while Serpilin sat facing him on the bed of the chief of staff, who had been killed that evening. They were summing up the day's action, patching up the day's losses in the regiment and discussing whom to send where so as to plug the gaps. By nightfall, they had to appoint one battalion commander, two company commanders and three political instructors to replace those lost during the day. Shmakov had only got to know the men in one battalion. Nearly all the candidates were nominated by Serpilin. When it came to the political instructors, Serpilin mentioned Sintsov.

"But what's the point," said Serpilin when Shmakov shrugged his shoulders, "what's the point of him trailing after me all the time until he gets killed? Seeing he's political instructor by rank, let him be political instructor for a company. He won't be any worse than the others, and even if he is, there's nobody else anyway."

Five minutes later, Sintsov, who had been woken up by Serpilin's orderly, stood blinking sleepily in front of Serpilin and Shmakov, whom he certainly hadn't expected to meet here, and listening to a cursory briefing. They were sending him, while it was still dark, to a company—to the Khoryshev with whom he had sat in his bare feet the day before on the railway embankment while they sunbathed and ate dried fish.

"It's just that I've never been in command," he replied hesitantly when Serpilin faced him with the obligatory, but in these circumstances no doubt meaningless, question: "Well, now—will you cope?"

"Now you'll have to take command," said Serpilin. "You've got a star on your sleeve and you're a Senior Lieutenant and I expect you to live up to this." He said all this in a fairly angry voice, not because he was actually annoyed with Sintsov, but because he wanted to drive home his change of status. "You're not allowed an escort now, and if you don't get there, you'll be a deserter!" And Serpilin grinned, making it clear that the last remark was just a joke.

Sintsov, who still hadn't fully collected himself, shook hands with Serpilin and Shmakov. He now saw them in a totally different light. Only yesterday, he had been a guest in the regiment of this lanky brigade commander with the good-natured, horsey face. Until only recently, he had been a chance front-line travelling companion of this little grey-haired battalion commissar. Now they were his CO and his commissar, and he was the political instructor of a company under their command. They no longer expected him to describe how other men were fighting; they expected him to fight like the rest. Never in his life had he experienced such a sudden and shattering change of circumstances. He recollected Junior Political Instructor Lyusin, who hadn't wanted to stay with the tankmen, and without sympathy, but with belated understanding, he realised that Lyusin hadn't found it easy either.

After Sintsov had left, Serpilin and Shmakov exchanged glances.

"I moved up from medical assistant to battalion commander," said Serpilin, "and I made out. So why should I have doubts about him?" He nodded towards the door. "D'you suppose they've turned out any worse than us after twenty-three years of Soviet power? Or that we just talked their heads off and never made men of them? I don't believe it! Even in spite of the black times we're going through now, I still don't believe it! Perhaps we didn't always train them as well as we should have done, but we didn't do too badly, and we've made them tougher than the nazis have made their own men! No, we didn't train our men too badly. I've realised this in prison more than once. You're not surprised about me having been in gaol?"

"No, Zaichikov told me about you," replied Shmakov uneasily.

But Serpilin took Shmakov's stiffness the wrong way. "You were out of luck when fate sent you as a commissar to an old lag like me, Comrade Shmakov," he said with bitter irony.

Shmakov could have said a great deal in answer to this. He could have pointed out that fate never threw him into the army at all, since he had volunteered. He could have replied that he had asked Zaichikov to use him in any capacity after, and not before he realised that the division was in a serious predicament. Finally, he could have replied that he had every bit as much faith as Serpilin in Soviet power and in its ability to rear people to support it till their dying breath, and that therefore he had as much faith in him, Serpilin, as he had in himself.

But Professor, and now Battalion Commissar, Shmakov, who was normally a chatty person, could not bear explaining himself when he felt he was being forced to. And so he gave Serpilin none of the answers that he could have done. He remained silent, looked Serpilin straight in the eye, and merely said:

"Comrade Serpilin, I am afraid I must seem a bit of a dry stick to you. Please, don't let this put you off."

And by this he made it clear to Serpilin that the latter's reproach was unjustified.

"If I've understood you rightly, you're not concerned with my recent past," said Serpilin, who liked to take the bull by the horns.

"Yes, you've understood me rightly."

"Well, it still concerns me. Can you understand that?"

"Yes, I can."

"Your name and patronymic?"

"Sergei Nikolayevich."

"I'm Fyodor Fyodorovich."

"So we've been introduced at last!" laughed Shmakov, glad that the crisis was over. "And it's just as well. If one of us suddenly died, it could be most inconvenient: they wouldn't be able to fill in our initials on the burial form."

"Sergei Nikolayevich, my brother in Christ and in regimental harness!" exclaimed Serpilin, shaking his head. "Knowing how to die—that's only half of the army's business. It's the Germans that should do the dying: that's what's wanted of us." He rose to his feet and, stretching up to his full height, said that it was time to go and report to the divisional commander.

"Maybe we should leave him alone. He's in a bad way," protested Shmakov.

"If we report to him, he'll feel better," said Serpilin. "His wound's too serious for him just to lie there like that waiting to die. As long as he's giving orders, he'll stay alive!"

"I don't suppose the doctors will agree," said Shmakov, also rising.

"I'm not asking them to agree. I'm a medical assistant myself."

Shmakov smiled in spite of himself. Serpilin also grinned at his own joke, but suddenly turned serious again.

"You mentioned death just now, and let me tell you once and for all so that you should understand me completely. I'm not scared of dying in front of everybody. But I cannot afford to be posted missing. Understand?"

He kicked the door open and left the dug-out first.

Once again, the fighting next day lasted from dawn to dusk. Most of the field and anti-tank guns were gradually knocked out of action, and the German tanks, often penetrating deep into the regiment's positions, rolled for some time in and out among the trenches, crushing dug-outs with their caterpillar tracks, pounding away with their guns and enfilading the trenches with machine-gun fire. Sometimes it looked as though the regiment's positions had already been taken; but throughout the whole of that day the German infantry were unable to break through after the tanks, and without the infantry the tanks couldn't finish off the job, some of them withdrawing from action with their ammunition spent, others, showered with bunches of grenades and bottles of petrol, bursting into flames deep inside the positions.

Due to the lack of artillery and shells, fewer tanks were set on fire than on the previous days, but nine were burned out at various points notwithstanding. One of them even crowled onto Serpilin's dug-out while Zaichikov was lying inside. It was set on fire, and stood right there on top of the dug-out like a monument, its rear end in the trench and the muzzle of its gun sticking up into the air.

There were eight successive German attacks altogether that day. Sintsov, who had joined Khoryshev's company the evening before, only glanced twice at his watch in twenty-four hours. He hadn't time to wonder whether he had proved himself a good or bad company political instructor. He simply spent the whole day in the trenches with the men and tried to give the most suitable orders to the few soldiers in his immediate vicinity. He ordered them not to shoot when he felt that the attacking Germans should be allowed to come nearer, ordered the men to open fire when he realised it was time, and fired himself, no doubt killing some Germans. There were moments when it seemed to him that it was not himself giving orders to the men, but his pips and the commissar's stars on his sleeves: it was them that the soldiers saw, respected, and obeyed.

Consequently, when the eighth and last German attack was over and it began to get dark, and Khoryshev, with his head bandaged under his forage cap, came up to Sintsov and bellowed into his ear as if he were deaf: "Well done, Political Instructor!", Sintsov merely shrugged his shoulders. He didn't know himself whether he had done well or not. He only knew that they had held onto the trenches they had been occupying since morning; and that, no doubt, was a good thing.

He was suddenly astonished to realise that he was still alive. Too many had been killed or wounded round him during the day. While each man was being killed or wounded, he had not thought of himself; but now, when the battle was over and he could think of all the killed and wounded together, it seemed strange to him that all those men had been unlucky, while he himself had escaped without a scratch.

"D'you think they'll be back again tomorrow?" he asked Khoryshev.

The latter couldn't hear him and asked him to say it again. Sintsov wearily repeated his question, and Khoryshev replied in an equally tired voice:

"Of course they'll be back! What else d'you expect?"

It was already quite dark when Serpilin went back to the divisional commander in the dug-out. The upper layer of roofing had slipped sideways, and one beam had come adrift and was hanging down at an angle. The floor near Zaichikov's cot was covered with mounds of soil that had trickled down from the roof.

"I nearly got squashed by that tank," joked Zaichikov. "I thought the Germans were here and I was just about to start shooting." He touched the pistol poking out from under his pillow. "Anything been heard of Loshkarev?"

"Nothing for the last few hours," said Serpilin. "It's dead quiet over there."

"I've been listening all the time. After midday, it began to get quiet. I'm worried about Loshkarev," said Zaichikov uneasily.

Serpilin said nothing. He wasn't worried about Loshkarev any more. It had become so quiet out there that it was too late to worry any more.

"The commissar will be back shortly. We can ask him," said he. "They've spotted something from the grain elevator. He told me over the telephone that he wanted to go up there and have a look."

Half an hour passed, and there was still no Shmakov. At last he returned, perspiring after his hurried walk, his tunic black with sweat. Before saying a word, he drank two mugs of water straight off from a bucket standing in the corner. The water was cloudy, with a yellow sediment: some clayey soil had trickled down into it from the roof. He poured himself a third mugful, took off his cap, and poured the water over his burly red neck with its grey, close-cropped hair.

"Have you had a hot time of it today?" asked Serpilin, half in jest and half in earnest.

"Yes, it's hot. Beginning to feel my age," said Shmakov apologetically. He sat down on the stool and told how the Germans hadn't fired once on the elevator all the time he had been up there.

"The tower's riddled like a sieve," he explained. "They probably think we've moved the observation post out by now. But I've got some bad news for you. It's all quiet on our right—not a shot. An hour ago—true, I can't swear by my own observations as it was already getting dark, but the men confirm this—they can see better than I can—," he took off his spectacles, wiped them with his finger-tips, and replaced them—"the Germans have marched a column of prisoners westwards down the road from Mogilev."

"Many?" asked Zaichikov.

"The men say about three hundred."

"So that's the end of Loshkarev's regiment," said Zaichikov and then, after a pause, repeated: "That's the end of Loshkarev's regiment."

There was a long silence in the dug-out. Nobody spoke. All three were thinking the same thing: their turn was bound to come tomorrow or the day after. The shells were running out; they still had some grenades, but those would soon be finished too, and they were already out of petrol bottles. The Germans would renew their attacks tomorrow, and granted they could hold out for another day, what would happen then? They could, of course, try to get away in the night and break through to the east, beyond the Dnieper. But how they would succeed, and whether they would do so, and what their losses would be if they did.... The prospects were not encouraging. It was a shame, a crying shame, to leave these positions where they had successfully held out for several days and destroyed nearly seventy German tanks. They wouldn't knock out many tanks if they abandoned the trenches....

Although all three were thinking the same thoughts, no one cared to speak first. Serpilin was waiting for the divisional commander's comments; Zaichikov wanted to see what Serpilin would have to say; and Shmakov, turning his round grey head from side to side, was looking alternately at the other two, evidently of the opinion that, as a new arrival in the regiment he should be the last to speak up on such matters. And so none of them said a word and all tacitly postponed the decision till tomorrow.

In the middle of the night there were sounds of intensive fighting on the far side of the Dnieper. The Germans were unlikely to be launching a night attack. Serpilin had already noticed that they didn't like night battles as a rule. "They do well enough in the daytime." And he smiled bitterly at his own thoughts. Most likely it was Yushkevich breaking through to the east with his remaining units.

It was hard to tell whether Yushkevich actually succeeded. One way or the other, the left bank became quiet again. It was all over, and by the morning of the fifth day's fighting, Serpilin's regiment was completely isolated. After dawn, Serpilin was expecting fresh German attacks, never doubting that they would begin at any moment. But an hour passed, and then another, and still the Germans made no move. On the contrary, observers reported that the German battle outpost had been withdrawn into the forest during the night. This was baffling, but an hour later the riddle solved itself.

The Luftwaffe reappeared in the sky. During the last four days, they had only made one strike: that had been when the tanks had cut Serpilin's regiment off from Loshkarev's. Evidently they had been busy in more important sectors elsewhere; but Serpilin and his regiment were now to feel the full weight of their striking power.

After leaving the regiment in peace for the first three hours of daylight, the Germans spent the rest of the day compensating for it. For exactly twelve hours—from nine in the morning till nine in the evening—waves of German aircraft dive-bombed the regimental positions and never once ceased their deadly hammering for more than half an hour at a time. Heavy half-ton and quarter-ton bombs, bombs weighing a hundred, fifty and twenty-five kilogrammes, canisters of three- and two-kilogramme bombs that scattered all over the place like peas—all these came raining down on Serpilin's regiment from morning till evening. The Germans may not have thrown in all that many aircraft—perhaps only twenty or thirty—but they were coming from an airfield quite close by and so were able to operate non-stop. No sooner had one formation of nine flown away than another appeared in its place and continued the relentless hail of bombs.

It was now clear why the Germans had withdrawn their battle outpost: they didn't want to waste any more tanks and infantry on Serpilin. Their air force was available now, and they had given it licence to kill, having decided to flatten Serpilin into the ground without cost to themselves and then pick up with their bare hands what was left of the regiment that had made such a nuisance of itself. Even tomorrow they would probably refrain from attacking and would continue their relentless bombing. The thought frightened Serpilin. Nothing is harder than to perish without paying for death with death. But that was exactly what they were in for. When the last raid was over and the Germans had flown home to supper and bed, the regiment's positions had been so badly mangled by the relentless hail of iron and steel from the sky that it was impossible to find a fifty-metre length of telephone cable intact anywhere. Only one Junkers had been shot down, and the losses in the regiment had been as heavy as those yesterday—till then the bloodiest day of all.

When the fighting had started, the regiment's numerical strength had been two thousand one hundred. Now, at a rough estimate, there were barely six hundred left. Serpilin visited Zaichikov in the dug-out with this uncomfortable report. Several times that day he had expected to find the divisional commander dead. At least ten bombs of various calibres had burst round the dug-out which, by some miracle, had been left unscathed in that ring of death.

"Comrade Divisional Commander, my opinion is that we should try and break out tonight," said Serpilin immediately on entering. He was convinced today that there was no alternative and, once convinced, was anxious to give his opinion without further ado. "If we don't break through, they'll go on wiping us out from the air tomorrow."

White-faced, his wound beginning to fester, Zaichikov, in a voice notably much weaker than yesterday, said that he agreed, and when Shmakov joined them, the three of them discussed which direction they should take so that, on breaking through, they would emerge as near the Dnieper as possible.

Within half an hour, everything had been settled. Shmakov, who spoke German, went to his dug-out in order to interrogate an air-gunner who had baled out of his Junkers, and Serpilin left to do the rounds of the trenches. In order to facilitate control over the men during the night battle, he decided to reform all the survivors into one battalion and proceeded to do so at once, making his appointments there and then in the trenches and indicating the assembly points before the break-through. It couldn't be postponed for another twenty-four hours, and there was no way of prolonging the short July night. Reducing Plotnikov's battalion to a company and appointing Khoryshev platoon commander accordingly, Serpilin glanced briefly at Sintsov, who was now free of his duties, and ordered him to come along.

They returned to the command post, and Serpilin went past Zaichikov's dug-out and looked in on Shmakov.

Bristling with anger and with an ugly expression on his face, Shmakov was sitting at the table. Facing him at attention stood a tall young German in Luftwaffe uniform. His face was twitching nervously, as if he was being bothered by flies. One cheek was pale, the other was covered with red blotches.

"What's this? Haven't you finished yet?" demanded Serpilin from the doorway.

"I've just had to clout him one and make him stand up," said Shmakov. He was obviously angry with himself. "There he was, sprawling on the chair and promising my life would be spared when I was their prisoner if I escorted him personally through our lines! One good turn deserves another, you might say! Decided to enlist me, the lout!"

"Any practical results from the interrogation?"

"Not much. He hardly knows anything about the situation here. They were only posted from Brest this morning. He claims he bombed the Brest-Litovsk fortress only two days ago.

Shmakov paused. He and Serpilin exchanged glances, and once again they realised how well they understood one another.

"He doesn't know the set-up. They had no maps. He says the air-gunner isn't allowed one." Shmakov remembered his own son and added: "That's probably true. In general, a dead loss to us in practical terms. But psychologically...."

"We haven't time for psychology now, Sergei Nikolayevich," said Serpilin impatiently. "The position's clear and time's precious. I'm off. I'll be waiting for you at Zaichikov's."

It was barely a hundred paces from Shmakov's dug-out to Zaichikov's.

"Comrade Brigade Commander," asked Sintsov hurriedly, afraid of missing the opportunity. "D'you think that's true ... about Brest?"

Serpilin was in a great hurry, but Sintsov's question angered him and brought him to a halt.

"As far as I'm concerned, it's true a hundred times over!" he said abruptly. "Why have doubts? If you imagine that we're the only ones who don't like the idea of throwing up their hands and surrendering, then you're a fool! It's an insult to the Red Army!"

After this reprimand, both men walked on another forty paces or so in silence.

"You're an educated man," said Serpilin finally, breaking a silence which Sintsov had been finding very uncomfortable, "although not quite educated enough, I can see." In these words and in the unexpected stiffness of Serpilin's attitude there was an undertone of still active rage. "I am taking you on as adjutant. When we start breaking out of encirclement, you'll have to keep a strict daily record of personnel—those leaving and those arriving; so you'll be with me all the time."

"So that's it! We're going to try and break out after all!" thought Sintsov; and he regretted that Serpilin had taken him on. During the last two days he had become used to the idea that he would fight to the bitter end with Khoryshev and the men from that company.

"We're moving in an hour," said Serpilin, as he and Sintsov entered the dug-out.

"You'll be moving," said Zaichikov, "but I'm not exactly mobile. I'll be so much baggage. I'll only be a burden...." And he weakly clenched the fist lying on the greatcoat.

"Never mind, if we make it, we'll carry you out too.... There's only one of you, and there's six hundred of us."

"Has that been confirmed—six hundred?"

"We even have a few over," said Serpilin. "If we penetrate successfully, then we'll get through. We can deliver the necessary punch," he added.

"Well," said Zaichikov, "we can't postpone it any longer. Sit down, Serpilin, and write the order appointing you divisional commander. Whether you get me out of here or not, you'll be in charge. I can't stay in command any more."

Serpilin shrugged his shoulders.

"Orders are orders." He didn't want to object—Zaichikov was right—it was time to get on with it.

"All the more so," said Zaichikov, "seeing that when we break through, we may meet men from other units in the division, and you need a firm hand in encirclement. As nowhere else!"

Serpilin nodded silently. In his opinion, this was also true.

"Sit down and write out the order," said Serpilin to Sintsov, his friendlier tone of voice virtually cancelling out their recent conversation. He didn't want the order of appointment to be made out in his own handwriting.

"How am I to do it?" asked Sintsov, settling himself at the table.

"In black and white," said Zaichikov, and he gritted his teeth at a sudden stab of pain.

"I'm asking because I've only got a pencil," said Sintsov, taking one out of his tunic pocket and looking at it dubiously. The point was broken.

"Sharpen it," said Serpilin, handing him a pen-knife.

While Sintsov was sharpening his pencil, Zaichikov lay staring in silence at the ceiling. As soon as Sintsov had finished, he immediately began dictating:

"Order Number..." he frowned as he tried to recall the number of the last divisional order, then remembered, and said: "Number Eleven. 'As a result of my being incapacitated by a wound, I hereby order Brigade Commander Serpilin, CO of 526 Rifle Regiment, to take over command of all units of the division entrusted to me.' Put my initials!"

Sintsov was expecting more dictation, but Zaichikov merely said: "That's all", and, wiping his forehead which was damp with exhaustion, fell back on the pillow.

"Give it me to sign—no, wait: there's a red pencil in my map-case. Get it!"

Zaichikov's map-case was hanging from a nail in the dug-out wall. Sintsov took out of it a red, well-sharpened pencil and, laying the order on the map-case, went up to Zaichikov.

Zaichikov half-raised himself up on one elbow, took the pencil in his enfeebled fingers, and began signing his name. At the second letter, the pencil shook and the point snapped off, leaving an unwanted red smear on the paper."

"Oh, damn!" swore Zaichikov. "Sharpen it!"

Sintsov took the pen-knife from Serpilin again, sharpened the pencil, and Zaichikov, holding it in his fingers with an effort, carefully finished signing his name and put the date underneath.

"Take it, Serpilin," he said.

Serpilin read through the order, folded it in four, and put it away in his tunic pocket. On leaving for the front to take command of a regiment, he had believed that the time would come when everything in his life would sort itself out and he would be ordered to give up his regiment and take over a division. But who would have imagined that he would have to take over this particular division, and in such circumstances?

"Request permission to go and prepare for departure," he said to Zaichikov and saluted, not out of habit, but because he wanted to say this for the last time.

Zaichikov understood what he meant and, instead of replying, greatefully held out his weak, damp hand. Serpilin shook it firmly and left the dug-out.

"Are the company commanders assembled? Come to me, please!" It was his peremptory falsetto making itself heard outside.

CHAPTER SIX

It was a sunny morning. One hundred and fifty men, all that was left of Serpilin's regiment, were walking through dense forest on the left bank of the Dnieper in an attempt to get away as quickly as possible from the point where they had made the crossing. Of those hundred and fifty, every third man was slightly wounded. Five seriously wounded, who had been brought across to the left bank by some miracle, were being carried in turns on stretchers by the twenty fittest soldiers, handpicked for the purpose by Serpilin.

One of the stretcher-cases was the dying Zaichikov. He kept losing consciousness and then waking up to stare up at the blue sky and the tops of the pines and birches swaying overhead. His mind was confused, and he thought that everything was swaying—the backs of the stretcher bearers, the trees, and the sky. With an effort, he listened to the silence. Sometimes he imagined he heard the noise of battle, and then, suddenly coming to his senses, he could hear nothing at all; and then he imagined he had gone deaf, although, in fact, the silence was real.

It was quiet in the forest, save for the gentle creaking of the trees in the wind, the footsteps of the weary men, and the occasional clatter of mess-tins. The forest was so quiet that the others found it strange too, and not just the dying Zaichikov. They had become so unaccustomed to silence that it now seemed somehow ominous. As a reminder of the appalling hell of the river crossing, the fine and scarcely visible steam from the uniforms drying on the march was still hovering over the column.

Serpilin had sent scouts ahead and out on both flanks, had left Shmakov to bring up the rearguard, and was himself walking at the head of the column. It was costing him quite an effort to keep his legs moving, but to those behind it seemed that he was walking easily and quickly, with the confident gait of a man who knew where he was going and was ready to carry on like this for days on end. But Serpilin was not finding it easy to create this impression. He was no longer young, had been battered and bruised by life, and was terribly exhausted after the battles of the last few days; but he knew that from now on, in encirclement, nothing was unimportant or insignificant: everything mattered, including the way he marched at the head of the column.

Amazed at the light and rapid gait of the brigade commander, Sintsov followed behind, shifting his sub-machine gun from the left shoulder to the right, and then over to the left again. Every muscle in his body seemed to be aching with fatigue. The sunny July day was incredibly beautiful. The air was redolent of resin and sun-warmed moss. The sun-beams slanted down through the swaying branches of the trees to cast dancing patches of warm, golden light on the ground. Amid last year's pine-cones and needles were the green bushes of wild strawberries with the gay red globules of their berries. From time to time the soldiers bent down to pick them as they marched along. For all his fatigue, Sintsov never ceased marvelling at the beauty of the forest.

"Alive," he thought. "Alive in spite of it all!" Three hours previously, Serpilin had ordered him to list the names of all who had made the river crossing. He had drawn up the list and knew that one hundred and forty three men had survived. Of every four who had attempted to break through during the night, three had died in battle or had been drowned; only the fourth had survived, and he was one of the lucky few.

To walk on like this through the forest and, by evening, to rejoin one's own troops without having run into the Germans—that would be real bliss! And after all, why not? The Germans weren't everywhere, when all was said and done, and it might be that our forces hadn't retreated as far as all that.

"What d'you think, Comrade Brigade Commander—will we meet up with our own crowd today?"

"I don't know," said Serpilin half turning round without stopping, "but I know we will sometime or other. So we'll leave it at that, shall we?"

He had begun seriously but had ended on a note of grim irony. His thoughts were the direct opposite of Sintsov's. Judging by the map, if they kept to the dense forest and avoided the road, they could carry on for another twenty kilometres at the most, and he hoped to have covered that distance by evening. But to proceed further eastwards, they would have to cut across the road, and that meant they would run into the Germans. It was too much to expect that they might again be able to penetrate into the forest area, coloured green on the map, without encountering the enemy. Serpilin didn't believe it possible, and this meant that when they came out on to the road at night they would have to fight again. As he walked along, his mind was very much on the battle soon to take place amid the green hush of the forest which had inspired Sintsov with such happiness and faith.

"Where's the brigade commander?"

A Red Armyman from the forward patrol ran up, caught sight of Serpilin, and shouted cheerfully: "Comrade Brigade Commander! Lieutenant Khoryshev sent me! We've met our own people—from the Five Hundred and Twenty Seventh!"

"You don't say," exclaimed Serpilin joyfully. "Where are they?"

"There! Over there!" The Red Armyman stabbed his finger ahead to where soldiers could be seen approaching through the undergrowth.

Forgetting his fatigue, Serpilin quickened his pace.

The men from the 527th Regiment were headed by two officers—a captain and a junior lieutenant. All were in uniform and carrying rifles. Two of them were even armed with automatic rifles. The captain, a curly-haired young man in a rakishly tilted forage cap, stopped and said with a dashing air: "How'd'you do, Comrade Brigade Commander!"

Serpilin remembered having seen him at Divisional HQ. If his memory wasn't playing him false, this was a representative from the Special Department.

"Hullo, my dear fellow!" said Serpilin. "Welcome to the division on behalf of us all!" And he embraced the captain with fervour.

"Well, here we are at last, Comrade Brigade Commander," said the captain, touched by this gesture of affection, although it was not exactly in conformity with army regulations. "Is it true that the divisional commander is with you?"

"Yes," said Serpilin. "We got him out, only..." he broke off. "We'll go and see him now."

The column halted, and all looked joyfully at the new arrivals. There were not many of them, but everybody thought that this was only the beginning.

"Keep moving," said Serpilin to Sintsov, "until the pre-arranged halt." He glanced at his big wrist-watch. "Another twenty minutes to go."

The column moved on reluctantly, and Serpilin, indicating that not only the captain and the junior lieutenant but all the Red Armymen with them should follow as well, slowly walked back down the advancing column. The wounded were being carried in the middle.

"Put him down," said Serpilin quietly to Zaichikov's stretcher-bearers.

The soldiers lowered the stretcher to the ground. Zaichikov was lying motionless, his eyes closed. The happy look on the captain's face faded. Khoryshev had said immediately on meeting him that the divisional commander was wounded, but Zaichikov's appearance shook him. The once full and sun-tanned face of the divisional commander was now gaunt and deathly pale. His nose was as sharp as that of a corpse, and there were black indentations where he had been biting his bloodless lower lip. A weak white hand rested lifelessly on the greatcoat. The divisional commander was dying, and the captain realised this at a glance.

"Nikolai Petrovich. Nikolai Petrovich," called Serpilin softly, bending his tired legs with an effort and going down on one knee beside the stretcher.

Zaichikov's hand stirred on the greatcoat; he bit his lip, and only then did he open his eyes.

"We've run into our own forces from the Five Hundred and Twenty Seventh!"

"Comrade Divisional Commander! Captain Sytin of the Special Department reporting to you for instructions! I've brought with me a section consisting of nineteen men."

Zaichikov looked up without speaking, and his white fingers stirred feebly on the greatcoat.

"Bend down lower," said Serpilin to the captain. "He's calling you."

Then, like Serpilin, Sytin went down on one knee, and Zaichikov, releasing his bitten lip, whispered something that the captain could not hear. Zaichikov repeated himself with an effort.

"Brigade Commander Serpilin has taken over the division," he whispered. "Report to him."

"Permission to report," said Sytin, not getting up, but turning to address Zaichikov and Serpilin together. "We've brought the divisional colours with us."

One of Zaichikov's cheeks twitched feebly. He wanted to smile, but couldn't.

"Where is it?" his lips whispered. The words were inaudible, but his eyes seemed to be imploring: "Show it to me." Everyone knew what he meant.

"Sergeant-Major Kovalchuk brought it out on his person," said Sytin. "Kovalchuk, take off the colours."

But Kovalchuk, without waiting to be told, was already unbuckling his belt. He threw it to the ground, pulled up his tunic, and began to unwind the colours, which he had been wearing round his waist next to his skin. Having unwound the banner, he took it by the upper edge and held it out so that the divisional commander could see it clearly—creased, soaked in sweat, but intact, with the familiar legend embroidered in gold on the red silk: "176th Red Banner Rifle Division of the Workers' and Peasants' Red Army".

As he looked at the banner, Zaichikov wept. He wept as only an enfeebled and dying man can weep—quietly, without moving a single facial muscle. Tear after tear slowly trickled from his eyes. And the stalwart Kovalchuk, as he stood there holding the banner in his huge, burly fists and looked over the top of it at the face of the divisional commander who was lying on the ground and weeping—he too burst into tears, as only a healthy, powerful man shaken to the core of his being can weep: his throat contracted spasmodically as he choked on the tears, his shoulders heaved, and his big hands shook. Zaichikov closed his eyes and shuddered. Serpilin took his hand in alarm. No, he was not dead: the weak pulse was still throbbing in his wrist; he had merely lost consciousness, and by no means for the first time that morning.

"Pick up the stretcher and carry on," said Serpilin quietly to the soldiers who were standing and watching Zaichikov in silence. The men took hold of the stretcher, lifted it carefully, and bore it away.

"Put the banner back on again," said Serpilin to Kovalchuk, who was still standing with the colours in his hands. "Now that you've brought it out, you can carry it further."

Kovalchuk carefully folded up the banner, wound it round his body, lowered his tunic, picked up his belt off the ground, and buckled it on again.

"Comrade Junior Lieutenant, form up with your men on the rear of the column," said Serpilin to the lieutenant, who had also been weeping a moment before, but now stood beside him, sniffing in embarrassment.

When the rear end of the column had passed, Serpilin took Captain Sytin by the arm and set off with him, leaving an interval of about ten paces between themselves and the tail-end of the column.

"Now report what you know and what you've seen."

Sytin began describing the previous night's battle. When Divisional Chief of Staff Yushkevich and Yershov, the CO of 527 Regiment, decided to break through to the east during the night, the fighting had been heavy. They had broken through in two groups with the intention of joining up again, but had not succeeded in doing so. Yushkevich had run into some German sub-machine gunners and had been killed in front of the captain's eyes, and Sytin didn't know whether Yershov, who had been in command of the second group, was still alive, or, if he was, where he had broken through. By morning he had himself broken through and had ended up in the forest with twelve men. He had then met another six led by the junior lieutenant. That was all he knew.

"Well done, Captain!" said Serpilin. "You got the divisional colours out. Who thought of them? You?"

"Yes," said Sytin.

"Well done," repeated Serpilin. "You made the divisional commander happy in his last hours."

"Is he going to die then?" asked the captain.

"Can't you tell?" asked Serpilin in his turn. "That's why I've taken over command. Let's walk faster. We must catch up the head of the column. Can you put on speed, or haven't you the strength?"

"I can," smiled the captain. "I'm young."

"What year were you born in?"

"Nineteen sixteen."

Serpilin whistled. "So you're twenty-five, then. You fellows certainly get your promotion quickly!"

Hardly had the column had time to fall out for the first proper halt, when Serpilin's heart was gladdened by yet another encounter. The watchful Khoryshev, still moving ahead with the forward patrol, noticed a group of soldiers in the thick undergrowth. Six were sleeping side by side, while two more—a soldier with a German sub-machine gun, and a woman doctor sitting in the bushes with a revolver on her lap—were mounting guard over the sleeping men and not making a very good job of it.

Khoryshev decided to play a practical joke: he crawled out of the bushes right in front of them and shouted "Hands up!"—and was nearly mowed down by a machine-gun as a result.

As it turned out, these people were also from the division, only from the rear units. One of the sleeping men was a supply technician. In charge of food stores, he had brought out the whole group, consisting of himself, six storesmen and waggoners, and the woman doctor, who happened to have been spending the night in a neighbouring hut.

When they had all been taken to Serpilin, the supply technician, an elderly, bald-headed man who had been called up after the outbreak of war, described how German tanks carrying assault troops had burst into the village where they were stationed. He and his men had escaped through the back yards into the kitchen gardens. Not all of them had been carrying rifles, but they hadn't wanted to surrender to the enemy. Himself a Siberian and a Red partisan in the old days, he had taken it upon himself to lead his men out through the forests to rejoin our own forces.

"And I did it, too," he said. "True, I didn't get them all out—I lost eleven men. We ran into a German patrol. But we killed four of them and took their weapons. She shot one German with her revolver." And he nodded towards the woman doctor.

She was so young and so tiny, that she seemed no more than a child. Serpilin and Sintsov, who was standing beside him, and, indeed, everybody around, looked at her with astonishment and affection—and all the more so when, as she chewed at a hunk of bread, she began telling them about herself.

She talked about everything that had happened to her as of a chain of actions, each of which it had been absolutely essential for her to perform. She told how she graduated from an institute of dental surgery; then they began accepting Komsomol girls for the army, and she naturally joined. Then it turned out that nobody wanted their teeth attended to during the war, and so she changed from dental surgeon to nursing sister, because there was nothing else for it. When the doctor was killed in an air-raid, she became a doctor because a replacement had to be found; and she went into the rear herself for medical supplies were needed for the regiment. When the Germans broke into the village where she was spending the night, she naturally got out with all the rest because she certainly didn't want to stay behind with the Germans. Then, when they ran into the German patrol and the shooting began, a soldier was wounded in front of her. He was groaning heavily, and she crawled up on her hands and knees to dress his wound. Suddenly, a big German jumped up right before her. She drew her revolver and killed him. The weapon was so heavy that she had to hold it with both hands while she fired it.

She ran through all this quickly, chattering away ten-to-the-dozen like a child and then, having finished her piece of bread, she sat down on a tree stump and began rummaging in her first-aid kit. First she pulled out several emergency dressings, and then a tiny black patent—leather ladies' handbag. Sintsov, who was leaning back against a neighbouring tree, could see from his superior vantage point that the handbag contained a powder-puff and lipstick, black with dust. Hastily tucking away the powder-puff and lipstick in case anyone noticed, she drew out a mirror, took off her forage cap, and began combing her girlishly soft and fluffy hair.

"There's a woman for you!" said Serpilin, after the little doctor had finished combing her hair and, with a glance at the soldiers round her, had somehow inconspicuously retired and disappeared among the trees. "There's a woman for you!" he repeated; and he dealt a slap on the shoulder to Shmakov, who had caught up with the column and had sat down near him. "That's the real goods! You'd be ashamed to show cowardice with someone like that around!" He grinned broadly, his steel teeth gleaming, flung himself down on his back, closed his eyes, and instantly fell asleep.

Sintsov slid his back down the trunk of the pine-tree, came to rest on his haunches and, with a glance at Serpilin, yawned luxuriously.

"Are you married?" asked Shamkov.

Sintsov nodded and, putting off his sleepiness, tried to imagine how things would have turned out if, when he was still in Moscow, Masha had insisted on leaving for Grodno with him and they had been given permission.... They would have left the train at Borisov together.... And then what? Yes, it was hard to imagine.... And yet somewhere deep down he knew that she had been right and he had been wrong on that bitter last day together. A month ago, he had feared more than anything else that she would leave for the front. Now he was no longer troubled by the thought that she might already be there somewhere.

After all he had been through, the violence of his hatred for the Germans had erased many boundaries that had previously existed in his consciousness. He had long been unable to think about happiness or the future without the fascists wiped out first. Why shouldn't Masha feel the same as he did? Had they taken less from her than from him? Was she any worse than him? Or weaker? Why had he wanted to deprive her of the right which he would allow no one to take away from him? The right which you wouldn't even dare try to take away from that little doctor!

"And have you any children?" said Shmakov, interrupting his thoughts.

Every time he had thought of his family during the past month, Sintsov had managed to convince himself that everything was alright and that his daughter had long been in Moscow. He explained curtly and glumly what had happened to his family; but the more emphatically he convinced himself that all was well, the less he believed it.

Shmakov noticed his expression, which had suddenly become gloomy and withdrawn, and realised that he would have done better not to ask.

"Well, get some sleep now," said Shmakov. "It's only a short rest, and you'll be up again before you've closed your eyes."

"What sleep can I get now?" thought Sintsov angrily. But, after sitting there for about a minute with his eyes open, he suddenly let his nose drop onto his knees, started, opened his eyes again, tried to say something to Shmakov and, instead bowed his head on his chest and fell fast asleep.

Shmakov looked at him enviously, took off his glasses, and began massaging his eyes with his thumb and index finger. His eyeballs were sore from lack of sleep; the daylight seemed to sting them even through his tightly closed eyelids. But he still couldn't get to sleep.

During the last three days and nights, Shmakov had seen so many dead young men of his own son's age, that his grief as a father, which he had pushed out of his mind by sheer will-power, had come to the surface again and had grown into an emotion which concerned not just his own son, but all the others who had died in front of his eyes, and even those whose deaths he had only heard about. This emotion had grown and grown, and had finally become so violent that it had changed from grief into wrath. This wrath was now choking him. He sat and thought about the nazis. Everywhere, on all the roads of war, they were at that very moment trampling to earth under their iron heels thousands upon thousands of young Soviet people like his son—killing one after another, destroying life after life. And he had now come to hate those Germans as he had once hated the whiteguards. Never in his life had he felt such hatred, and it seemed unlikely that a greater hatred than his could possibly exist on this earth.

Only yesterday it had cost him an effort to give the order for the German airman to be shot. But today, after the heartrending scene at the river crossing, when the German machine gunners had in cold blood lashed the water round the heads of drowning, wounded, yet not completely slaughtered men, something had finally snapped inside him in spite of his better self, and he had vowed, in the heat of the moment, never to spare those murderers anywhere, or under any circumstances neither during the war nor after!

Shmakov's was the normally calm face of a no-longer-young man who was by nature kind and intelligent; but while he was thinking these thoughts, his expression must have been very unusual for him indeed, because he suddenly heard Serpilin's voice:

"Sergei Nikolayevich! What's the matter? Is something wrong?"

Serpilin was lying on the grass and staring at him wide-eyed.

"Nothing at all." Shmakov put on his glasses and his face resumed its normal expression.

"In that case, what's the time? Aren't we due to move off? Can't summon up the energy to look at my own watch," joked Serpilin.

Shmakov glanced at his watch and said that they had another seven minutes' rest to go.

"I'll get some more sleep, then," said Serpilin, shutting his eyes.

After the hour's halt, which Serpilin refused to prolong by a single minute, although the men were terribly tired, the column continued on its way, gradually swinging round to the south-east.

Before the evening bivouac, the detachment was joined by another thirty men who had been wandering through the forest. No more turned up from their own division. All thirty men, whom they met after their first rest, were from a neighbouring division which had been positioned to the south along the left bank of the Dnieper. They were all from different regiments, battalions and rear units; and although they included three lieutenants and one senior political instructor, not one of them had a notion where their own Divisional HQ was, or even in what direction it had retreated. However, from the various disjointed and often conflicting accounts, it was possible to build up a general picture of the disaster that had overtaken them.

Judging by the names of the places from which the scattered men had come, the division had been extended along a thirty-kilometre front at the moment when the Germans broke through. Moreover, it had not had the time, or else had not been able, to dig in properly. The Germans had launched a huge and murderous air-strike, bombing the division for twenty hours non-stop and then, after making several airborne landings in the rear and destroying control and communications, had, under cover of their air force, begun a massive crossing of the Dnieper at three points. The division's units had been completely disorganised: in some places they had fled, in others they had fought desperately; but it had been too late to stem the general tide of events.

The men from this division had been proceeding in small groups of two or three. Half of them were unarmed. After a talk with them, Serpilin formed them all up on the column, mixing them with his own men. He formed up the unarmed soldiers as they were, saying that they would have to get their own weapons in battle, since he had none to spare.

Serpilin spoke sharply to them, but not rudely. To the senior political instructor, who excused himself on the grounds that although he was unarmed, at least he had kept his full uniform and Party card, Serpilin sourly objected that a Communist at the front should respect his arms as much as his Party card.

"We're not going to Golgotha, my dear comrade," said Serpilin. "We're in battle. At least it's in your favour that you have a conscience. You'd rather be stood up against a wall and shot than tear off your commissar's insignia. But that's not enough for us. We don't want to be stood up against a wall: we want to stand the nazis up against one. And you won't do that without arms. That's the way it is! Now join the column, and I hope you'll be the first to get a weapon in the fighting."

After the embarrassed senior political instructor put several paces between himself and Serpilin, the latter called him back, unclipped one of the two pineapple grenades at his belt, and held it out on the upturned palm of his hand.

"That's to give you a start!"

Sintsov, who was, in his capacity as adjutant, writing the names, ranks and unit numbers down in a notebook, was inwardly pleased at the inexhaustible reserve of patience and cool-headedness shown by Serpilin in dealing with the men.

It is impossible to read another man's mind, but more than once during the last few days Sintsov had formed the impression that Serpilin had no fear of death. This may not have been so, but it certainly looked like it.

At the same time, Serpilin didn't pretend not to understand that men could lose their nerve, run away, go to pieces, and throw down their weapons. On the contrary, he did not hesitate to make it clear that he understood all this, but at the same time he firmly implanted in their minds the notion that their fear and their recent defeat were already things of the past. What had happened couldn't happen again: they had lost their weapons, but they could acquire new ones. That is probably why the men left Serpilin without feeling crushed, even when he had spoken sharply to them. He quite rightly didn't relieve them of their guilt, but he didn't make them feel totally to blame either. They sensed this and wanted to prove that his faith in them was justified.

Before the evening bivouac, there was another encounter, quite different from all the previous ones. A sergeant and a Red Armyman returned from the flank patrol, which was proceeding through the very densest part of the forest, with two armed men under escort. One was a little private with a worn leather jacket over his tunic and a rifle on his shoulder. The other was a tall, handsome man of about forty, with a big, aquiline nose. The aristocratic grey hair protruding from under his forage cap lent an air of distinction to his youngish, clean, unlined face. He was wearing good-quality riding-breeches and patent leather boots, and slung over his shoulder was a brand-new submachine gun with a circular ammunition drum; but his forage cap was soiled and greasy, and the equally soiled and greasy private's tunic looked awkward on him, didn't fit round the neck, and was too short in the sleeves.

The sergeant came up to Serpilin with these two, glanced at them and, with his rifle at the ready, said: "Permission to report, Comrade Brigade Commander! I've brought two detainees. I arrested them and brought them under escort because they won't give an account of themselves and because of their appearance. They refused to be disarmed, and we didn't want to open fire in the forest unnecessarily."

"Colonel Baranov, Deputy Chief of the Operational Department of Army HQ," rapped the officer with the submachine gun, bringing his hand smartly up to his forage cap and springing to attention in front of Serpilin and Shmakov. He sounded angry and irritated.

"Our apologies," said the sergeant who had brought the detainees, also saluting.

"Why apologise?" demanded Serpilin, turning to him. "You did right to arrest them, and you did right to bring them to me. Continue to act that way in future. You may go! Your documents please." And, having dismissed the sergeant, he turned to the colonel without addressing him by rank.

The latter's face twitched in an embarrassed smile. Sintsov realised that this man evidently knew Serpilin, but had only just recognised him and had been shaken by the encounter.

This, in fact, was so. The man who had called himself Colonel Baranov and who indeed bore this name and rank and held the appointment which he had mentioned, was so far from expecting to find Serpilin in front of him, here, in the forest, in military uniform and surrounded by other officers, that at first he had merely noticed that the tall brigade commander with the German submachine gun slung over his shoulder seemed to remind him of someone.

"Serpilin!" he exclaimed, flinging open his arms—it was hard to say whether in extreme astonishment or because he wanted to embrace Serpilin.

"Yes, I'm Brigade Commander Serpilin," said the latter in an unexpectedly dry, metallic voice. "I'm the commander of the division entrusted to me; but I can't tell who you are at the moment. Your documents!"

"Serpilin, I'm Baranov! What's the matter with you? Have you gone mad?"

"For the last time, please produce your documents," said Serpilin, still in the same metallic voice.

"I have no documents," said Baranov after a long pause.

"And how come you have no documents?"

"It just happened that way. I lost them accidentally. I left them in the other tunic when I changed into this soldier's one...." And Baranov ran his fingers over the greasy tunic that was too tight for him and didn't fit.

"You left your documents in the other tunic? And are your colonel's insignia also on the other tunic?"

"Yes," sighed Baranov.

"Then why should I believe that you are Colonel Baranov, Deputy Chief of the Operational Department of the Army?"

"But you know me! We were at the academy together!" muttered Baranov, now very much at a loss.

"We'll assume that," said Serpilin, not in the least mollified and still with the same metallic hardness that Sintsov found so unusual. "But if you hadn't met me, who would be able to confirm your identity, rank and appointment?"

"He would," said Baranov, pointing to the little Red Armyman in the leather jacket beside him. "He's my driver."

"Have you your documents with you, Comrade?" said Serpilin, turning to the driver without looking at Baranov.

"Yes..." stammered the soldier, at first not quite sure how to address Serpilin. "Yes, Comrade General!" He opened his leather jacket, took out of his tunic pocket a Red Armyman's book wrapped up in a piece of cloth, and offered it to Serpilin.

"Ah," said Serpilin, and he read aloud: "'Red Armyman Zolotarev, Pyotr Ilyich, military unit 22/14.' That's all right." And he gave the soldier back his book. "Tell me, Comrade Zolotarev, can you confirm the identity, rank and appointment of this man whom you have been detained?" And, still not turning to Baranov, he jerked his thumb at the colonel.

"Yes, Comrade General, that really is Colonel Baranov. I'm his driver."

"So you confirm that this is your commander?"

"Yes, Comrade General."

"Stop playing games, Serpilin!" shouted Baranov in exasperation.

But Serpilin never even glanced at him.

"It's just as well that at least you were able to identify your commander, otherwise, in different circumstances, he might have been shot. No documents, no badges of rank, someone else's tunic, and an officer's breeches and boots...." Serpilin's voice grew grimmer and grimmer at each word. "Under what circumstances did you get here?" he asked after a pause.

"I can explain everything..." began Baranov, but Serpilin, turning to him at last, cut him off short.

"I'm not asking you at the moment." He turned back to the Red Armyman. "Report...."

Hesitantly at first, then gaining confidence and trying not to forget anything, the Red Armyman told how they had arrived from the Army three days back and had spent the night in Divisional HQ. In the morning, the colonel had gone to HQ, but the Germans began bombing the whole area. Shortly afterwards, a driver arrived from the rear with the news that the Germans had made an airborne landing with tanks back there. Hearing this, the driver had started up his engine in case of emergency. An hour later, the colonel had hurried back, congratulated him on having his engine running, jumped in, and ordered him to head back to Chausy as quickly as possible. When they had driven out on to the highway, there had been heavy firing and smoke in front of them, so they had turned off on to a side-road and proceeded along it; but they had heard firing again and had seen German tanks at the cross-roads. They had then turned off down a side-track leading into the interior of the forest, had swung off the road under the trees, and the colonel had then ordered him to stop the car.

As he was recounting all this, the driver glanced at his colonel from time to time as if seeing confirmation from him; but the latter stood in silence with his head bowed. The most painful part of the story for him was about to begin, and he knew it.

"Then the comrade colonel ordered me to take out my old tunic and forage cap from under the seat—I'd lately been issued with a new uniform, and I'd kept the old tunic and cap, just in case, say, I had to crawl under the car. The comrade colonel took off his tunic and forage cap and put my things on instead, and then he said that we'd have to get out of encirclement on foot now, and he ordered me to throw petrol over the car and set it on fire. Except that I..." the driver hesitated, "except that I didn't know, Comrade General, that the comrade colonel had left his documents in his own tunic, otherwise I'd have reminded him, if I'd known; but as it was I set them on fire with the car."

He felt himself to blame.

Serpilin was visibly shocked.

"You hear that, Baranov?" he said, turning to the latter. "Your driver regrets not reminding you about your documents." There was a marked sneer in his voice. "It would be interesting to know what would have happened if he had reminded you about them, wouldn't it?" He turned back to the driver. "And what happened next?"

"We carried on for two days, keeping under cover. Until we met you...."

"Thank you, Comrade Zolotarev," said Serpilin. "Enter his name in your lists, Sintsov. Catch up with the column and take your place in the line. You'll get your food rations on bivouac."

The driver was about to go, then stopped short and looked inquiringly at his colonel. But the latter was still standing with his eyes on the ground.

"Go!" said Serpilin authoritatively. "You're free."

The driver went away. There was an uncomfortable silence.

"Why did you have to question him in my presence? You could have asked me without compromising me in front of a private."

"I asked him, because I trust the version of a soldier who has kept his documents more than I trust that of a colonel who has changed his clothes and has no insignia of rank or documents," said Serpilin. "At least I've got the whole picture now. You arrived at the division with orders to check that the Army commander's orders were being carried out. Yes or no?"

"Yes," said Baranov, still staring stubbornly at the ground.

"And instead of doing so, you cleared off at the first sign of danger! You dropped everything and you cleared off. Yes or no?"

"Not quite," said Baranov.

"How d'you mean, 'not quite'?"

But Baranov stayed silent. However insulted he may have felt, here was nothing he could say.

"I compromised him before a private! You hear that, Shmakov?" said Serpilin, turning to him. "What a laugh! He got the wind up, took off his officer's tunic in front of a private, threw away his documents, and now it turns out that I've compromised him. I didn't compromise you in front of a private. Thanks to your disgraceful conduct, you compromised the headquarters staff of the Army in front of a private.

If my memory doesn't play me false, you were a Party member. Did you burn your Party card as well?"

"I burnt the lot." And Baranov shrugged his shoulders.

"You say that you accidentally left your documents in your tunic?" It was Shmakov, white with anger, intervening in the conversation for the first time.

"Accidentally," said Baranov.

"In my opinion, you're lying. In my opinion, if your driver had reminded you, you'd have got rid of them just the same at the first suitable opportunity."

"What for?" asked Baranov.

"You know better than I do."

"But I was still armed," said Baranov.

"If you burnt your Party card before there was any real danger, then you'd have thrown down your gun at the sight of your first German."

"He hung on to his gun because he was scared of the wolves in the forest," said Serpilin.

"I kept it in case of Germans!" shouted Baranov shrilly. "In case of Germans!"

"I don't believe you," said Serpilin. "You, a staff commander, had a whole division under you, and yet you left it in the lurch! How were you going to fight the Germans single-handed?"

"Fyodor Fyodorovich, what's the point of going on like this? I'm not a schoolboy. I understand everything," said Baranov, suddenly quiet.

But Serpilin only reacted with distrust to this unexpected humility on Baranov's part. It was as if the colonel, who had hitherto been frantically trying to justify himself, had suddenly decided it might pay him to change his tune.

"What do you understand?" he asked.

"My guilt. I'll wipe it out with blood. Give me a company, or even a platoon. After all, I was heading for my own people, not the Germans. Can you believe that?"

"I don't know," said Serpilin. "In my opinion, you weren't proceeding anywhere in particular. You were just proceeding according to the circumstances and letting things take their own course...."

"I curse the moment when I burnt my documents and I'm sorry..." began Baranov. But Serpilin cut him short:

"I believe you're sorry now. You're sorry now that you were in such a hurry, because you ended up with your own people. But if things had turned out otherwise—well, I don't know whether you'd have been so sorry. What do you think, Commissar?" He turned to Shmakov. "Shall we give this ex-colonel a company?"

"No," said Shmakov.

"A platoon?"

"No,"said Shmakov.

"I'd say the same. After the way you acquitted yourself, I'd sooner trust your driver to command you, than you to command him!" said Serpilin, and for the first time he spoke to Baranov a shade more gently than before. "Go and get in line with that fancy little sub-machine gun of yours and see if you can, as you say, wipe out your guilt with blood. German blood," he added, after a pause. "And with your own too, if need be. By virtue of the authority invested in myself and the commissar, you are hereby reduced to the ranks until we join up with our own forces. You will then account for your own behaviour, and we for taking the law into our own hands."

"Is that all? Have you nothing more to say?" asked Baranov, raising his head and looking resentfully at Serpilin.

Serpilin winced at this, and he even shut his eyes for a second to hide his feelings.

"You can thank us for not having you shot for cowardice," put in Shmakov instead of Serpilin.

"Sintsov," said Serpilin, opening his eyes, "enter Private Baranov on the unit rolls. Go with him," he nodded towards Baranov, "to Lieutenant Khoryshev and tell him that Private Baranov is now under his command."

"You're in command here, Fyodor Fyodorovich, and I shall obey your orders. But don't expect me to forget this."

Serpilin clasped his hands behind his back and cracked his fingers, but said nothing.

"Let's go," said Sintsov to Baranov, and they began to catch up with the column, which was now ahead of them.

Shmakov looked intently at Serpilin. Himself upset by what had just happened, he sensed that Serpilin was feeling even more badly shaken. The brigade commander was apparently deeply pained by this disgraceful conduct on the part of someone he had once respected.

"Fyodor Fyodorovich!"

"What?" replied Serpilin, as if waking up out of dream, and even starting slightly. He had become lost in his thoughts and had forgotten that Shmakov was beside him.

"Why are you so upset? Were you in the service together a long time? Did you know him well?"

Serpilin looked at him vaguely and surprised the commissar by answering with uncharacteristic evasiveness:

"Does anybody ever know anybody really well? Let's get a move on until it's time for a halt!"

Shmakov didn't like to force confidences out of people, so he fell silent. Both men quickened their pace and walked side by side until it was time for a halt, neither of them saying anything and each wrapped in his own thoughts.

Shmakov had got it wrong. Although Baranov had indeed been with Serpilin at the Academy, Serpilin, so far from having a high opinion of him, had actually despised him. He had regarded Baranov as an out-and-out careerist, interested purely in his own self-advancement and not in the good of the service. Baranov was ready to support one doctrine today and another tomorrow—to say that white was black and black was white. Skilfully adapting himself to what he thought might please his superiors, he was not above supporting blatant errors of judgement based on ignorance of facts of which he was perfectly well aware.

His hobby-horse was reports and information about the armies of hypothetical enemies. While emphasising the real and imaginary weaknesses, he obligingly kept quiet about all the strong and dangerous sides of the future enemy. Although well aware that he was treading on very thin ice where such matters were concerned, Serpilin condemned Baranov for this on three occasions—twice to his face in private, and the third time in public.

He had later been reminded of all this in quite unexpected circumstances, and goodness only knows what it had cost him, during the conversation with Baranov, not to come out with everything that had suddenly been stirred up in his heart.

He didn't know whether he was right or wrong to think as he did of Baranov, but he knew well that this was not the time or the place for remembering old grudges. They just didn't matter!

The most difficult moment in their conversation had been when Baranov had suddenly looked Serpilin inquiringly straight in the face. But he had withstood even that look, and Baranov had gone away reassured—at least if that parting shot of his was anything to go by.

Well, so be it. He, Serpilin, had neither the inclination nor the right to become personally involved with his subordinate, Private Baranov. If the latter fought bravely, Serpilin would thank him in front of the unit. If he died an honourable death, Serpilin would send in a report. If he turned yellow and ran for it. Serpilin would have him shot, just as he would have anyone else shot in the circumstances. He would be completely fair. But what a painful business nevertheless.

They bivouacked near a human habitation—the first they had seen in the forest. There was an old woodman's cabin on the edge of a clearing that had been ploughed up to serve as a kitchen garden. There was a well close by—a joy to the men, who were enervated by the intense heat.

Sintsov handed Baranov over to Khoryshev and went into the cabin. There were two rooms inside; the door into the second one was shut. From behind it came the fretful, interminable sound of a woman weeping. The walls in the first room had been papered with yellowing news-sheets. In the right-hand corner hung an ikon-stand. On the broad bench next to two commanders, who had preceded Sintsov into the cabin, sat a grim, unmoving, silent eighty-year-old man in a spotlessly clean white peasant blouse and linen breeches. His face was etched with deep wrinkles, and a little cross hung from his scrawny neck on a worn copper chain.

A tiny, brisk old woman, evidently of the same age as the man, but seeming much younger owing to the quickness of her movements, greeted Sintsov with a bow, took another glass tumbler from the wall-cupboard, which was draped with an embroidered hand-towel, and put it in front of Sintsov near the two tumblers and the milk-can already standing on the table. Before Sintsov arrived, the old woman had been giving a drink of milk to the two commanders.

Sintsov asked her if she could fix a meal for the CO and the divisional commissar, adding that they had their own bread.

"What can I give you except milk?" The old woman threw up her hands in distress. "I could light the stove and boil some potatoes, if you have time."

Sintsov didn't know whether there was time, but he asked her to boil some potatoes anyway.

"We've still got some old one's—last year's..." she said; and she busied herself at the stove.

Sintsov drank the milk out of the cold, blue-tinged tumbler. He would have liked more but, after glancing into the can, which was less than half-full, he hesitated. The two officers, who would evidently also have liked another glass each, took their leave and went out. Sintsov was left with the old couple. The woman fussed about at the stove, put a spill under the logs, went into the next room, and returned a moment later with some matches. Each time she opened and closed the door, the sound of wailing surged in from the other room.

"Who's that crying?" asked Sintsov.

"It's Danya," said the woman. "My granddaughter.... Her boy friend's been killed. He was crippled in one arm, so they didn't take him into the army. They were driving the kolkhoz herd from Nelidovo. Just as they were crossing the main road, the Germans dropped some bombs and he was killed. That's the second day she's been wailing like that," added the old woman.

She lit the spill, put on the stove a pan of potatoes already washed—probably for herself—sat down on the bench beside her husband, rested her elbows on the table, and began to tell Sintsov her troubles.

"All our men are away fighting," she said, looking at Sintsov. "Our sons are away figting, and our grandsons are away fighting. Will the Germans be here soon, d'you think?"

"I don't know," said Sintsov.

"Some people from Nelidovo have been saying that the Germans have already got as far as Chausy."

"I don't know," repeated Sintsov. And, in fact, he didn't know what answer to give.

"It can't be long now," said the old woman. "They've been driving off the herds for the last five days, and they're not doing that for nothing. As for us folks," she pointed a withered hand at the can, "that's our last milk we're drinking. We've given up the cow, too. Let them take her away. God willing, they may bring her back again. I was talking to a neighbour, and she was saying that there's hardly anybody left in Nelidovo—they're all going away...."

While she was speaking, the old man just sat there saying nothing. All the time Sintsov had been in the cabin, he hadn't uttered a single word. He was very old, and it was as if he wanted to die there and then, before, following these men in Red Army uniform, the Germans walked into his home.

And Sintsov was overwhelmed by such sadness at the sight of him, and there was such despair in the weeping behind the door, that he couldn't stand it any longer. He went out, saying he would be back soon.

As he stepped down from the porch, he saw Serpilin approaching the cabin.

"Comrade Brigade Commander..." he began. But the little doctor ran up to Serpilin ahead of him and, deeply agitated, said that Colonel Zaichikov wanted him urgently.

"I'll come later if I have time," said Serpilin with a wave of the hand to Sintsov in reply to his invitation to go inside the cabin for a rest, and he went off after the doctor.

Zaichikov was lying on the stretcher in the shade under a dense clump of hazel bushes. He had just been given a drink of water and had clearly had some difficulty in getting it down. His tunic collar and his shoulders were wet.

"I'm here, Nikolai Petrovich," said Serpilin, sitting down on the ground beside Zaichikov.

Zaichikov opened his eyes so slowly that it was as if even this movement cost him more strength than he could summon.

"Listen, Fedya," he whispered, addressing Serpilin in this way for the first time. "Why not shoot me, eh? I haven't the strength to suffer like this. Do me a favour."

"I can't," said Serpilin, and his voice shook.

"It's not just that I'm suffering—I'm a burden to you all," said Zaichikov, enunciating each word with an effort.

"I can't," repeated Serpilin.

"Give me a pistol, then, and I'll shoot myself."

Serpilin said nothing.

"Scared of the responsibility?"

"You mustn't shoot yourself," said Serpilin, pulling himself together. "You haven't the right. It'll have a bad effect on the men. If it was just the two of us...."

He didn't finish; but the dying Zaichikov believed, that were they alone together, Serpilin would not refuse him the right to shoot himself.

"I'm in such pain," he said, closing his eyes, "in such pain. Serpilin, if only you knew—I can't bear it any longer. Put me to sleep. Order the doctor to put me to sleep. I keep asking her, but she won't give me the stuff. She says she hasn't got any. Couldn't you check and see if she's telling the truth?"

He was lying motionless again, his eyes closed and his lips shut tight. Serpilin stood up and, stepping aside, called the doctor over.

"Is it hopeless?" he asked quietly.

She merely shrugged.

"What's the use of asking? Three times I've thought he was going. He has a few hours left at the most."

"Have you something to put him to sleep with?" asked Serpilin quietly but firmly.

The doctor looked at him in fright with her big, child-like eyes.

"It's not allowed!" she said.

"I know what's not alowed. It's my responsibility," said Serpilin. "Have you got anything or haven't you?"

"No," said the doctor; and he felt that she was telling the truth.

"I can't bear to see him suffer like that," he said.

"D'you think I can bear it, then?" she replied and, to Serpilin's surprise, she began to cry, rubbing the tears all over her cheeks with her fists.

Serpilin turned away.

He went back to Zaichikov, sat down beside him, and studied his face intently.

With the approach of death, his cheeks had sunk in and emaciation made him look younger. Serpilin suddenly remembered that Zaichikov was all of six years younger than himself and had still been a young platoon commander towards the end of the Civil War when he, Serpilin, was already in command of a regiment. And at this recollection of the distant past, Serpilin was overwhelmed with bitterness that he, no longer a young man, should be watching over the death-bed of a man so much his junior. "Oh, Zaichikov, Zaichikov," thought Serpilin, "you didn't exactly set the world on fire when you were under my command; you served better than some and worse than others; then you fought in the Finnish campaign, and bravely too, I'm sure; they don't give two Orders for nothing; and you didn't funk it near Mogilev either, you kept your head, you stayed in command as long as you could stand on your own two feet, and now you're dying here in this forest, and you don't know, and you never will, when this war's going to be over that's cost you so much grief from the day it started...."

"At least keep the divisional number," whispered Zaichikov, suddenly opening his eyes and seeing Serpilin seated beside him.

No, he wasn't unconscious. He was lying and thinking about the same things, or almost the same things, as Serpilin.

"Why shouldn't we keep it?" said Serpilin confidently. "We'll get out with the colours, we'll get out with our weapons, and we'll report what sort of a fight we put up. Why shouldn't we keep it? We haven't dishonoured it, and we're not going to dishonour it either. I give you my word as a Communist...."

"Good..." said Zaichikov, closing his eyes. "But I'm in great pain. Go away, you've got things to do!" he said very quietly but with great effort, and once more he bit his lip in pain.

At eight o'clock in the evening, Serpilin's detachment reached the south-eastern fringe of the forest. Ahead of them, according to the map, lay another two kilometres of sparse woodland, and beyond that the highway, which they had no means of avoiding. On the other side of the road lay a village, a strip of ploughed land, and only then did the forest begin again. Halting short of the woodland, Serpilin ordered his troops to fall out for a rest, anticipating a battle and then a night crossing to follow. The men needed the chance to regain their strength and get some sleep. Many had been at their last gasp for some time, but had kept going, aware that if they didn't come out onto the highway and cross it during the night, then all their efforts hitherto would have been pointless: they would have to wait until the following night.

Serpilin did the rounds of the detachment, checked the sentry posts, and sent a patrol ahead to reconnoitre the highway. While waiting for it to return, he decided to have a rest. But he didn't get the chance to do so immediately. He had just sought out a likely spot for himself on the grass under a shady tree, when Shmakov came up and sat by him, thrusting into his hand a discoloured German leaflet which had evidently been lying about in the woods for several days.

"Here, take a look at this. The men found it and handed it in. Must have been dropped by air."

Serpilin wiped his eyes, gummy with lack of sleep, and conscientiously read the whole leaflet from beginning to end. It announced that Stalin's armies had been smashed, that six million prisoners had been captured, and that German troops had taken Smolensk and were approaching Moscow. Then followed the conclusion: further resistance was useless. After this came a promise to "preserve life for each who voluntarily surrendered, including command and political staff"; also to feed POW's three times a day and keep them in conditions universally accepted in the civilised world. A sketch map had been printed on the back of the leaflet. The only cities actually named were Minsk, Smolensk, and Moscow; but according to the general scale, the northern arrow of the advancing German armies reached well beyond Vologda and the tip of the southern one lay somewhere between Penza and Tambov. The middle arrow, incidentally, almost touched Moscow, but the authors of the leaflet had evidently drawn the line at taking the capital itself.

"Hm ... yes," drawled Serpilin derisively and, folding the leaflet in half, he returned it to Shmakov. "Even you're apparently promised your life, Commissar. What d'you say? Shall we surrender, eh?"

"Even the Denikin lot were better at churning out this sort of bumph," replied Shmakov and, turning to Sintsov, he asked him if he had any matches left.

Sintsov took a box out of his pocket and was going to burn the leaflet without even bothering to read it, but Shmakov stopped him.

"Go on, read it! It's not infectious!"

Sintsov read it through and was surprised at his own lack of emotion. Yesterday and the day before he had personally killed two nazis, the first with a rifle and the second with a German submachine gun. Perhaps he had killed more, but he was certain of those two. He wanted to go on killing Germans, and this leaflet had nothing to do with him....

"To preserve life for each.... For each! That's no way to write Russian," he thought and, striking the match on the still damp box, he applied the flame to a dog-eared corner of the leaflet.

Meanwhile Serpilin, like a true soldier, was settling down without further ado for a rest under the tree that had taken his fancy. To Sintsov's amazement, the few absolutely essential items in Serpilin's kitbag included a rubber pillow folded in four. Comically puffing out his gaunt cheeks, Serpilin inflated it and laid his head on it with gratification.

"Never go anywhere without it. Present from my wife!" he said with a smile to Sintsov who was staring at these preparations. But he did not add that the pillow was also of sentimental value. It had been sent to him by his wife from home several years ago and had travelled with him beyond the Arctic circle and back again.

Shmakov didn't want to go to sleep while Serpilin was having his nap, but Serpilin talked him into it.

"We won't be able to take turns today anyway," said Serpilin. "We've both got to stay awake tonight, because we're almost certainly going to have to fight. And no one can fight without some sleep first—not even a commissar! So be a good fellow, shut your eyes and roost awhile, even if only for an hour."

Serpilin gave orders that he was to be woken as soon as the reconnaissance patrol returned and then blissfully stretched himself out on the grass. After tossing from side to side for a while, Shmakov also dozed off. Sintsov, who had received no instructions from Serpilin, with difficulty resisted the temptation to lie down and go to sleep too. If Serpilin had told him that he could go to sleep, he wouldn't have been able to resist and would have lain down. But Serpilin hadn't said anything, and so Sintsov, struggling to keep awake, began to pace to and fro across the little glade in which the brigade commander and the commissar had gone to sleep. Previously, he had only heard stories of people dozing off on their feet; but now he experienced it himself, suddenly stopping from time to time and losing his balance.

"Comrade Political Instructor," said a quiet and familiar voice at one such moment.

Khoryshev was standing in front of him.

"What's happened?" asked Sintsov, noticing with alarm the signs of great agitation on the lieutenant's boyish face, usually so calm and cheerful.

"It's alright. They've found a gun in the forest. I want to report to the brigade commander."

Khoryshev was still keeping his voice down, but Serpilin must have been woken by the word "gun". He propped himself up on his hands, looked at the sleeping Shmakov, and quietly and quickly got to his feet, indicating with a gesture that Khoryshev should not report at full voice, otherwise they might wake the commissar.

Straightening his tunic and signalling Sintsov to follow him, he walked several paces into the forest interior. Only then did he allow Khoryshev to make his report.

"Well, what kind of gun have they found there? German?"

"Ours. And five men with it."

"What about ammunition?"

"One round left."

"Not a lot. Is it far from here?"

"About five hundred paces."

Serpilin shrugged off the last traces of sleep and told Khoryshev to take him to the gun.

On the way, Sintsov felt like asking why the usually calm lieutenant was looking so agitated; but Serpilin covered the whole distance in silence and Sintsov couldn't bring himself to disturb him.

After about five hundred paces, they saw a 45-mm anti-tank gun standing in the middle of a copse of young fir-trees. Near the gun, on a thick carpet of old, russet fir needles, the five artillerymen already mentioned by Khoryshev were sitting with Khoryshev's own platoon.

As soon as the brigade commander appeared, all jumped to their feet—the artillerymen somewhat later than the rest, but nevertheless before Khoryshev had given the command.

"Good evening, Comrades!" said Serpilin. "Which of you is acting as senior?"

A sergeant-major stepped forward. The peak of his cap, with its black artillery band, was split in two. One eye was nothing but a swollen wound; the upper lid of the other was twitching nervously. But he stood firm and steady, as if his feet in the tattered boots were nailed to the ground, and his hand snapped to the split peak of his cap as if the arm in the ragged, scorched sleeve was worked by a spring. His voice deep and strong, but quivering slightly with excitement, he reported that he, Sergeant-Major Shestakov of the Ninth Independent Anti-tank Battalion, was at present the senior in command. He had fought his way out from near Brest, bringing with him what was left of the equipment.

"From where did you say?" asked Serpilin, wondering if he had heard right.

"From near Brest, where the full battalion was engaged in its first battle with the nazis," replied the sergeant-major, rapping the words out rather than just saying them.

There was a silence.

Serpilin stared at the artillerymen, wondering if what he had heard could be true. And the longer he looked at them, the clearer it became that this incredible story was the real truth, while what the Germans were writing in their leaflets about their victory was nothing but a plausible lie.

... Five blackened and starved faces, five pairs of tired, overworked hands, five soaked and dirty tunics, torn by tree branches, five German submachine guns captured, and a gun, the battalion's last gun, dragged by these soldiers all the way from the frontier, a distance of over four hundred kilometres. No, Messrs Germans, you're not going to have it all your own way!

"With your bare hands?" asked Serpilin, swallowing a lump in his throat and nodding at the gun.

The sergeant-major replied, and the others, unable to restrain themselves, chorused their support, to the effect that they'd towed it in various ways: by horse, then by hand, then they'd come by some horses again, and then they'd had to tow it along by hand once more....

"What about the rivers—how did you get it across the Dnieper?" asked Serpilin.

"On a raft, the night before last...."

"And we never managed to bring over a single one," said Serpilin suddenly. But although he ran his eyes over all his own men as he spoke, they felt that he was only reproaching one person—himself.

Then he looked at the artillerymen again.

"Is it true that you have shells with you?"

"One round ... the last," said the sergeant-major apologetically, as if guilty of negligence in failing to replenish the ammunition supplies in time.

"Where did you expend the round before the last?"

"Here, ten kilometres away." The sergeant-major jerked his thumb to the rear, where the highway ran behind the forest. "We rolled the gun last night up to the road, into the bushes, at point-blank range. We hit the leading lorry in a convoy smack in the headlights!"

"Weren't you scared of them combing the forest?"

"We're sick of being scared, Comrade Brigade Commander. Let them be scared of us for a change!"

"So they didn't comb the forest after all?"

"No. They just lobbed some mortar bombs round us. The battalion commander was fatally wounded."

"Where is he?" demanded Serpilin quickly; but he already knew where before he had finished speaking.

He had followed the sergeant-major's eyes to a spot nearby where the yellow mound of a freshly-dug grave stood under an enormous pine-tree, bare to the very summit. The broad German sword with which they had cut the turf to lay round the grave had not yet been removed and was sticking up out of the ground like an unwanted cross.

A rough criss-cross, still oozing resin, had been slashed into the bark of the pine-tree over the grave. To the left and right of it were two more gashes, just as evil-looking, like a challenge to fate or a silent promise to return.

Serpilin went up to the grave and, removing his cap, looked long and silently at the ground, as if trying to stare through it at something no one would ever see again—the face of the man who had fought his way from Brest, bringing to this forest by the Dnieper all that was left of his battalion: five men, a gun, and one last round of ammunition.

Serpilin had never seen him, but he felt that he knew just what sort of person he had been: the kind of man for whom soldiers will go through fire and water; the kind of man whose dead body is carried away from the battle by soldiers at the risk of their own lives; the kind of man whose orders are obeyed even after his death; the kind of man it took to rescue this gun and these soldiers.

But these men, whom he had brought out, were worthy of their commander. He had been what he had been because he had marched with them....

Serpilin replaced his cap and silently shook hands with each artilleryman in turn. Then he pointed to the grave and asked abruptly:

"Name?"

"Captain Gusev."

"Don't write it down; I'll remember it till my dying day," said Serpilin, noticing that Sintsov had reached for his map-case. "No—write it down. We're all mortal! And enter the artillerymen on the unit rolls. Thanks for everything you've done, Comrades! As for your last round—I think we'll be firing that off in action tonight."

Serpilin had already noticed Baranov's grey head among Khoryshev's soldiers and the artillerymen; but it was only now that their eyes met. Shuddering with contempt, Serpilin read terror in the other man's eyes at the thought of the impending battle.

"Comrade Brigade Commander!" said the little doctor, coming up from behind the soldiers. "The colonel wants you!"

"The colonel?" asked Serpilin. His mind was on Baranov, and it took him a moment to grasp which colonel was sending for him. "Of course, let's go, let's go," he said, realising that the doctor meant Zaichikov.

"What's happened? Why wasn't I sent for?" exclaimed the doctor when she saw the soldiers gathered round the new grave.

"It's alright. Let's go. It was too late to send for you!" said Serpilin, and with rough gentleness he put his big hand on her shoulder, almost forcibly turned her round and, his hand still resting on her shoulder, went away with her.

"No faith, no honour, no conscience." He was still thinking of Baranov as he walked beside the doctor. "As long as war seemed a long way off, he used to shout that it would be a walk-over when the time came. But now it's arrived, and he's been the first to run for it. If *he*'s scared, if *he*'s terrified, then he thinks it's all up with us and we can't win! The hell it does! Apart from yourself, there's Captain Gusev, and his artillerymen, and us sinners, the living and the dead, and this little doctor here, who has to hold a revolver with both hands...."

Serpilin suddenly realised that his heavy hand was still resting on the doctor's thin shoulder—was not just resting on it, but even using it for support. She carried on as if unaware, however, and was even deliberately giving him that support. She probably never even suspected that there were people like Baranov in this world.

"Sorry, I forgot my hand was on your shoulder," he said to the doctor gently. And he removed it.

"I don't mind. Lean on me if you're tired," she said. "I'm pretty strong, you know."

"Yes, you're strong," thought Serpilin. "We can't lose with people like you, and that's a fact." He wanted to say something affectionate and confident to this little woman as an answer to his private thoughts about Baranov; but he couldn't find the words, and so they continued in silence to where Zaichikov was lying.

"Comrade Colonel, I've brought him," she said softly, going down on her knees and bending right down to Zaichikov's face.

Serpilin kneeled beside her and she moved aside so as not to prevent him also bending closer.

"Is that you, Serpilin?" asked Zaichikov in a scarcely audible whisper.

"Yes."

"Listen to what I'm going to tell you," said Zaichikov even more quietly, and he fell silent.

Serpilin waited a minute, then two, then three; but he was not destined to know what his former commander had wanted to say in the last moment of his life to the new divisional CO.

"He's gone," said the doctor almost inaudibly.

Serpilin slowly removed his cap, remained bareheaded for a few moments on his knees, straightened them with an effort, stood up and, without saying a word, went back.

The scouts returned with the information that there were German patrols on the highway and that there was traffic heading towards Chausy.

"So we're going to have to fight our way through," said Serpilin. "Rouse the men and form them up!"

Now that he knew that his suppositions had been confirmed and that they were unlikely to get across the road without a fight, he finally shook off the feeling of physical weariness that had dogged him since morning. He was full of determination to take these men, now getting up from their sleep with their rifles in their hands, where he was supposed to take them—to join up with the main Soviet forces! He was not even prepared to consider an alternative.

That night he did not, and could not, know the full value of what had already been achieved by the men of his regiment. And, like him and those under his command, the full value of what they had done and were doing was not yet known in thousands of other places to thousands of other men who were fighting to the death with a stubbornness never anticipated or envisaged by the Germans.

They did not, and could not, know that the German army generals who were still advancing in triumph on Moscow, Leningrad and Kiev, would, in twenty years' time, call that July of Forty-One the month of deceived hopes, of successes that did not culminate in victory.

They themselves could not have foreseen the enemy's future bitter admissions; but almost each and every man at that time, in July, did everything humanly possible to ensure that things should happen exactly as they did.

Serpilin stood and listened to the subdued commands. The column was stirring raggedly in the darkness that had descended on the forest. A flat, ruddy moon was rising over the jagged tree-tops. The first day of encirclement was nearly at an end....

CHAPTER SEVEN

After the successful, for us, counter-offensive in August and October near Yelnia a relative lull set in on the Western front. Lieutenant-Colonel Klimovich's tank brigade was positioned in the woods south of Yelnia. Its reconnaissance battalion; functioning as infantry, had taken up a four-kilometre-long defensive sector on the front line.

Before the war, Klimovich had been in command of a tank brigade stationed outside Slonim. There were about seventy men left of those with whom he had begun the war. Some had been killed when the brigade was breaking out of encirclement through the woods towards Slutsk and Bobruisk, others had fallen while covering Mogilev, and yet others had been put out of action as late as in August and September near Yelnia.

Before the battles outside Yelnia, the brigade had been equipped half with old BT-7 tanks and half with the new

T-34's. These latter had proved to be first-class, and so it had fallen to their lot to bear the main brunt of the fighting outside Yelnia. Each battalion had sustained serious losses, but the brigade, instead of being withdrawn to the rear, was promised replacements of men and also tanks—this time T-34's only. Klimovich, who had fallen in love with these machines during the Yelnia battles, awaited their arrival with an impatience which can only be understood by a tankman, who, since the war broke out, had already twice miraculously escaped from a BT-7 blazing like a match-box. That these light machines, for all their speed, were weak in armour and fire-power had already become clear towards the end of the Khalkhin-Gol fighting. But it was with the obsolete BT-7's that Klimovich had met the war on the Western frontier, since the promised T-34's had not yet arrived.

On the fifth day of the war, he had nearly shot his company commander in front of the assembled troops for flying into a blind rage and shouting, in front of the crews, that no one could fight in those match-boxes. An hour later, that officer went into battle, destroyed a German tank, and was himself burnt out right before Klimovich's eyes.

Outside Yelnia, Klimovich fell victim to two conflicting emotions: pride in his crewmen who, in their new machines, cracked the German tanks like nuts, and bitterness because he hadn't had a single one of them at the outbreak of the war and had been forced to sacrifice two of his own tanks for every one of the enemy's, when it should have been the other way round.

Now, during the lull, he had repaired all the BT-7's left in the brigade, and was stubbornly driving it home to his subordinates that it was possible to fight even in these machines, but secretly he was waiting for the new tanks with a passion unlike anything he had ever experienced for anything else in this world.

He had always been a soldier to the core; but now that military service had become warfare, it obsessed him to the exclusion of everything else. He thought only about his brigade, because he had nothing else he could call his own. Before the war, he had lived under the same roof with four people. Three of them he had loved, and the fourth he had considered himself obliged to take care of. These were his daughter, his son, his wife, and his mother-in-law. On the third day of the war, all four were killed by a bomb while they were driving along the road in a car and he thought them already out of danger. When the news was broken to him, there was a battle in progress. He was not even able to go and see to the burial of their remains.

He was only thirty years of age, and if it had ever occurred to anyone to ask him: "The worst that could happen has happened to you, but you have your life before you. Surely there will be something to replace what you have lost?", then, despite the intensity of his grief, he would probably have replied: "Yes, there will be something." But during all those months, no one who heard his steady voice and saw the deadpan expression on his face ever thought of asking him how he proposed to live after the war. Nor did he ever think about it himself. He was now part of the war and, as long as it lasted, there could be no place in his soul for anything or anybody else, now that his family were dead, except for war and its immediate interests and demands.

On the evening of October lst, Klimovich was sitting alone at brigade HQ in a cabin which was ramshackle and filthy to look at from outside, but had been scrubbed as clean as a new pin inside—he was a pedant and loved cleanliness—and was reading *New Tales of the Good Soldier Schweik* by a front-line satirist. Most of the men at the front used to enjoy these stories, but Klimovich didn't like them. The Germans were hitting us harder than we were hitting them, which meant that it was still too early to laugh at them. Even so, he was reading the stories because it was his habit to study the whole front-line newspaper from beginning to end in case he found something likely to be of practical value in army life.

The telephone whirred on the table. Folding the newspaper so that the place he had reached was on the crease and he wouldn't have to hunt for it again, Klimovich picked up the handset. It was the reconnaissance battalion commander ringing to report an unusual occurrence. Frequent machine-gun. submachine gun and rifle fire, accompanied by grenade explosions, had broken out ahead of the batallion's front line and in the enemy's rear. Klimovich snatched the phone away from his ear, pushed the windows open, and listened intently. His practised ear detected the scarcely audible echoes of a distant battle.

"I'm coming over. Wait for me," said Klimovich.

There had been a brief shower of rain and it was dark and damp in the forest. A lieutenant who had been sent out to meet Klimovich was walking ahead of him, his hands on a submachine gun and his elbows bulging under the wet cape. As he passed a BT-7 camouflaged in a deep trench,

Klimovich again thought about what was constantly on his mind these days: "The sooner we get those Thirty-Fours, the better!"

The observation post had been set up on the very fringe of the forest. It commanded an excellent daytime view of the flat, unmown meadow sloping down to the stream, and of another meadow like it rising towards the forest on the German side. On the meadow stood two burnt-put tanks side by side: one of our BT-7's and a German T-4. They had been standing there like that for nearly a month, inseparable as twins.

White and red signal flares kept soaring up in front here and there over the German forest, accompanied by the flickering flashes of explosions. The machine-gun and rifle fire was no longer a kilometre and a half behind the German front line, as the Reconnaissance Battalion commander had reported half an hour previously, but was now quite near. It was four hundred metres to the German forward positions, and the fighting was in progress some five hundred metres behind them, at a point where, according to intelligence reports, the second line of German trenches was located.

Klimovich was infected by the general excitement at the observation post. All were thinking the same thing, afraid to believe what they had guessed.

"Ivanov, get the crews to their tanks!" said Klimovich to the Reconnaissance Battalion commander after he had listened to a report of observations made during the last half hour.

"Right away!" said Ivanov; but he couldn't resist asking: "Are we going to fight our way through to meet them, Comrade Lieutenant-Colonel?"

"We'll decide according to the circumstances. Get on with it!" said Klimovich. He went down into the dug-out and ordered the operator to connect him with Army HQ.

He had already rung the Army before leaving, but it was now time to call them again. Hardly had the operator begun turning the handle, when the bell rang: Army HQ was asking for the brigade commander.

"What can you see there? Report!" said the voice of the Army Commander.

Klimovich reported that he could see flares and the flashes of explosions, that there was fighting in progress behind the German lines, and that the interval between themselves and the battle was between eight hundred and nine hundred metres.

"Your neighbour on the left reports the same," said the Army Commander. "But the fighting's on his right, so it's all happening on a narrow sector in front of you. How do you evaluate the situation and what action do you propose to take?"

Klimovich told him what he and all the reconnaissance people with him thought: a unit was breaking out of encirclement and was fighting its way through the German front line on their sector. He asked for permission to bring up the tanks and carry out a battle reconnaissance operation to the left and right of the sector where the fighting was in progress.

The telephone was silent for several seconds, and then the Army Commander said that according to his information no units had been cut off in the German rear for some considerable time, and it might be a clever ruse: they would force us to rush forward, and then they would overrun our positions.

"I'm reckoning with that possibility, Comrade Commander," said Klimovich. "I'm taking precautionary measures and leaving the Thirty-Fours behind me in ambush."

"How many of those have you got in action now? Eleven?" interrupted the Commander.

Each Thirty-Four was precious to the army in those days. The Commander had remembered the number correctly.

"Eleven," confirmed Klimovich. "Still, if it is our own people breaking through, we've got to help them, haven't we, Comrade Commander?"

Again the handset fell silent. Klimovich could hear voices, but was unable to distinguish the words. The Army Commander was evidently talking to a member of the Military Council or to the Chief of Staff.

"Go ahead," he said a minute later. "Report every half hour."

Klimovich replaced the handset and, without losing any more time, began preparing for the attack. He picked up the telephone again, spoke to the battalion commanders and gave them his instructions. Meanwhile, the battle raged on in front of them, moving now to the left, now to the right, now gaining ground, now uneasily backing off. No, it couldn't be a ruse. Eight hundred metres away, between the first and second lines of the German positions, men were dying, breaking through and falling back, hemmed in on all sides by a ring of German fire that was also moving and was intensifying every minute. It was as if a live, bleeding heart was pulsing between the enemy lines, and the Germans were stinging it from every side with shell-bursts, stabbing it with machine-gun fusillades, and ripping it apart with mortar fire....

If the Army Commander had refused Klimovich permission to go and help the men, who had probably covered hundreds of kilometres and were now dying a stone's throw away from their own forces, it would have been the blackest day in Klimovich's life as a soldier. Had he been told beforehand that if he went to their assistance he would surely be killed, he would have still gone into battle without a moment's hesitation.

And when that wounded and mangled heart out there in the middle of the German positions made a last, desperate, bloody, two-hundred-metre bound towards the forward lines of the German trenches, and when eight BT-7's and a hundred and fifty men from the Reconnaissance Battalion rushed the German positions in the dark and went to meet it, this was not just a daring night attack, but a single coordinated and unswerving act of the spirit by all the men in the Reconnaissance Battalion, already thinned down considerably during a series of prolonged battles.

Klimovich's plan—to strike to the left and right of the sector where our troops were breaking through from the German rear—proved to have been the right one, and it brought immediate results. The Germans had been assembling along the trenches and communications trenches towards the anticipated breakthrough point in order to plug the narrow bottleneck with a human cork; but when they heard the roar of tank engines on both sides and shouts of "Hurrah!", they hastily turned round and moved out to the left and the right again. This two-way movement at night-time was bound to result in confusion, and the confusion was aggravated by the fact that the breakthrough from the rear and the attack from the front were a double surprise for the Germans.

The battle subsided in an hour. It flared up here and there for a while, then died down entirely; then a few belated bursts of submachine-gun fire reverberated somewhere in the dark again as if in an empty bucket. Klimovich lost two tanks to German mines and fifteen men shot down on both sides of the stream. Even so, at a rough estimate made that night, a whole battalion—over three hundred men—had burst in the confusion of battle through the German positions and now, dazed with happiness, ragged and hungry, still clutching their weapons, were streaming, fit and wounded alike, along the tank battalion's trenches and dug-outs.

Radio stations all over the world watched ice-breakers and aeroplanes from six countries rescue the twelve men of the Nobile expedition. Newspapers all over the world described how airmen saved the *Chelyuskin*'s crew when they were trapped in the ice. With bated breath, tens of millions of people waited for the news as three expeditions simultaneously raced to pick up the four men marooned on the "North Pole" ice-floe.

What happened that night on the Reconnaissance Battalion's sector of the 17th Tank Brigade only took up half a page in the Front operational report and did not even get into the Informburo bulletin. But the greatest of all the joys known to man—the joy of those who have saved the lives of their comrades—was in no way diminished. And that joy sang in their hearts all night, shone on their faces, was felt in the warmth of the handshakes in each dug-out and shelter of Klimovich's tank brigade—wherever rescued and rescuers were sitting side by side, embracing, interrupting one another, incoherently describing how it had all happened, eating bread, kasha and tinned meat, and falling fast asleep on cots, on shelves, on the earth floor, and on prickly carpets of pine fronds.

During the recent battle, Brigade Commander Serpilin, in charge of the group which had broken through, had been wounded in both legs. An adjutant and two submachine gunners carried him on his greatcoat into Klimovich's cabin and put him down on a country bed covered with a pale blue quilt. Lanky, dirty, unshaven, his grey hair matted on his balding head, Serpilin lay there propped up against a mound of white pillows. But he was in full uniform, with the Order of the Red Banner and the "Twenty Years of the Workers' and Peasants' Red Army" medal on his tunic, and with the insignia on his dirty tunic: on one side there was a real one with the enamel peeling off; the other was of wool, having been cut out of the cap-band.

Serpilin's breeches had been cut open above the knees and his legs were resting on the pale blue quilt. Blood was seeping through the grimy bandages.

The submachine gunners put him down on the bed and left the cabin with Klimovich's orderly, who rushed them off for something to eat, while Serpilin's adjutant—an extremely tall and emaciated political instructor—hovered over his commander like a guardian angel and, resting his elbows on the head of the bed, looked steadily down at the face below.

Klimovich sat on a stool by the bed.

"Comrade Brigade Commander, I've sent for the doctor. He'll be here any moment. D'you mind if I bandage you up before we talk?"

"Never mind the doctor, Lieutenant-Colonel," said Serpilin, speaking with an effort in a quiet but firm voice. Send me straight to the field hospital. They won't operate in here anyway. But put me in touch with the Army Commander first. Have you a direct line?"

"Yes."

"Who's your CO?"

Klimovich told him the Army Commander's surname.

"Sergei Filippovich?" asked Serpilin. And a faint smile appeared on his tired face.

"Yes."

"An old academy colleague," said Serpilin. "Put me through to him!"

Klimovich raised no objections and rang for the Army Commander. He had to put in a report anyway, and was already ten minutes late with it owing to the general excitement.

"Lieutenant-Colonel Klimovich reporting," he said, when the Army Commander came to the telephone. "As a result of the battle, a group of nearly three hundred men carrying arms has broken through to me. The commander of the group wishes to speak to you."

"Let him have the phone," said the Army Commander and there was the same tremor of excitement in his voice as in Klimovich's.

Klimovich went round the table, pulled the flex out from underneath, and carried the telephone over to the bed. The brigade commander tilted his head back, saw his adjutant's face above him, and signalled with his eyes for the latter to adjust the pillows so that he could sit up.

"Comrade Commander!" said the wounded man into the mouthpiece, not quietly, as he had just spoken to Klimovich, but loudly, at the top of his voice. "Brigade Commander Serpilin reporting! I've brought out into your sector the Hundred and Seventy Sixth Rifle Division under my command.... How d'you do, Sergei Filippovich. This is Serpilin...."

It was only at these last words that his voice failed, a spasm of sobbing convulsed his throat, and he rolled over sideways with the pillows too suddenly for the adjutant to be able to hold him. The handset fell onto the floor. As he picked it up, Klimovich heard the Army Commander speaking under the impression that Serpilin was still listening.

"... Serpilin? Which Serpilin? Is that you, Fyodor Fyodorovich?" said the Commander's voice in the handset which Klimovich was now holding to his ear, since Serpilin himself had lost consciousness.

The doctor had hurried in and, stooping over the wounded man, was already cutting open the dirty bandages with a pair of scissors, while the nurse hurriedly laid out ampoules and a hypodermic syringe on the stool.

"Why don't you say something, Serpilin? Is that you or isn't it? What Serpilin? Why don't you say something?" shouted the Army Commander into the phone, and Klimovich stared at the unconscious Serpilin, forgetting that he should have told the Army Commander by now that it was he, Klimovich, at the phone, not Serpilin.

"Comrade Commander," he said finally, tearing his eyes away from Serpilin. The doctor was wiping his arm with a cotton-wool swab soaked in ether prior to injection. "This is Lieutenant-Colonel Klimovich. I'm at the telephone. The brigade commander is wounded and has lost consciousness."

"What does he look like?" said the Army Commander's voice. "Tall, thin, going bald?"

"That's the man," said Klimovich. He didn't bother to look at Serpilin again, because he had already committed it to memory for the rest of his life that Serpilin was tall, thin and going bald; that he had one bar with the enamel peeling off and the other had been improvised out of a cap band; that he wore the Order of the Red Banner and the "20 Years of the Workers' and Peasants' Red Army" medal; and that he was the kind of man thanks to whom the army would always be an army, even when retreating from the frontier as far back as Yelnia—the kind of man you didn't have to look at twice to understand and memorise what sort of a person he was.

"That's him! Serpilin!" shouted the Commander joyfully into the phone. "How did he manage to get here? He's been in ..." In the heat of the moment the commander nearly said something that Klimovich had no business to know, and after a short pause he added that he would be visiting the brigade at once.

"Have you a doctor there? What does he say?"

"He's here now, Comrade Commander. I'll ask him." Klimovich turned to the doctor. "The Commander's coming right away. He wants to know your opinion of the brigade commander's condition."

The doctor was standing over Serpilin, still holding the syringe.

"He shouldn't come here," said the doctor to Klimovich's astonishment, not even looking round. "We're going to put on another tourniquet, and then we'll have to take him to the field hospital, straight on to the operating table. Every second counts. Tell that to the Army Commander."

"Comrade Commander," said Klimovich, picking up the telephone again. "The doctor reports that the brigade commander must go straight on to the operating table in the field hospital." He heard the Commander sigh at the other end and then swear softly and bitterly.

"Tell the doctor to take him, then. Tell him I'll come to the hospital myself. I might even manage to get there before the operation.... No, don't say that. They'll get nervous and mess things up. Say I'll be at the hospital immediately after the operation. When you've sent him off, report to the Chief of Staff about the breakthrough. That's all for now."

Ten minutes later, a stretcher was brought in and Serpilin was laid on it. Klimovich saw him out to the field ambulance. Behind him came Serpilin's adjutant, who wanted to get into the ambulance after the doctor and the nurse. The doctor said there was no room and it was unnecessary in any case....

"I dare say, Comrade Doctor, but I'm going," said the adjutant; and he put his hand on the side of the ambulance.

"Comrade Lieutenant-Colonel!"

But, to the doctor's surprise, Klimovich sided with the adjutant. He considered it right and proper that the latter should want to go to the field hospital with his brigade commander.

"Never mind, get in! They can make room. Then you can come back in the same ambulance."

"If the brigade commander orders me to," said the political instructor.

"I understand. But if you do come back, report straight to me."

"Comrade Lieutenant-Colonel, please tell our Commissar Shmakov that I've taken the brigade commander to the hospital!" shouted the political instructor from the ambulance, which was already moving off.

The ambulance drove off.

Wondering vaguely where he had seen that lanky political instructor before, Klimovich returned to the cabin, put the telephone back in its former place, and rang the rear assistant to tell him not to overdo the celebrations or give the exhausted men too much food or vodka.

"There's no limiting tankmen's hospitality," said the other over the telephone in an attempt at a joke.

"Limit it just the same," snapped Klimovich, "and see they all get a bath overnight. That'll be real hospitality."

He then rang the brigade commissar and asked him if Commissar Shmakov was there from the group that had just broken out of encirclement.

"Yes, he's here. He has a slight graze on the head. We've bandaged him on the spot. He's had a bit of a lie-down, and we're about to have supper."

"Very well, go ahead. I'll join you immediately," said Klimovich, and he left the cabin, having first given instructions to his orderly in the event of the political instructor coming back to spend the night there.

Driven by the wind, ragged grey clouds were scudding low over the horizon, and the pale autumn stars twinkled through from time to time. It was so deathly quiet over the front that the recent battle already seemed erased from living memory.

Meanwhile, Sintsov, squatting at Serpilin's side, was being jolted in the ambulance over a pitted forest road.

When they were halfway to the hospital, Serpilin recovered consciousness, but did not speak, only grunting through his clenched teeth as the lorry banged over the pot-holes.

Finally he asked:

"Where are we going? Hospital?"

And, recognising Sintsov's voice, he told him that when they reached their destination he should return to the "division", as he had stubbornly been referring for more than two months to the men who had broken out of encirclement with him, and as he continued to refer to them now.

"I wouldn't want to leave you," said Sintsov, thinking of the forthcoming operation.

But Serpilin mistook his meaning.

"Ah, my friend, surely you don't intend to follow me all the way to the Urals, do you? Goodness only knows where I'll be sent for treatment! So when are you going to do your fighting? The real war hasn't even started yet!"

"I only wanted to wait until the operation...." Sintsov sounded hurt.

"All right then, wait!" said Serpilin, understanding him at last. "In my opinion as a medical assistant, I'm not badly wounded; it's just a damned nuisance losing so much blood."

He sighed, and then suddenly asked:

"D'you remember how our little doctor cried because she couldn't do any blood transfusions for the wounded while we were in encirclement? The men would gladly have donated their blood: she was a marvellous doctor; but there was no way of doing the job! No instruments, no laboratory.... Yes, my friend, it's a bad thing not to be properly armed—it's the worst thing that can happen to anyone! By the way, don't forget her.. Look after the girl.... Tell Shmakov. As for you, do what you can for her...." At these words, Serpilin touched Sintsov's hand with his own, ice-cold with loss of blood.

"Comrade Brigade Commander..." said Sintsov with a tremor in his voice, conscious of that touch and not knowing how to continue.

He feared losing no one in this war more than Serpilin, but he could hardly ask him outloud: "Comrade Brigade Commander, please don't die!"

The whole field hospital was on its feet. Many seriously wounded had already been brought in before Serpilin arrived. There wasn't an inch of space in the reception and allocation department, or in the pre-operation section.

The stretcher-bearers hurriedly removed Serpilin from the ambulance, folded back the tarpaulin flaps, and carried him into the reception tent.

Sintsov pushed his way in behind the stretcher and, in the feeble yellow light of the lamps, took a last look at Serpilin's bluish-white, bloodless face.

"You needn't worry, I'm not going to die. That's not what I've tramped all these miles for," said Serpilin, as if in answer to Sintsov's unspoken question.

The tired orderlies were carrying the stretcher on shoulder-straps improvised out of puttees; their shoulders were quivering, and Serpilin's face was quivering too as a result.

Someone, covered with a sheet and apparently dead, was being brought the other way. The stretcher-bearers moved aside in the passage, jolting the stretcher as they did so, shifted their grip, and carried Serpilin into the operating section.

For nearly two hours, a worried Sintsov cooled his heels outside. Finally, the army doctor who had brought Serpilin from the tank brigade came out and said that Serpilin had been given a blood transfusion, two bullets had been taken out of his legs, his heart had withstood the strain, and there seemed to be no immediate danger.

"At this moment in time..." added the doctor pedantically. But Sintsov wasn't listening any longer. He understood one thing only: Serpilin had pulled through!

Now that he no longer need worry about Serpilin, Sintsov felt almost delirious with relief and joy at the thought of returning to his unit.

He talked the army doctor into delaying his departure for another ten minutes and went to the hospital commander in order to ring Shmakov at once.

The commander tried to dissuade him. Lieutenant-Colonel Klimovich had already phoned through. He had been given all the details, and so had the Army HQ. But Sintsov was deaf to all arguments, insisted on having his way, and so in the end they got through to Shmakov by telephoning the tank brigade indirectly through the HQ of the rifle division to which the field hospital was attached.

Sintsov reported to Shmakov, who had already heard it all from Klimovich, how the operation had gone and what Serpilin's condition was at present. Then, since his mind was still not at rest, he added that he would be returning presently and would describe it all in person.

"Good, but better put it off till morning," said Shmakov, tactfully interrupting Sintsov's burst of enthusiasm. "I'm afraid I've already taken my boots off. I want to lie down. Anyway, it's time you had a rest too."

Sintsov's happy voice sounded over-excited to him. They'd probably given him a glass of something at the hospital by way of celebration. "It wouldn't take much for a man as tired as he is," he thought without condemnation, and once again he advised Sintsov to get back as soon as possible, lie down, and cool off.

But Sintsov couldn't calm down. He was virtually drunk with happiness and over-exhaustion.

After a hasty snack of tea and army biscuits, he said that he was in a hurry and leapt to his feet; but, as he took his leave, he suddenly grabbed the hospital commander by the sleeve and spent another five minutes happily telling him what sort of a man Serpilin was and what a good thing it was that he had pulled through.

Then, still in the same exalted mood, he spent the whole of the return journey telling the army doctor, who was nodding with fatigue, how they had broken out of encirclement.

Even when he arrived back at Klimovich's cabin, he still felt disinclined to lie down on the cot that had been made up for him.

Klimovich himself was away. The sleepy orderly said irritably that the lieutenant-colonel had gone to the front line. He was personally supervising the recovery of the tanks knocked out by enemy mines.

Sintsov, still happy and over-excited, decided for some reason to await Klimovich's return. Then, pacing up and down inside the cabin, he asked the orderly whether their tank brigade had been forced to break out of encirclement too, and, if so, where from. Finally, he asked him to find out if the water was still hot in the bath-house, and whether it mightn't be possible for him to have a bath right now instead of waiting till morning.

"What the blazes d'you want with a bath now, you skinny devil? You'd do better to lie down at once, before you go off your nut!" thought the orderly, half angrily, half sympathetically. He said nothing, however, turned his back on Sintsov, grunted, took his forage cap off its nail, and went off to inquire.

When he returned, Sintsov was sitting on the cot fast asleep. With his eyes shut and his head lolling on one shoulder, he looked like a shot bird.

The orderly shook his head, drew off the political instructor's wet, holed boots, unwound the dirt-blackened foot wrappers, and, taking him by the shoulders, lowered his head onto the pillow.

When Sintsov opened his eyes again, it was daylight. Klimovich, in boots, breeches and undervest, with a towel tucked under his chin, was seated on a stool opposite the wall mirror, shaving his head.

"So you've woken up at last," he said, turning round, razor in hand. One half of his head was shaven, the other was covered in lather.

"Comrade Lieutenant-Colonel," said Sintsov, hanging his feet over the edge of the cot and looking intently at his host. "I did hear right yesterday, didn't I? Your name is Klimovich?"

"Yes. What of it?"

"But I'm Sintsov. Don't you recognise me?"

Klimovich put the razor down on the window-sill, and, as the gaunt, broad-shouldered, bearded man got up from the bed, looked him up and down quickly as if to make absolutely sure that he was not mistaken, and then went quickly across to meet him.

They embraced, and a tear actually started in Sintsov's eye—the result of fatigue and excitement.

"I was actually thinking yesterday that I'd seen that political instructor somewhere before!" said Klimovich, hurriedly summoning up a grin, since he was not given to sentimental scenes.

"If it weren't for your name, I'd have never recognised you with your head shaven like that!"

"Only half shaven," corrected Klimovich, and he went back to the mirror to finish.

It is possible that under different circumstances they would have been more demonstratively pleased to see one another; but yesterday's meeting in battle had already given them the greatest joy which human beings can cope to experience.

Yesterday they had been truly happy. Today they were simply pleased at having met for the first time since their schooldays, and yet having still recognised one another, and so they chatted away like old friends.

"Your brigade commander's in good shape," said Klimovich, relathering his head. "They've already picked him up from the field hospital. They say he'll be put on a plane for Moscow! Front HQ's been asking about him. It'll be the Supreme Command next! The Army Commander visited him this morning. Why is he a brigade commander? Didn't they have time for the formalities?"

"No," said Sintsov, without going into the details. He had heard about Serpilin's past; but now, after two months' fighting, it simply never entered his head to discuss the matter.

"That means," he said after a pause, "that our division's without a commander for the time being."

"As long as the division's there, they'll find a commander!" replied Klimovich. "Have you been with it from the start, then?"

In a few words—so briefly that he even surprised himself—Sintsov told his story up to the time when he joined Serpilin.

"So you went adrift and became a soldier," said Klimovich with a smile of approval. "I picked up more than my share of drifters when I was breaking out of encirclement; and there are so many real fighters among them that I can't imagine how I ever managed without them!"

Sintsov's heart warmed at this indirect praise and he said what had been very much on his mind when he was coming out of encirclement: that he wouldn't be asking permission to go back to his newspaper, but would stay with the division.

"Provided they keep it on and don't disperse you all. They've come from the Army and Front Headquarters to sort your lot out. I don't know what their intentions are...."

"Sort us out? What for? We came out as a military unit, in uniform, with arms, and with our colours."

"If you hadn't, it would be a very different story. They'd send you off to be vetted, as required by law, and they'd give you a thorough grilling. Who are you? Where are you from? Why did you get yourselves cut off? Why did you break out?" At these last words, Klimovich smiled mirthlessly.

"What is there to smile about?" said Sintsov, suddenly angry. "Is it a good thing, then?"

"What d'you mean, 'good'? It would be a good thing if we were fighting outside Königsberg, not Yelnia. It would be a good thing if the Germans were breaking out of encirclement, not us! It's entirely possible that your Serpilin will convince them that they should let the division retain its number and be supplemented, instead of splitting up the survivors. It's entirely possible," repeated Klimovich. He wanted to reassure Sintsov, whose mood had darkened noticeably. "All the more so, seeing you got the colours out. They recently mentioned in the paper how some men broke out of encirclement without a thing except their colours. What a fuss they made of it!"

"What's so bad about that?" demanded Sintsov touchily.

"What's so good about it?" demanded Klimovich in his turn. "The thing is to try and get out not just with the colours, but with tanks, and guns, and people who'll fight again. It's your duty to save the colours, unless you've lost all conscience. We got our colours out of Slonim, but we didn't pat ourselves on the back for it. What else should we have done? Bringing out seven tanks out of a hundred and forty's nothing to boast about! And yet your newspaperman makes a big thing of it: 'The banner! The banner!' He might have said a word or two about what else they brought with them, and how many men they got out of it alive! As if that didn't matter in the least! Some blabbermouth feels happy because he's still alive and shoots a line to the pressman, who duly toddles off to write his piece...."

"You don't like newspapermen, I gather," said Sintsov.

"And why should I? If they know what it feels like to come out with the colours but no tanks, they'd write it up differently, believe me!"

"I know what it feels like," said Sintsov.

"You don't come into this, you're a soldier now," interrupted Klimovich. He pulled out from under the table a pair of new boots tied together with cord and smelling of tar, and threw them down at Sintsov's feet. "Here, try them for size!"

They were too small, and Klimovich was disappointed. He had no other boots with him.

"You've certainly grown a fine pair of hooves there," he said, glancing at Sintsov's bare feet. "Just the job for footslogging."

"I have done some footslogging...."

"D'you think I haven't?" demanded Klimovich. "When I lost my tanks, I did some footslogging too, thank you very much. 'Vast is my native land', as the song has it. And I know it too from personal experience! Never mind, Sintsov." He sprinkled his towel with eau de cologne, wiped his head and face, and, planting his legs wide apart, as if challenging someone to battle, stood in front of Sintsov—small, broad-shouldered, with the iron muscles bulging under his vest. "Don't worry—you just wait. I'll ride into Germany in my Thirty-Four one of these days. And I'll put you on top of it—that is, provided it isn't R.I.P. for the two of us and a plywood obelisk with a star. Well, Khaustov, have you brought us breakfast?" he asked, hearing the door creak behind him.

"Yes," said the orderly, putting down on the table a teapot and some plates covered with napkin.

"How about the baths? Any room?"

"I wouldn't say there is much room, Comrade Lieutenant-Colonel...."

"We'll have some tea, and then you can escort the political instructor to the baths. Did you find some fresh linen for him?"

"Yes! Only I'm afraid...." The orderly didn't finish, looking doubtfully at Sintsov's tall figure.

"Let's have breakfast now," said Klimovich, pulling on his tunic, "otherwise I'll be late. Anyway, you've got to have a wash and get rid of that beard. The brass hats want all your officers assembled for eleven o'clock. And you're as hairy as a priest. All you need is a cross on your chest!"

Klimovich avoided serious conversation at breakfast. He was in a hurry.

Advising Sintsov to eat more slowly and masticate his food thoroughly after his spell on short rations, Klimovich gulped down two glasses of tea and stood up.

"Excuse me. My time's up. If you want to tell the old folks at home that Christ is risen, write your letter and give it to Khaustov. He'll send it off today through our field post."

"By the way, how is your family? Where are they?" asked Sintsov suddenly. He could not have asked a more awkward question.

"I have no family," replied Klimovich abruptly in a strange, stony voice, and he went out without saying good-bye.

At first, Sintsov couldn't understand this, and for a whole minute he stared blankly at the door that Klimovich had just slammed behind him.

"Why did he react so strangely? What's wrong with his family? Quarrels? Unfaithfulness? Divorce?" he wondered; and only when he caught the orderly's gloomily reproachful eye did he realise that Klimovich hadn't meant quarrels, or unfaithfulness, or divorce, but death.

The thirty commanders and political instructors who had escaped from encirclement under Serpilin were assembled in the big tent of the brigade's political department. During the night they had all shaved off their beards, washed, and spruced themselves up. Some, who had come out the evening before almost in rags, were now wearing the grey uniform of the tank corps. Klimovich had considerately ordered his rear assistant to issue ten sets of uniform.

As they all went into the tent and exchanged greetings, they hardly recognised one another. It was hard to imagine that one night in human conditions, a bath, and a shave could change people so much.

Battalion Commissar Shmakov introduced his comrades from encirclement to the commission and laid on the table a list of three hundred and twelve men who had fought their way through the German lines.

There were three officers in the commission: a regimental commissar from the Army Political Directorate — a pleasant black-haired, kindly man who had not had enough sleep and yawned incessantly; a lieutenant-colonel from the Front Personnel Branch no longer young, and sitting bolt upright as stiff as a ramrod ("A dry old stick, that one," thought Sintsov as soon as he saw him); and a small, stony-faced, thin-lipped major from the Special Department, who for some reason was wearing the uniform of the Frontier Guards.

That morning's conversation with Klimovich had put Sintsov on the alert. He had dreamed that all the men who had broken out of encirclement with their weapons and with the divisional colours would be ceremonially drawn up on parade and thanked for what they had done; but for some reason the officers had been assembled in a tent away from the rest of the men.... It suddenly struck Sintsov that things were going to turn nasty, and quite differently from what he would have liked.

In actual fact, the discussion opened quite inoffensively.

The pleasant regimental commissar from the Army Political Directorate was the first to speak. He said that it would be out of place to hold a ceremonial parade here, so close to the front line. They would still have time for that when they arrived at their destination in the Yukhnov area, to which they were to be transferred on that same day. The commanders and political instructors, whom he wished to congratulate on behalf of the Army Command on breaking out of encirclement, must understand that the decision to retain or not to retain their divisional number, and whether the division would continue to exist and would receive replacements as such—this matter, which had already been put to them by Comrade Shmakov, could not be settled in a day, and, in any case, not by them or even by the Army Command. Until the matter had been settled at a higher level, it would be necessary to regard all who had escaped from encirclement not as a military unit, but as a group which had been temporarily formed in conditions of encirclement and which, as such, had already discharged its obligations. This being so, it no longer existed as a group, and those responsible would henceforth examine the case of each man individually, due allowance being made for rank and appointment and for the manner in which each had conducted himself when in encirclement.

"All the more so," added the regimental commissar, "since, according to preliminary data, there are now only one hundred and seven left in the group out of the original Hundred and Seventy Sixth Division, and the other two-thirds are men who joined the nucleus at various times."

While he was speaking, Shmakov, continually poking the corner of his handkerchief behind his spectacles and wiping his eyes, which were watery with lack of sleep, was watching the regimental commissar closely. Before this general discussion, they had already had a preliminary talk, and Shmakov had been waiting with some anxiety to see whether the regimental commissar would speak as, in Shmakov's opinion, he should.

The regimental commissar then turned to the lieutenant-colonel from the Personnel Branch, and the lieutenant-colonel said in a squeaky wooden voice that he would discuss the matter further when the men had been placed at his disposal in the new place; but the commanders must now form up their troops, march them to the lorries, which were in a small wood about a kilometre away, and put twenty men and two officers on each lorry. Their destination was the village of Lyudkovo near Yukhnov — a distance of about one hundred and forty kilometres — and their itinerary would take them south-east along the Yelnia-Shuya road, then east along the Yukhnov highway. The lorries were to proceed at thirty-metre intervals. In the event of air attacks, the men should disperse as far away from the road as possible. Incidentally, they were hardly likely to need instructions as how to do this. He himself would be in a passenger car at the head of the column. Having drummed all this out, the lieutenant-colonel stopped. He evidently had no intention of adding to what he had already said.

When the lieutenant-colonel had finished, the regimental commissar turned to the Frontier Guards major from the Special Department.

"Well, Comrade Danilov, have you any riders to add, or shall we get moving?"

The major with the tightly compressed lips, evidently in no hurry to reply, sat without speaking for several seconds then finally opened his mouth and said in a stiff, light bass voice that he had no riders to add, but that he would like to put one question to the senior officer of the group. So saying, he turned to Shmakov.

"Have the arms been handed in yet?"

"What arms?" asked Shmakov.

"The captured weapons in possession of personnel."

"Why should we hand them over?" said Shmakov. "Captured or otherwise, they're ours. We fought our way through with them. What's the point in handing them over?"

There was a general uproar. The Frontier Guards officer waited until it had subsided and then said without raising his voice that as far as weapons were concerned, there could be no "ours" or "yours" in the Army. There were only arms as permitted by the regulations and issued to personnel when they were supposed to be issued. Servicemen, when en route for reclassification and remustering, were not allowed to carry arms, and certainly not captured ones. These must be handed over and not taken by the men into the rear. There was nothing more to be said on the matter.

"We shall see about that!" intervened Shmakov sharply. "We are going to hand in a formal application for our division to be retained." In the heat of the moment he had completely forgotten that he had never been registered on the divisional strength in the first place.

"We are not going to go further into this issue with you, Comrade Battalion Commissar," said the major, and although he was refusing to give way to Shmakov, there was a glimmer of sympathy in his eyes. "Whether the division will continue to exist is not for you and me to decide; but independently of how this matter is settled, all captured weapons must be handed over in the meantime."

"Apart from officers' personal arms!" This was said quite unexpectedly and loudly, even aggressively, by the wooden-faced lieutenant-colonel from the Front Personnel Branch who had hitherto maintained a dispassionate silence.

This dry stick of a man had clearly been touched to the quick by something just said. Perhaps he imagined himself having to unholster and hand in the Mauser which he had captured from the Basmachi * in the Twenties and which he knew down to the last burr on the stock.

"This is an insult!" said Shmakov, standing up and clenching his fists with rage. "An insult!" he repeated loudly, his voice reverberating. "A real insult, and I'm ashamed to look my men in the face. Aren't you ashamed too?" he suddenly shouted at the major.

The latter also stood up and, going rather pale in the face, slowly fastened one stud on his map-case and then the other.

"Orders have been promulgated," he said very quietly, and all sensed that it was costing him an enormous effort of will to keep his voice down, "we asked for an explanation, and the explanation given was that these orders must be obeyed; and therefore, Comrade Battalion Commissar, captured weapons must be handed over."

Klimovich, who had been absent some time, almost since the beginning, suddenly walked into the tent when the

* *Basmachi*— White bandits in Central Asia.— *Ed.*

altercation was at its height. He waited for the right moment and, stepping forward, asked the regimental commissar's permission to make a report.

"Comrade Regimental Commissar! The Army Commander has just called me to the telephone and has instructed me to inform you that by order of the Army Military Council, the ceremonial parade of the group which broke through under command of Brigade Commander Serpilin, and also the short meeting in connection with this, are to be held here in the disposition of the unit entrusted to me."

All present exchanged glances. The regimental commissar was much relieved. Before setting out that morning, he had reported to the head of the Political Department that in his opinion a parade and a meeting should be held on the spot, with the tank brigade present. The chief of the Political Department, however, had declared that this was not the time or the place to do so: they would only be asking to get themselves bombed!

"So I got my way, and he didn't get his. That means the Military Council have changed their minds!" thought the regimental commissar, all the more pleased because throughout the whole of the foregoing discussion he had suffered from being unable to act as he would secretly have preferred.

The lieutenant-colonel from the Personnel Branch and Major Danilov were subordinate to the Front and had no direct instructions where and how to conduct the meeting; but they could not venture to contradict the officer commanding the Army in whose disposition they happened to be. They merely exchanged glances in silence.

Shmakov was openly triumphant.

"Your permission, Comrade Regimental Commissar?" he requested before anyone else had time to speak after Klimovich.

"Go ahead."

"Captain Muratov! Political Instructor Sintsov! Order the ... order the division to fall in!" He had paused for a moment, and had then used the word which had etched itself into everyone's consciousness.

"That's a good thing!" said Klimovich, sitting down at the table. "True, I've already given the orders, but let them get a move on. We haven't any time to spare, and the Army Commander's orders were to get on with it and not hang about!"

As he sat down, Klimovich glanced sympathetically at the battalion commissar, who was now looking much more cheerful. He liked this stubborn old man, as he privately called Shmakov, who hadn't a single black hair left on his head. He had been driven to take the initiative, because he sympathised deeply with Shmakov's distress for his men. He had lied in saying that the Army Commander had called him to the telephone. He had, in fact, left the tent and had personally rung the commander, requesting permission to hold a ceremonial parade and a short meeting with the tank brigade present.

"Of course," the Army Commander had said irritably. He had evidently been very busy. "We've already sent you the Deputy Head of the Political Department. What are you interfering for? Can't he handle it himself?"

"I don't know, Comrade Army Commander. He evidently has other instructions."

"What other instructions could he have! Anyway, get on with it! Only don't be too long about it."

"Well then," said the regimental commissar, resting his fists on the table. "Any more questions?"

"The old one—about the weapons," said Shmakov.

"Comrade Lieutenant-Colonel," said the major turning to Klimovich and interrupting Shmakov."The Army Commander hasn't given orders for the captured arms *not* to be handed over, has he?"

"No," said Klimovich.

"Then the decision rests," said the regimental commissar quickly, not risking the chance of another altercation. "After the parade and the meeting, the captured weapons are to be handed over and the men are to board the lorries!"

"One moment, Comrade Regimental Commissar," said the wooden lieutenant-colonel from the Personnel Branch rising to his feet. He looked at Shmakov and, drily rapping the knuckle of his index finger on the table in the ensuing silence, said angrily: "I must ask you, Comrade Battalion Commissar, not to use the word 'division' at the meeting, since the question of retaining the number has not been decided, and you are not a division, but a group which has broken out of encirclement and which consists of men and officers from four different divisions and from other separate units."

"You old pedant!" Shmakov felt like shouting; but he controlled himself and said:

"Very well."

Things had worked out in his favour, after all. They were going to parade the men and thank them. That was what mattered most. As for the rest—to hell with it! They could sort that out later.

He got up from the table and followed the others to the exit; but the major from the Frontier Guards suddenly appeared beside him and gently touched his sleeve.

"May I detain you for a word or two, Comrade Battalion Commissar?"

"Certainly, Comrade Major," said Shmakov, somewhat puzzled. He would have thought there was nothing more to discuss.

"This is the problem," said the major, patiently waiting until all the others had gone outside and he and Shmakov were alone together. "We don't know your men at present, but you do. What's your opinion," and he stressed the word "your", making it clear that Shmakov's opinion was anything but final as far as he was concerned, "can you answer fully for each of the men who came out with you?"

"Answer for them?" snapped Shmakov. "In my opinion, they've already answered your question by not staying with the Germans and by fighting their way back to their own forces."

"I realise that, Comrade Battalion Commissar," said the major, swallowing Shmakov's reprimand. "That they came out to rejoin their own troops is as much a fact for me as it is for you. But your people broke through under command, and in such conditions it sometimes happens that one man comes out with the rest who had no intention of breaking out of encirclement on his own, but, since he found himself under command, was forced to go along with everybody else. However, for one reason or another, he still enjoys the confidence of his commanders. Have you any such men?"

"Firstly, in my opinion, no," said Shmakov quickly, "and secondly, we've crossed the front line, we're home at last, and I don't understand what you're worrying about."

"I'm not worried about anything, Comrade Battalion Commissar," said the major, pretending not to notice Shmakov's exasperation and speaking with a patience which testified to remarkable self-restraint. "As a man with a job to do, I'm only interested in one thing: isn't it possible that among the people who came out with you, there are persons who attached themselves to your group with motives of their own, who partially achieved these aims by crossing the front line with you, and who will achieve them fully at a later date, disappearing somewhere en route before they can be checked? I don't know whether there are any such men among you, but we know from experience that there might be. And it would be better to think about that now, before it is too late."

"I have no such persons with me," repeated Shmakov stubbornly. "We found one scoundrel out and shot him without waiting for your advice. The other scoundrel shot himself. As for sooner or later...." He wanted to say, "My dear comrade, you and I have recently taken to mistrusting a man too soon and then deciding too late that he was reliable after all!" This is what he wanted to say, but he broke off in mid-speech and merely remarked that in his time he had worked for a year in the Cheka and knew every bit as much about vigilance as the Comrade Major.... "Provided, of course, that you look on it as a sword and not as a broom...."

"What d'you mean by that?" asked the major drily.

"Exactly what I say," said Shmakov, who still hadn't calmed down yet. "One must have faith in one's own men. Without faith, there's no vigilance, there's just suspicion and panic!"

There was a challenge in this last remark, but the major saw fit not to take it personally, and coldly said that this was all true, but at the present time one had to come to terms with the circumstances. The circumstances were extremely complicated, and one could not turn a blind eye to the fact.

"I have not been turning a blind eye, and I'm not doing so now!"

"Then I have no more to say," said the major. "I shall be travelling in the rear of the column. I have two spare seats in my car. I should like to offer you one," he suddenly added, as if stressing by this unexpected invitation that he, Major Danilov, was doing his job, considered himself in the right, and did not attach the slightest importance to this battle of words with the excitable battalion commissar.

The lane through the tall pine-trees stretched as far as the horizon. The autumn sun, peering through the clouds, threw faint patches of light on the carpet of pine needles, still damp after yesterday's rain. Wherever the sandy topsoil showed through, it was covered with fine dimples after yesterday's rain. Every time a breeze blew up, the pines shook what remained of yesterday's raindrops out of their branches, and the men on parade grinned, shivered, and dug their fingers down inside their tunic collars....

The men had only just formed up and were standing at ease, the commanders not yet having arrived.

During the night and the following morning, thirty more who had thought themselves fit in the excitement of the moment had been sent off to the hospital. Two hundred and eighty-two men were now drawn up along the forest lane—exactly half of those listed as being on the strength before yesterday evening's battle.

All the men on parade were carrying arms. Fifty had Soviet rifles; the others, after two and a half months' fighting, had gradually accumulated German weapons—rifles and sub-machine guns. Some had German grenades, the long handles sticking up out of their belts.

On the left flank stood six automatic rifles brought out of encirclement—two of them Soviet and the other four German. Further away, on the same flank, stood a big German regimental mortar with two unexpended bombs lying on the ground beside it. At the mortar stood its crew—three of the artillerymen who had come from near Brest and who had joined Serpilin on the first day of encirclement. It was still a secret how they had managed to bring the stout barrel, the base-plate, and even a few rounds of ammunition out of last night's hell, when towards the end it had been almost impossible to know what was happening; but they were now feeling proud of themselves, and they stood there without attempting to hide the fact.

On the right flank stood Sergeant-Major Kovalchuk, towering half a head higher than the rest and looking as impressive as he had once seemed to Colonel Zaichikov, the late commander of the division. Three times wounded while in encirclement—twice only slightly and once rather more painfully—his head bound in a clean bandage and his shoulders bravely squared, he stood holding the divisional colours.

In spite of everything, he had personally carried it from beginning to end and had brought it out safely with him!

When, half an hour previously, the order had been given to fall in and they had begun looking for Kovalchuk, he was finally found at the edge of the forest; sitting on a tree-stump and whittling a new flag-pole with his jack-knife. He was now standing with the banner attached to the freshly-cut pole, and all could read on the once red, now sweat-soaked and frayed silk the legend spelt out by the late Colonel Zaichikov two and a half months ago: "176th Rifle Division of the Workers' and Peasants' Red Army"....

Sintsov, waiting impatiently like the rest for the ceremony to begin, was standing a short distance away from the banner and talking happily to the last man he had expected to meet there. Even before ringing the Army Commander, Klimovich had already asked the commander of his Reconnaissance Battalion and the tankmen who had distinguished themselves in the night's battle to stand by for the ceremony. The battalion commander had arrived in a lorry. The men with him had swarmed out of the back. As he had jumped down from the cab, he had bumped into a tall, lean political instructor with a German submachine gun slung round his neck. The tank captain and the political instructor had stared at one another for several seconds in silence.

"Near Bobruisk, wasn't it?" said Sintsov at last, the first to speak. He spoke first, because he remembered the encounter better than the captain. "You detained me and you commandeered Lyusin, my junior political instructor.... And the pilot stayed with you...."

"That's right!" replied the captain gaily. "Pity you didn't stay on too. We could have done some fighting together!"

"I was wounded at the time," Sintsov reminded him.

"Are you fit now?"

"Yes."

"You haven't collected any bonuses?"

"No, not so far."

"You're in luck, then. I copped one in the shoulderblade afterwards, and had a piece torn off my ass, if you'll excuse my language."

"So you've been with the same brigade all this time?" asked Sintsov.

"Where else?"

"It turned out that your CO — " Sintsov wanted to say "is a schoolfriend of mine", but said instead: "is an old comrade of mine."

"Well, what d'you know!" said the captain with a grin. "And there was I talking to him over the telephone while you were right beside me. Why didn't you say so? I'd have put you on to him there and then!"

"Like hell you would! Tell me another!" And Sintsov burst out laughing.

"Perhaps not," grinned the captain. "When things get tough, you have to screw on your own bolts. Anyway, you were welcomed with open arms here. You broke through straight into my Reconnaissance Battalion!"

"But weren't you rear assistant before?"

"What of it!" And the captain waved his hand. "When you're fighting your way through the Germans, you forget which is the front and which is the rear. One minute you're bashing them in the face, and the next minute you're kicking like a horse. I was rear assistant, then I became a reconnaissance man—anyway, why tell you? You've just got out of encirclement yourself.... And what a nerve! What a nerve! No one's broken out for a whole month, and they were just beginning to wonder if that was the end of it. Your commander's got a nerve too, that's obvious," he added approvingly. "Is it true he's been wounded?"

Sintsov nodded.

"Pity!"

"Listen," said Sintsov, remembering Lyusin again. "How about that comrade of mine—the one who stayed with you?"

"What, the junior political instructor? In the swanky little forage cap?" The tankman laughed. "Interesting character, actually. Didn't want to stay at first and kicked up about it. Then, when he saw he wasn't going to wriggle out of it, he fought pretty decently for three days. On the fourth, when the position was a bit more stable, he went straight to the brass with a complaint: we'd forced him against his will, taken the law into our own hands, and so forth! And off he went back to his newspaper. We even wanted to put him up for a medal for those days he spent in action. But when he cleared off like that, we scrapped the idea, naturally."

"And the pilot—the major?"

"Now that I don't know," said the tankman. "He was wounded on the second day. Where he is now—in heaven, on earth, or six feet under—I've no idea."

"So your name's still Ivanov, and half Russia depends on you?"

"Not on me—on my name!" said the tankman with a smile. He gave Sintsov a friendly clap on the shoulder and, stepping back two or three paces, folded his arms and looked long and with delight at the banner that Sergeant-Major Kovalchuk was holding.

"That's the stuff!" he said after a moment's pause. "Makes you tingle all over!"

When Shmakov walked out into the middle of the forest lane and gave the command "Attention!", the two ranks levelled off, rattled their arms, and stood still. On the right flank, two paces away, the tankmen from the Reconnaissance Battalion were drawn up with their commander in front of them.

The regimental commissar stepped forward and said in a quiet, friendly voice that with the authority of the Army Military Council and on its behalf he wished to congratulate them on breaking out of encirclement so bravely with their arms and their colours. He avoided using the word "division" or "group" and simply began: "Comrades! I congratulate you...." In reply, there was a ragged but heartfelt response of "We serve the working people!"

The regimental commissar then stepped back one pace and Lieutenant-Colonel Klimovich came forward.

The regimental commissar had said nothing unusual—just a few friendly, fair words. But when Klimovich, before speaking, ran his eyes up and down the ranks, he was surprised to see tears in the eyes of many, and, strange as it may seem, the tears all but welled up in his own.

"Comrade Soldiers and Commanders!" he said in his loud, clear voice; and his small figure was as stiff as a ramrod. "The Seventeenth Tank Brigade will never forget your heroic achievement and our comradeship in last night's engagement at Point Two Hundred and Eleven, where we offered each other the hand of soldierly friendship. Our Reconnaissance Battalion—" and he indicated Captain Ivanov, who was standing in front of his tense and excited troops, "—will always be proud that you rejoined your own side in his sector. Captain, a salute in honour of comradeship on the field of battle!"

The tank crews raised their rifles and discharged a volley.

Silence fell. No one knew what was going to be said next by this little lieutenant-colonel who had suddenly discovered in himself a flair for the poetic. But he waited for another second in silence and then said the only thing that, in his opinion, remained to be said.

"Death to the fascist invaders!"

Shmakov spoke third. His was the most difficult task of all: to close the ceremonial meeting and make the last and utterly prosaic announcement about the handing over of weapons and the procedure for transit to the rear.

He really wanted to say a great deal, but he restrained himself, and for that reason was able to cope. Only once did his voice momentarily break, and that was when, as he stretched out his hand towards the banner, he said that under command of temporarily incapacitated Brigade Commander Serpilin and under that same banner of the 176th Division, they would yet be returning by the roads down which they had retreated. But he pulled himself together with an effort of will, because tears were of no avail at a time like this and, like a man inspired, he fervently shouted the very words which Stalin was to say to the whole world some months later: "Comrades, we'll be celebrating on our street too one of these days!"

A ragged cheer rose from the ranks. Many were in tears.

Shmakov paused. He seemed outwardly calm, although this calm was costing him great inner effort. He then announced, as if it were a matter of course, that since they were being sent to the rear they would have to hand over all captured weapons and also the ammunition with them. After a rest and remustering procedure, all would be issued with arms in accordance with normal procedure. The captured weapons were needed here, at the front.

"But, Comrades, we shall keep lists of everything we've handed over," he added gaily, raising his voice for emphasis, since he sensed a slight restlessness in the ranks. "This will help us to remember who disarmed whom when we were breaking out of encirclement—the Germans us, or we the Germans."

He then said that the lorries for transit to the rear had already arrived and they would be boarding them as soon as they had handed over their weapons. He then gave the command "Stand at ease!" Company and platoon commanders left to supervise the handing over of the weapons, and Shmakov turned round and looked at the regimental commissar as if to say: "How was that? Was everything done as agreed?"

The regimental commissar nodded.

"Still, you couldn't hold back about the division. You mentioned it!" creaked the wooden lieutenant-colonel reproachfully.

"Not the division—the divisional colours!" snarled Shmakov. But in the next moment he smiled agreeably. "You'd better not tangle with me, Comrade Lieutenant-Colonel. I'm an old hand at dialectics. I even have a degree in that subject. If we begin arguing about definitions, you'll get the worst of it. I'll make mincemeat of you!"

The surrender of the captured weapons took an hour. Some of the men handed them in quite calmly. Orders were orders after all. Others were upset and swore under their breath. Still others hid their captured pistols somewhere or other: they were particularly sorry to part with them.

Sintsov, who had no pistol, only a sub-machine gun, handed it in—which left him totally unarmed. Many of the other commanders found themselves in the same predicament. While coming out of encirclement, they had not regarded a pistol as a serious weapon and had settled for a sub-machine gun and a couple of grenades at their belts.

"Get a move on, Comrades," said Klimovich, suddenly going up to Shmakov. The operations duty officer had only just hurried up to tell him something that had suddenly changed his mood. "Get a move on! I want you out of here in five minutes!" he concluded.

Without going into explanations, he shook Shmakov's hand, touched the peak of his cap in acknowledgement to the others, and called Ivanov over.

"Let's go, Captain!"

Sintsov ran after him to say good-bye.

"Comrade Lieutenant-Colonel!" he shouted after Klimovich.

Klimovich halted abruptly, turned to him, and shook his hand.

"Good-bye, Vanya! Get moving. Don't hang around. Please excuse me. I'm in a hurry." And he went on his way.

CHAPTER EIGHT

The convoy, consisting of thirteen lorries and two staff cars—one at the front and one in the rear—had been travelling for more than an hour along a forest road which, according to those who knew the region, came out on the Yukhnov highway.

After yesterday's rain, the weather was dry and windy once more. On either side of the road, kilometres of red and yellow autumn forest alternated with autumn-grey fields stretching far away towards the horizon. Driven by the wind, the dry leaves kept blowing across the road under the wheels of the lorries; but from time to time the sun shone through the clouds and it became quite warm and cheerful.

As he was handing over his arms before they embarked, Sintsov had asked Shmakov what his duties were now and which lorry he should board.

After so unexpectedly losing Serpilin, for whom he had been adjutant, orderly, and clerk all rolled into one, he had been feeling at a loose end.

"There's no hurry," said Shmakov amiably. He had been in a better mood since the meeting and was taking a kindlier view of the world in general. "Wait till we arrive, and then we'll sort it out. Any lorry will do. There's plenty of time—you'll be a commander yet!"

Sintsov got into the first vehicle that came his way. It was in the middle of the convoy.

He found himself sitting in the back next to Zolotarev, Baranov's driver. He was still wearing the same leather jacket, only it was now bleached, frayed and full of holes, and he still had the rifle he had been carrying when he had met them. While in encirclement, he had not had any ambitions to possess a captured weapon, and so he had gained as a result.

Next to Zolotarev, on the other side, was a driver from the tank brigade who had asked permission to come along as far as the repair depot, where his lorry was waiting to be picked up.

At first, the only subject of conversation was the captured weapons. The driver from the tank brigade never seemed to tire of joking about this topic.

"Of course," he said, "that captured mortar of yours, and the machine guns, and even an artillery piece—if you'd taken one—no one's going to grab those. But they'd start a war over the sub-machine guns. How come your command agreed to turn in such valuable trophies? If I'd been in charge, I'd have refused to hand over a thing!"

"D'you want them taken into the rear? They're needed more at the front," objected Sintsov out of a sense of duty rather than because he felt that way.

"At the front? But you're not going to Siberia! You'll be back at the front yet!"

"May be, but not straightaway."

"You're right, Comrade Political Instructor," said the driver, outwardly polite, but with a glint of amusement in his cunning eyes. "Except that personally I wouldn't hand in a thing! Oh yes, there'll be a war over those sub-machine guns of yours!... Our brigade commander's bound to try and get his hands on them: 'Save them for the brigade!' And they're sure to come from the rear of the Army and say: 'Give us those!' And they'll pop round from the neighbouring division, and they'll ask very politely and very neighbour-like: 'Could you maybe let us have a few?' As for the Army HQ, they'll come round, and then it'll be 'Cough up!' They'll just drive up and help themselves. All the more so, they'll say, seeing you tankmen did well for trophies at Yelnia. Yes, Yelnia ... it was tough fighting, but the trophies were nothing to write home about.... No, nothing to write home about at all...."

The conversation changed to the recent fighting outside Yelnia. As far as Sintsov could make out, the driver had not taken part but, probably repeating accounts he had heard from others, he said airily that the Germans had thrown in up to eight divisions there—a whole army, in fact—and they'd been given something to think about; but towards the end things had turned nasty for our side. According to the driver, if our "neighbours" hadn't let us down (he didn't go into details over who precisely these neighbours were and in what way they'd let us down), then we'd have had the Germans completely bottled and corked up.

But the men were being bounced up and down so violently as the lorry went over the pot-holes in the road that they kept missing whole words and phrases and having to ask for them to be repeated.

"So you let them get out?" asked someone bitterly when the driver mentioned the bottle.

"It's not that we let them out entirely," replied the driver, "but they brought up a lot of heavy stuff.... As I was saying, the trophies were nothing special."

And although everyone was pleased that the Germans had been given a rough time of it at Yelnia—eight divisions, what's more—it was taken as a personal insult that we hadn't finished the job off and corked them up. The men in the lorry would have loved it if the Germans had been encircled and given a dose of their own medicine.

Then, after a pause, someone asked whether the losses had been heavy in the fighting near Yelnia.

"How shall I put it?" replied the driver vaguely. "There were some here and some there; but then if you take the human losses, or the equipment side of it, then it's a question of how you reckon them up...."

Then Sintsov realised that the losses had been heavy, but that the driver didn't want to talk about them now.

"What about the air force?" asked someone.

"Look! It's just not there!" replied the driver, letting go of the side and pointing up at the sky. "Here we are, riding along, and nothing's happening. We didn't dare show our noses before. I'd say we're running too much of a risk right now. True, it's been quiet the last few days. Not many planes about. Even makes you get the wind up wondering what it's all in aid of."

"But what were the losses?" persisted the soldier who had already raised the subject. "Your brigade, for instance—how many of you were there when the war started, and how many of you are there now?"

"It's hard to say..." said the driver, evading the issue again. "We lost men in the first battles, then we broke out of encirclement and lost some more. True, we picked up more on the way...."

"That goes for us too," said several voices at once.

"Yes, but the people we lost may have joined up with others," continued the driver logically, "so it works both ways. Then we re-formed—that meant a new count. Then there was the fighting outside Yelnia, and now we're waiting for fresh replacements. So how d'you work out the figures? Me, for instance—I've been with the brigade right from the beginning, ever since Slonim."

"And are there many like you?"

"I haven't counted them. I don't know!" snapped the driver.

And again Sintsov thought: "Not many!"

"What about mail? Are you getting any?" he asked. "Is the field post working alright?"

"Hard to say.... The letters arrive—I won't say quickly, I won't say slowly. Generally speaking, it depends on where your folks are. Where's your family, for instance, Comrade Political Instructor?"

"I don't know!" said Sintsov glumly. He didn't want to dwell on the subject. But, as it turned out, the other was equally reluctant.

"There's nothing worse than being without news, that's a fact," he said. He heaved a sigh and fell silent.

"Perhaps he's lost his family too," thought Sintsov on hearing him sigh. "Or maybe he's lost his, and mine's been found in the meantime. After all, there's happiness in war as well as misfortune!"

Resting his elbows on the side of the lorry and looking down at the grey ribbon of road speeding under the wheels, he began wondering what was in store for him: happiness or unhappiness? How was his daughter? Perhaps his mother-in-law had brought her back to Moscow after all when he was already at the front. Or perhaps they had been left behind in Grodno, which meant that nothing was known or would be known.... And what about Masha? He was now almost convinced that she had joined the Army as she had intended to, back in June. He hadn't had the chance to write to her today. And how was he to address the letter in any case? How was he going to trace her? He could write to her brother in Chita; but the time it would take for the letter to get there and back didn't bear thinking about.

"Even so," said Sintsov, "if my family's in Moscow, will a letter from here get there in a week?"

"About a week and a half."

"How about Vyazma?" asked Sintsov, thinking of his father and his brother.

"It'll take longer to Vyazma," said the driver. "It's nearer, but it has to go the long way round, through Moscow... Vyazma's in Smolensk Region, and Fritz has taken Smolensk."

Sintsov nearly asked him what he meant. It was the first time he had heard the word "Fritz". When they had been left behind in encirclement, the word had not yet been current in Army slang.

"'Fritzes'—that's what we call the nazis now," explained the driver readily. He had noticed the flicker of bewilderment on Sintsov's face. "Didn't you ever hear it when you were in encirclement?"

"No," said Zolotarev instead of Sintsov.

"So you've been completely cut off from the world," said the driver, laughing.

"You're dead right there. We've lost touch with the world," said Zolotarev, slapping the tank brigade driver on the knee. "Take me, for instance: I haven't laid hands on a driving wheel for nearly three months."

"You're not the only one who hasn't laid hands on anything for three months or more," said a thin, cheerful voice in the corner. "But we're not complaining. We keep our chins up. And he's weeping for his driving wheel...."

The others laughed and cracked some even bluer jokes. The conversation warmed up, with everybody joining in for a few minutes. Then it quietened down again, and the men talked among themselves in the corners.

"I certainly miss being behind the wheel," said Zolotarev, still harping on the same subject, and he took hold of the tank brigade driver by the sleeve. "I wouldn't mind getting in there and taking over right now!" And he nodded at the cab.

"Were you on lorries?"

"No, a car. Brand-new. They'd only just finished running it in when the war started."

"What happened? Was it bombed, or did you abandon it?"

"I burnt it.... On orders...."

Zolotarev remembered how he had set fire to his car and shut up like a clam.

"Who were you driving for?" asked the tank brigade driver.

"Why, for a..." said Zolotarev, caught Sintsov's eye, and stopped short. They had both witnessed the death of the man Zolotarev was reluctant to mention by name.

One evening in the second month of encirclement, Sintsov had stalked over on his long legs to Khoryshev's platoon with the latest order from Serpilin.

The situation had been shaping out much as during the first twenty-four hours of encirclement. The road had to be crossed during the night and a battle was unavoidable.

After speaking to Khoryshev, Sintsov sat down for a smoke before returning. Khoryshev made a truly noble gesture, giving him a pinch of *makhorka* dust mixed with powdered leaves.

The platoon was dispersed round them in the undergrowth. Those whose weapons were in order relaxed, while the others cleaned theirs and made ready for battle.

Zolotarev was sitting beside Sintsov and cleaning his rifle, grumbling that pulling the barrel through without oil was like trying to swallow a mouthful of stale bread.

Baranov was sitting on a hummock about twenty paces away and cleaning a captured automatic pistol.

On Serpilin's instructions, Sintsov had been inquiring about Baranov, and Khoryshev had replied with dissatisfaction that Baranov had not been putting up much of a show. He was always on the lookout for a chance to skive off.

"Not long ago, he made a bad bargain. He swapped a sub-machine gun for a pistol," he added, to make his meaning clear. "Too heavy for him, a sub-machine gun! But would you or I make such a swap? Me, I'd drop dead first! If people mean to fight to the last, do they go and swap the real thing for a toy?"

And so there was Baranov, sitting on a hummock a little way off from the others and messing about with that same automatic pistol.

"Why is he on his own?" wondered Sintsov, and then he answered his own question. Baranov hadn't become reconciled to his position. He hadn't admitted that after all he had done, things could hardly be otherwise. And the men sensed this and were avoiding him.

After thinking thus about Baranov, he pulled at his cigarette, glanced at Zolotarev, realised that the latter was actually looking the other way in order to fight his craving, and offered him the hand-rolled cigarette. "Here, have a drag!"

Zolotarev carefully took the cigarette between two fingers, pulled deeply but quickly in order not to take too much, and handed it back to Sintsov.

It was just then that the shot rang out. Khoryshev sprang to his feet.

"Who's shooting?" he demanded, hissing with fury. They had fallen out much too near the road to be able to allow themselves such a luxury.

But it turned out that there was no point in asking. Baranov was lying there dead. The shot had come from his pistol, hitting him full in the face and blowing half his head off.

At the time, Sintsov assumed that Baranov had shot himself because he was tired of the daily hazards, or because he was afraid of the impending battle, or perhaps because—but who would ever know? No use asking him now....

But when Sintsov reported the incident, Serpilin shook his head.

"I don't believe he shot himself," he said. "It was an accident, though accidents sometimes have causes, mind you. He'd gone to pieces and he just didn't care any more; and he was cleaning the gun carelessly; and the weapon was a strange one. So there's your bullet in the forehead. Figure it out for yourself: accidental or intentional."

Sintsov held to his former opinion and gave the matter little further thought. The heavy night battle, in which many men were killed, wiped the incident completely out of his mind.

As always when there were losses, Sintsov struck Baranov's name off the list. And there the matter ended....

It was only now, as he and Zolotarev caught one another's eye, that both remembered the dry crack of the shot in the forest that had cut off the life of the man Zolotarev didn't want to mention by name.

"Home, sweet home!" shouted the driver from the tank brigade gaily, standing up in the back of the lorry and banging on the roof of the cab.

The lorry driver poked his head out.

"What's up?"

"Slow down a bit. I've got to turn off for the repair depot."

The driver shook Zolotarev's hand, waved to the others—"Keep well, look after yourselves"—and, as soon as the lorry began to slow down, picked his way over the feet of the seated men till he reached the tailboard, and then jumped down on to the road, nimbly dodging the front wheels of the lorry behind.

At the spot where he had jumped off, a newly-worn road led into the depths of the forest. There were anti-aircraft guns on the outskirts. They had been mounted in square pits and masked with camouflage netting, and two T-34 tanks, their engines bellowing, were crawling into the interior, leaving jagged twin ruts in their wake.

"They're probably putting them through their paces after repairs," thought Sintsov, remembering what the driver had said about the depot.

They left the forest road behind them and carried on, passing a convoy of brand-new green lorries coming the other way and piled high with boxes of shells. They had already met once such convoy on setting out. Nor was it their first sight of AA guns: they had caught a glimpse of some in a copse half an hour previously near one of the bridges they had crossed.

Smoke was rising over the trees here and there. At one spot, Sintsov noticed a battery of heavy guns. There were sentries on duty at the bridges.

Three squadrons of nine Soviet bombers with fighter escort sailed high overhead on their way westwards. If you had asked Sintsov what had done most to reassure him after all he had been through in encirclement, he would have probably replied that nothing had brought him greater relief than those signs of the army and of military order imposed on the peaceful rural landscape. They seemed to promise that what he and his comrades had witnessed would never happen again: the army was established here, had been established here for a long time, was going to stay, and was not going to retreat any more.

Remembering the Germans, Sintsov had only one desire: that they should be hunted down as they had hunted us down; that they should be bombed and strafed from the air, outflanked with tanks, surrounded and crushed to death without food or ammunition, taken prisoner and given no mercy. That is what he wanted, and he wanted it so passionately that he would have laughed in the face of any man who had dared to tell him that his thirst for vengeance would be assuaged one day and his hatred would pass.

As he rode along, looking at the signs of the army and of military order scattered over the landscape, he thought of our future offensive: surely there would be an offensive some day!

But alongside this there was another feeling—a feeling of relaxation and carefree happiness. For two and a half months, he had seen enough of the earth, and the sky, and the pines and birches, and the forest glades and dells, and the sort of fir thicket that now came up to the roadside. And it had sometimes been so quiet in encirclement that you could hear yourself breathing....

Even so, it wasn't the same behind the German lines: the birches, the pines, the earth, and even the silence—all were different....

But at the present time, all these things brought delight and joy to his heart as they flashed past. Everything was a joy: the lorry in which they were riding, Khoryshev's familiar flaxen locks waving in the breeze—he had pushed his head out of the cab of the lorry in front—the dark blue firs, the yellow birches, the copses, the smoke from the chimneys, the men, the AA guns, our own planes in the sky, the snatches of song floating back from the leading lorry....

Sintsov luxuriated in all this happiness, looking eagerly at everything with wind-reddened, joyous eyes, smiling for no particular reason, and conscious of the autumn cold creeping inside his greatcoat collar.

Smiling, like Sintsov, at his own thoughts, Battalion Commander Shmakov sat between Major Danilov and the little doctor and looked out of the side window. Sometimes he would tear his eyes away and look timidly at the broad backs of the driver and the orderly in front, both wearing the same Frontier Guards uniform as their major.

If Shmakov's sense of outrage at handing in the captured weapons had not entirely evaporated, at least it was beginning to do so because it was already a thing of the past and no longer seemed to matter so much, and because when it actually came to handing over the weapons, the men had taken it more calmly than Shmakov had expected. And since the fear of offending the troops had been uppermost in his mind and had been the reason for his putting up such a fight, the matter had somehow settled itself of its own accord.

The little doctor, who had never uttered a murmur all the while they were in encirclement, had suddenly felt ill that morning and had slept throughout the journey, curled up into a warm, feverish ball in the corner. As Shmakov rode along, he looked out of the window, enjoying one "Kazbek" after another from the cigarette-case that Danilov repeatedly and obligingly kept flicking open in front of him.

At first, when the major had invited him to sit in his car, Shmakov had wanted to refuse—he was still seething with a sense of injury. Then, after they had taken their seats and had moved off, he had wanted to continue the argument with Danilov about true vigilance and false suspicions, but had postponed it because they were not alone. The doctor was there, and the two soldiers with the major. Within half an hour, he had lost all desire to argue anyway.

The further they travelled, the greater became the feeling of joy and even tenderness in his tired soul and his tired body because, by some miracle, they had come out of it alive and in one piece, had come out fighting and with honour.

Finally, after nearly an hour on the road, he gave up feeling angry with Danilov and broke the silence. It had been established in the car on his initiative, but he was the first to find it a strain.

"It's rather a long way back to the rear," he said.

"Not as far as all that," objected Danilov, pleased that this battalion commissar, whose justifiable outburst that morning had made a good impression on him, was not nursing his grievance any more. "It's normal! It's a big front, and we're on the flank. If the rear units are put nearer one flank, it means they'll be that much further away from the other."

"Well, never mind the rear units," said Shmakov, letting it be understood by this comment that they were merely an opening conversational gambit. "Tell me the news about Moscow. Has it been badly mauled?"

"I haven't been there myself," said Danilov. "But a couple of days ago I was talking to someone who has. Not much damage. They're not letting the Germans get through!"

"That's marvellous!" said Shmakov joyfully. "You know, when I came to the front in the middle of July, I was reassuring the Muscovites myself—and not just the Muscovites either. No, I kept telling them: they're not flying that way, and if they do, we won't let them through! Then, while we were in encirclement, I read all kinds of leaflets.... Where did they end all up? With the Commissar.... I read my bellyful!" he grinned. "And I sometimes felt worried sick about Moscow! According to them, they hadn't left a stone standing. I realised that they were lying, of course, only how much—that was the question."

"A great deal," said Danilov. "They say the damage in Moscow is less than two per cent."

"Well, that's marvellous!" repeated Shmakov joyfully.

Having started by asking about Moscow, he went on showering Danilov with various other questions: about the rear, about the front, about losses, about morale—about everything that came into his head and about which he hadn't had the chance to satisfy his curiosity during his sleepless night with the tank brigade.

"You've taken me by storm. You haven't even given me the chance of getting myself into a state of military preparedness," said Danilov, unable to hold out any longer and smiling in spite of himself.

"Never mind, stick it out!" said Shmakov cheerfully. "I've stuck it out longer. I haven't seen a word of print for two and a half months, except for that fascist junk!"

He asked Danilov a few more questions—the last was to enquire how long it took a letter to get to the front and back. He was only human, after all.

But suddenly, when, after replying to the last question, Danilov tipped his cap over his eyes and scratched the back of his head while waiting for the next one, all he heard was a gentle, tired snore. Shmakov had dozed off in mid-speech. Even he had finally succumbed to happy fatigue....

"Come on, get out, get out! Wake up!"

Shmakov could hear a voice in his sleep, but just couldn't wake up.

"Wake up, I tell you!..."

He opened his eyes. The car was stationary. The driver and the orderly who had been sitting in front were nowhere to be seen. There was no sign of the doctor either, and Danilov, standing outside and holding the door open, was pulling him violently by the arm.

"Get into the ditch!... Aircraft!" Danilov was shouting, angrily but without any particular nervousness.

Shmakov got out onto the road and jumped down into the ditch. The doctor was already sitting there, smiling apologetically and rubbing her eyes with her fist. She was still only half awake and had no idea how far they had come or how long she had been asleep.

There was forest all round them. The whole convoy had stopped dead on the road. The men had left the lorries and were already scattered along the roadside. Only one or two men in front were still sprinting across the road.

The planes were approaching from the west. They were quite close and flying very high, but were not yet directly overhead.

"Perhaps they're ours coming back," said Shmakov uncertainly, mainly to reassure the doctor, although the familiar oppressive, throbbing drone already told him to the contrary, and the doctor was not in the least nervous anyway.

"We shall soon see," said Danilov drily. "Perhaps we could sit down for a while?"

With a smile at Shmakov, he was the first to sit on his haunches and, barely touching the ground as he did so, he meticulously brushed off a few grains of sand that had adhered to his fingers.

A few more agonising seconds passed. The aircraft were German, but they were already overhead and any bombs they dropped would overshoot. Shmakov explained this to Danilov.

"That's if they haven't noticed us and don't mean to turn round," said Danilov. "Better wait two or three more minutes."

But the aircraft didn't turn round. They continued on their former course and at their former altitude, and the AA guns began thumping somewhere ahead of them, firing quite accurately, if not very rapidly. The white balls of flak at first blossomed out into a few small clouds underneath the planes, then appeared above them and on both sides. One of the planes began trailing smoke and, in a long curve, belching more and more smoke as it did so, veered off to one side. Again the white puffs of shell-bursts leapt up in the sky, but they were now a long way behind the planes.

"Oh, they're miles out! Why couldn't they watch what they were doing?" cried the doctor in disappointment, and she was the first to jump out of the ditch. The happiness on her face had given way to exasperation with childlike suddenness.

"There's a bloodthirsty one for you! They've dealt with one, and that's something," said Danilov. "Well, we could be getting back to the lorries now!"

He took off his green cap and began waving it as a signal for the men to climb aboard.

"You know what..." said Shmakov, who had recovered from his mood of unclouded joy after the German planes appeared, and who was again conscious of his responsibility towards the men. "I'm going to leave you. I'll ride in one of the lorries somewhere in the middle of the column. The regimental commissar at the head, you in the rear, and me in the middle. It'll be better that way. I'll leave the doctor in your care." He smiled and ran along the column of lorries, which were already being boarded by the men.

Sintsov was sitting in the back of his lorry when Shmakov went past, stocky, grey-haired, running at a steady pace like an athlete, and faster than his years would suggest.

"I'm still fit!" he shouted gaily, without stopping for breath, to Sintsov and all the others watching him from the lorry. "I may be fifty-two, but so what?"

He ran past one more lorry and climbed into the next—not into the cab, but into the back, to the delight of the men sitting there. He must nevertheless have been feeling hot by now, because, when the convoy moved off, Sintsov could see his hatless grey round head in front all the time: it seemed from where he was sitting even whiter than usual, because it had been bandaged on the slant after yesterday's scratch.

When the convoy was already in motion again, the ground and the air were shaken several times by bomb explosions somewhere ahead.

All waited for more explosions, but there were none.

"They're unlikely to have dropped all their bombs," said Zolotarev. "That was a piddling effort! What d'you make of it, Comrade Political Instructor?"

Sintsov was thinking the same. The men were still in a good mood. That their AA guns had been firing and that they had actually seen an aircraft shot down had compensated for the alarm caused by the appearance of the German bombers.

There was a hitch a few kilometres on. The convoy had reached the exact spot where the bombs had recently fallen. Infuriated by their loss, the Germans had dropped several bombs on some AA battery positions near a bridge across a narrow river.

The AA guns had been undamaged, but one of the bombs had fallen right by the bridge itself, blocking the approach. The blast had carried away the parapet and part of the deck. The convoy halted at first; but then, from a distance, Sintsov saw a car cautiously lead the way across, with the lorries following one after the other.

When their lorry had reached the bridge, Sintsov stood up in the back, curious to see how the ones in front were getting across. At that moment, Shmakov's lorry was crossing the bridge.

About four metres of deck had been torn off, and the lorry was going slowly and carefully over the two heavy timber beams that formed the base of the deck. The front or rear wheels only had to stray an inch to one side, and the lorry would fall through.

This is precisely what happened to the next lorry, with Khoryshev sitting in the cab. The driver, evidently not as experienced as the others, misjudged his steering, the back wheel rolled off the beam, and the lorry slid off and came to rest with its transmission shaft on one of the beams. Luckily, its front wheels caught on to the other.

No one was hurt. One of the soldiers was thrown over the side by the sudden jolt, fell into the river and, dripping wet from head to foot, climbed out again to the general merriment of his comrades.

A minute later, Khoryshev was already directing operations on the bridge, while the men who had jumped out of his lorry and Sintsov's were working out the best way of combining their efforts to get the lorry back on to the beams.

On the far bank, Shmakov, his hands cupped to his mouth, asked whether they should wait or not. But Danilov, who had driven up past the convoy along the verge and was already standing by the bridge, waved his green cap and answered that there was no need. Why cause an unnecessary jam?

"Carry on! It's five kilometres to the Yukhnov highway. Turn left at the crossroads. We'll be behind you. You've got a car there in front—it'll lead the way!" he shouted.

Shmakov got back into his lorry and moved on to catch up with the other lorries. The men on the bridge worked away for another fifteen minutes.

The lorry was finally heaved back up again, and this time it negotiated the bridge successfully. Danilov ordered everyone except the drivers to get out, and he let the lorries through one at a time under his own personal supervision.

Only after the last lorry had reached the other side did he move off after it in his car, and the tail-end of the convoy, with the intervals between the lorries gradually increasing, moved on towards the Yukhnov highway.

Neither the regimental commissar from the Army Political Department, nor the lieutenant-colonel from the Personnel Branch, nor Shmakov, who were travelling at the head and in the middle of the column, respectively, nor Danilov, who was bringing up in the rear, not one of them knew that a few hours ago German tank corps had broken through the Western Front to the south and north of Yelnia and, pressing in on our Army rear units, were driving a wedge tens of kilometres deep. Not one of them yet knew that the bottleneck at the bridge, by dividing their convoy into two parts which were now travelling with a twenty-minute interval between them, had in fact divided all of them, or nearly all of them, into the living and the dead.

Shmakov could not know that the lorry to which he had changed would be the last vehicle to turn safely off the Yelnia forest lane on to the Yukhnov highway. And Major Danilov could not know that in ten minutes' time the forest lane, which ran almost parallel to the front would bring the tail-end of the convoy out on to the intersection with the Yukhnov highway and straight into a spearhead of German tanks and armoured troop-carriers, which had penetrated our rear.

He did not know this, and rode calmly on to his doom.

"Another four kilometres or so to the crossroads, and we'll be a third of the way there," said Danilov to the doctor. "How are you feeling?"

"All right," she said. She touched her burning forehead. "A bit of a temperature, but it'll pass. No, go on, smoke," she added, noticing that Danilov had taken out his cigarette case and put it back in his pocket. "I don't smoke, but I love the smell," she lied, self-sacrificing as always. As if to convince the major, she closed her eyes, although she was not feeling sleepy any more.

The doctor sat with her eyes closed, and Danilov smoked and once again ran over in his mind the morning's altercation with Shmakov. Order is order, and once it has been established, then it is not violated in the army; although in this case, to tell the truth, it had really gone against the grain, having to confiscate those weapons. He put himself mentally in Shmakov's place: he wouldn't have liked it either that morning. It's one thing when you're breaking out on your own, or in twos and threes without uniform or documents; but it's another matter entirely when a whole military unit breaks out of encirclement with weapons, documents, and badges of rank. In this case, it would only have been fair to let those men keep their weapons. Why shouldn't they take them into the rear? Why shouldn't they take them and feel duly proud of themselves. Afterwards—and this would be where his department stepped in—they could make a proper check without offending anyone's self-respect, and if, contrary to expectations, there should prove to be some bad elements amongst them, then they could be weeded out.

Today's scene had not been to Danilov's liking. And it wasn't the only thing he hadn't liked since he had transferred from the Frontier Guards to the Special Department. What a job!

Toughened by a long spell of service with the Frontier Guards, he had been seriously wounded at Khalkhin-Gol and had fallen back from Lomzha with the remnants of his detachment. Keen-eyed, retentive of memory, thorough, able to trust and not to trust, Danilov was one of those people who naturally fit into a Special Department. Although not conceited, he felt that he belonged there. As a man who had been catching real spies and saboteurs for many years, he was conscious of his own superiority over certain of his colleagues who could not tell fact from fiction and, as sometimes happened, were not even particularly worried about this. Danilov used to "turn nasty", to use his own term, on such colleagues, and he hadn't been in the Special Department long before he showed one of them up for what he really was.

And so there he was, quite unaware that he was taking to their death a group of men who had only just escaped from its clutches.

"We're nearly at the crossroads I mentioned," said Danilov. He looked round at the doctor and, realising that she wasn't asleep, opened the window.

At that moment the first shell exploded, and Danilov saw German tanks cutting across the Yukhnov highway and heading straight over the fields. It was too late to turn the car round. Nor would Danilov have abandoned the column in an attempt to escape. He flung the door open and jumped out first on to the road with the submachine gun which he always had with him in the car. His Frontier Guards jumped out after him, also carrying submachine guns.

"Get out!" yelled Danilov at the doctor, and he pulled her out by the hand.

All hell was let loose. Slewed across the road, the leading lorry was in flames. Those behind were braking and crashing into each other. Shells were bursting on and near the road. Men were jumping out of the lorries, diving into the ditches, running across the fields. The tanks were spraying them with machine-gun and cannon fire. One drove straight on to the road and went along the convoy, sending one lorry after another crashing into the ditch and running over the men as they leaped down. German submachine gunners were already piling out of the armoured troop-carriers and, fanning out on all sides, were shooting from the hip at every living soul in sight.

It was too late to rally the men, three quarters of whom were unarmed. All that one could do was to give the fleeing men covering fire as far as was humanly possible and sell one's own life as dearly as possible. And this is what Danilov and his two Frontier Guards did.

He lay down in the ditch behind his car, overjoyed—if one can talk of being overjoyed at such a moment—at one thing: that the Germans, drunk with easy victory, were jumping down out from their armoured troop-carriers and as they ran up closer he would be able to mow down at least some of them.

Danilov glanced round. There was scrub behind him, beyond the road. Several men had already dashed into it under fire.

"Run into the bushes behind, you'll be safe!" said Danilov, nudging the doctor as she lay beside him in the ditch. "Quick, before it's too late!"

But the doctor only looked at him in silence and turned away. She didn't want to run or seek cover. She wanted to be able to shoot at the Germans with her revolver, and then die and never know or see anything again. She was at the end of her tether!

Danilov then pulled her up by the shoulders, swung her round, and hurled her out of the ditch.

Once on top, she looked round helplessly. Two Red Armymen ran past. Caught in the general stampede, she ran after them.

May no one in the last moments before he dies ever see what Danilov saw or think what he thought! He saw helpless men whom he, Danilov, had disarmed, darting about the road and being mown down at point-blank range by the Germans. Only a few managed to fire two or three desperate shots before falling down dead. Most of them died unarmed, deprived of that last bitter human joy: to be able to sell one's life dearly. They ran away, and they were shot in the back. They put up their hands, and they were shot in the face.

Even in the most terrible nightmare it would be impossible to imagine a more appalling responsibility than the one which Danilov was now fated to bear. His sincere and brave heart nearly burst with a grief so intolerable that death itself seemed simple and unterrifying in comparison.

And he faced death without a trace of fear. After pushing the doctor out of the ditch, he opened fire on the Germans and shot five of them before a German bullet smashed into his head.

The last thing he heard on earth before he died was his orderly, who was to outlive him by a second, delivering a burst of submachine gun fire point-blank at the Germans only three paces away.

Seconds later, German submachine gunners were already standing over the three corpses in the ditch, and a German Oberleutenant, applying a blood-soaked handkerchief to his bullet-slashed cheek, was stooping down and looking at the bright green tabs of the Russian major lying dead at his feet.

CHAPTER NINE

On the third evening after the incident on the Yukhnov highway, three people were walking through dense forest some fifty kilometres from the scene of the catastrophe. It would be more exact to say that only two of them were proceeding on foot: Political Instructor Sintsov and Red Armyman Zolotarev. The third member of their party, Ovsyannikova, or "the little doctor" as they had called her in Serpilin's group, or simply Tanya, as Sintsov had begun to call her during their march, had been unable to walk since midday. The two men were taking it in turns to carry her pick-a-back in a ground-sheet slung sack-wise over one shoulder.

It was now Sintsov's turn. He trudged along, bending low under his burden and mentally counting the last thousand paces until the next halt. He had wound the corner of the ground-sheet round his fist to prevent it from slipping out of his weakened fingers. Her feverish head lay on his shoulder, lolling like that of a corpse every time he missed his footing. Sometimes, as he bent right down to wipe the warm sweat from his eyes with his fist, he could see under his right arm the doctor's legs dangling down from the ground-sheet, one in a boot and the other unshod, bare, and swollen. It was quite tiny, like that of a little girl. At any other time, such a burden would not have been too much for Sintsov, but after four hours of this, the two exhausted men were nearly at the end of their tether, and Sintsov was regretting that they hadn't stopped at the very beginning to lop off some branches and lash them together to make a stretcher. They would have to do this anyway as soon as they stopped for a rest.

For those who escaped during the first few minutes back there on the highway, every step in one direction or the other now meant fresh chances and hazards.

Those who forced their way into the depths of the forest to the left of the road with the intention of waiting for nightfall there, were mown down at dawn by submachine gunners combing the terrain. Under different circumstances, the Germans might have taken prisoners; but a stray or perhaps carefully aimed bullet had killed outright the commander of an SS tank regiment as he was observing the slaughter from the turret of his tank, and the Germans were exacting a merciless revenge for this unexpected loss.

On the other hand, those who ran off into what might have seemed the most unreliable place—the sparse bushes to the right of the road—survived. The Germans did not hunt for them there, and they emerged to join up with their own forces outside the German ring that very night.

Several soldiers who had assembled round Lieutenant Khoryshev an hour after the catastrophe headed straight back under his command. Towards evening they met the tank crewmen with whom they were to break out of encirclement a second time.

The ones who ended up in the forest moved off through it directly northwards, reckoning that this would take them further away from the Germans; but they merely found themselves in the path of tank and infantry columns racing to close the huge ring round Vyazma. Sintsov was one of them. On jumping down from his lorry, he dashed into the forest and kept going for the next hour after his escape with only one aim in mind—to get as far away as possible. As soon as he heard the shooting and saw tanks, with German soldiers jumping down from their armoured carriers, he had clutched empty air where the submachine gun usually hung across his chest.... He had nothing, not even a revolver. And so he jumped down from the back of the lorry and ran into the forest.

He met Zolotarev an hour later. After alternately running and walking for several kilometres, he finally stopped and leaned up against an old pine-tree to recover his breath. At that moment, Zolotarev came up to him in his torn leather jacket and, most important of all, with his rifle over his shoulder.

"What are your orders, Comrade Political Instructor?"

These first words of Zolotarev's did more than anything in this world to re ive a crushed and disarmed man who had forgotten for a whole hour that he had not only been a commander, but must remain one.

"We'll decide that in a moment," replied Sintsov, trying to seem calm and looking not so much at Zolotarev as at his rifle.

"That's two of us now, and at least we have a rifle," he thought, and in order to calm himself properly, he suggested to Zolotarev:

"Let's sit down and have a smoke."

They sat down under the pine-tree. Sintsov pulled out an almost full packet of "Kazbeks" from his pocket, and both men lit up.

On Klimovich's orders, his rear assistant had issued all the commanders just out of encirclement with "Kazbeks" while the weapons were being handed over.

"Lap of luxury, Comrade Political Instructor," said Zolotarev, drawing at his cigarette with enjoyment.

"More than that!" said Sintsov. "A rifle between the two of us!"

"Haven't you got a pistol?" asked Zolotarev.

"I've got a receipt for a submachine gun from the Chief of Military Supplies!" said Sintsov as bitterly as before. "If anything happens, I'll fire that!"

"Never mind, we'll get hold of something, Comrade Political Instructor!" said Zolotarev sympathetically, and he explained that he had been following in Sintsov's tracks for the last half hour. Wherever the Comrade Political Instructor went, he meant to go too, except that he hadn't approached straightaway, but had waited a while.

While they sat and smoked, Sintsov remembered how they had both sat like this together a fortnight ago, smoking and looking at Baranov.

"That's the second time this soldier's had to break out of encirclement with his commander," he thought with an involuntary feeling of responsibility for the behaviour of that confounded Baranov. "But why just two of us?" he thought almost immediately afterwards. "We're not the only ones in this forest. We might get together a whole group before nightfall."

His hopes proved vain, however. An hour after their smoke, they ran into the little doctor but never met another soul after that.

"Yes, here's someone we really must look after," thought Sintsov, remembering what Serpilin had said when he first saw her.

Every human being can endure so much, and then there comes a point of total exhaustion. That's how it was with the indefatigable little doctor. She had done so much during the time in encirclement, she had done so much crawling about on her hands and knees to bandage the wounded in places where it was fatal to lift one's head!... Now she could hardly walk. She was limping painfully along, her face drawn and glowing with fever. Even her revolver, slung at her side as always, seemed intolerably heavy. That morning, Shmakov had wanted to send her to the field hospital, but she had insisted on having her own way and travelling with all the rest. And now look where it had got her!

When she caught sight of Sintsov and Zolotarev, she was overjoyed and hobbled to meet them so fast that she nearly fell down.

"Oh, I'm so happy!" she kept saying like a child, clutching the lapel of Sintsov's greatcoat. "Isn't there anyone else? Just the two of you? Haven't you seen any of the others?"

"Have you?" asked Sintsov in his turn.

"Me? No," she said. "I saw men running through the forest. And then I twisted my leg, and so I carried on alone. What a good thing Shmakov changed to a lorry in time!" she suddenly exclaimed joyfully.

"Alright for him, maybe; but you didn't change over...."

"He wouldn't have if he'd known," said the doctor, as if scared that Sintsov might think badlv of the commissar.

"I'm sure he wouldn't," said Sintsov smiling. "If we'd known, then things...." He dismissed the bitter thought with a wave of his hand and said that in any case it was a good thing that she was alive and that they had met her.

"What's good about it?" she said, pointing downwards. "I've twisted my leg and I've got a temperature." She laid the palm of Sintsov's hand on her forehead. "Can't you feel it?"

"Never mind, lass!" said Zolotarev. Doctor Ovsyannikova seemed too young and too small to be called "Doctor". "Never mind, lass!" he repeated sympathetically. "We'll get you there, even if we have to carry you piggy-back! After what we've seen you doing for other folks, anyone who didn't get you out of this would be a real swine!"

And now, on the third day, everything had turned out as Zolotarev had prophesied with the best of intentions. In the afternoon, the doctor had stumbled on her twisted leg and dislocated her ankle, and for the last five hours the other two had been taking turns at carrying her on their backs.

True, after her accident she still had hopes of carrying on. She made them take off her boot and asked Sintsov to try and replace the dislocated joint. She sat down and took hold of some roots protruding from the ground. Zolotarev held her from behind by the waist and Sintsov did as she told him. Streaming with sweat, he twisted and pulled her leg. But in spite of all her instructions, given in a stifled whisper because of the pain, he failed to replace her ankle. All her suffering proved in vain. They had to adapt a ground-sheet and heave the doctor up onto their backs.

And so Sintsov was carrying her along and counting the steps. There were less and less to the halt that they had set for themselves—three hundred... two hundred... a hundred and fifty....

Recovering consciousness and sensing what a burden she was to him, she whispered feverishly in his ear:

"Leave me!... D'you hear, leave me!... It's only worse for me when you suffer like that!... I'd feel better if I could stay behind...."

He couldn't reproach her for saying this, because she was telling the truth. Even now she was thinking of others more than of herself.

Finally, they called a halt. Zolotarev spread out Sintsov's greatcoat, which he had worn slung over his shoulders while Sintsov was carrying the doctor, and helped him to put her down.

The sick woman stirred slightly. While they had been carrying her like a sack, her whole body had gone numb.

"Are we going to spend the night here?" she asked softly.

"Not yet," said Sintsov. "Lie there while we'll talk it over."

He signalled to Zolotarev and they went off to one side.

"What are we to do? We needn't have been in such a hurry. We should have made up a stretcher on the spot."

"What d'you mean by 'needn't have been in such a hurry', Comrade Political Instructor?" objected Zolotarev. "You could see the road through the trees, and there was traffic. If we'd stopped there to fix a stretcher, we'd have had the nazis dropping in to say 'Guten Morgen' in no time!"

"Granted," said Sintsov. "But now what? We must still lash up a stretcher."

"No, not lash up a stretcher, Comrade Political Instructor, but find some local people by nightfall and leave her with them," said Zolotarev with conviction. "If we carry her much further, she'll die."

"What about the Germans?" said Sintsov. "We've seen three villages so far, and the Germans are driving about all over the place."

"Well then, let's carry on through the forest. We might find a lodge or something."

"It seems terrible leaving her on her own."

"Not on her own. With people."

"It still seems terrible."

"And supposing she dies on us? Wouldn't that be terrible, then?" asked Zolotarev. He listened, and added: "She's calling us."

And so, without having arrived at an agreement, they went back to the doctor. Her face on fire, she had propped herself up on her elbows and was looking at them anxiously.

"Why did you go away so suddenly?" she asked.

"Don't worry, we won't leave you, Tanya," said Sintsov.

But that was not what was worrying her.

"Why are you taking decisions without me?" she said. "Since we're going together, let's decide together."

"Very well, then," said Sintsov, resolving to be perfectly frank with her. "Zolotarev and myself were talking about a stretcher, and how to carry you further. Then we thought that you wouldn't be able to stand a long journey."

"That's right," she said, still not understanding what they wanted, but ready to make any decision easier for them.

"So we decided to find some people, leave you with them, and then carry on further without you."

She sighed:

"You damned fool! Oh, you damned fool!..."

She was cursing herself for dislocating her ankle and for being unable to go with them. She realised that they were right, but even death seemed less terrible to her at that moment than being left behind.

They had a short rest, continued on their way, and not long before dark came upon a little-used road leading into the interior of the forest.

Sintsov decided to turn off down it, and they did so, not losing sight of the road, but keeping some distance from it.

An hour later, the road led them to a forest glade in which stood a few small houses and the long shed of a sawmill. There were no vehicles or people to be seen. The mill was idle; but the stacks of logs and planks told them that work had recently been going at full pitch.

Zolotarev went ahead to reconnoitre while Sintsov stayed behind with the doctor.

"Ivan Petrovich," she said softly. "If they're bad people, don't leave me. Better give me back my revolver, and then I can shoot myself. Much better," she repeated.

"Why bad people?" retorted Sintsov angrily. "Are they all bad except us, then?"

"You and Zolotarev are good," she said. "Look how far you've carried me! I feel ashamed."

"You can stop that!" said Sintsov, still angry. "Say that to anyone you like, but not me! You've been with us for three months, and we know what sort of person you are. So you needn't try pulling the wool over our eyes! If I'd dislocated my ankle instead of you, wouldn't you have carried me?"

"You're a difficult one to handle, you're so tall!" she said; and she smiled, not because Sintsov was tall, but because this usually gloomy political instructor was speaking so crossly to her out of the goodness of his heart and for no other reason.

"Are you married?" she asked, after a pause. "I've been meaning to ask you for ages. But you're always so cross...."

"Have I become good-tempered all of a sudden?"

"No, I just felt like asking."

"I'm married. And I have a daughter. Her name's Tanya, the same as yours," he said glumly.

"Why are you so cross?" she asked. "I'm not after you, you know."

He looked long and intently at her tired face and thought how often people fail to understand one another. Then he said gently, as if to a little girl:

"You're silly, that's what you are—silly!... It's just that I don't know where my daughter is or my wife either. Most likely as not, my wife's at the front, like you. And it all suddenly came back to me. As for you, I think you're the nicest woman in the world—and the lightest," he added, smiling. "D'you think you're hard to carry? Why, you're hardly any weight at all!"

She didn't answer, but just sighed, and a tear glistened in the corner of her eye.

"Now look at you!" said Sintsov. "I meant to cheer you up, and you have to go and—here's Zolotarev!"

Zolotarev confirmed their original impression: there were no Germans in sight, but there were some people in the sawmill. During the fifteen minutes that he had lain watching from the fringe of the glade, he had twice seen a man hobble out of the end house on crutches to look at the sky and listen to the aeroplanes. Then a little girl had run out of the house and back in again.

"I didn't see anyone else!"

"Well then, let's go," said Sintsov.

He picked up the doctor, ground-sheet and all, and, without attempting to settle her on his back, carried her along in his arms like a babe.

"Maybe I should go into the house first and check," said Zolotarev warily.

But Sintsov was insistent.

"If there aren't any Germans, let's walk straight in. We're among our own people, aren't we?"

It suddenly seemed degrading that they should have to carry out further reconnaissance here, on their own soil, of a house which he or any other man wouldn't have hesitated to enter before the war with a sick woman in his arms.

"I suppose they're all right," he said. "And if they aren't, we have a rifle to deal with the likes of them."

And so, with the doctor in his arms, he went up to the end house and kicked the door.

A frightened fifteen-year-old girl drew back the latch and saw a tall, broad-shouldered man with a gaunt, fierce face carrying a woman swathed in a ground-sheet. His big hands were trembling with exhaustion, and both his sleeves—as she noticed at once—bore the red stars of a commissar.

Behind the tall man stood a second, small in stature, wearing a torn leather jacket and carrying a rifle.

"Let us, in, girl," said the tall one in a commanding voice. "Show us where to put her." And, noticing the fear in her eyes, he added more gently: "We're in trouble, as you see!"

The girl threw open the door. Sintsov carried the doctor into the cabin and glanced round quickly. The room was half rural, half urban: a Russian stove, a wide bench along the wall, a sideboard, an oilcloth-covered table, wall-shelves draped with paper doilies....

"Is there someone here besides you?" he asked the girl, still holding the doctor in his arms.

"I should say so," said a husky voice behind him.

Sintsov half turned and saw the one-legged man on crutches already mentioned by Zolotarev standing in the door that led into the adjacent room. He was elderly and heavily built, with his hair untidily plastered down on his head and a thick blonde stubble on his flabby face.

"How d'you do," he said hoarsely and without cordiality.

Seeing that Sintsov was about to put the doctor down on the bench, he stopped him with a gesture.

"Wait.... Lena, go into the bedroom and take the mattress off the bed, but leave the blanket and the sheet—just bring the mattress!... Look lively! He can't stand there holding her for ever!"

Sintsov looked straight at his unfriendly host, and his face must have reflected his mood—a determination, in spite of war and encirclement, to demand everything that a Soviet citizen in trouble has the right to ask of another.

"Why are you staring? Because I'm not pleased to see you?" demanded the host. "What have I got to be pleased about? If the Germans drive up—and we're right on their route—we're all sunk. So what am I to do? Can't throw you out—I'm not that hard-hearted.... Here! Here! Put it on this end, tuck up the bottom and make a pillow, it's long enough." He turned to the girl, who was hurriedly laying the mattress on the bench.

Sintsov put the doctor down and straightened up again painfully. He felt as if he had wrenched every sinew in his body.

"You've got a nerve!" said the host, half-mocking, half-respectful, when he noticed the stars on Sintsov's sleeves. "The Germans have been all over the place for two days, and you're still commissarring.... Lena, bring a drink of water! These people are tired, they need a drink!... Come on, sit down, be my guests." He stood his crutches up against the wall and, taking hold of the table, sat down first, the stool creaking noisily as he did so. "I should hide you in the cellar, but what the hell! Either I'm scared or I'm not scared! Will you be staying overnight?"

Sintsov nodded.

"And then what?"

Sintsov said that at dawn they would leave for their own forces, but they would like to leave the sick woman—a doctor—here. She had a fever and had hurt her leg. She must rest until she was better. Even if the Germans came, a woman was hardly likely to arouse suspicion, especially since she was ill, not wounded.

"So she's a doctor, then," said their host, "I was thinking she was your wife."

"Why?" asked Sintsov.

"It's not every man that carries every woman around in his arms like that. So she's a doctor, then," repeated their host and, taking up his crutches, he went to the sick woman's bedside. "My word, you've caught something there!" he said, and he laid his hand on her forehead. "You're hot. Not typhus, is it?"

"No, pneumonia probably," said the doctor, swallowing with an effort.

"Even if it's typhus, I'm not scared. I've had every kind of typhus going. What's the matter with your ankle?

"Dislocated."

"We'll have a look at it tomorrow. Maybe it needs hot compresses. Mustn't neglect your feet. Neglected mine once, and I've been hobbling around ever since. Let's get acquainted: Biryukov, Gavrila Romanovich." He pressed the doctor's hot hand, then shook hands with Sintsov and Zolotarev.

The girl came in with a pail and a mug.

"Her first..." said the host nodding towards the doctor with his typical rough solicitude. "Where have you come from? How many days have you been on the move?"

With a bitter smile at the thought of his own fate, Sintsov said that they had been on the move seventy-three days all told.

And in reply to the question: "Why is that?", Sintsov explained briefly.

Biryukov whistled.

"You've had a rough time, for sure! No sooner home, so to speak, than everything's topsy-turvy again. Listen, Lena, you know what," he said, in a good mood now. "Leave the mattress here and share the bed with her. We men can fix ourselves up in here."

The girl joyfully dashed off to make the bed. She was proud of her father for having made this decision. A few minutes later, Sintsov carried the doctor into the next room and put her on a wide double-bed with a feather mattress.

"Oh, isn't it lovely! I can't believe it!" whispered the doctor. "Help me to undress, girl!" She thought the men had already left the room, but they were still there and went out as soon as they heard.

"Lena, come here a minute!" called Biryukov when they were back in the kitchen.

"What is it?" The girl stuck her head impatiently round the door.

"Don't you what-is-it me! Come here! And shut the door behind you!"

The girl went over to him.

"If she's got army underclothing on, take it off as well when you undress her. Get your mother's night-dress. Collect up all the army things and take them into the woodshed. You know where, don't you? Where we put the uniform of the fellow that was here yesterday. Being a woman won't help her any. Take out her papers and give them to me. I'll look after them. Or maybe you'll take them with you?" he said, turning to Sintsov.

"They'd better stay with her. She might need them later."

"You don't say!" grinned Biryukov. "There was a chap stopped off here yesterday.... I'm not going to mention his rank—to hell with him.... Didn't even ask for something to eat. All he was worried about was getting out of his uniform. Took his money out of his pocket, everything he had, and shoved it under my nose: "It's all yours. Just give me something with holes in!" I gave him a shirt and breeches—true, they were all in one piece—I didn't have anything with holes in—and let him go. Let him go where he wants. What can you take from a man when his teeth are chattering with fright and he can hardly speak? I hid his uniform along with his papers. Are you aiming to go on as you are?"

Sintsov nodded.

"And what about the Germans?"

"We'll take them on," said Zolotarev, entering into the conversation for the first time.

"A lot of fighting you'll be able to do with that!" And their host nodded at the rifle propped up against the wall. "But I must say the Germans have put the f ar of God into a lot of people, there's no two ways about it!"

"Well, it is a frightening business, after all!" said Sintsov.

"That's true," said their host thoughtfully. "Frightening at close quarters, and even more so from a distance." Then, as his daughter ran across the room, he called to her to get something to eat as soon as she had finished with the doctor.

While the girl ran to and fro, and then, after draping the window with sack, started laying the table, Sintsov and Zolotarev listened as their host told them in brief what he called "the story of his life".

"As a matter of fact, you are not entitled to ask who and what I am," he said, broaching the subject himself. "I'm not in your house, you're in mine. But you're leaving someone here. So you must want to know what sort of a person you're leaving her with. Am I right?"

Sintsov said that was precisely it.

"There you are—'precisely'!" laughed their host.

During the Civil War he had fought and been discharged into the reserve as platoon commander. He had been a Party member and had worked for a long time as foreman of a team of lumbermen. While there, he had got frost-bite when drunk and had lost a leg. There had been no surgeon available, and the medical assistant had sawn off his leg for all the world as if it had been a wooden beam. Then, demoralised by his disability, he had started going downhill, had begun drinking, had spent all his money, and had been expelled from the Party.... He had even taken to hanging about the markets, begging.... And then, six years ago, he had come here to visit the widow of an old fellow workman.

"Her mother," he nodded at the wall of the room where the girl was busy. "Two children, and neither of them mine."

The woman had rescued him from the hopeless degradation into which he had sunk, and he had stayed on with her. He had become a mechanic at the sawmill and the stepfather of both her children.

Four days ago, disaster had struck the family. The host's fourteen-year-old stepson, who had been listening eagerly to the soldiers at the sawmill talking about the war, had suddenly disappeared. He had probably tagged on to a unit passing through that day. The mother had been in a dreadful state all day, and at night, without saying anything to anybody, had gone to find her son and bring him back home.

"And now look what's happened! Germans all round us, and she's been missing for three days. When you banged on the door, I thought it was her. I haven't had a drink for ages, but I did yesterday, to cheer myself up. There was a bottle left over by the soldiers. Lena tried to take it away from me, and I've got a suspicion I hit her.... I was too drunk to know what I was doing. She hasn't said anything, but I've a feeling

I hit her. And she's not used to it.... Now then, Lena, lay the table; and there's a little vodka left in the bottle you took away from me yesterday...."

There was indeed a little vodka. The men each drank half a tumblerful and had a snack of cold, heavily salted potatoes.

"What about her?" asked the host, nodding at the door. "Did you take her something to eat?"

"Before I brought yours in," replied the girl.

"You did right, then," said the host.

Zolotarev grunted contentedly after his food and drink, but otherwise said little, laid his rifle down beside him, and, covered with his leather jacket, lay down to sleep by the wall on some hay brought in by the girl. Sintsov wanted to visit the doctor, but the girl stopped him at the door. The sick woman had just fallen asleep.

"Maybe you'd like something else to eat?"

"No, thanks. I don't want to eat too much on an empty stomach."

"You've got a point there."

Biryukov turned down the wick slightly and rested his elbows on the table.

"Tell me, Comrade Political Instructor, just what's going on? Here you are, sitting in front of me, Workers' and Peasants' Red Army and all that, and I can respect you for not getting rid of your uniform, so that's why I'm asking you. Just exactly what's going on and how long is it going to last? Don't think you're the first I've asked. I've talked to soldiers too, and there was a senior lieutenant staying here in charge of the sawing—though he didn't know much.... Then there was a general, in command of a division. It was right in our forest waiting to be sent to the front. A real fighting general, no two ways about it. He'd broken through from the frontier with his men, and he'd collected up another division, and he was off back to the front.... So I asked him: 'Comrade General, I know you never dreamed you'd retreat this far—you don't have to tell me, I know you didn't! But things haven't worked out well for you. So what d'you think now? Tell me honestly—won't you be leaving? And won't the Germans be coming into my house?'"

At these words, Biryukov lifted his head and, as if saying good-bye, slowly ran his eyes round the cabin.

"And what did he answer? 'Nothing of the kind! We'll advance tomorrow', he says, 'and we'll go into battle, and we'll give the Germans a thrashing, and the first thing we do'll be to kick them out of Yelnia.' So what happened? Sure enough, the general went ahead and took Yelnia. But yesterday the Germans had already by-passed us. And they've gone a long way! They say the telephone operator rang Znamenka from Ugra, and they were jabbering in German at the other end, and that's fifty versts east of here!"

"Impossible!" said Sintsov.

"May be so, but it's a fact. The general took Yelnia, and the Germans are in Znamenka. Where's that general now? Can you tell me?"

"Where? Where?" said Sintsov, suddenly losing his temper. "He's fighting it out somewhere in encirclement, that's where he is. And we'd be doing the same, if they hadn't caught us napping like that.... We got from Mogilev to Yelnia. We had good cause to surrender plenty of times and in plenty of places, but we didn't. D'you think the others are any worse than us?"

"Maybe they're no worse; but the Germans have got you surrounded again, haven't they! Did you have to wait for it to happen? Couldn't you have hemmed him in from both sides? And now we're standing and waiting for him to hit first. And here's another question: are you going to stand up to him? Because if you don't stand up to him, then you're down and he's thrashing you. You and that soldier of yours—where are you? You're down, you are, and no mistake."

"No, we aren't," said Sintsov.

"Then you're crawling, anyway...."

"No, we're not crawling either. We're heading for our own side and we'll get there!"

"And if you meet any Germans?"

"We'll kill them."

"And if you meet a tank? Will you kill that too?... In my opinion, you'd do better not to meet anybody. Just keep out of trouble till you get to your own side. Because if you do meet the Germans, they'll kill you more likely than you'll kill them."

"I don't know," said Sintsov, "but one thing I do know." He paused, mentally running over everything he had been through since the day he had driven across the Mogilev bridge and joined Serpilin. "I do know one thing. The men in our army will never forgive themselves if we lose the war."

"That's something you know. But what is it you don't know? You started off by saying 'I don't know'."

"I don't know where all our matériel is. It seems to have vanished into thin air."

"And their planes," said Biryukov after a pause, "fly over us on the way to Moscow—drone, drone, drone. They head that way in the evening, and back again in the middle of the night. I go out onto the porch and I listen: are there many coming back? How many does it sound like up there?... Anyway, get some sleep. Don't hold it against me for keeping you up talking. You're maybe the last political instructor I'll ever talk to. I shall have to talk to the Germans tomorrow. When you get to our people and report, tell them from me: maybe you've got plans of retreating to Moscow, like Kutuzov; but you've got to think about people too. Of course, not every grub in the woodwork loves the Soviet system, but I'm not thinking about grubs, I'm thinking about people. If they had told me in all conscience that they were going to pull out and that it was part of the plan, I'd have been up and off myself. But now what? Have I got to stay here and eat humble pie in front of the Germans? Have I got to whine that I'm a decent fellow really, got chucked out of the Party, and don't agree with Soviet power.... You think I'll do that? Why leave me to such a fate? I'd rather have left as well. You tell them that, Political Instructor. Ah, but you won't! When you get there, you'll say: 'Reporting for duty.' And that's all you'll say."

"Why?"

"Because you will, that's why. Anyway, don't worry about the doctor. We won't hand her over to be killed."

"I'm not afraid of that, I trust you," said Sintsov.

"You've got no alternative," said Biryukov, his gloomy smile returning again. He turned the wick right down, lay down heavily on the bench, turned over several times, and began snoring loudly.

Sintsov lay staring at the ceiling and imagined that there was no ceiling there, just the black sky; and he could hear the throbbing drone of bombers on their way to Moscow.

He was just beginning to doze off, when a child's hand touched his face.

"Comrade Political Instructor," said the girl, squatting down on her haunches, "you're wanted."

Sintsov got up and, without bothering to put his boots on, followed the girl into the next room on his bare feet.

"What is it?" he asked, stooping over the little doctor. "Feeling bad?"

"No, better. But I'm scared I'll lose consciousness or fall asleep, and you'll go without saying good-bye."

"We won't go without saying good-bye," said Sintsov.

"Leave me my revolver. I want it under my pillow. All right? I'd give it to you, but I need it myself."

But Sintsov replied without hesitation that he would not leave the revolver there, because he really needed it, whereas it could mean the end of her.

"Think about it: they've hidden your uniform, they've even dressed you in another nightgown—and then the Germans find a revolver under your pillow! If the Germans don't come, you won't need it. If they do, then it could mean death for you—and your hosts," he added. It was this that put a stop to any possible objections. "Get some sleep. Are you really feeling better?"

"Yes.... If you see Serpilin, tell him about me. Alright?"

"Alright."

He pressed her hot hand.

"Your fever seems worse to me."

"I feel thirsty all the time, but otherwise I'm fine," she said.

"Comrade Political Instructor," said the girl, stopping him on the threshold. "I want to tell you something...." She paused and listened intently to her stepfather snoring. "Don't you worry about Tatyana Nikolayevna. Don't think my father—" she called him "father", not "stepfather"—"is a bad man. He's worried about my mother and my brother.... Take no notice of what he tells you about being thrown out of the Party. It was a long time ago, I don't even know when! But when the war started, he went straight to the Regional Committee and asked them to take him back again. They'd even considered his application in the timber works, and then they all started leaving to join the army, and so they didn't hold a proper meeting. Don't you worry about him!"

"But I'm not worried," said Sintsov.

"I'll do all I can too!" whispered the girl passionately. "I'll make out that Tatyana Nikolayevna's a relative of ours! We've arranged that already between us. I give you my word as a Komsomol!"

"Are you a Komsomol already?" asked Sintsov.

"Yes, since May."

"Where's your card, then?"

"D'you want me to show it to you?" asked the girl eagerly.

"No, there's no need," said Sintsov. "Only you know what—it would be a good idea to find a doctor or nurse and get her leg put right. I failed. It takes skill."

"I'll find a doctor and I'll bring him here!" said the girl with the same eagerness. "I'll do everything!"

And Sintsov felt that she would indeed find one, and bring him to the house, and do everything, and give her life for that little doctor.

He lay down again and this time fell asleep instantly, without a single thought in his head.

He was woken up by a sensation of light shining into the cabin. While still half-asleep, he thought that it was daybreak; but when he opened his eyes, it was still dark inside. He was about to close his eyes again, when a broad beam of light suddenly lit up the window. It could only be one thing: the headlights of some vehicle driving up to the sawmill.

Sintsov jumped up and, without stopping to pull on his boots, shook Zolotarev and his host awake.

There was another flicker of light in the window.

"It's the Germans!" said Biryukov hoarsely. "Run for it!"

Hopping on one leg and feeling his way along the wall with his hands, he went to the window that looked out on to the yard and flung the casement wide open.

"Out you go! Get across the yard, and then through the kitchen gardens into the woods. They won't see you! Hurry up!"

The noise of several vehicles could be heard through the open window. Sintsov let Zolotarev go through first, and, still in too much of a hurry to put on his boots, snatched them up in one hand and climbed over the window-sill.

He was only just in time. Other vehicles were already moving up, and one had already stopped outside the house. They could hear loud voices speaking in German. It was a lorry full of soldiers.

Sintsov and Zolotarev crossed the kitchen garden, ran in between the timber stacks as far as the outskirts of the forest, and sat down to recover their breath.

The German lorries were turning round, their headlights blazing in all directions, and a light appeared, first in one window and then in the other of the house which they had only left five minutes ago. The light filtered through the sacking loosely draped over the casement and was visible even from where they were sitting.

When he saw that light, Sintsov had a sudden, acute feeling of helplessness. An hour ago, they could have somehow protected the doctor with their rifle and revolver. But now she was totally defenceless and alone, a responsibility to those people and at the mercy of the enemy.

Zolotarev was thinking the same.

"Just so long as she doesn't talk too much in her fever," he said, and added: "Perhaps we could have a smoke, eh, Comrade Political Instructor? I'm feeling a bit shaky."

"And if they spot us?"

"Don't worry, they won't. We'll hide under our greatcoats."

And so there were no longer three of them, but two. They carried on together for another six days and nights until fate broke up their partnership too and sent them in different directions.

During that time, they experienced everything that can befall two men in uniform with a rifle and pistol making their way to their own side through an enemy armed camp. They knew cold, and hunger, and starvation, and the oft-recurrent fear of death. Several times they were within a hair's breadth of death or captivity, hearing German voices and the clash of German arms only twenty paces away, or recognising the roar of German lorries and the stink of German petrol.

Four times, they spent the night stiff with cold in the chilly October woods, and twice they called at houses to spend the night.

In one house, the people welcomed them. In the other, they were afraid—not of Sintsov and Zolotarev, but of what might happen if the Germans knew that the two of them had stayed overnight. In both houses the inhabitants took particular notice of their uniforms. On the first occasion, they were proud of Sintsov and Zolotarev; but on the second, they feared for their own skins.

When they left the first house at daybreak, Zolotarev said to Sintsov:

"Now that's what I call real Russians! True, Comrade Political Instructor?"

And Sintsov said:

"Yes!"

But when they left the second house at daybreak, Sintsov told Zolotarev:

"No, we'll keep these uniforms on until the end, just so long as it gives those cowards something to think about!"

Zolotarev replied that Sintsov was a fool to agree to give them a hundred rubles for food. He'd have done better to spit in their faces!

"But I did!" said Sintsov, "just by giving them those hundred rubles. They can stick them down their throat!"

"And they were saying they had a son in the Army!" continued Zolotarev, who hadn't calmed down yet. "Bad luck, having to go and fight for parents like that!"

"There's the Soviet way of life to think of, not just parents," said Sintsov.

"Yes, but it's still rotten shame!" said Zolotarev.

This was nearly their last conversation together, because half an hour later, while climbing up out of a steep forest gully they ran head-on into two German signals men. The meeting was equally unexpected for both pairs, but the Russians, who were coming out of encirclement and were as wary as wild beasts, reacted faster than the Germans, who had just had morning coffee and were whistling a tune on a full stomach.

Zolotarev threw up his rifle and fired at one of the Germans before the latter was able to unshoulder his own. The second German panicked and ran off into the undergrowth. Sintsov dashed after him firing his revolver, but only brought him down with the seventh and last round.

Then they took one rifle and an ammunition pouch and ran through the forest to get as far away as possible from the scene of the shooting. They kept on running until they finally collapsed in a dense thicket. Only then, as they lay there, did they consider the incident in retrospect.

"So we killed them," thought Sintsov, remembering the question back at the sawmill—"And if you meet any Germans?"—and his answer—"We'll kill them."

"Let's get going," said Zolotarev, "in case they start combing the forest. We haven't come all that far."

"Very well," said Sintsov, adding, as he slung the German rifle on his shoulder: "Feels heavy. I've been without a rifle so long that I'm not used to it any more."

Zolotarev advised him to throw away the revolver since he'd used up all the ammunition anyway; but Sintsov was reluctant to do so and hung on to it just the same, saying that they would find more.

As it happened, he was soon to be left with the empty revolver again. They were fording a river at night, and as he made his way across with the water up to his chin, he stepped into a deep hole and was so taken by surprise that he lost his greatcoat and the German rifle, both of which he had tied together with a strap and was holding over his head. No matter how often he dived down and felt for them, he couldn't find anything. And so they were left with one rifle and one leather jacket between the two of them.

They had some tough breaks during those six days, and the toughest of all was that they were unable to get through to their own side no matter how hard they tried. The deeper they penetrated towards the east, the further the Germans seemed to have advanced.

Their chances of reaching the front line finally began to seem hopeless. The solitude oppressed them more than anything else, and the hard times on the march from Mogilev to Yelnia with Serpilin began to seem sheer bliss compared with what they were going through now. If they could only meet a unit fighting its way out and join up with it!

True, they did meet a senior lieutenant in uniform with seven armed soldiers one early evening. Sintsov and Zolotarev wanted to join them, and the senior lieutenant raised no objections. But during the night he changed his mind; perhaps he didn't believe Sintsov's story that they had been making their way out of encirclement since July. Near daybreak, Zolotarev heard the bushes, which had been caught by the early frosts, crackling in the distance. The eight men had risen and moved off without waking the two of them.

"Shall we catch them up?" asked Zolotarev.

But Sintsov said:

"If they don't trust us, let them go."

There was still no sign of a unit fighting its way out which they could join. The troops leaving the Vyazma area were evidently proceeding by other routes.

They spent their last night in a forest skirted by a highroad along which flowed an endless stream of German transport.

They waited for the right moment, sprinted across the road, penetrated into the forest for another two kilometres or so, broke off some fir branches, piled them up, and lay down in them, covering themselves with Zolotarev's holed leather jacket. It was too damp and cold to sleep there, although they huddled close together for warmth. They were tormented by hunger into the bargain. That morning they had finished up the food they had brought after their last night with a roof over their heads.

Neither of them could sleep.

"Pity I lost my belt," said Sintsov with a mirthless smile. "At least I could tighten it round my stomach. It wouldn't be so bad then."

"We were fools not to search those Germans' packs for food," said Zolotarev.

It wasn't the first time he had regretted this.

"That road we just crossed was cobbled," said Zolotarev after a pause. "What road would that be?"

"Looks like the one to Vereya," said Sintsov. "We've left Medyn behind to the south. That could well be the road from Medyn to Vereya."

"And how far is this Vereya from Moscow?"

"About a hundred kilometres," said Sintsov.

"I see..." said Zolotarev thoughtfully. "So we're just within a hundred kilometres of Moscow, and we still haven't crossed the German lines. It's hard to believe...."

He listened intently to the low, heavy carpet of sound unrolling across the sky. "They're heading for Moscow!"

"And every night at the same time," said Sintsov.

"So they're flying to Moscow," said Zolotarev. "It means they haven't taken the city, if they're still flying!"

They lay there in silence for several minutes.

"Vanya!" said Zolotarev, "Vanya!" They belonged to the same generation. Political Instructor Sintsov was twenty-nine and Zolotarev was twenty-six. Disaster had brought them very close to one another, and in the midst of the life which they were living now and which, they sometimes felt, had left them all alone in the world, they had become close friends without even realising it.

"What's the matter?"

"We left the doctor behind. We didn't save her!"

"How could we? Even if we'd been drowning, we'd have lifted her up over our heads somehow! But what could we do? Would she have been any better off dying on the way?"

"You've got a point there," agreed Zolotarev. Then, with a sigh, he repeated: "We still left her behind!"

"Well, what do you want, then?" retorted Sintsov irritably.

"Oh, lots of things.... I want them, but I can't have them. That's what hurts.... D'you know what I want?"

"Well, what?"

"If they said to me: 'Zolotarev, would you agree to being dropped on Hitler instead of a bomb, knowing you'd kill him but be smashed flat as a pancake?', then I'd only ask one question: 'Will you hit the target?' And if they promised: 'Yes, we'll hit it', then I'd say: 'Drop me, then!' D'you believe me?"

"Yes, I do."

"And another thing, I sometimes wonder why did I have to end up as a driver. I could easily have been in tanks!"

"Well?"

"Nothing. Except that I'd like to have at least one crack at the Germans with a gun, not just a rifle. Smash something to smithereens all by myself—a tank or a lorry! When we get out of this, I'll never be a driver again. To hell with that!"

"If they find out you're a driver, you'll be posted as one."

"I won't tell them. Vanya, I say, Vanya!"

"What?"

"Tell me, will the Germans take Moscow?"

"I don't know."

"But what's your opinion?"

"I don't think they will."

Another low carpet of sound unrolled across the sky.

"More of them on their way."

"Where did you study, Vanya?"

"At seven-year school first, then in a trade school."

"Me too. Which kind were you at?"

"A Woodwork School. At home in Vyazma. And you?"

"I studied at Rosselmach, in Rostov."

"Then what did you do?"

"I got a job. Then I left to take a course."

"Where?"

"At CIJ."

"CIJ? What's that?

"The Communist Institute of Journalism."

"I just kept on working. On a tractor and a lorry. I didn't change over to cars until after I joined the army. What do you think?" he asked suddenly. "Will Serpilin pull through?"

"I don't know. The doctor said he would."

"It would be nice to end up in his unit again, eh?"

"Well, if we get out of this, we'll write an application."

"Is your family in Vyazma?"

"My father and brother were. But I don't know whether they're still there or not. They might have left."

Sintsov fell silent and estimated how many kilometres it was to Vyazma, and thought that if they failed to break out of encirclement, they could go there instead, find people they knew, and join the partisans.

Sintsov and Zolotarev thought that Vyazma, deep behind the German lines, had already fallen. It would no doubt have been less painful for both of them, in spite of everything, if they could have known what was actually happening there. That night, the ring round Vyazma was tightening inexorably, but it could not strangle the encircled Soviet forces which were making a last desperate stand against German tank and infantry corps. In a few days' time, those same enemy tank and infantry corps would still be delayed at

Vyazma, instead of being outside Moscow, where Hitler needed them.

The tragically large-scale October encirclement and the retreat on the Western and Bryansk fronts consisted of a series of incredibly stubborn defensive actions which, now in grains and now in hills of sand under the wheels of the German armoured vehicles, did not give them the chance to gather the necessary impetus for the advance on Moscow.

And the two men lying in the forest that night near Vereya and feeling so insignificant, unhappy, and defenceless, were nevertheless two more grains of sand thrown by their own volition under the wheels of the German military machine.

They also helped to prevent the Germans from reaching Moscow, although that very night they had been shuddering at the thought that we might surrender it, unaware that Moscow was not going to fall.

They were woken towards daybreak by the noise of a violent battle nearby. The bluish glimmer of dawn was only just visible in the forest. They got up and went towards the noise, knowing that if this was a battle then our troops were there as well as the Germans and, if they were lucky, they had some chance of getting through to their own side.

War has its own values, and they headed for the lethal shell-bursts and the stuttering machine-gun fire as eagerly as, in other times, men make for the voice of life, the beacon, the light shining in the steppes, the human habitation amid the snowy wastes.

"D'you suppose there's a front line ahead?" asked Zolotarev.

Sintsov wanted to believe this too, but he thought a second and said that it was unlikely. If the front line cut across this sector, it would hardly have been so quiet during the night. It was probably our own men breaking through the German rear.

They pressed forward, and the battle seemed to be coming to meet them halfway. They could already tell that it was not just any machine gun, but one of our own Maxims delivering short bursts quite close at hand.

"Saving his ammunition," said Zolotarev.

Sintsov nodded.

They covered another two hundred paces. It was getting lighter in the forest, and they began to proceed more carefully, afraid of running into the Germans first.

Suddenly, a shell burst a hundred metres away, to be followed by another. They dashed across and lay down in a still smoking crater, and the shells began to burst one after another round them, and also far to the left and right.

Several batteries at least must have been firing.

At first, Sintsov thought that the Germans had miscalculated and were shelling empty ground. He was so delighted at this that for a moment he lost all sense of danger.

But the shells continued landing in the same strip, and Sintsov realised that the Germans were laying a screen of fire to cut off the line of retreat for our people.

"Shall we stay here awhile, or push on?" he asked Zolotarev.

They could hear machine guns again.

"Let's go," replied Zolotarev.

They began running across, taking cover in craters or hollows, or simply flattening themselves on the ground.

"We'll never make it," said Sintsov when they had thrown themselves down, at the foot of a big pine-tree.

Those were the last words that Zolotarev was to hear from him.

A shell exploded. Both men flattened themselves on the ground, and when Zolotarev half rose again, he saw the political instructor lying with his arms flung out and his head and forehead so bloody that he seemed mortally wounded.

"Vanya! Vanya!" He shook Sintsov by the shoulders. "Vanya!"

But Sintsov did not react.

Zolotarev heaved his lifeless body on to his shoulders and went on towards the sound of machine-gun fire.

After a hundred paces, he fell, unable to support the weight, got up again, heaved Sintsov up on to his shoulders, and again fell down. And there he lay, feeling that he would never be able to carry such a weight as far as his own troops.

Meanwhile, the seconds were racing by and he had the impression that the sound of machine-gun fire was beginning to recede.

He then decided to run to his own people as fast as possible, get someone to help him, and come back for Sintsov.

He pushed Sintsov's documents with trembling fingers into his own pockets and, after a moment's hesitation, pulled off the political instructor's torn tunic with its missing buttons.

He was determined to come back if he reached his own people; but he might fail, and he didn't want the Germans to identify Sintsov as a political instructor by his tunic, in which case they might torture him if alive and mutilate his corpse if dead.

After covering two hundred metres at a run, he hurled the tunic into a copse of small fir-trees and then, after another three hundred metres, stumbled upon four men running to a new fire position and dragging a Maxim behind them. Three of them were in tank corps uniform, and the fourth was none other than Lieutenant Khoryshev, his forage cap askew and the blond forelock protruding from underneath.

Zolotarev had run into his platoon commander just as the latter had reached the new position and was ordering the machine gun to be turned round. He was the first to see Zolotarev coming at him and, not in the least surprised and with a smile, as if expecting this, he shouted:

"Well, if it isn't Zolotarev come down from the blue! Got some ammunition?"

"Yes!"

"Then lie down and get ready to fire. Fritz'll show up any moment now."

Several soldiers in tank corps or infantry uniform ran past and lay down among the trees. All were staring intently into the depths of the forest on which Khoryshev had trained the muzzle of his machine gun.

"On your own?" he asked, without looking at Zolotarev.

"I came with Sintsov."

"Where is he, then?"

"Badly hit. Not far from here. Give me someone. We'll carry him back with us."

"Where did you leave him?"

Zolotarev pointed vaguely towards where, according to his estimate, he had left Sintsov.

"Where's he been hit?" asked the platoon commander, perhaps already working out the best way of rescuing Sintsov; but he broke off suddenly and went down beside his machine gun. Submachine guns had opened up and were whipping the russet leaves off the branches overhead... swore Khoryshev, and he fired the first burst before Zolotarev could see what he was aiming at.

Then Zolotarev saw them too. Germans were darting about among the trees about two hundred metres away.

As soon as the machine gun began firing, an automatic rifle to the right and a mounted machine gun further off also opened up.

Bursts of German submachine gun fire were lashing the branches overhead.

Zolotarev managed to fire several rounds at the Germans as they ran across his field of vision. Then they went down under cover.

Khoryshev gave the signal for another dash. They sprinted a hundred and fifty metres and took up a new position.

The Germans didn't keep them waiting here either. Small mortar bombs began exploding between the trees, and figures could be seen running across again.

Khoryshev's machine guns and the others to the right of him re-opened fire and, pinning the Germans down, again changed their position.

"What am I to do?" asked Zolotarev, crawling up to Khoryshev. "Give me one man and I'll go and find the political instructor...."

"Where?" interrupted Khoryshev. "You damn fool! Where? Show me where!"

And Zolotarev pointed his finger hopelessly, realising that Germans had appeared during the fighting between them and the place where he had left Sintsov.

"You should have brought him in at once. It's no use now!" said Khoryshev angrily.

"Then I'll go on my own!" said Zolotarev.

"You want to commit suicide? Lay on some fire! Look, the Fritzes are coming!"

And, indeed, the Germans had started running through the trees, only nearer this time than before, and Zolotarev, with despair in his heart, but calmly and ably, like the soldier he was, opened fire on the green figures running across in front of him.

Lieutenant Khoryshev, with ten of his own men and ten tankmen was covering one tiny sector on the flank of Klimovich's tank brigade, which was cutting its way through the German rear that night.

Klimovich's brigade, in its turn, was only a part of the forces on the Western Front which had made their way through the German rear, had bunched up into a fist and, strewing the fields of the Moscow region with their own and the enemy dead, had spent all that night, the next day, and half the following night battering at the German ring. In the end, after losing half their men, they had broken through notwithstanding.

They had accomplished this miracle on little fire-power, with much loss of blood, and with a courage that defies description; but after they had broken through, they were not sent away to rest and be replenished, but were left at the point where they had broken through.

The front line, which was steadily moving back towards Moscow, continued to give way here and there under the German pressure.... One of these breaches was immediately filled by units which had only just broken out of encirclement, after they had been hurriedly sent food, a few artillery batteries, and ammunition for the rifles and machine guns.

On the evening of the day when they burst out of encirclement, these troops were fighting again, but this time with their front facing west and not east. Moscow was behind them, not in front of them, and they now had some artillery, and neighbour units on their right and left flanks. Exhausted beyond the limits of human endurance, they were happy about this nevertheless.

But Zolotarev himself was not feeling happy, and although he was of no importance, nothing more than a private with extended service to his credit, he proved on the second morning after the breakthrough that it was essential for him to see Lieutenant-Colonel Klimovich, commander of the tank brigade.

Klimovich, who had by sheer good luck slipped unscathed out of a dense barrage, had returned from the observation post to the command post and was standing near a school building which had been damaged by artillery fire. He took off his helmet and, with obvious pleasure, as if taking a shower, exposed his round, shaved head to the autumn rain drizzling down from the cloudy sky.

"A week of this rain and the roads'll be waterlogged. It'll be tough for us all, but worse for the Germans," he said to the tank corps captain standing beside him. Then he looked at Zolotarev who was approaching.

"What is it?"

Zolotarev put it in a nutshell. He knew that the brigade commander could spare him very little time, and so he had been rehearsing in advance. But Klimovich listened to him without showing the least sign of impatience.

He only interrupted once, and that was when Zolotarev said he had heard from the political instructor that the latter knew the comrade lieutenant-colonel.

"Friendship doesn't come into it!" interrupted Klimovich. "Thousands are being killed every day for friends and strangers alike! What price friendship in wartime?"

His voice betrayed the bitterness of a man who had seen so many fine men killed that he could no longer feel sorrier for one than for the others—and this not out of callousness, but from a sense of justice.

He spoke again, and only a few words at that, when Zolotarev finished and took Sintsov's documents out of his tunic pocket.

"So you're feeling bad because you didn't go back for him, is that it?"

"Yes," said Zolotarev.

"You meant to go back when you left him?"

"Yes."

"Don't take it too much to heart. You wanted to do your best, but war dictated otherwise. There are times when even God doesn't know the answer!" And then he ground his teeth, suddenly remembering that if he hadn't lived to do his best for his family by sending them from Slonim to Slutsk by car, they wouldn't have been hit by a bomb, would have left six hours later by train, and would still be alive, like so many other families.

"Let me have those!" he said, nodding at the documents.

He took Sintsov's Party card from Zolotarev, opened it, and when he saw the photograph of that quite young face, he was suddenly reminded of their youth together. He snorted angrily to hide his feelings and passed the documents to the captain beside him:

"Ivanov, put them in with all the others."

He did not make it clear what he had in mind by this. There was no need. All the time they had been breaking out of encirclement, the iron box that accompanied them on their travels had, like a common grave, been steadily filling up with the documents of all those killed in action.

CHAPTER TEN

Sintsov didn't know whether he lay unconscious for five minutes or an hour. His first impression on recovering consciousness was of silence.

He lifted his head, propped himself up on his hands, and sat up, rubbing the congealed blood out of his eyes. Then he looked round. There was no one in sight.

"Zolotarev!" he shouted feebly, and then more loudly: "Zolotarev!"

He thought that Zolotarev must have been killed and, still sitting on the ground, looked round to try and find him. But he could see no sign of Zolotarev anywhere, dead or alive.

Sintsov touched his head. It was covered in blood, but was only hurting on one side, over the temple. He incautiously touched a loose flap of skin with his fingers and cried out. A trickle of blood coursed down his forehead.

He lifted himself to his feet. He was feeling dizzy, but he reckoned he wasn't as weak as all that and should be able to walk. Pressing the palms of his hands instinctively to his chest and taking them away again in fright, he saw two bloody marks on his dirty undervest, and only then did he realise that he was without his tunic.

It never occurred to him what had actually happened. He thought, wrongly, that he had torn off his tunic while still half-dazed and had hidden it somewhere with his documents. Many times he had thought how, if death should be inevitable, he must find time to tear up or hide his papers. Perhaps he had even dreamed it all while he was unconscious.

He lowered himself to the ground, began feeling about him, and saw a trail of black stains on the limp grass. It was his own blood. Still on his hands and knees and parting the small bushes in his path, he set off back along this trail of blood, but could find neither his tunic nor the discarded documents anywhere in the undergrowth.

He finally made his way to a pine-tree which he recognised beyond all possible doubt. When the shell had exploded, he had fallen here, pricking his cheek painfully on something and even noticing it at the time. This was the place alright. And a big stain of blood which had already soaked into the ground. He again pressed his hands to his chest as if he had only dreamed that he was in his undervest. But he was without his tunic.

"Maybe Zolotarev decided I was dead and took it off for me..." thought Sintsov uncertainly for the first time.

He could hear the noise of battle behind him. They were still shooting over there. He must head that way!

He listened again, rose unsteadily to his feet, and saw two Germans approaching. One, armed with a rifle, was some thirty paces away; the other, quite near, was pointing a submachine gun at him.

"Halt!"

Sintsov saw that the German, his mouth distorted in a snarl of fury, was about to shoot him in the stomach. He absently remembered the long-empty revolver in his breeches and raised his hands, feeling that if he was made to stand like this for long, he would collapse.

Over an hour had passed since the time that Sintsov had been knocked unconscious. The Germans had methodically been combing the forest after the battle, which had rolled past and had receded towards the east.

The German with the rifle and other Germans visible further off continued on their way through the forest. The German with a submachine gun took Sintsov back in the direction from which he and Zolotarev had come that morning.

Sintsov walked slowly, although the German shouted at him in annoyance and once even thrust his submachine gun into the small of his prisoner's back.

Sintsov wasn't feeling quite so dizzy and he could have walked a shade faster, but didn't do so because he was not afraid of the German behind him.

"To hell with him, let him shoot," he thought calmly as he listened to the gradually receding noise of battle.

The German with the submachine gun took Sintsov to a group of other prisoners sitting on the outskirts of the forest and guarded by two elderly Germans with rifles, and said something to them, pointing at Sintsov. One of the two Germans with rifles took out an exercise book, put a cross in it, and then wrote something—perhaps the name of the German who had brought Sintsov. Sintsov's captor went away with a last glance round. The elderly German with the notebook looked at Sintsov's bloody head and said:

"Setz dich!"

Sintsov sat down with the other four prisoners. One of them was wounded in the arm, one had his neck swathed in a dirty bandage, and the third kept spitting blood: his cheek and mouth were a mess.

Sintsov thought he knew the soldier wounded in the arm, and this proved to be so.

"Comrade Political Instructor," whispered the soldier, moving up closer, "This is a fine place to be meeting again! A good thing you at least got rid of your tunic!"

"I don't remember taking it off," said Sintsov.

"Never mind, at least you got rid of it," said the soldier in the same sympathetic whisper. "What's the point of getting yourself shot when there's no need?"

Sintsov was subsequently to remember these words on more than one occasion.

"We thought we were quite safe!" continued the soldier after a pause. "Now look at us!"

It turned out that after the incident on the Yukhnov highway, he had returned to the tank brigade with Khoryshev and had spent nine days breaking out of encirclement with them. He had fallen behind in today's battle while dressing his wound and had been captured by the Germans.

"Far from here?"

"About three kilometres."

"That means Klimovich got his tanks away from Yelnia," thought Sintsov, half respectfully and half enviously.

"I shan't address you by your rank any more," said the soldier, again in a whisper. "They're listening."

The Germans were indeed listening, although it didn't look as if they could understand anything.

"Schweigen! Schweigen!" shouted one, trying to look fierce.

They didn't want the prisoners to talk among themselves.

Within three hours, they had assembled on the outskirts all the men taken prisoner in the forest after the Russian breakthrough. They marched them off in column, first along a forest road, then down the Borovsk highway.

There were forty men in the column, half of them slightly wounded. There was not a single stretcher-case. It was whispered round among the prisoners that the Germans had shot all the seriously wounded on the spot in the forest. In spite of this, the guards escorting the column were not unduly cruel, merely urging the column on and shouting "Schweigen! Schweigen!" whenever they noticed someone talking.

At this stage the exercise book with the little crosses and, above all, with the total number of prisoners began to play its part. This exercise book now passed from the elderly German soldier to a middle-aged, long-legged German lieutenant who was stalking gloomily along the side of the road, ignoring prisoners and guards alike.

"They'll herd us along like this till evening to their distribution point," whispered the sickly-looking soldier with the bandaged neck as he limped along beside Sintsov. "Then they'll line us up and start: 'Nicht Offizier? Nicht Politruk? Nicht Jude?...' That's German for Jews."

"How do you know?" asked Sintsov.

"I've been through it once before. I got away, but here I am again! And they won't give us a thing to eat until they've questioned us all."

The soldier with the bandaged neck was one of the four to whom Sintsov had been taken in the forest. While they had been sitting there, Sintsov had managed to sneak the empty revolver out of his pocket unnoticed and hide it under a big pine-tree root; together with his missing tunic, it could have given him away. But mightn't he be given away by any of those four men? One of them knew that he was a political instructor, and the other three had heard him addressed as such.

Sintsov only thought of this when the soldier with the bandaged neck mentioned the distribution centre. He considered it for a moment, then dismissed it from his mind. "They won't say anything, and this man with the bandage on his neck won't talk either. He's not bothered about the distribution point, he's only warning me to be on my guard."

After two hours' marching, the column turned off the main road onto a side-road, and then turned off that road too. An anti-tank ditch had been dug across it. A whole crowd of women were filling in the trench with shovels or with their bare hands.

"Slave labour!" shouted someone in the column.

"They're being punished!" responded another, also in a loud voice. "You dug it against us—now you can fill it in with your bare hands!"

"Schweigen!"

The women looked up from their forced labour and glanced over their shoulders at the prisoners. Their guards noticed this and shouted at them in coarse, rasping voices.

"Swearing in their own language, probably," said the soldier with the bandaged neck to Sintsov.

The guards halted the column a kilometre beyond the anti-tank ditch at an abandoned village badly knocked about by artillery fire and on the edge of which stood a stone building, almost intact, with the inscription "Hospital" on its façade.

In spite of the war and the devastation all round, there was still something indefinably new about the hospital. Perhaps it had only been finished that spring or at the beginning of summer, before war broke out.

As it turned out, they had stopped the column at that building with two humane aims in mind: to feed and bandage the wounded. Both operations were being performed by Russians. There were mounds of potatoes and beetroot on the floor of the hospital kitchen. Two women were boiling soup on a stove in a bucket and a big enamelled pan. The kitchen smelt of peelings, earth, and smoke. They were not cooking for the prisoners, but for the women who had been brought here to the road-works. But the lieutenant in charge of the column evidently knew the set-up and stalked straight in with the column of prisoners.

There were ten aluminium mess-tins in the kitchen altogether. The prisoners stood in line, and the cook served each one with a mixture of half-cooked, soggy potatoes and beetroot, and when she saw anyone particularly emaciated among the men filing past, it was as much as she could do not to burst into tears of compassion.

The hash was piping hot, but all ate hurriedly, scalding themselves rather than hold up their comrades. A German stood near the cook and kept an eye on her in case she served too much or any of the prisoners tried to get a second helping.

Sintsov also scalded himself on his hash and was nearly sick. He clamped his hand over his mouth, somehow managed to swallow down the gorge that rose to his throat, and went into the next room where the wounded were being bandaged.

It must have originally been the maternity ward, but it was now bare except for a table and two stools. On the floor along one of the walls, hay had been strewn covered with dirty sheets, on which lay several shapes covered with anything that had come to hand. Someone, apparently a woman, was groaning incessantly.

Two people were bandaging the wounded: an old, crippled nurse, and a doctor—a huge old man with a leonine face and hands that were still strong and skilful, but that trembled now and again, either because of old age or because here too, as in the kitchen, there was a German breathing down his neck. The only difference was that the other German had kept saying "Genug! Genug!", whereas this one kept repeating "Schneller! Schneller!"

"Take it easy," said the doctor to Sintsov as he sat on a stool and held back his head.

He dabbed the wound with hissing hydrogen peroxide and then, roughly taking hold of the flaps of skin, cut the hair round the edges with a few snips of the scissors, daubed them with iodine so that Sintsov yelped with pain, laid something on top, pressing it down with his fingers so that it hurt again, gave Sintsov a push to indicate that he should sit on the next stool, and said to the nurse: "Bandage!"

The next case, a soldier with crushed fingers, had already taken Sintsov's place.

The nurse, one shoulder hunched higher than the other, began bandaging Sintsov's head, whispering angrily to herself. At first Sintsov couldn't understand what she was talking about, but he then realised that she was cursing the Germans for standing over Nikolai Nikolayevich and not letting him get on with his job in peace. Both these old people—the doctor and the nurse—had probably been working together here for ages, and she was suffering even more for her surgeon than for the wounded.

Sintsov could now see the doctor's face, which he had been unable to study while seated before him on the stool, and he realised the torture it was costing this man to be compelled to work like an animal doctor. His guard had no intention of waiting, but he wanted to treat as many of the wounded as possible with his rough but skilful hands. His leonine face, with its grey brows, broad, flattened nose, and stiff, bristling, almost cat-like whiskers, was perspiring with strain and looked grim and unhappy. Given the opportunity, he would no doubt have run his scalpel across the throat of that confounded German who kept drumming "Schneller! Schneller!" in his ear like an automaton.

Exactly an hour later, the column was made to fall in again. There hadn't been time to treat some of the wounded, but the long-legged lieutenant glanced impatiently at his watch, and nothing else mattered any more after that. The guards were in a hurry to get the prisoners to their destination, shouting at them even more harshly and making them get a move on.

But all this ended suddenly when the column ran into a German traffic jam which seemed endless from where they were standing. The prisoners could, of course, have made a detour; but the trees crowded right up to the road, and the long-legged lieutenant evidently didn't want risk entering the forest in order to by-pass the vehicles.

"Well, we're stuck!" said the soldier with the bandaged neck to Sintsov. They had been marching along side by side.

"Didn't they have time to bandage you?" asked Sintsov.

"I'm not wounded. It's a boil.... Now we're going to have to stand and wait," he added. "You think they're organised? They're disorganised too. The last time they drove me into camp, I had my bellyful of these bottlenecks—before I escaped—and every time I used to think: where's our air force?" He paused and then said dreamily: "Oh for a smoke to cheer us up!"

Sintsov didn't answer, but his neighbour went on talking. "Did you see some people lying on the floor when they were bandaging you up?"

"Yes," said Sintsov. "One of them was a woman, I think...."

"Not just one—all of them! The cook told me when she was ladling out my soup. All women, with their hands blown off. Our people managed to lay some mines near the anti-tank ditch, so they made the women dig them up with their bare hands. There's only a few lying in the hospital. The ones that got it real bad or were killed were just chucked straight into the ditch and buried."

"The swine!" thought Sintsov. "Honestly, the swine!"

He had been in a state of extreme depression ever since being taken prisoner, but he was now no longer indifferent to whether the Germans shot him or not, or whether he arrived at his destination, or whether he collapsed on the way and they finished him off.... Once again, he wanted to escape at all costs so as to kill Germans for the anti-tank ditch that those women had been filling in and for those severed hands....

When the first Ilyushins swept over the road with a roar, neither Sintsov nor the other prisoners understood what was happening. It was the Germans who brought it home to them. The troops began jumping into the ditches straight from the back of their lorries and the guards threw themselves prone on the ground while more and more aircraft came sweeping over the road....

A man screamed shrilly in his death agony. Some of the prisoners were falling on the roadway, and several others stood where they were, staring up into the sky as if petrified.

"Nieder! Zu Boden! Legt euch!" It was the German lieutenant, who had flattened himself on the ground and was yelling frantically at the prisoners.

He had completely lost his composure, shouting and tugging at his revolver which had stuck in its holster. No doubt he felt horribly ashamed to be grovelling on the road with the prisoners towering over him. But the planes went on flashing across with their machine guns blazing, and he hadn't the strength either to make himself stand up or these prisoners lie down. But he would force them to lie down!

"Zu Boden!..." he shouted, and began firing his revolver at a knot of prisoners still standing on the road.

"Comrades, let's run for it!" shouted Sintsov, surprising even himself. He had just seen the soldier with the bandaged neck clutch his head and fall at his feet. "Let's run!" he yelled again. He leapt over the ditch and, crashing through the bushes, charged into the forest, hearing the branches snap behind him as several more made a dash for it. There was the rattle of machine-gun fire overhead, and he heard explosions and submachine gun bursts behind him.

Sintsov never found out how many managed to escape. They scattered through the forest in different directions and never met again. He carried on, carried on almost without stopping, and several times he sat down for a few minutes to recover his breath. He kept going for the rest of that short October day until it finally grew dark, and then he kept going all that night. He kept going through forest, through a village burnt to ashes, and again through forest; he climbed over two anti-tank ditches and some abandoned trenches. He stumbled on some corpses in one of them, and this was his salvation, for he would have frozen to death otherwise. From one body he took a tunic, and also a quilted jacket, almost new except for some bloodstains on the edges, and near one of the other dead bodies he picked up a fur hat with ear-flaps: it had rolled a short distance away from its owner. Gritting his teeth, he pulled it down onto his head over the bandages. He wanted to take a rifle that was lying there too, but the bolt was missing and he was unable to find it however much he groped round for it. Then he cut across two roads; one was deserted, and a column of German motorcyclists drove down the other a minute after he had crossed it. He could smell the reek of fires, saw glows now to the left, now to the right, and heard shooting which at one moment seemed to be coming from all sides. At this point he imagined that he was crossing the front, and, indeed, he was doing just that....

But when, completely done in, he collapsed in a forest thicket, he heard the thunder of artillery again, only not to his right, nor to his left, and nor behind, but a long way in front. He was too exhausted to think clearly, and it never entered his head that these distant explosions could be a German air-raid in our rear. On the contrary, he thought that he had only imagined crossing the front, and that the lines were still ahead of him.

Since he had decided to escape at all costs and didn't want to take any risks, he drank a few cupped handfuls of marsh water and crawled into a clump of bushes. It would be better to wait for dusk and try to cross the front at night, when he would have a better chance of succeeding than by day. Once he had made up his mind about this, he slept like a log for several hours and only awoke when the sky was beginning to turn grey.

He got up, set off once more and covered another five kilometres through seemingly endless forest. Once, he heard voices and a shot that made him nearly jump out of his skin. Had he gone towards the voices and the shot, he would have walked straight into a field hospital stationed there. But he still thought that he had yet to cross the front, that the voices and the shot were German, and that he must carry on further.

Finally, when it was getting quite dark, he came out of the forest into a field crossed by an anti-tank ditch. He clambered over it and came to a hamlet—three cottages with wattle fences running from behind them. He went to the end cottage.

It was quiet all round. The cottage seemed deserted, but as he drew nearer, a middle-aged Red Armyman came round the corner towards him, bucket in hand.

It was a miracle! That the soldier should have been calmly going to the well with a bucket left no doubts in Sintsov's mind he was with his own side again!

Sintsov stared at the soldier, and the soldier stared back. Sintsov was younger than the man with the bucket—the other looked about forty—but Sintsov could not imagine what his own appearance was like, so he was quite startled when the soldier with the bucket looked at him intently for another two or three seconds and then asked:

"What d'you want, Dad?"

Sintsov knew that he had a twelve-day growth of beard, but what he didn't know was that it was half grey.

He stepped two paces towards the soldier without saying anything, so that the latter even backed away and asked:

"Who d'you want?"

But Sintsov still said nothing, reached out, and began to shake the soldier's hand so vigorously that the bucket rocked from side to side.

"I've come through at last..." was all he managed to say in the end.

"I'll say you have," said the soldier, the bucket swaying from side to side because Sintsov was still pumping his hand. "I'll say you have. And then some! It's twenty kilometres from there back to the front. You mean to say I'm the first you've run into?"

"Yes," said Sintsov. "I've been travelling at night and lying low in the forest in the daytime. I thought I had another night on the move ahead of me...."

"And what rank might you be?" asked the soldier a shade more respectfully after a closer look at Sintsov's half-grey beard. "A colonel, maybe? Or higher?" There was even a pleased twinkle in his eye. Had a real live general come to him out of encirclement?... For all the seriousness of the general situation, such an incident would have delighted him.

But Sintsov disappointed him.

"I'm a political instructor," he said.

"In that case, Comrade Political Instructor, wait for me here while I go to the well, or come with me and then I'll take you to our senior political instructor. You came out right by his hut!"

Sintsov went with him to the well and, still unable to believe that he had really found his own people again, waited while the soldier filled his bucket, and then went back with him to the house.

"Yes, you've grown a likely beard there. A right beaver!" joked the soldier as he led Sintsov into the passage. He put down the bucket, opened one of the two doors in the passage, and said in a quite different, precise and official-sounding voice: "Excuse me, Comrade Senior Political Instructor! I've brought you a political instructor just out of encirclement!"

A middle-aged man was sitting inside and spooning soup out of a mess-tin stood on a newspaper.

He was evidently about the same age as the soldier, being also this side of forty. He was eating his soup with a miserable air, his cheek resting on his hand woman-fashion. Without changing his pose, he turned and looked at the door.

His face was good-natured, soft, and rather full. His tabs with their one pip were pale blue, from which Sintsov deduced that he had come to an air force unit. The senior political instructor was only wearing one boot. His other foot was clad in a woollen sock. The discarded boot was lying on the floor, and a home-made, skilfully cut walking-stick stood propped up against the table.

"This soldier probably cut it for him," thought Sintsov for some reason, although there were a thousand far more important matters which could have occupied his mind at that moment.

"Well, come in," said the senior political instructor and, half rising from his seat, he offered Sintsov his hand. "My word, you look haggard!" he said sympathetically "Hungry?"

"I'd like some tea more than anything else," said Sintsov. Although he hadn't eaten for two days, he wanted above all to get warm.

"Tea by all means," said the senior political instructor, nodding at the teapot on the table. "Have some soup in the meantime." He wiped his spoon on some bread and pushed the mess-tin, newspaper and all, over to Sintsov.

Sintsov took the spoon and started eating, and the senior political instructor sat opposite and watched, not how he was eating, but Sintsov himself.

When there were only a few spoonfuls, Sintsov caught his eye and realised that he was still wearing his hat. Reluctantly tearing himself away from the spoon and the pan, he took hold of his hat with both hands and, groaning with pain, removed it. It had become partly stuck to the bandages in one place.

"Wounded?" asked the senior political instructor when he saw the dark bloodstain on the bandages.

But Sintsov finished the last two spoonfuls before replying:

"Nothing serious. It knocked me out so badly I nearly didn't come round again. But the wound's nothing—tore off a bit of scalp...."

"Where did they treat you?" The senior political instructor poured a mug of tea and pushed it over to Sintsov.

It was a natural question to ask. Sintsov had not taken off his hat while on the move, and the bandages were still almost fresh. He told how and where he had been attended to, and, having once started, told the whole story.

The senior political instructor sitting opposite him had also been fighting his way out of encirclement in June and July, and this had meant a long march from the frontier. He had then had a spell in hospital and, after discharging himself prematurely, had only been three days at the front again. He listened to Sintsov sympathetically and found nothing surprising in his story except that the man who had been through all this should be sitting in front of him alive and in fairly good shape.

"I certainly never thought I'd miss the front by twenty kilometres and walk straight into the air force!" said Sintsov, pushing away the empty mug.

It was evidently not the first time that the senior political instructor had come against this kind of misunderstanding, and he grinned.

"Don't take any notice of my tabs. I was commissar of an Airfield Servicing Battalion at the beginning of the war. We're not air force, we're a Construction Battalion. The Germans wiped out the former CO and commissar with the same bomb. They sent me here straight from hospital and a new CO from the Regional Military Commissariat. We've been digging for three days and nights non-stop. We've already abandoned the line we dug on the first day." He shook his head angrily. "They'd do better to send me as an infantryman to fight for Moscow, instead of leaving me to plough and then quit like this! True, not everyone here has a rifle—two among three. They're lying around somewhere, and we're screaming for them!"

"Does that mean things are going badly outside Moscow?" asked Sintsov with distress. He had thought so many times during this war that the worst was behind him, and now it seemed that it was yet to come! Even the words "outside Moscow", which he had just heard spoken for the first time, suddenly shook him, although he had said them himself. Outside Moscow! Things couldn't be worse than that!

"We're moles, of course, and our job's digging. But it really does look as though things are going badly," admitted the senior political instructor reluctantly and with an effort after a pause. "My battalion commander heard this morning that there's been another call-up in Moscow. It doesn't matter who they are in civil life—they're all going off as privates!" He looked at Sintsov's pale face and at the dressing on his head, and added: "There's a field hospital not far from here. You say it's nothing serious, but you ought to go there for a check-up anyway. They may think otherwise."

Sintsov shook his head.

"No, I want to fight, if things are serious! If you'll give me permission, I'll get some sleep somewhere here and leave in the morning."

"Where for?"

"The front, with any reinforcements and to any unit, as ordered. I can't count on more than that without documents, but I think they'll take me as a private!"

The senior political instructor was not surprised. He had been expecting Sintsov to make this admission, because those who had broken out of encirclement with documents usually began by proudly producing them for inspection.

"Without any documents at all?" he inquired.

"Not one."

"That makes things worse." He shook his head sympathetically rather than reproachfully. "Now me, for instance—I brought mine out, though things were tough."

"I brought them out too, the first time. But the second time...." Touched on the raw, Sintsov explained exactly how he had come to be without documents. He told the whole story, and suddenly felt that the other was looking at him with suspicion for the first time, as if to say: "What are you trying to wriggle out of it for? All right, you tore them up or you buried them when the Germans approached.... Well, it's understandable!... That's the way it happens. So why tell lies?"

"Well," said the senior political instructor. "That being the way things are, stay overnight with Yefremov—that's the soldier who met you. But I'm leaving. I think I heard my lorry—it's come to pick me up."

And, indeed, a lorry had roared up several minutes ago, and then the engine had been switched off.

"Everything's topsy-turvy. Ditches here, breastworks there.... I left at dawn, came back for an hour, and I'm off again till dawn. There's nothing else for it...." He was going to continue, but stopped. Now that Sintsov had told him something he didn't believe, he was not disposed to further confidences. "Yes, you get some sleep," he continued. "In the morning, the battalion commander and I will send you off to HQ.... Yefremov! I say, Yefremov!..."

"I'm here, Comrade Senior Political Instructor!" said the latter, looming up on the threshold.

"Help me on with my boot, please, Yefremov.... After that wound.... Quite a process." This last sentence was still addressed to Sintsov. The senior political instructor was embarrassed at having to ask for help.

Yefremov bent down and held the boot while the senior political instructor, wincing with pain, pushed his foot into it. Then he took the stick from its place against the table and limped out.

Sintsov followed the political instructor, but the latter only said a few words to Yefremov on the way and climbed into the cab of the lorry without looking round.

"D'you use a cut-throat razor?" asked Yefremov, watching the lorry as it drove off.

"Yes," said Sintsov.

"I could give you a shave, perhaps?"

Sintsov had neither the strength nor the inclination to refuse. A strange feeling, to sit on a stool with your head held back and feel yourself being shaved!

As Yefremov shaved him, he felt more and more drowsy, and, collecting his thoughts with an effort, heard through his drowsiness how the battalion was already digging its third line of defences, and how we kept on retreating and retreating, and how it was a good thing that he, Sintsov, had run into the commissar and not the battalion commander, and how the Germans had bombed the anti-tank ditch in the afternoon and had wounded twenty semi-disabled men. A bomb isn't choosy, it doesn't care what it gets as long as it gets something....

Then Sintsov suddenly dropped right off, his head jerked, and he felt a painful cut on his cheek.

"Now then! You mustn't doze off—I might cut your throat," said Yefremov reproachfully. He tore off a scrap from the newspaper under the mess-tin and stuck it onto the gash.

He finished shaving Sintsov, went outside, and poured several mugfuls of water over Sintsov's hands. Sintsov washed himself, trying not to wet the bandage.

"Would you like me to bandage you up again?" asked Yefremov.

But Sintsov declined:

"I'm afraid of touching it," he said, yawning wearily.

He couldn't shake off his fatigue. It would take twenty-four hours of solid sleep to do that, evidently. They went into a cubby-hole which was being used as a makeshift storeroom for domestic utensils and sacks of potatoes and cabbages. A mattress lay on a bench too narrow for it.

"Lie down," said Yefremov, pointing to the bench.

"What about you?"

"Duty's duty. The battalion commander could still arrive."

Sintsov was asleep before his head touched the bench, and when he awoke it was late at night.

"Get up! Get up!" urged Yefremov. "Get up! The battalion commander's sent for you!"

Sintsov began putting on his boots. Yefremov went into the next room.

"Orders carried out, Sir!" Sintsov heard him report even as he was crossing the passage.

"Very well. Let him come in," said a young, irritable voice. "I'm dog-tired, and now I've got this business...."

At the table by a paraffin lamp sat a small, sturdy senior lieutenant with a pale, round face, handsome eyebrows that looked as if they had been pencilled on, and slightly protuberant eyes. A greatcoat, mud-splashed to the collar, hung loosely from his shoulders. A peaked cap, also mud-splashed, was lying on the second stool.

"May I come in?" asked Sintsov, crossing paths in the doorway with Yefremov, whom the senior lieutenant at once dismissed. "How d'you do?"

"Use the correct form of address!" snapped the senior lieutenant.

Sintsov looked at him without saying anything, took the cap off the stool, placed it on the table, and sat down.

"Stand up!" yelled the senior lieutenant.

Sintsov sat where he was and looked at him without saying a word.

"Stand up!" yelled the senior lieutenant again.

Sintsov remained seated.

The senior lieutenant reached for the pistol in his holster.

"Don't you shout at me," said Sintsov without moving a muscle. "I am a political instructor and your equal in rank, and I find it hard to stand. So I've sat down. All the more so, since you're sitting too."

"Where are your documents?"

"I have no documents."

"Then while you have no documents, as far as I'm concerned you're no political instructor! Stand up!"

It was an ominous beginning to the interview. They stared at one another for some time, and the senior lieutenant must have realised that he would have to shoot this man before he could ever make him stand up.

The senior lieutenant was the first to look away.

"I've heard about you from my commissar," he said casually, as if speaking of a subordinate, "but unlike him, I happen to be a Doubting Thomas. Go through that fairy-tale of yours again!"

This was so unexpected that Sintsov failed to understand at first.

"Very well, I'll go through that fairy-tale of mine again," he said with suppressed fury, after a long pause. Fortunately for himself, he remembered just in time that, whatever the circumstances might be, they were both on active service and he had come out into the disposition of a unit under the command of this senior lieutenant. Although he had told everything to the unit's commissar, its commander had the right to demand a repetition. Sintsov controlled himself and conscientiously retold the whole story from beginning to end.

While Sintsov talked, the senior lieutenant sat and didn't believe a word. He was young, bad-tempered, and very confused. As often happens with weak and selfish people, his evil-minded reluctance to trust others was born of a shameful and painful awareness of his own confusion. He had himself volunteered for the front, but when he found himself in the appalling chaos near Moscow, he had been so terrified on the first day under air attack in the open fields that three days and nights later he still hadn't recovered. He had been doing his level best to conduct himself as before and as was expected of one in military uniform. Hiding his personal terror, he had been goading his subordinates and accusing them of cowardice. But he could not deceive himself. And now, sitting opposite Sintsov, he felt deep down inside that he would never have withstood all that this man was describing to him. He would never have withstood three months of encirclement, or have stayed in commissar's uniform until the end, or, though wounded, have escaped under fire from imprisonment. Knowing that he would not have done this himself, he resented, out of a feeling of self-protection, the idea that others might be capable of such conduct.

The senior lieutenant listened to Sintsov and didn't believe him—not because Sintsov was untrustworthy, but because he very much wanted to convince himself that the man sitting before him was a liar—more than that, was maybe a German saboteur, and this saboteur would have been detained by none other than himself, Senior Lieutenant Krutikov, who may have only arrived at the front three days ago, but who knew how to handle the situation better than certain others who had been at the front and in hospital.

More than once during the last few days, overcome by inner trepidation, he had winced under the good-natured but fully understanding look of his commissar, and he was glad of the chance to get the better of him, just this once, with the keenness, severity and ruthless zeal which is liberally practised by men of his kidney when they are not in fear of their own lives.

He interrupted Sintsov several times with openly suspicious questions.

"How come, not a single document? Alright, so you lost your tunic by some miracle. But you could have at least left one piece of paper in your breeches in case the worst came to the worst."

Then he had doubts about the quilted jacket.

"You mean to say you walked all that way and your jacket is almost brand-new?"

Sintsov held himself in check this time too, patiently explaining that he had taken it from a dead man.

But when the senior lieutenant suddenly said:

"A likely story! You're wounded in the head, you fall down unconscious, and after that you walk nearly forty kilometres!"—Sintsov could stand it no longer.

He rose to his feet, drew himself up to his full height, took off the jacket, and pulled up his tunic and undervest.

"See that?" He jabbed his finger at the dark blue double scar on his side. "I poked myself with a nail there specially for your benefit! And this—" he pointed to his bandaged head "—this is only camouflage too. There's nothing there! Want me to unbandage it?"

"I'm not a doctor, don't play the fool!" exclaimed the senior lieutenant in confusion, saying the first thing that came into his head.

Sintsov looked at him expectantly for a few more seconds and said: "You're a fine one, you are!" and, pulling down his tunic again, began putting on the jacket as unhurriedly as he had taken it off.

With an effort, the senior lieutenant banished the sudden decent thought that everything this man had told him so far was the pure and unvarnished truth. He drove it out of his mind because it was unpleasant to him.

He would not have been at fault if he had simply been unable to believe Sintsov. He was at fault because he didn't want to believe, and Sintsov felt this instinctively.

"All right, go and get some sleep. We'll get this out tomorrow!" said the senior lieutenant at last.

Sintsov rose to his feet in silence, looked at the other from his full height and, without saying a word, went out.

Left on his own, Senior Lieutenant Krutikov rose to his feet, stood in the silence of the empty room, listened as Sintsov settled himself down on the other side of the wall, and then began pacing up and down the room while considering the next move.

He must send Yefremov immediately with a note to the next village, where the Special Department of a division moving up to the line had been quartered in the two end houses, much to the inconvenience of the Construction Battalion. He must send Yefremov without a moment's delay so that the Special Department could come for that type this very night!

This could, of course, easily have been postponed till the next day; but Senior Lieutenant Krutikov was goaded on by the demon of vanity combined with his accursed lack of self-confidence. He couldn't get his suspicions confirmed soon enough.

He picked his map-case up off the table, took out his field book, wrote a note to the Special Department, folded it up, and called Yefremov.

Yefremov, who had been snatching forty winks on a stool in the passage, came in looking sleepy and bad-tempered. Even before he had dozed off, he had sensed that the senior lieutenant's pacing from one end of the room to the other boded ill.

Yefremov listened to his instructions, took the note, sighed, and said: "Yes, Sir!" As far as he was concerned, the whole scheme was futile. He glanced disapprovingly at the senior lieutenant, slung his rifle over his shoulder, and went out, slamming the door angrily behind him.

Krutikov, who had suddenly had enough of charging up and down the room, sat down at the table and let his round, tired head drop onto the map-case.

He had hardly slept for three days and nights and, enervated by his battle with fear, had still been zealously building ramparts, digging trenches and ditches, and setting up anti-tank obstacles. He was now tired, as all must tire eventually, and no sooner had he closed his eyes than he fell fast asleep as a young man will.

And in his tired dreams there were no trenches, or bombs bursting before his eyes, and there was no haggard, mean-looking political instructor offering to tear the bandages off his head. All he saw in his dreams was the pretty, pathetic, face of his wife, frightened at their sudden parting, and he murmured something with sluggish, sleepy lips.

He dreamed of his wife's face and smiled, hugging the table with his plump cheek; and his expression was quite different from the one Sintsov had seen....

"Permission to report, Comrade Senior Lieutenant!..."

The senior lieutenant started out of his sleep. Yefremov was standing in front of him, his hand applied to his fur hat and his rifle on his shoulder. He was standing at attention, but there was a mocking twinkle in his eyes.

"Permission to report! They said that seeing he'd come in of his own accord, he'd hardly run away, so let him stay with us till morning. Then they said that they've got enough to do as it is. If we want, we can take him in tomorrow, and if we don't, that's up to us. 'You've got your own superiors,' they said, 'so you can go to them for orders!' And then they said: 'Tell your Comrade Senior Lieutenant—' and Yefremov could no longer hide the twinkle in his eye—'this case doesn't look like a saboteur, so let him sleep in peace and stop worrying!' "

"Dismiss!" said Senior Lieutenant Krutikov angrily.

But Yefremov didn't leave straightaway. He slowly removed his hat, took out the sheet of paper from the senior lieutenant's field book, and put it on the table.

"They ordered me to return the note. They said: 'Put it on your own files, ours are full up as it is!'"

"I told you to dismiss!" shouted Senior Lieutenant Krutikov, sensing the mockery in Yefremov's words but unable to put his finger on anything.

Yefremov went out into the passage, grinned to himself in the darkness, and went into his cubby-hole.

"Must tell the political instructor! What a laugh!" he thought, still grinning. "Pity he's asleep."

But Sintsov wasn't asleep, and when Yefremov told him how the senior lieutenant had sent him to the Special Department, Sintsov considered it well beyond a joke.

Red Armyman Yefremov wouldn't have had any qualms about despatching to the other world any man he considered a saboteur. He had faith in this political instructor, couldn't understand why Senior Lieutenant Krutikov was unable to trust him, and was delighted that the latter had been given such a dressing-down in the Special Department.

Yefremov refused the bench that Sintsov offered to vacate. He settled down on the floor beside him, and from there, in a mocking whisper, gave the details of his visit to the Special Department and his report to the senior lieutenant, to whom he had taken a hearty dislike during three days' service under him. To tell the truth, he considered himself subordinate, not to Krutikov, but to the commissar with whom he had served in the Airfield Servicing Battalion, with whom he had broken out of encirclement, with whom he had been in hospital, and with whom he had obtained his premature discharge in order to fight outside Moscow.

"That's the way it goes, Comrade Political Instructor," he said, and he settled his head more comfortably on a sack of potatoes. As he went off to sleep, he grinned once more at the cheering recollection of how the senior lieutenant had put his foot in it.

But Sintsov was not in the least amused. In spite of his tiredness, he had lain there unable to sleep ever since he had left Senior Lieutenant Krutikov.

Great distress can be caused to one man by another who has so far been a complete stranger. The senior lieutenant had not believed Sintsov, and Sintsov was miserable, although he neither liked nor respected this senior lieutenant and felt guilty before no one, him least of all.

"Where are you, where are you, Petya Zolotarev, my friend?" thought Sintsov, lying there with his eyes open. "Are you alive or have you been killed? No one except you can tell me or anyone else what happened in the forest when I lost consciousness. Did you do it for my sake, or did I take off my own tunic and bury it without knowing what I was doing and then forget where it was? Or was there something else I don't know and can't even guess at?... And what am I to say to people when they don't believe me?... Should I tell them what I know, or should I give up and invent something I don't know?..."

As he asked himself these questions, and was reminded of an unforgettable remark made by Serpilin after the river crossing on the first day of encirclement: "Better to be stood up against a wall and shot than to tear off one's own commissar's stars". No! He, Sintsov, hadn't torn them off! But what if people thought he had? And what if they thought that not only had he torn them off, but he hadn't even the decency to admit it?

He remembered what that soldier had said to him in the first few hours of captivity: "A good thing you got rid of your tunic." Then he remembered the sudden look of suspicion in the senior political instructor's eyes; and then, with still unabated fury, he remembered the questions of the senior lieutenant and, with a sudden, calm, inner surge of determination, he decided that the Special Department was the place to which he should report if even decent people were unwilling to take him entirely at his word. The conversation with the senior lieutenant had come as such a slap in the face that he was already beginning to imagine further suspicious faces, more suspicious questions, and more foolishly triumphant eyes: "Aha! Now I've caught you out!" No, he would go where the duties of the service demanded that they should check everything from beginning to end, and he would go right this minute, without delay, as a matter of urgency! Let them check! If they could, that is. And if they couldn't, let them send him into action and check in battle! That was the only answer, especially now, with the Germans near Moscow.

He let his feet down from the bench, put on his boots, jacket and hat and, stepping past Yefremov, who was whistling lightly in his sleep, went into the passage.

A faint strip of light was showing under the other door. Sintsov determinedly flung it open and went inside. The senior lieutenant was sleeping with his face buried in a pillow, his dirty boots standing on a sheet of newspaper. His holster and belt were lying beside him on the stool, and the map-case was on the table. The lamp was still burning, and the smoky wick was almost burnt out.

"Senior Lieutenant!" called Sintsov and, without lowering his voice, repeated: "Senior Lieutenant!"

But the senior lieutenant was dead to the world.

At first, Sintsov wanted to wake him and tell him that he had himself decided to go to the Special Department immediately—whether with or without an escort would be at the discretion of the Comrade Senior Lieutenant. But after calling him twice and eliciting no response, he changed his mind. He went up to the table, calmly opened the map case, tore a sheet out of the field book, took out the neatly sharpened pencil from its groove, wrote a few words and, picking up the pistol which the senior lieutenant had reached for during their conversation, laid it on top of the sheet of paper. As he approached the door, he threw a last mocking glance back at the whole picture: the senior lieutenant sleeping like a log, the lamp nearly out, the note with the pistol on top of it....

"If a real saboteur came your way, you'd be in serious trouble!" thought Sintsov.

It was already growing light outside. The road sloped from the settlement up a hillside, and he could see the grey roofs of a village up there about a kilometre and a half away. Yefremov had recently told him how he had trudged up that hill. Sintsov knew exactly where to go.

After covering about a kilometre, Sintsov stood aside to make way for an approaching lorry.

"Probably to pick up the senior lieutenant," he guessed, grinned at the thought of the uproar when that officer woke up, and continued on his way.

Yefremov woke up to the sound of a lorry hooting outside. He stretched himself, jumped up sleepily, pulled aside the sack hung over the window—it was light outside—turned round, and saw that the political instructor was no longer there. He looked into the next room. Perhaps the political instructor had gone in to the senior lieutenant. But the latter, who had also heard the lorry hooting, was lying alone in the room, still mumbling sleepily and rubbing his eyes with his fists.

Yefremov dashed outside, thinking that perhaps the political instructor had just gone out to obey a "natural call", walked round the building, and even said several times, but not too loudly: "Comrade Political Instructor! Comrade Political Instructor!" But there was no answer.

Then, after hesitating in the passage awhile, but not too long, because he had to make his report—there was no alternative—he went into the room.

The senior lieutenant was sitting on his cot and still rubbing his eyes.

"Well, has the lorry come? I did hear it, didn't I?"

"The political instructor's gone," said Yefremov, drawing himself up to attention.

"What d'you mean, gone?"

"He's gone. He's not outside, he's not anywhere," said Yefremov.

"So! And they call themselves a Special Department! Gone! Gone, the filthy saboteur!..." shouted Senior Lieutenant Krutikov in a voice triumphant with a sense of his own rightness, and his face at that moment was as happy as Yefremov's was miserable....

Neither of them was yet aware of Sintsov's note.

The note was discovered when a much-berated Yefremov had gone out of the room and Senior Lieutenant Krutikov reached for his pistol. Distractedly moving it to one side, he read the note several times over, glad at only one thing: that Yefremov, thank goodness, had already left. The note consisted of only four words: "Gone to Special Department." But Krutikov's own pistol on top of it was such a stinging postscript, that the senior lieutenant nearly wept with humiliation.

Meanwhile, Sintsov was walking along the road. In spite of the early hour, he had met a number of servicemen, but no one had paid him any particular attention because he was dressed much as they were. He was wearing a fur hat with ear-flaps and a star, with just a glimpse of the white bandage under the brim on one side, a quilted jacket, and badly worn boots; but not everyone was wearing new ones. He had no rifle; but not everyone was carrying a rifle. In a word, he was hardly distinguishable from the other military personnel walking or riding along that road at that hour.

It's a great thing to make up one's mind once and for all. Even one's gait is not the same any more.... Seen from the house he had just left, the village for which Sintsov was heading had apparently been situated by the road, but it was actually some distance to the right. In front of him was a bombed bridge and a detour. After the detour, the road carried straight on, but to reach the village meant turning off to the right.

Sintsov walked up to the detour just as a staff car, which had recently overtaken and passed him on the road, became stuck in a deep rut gouged out by the lorries.

The driver and the commander jumped out of the car and started heaving it out—the driver opening one door and guiding the steering wheel with one hand, the commander pushing on the rear bumper.

"Hey, soldier!" shouted the commander, turning and noticing Sintsov. "Give us a hand here! Help us get it out. Come on, quickly!"

Sintsov reluctantly obeyed this peremptory summons, went up, and took hold of the rear bumper. They pushed together, and the car rode up out of the rut.

"That'll do, thanks," said the commander, straightening up and brushing down the skirts of his greatcoat.

Sintsov also stood up and their eyes met. Before him was Lyusin, alive and well, looking exactly the same as before, only with three pips instead of two!

They were both astonished—Lyusin, apparently, even more so than Sintsov.

"Lyusin! How are you?"

They shook hands, still very much surprised.

"And we'd already written you off as missing...."

"Was my wife informed?"

"That I can't tell you.... Where've you been?"

"I only got out of encirclement yesterday.... Where are you going? The editorial office? Where is it now?"

Lyusin finally released Sintsov's hand. A shade agitated at first, his expression was now faintly condescending.

"When I went to the front line, it was at Perkhushkovo."

"But that's right near Moscow!" exclaimed Sintsov, who even now found it hard to realise that the front had moved up to the capital.

"It is indeed!... Where else? I spent five days at the front line, and last night they told me in the Army Political Department that the editorial offices weren't at Perkhushkovo any more. They were either in Moscow, at the *Gudok**

* *Gudok*—a Moscow newspaper.—*Ed.*

building, or even on the other side of Moscow, somewhere along the Gorky railway line. For the last few weeks, the editorial offices were on a train, so maybe they moved the train further east. But it may be in Moscow itself. That's the way things are!" said Lyusin cheerfully. His cheerfulness was due to the fact that he had been at the front line for several days running, was now recovering from the sense of instant danger, and was driving back to the editorial offices with a map-case full of copy.

"Where were you going just now?" asked Lyusin. He looked at Sintsov's sunken features and added: "Yes, one could say you're only half the man you were!"

"Where?" echoed Sintsov. "Well, now that I've met you I'm going where you're going—to the editorial offices. Will you take me along?"

Only five minutes ago he had been completely certain that his destination was those two houses at the end of the village. But now he would have thought it strange to have any intention other than that of going to his own editorial offices with Lyusin, who had turned up so unexpectedly. The meeting with Lyusin was a fluke. Who in his place would have doubted this?

"Of course. Take a seat," said Lyusin after hesitating for just a fraction of a second. "Mind you, this car isn't mine, it's going from the Army Political Department to Moscow, but it'll take us there.... True, there's a Draconic law just come out affecting the drivers. They're not supposed to give any lifts—still, I think it should be all right, eh?..." And he turned to the driver, who was standing nearby and wiping his hands on a rag.

"Of course it'll be all right!" smiled the driver, pleased at Sintsov's good luck. "Especially if you take the responsibility!" he added, opening the door and clearing a space for Sintsov beside the odds and ends cluttering up half the back seat.

The driver took his place at the wheel, Lyusin sat beside him, and Sintsov, hunching his shoulders, squeezed into the back. A saucepan containing some warm left-over kasha, a spoon, and a car headlamp crashed down on to his knees from a pile of things covered with a ground-sheet.

"Shove them under your feet," said the driver, turning round at the noise. "A lorry was hit by a bomb nearby, and I salvaged a few odds and ends."

They travelled fairly fast, and Sintsov estimated that at this rate they would be in Moscow within three hours. He found it incredible that only two days ago, at the very same time in the morning, he had felt such a long way from Moscow when he had been taken prisoner.... And yet they would be in Moscow in three hours.... He could hardly believe it, just as he could hardly believe that Lyusin was sitting in front of him and that the car was taking them to their own editorial office. He even had a tantalising glimmer of hope, probably too good to be true, that Masha had not gone anywhere, was still in Moscow, and he would be seeing her in a few hours' time.

"Listen!" said Sintsov to Lyusin. Although they had known one another less than twenty-four hours in all, everything they had been through since they had met in the war had brought them so close during those twenty-four hours that both felt impelled to speak to one another without formality as man to man. "Listen!"—Sintsov had always been direct in such matters as this—"You didn't take offence that time near Bobruisk, did you?"

He had been through far too much since then to feel in retrospect that he had wronged Lyusin, but he now realised better than he had at the time how hard it had been for the other near Bobruisk, and he didn't want to leave so much as a trace of bad feeling between the two of them.

Lyusin roared with laughter without turning round. He laughed perhaps a little too long for a man who was not supposed to be in the least offended.

"A fine thing to talk about now!" said Lyusin, still laughing. "First, I forgot about that ages ago. I've been in so many scrapes since then. Secondly, it's thanks to you I got my baptism of fire."

The phrase "thanks to you" in itself betrayed a still latent resentment, but Sintsov didn't notice it at the time.

"I met that tank captain again later, you know."

"A brave fellow, but a menace!" interrupted Lyusin.

"No, listen! He even said they'd put you up for a medal, but when you went back to the editorial office, they scrapped the recommendation."

"I don't care!" said Lyusin, although he actually cared a great deal. He turned round to Sintsov and opened the lapels of his greatcoat. "See that?"

He was wearing a brand-new medal "For Valour" on his chest.

"And I got it without their help, too!"

"What for?" asked Sintsov with a slight twinge of envy, but still glad for Lyusin's sake.

"The Yelnia battles. I was with the same division from beginning to end. I played it right—it took Yelnia; the divisional commander was made a Hero and I got a medal!"

He spoke of the divisional commander and himself as if they were the only two worth mentioning.

"So the tankmen didn't find much wrong with me, then!" said Lyusin, unable to resist returning to a theme so pleasing to him.

"No."

"What else did they say?"

"Nothing else. You just happened to come up in the conversation," said Sintsov, not noticing how "come up" rattled Lyusin. "There wasn't time for talk. We ended up in encirclement again two hours later."

He began describing his own encirclements, alternating between the two of them.

Lyusin interrupted him several times, half-turning round to ask questions or pass comments, and only when Sintsov came to the letters sent with Mishka Weinstein did Lyusin turn right round again.

"Really? So that's where he ended up! They looked for him everywhere.... Not a trace! Vanished!"

"Vanished..." echoed Sintsov dully, and for a second he saw Mishka as if he were there alive in front of him, carefully putting into his tunic pocket the pages of the letter that had evidently never reached its destination. Vanished.... And yet at the time things had looked as if they were going to turn out otherwise....

"Vanished!" repeated Lyusin. "Didn't you know?"

"How could I?"

"But of course."

"To blazes with those fairy-stories of mine!" said Sintsov, suddenly breaking off in mid-narrative, remembering what the senior lieutenant had said, and thinking with relief of the difference between the Sintsov who had been sitting that night in the house and listening to the senior lieutenant's suspicious questions, and the Sintsov who was now riding with Lyusin towards Moscow.

"Tell me how things are at the editorial office, and at the front, and in Moscow, and in general...."

"As far as I can make out, they're fighting at the front," said Lyusin. "The Germans are pushing hard, and we're fighting back. What else can we do?"

Although the army he had just left was actually in a serious predicament, and although it was retreating under the

German onslaughts, Lyusin, who had spent the last few days at the front line, was nonetheless returning to the editorial offices in a better mood than when he had departed. Leaving Moscow, he had been travelling forward into the unknown, into a vortex of rumours about some disaster that had occurred, and the grim realities of the retreat had proved more reassuring than what he had imagined from a distance. Moreover, he was going back alive and well.... He answered Sintsov truthfully, although with the slight casualness of a man who is anxious to impress with his experiences.

"As for Moscow, I don't know. Some people may be in a blue funk. There was that sort of feeling in the air when I left. We'll see when we arrive," he added grimly.

In the meantime, they drove across a bridge flanked on either side by concrete pill-boxes sunk into the ground, and then they passed an anti-tank ditch and a strip of anti-tank obstacles, consisting of welded iron rails, that receded as far as the horizon and beyond, and then several rows of stakes put up for barbed wire, and then more concrete pill-boxes not yet sunk into the ground.

"They're building defences everywhere. When I came out of encirclement yesterday, I walked straight into a construction battalion," said Sintsov.

There is no telling how things would have turned out if he had not begun this conversation, but begin it he did and, having done so, he inevitably came to the point at which Lyusin finally realised that he was taking a man with no documents to Moscow.

Such cases were, of course, nothing new to Lyusin, who had been at the front since the first days of the war; but what was new to him was that he, Lyusin, and no one else, at a time when the Germans were outside Moscow, was on his own responsibility taking to Moscow a man who had come out of encirclement with no documents. This possibility had occurred to him immediately Sintsov had asked: "Will you take me along?", and it had been behind Lyusin's slight pause before he had said: "Of course!" But he hadn't had the heart to ask about it straightaway. There had been something so self-assured about Sintsov's bearing that he couldn't bring himself to raise the matter. And now Sintsov himself was openly saying that he had no documents. What is more, he was cursing a senior lieutenant who, in Lyusin's opinion, may have been something of a fool, but who had, on the whole, acted entirely within his rights.

Sintsov went on talking, not noticing that Lyusin's neck in front of him had suddenly stiffened. Lyusin no longer turned his head to look round, and during the pauses, instead of his former exclamations and questions, he merely forced himself to say a brief "I see" each time.

Still unaware of this, Sintsov went on talking. That he had no documents, especially after yesterday's episode with the senior lieutenant, seemed to him a major disaster for which he would have to take the consequences. But the fact that he was now travelling with Lyusin who, unlike the senior lieutenant, knew who and what he was, and was travelling to the editorial office where they also knew him and where he might have been working to this day had they not left him behind in the Mogilev hospital—all this went to alleviate somewhat his resentment at the predicament his lack of documents had landed him in.

He went on talking and talking, carried away and completely failing to notice that Lyusin had ceased to react. It never even have occurred to him what Lyusin was thinking just now, and meanwhile Lyusin was thinking of matters which were to affect Sintsov's whole future.

They had already been through one checkpoint before the documents came into the conversation, and they had been let through without detailed verification. A soldier with flags had merely glanced at the car when the driver braked and, on seeing that all inside were army personnel, he had waved them on.

But at the nineteenth kilometre, directly ahead, they would soon have to stop at the first Moscow checkpoint, which was notoriously strict.

Lyusin remembered this from his departure from Moscow, and he was now cursing himself bitterly for having been so irresponsible as to take Sintsov in the car. "You fool! You should have asked him straightaway," he thought, so furious that he could have kicked himself. "You should have asked him first and then refused to take him. You should have advised him where to report and promised to inform the editorial office. What on earth's going to happen now?..."

"Comrade Political Instructor!" said the driver, as if in answer to Lyusin's thoughts. He too had been disturbed by Sintsov's story, and even more by the grim expression on Lyusin's face. "We've passed the twenty-second kilometre, soon it'll be the twenty-first, and then there's the checkpoint at the nineteenth...."

Lyusin didn't answer, rode on another half a kilometre in silence, still struggling with himself, and then suddenly said sternly:

"Stop the car! Let's get out for a moment," he added, turning to Sintsov.

Sintsov got out, puzzled that they should have stopped here, of all places. There was no one on the road at that spot. There was a forest on the right, and fields and summer villas on the left. He tried to remember the name of the spot—it was in the Moscow district—but couldn't.

"Let's go a little further, over there," Lyusin took him by the arm and led him several paces away from the car. He didn't want to talk in front of the driver, because although he felt himself to be in the right, deep down inside he was ashamed at what he was going to have to say.

"Listen!" said Lyusin in embarrassment. "There'll soon be a checkpoint, and you have no documents."

Sintsov had already guessed what Lyusin was driving at before he had even finished speaking. He looked him straight in the eye and said nothing.

Lyusin was expecting the other to answer, but Sintsov just looked him grimly in the eye, leaving it to him to say more if he wished, or to let it rest at that if he didn't.

"Well, why don't you say something?" asked Lyusin at last.

"What is there for me to say?" asked Sintsov.

"If you'd told me right away that you hadn't any documents, when you were getting into the car...."

Sintsov said nothing, but there was such a look on his face that Lyusin thought: "He's going to hit me!"

Lyusin backed off a little and shifted his weight from one foot to the other before he asked:

"What about it?"

"Very well," said Sintsov dully. "Take me to the checkpoint and I'll get out."

"It's not far from here," said Lyusin falteringly. "I could take you on a bit further, of course, but not right up to the checkpoint—at least half a kilometre short...."

"Why half a kilometre short? Why not to the checkpoint?" Sintsov was already beginning to realise why not to the checkpoint, but there was no reason why he should spare Lyusin's feelings.

"Because..." Lyusin broke off. Now came the most difficult moment. "Because it is strictly forbidden to carry unauthorised persons, especially if they haven't any documents. Think about it yourself—we'll get the driver into trouble too, and it'll mean a lot of unnecessary unpleasantness for me. They'll detain you anyway. With me or without me, they'll stop you at that checkpoint.... And I'm carrying newspaper copy. I'm not in a hurry for my own sake. And they could give me five days on the spot just for taking you through without documents.... They have the authority! As for you, what difference does it make whether you ride to the checkpoint or walk to it?"

"Well, imagine that—five days!" Sintsov sneered with contempt despite the gravity of his position. "You think it makes no difference, but I think it makes a hell of difference whether I arrive with you and am handed over by you, or whether I arrive out of encirclement alone, on foot! How the hell am I to explain how I ended up here just outside Moscow? Where have I come from? Why? How can I convince them that I'm not a deserter?"

"Never mind," said Lyusin. "While you're under detention and being investigated, I'll already be at the editorial office and we'll get on the phone straight to this checkpoint...."

"Like hell you will!" said Sintsov contemptuously. "All right, drive on!" he snapped. And he stared fixedly at the ground.

"Try to see my point of view," said Lyusin in an attempt to soften the blow.

"You didn't have to take me," said Sintsov, speaking with an effort and still not looking at him. "But if you did, you should've been prepared to take me all the way without worrying about getting five days. But if you really are worried about that, then you shouldn't have taken me...."

Lyusin no longer thought that Sintsov was going to hit him, and yet at that moment Sintsov was very near to doing so.

"You bastard! That senior lieutenant didn't know me after all, but you, you're just a bastard! Scum!"

For one second he raised his eyes and stared at Lyusin with real loathing, then looked away, turned his back on the other and, putting his hands behind his back, clasped them so hard that the bones cracked.

"All right, if you want it that way!" shouted Lyusin, unable to think of anything to say. It was as if he had been offering Sintsov some kind of choice which the latter had refused to make.

Lyusin climbed back into the car, slammed the door, and the car moved off.

Sintsov, with his back to it, heard it drive away.

Never before in his life had so many hopes collapsed in a single moment!

He turned round and, his hands still behind his back, watched the car until it finally disappeared from view.

CHAPTER ELEVEN

The signals school at which Masha had been training for the last three months — since the beginning of July — was quartered in what had originally been a children's sanatorium thirty kilometres along the Kaluga highway.

On the evening of October 16th, Masha and her friend Nusia Zhuravskaya were granted permission to spend the night in Moscow in order to pick up from home a few clothes that they might need behind the German lines.

It was cold and windy. Both women rode all the way in the back of a lorry which was going to Moscow for groceries. They lay on the straw, shielding themselves with the heavy tarpaulin normally used to cover the provisions. Masha was feeling warmer now, and in the darkness under the tarpaulin she imagined that she was not in a lorry going to Moscow for groceries, but lying on the floor, likewise in darkness, of the night place in which she would cross the front and from which she would be parachuted down behind the German lines. Their course of training had finished a week ago, and any night they were expecting their final briefing and despatch.

She already knew that she was to be dropped with her radio transmitter on one of three possible points near Smolensk, and that she would then have to make her way to the city. According to the cover story which had been built up to back her false passport, she had been in Smolensk as a child with her mother. Unable to leave Vitebsk in time, she had lost her mother in an air-raid and had wandered about for several months in search of shelter. She had decided to make her way to an aunt in Smolensk. The address of this aunt, a living person who had, unlike Masha, a real name, was the rendez-vous which she had to commit to memory at the last moment before take-off.

Masha lay in the back of the lorry, pressing against Nusia's warm back and, her lips scarcely moving, repeating to herself: "Veronika, Veronika...."

Veronika was to be her name, and she didn't like it. She felt that she would never be able to respond to it naturally, without showing surprise.

"Veronika, Veronika..." her lips repeated soundlessly.

The minute the evening roll-call was over and the company commander had given the order: "All dismiss! Artemyeva and Zhuravskaya, report to me!", Masha had felt that the future had moved up and was now part of the present.

She had not been mistaken. The company commander had given them leave till morning so that they could pick up at their Moscow flats what he described as "civvies". This meant that Masha and Nusia were both going to be dropped behind the lines as agents. Radio operators going to work for partisan detachments were usually sent in uniform and sheepskin jackets.

"It's mistake sending her there..." thought Masha of her friend, and by no means for the first time. She felt that Nusia was no use for such work, since she had been a spoilt child, was too inexperienced, and had not yet seen enough of the outside world. Furthermore, her appearance was much too striking and could attract attention to her at once.... Masha didn't think this applied to herself. What she feared more than anything else was the air trip, especially since her parachute had failed to open during a practice jump and she had only pulled the emergency ring just in time.

She turned over on the straw, pressing her cold back to Nusia, and lifted the tarpaulin a little way in order to catch at least a glimpse of the sky as it flew over the lorry. It was a cold autumn evening sky, sunless, moonless, and starless, monotonously grey, at which you could stare as hard as you liked without being able to see a thing—not even a cloud shape or formation.

"There are people in this world who at least have some news about their families!" thought Masha. "Nusia here knows that her father escaped from encirclement and is now the chief surgeon of a field hospital on the Western Front. He writes to her, and she writes back to his field post number.... And her brother was wounded and they amputated his foot, and he's in hospital in Kazan, and he writes to her too.... And lots of other people write and receive letters, or meet people who've either seen or heard something about their families.... But I haven't had any news at all, good or bad. Not a word.... I don't know anything about my daughter, or my mother, or my husband, and I have to keep wondering all the time: are they alive or not?"

During her first week at the school, she had asked—naively, as she now realised—if they could possibly use her somewhere in the Grodno area after she had finished her course.

"Why d'you ask?" demanded the school commissar sharply. He knew all the circumstances of Masha's life from her application form and her autobiography, but he considered it unnecessary and possibly even harmful to spare her feelings. "Why?" he repeated. "So that you can rescue your family single-handed? They'll try to do that without you and if you turn up there you can only bring disaster on them. And on yourself too.... No, it's not a very good idea!" He smiled grimly. "A political instructor's wife who's lived for a year and a half in Grodno now goes back there on an underground assignment! Did you come to our school out of personal motives? If you did, then you've been wasting your time."

"Of course I didn't," said Masha. This was not quite true, because the forlorn hope that, once across the front, she might be able to trace her mother and her little daughter, or, if not, at least find out something about them, had also played its part in her decision to come to this particular school.

That had been three months ago, and she had since become used to the idea that her mother and Tanya were "there" and that, if they were alive, it would be a long time before she had any news of them. But the thought of flying behind the German lines with still no news of her husband was still unacceptable and intolerable to her.

In June, at the railway station, he had pressed her hand through the railings, had wound the strap of his kitbag round his wrist, and had leapt on to the moving railway carriage.... Then someone else had jumped on and blocked him from view.... And with this, everything, absolutely everything had been cut off.... She still found it hard to believe.

Three times she had sent in written enquiries which had simply not been answered. Twice, by sheer persistence, she had got as far as the Political Directorate; on the first occasion immediately after entering the school in July and the second time quite recently, in September, after obtaining a special twelve-hour leave pass for the purpose.

The first time, in June, they had told her they had at present no information concerning the whereabouts of the Army paper *Battle Banner* on which her husband was serving. This answer both alarmed and reassured her. They knew nothing about Sintsov, but they also knew nothing about the editorial office either, and an entire editorial office could hardly vanish into thin air! They didn't know, but they would eventually. She left her school postal number and asked the battalion commissar who had granted the interview to drop her at least a line as soon as there was news of the editorial office. The battalion commissar promised to do so, but she had heard nothing from him for two months.

Apart from the battalion commissar, she had left her address with a comrade of her late father's who lived in the same house—Zosima Ivanovich Popkov. Old Popkov took her letter-box key and promised to pay a daily visit to the Sintsovs front entrance and, if a letter should arrive, to forward it to her immediately. But since then not one letter had arrived from the front.

When she had called at the Political Directorate for the second time, in September, she had been received by a different battalion commissar—the first one had left for the front—and the new battalion commissar had said: "Yes, yes, the editorial office of *Battle Banner* has successfully broken out of encirclement and is now operating in the appointed place, and the editor is the one who was in charge before the war, Gureyev, but unfortunately in answer to our enquiry we have had an official reply from them to the effect that Political Instructor Sintsov, the editorial secretary, did not report to his place of service after leave."

Two months ago, Masha would no doubt have tried to convince the battalion commissar that this was impossible and that she had seen her husband off personally when he left for Grodno.... But now, in September, when she could understand much of what she could not possibly have understood in June and July, she merely sighed and went away, even forgetting to say good-bye.

"Didn't report back from leave. Which means he didn't get that far. But what does 'didn't get that far' mean? If he had ended up in hospital or had been fighting with some other unit, he would have written. That means he's in encirclement somewhere.... What else could it mean?"

So she reasoned, trying to reassure herself, trying to be firm and not to believe the worst. But deep down inside she was troubled by an almost maternal heart-ache, much like what she felt whenever she thought of her daughter. And as soon as she weakened and gave free reign to this feeling, her husband—a big, strong, broad-shouldered man that he was—seemed smaller than a little boy....

Earth and war then seemed unimaginably vast, and lost somewhere in that war was one man known to no one and needed by no one except herself—one little man, her husband.... And at such moments it seemed nothing less than a miracle that a kind of thread should ever reach from him to her over that enormous distance.

This was her feeling now as she watched the vast grey sky rushing over the lorry. That sky didn't want to answer a single one of her questions, although it seemed to know everything. Someone somewhere must know, even if she didn't, what he was doing, what he was thinking, where he was!... That was what mattered most. Where was he?

"Love..." thought Masha suddenly. "What is love? Being happy together, and missing him, and sometimes crying at nights? Not wanting to look at another man? Or writing him letters without knowing where to send them? Yes, it's all these things, and yet it's all so little compared with what I feel, and what I want, and what I can't put into words. I don't know, I don't know.... What do I want most of all now?" she asked herself again. "Most of all, I want...." She thought again and firmly told herself that most of all she wanted to be where he was....

"And if it's terrible there, and I could be killed? I still don't care! And if we're wounded? I still want to be with him: let them wound us both! And if we die? It doesn't matter, as long as we die together...."

Who knows, perhaps at that very time, in the holocaust of war, these thoughts were the answer to the question which was troubling her most and over which she had just been whispering: "I don't know ... I don't know...."

... Masha once more pulled the tarpaulin over her head as a protection against the wind blowing into the back of the lorry and turned over again. As she thought about her husband, she sighed straight into her friend's ear. Nusia pulled her hand out of her glove and rubbed her ear: it had begun tickling her.

"Crafty! You're warming yourself against me!" said Nusia, and she yawned luxuriously. "It would be nice if the gas was on. You could come and have a wash at my place...."

"Who knows, maybe it is on," said Masha.

"Hardly," said Nusia. "You should have heard the news bulletin. It's awful!"

And although she said "awful", and although both of them, like the rest of the trainees at the school, had been appalled and shaken by what they had read in the evening bulletin—"The position on the Western sector of the front has deteriorated"—they had not yet grasped the full horror of the statement.

Their school lived in a world of its own, dedicated to thoughts of a not-far-distant and dangerous future on the other side of the front line. As she wrapped herself round for the night in the stiff cotton sheet and the army blanket, Masha used to wonder only about one thing—what would be the sequel to those quiet days at school, with exercises at the blackboard, with the assembly and stripping down of radio transmitters, with the breakfasts, dinners and suppers at set times, with the nocturnal whisperings about the future, and how that future would begin there on the other side of the lines. She wondered how she would arrive at her rendez-vous for the first time and what sort of people she would have to work with: loyal and reliable? Or would one of them suddenly turn out to be a traitor? She thought how, if she fell into the hands of the Germans, they would torture her; but whatever they might do to her, she must not say a word about what she had learnt in the quiet little villas of the children's sanatorium which was not a sanatorium any longer.

The logic of their life was such that these speculations sometimes involuntarily drove out any thoughts Masha and her friends might have had about what was happening at the front. They paid particular attention to reports from behind the lines about how Comrade S. or Comrade K. and their partisan detachment had wiped out so many nazis in the forest, or had raided a German headquarters, or had set a fuel tank on fire, or had mined a road, or had burned down the house occupied by Baron von Biederling, a returned landowner.... They were less concerned with bulletins from the front than with what was happening on the other side, where they would themselves soon be operating. And the touch of egoism in all this was probably excusable, in view of what lay in store for them....

The lorry braked sharply. Masha heard the familiar "Please produce your documents" right in her ear. Burylin, the school's quartermaster, rustled some papers in the cab, and then those same papers rustled in the hands of the man who had taken them. The dry voice that had requested the documents then demanded:

"What have you got in the back?"

"Two of my service personnel. But I'm the senior in command."

"That doesn't mean a thing," said the voice.

Masha and Nusia sat up and threw the tarpaulin back.

A tall, gaunt lieutenant looked over the side of the lorry. There were no less than three patrolmen standing behind him.

"Your documents!" said the lieutenant.

Masha and Nusia got out their leave passes and handed them over. He looked at them closely, handed them back, and turned away without even a second glance at Nusia, which was very unusual indeed.

"You may proceed."

"There's a bad-tempered one for you!" said Nusia.

"A whole four of them," said Masha, looking back.

She again remembered yesterday's evening bulletin: "The position on the Western sector of the front has deteriorated." This and the four patrolmen, instead of the two she had seen standing there in September, gave her a sinking feeling in the pit of the stomach.

The road was flanked with huge piles of anti-tank obstacles welded out of girders. The lorry then bounced past a barricade that left only enough room for one vehicle to pass at a time. In the last few days, they had known at the school that Moscow was being fortified and that barricades were being erected. Knowing, however, was one thing, but seeing them, almost within the city limits, was another matter entirely.

"Lie down or you'll freeze," said Nusia, who had already lain down on the floor of the lorry.

Masha tore her eyes away from the road with an effort, covered herself with the tarpaulin, and lay down again next to Nusia.

It's hard to say whether it was for the better or not, but because they lay under the tarpaulin for another half hour to get warm while the lorry drove from the city gates to Pirogovskaya Street, they didn't get a real look at the outskirts of Moscow or at what was happening there that evening.

The lorry stopped.

"D'you want to get out here?" asked Burylin, half-opening the cab door and banging the coachwork with the flat of his hand.

Masha and Nusia crawled out from under the tarpaulin one after the other, stepped on to the wheel, and jumped down.

A ragged column of civilians, badly out of step, was marching past down the middle of the road. They were of various ages and dressed any old how: some in overcoats and cloth caps, some in fur hats and quilted jackets. They marched along glumly, without singing, and some were smoking as they went.

"This is a fine state of affairs, girls!" sighed Burylin, not getting out of the cab. There was a dazed expression on his fat and usually jolly face. Although they had only driven down a few streets after turning off the old Kaluga highway, he had seen what the girl trainees had missed while they were lying under the tarpaulin in the back.

"Yes, girls, this is a fine state of affairs!" he repeated, and he thought of his own family—a wife and two children living on the other side of the city at the Semyonov Gates. He must find the time overnight to squeeze them into a train going east. "I'll get the groceries at the warehouse and I'll be back here with the lorry at seven hundred hours. Be ready and waiting outside."

The lorry drove off, leaving Masha and Nusia alone on the pavement at the junction of the road and a side-street.

"Let's go straight to my place, shall we?" suggested Nusia, shivering in the cold wind. "After all, you haven't got anyone waiting for you."

Masha was still watching the ragged column of civilians as it marched away down the road and, wrapped up in her own troubled thoughts, she didn't answer Nusia straightaway.

"Well, how about it?" asked Nusia.

Masha's house was quite near, round the corner; but Nusia's was five blocks away, and Nusia didn't at all like the idea of going there on her own.

"No, I'll collect my things first, and then I'll come over to your place," said Masha.

"Alright, I'll wait."

"No, don't wait. Off you go. I'll join you later."

Masha didn't want to go straight over to Nusia's for the night, not just because she had to collect up her things that evening, but because she couldn't go to bed without first calling on old Popkov and finding out whether a letter had arrived for her during the last few days and not yet been forwarded. But she didn't want to explain all this to Nusia; it would have meant talking about her husband and about her fears for him. It would have meant seeking moral support from a person who was herself in need of such support, being the weaker of the two.

"Alright, I'll go," said Nusia humbly, intimidated by Masha's firmness. But, as if still waiting for Masha to change her mind, she nervously lit a cigarette.

She stood in front of Masha, scared to leave her—tall, beautiful and graceful, even in the army greatcoat and the rough soldier's boots that were too big for her. Masha looked at her closely and felt a heart-rending, affectionate pity for this Nusia with her beautiful and, as it seemed to Masha, weak-willed face—the cigarette didn't suit it at all—and with her tall, willowy, girlish figure that was so strong and yet so frail.

As she looked at Nusia, Masha thought of something that had occurred to her many times: she was older and stronger than Nusia, older and stronger, especially since she was married and had a husband and a child.... Yes, she had a family, even though she knew nothing about them.

Masha thought of something that Nusia and the other girls had often discussed together: what lay in store for them if they should fall alive into German hands before they had had the chance to commit suicide. Masha nearly cried out at the thought, but controlled herself, and instead of saying what was on her mind, said in her clear, calm, sad voice:

"You are beautiful, Nusia!" Then she recalled how Sintsov had often said just that to her, had said it in admiration, though she was not as beautiful as Nusia. He had even said it to her when she was carrying Tanya and when—Masha knew this for a fact—she had been anything but beautiful to look at. And when this occurred to her, she thought with alarm about herself, about her future mission behind the German lines and, angry with herself at her own cowardice, said sharply and almost rudely to Nusia: "Well, off you go, what are you standing there for?" So saying, she went down the side-street that led to her house.

As she passed the familiar front entrance, she noticed that the doors were wide open. She went through into the courtyard. There was not a sign of anyone there, and all the windows had been masked with black-out paper. Popkov lived on the top floor over entrance Number Seven, which was some distance further on. Masha tripped over a mattress left lying out in the courtyard there and nearly fell.

It was pitch dark on the staircase. She climbed up to the top floor, fumbled around for some time trying to find the bell-push without success, and then began knocking on the door. There was no answer. Then she heard Popkov's hoarse voice:

"Who's that?"

"It's me, Zosima Ivanovich! It's Masha!" she said. To this day, out of childhood habit, she was scared of the cantankerous old man.

He said no more, and she heard his footsteps slapping into the interior of the flat and then back to the door again. He was a long time fiddling with the bolt and chain. Finally, he opened the door.

"Come in. I'm on my own. I'm not well."

There was no light in the passage, and Popkov took Masha straight into the sitting-room, where there now stood a big nickel-plated bedstead with rumpled bedding. After the death of his wife, Popkov had moved in here and made the other room available for his married son.

"Sit down! What are you standing there for?" said Popkov and, straightening the bed clothes as he passed, he sat down at the table first. He was wearing an old, once best fur coat directly over his underclothes.

Masha sat opposite him at the familiar table. She remembered that they had the same kind of table in their own flat. Masha's father and Popkov had bought two identical folding-leaf tables in the same shop at the same time when they had moved into these first workers' flats at the end of the 'twenties.

"Well, what have you got to say for yourself?" asked Popkov, looking at Masha and passing the palm of his hand over his shaven head with the bristly grey hair on either side of his bald patch. It was chilly in the flat, and his head was feeling the cold.

"What have I to say for myself?" Masha shrugged her shoulders. "I thought maybe you'd have something to tell me."

"I would if I had, but I haven't. Your letter-box is empty. I went out and had a look yesterday."

Masha sighed as if she were blowing out a candle.

"What are you sighing for?" asked Popkov fretfully, and then heaved a sigh himself. "I haven't looked in your letter-box for two weeks. I've been in hospital with a hernia. But I had a look yesterday, and it's empty."

"Where are the rest of the family?" asked Masha.

"They've left. The factory's been evacuated...."

"What about you?"

"I tell you, I've been down with a hernia! I was lifting heavy weights and overdid it...."

Popkov had retired on pension three years ago, but had gone back to the workshop after war broke out.

"So what now? Will you follow them?" asked Masha.

But the old man shook his head.

"There's nothing worse than waiting for somebody or trying to catch them up. I'll get fixed up somewhere here—some little factory that's staying on where I can do munitions work. Earlier on, I'd have left, but I don't feel like it now. There's enough refugees from Moscow without me. Anyway, you've been out in the streets, you've seen for yourself. I went to buy some bread this morning, then I took a look at all the people running away and thought: oh, to hell with it!"

Popkov believed in calling a spade a spade.

"It's disgraceful, but there's mattresses lying about in the yard. There's so much fluff flying about, you'd think it was a Jewish pogrom. No, I won't budge a step out of Moscow now, on principle!" He began coughing, slid his hand under his fur coat, and rubbed his chest.

"In my opinion, you're not well, Zosima Ivanovich," said Masha.

"It's only a slight chill. I was discharged from hospital and caught a chill straight off. It never rains but what it pours. The factory's gone to Miass," he said after a pause. "They say there's a town of that name in Chelyabinsk Region. My son told me when he visited me in hospital. But goodness knows exactly where it is—I've hunted and hunted all over the map and I still haven't found it. What have we come to? Our old Moscow factory dumped in such a hole that you can't even find it on the map.... Why did you come here?" He suddenly looked up at Masha. "If it's about mail, then I—if there are any letters, I'll forward them. Don't worry, I'm not going to bolt for it. I'm going to stick here like a rusty nail in a plank and wait till victory. Or d'you think the Germans'll take Moscow?"

"Whatever are you talking about, Zosima Ivanovich?" Masha actually cried out at the unexpectedness of this question, and the old man realised that the thought had never entered her head.

"And why not, may I ask?" said Popkov, glad at her confidence but teasing her out of habit. "You want to see the way some of them have been making themselves scarce! I stopped one fellow—a big, burly chap he was—and asked him: 'Have you authorisation to leave?' You should have seen him dive into all his pockets. He covered half the pavement with bits of paper. And who was I to him? Why was he scared? It means he was yellow through and through!"

The old man pulled his hand from under his coat and angrily swept it over the table, as if brushing away invisible crumbs....

"Well, what about it? If you didn't come for your mail, what did you come for?"

"They're sending us to the front soon. I just dropped in to pick up a few odds and ends," said Masha. She had to abide by school regulations and not give away any secrets, but she wanted to be as truthful with the old man as she dared.

"So they're sending you to the front too? What are you up to, then?"

Masha looked at him but said nothing.

"All right, you don't have to answer if you're not supposed to!" said Popkov without taking offence. "But clear up one thing for me. Tell me, have you got a whole women's battalion, same as under Kerensky? Or d'you have menfolk with you as well?"

"We do," said Masha, smiling in spite of herself.

"Thank goodness! At least we haven't come to that yet!" Popkov sighed and paused for a moment. "There was a colonel with me in hospital. From the front. But he wasn't wounded, he just had a hernia, like me. They still have hernias, even at the front.... So I asked him: 'Now you tell me something: what's all this "unexpectedness" about? Where were you?' says I, 'you army people? How come you didn't tell Comrade Stalin about this, even if only a week or three days before it happened? Have you no conscience? Why didn't you report it to Comrade Stalin?'"

"So what did he say?" inquired Masha, who had asked herself the same agonising question many times but had never put it as bluntly and fearlessly as Popkov.

"What did he say? He didn't say anything. He was rude to me, an old man. But I suppose *you* know what it's all about?" grinned Popkov. "Last month, one young lady from our yard gave me an earful. She knew it all, she did! But you should have seen her today, running across the yard with a suitcase as fast as her legs could carry her, poor thing. So if you know what it's all about, then good luck to you, and better keep it to yourself."

"I don't know, Zosima Ivanovich," said Masha. "We lived almost on the frontier for a year and a half right in Grodno, and d'you think we weren't all worrying about war? Of course we were! And then I must have gone mad, leaving mother there with Tanya like that! I don't know how it is with other people, but I think about myself and my husband, and how we could have done a thing like that I don't know. I still can't understand it when I think about it."

"Now let me tell you how I understand it," said Popkov sternly, even solemnly, after a long pause. "Just what all that 'unexpectedness' was about I don't know—it's beyond me. When they've got visitors in the next flat, they lay the table and people can hear! But how was it that the Germans collected up a whole army under our noses without us hearing about it? It's beyond me! And let me tell you something else. It's true we didn't know how strong the Germans were. It's true they're tremendously strong. That's why they overran us straight from the frontier." Popkov put his hands on the table in front of him and leaned right over towards Masha. "You're not a little girl. You can remember a thing or two in your time. So tell me this: no matter how hard it was for us, did we ever grudge the Red Army anything? Was there ever a time when the Red Army needed something that the people wouldn't give them? Answer me! Was there ever such a time, or wasn't there?"

"There wasn't—ever," said Masha in a subdued voice.

"As I see it now, the Red Army hasn't got everything it ought to have! Look at the time that's gone by, and we haven't stopped the nazis yet! And now I'm asking you and I want an answer. Why didn't they tell us? If the worst came to the worst, I'd even give up this flat, I'd live in one room, I'd live on a crust of bread and boiled turnips as I did in the Civil War, if only the Red Army had everything it needed and didn't have to retreat from the frontier.... Why didn't they have the decency to tell us? Why did they hush it up? Am I right or wrong to ask?"

Masha didn't know whether Popkov, as he sat opposite her talking, or rather shouting, was right or wrong. But in spite of all the bitterness of his tirade, she felt a spiritual strength in him that made her physically strong too and ready for anything—the boiled turnips, the crust of bread (what did a crust of bread matter anyway?) and ready for any battle, for any kind of death, just so long as it would put things to rights and change the situation so that the Germans wouldn't advance on us, but we would advance on them!

"Never mind, Zosima Ivanovich!" said Masha cheerfully, happy at this sudden overwhelming feeling of confidence. "We'll wring those nazis' necks yet—we'll wring them yet before we're done!"

"Now hark at you!" replied Popkov in exasperation. "We're talking at cross purposes! I know just as well as you who's going to be on top and who's going to be down in the end! But why have we been down all these months?..."

"Why down? Why?" said Masha, disconcerted at this fresh onslaught. "There's heavy fighting going on, naturally."

"I know there's fighting, I can read that in the bulletins," said Popkov, still hammering home his point. "They've killed some here, and taken some prisoners there, and halted them somewhere else.... And yet Bryansk and Vyazma fell two days ago! So where does that put us: up or down? How d'you sum that up, in military terms? You're in the Army—you tell me!"

Masha had no chance to reply. Hundreds of anti-aircraft guns suddenly opened up, distinctly and indistinctly, quite close at hand and far away.

"I was wondering why they were late today," said Popkov calmly. He glanced at the old pre-revolutionary clock on the wall and stood up. "Are you going down to the shelter?"

"What about you?"

"Can't be bothered. You only sit stewing there while they bang-bang away upstairs. So I've come to the conclusion it's better to stay in the flat.... Well, are you going or not?"

"No, I'll wait here with you till it's over," said Masha, hesitating slightly—not because she really wanted to go down to the shelter, but because she had decided to go to her own flat and had then changed her mind: there was nothing to hurry there for.

"Let's put the light out then and pull up the blind," said Popkov, delighted that Masha was going to stay. "I was sitting here and looking through the window last night. An interesting spectacle!"

Clutching the fur coat round his throat, he went to the light switch, turned it off, shuffled across to the window in the dark, and lifted the paper blind.

Masha sat on the window-sill beside the old man. The flat was on the top floor, the buildings round them were not high, and they could see the whole sky, which was thumping, booming and banging away as if under thousands of hammer blows. Stretched over the city like an enormous black sheet, it kept ripping open in hundreds of different places, and the rents were filled with the fireballs of exploding anti-aircraft shells.

There was an anti-aircraft battery booming away behind the house and drowning all the other noises with its thunder. Between salvoes, as in a faulty radio, could be heard the intermittent droning of aircraft high in the sky. The house was shaken by bomb explosions several times. Tongues of flame were flaring up and sinking down again somewhere in the heart of the city.

Then Masha heard something clang quite close by.

"Shrapnel," said Popkov. "It hit the balcony. We'd better move away in case a fragment flies in," he added, turning to Masha. "We could get cut by broken glass...."

Masha said nothing and went on staring at the sky.

"Yes, our anti-aircraft defences take some getting through," said Popkov during a relative lull. As if in confirmation, a bright and particularly vivid blob of flame flared up high in the sky among the yellow balls of flak, then changed from a formless blob into a triangle, then became a half-cross and, disintegrating, plummeted fierily down into the darkness.

"They've got one!" shouted Popkov.

The anti-aircraft barrage quietened down, the yellow balls burst less and less frequently, and the long arms of the searchlights criss-crossed against the dome of the sky began to sink down towards the horizon one after the other.

"That's one wave gone over," said Popkov, still looking out of the window. "It's like Sodom and Gomorrah here at night. But when you go out in the morning, all you see is a few wisps of smoke in places. A house here, a house there, but Moscow's still in one piece!"

So saying, Popkov let down the blind and for a moment they were left in total darkness.

"Oh well, war's a temporary thing," said Popkov, and he put on the light. "Shall we have some tea?"

Masha thanked him and declined. Nusia was waiting and might even be getting worried. She must pick up her things as soon as possible and go to her place for the night.

"Thank you, Zosima Ivanovich! I'll look in again sometime!"

"When will that be?" asked the old man grimly.

She shrugged her shoulders.

"I don't know."

Letting go of the collar of his fur coat, Popkov passed his rough hand with unusual tenderness over Masha's head by way of farewell.

"All right, off you go!" He shut the door after her, and the chain rattled.

Masha crossed the yard again and went in by her own entrance. There was a wind, and the doors had been wedged with bricks against which they creaked forlornly. And Masha thought: "Supposing there's a letter waiting for me behind the round hole in the letter-box on the door of our flat on the second floor, and it's only come today, and it's not from Sintsov, but just to inform me that he's been killed?"

Holding on to the banister, she felt her way up the dark staircase, took the key out of her tunic pocket, and felt for the keyhole. But her hand touched something that jingled unexpectedly. She started, first withdrew her hand, and then felt a metal ring with a bunch of keys attached. The ring passed through a key inserted into the keyhole. Masha touched the door handle and the unlocked door opened uncannily. Masha stood motionless in the dark for a minute, frozen with indescribable terror at the door and the keys. Then, annoyed with herself, she abruptly pushed the door open and went into the flat. At first everything seemed quiet, but then she heard the sound of irregular breathing coming from the second room. She stepped through the bedroom doorway and pulled a torch out of her greatcoat pocket.

In fur hat, quilted coat, and tattered boots, Sintsov was lying face down on the bare mattress, his head hanging over the edge of the bed. He was fast asleep and not moving at all. His breathing was laboured and feverish.

As she stood there petrified, holding the torch, Masha suddenly noticed that the window hadn't been blacked out. She switched off the torch and felt her way hurriedly across the room to let down the paper blinds in both rooms, then ran into the kitchen, lowered the blind in there too, hurried out on to the landing, took the bunch of keys out of the lock, went back inside again, shut the door behind her and, snapping on one light switch after another, turned on the two remaining lights in the passage and the kitchen.

Only then did she return to the bedroom. A weak light was filtering in from the passage. Sintsov was still lying prone with his head hanging over the edge of the mattress. Masha knelt down, pressed his head to her breast and, still holding it there, lifted it up a little way and laid it on the mattress. She then reached for the pillow, again lifted her husband's head, and put it down on the pillow. She noticed the edge of a dirty bandage under the tight-fitting fur hat, but was afraid to take it off. Sintsov didn't wake up. He seemed feverish. She put her lips to his temple, but it wasn't hot, just damp and bedewed with fine drops of perspiration. Masha threw off her own hat and greatcoat with feverish haste and, taking off her boots as if the noise of them hitting the floor might wake this man who was completely dead to the world, she ran into the kitchen, lit the gas, which barely glimmered with a weak violet flame in the burner, took a large saucepan off its nail, ran some water into it, and put it on the stove.

She then rummaged around in the kitchen table drawer for soap and a sponge, took them out, unlocked the sitting-room wardrobe, took out some clean underwear, socks, a towel, two sheets and a blanket and, hanging everything else over the wardrobe door but tucking the sheets and blanket under her arm, she went back to the bed. She sat down on the edge, careful not to drop the sheets, and only then, as she snuggled up to her husband, holding him by the shoulders and pressing her breast up against his back, did she burst into tears of joy, sniffing, gulping, now drawing back from him for a moment, now again convulsively embracing her husband who was motionless and still fast asleep.

CHAPTER TWELVE

To sleep as heavily as Sintsov, a man would have to be reduced to the last stage of exhaustion—as, indeed, he was.

He had arrived home and had fallen asleep, collapsing on to the bare mattress two hours before his wife came in.

But eight hours had elapsed between the moment when he had fallen asleep and the moment when, after being turned out of the car by Lyusin, he had been abandoned on the road within twenty kilometres of Moscow. Those eight hours were to cost him dear.

Standing there alone on the road, he had regretted that he had kept control of himself and not hit Lyusin. What was he to do now? In spite of everything, the right thing would probably be to go to the checkpoint and try to explain how he came to be there and where he was going. But people do not always do the right thing.

Alone on the highway, Sintsov had cursed himself for getting into Lyusin's car. And yet he hadn't wanted to turn back. With Moscow not far away, he would get to his former editorial office in any case and he would get to it from this very spot where he had been abandoned by Comrade Lyusin. He would get there, and he would find his place in the fighting line!

In his despair and fury, he had rashly decided to try and reach his editorial office by avoiding all the checkpoints. If he failed, if they held him up, it would make little difference. One way or the other, he would have to prove that he wasn't a deserter and had no intention of being one.

He would almost certainly not have reached Moscow had it been one day earlier or one day later. But on that particular day, the sixteenth of October, the incredible had happened. Leaving the main road and by-passing the checkpoints, he had come to the familiar outskirts of the city and then, still unnoticed and undetained, had reached the very centre of Moscow. Later, when all this was a thing of the past and when anyone in his presence spoke of the sixteenth of October with venom or bitterness, Sintsov would maintain a stubborn silence. He found it intolerable to remember Moscow as it had been on that day, even as it is intolerable to see a loved one's face distorted with terror.

There were, of course, enough people doing everything in their power to prevent the surrender of Moscow—not only outside the city where troops were fighting to the death, but in the city too. And that is precisely why Moscow did not surrender. The position at the front outside the city, however, seemed to be taking the worst and most disastrous turn since the beginning of the war, and there were other people there that day ready in their despair to believe that the Germans were going to enter tomorrow.

As always at such fateful times, the firm faith and inconspicuous efforts of the first kind of people were not obvious to all, whereas the distraction, grief, horror and despair of the second were very much in evidence everywhere. This was what showed on the surface, and it could not have been otherwise; for tens of thousands of people, trying to escape from the Germans, streamed away from the city that day, inundating its streets and squares with a dense tide that surged to the railway stations and to the highroads leading to the east—although, to be fair, only a few thousands of those tens of thousands could rightly be condemned afterwards by history....

Sintsov walked along the streets of the city, where no one wanted anything to do with him on that terrible Moscow day, and when people were hunting their lost ones without success, banging at the locked doors of apartments, desperately waiting at cross-roads under clocks that had stopped, and screaming and sobbing in the turmoil of the squares outside the railway stations.

Sintsov had long since forgotten about Lyusin. His fury against the man now seemed insignificant and petty in the flood of grief which had overwhelmed him and was now sweeping him like a cork along the streets of Moscow. It was he himself he was cursing now, not Lyusin. If he had gone to the Special Department as he had originally intended, perhaps they would have given him a rifle back there, a hundred kilometres from Moscow where the city's fate was being decided. But to gain hope of this, he had to finish what he had begun and find the editorial office.

He finally turned off at the Nikitsky Gates, which were jammed with vehicles and people, into a cul-de-sac called the Khlynov Tupik, and went to the editorial offices of *Gudok*, which he had visited on occasion before the war.

Here, as everywhere else, there was a smell of burning, and charred paper was being whirled through the air by sudden gusts of wind. All the windows of the editorial office were completely masked by black-out blinds, and an old watchman in a black railway-workers' greatcoat was sitting at the padlocked door with a small-calibre rifle. He was taking no notice of the people as they scurried and bustled past him down the cul-de-sac with their possessions.

Sintsov went up to him and, although a negative reply seemed inevitable, he nevertheless asked the watchman whether a Front newspaper had arrived there. The watchman silently shook his head.

"Has *Gudok* left?" asked Sintsov, although it had clearly done so.

"What's it to you?" asked the watchman, looking up at last. "What papers have you got? Let's see them."

"What d'you want my papers for?" asked Sintsov.

"So that I'll know if it's alright to answer your question!" said the old man irritably.

Yes, *Gydok* had left, and the Front newspaper had not arrived yet, and there was no knowing when it would. That was clear. And if Sintsov continued to hang around the cul-de-sac and stare at the office windows, even although he knew the answer, it was only because he hadn't the slightest idea what to do next.

It suddenly occurred to him that if the editorial offices weren't in Moscow, then he should at least try to look up Serpilin. He had, after all, been taken to hospital here, in Moscow....

"But how are you going to find him?" asked another, more sober voice. "What hospital? With all this going on here, who's going to tell you where Serpilin is?"

The Army Political Directorate building stood not far away, on the corner of Arbat Square. He remembered how he had been there in 1940 before being posted to Grodno, and thought: "Go there, perhaps?" But who would let him in without documents? And were the staff still in occupation? Hardly...."

Then there flashed through his mind again the impossible thought which he had long since pushed away: "What if Masha's still in Moscow in spite of everything?" And this impossible thought, although he fought it stubbornly, drew him from the Khlynov Tupik towards the Usachevka, to the house which he had left to go to war.

Halfway there, he again forced himself to stop thinking about the impossible: there was no one in the flat, of course. He wasn't deluding himself. He just needed somewhere to sit down for an hour and pull himself together. If no one had the key, he would sit on the staircase! Then he would get up again and go.... Yes, but where? Straight to the Military Commissariat. He would go and tell them, without going into details, that he was a volunteer, that he wanted to be signed on.... After all, they were forming units of some sort: they were sending people straight to the front!... He could explain himself after the first battle! It wouldn't matter any more then. All that would matter would be that they had accepted him and sent him to the front! Of course, that was the thing to do!

But at the last moment, when he had already reached the house doors and had suddenly remembered all the details of how Masha, in June, behind that window on the second floor, had helped him pack for the front, everything else went out of his mind except his thoughts of her and how she might suddenly be there.

The entrance doors had been wedged wide open with bricks, and the pavement was littered with what had once been an armchair. After all that Sintsov had seen on his way through Moscow, this could hardly surprise him.

He kicked aside the bits of wood, went up to the second floor, and banged on the door with his fist. Long after he had realised that there was no one at home, he went on thumping at the door with his face pressed up against it, and all his sudden, overwhelming despair went into that desperate and frenzied banging on the door.

Finally, he straightened up, turned round with a gesture of resignation, and stumbled his way down the staircase.

A lorry was backing out of the gateway with a load of household possessions and bags. It was piled so high that the articles on top were catching the underside of the arch. A man was hopping about feverishly on the roadway, throwing his hands into the air and shouting: "Left, left, now straighten out, straighten out!..." The lorry finally drove through. The man stopped dancing about on the road and wiped his perspiring face with the sleeve of his jacket. Sintsov recognised him. It was the local house supervisor—Klyushkin or Kruzhkin. Sintsov had known him ever since he had begun courting Masha but couldn't quite remember his name.

"Listen!" shouted Sintsov. "Listen!" he repeated even more loudly, and, going up to the house supervisor, he seized him so roughly with his weakened, but still strong, hand by the collar that the man's jacket ripped open at the seam.

"What's the matter with you? Have you gone mad?" yelled the house supervisor, wrenching himself free. He was about to hit Sintsov, then recognised him and said: "Was that you banging up there?"

"Yes."

"Your wife's gone away!"

"Where?"

"How should I know where everybody's gone!" said the house supervisor, and he climbed into the lorry. "They've burned the registers, they've burned everything today, they've even burned the telephone books! Everything!" he repeated almost frantically from the lorry. "Your wife left in July. She was in Army uniform."

"Where is she then?" shouted Sintsov, following behind the lorry as it moved off.

"Hey, hey, stop a moment!" shouted the house supervisor suddenly, banging the cab roof with the flat of his hand. "Hey!" he shouted to Sintsov as the lorry braked. "I've got a duplicate of your key!"

He tore open his briefcase and pulled out a large ring of bent wire holding about two dozen keys.

"Which is yours? Take it, only hurry up!"

Sintsov went up and began sorting uncertainly through the keys.

"Come on, come on," urged the house supervisor with a glance round at the driver who had poked his head impatiently out of the cab. "Oh, go on, take the lot!" he shouted, and he dropped the whole bunch.

Sintsov missed it, and it fell on to the road with a crash.

"Where are you going?" asked Sintsov as the side of the lorry slid past.

"Where everybody else is!" shouted the house supervisor. "I'm a Party member. D'you expect me to stay here and wait for the Germans to hang me?"

"A fine Party member you are!" thought Sintsov, picking the keys up off the road. The image of that strong, hairy hand handing the keys down over the side of the lorry was to leave a profound and bitter impression on his mind.

As he examined each of the keys in turn, it suddenly occurred to him that Masha might have left a note for him in the flat just in case.... This thought of a note so obsessed him that he dashed up the stairs, unlocked the door and ran into the flat, leaving the bunch of keys in the lock.

There was no note—neither on the dining-room table with the familiar folk-craft ash-tray—a wooden boat with a swan's head—nor in the other room on the bed, on which lay nothing but a bare striped mattress and an uncovered pillow with the feathers sticking through.

The wardrobe was locked. Sintsov tugged at the handle, but it refused to budge. There was a thick layer of dust on everything—the floor, the chairs, and the bare table. The sitting-room ventilation window, with the pane cracked, was swinging loose in the wind. He shut it, sat down, and let his big, worn hands slump heavily on to the table top.

Everything that he and all his comrades had been through so determinedly ever since Mogilev made sense or failed to make sense depending on the answer to one simple question: were we or were we not going to win this war that had begun so badly for us? Apart from the roll of honour that he had given to Shmakov as they broke out of encirclement near Yelnia, he had inwardly noted the long list of sacrifices made before his eyes, usually without a moment's hesitation, by men paying for victory with their lives. And now, before his very eyes again, in contrast to all those sacrifices, there was a question mark looming over Moscow as tremendous and as black as tragedy itself!

Perhaps in some other state of mind he would have distinguished between the likelihood, appalling as it may have been, of losing Moscow and the possibility of an irrevocable defeat which would mean the end of everything. But at the present moment, his soul was like a boat which has been so heavily overloaded that it has finally begun to founder. And on top of all that, this silent, empty flat—no wife, no child, no father, no brother—no one!

The key to the flat had been flung at him by a man who was leaving because tomorrow, as he thought, the Germans would be entering Moscow. And that man was running away from Moscow—Sintsov was ready to swear it—and was certainly running away without orders, for all his bull-like neck, and his strong, hairy hands which would have been better employed holding a rifle....

No, Sintsov was not envious of that big brute who was so anxious to save his skin; but he was oppressed by the thought that he himself had no Party card in his pocket and couldn't cross three streets right now to go to the District Party Committee where he had once received his Party card, and say: "I am Communist Sintsov. I've come to defend Moscow. Give me a rifle and tell me where to go!"

He thought about this with acute distress, and went on thinking about it until, as often happens with the most crucial decisions in our lives, it suddenly occurred to him: "But why can't I? Why? Why can't I go to the District Committee and say: 'I'm Communist Sintsov and I want to defend Moscow'? Have I stopped being a Communist, or something? That dumb ox on the lorry has the nerve to call himself a Party member. But I daren't call myself one! Even if they didn't believe me then, even if someone else refuses to believe me now, at least I know who I am. At least I know that I haven't stopped being a Communist! Why am I thinking of going to the Special Department, to the editorial offices, to the Military Commissariat, and why am I afraid of going to my own District Committee, where I joined the Party? Who can stop me from doing so? Who has the right? And, above all, who has deprived me of the right to go?"

He got up from the table, swaying with weakness. He went into the kitchen and spent some time fumbling about on the shelves in the dark until, to his joy, he found a half-loaf of bread as dry and as hard as a brick. He went to the sink to see if the water was on. It was. Leaning against the wall, he began softening the bread under the tap and hungrily devoured the wet pieces one after another as they crumbled in his fingers.

He was just finishing the last morsel when the anti-aircraft guns opened up outside. A searchlight beam flashed across the window and the house was shaken by an exploding bomb. Sintsov turned off the tap and, listening to the anti-aircraft fire, again fell prey to the horrible thought that had occurred to him several times that day already and compared with which his own plight seemed utterly insignificant: "Are we really not going to stop them? Are we going to surrender Moscow?"

"I must go now!" he whispered to himself, thinking of the District Committee again; but as he drew away from the wall, he felt that he hadn't the strength to get there. He must lie down for a moment. He must lie down and then go. Feeling his way along the wall with one hand, he went into the bedroom, caught hold of the cold, nickel-plated head of the bed, and fell full-length on to the bare mattress.

"I'll just lie down for a moment and then go," he whispered determinedly. "I'll lie down for fifteen minutes and then go...."

When Masha began waking him, he turned over and groaned in his sleep—threateningly and hoarsely at first, and then so piteously that it almost broke Masha's heart. She was prepared to sit over him like this for another hour without attempting to disturb him, but he was already waking up. Something that prevented him from sleeping any longer was surfacing from the depths of his tired consciousness. Still not awake, he stirred, flung his arms open, let them fall heavily on Masha's shoulders, and suddenly, as if something had hit him, opened his eyes. And in them she saw neither sleep nor surprise—only an infinite happiness such as Masha had never seen in anyone's eyes until that moment and such as she was never to see again.

Had Sintsov been asked what kind of happiness he wanted most in this life, he would still never have been able to think of anything other than that beloved, tear-stained face pressed to his cheek. All the horror of many days, and the most horrible of all—today—suddenly fled somewhere thousands of miles away. And he was not afraid any more.

He held Masha by the shoulders and, drawing her closer, he smiled. His smile was not agonised or pathetic, it was his ordinary, usual smile. As she looked into her husband's emaciated and horribly altered face, she decided that his appearance, which had frightened her so badly at first, didn't really matter.

With all the unreasoning directness and lucidity of which her mind, quite unaccustomed to vacillation, was capable, she had hastened to explain to herself everything that had happened. He had been in command of a partisan detachment and had been summoned to Moscow by aeroplane. She gave no further thought to why he had been in command, and why he in particular should have been sent for by aeroplane. Only yesterday at the school they had been discussing how several partisan commanders had been flown back to Moscow straight from behind the German lines and had been driven from the airfield to make their reports in the clothes they had been wearing.

Where hadn't Sintsov been, and what hadn't he been doing in her thoughts throughout all these months! But, having found this explanation for her husband's appearance, she thought of him further in no other way.

Sintsov released her shoulders, half sat up, and slumped sideways against the wall. The movement had cost him so much effort that his face went white.

"What's wrong with your head? Are you wounded?" asked Masha.

Tense in the expectation of pain, he removed his fur hat with both hands. But this time the bandages didn't stick to it, there was no pain, and so Masha, looking into his eyes, believed him when he said that it was nothing but a scratch.

"Perhaps I could change the bandage for you?"

He said there was no need. It was three days since the wound had been dressed and it would be best to leave well alone.

"How are Mother and Tanya?" he asked; but he had already seen the answer on her face before she could say anything. She had no more news, and knew nothing other than what they had both been aware of in June when they had parted at Byelorussky Station.

He didn't ask any more questions. What was there to ask? He merely held her hands for several minutes without speaking, just as he had done when they had said good-bye through the railings....

Masha looked thinner. Her hair was cut shorter than before, and in her army uniform with the rather broad, ill-fitting tunic collar she had changed from a woman back into a girl again.

"So you joined the army after all," he said at last.

"Yes."

"I thought you would. I didn't even expect to meet you here."

"So it was God who reunited us," said Masha in a broken voice.

"Have you been a believer long, then?" he asked in an attempt at a joke; but she didn't even realise that he was joking.

"As a matter of fact," she continued in the same broken voice, "I'm only free till morning. I haven't been here for a month. And for you and I, on the same day...."

"It means it was very important for us to see one another," said Sintsov, and his tired face lit up with the familiar, good-natured smile of a man older than her who knew so much more than she knew herself. "Don't be surprised. Tell me why you came, and why you haven't been here for a month, and what branch of the service you're in, and where...."

Masha made a half-hearted attempt to protest. All that had happened to her was of little interest. But he took her by the wrists and gently, but firmly, stopped her.

"I'll tell you all about myself, but it's a long story. Now you tell me at once, even if only in two words: where are you stationed? Haven't you been to the front yet?"

Masha looked at his gaunt, tired face, and at the sharp, unfamiliar lines near the cracked lips. She looked into his eyes, in which she also sensed something—she couldn't define it exactly, but it hadn't been there before—and she realised that she must either say nothing or tell him everything. Sparing of her words, because she felt it was more important to wash him and put him to bed properly, she told him briefly about herself, disobeying outright all the strict instructions she had received at school not to tell anyone, anywhere, under any circumstances.... The truth is that she never even gave them a thought, because neither the present circumstances nor the man to whom she was telling all this could have been envisaged in any instructions.

Sintsov listened to her, still holding her hands and conscious how they trembled every time she wanted to make some gesture or other while telling her story. She told him everything except for two items: she was to be dropped behind the enemy lines in the next few days, and there would be a lorry waiting for her round the corner tomorrow morning at seven.

He listened to her, his face expressionless but seeming a shade paler. If he had heard all this three months ago, let alone before the outbreak of war, he would no doubt have been horrified at the thought of what lay in store for Masha and would have said so forthwith, fearing neither to offend her nor quarrel with her.... But now, after all he had been through, although his heart was full of concern for her, he did not feel himself entitled to say a word. While in encirclement, he had seen women doing no less than what Masha herself had undertaken. Why shouldn't she have the right to this? Because he loved her, and not them?

"Well now," he said thoughtfully, pulling himself together when Masha had finished and was looking anxiously into his eyes. "Perhaps you might meet my father or brother somewhere behind the lines...."

"D'you think they didn't get away from Vyazma in time?" asked Masha.

"I don't think they did," said Sintsov brokenly, wincing at the memories her question had revived. "I don't think they did," he repeated. "Like so many others." He brought his face nearer to hers and, in a different tone of voice, said gently and calmly as if to a little girl: "You probably don't realise the full implications. It's not just something happening to you and me; it's happening to millions. It's the war that's done it, and only war can put things right again."

And a cruel expression, new to Masha, blazed up in his eyes and then died down again.

"Are you very tired?" asked Masha.

Sintsov shut his eyes and opened them again.

"Did you have a hard time of it?"

Sintsov nodded almost imperceptibly. His head was spinning and he was trying to pull himself together.

"When did you fly into Moscow? Today?" asked Masha softly. When he had closed his eyes, she had assumed he must be remembering something, and she was afraid of disturbing his thoughts.

And because she asked him so quietly, and because he had been fighting a spell of dizziness at that moment, he did not notice the word "fly", which would have startled him, but only heard the last word—"today"—and nodded weakly.

"I'm going to undress you now, wash you, and put you to bed," said Masha. Then she took fright at the word "wash", in case he should take it into his head that she found him unpleasant and disagreeable in his present dirty state—and she impulsively took his heavy, chafed, blood-stained hand and kissed it passionately over and over again.

"Let's get washed, shall we?" she asked, raising her eyes.

What could he say?

"Yes, of course, by all means!" What else could he want but for those small, strong and tender fingers, which he had thought about so many times, to undress him, wash him, and put him to bed?

"As soon as I saw you, I put some water on the stove to heat up," said Masha.

"Straightaway? You are a sensible one!" said Sintsov with a smile.

"I'm not sensible," said Masha. "I just want to help you. You seem very weak to me."

"Yes, I am very weak," said Sintsov. He took her clean little hand in his own big, grimy fist and felt a momentary desire to squeeze it until it hurt her.

"I completely forgot. Perhaps you want something to eat?" she asked.

"No, not at the moment," he said, amazed to find that he was indeed not hungry. "Go into the kitchen, and I'll get undressed and join you." Then, noticing through the doorway Masha's greatcoat draped over a chair, he added: "Just give me your coat and I'll put it over me."

He waited until she had brought him the greatcoat and gone out, and then, following her with his eyes, he put his feet on the floor and began pulling off his boots.

Then he stood up in the basin in the kitchen, and Masha washed him as a mother washes her children, or as old nurses in hospital wash the sick and wounded.

When Masha began washing him, she immediately noticed two white scars on his side.

"Were you wounded?" she asked softly. He nodded.

"Give me a mug of water, please," said Sintsov after Masha, holding him under the armpits like an invalid and supporting him with her shoulder, had led him up to the bed and set him down on it.

While Masha was fetching the water, he lay down. The sheets were clean, with the folds still showing, and Masha's greatcoat was spread over them in addition to the blanket. He touched the clean linen shirt that she had put on him after washing him, then sniffed it. After several months lying with Masha's things, it smelt of Eau-de-Cologne. Another shirt like it had been drawn over the pillow in lieu of a pillow-slip.

Masha brought him his mug of water, closed the door while he drank it, raised the window blinds, and then, taking the mug from him, undressed quickly and lay down beside him, shivering slightly and tucking the skirt of the greatcoat under her side.

"Why aren't you sleeping? You're tired out, I can tell!"

"Yes, but I can't sleep."

"Why are you sitting up?"

"I can talk better that way. I must tell you all about it ... I want you to know...."

"Later. Better lie down. You're tired. I'm scared for you, you're so tired. Are the searchlights bothering you? I'll get up and pull down the blind...."

"Nothing's bothering me."

"Well then, cover your shoulders. Here, take the greatcoat. You'll freeze. D'you really want to sit up?"

"Yes.... You don't know what it means to me, seeing you today...."

"Why don't I know?"

"You just don't know. And you won't either, until I've told you all I've been through. But when I tell you about it, then you will. If only you realised how grateful I feel to you just now."

"Grateful? What for?"

"For your love."

"Nonsense! Can anyone feel grateful for that?"

"Yes."

She sensed that he was disturbed by something else and not just by their reunion, but she couldn't guess what it might be. She was herself full of gratitude to him for being here, for having fought, for having been wounded, and for having survived, for being tired, yet for still having the same strong, good hands, and for loving her as before.... She was grateful to him for all this.... But she sincerely couldn't understand why he should be feeling grateful to her. Surely it wasn't because she had kissed his hands and washed his feet, or because she loved him as always, or perhaps even more than ever before?... After all, it was only natural. How could it be otherwise?

And he was indeed conscious of an overwhelming gratitude to her for the strength of her love and because, having experienced that strength anew he was now able to tell her about everything that had cost him so much mental agony that he had nearly reached the end of his tether.

He sighed and smiled in the dark, as if saying farewell with that smile to all that was good and tender, to all that had already passed between them that night. She didn't see him smile, but she sensed it, and asked:

"Are you smiling? What are you smiling at?"

"You," he said.

Then, suddenly serious, he said that the dearest thing to him on this earth was her faith and help at such a difficult time for him.

"Why difficult?"

"Difficult," he repeated. Then he suddenly asked: "What did you think when you saw me like this in someone else's tunic and jacket? You probably thought I'd come back from a spell with the partisans. Am I right?"

"Yes," she said.

"No, it's much worse than that." And he repeated, "Much, much worse than that!"

She shuddered, and her whole body tensed. He thought she was going to ask him what he meant, but she didn't. She only half sat up, like him. All the time he was speaking, she was trembling inwardly, whereas he talked for the most part in a steady, quiet voice which, had she not known him so well, would have seemed calm.

However difficult it may have been for him, he told her everything consecutively, right from the beginning, otherwise she would not have understood.

He told her about the night near Borisov and about the crazy Red Armyman he had shot; about the Bobruisk highway and the death of Kozyrev; about the battles for Mogilev and the two and a half months in encirclement. He told her everything that he had seen and thought about: the magnificent heroism of the men and their indescribable bewilderment at the horror and futility of what was happening; their fortitude and fearlessness, and the terrible questions that they were asking themselves and one another: why had things turned out like this and who was to blame? He told her everything, sparing her feelings no more than the war had spared his. He made her shoulder, in those two or three hours, all the weight of the bitterness and all the burden of the experiences which had descended on him in the last four months, and he did so without allowing for the effect of his words or the extent of her ignorance, which was very considerable, even though she knew about the war from the bulletins and newspapers, and had eyes, ears, and her own native common sense to tell her that events were probably far more terrible than might seem from what was being written and said. But this was all one thing, and what Sintsov was telling her was something else, infinitely terrible and infinitely shocking.

Masha sat there in bed and, in an attempt to control her trembling, sank her teeth into the corner of the pillow which she had covered with her husband's shirt instead of a pillow-case.

Had he been able to see her, he would have noticed that she was sitting up in bed as white as a sheet, her hands clasped and held to her breast as if she were silently imploring him to stop, to spare her, to give her respite. But he couldn't see her face. With his eyes fixed on the wall and, one hand gripping the back of the bed, the other balled into a fist and relentlessly beating the air in front of him, he talked and talked about everything that had accumulated in his soul and about which he had no one else to tell except her.

Only when he described the last battle outside Yelnia and his happiness on the night of the breakthrough—only then did her tense, frozen face relax as she breathed a sigh of relief. For the first time, she felt a little better.

"What's the matter?" he asked.

"It's all right, carry on," she said, controlling herself and thinking that the worst was already over.

But the worst was yet to come and, not noticing that she was on the verge of emotional exhaustion and without giving her any respite, he began telling her about the worst part of all. And now here he was, having endured what he had endured and having done what he had done, but having left undone what he had not been able to do. And if, after all that, he still had to answer for his confounded bad luck, then he would answer for it anywhere and before anyone without hanging his head in shame. Especially now that he had seen her!

"Fate, fate! To hell with that fate of mine!" he almost shouted, with a tremor in his voice. I can't be bothered with that when things are so desperate. Whatever my fate may be, I have to go and fight for Moscow, and that's all! Haven't I the right to, then? Yes, I have! And another question—" his voice finally broke, and for the first time in Masha's memory he completely lost his self-control. "When I went to that senior lieutenant and told him everything exactly as it had happened, why couldn't he believe me—and he a man who's seen nothing in his time, and never killed a single German, and has only just arrived from the Military Commissariat? Why didn't he want to believe me? I saw it with my own eyes—he didn't want to believe me! But why? Why don't they believe me?"

"Take it easy!" said Masha.

"I can't!" he shouted, and he snatched back his hand as she tried to stroke it.

She forgave him his rudeness. What else could she do but forgive him at such a moment?

"Take it easy," repeated Masha. Now that Sintsov had blown up and started shouting, she suddenly became calm, her own problems disappeared somewhere deep down inside, as did the questions which had risen to her lips: "How? Why?..."

"Take it easy," she said for the third time, feeling that, for all his terrible experiences in the war, she was now the stronger of the two and should try to help him. "What are you saying, my dear? Don't talk like that, please don't!" Instead of arguing with him, she began imploring him. And her tenderness mollified his fury. He quietened down, moved away from the wall, buried his face in the pillow, and lay motionless like that for a long time.

Masha reached out and touched his shoulder.

"Wait, don't touch me!" said he, his voice muffled by the pillow. "I'll be all right in a moment."

She thought he was weeping, but he wasn't.

He finally turned over, lay on his back, and gently touched Masha's hand.

"So what am I to do now?" he asked. His voice was quiet and steady again, as if he were a different man from the one who had been speaking three minutes ago.

"Why are you taking it like that, just because they don't believe you?" said Masha, instead of giving a direct answer. What he had said about not being believed had shaken her more than anything else. "What d'you mean they don't believe you? I do."

"Forgive me...."

"I didn't mean it that way."

"Forgive me anyway...."

He fell silent. So did Masha. He thought she was wondering how to answer his question about what he should do next. But her mind was elsewhere. She was thinking about all he had been through, and she was asking herself: put her in his place, and would she be able to endure it all? And she felt that the answer was no. He was asking her what to do next, yet he had done much for which she herself would never have had the strength. And this meant that there were two different sets of standards—the one that had existed before the war, and another, quite different, by which, although he was cursing those who refused to believe him, he felt himself at fault somewhere at the bottom of his mind. And what awesome and difficult standards they were!.. She remembered all the sleepless nights when she had wondered what was happening to him out there at the front. Many a time she had imagined that he had been taken prisoner, or was under fire, or had been wounded and was tossing about in delirium and crying out to her: "Masha! Masha!"—and his teeth had been chattering on the brim of his tin mug. And now nearly everything she had imagined had been the truth: he had been under fire, had been wounded, had been taken prisoner, had felt thirsty, and had cried: "Masha! Masha!", had nearly choked with thirst, and there had been no one to dress his wound.

"Why don't you say something? What d'you think I ought to do next?" asked Sintsov.

She moved up a little closer and, resting his bandaged head on her knees, said:

"I don't know. I should think you know best yourself."

And, indeed, she didn't know what answer to give him. But she knew what really mattered most: he must feel how much she loved him. This was the answer he needed most and, strengthened by her moral support, he suddenly told her simply and briefly that he had already decided before she arrived. He would go to the District Party Committee in the morning and he would tell them everything, and then they could decide for themselves what to do with him. He was only worried about one thing: something might go stupidly wrong at the last moment and he might be held up by a patrol on the way.

"I'll go with you," said Masha impulsively before she had time to remember that she couldn't do anything of the kind. The curfew was in force at night and that confounded lorry would be coming for her at seven o'clock precisely!

"You mean you'll take me by the hand and lead me there like a little boy?" He smiled gently in the dark. "All right, we'll see."

He was his former self again—big, strong, and calm.

"I completely forgot one thing," he said, apparently

smiling again. "Have you something to eat? I'm absolutely famished."

"Why didn't you say so when I asked you, silly?"

"I wasn't hungry then. I found a hunk of pre-war bread before you got here. I had to soften it under the tap."

"You poor dear!" said Masha. "I've got a few biscuits in my greatcoat and a tin of something, only I don't know what."

"What's the difference?" laughed Sintsov. "Even if they're only anchovies, we can wash them down with five mugs of water each and that'll be plenty."

"You stay there," said Masha, putting her bare feet down on the floor. "I'll go and fetch it."

"I'm coming too," he said, also putting his feet down.

They both stood up. She threw the greatcoat over her shoulders, he wrapped himself up in the blanket, and they both went into the kitchen and sat down at the table.

Masha produced a packet of biscuits that were already beginning to crumble, and Sintsov, with some difficulty, extracted a big can of meat from her other greatcoat pocket.

"I was wondering what that weight was on my legs all the time," he laughed.

"I completely forgot about it," said Masha.

Sintsov opened the can. They sat facing each other and ate the meat, digging it out on the end of a knife and spreading it on pieces of biscuit. Then Sintsov drank up the remainder of the gravy out of the can, smiled, and looked across at Masha.

"Well, we must look a real pair of idiots right now sitting barefoot opposite one another in the kitchen...."

He yawned and smiled apologetically.

"You know, I ought to be ashamed of myself, but now that I've had something to eat, I feel sleepy again, like a starved dog...."

"What is there to be ashamed about?" asked Masha.

And to make him feel better, she told him a white lie and said that she was feeling sleepy too.

They went back into the bedroom and lay down as they had always loved to when they were sleeping together—he on his back with his right arm thrown out, and she on her side with her cheek pressed to his big, strong, protective arm. But no sooner had they lain down than the anti-aircraft guns began banging with growing frequency in the sky.

"We won't get any sleep now," said Masha sadly, thinking of him and not herself. As before, she was not really feeling sleepy.

"Why won't we?" said Sintsov drowsily. "We'll drop off in a jiffy...."

And a minute later Masha sensed that he was indeed fast asleep. He had sometimes dropped off like that in the old days too, except that his breathing had been lighter and steadier; but now it was chesty and laboured.

"He's not feeling well at all," thought Masha uneasily.

During the whole of the air-raid alert and for an hour or two after, Masha lay awake, her cheek pressed up against her husband's big warm arm, thinking and thinking about what he had told her.

It wasn't that she hadn't already known about the realities of war. On the contrary, she had known a great deal, having heard bits and pieces at second or third hand; but she had probably needed to hear it all at once, and from the man lying at her side, in order to feel the full weight of the burden that had fallen not just on him and on herself, but on everybody else. Yes, everybody! That was the most horrible thing about it!

"What a tragedy!" she said aloud, not thinking of the two of them, but of everything in general, of the war as a whole. As she thought about the fall of Vyazma and the latest news bulletin, she reproached herself bitterly for having covered herself with the tarpaulin after the documents check at the gates and for having ridden through Moscow without even looking to see what was happening round her....

"Just as if I couldn't have cared less!"

She now realised from her husband's story that a great many people had died during those four months, thinking not of themselves, but of the need to stop the Germans. Yet the Germans had taken Vyazma and were approaching Moscow, which meant that if they were to be stopped, then a great deal more had to be done than had already been achieved by those who had died in the attempt but had failed! And she would have to do the same in the job which lay ahead of her. She was alarmed at herself for having been so badly shaken by her husband's story when she was going to see it all with her own eyes and, perhaps, have to witness worse things without a tremor!

Then she remembered that she hadn't yet collected her things together, and she must do this now so as not to rob him of a single minute.

She lifted her head away from him, and he flexed and unflexed his numb arm in his sleep.

21-825

She got up, went to the window, drew back the blind and, half opening the door into the passage and, still feeling incapable of doing anything else, went back to the bed, sat on the greatcoat which had slipped on to the floor, and stared at her sleeping husband's face.

His forehead was beaded with sweat, and his hands were resting feebly on the blanket. The two sharp, unfamiliar lines running from nose to chin had not been smoothed out even by sleep, as if something had rudely entered into the life of this good man, had entered into his life and might never leave it again.

Masha remembered the furious, spine-chilling hatred with which he had spoken about the Germans during his narrative; then she thought about this night, which was not yet over, and she sighed. Tomorrow, or the day after tomorrow, she would have to fly behind the German lines, and she hadn't told him to take precautions. She had thought about it, but hadn't bothered. But she should have done, because if, while working as an agent behind the German lines, it should suddenly transpire that she was expecting a baby, she would be in a fix! And however embarrassing it might be for her to mention it, she must nevertheless ask the school commissar that very day what she should do in such a contingency.

"Yes, today," she thought, glancing at her watch. "Today, and as soon as possible."

Her watch said six o'clock. It was time to get ready.

Masha opened the wardrobe and dug out from the back corner what she had already decided was the most suitable article of clothing—a rough old coat that she had brought back with her from the Far East and that she had been keeping in camphor. Then she rummaged about on the other shelves and fetched out a moth-eaten headscarf and some linen of her mother's that needed taking in a little.

She tied all this up in an old tablecloth and put it on the table. She then washed herself unhurriedly under the kitchen tap and dried herself with a Turkish towel until her skin glowed. Then, just as unhurriedly, she put on her uniform, combed her hair without the aid of a mirror and, glancing at her watch—it was now half past six—she sat down on the bed.

"Vanya!" She dug her nose into the pillow next to her husband's head and gently pushed her cheek against his. "Vanya!"

She thought it would take him some time to come to, but he awoke immediately and sat up.

"Ah! It's you!" And he gave her his good-natured smile.

Then he noticed that she was already dressed, and asked in alarm:

"Are you going? Where are you off to?"

She explained that a lorry was coming for her at seven and would be waiting round the corner and she mustn't miss it, because her leave only lasted till nine in the morning.

"Oh, well.... Maybe it's better that way," he said. "You go, and I'll wait till daylight, and then I'll go where I told you I would yesterday. I'll get dressed now. Leave the room for a moment, I'm still a bit shy of you."

"I'll turn my back," she said and, going up to the window, she partly opened the blind and looked outside. It was still dark.

"You're a funny one," she said. "You weren't embarrassed yesterday, and now look at you!"

"That's the way it is," he said as he put on his clothes.

He clumped into the kitchen in his boots. As she stood at the window, she heard him splashing his face under the tap.

"Well," he said, coming back into the bedroom and hanging the damp towel on the head of the bed. "Whatever happens there at the District Committee, whether they believe me or not, or whether they send me to the front or whether the worst comes to the worst—" he controlled himself in an effort to speak more calmly—"and they don't send me, I'll need your address anyway. I'll write and tell you how I get on."

Masha was in a quandary. What could she say to him? That she was flying off tomorrow or the day after? She didn't want to do that. Say nothing? She was incapable of that too.

"How much longer will you be at that school of yours?" he asked, and he glanced at the things bundled up in the tablecloth. "What's that?"

"Clothes. I've collected up a few things. That's what I got leave for," said Masha. Caught unawares, she hadn't the presence of mind to lie to him.

"Aha.... Now I get it. So you'll be off soon?"

She nodded.

"Give me your address anyway. What d'you have at the school—a mail-box, or a field post number?"

There was a yellowed newspaper lying on the window-sill. He tore off a corner and wrote down Masha's field post number with a pencil stub that was lying on the sideboard, put the piece of paper in his tunic pocket, smiled, and said:

"The only document I have."

He paused, and then, anxious to reassure Masha, said: "I might be able to trace Serpilin through the District Committee. I told you about him."

Masha nodded.

"Provided he's here and alive. Then things'll be much easier for me. I don't suppose he'll pat me on the back for turning up in Moscow like this, but I think he'll give me a reference for what happened before. I need everything I can get."

"I can't imagine anyone not believing you," said Masha.

"I can," said Sintsov, looking straight at her. And his eyes looked somehow strange—good-natured and yet evil at the same time. Then, not wanting to talk about himself any more, he mentioned her brother. "Where's Pavel? Still in Chita?"

"Yes, I had a letter from him not long ago."

"Is he still furious about not being in action?"

"Yes, he is.... Listen, Vanya," said Masha, again conscious of her emotional dependence on him. "What's going to happen to Moscow?"

"I don't know..." he said. "I'm not a prophet. I just can't imagine what's going to happen. But don't think we're going to lose the war. If that's what you're thinking, forget it! Everything I've told you is the truth. And I'm telling you this now: we're not going to lose the war! Not for anything!"

He said this with great force and, as it seemed, alarmed for Masha in case he should have given her cause for doubt.

"That's what I think too," said Masha, looking straight at him. "I just wanted to be sure of my own feelings."

Her face suddenly looked remote and preoccupied, and he noticed this at once.

"What's the matter?"

"The lorry's come. I can hear it."

She hurriedly put on her greatcoat, looked round, felt about on the table, found the torch, thrust it into her pocket, and only then, when she was fully dressed in greatcoat and fur hat, did she throw her arms round Sintsov's neck and stand clinging to him for a whole minute, unable to speak a word.

During that minute, as he stood holding her in his arms, he felt completely estranged from everything connected with himself personally, from all his troubles, past and present. All that remained was an infinite fear for Masha because she was flying behind the German lines, because she would be leaving soon, and because no power on earth would be able to tell him how she was getting on over there and he wouldn't be able to lift a finger to help her....

"Will you see me to the lorry?" she said, breaking away from him at last. "It's just round the corner."

"No," he said. "I don't want your people to see me. Don't let on to anyone that you've met me. Later, when I've got myself straightened out and can face the world again, you can talk about it if you want, but not now. Your job's a ticklish one. They could sack you for having a husband like me...."

"If only they *would* sack you," was the treacherous thought that flashed through his mind, but he suppressed it immediately.

"You mustn't talk like that!"

He embraced her, kissed her, let her go, and even pushed her towards the door. Without turning round, she picked up her bundle and went out into the passage. But just as she was opening the door, he caught up with her, turned her round to face him and asked:

"Tell me, where are you flying to? I want at least some idea of where you're going to be."

"Somewhere near Smolensk," she said.

"Be careful," he said in a choking voice. "Be cunning as a vixen, as a demon, as the devil, but don't let them get you, I implore you. D'you hear? I implore you. I don't want anything, nothing else matters ... nothing else matters except that you stay alive.... You understand?"

He was shaking her by the shoulders like a madman and saying things which at any other time would have sounded foolish to both of them.

Then suddenly his manner changed, and he smiled, offered her his hand and, after waiting until she had put her hand in his, he pressed it affectionately and firmly, but not so hard that it hurt.

"Till we meet again, Masha! Masha, my love ... Masha, Masha...."

And, letting go of her hand, he turned round and went back into the room.

She went out, hurriedly slammed the door behind her, and ran down the stairs.

Out in the courtyard, she involuntarily glanced back up at her window as she ran. It was wide open. In the faint grey light of the approaching dawn, she dimly made out her husband's face. He was not waving to her or shouting. He was simply standing at the window and silently watching her go....

At ten o'clock in the morning that day, Masha went into the tiny adjutant's room adjoining the office of the head of the school. The adjutant was not there. Masha waited for a few minutes, sighed, tugged her tunic straight, and knocked on the inner door.

"Come in!" said a voice.

Masha entered, closed the door behind her, and said what she was used to saying after three months at the school:

"Comrade Colonel, permission to speak."

"How d'you do, Artemyeva," said the man at the desk, looking up from his papers. "What can I do for you?"

"A personal matter, Comrade Colonel."

"Couldn't you go to the commissar?"

"The commissar's left for Moscow, Comrade Colonel, and I must see someone urgently."

"Sit down, then, and wait." And the head of the school, Colonel Shmelev, buried his nose in his papers again.

"Perhaps I'm in your way, Comrade Colonel? I'll go out," said Masha.

"If you were in my way, I'd say so," replied Shmelev without looking up. Masha sat on a chair by the wall and waited.

Colonel Shmelev was new to the school. The former head had left a week ago. Rumour had it that he had flown off on a special mission, and Colonel Shmelev had appeared in his place the next day. He had arrived from hospital after recovering from a wound, and had been prowling about the school corridors with amazing speed and agility for a man on crutches trying to walk with a wounded leg.

On the second day, he impressed everybody with his astonishing memory for names and faces, and yet in spite of all this, Masha had taken a dislike to him. In her opinion, he was too cheerful, garrulous and facetious for the job which they were being taught to do. When talking, he sometimes stuttered comically, jerked his head and winked. Masha knew that his wink was not in fun, but was due to shell-shock. She had seen two Orders of the Red Banner on the colonel's chest and knew that he had been wounded at the front in the present war. And yet she had been reluctant to come and see him. If what she wanted to say could have kept until the next day, she would certainly have waited for the return of the commissar, a rather gloomy individual who rarely smiled and said little. She found him more confidence-inspiring. She sat and waited, watching Shmelev. This time, he did not stammer, wink, smile, or crack jokes. He sat in silence and wrote with a pair of spectacles on his nose—Masha had never seen him wearing them before. His curly hair was heavily streaked with grey, and his evasive, animated, smiling face now looked tired, expressionless, and old.

Probably forgetting that Masha was there, Shmelev sighed heavily twice, frowned, rubbed his brow vigorously, as if driving away some unpleasant thought, and went on writing.

Masha had not yet told anyone that she had met her husband. In reply to the agitated Nusia, who had been waiting by the lorry, she had merely said that she didn't want to answer any questions.

Even now she had not quite recovered and was even glad that the head of the school was giving her this respite.

Shmelev finished writing, sealed the packet and, ringing the bell for his adjutant, ordered him to take it to Major Karpov, deputy head of the school, and inform him that he should leave in accordance with instructions already received.

Due to the deteriorating situation outside Moscow, Major Karpov had been ordered to take over emergency accommodation for the school at one of the railway stations on the Gorky line. Masha didn't yet know anything about this, but Shmelev had been working on the transfer of the school since yesterday evening and was in a thoroughly bad temper.

"Sit nearer, Artemyeva," he said after the adjutant had gone out, and he shifted his crutches from their place up against the right side of the desk to the left. Masha pulled up her chair and sat down again. "What can I do for you?"

Shmelev jerked his head and winked his left eye, only the wink wasn't cheerful, as usual, but tired and gloomy.

"I went to Moscow on leave yesterday and saw my husband..." began Masha.

"Your husband's name is Sintsov, isn't it?" said Shmelev, frowning slightly. "Ivan, Ivan...."

"Petrovich," said Masha, prompting him with a sinking heart. She had a feeling that Shmelev knew something dreadful about Sintsov that she hadn't yet heard of herself.

"A political instructor. Went to the front. You've had no news of him, and so now you've seen him, I gather, and he's back in Moscow," continued Shmelev.

"Yes, he's back," said Masha, agonisedly wondering what Shmelev knew about Sintsov that she didn't.

But Shmelev knew nothing about Sintsov that wasn't in Masha's personal dossier, at present lying inside the desk with all the other files. Three of the trainees were to be flown behind the lines that evening, and before talking to them prior to departure, he had been looking through their records once again.

"So your husband's back. Well, what about it?"

The young woman sitting before him with the girlish, pale and determined face did not look in the least as though she was going to ask not to be sent on an assignment because her husband had come back. But if so, then why had she come to see him, and why was she so upset, although she was trying to hide it?

"In the first place," said Masha, shakily launching out into the speech that she had rehearsed on the way back to Moscow, "what are my instructions if I discover I'm pregnant over there? I know I had no right, but what am I to do if it happens?"

"Well, well," thought Shmelev. "So she's scared after all and doesn't want to fly!" He prided himself on his knowledge of people. He was annoyed with himself for having made a mistake and he was ashamed for this woman who was either lying or deliberately contriving to be excused.

"You mean you're putting it to me that you can't go out on your mission?" he demanded stiffly.

Masha flared up.

"However could you think such a thing, Comrade Colonel?"

"I can think whatever comes into my head," said Shmelev, realising that his first assumption had been correct and his second one false, and duly delighted at the fact.

"I didn't volunteer to train here just to get out of it later!" said Masha, feeling her face turning bright red.

"I realise that," interrupted Shmelev. He wanted to help her now. "But if that's so, and if you're determined to do what you were trained for here, what are you asking me to do? I'm not a doctor and I'm not a clairvoyant."

"I'm asking," said Masha, reassured by the very sharpness of tone adopted by Shmelev, "because it could be a hindrance over there. What am I to do then? I'll act as is necessary."

"Anything can be a hindrance to an agent if he or she gives in to circumstances, and nothing can hinder that agent if the agent concerned subordinates the circumstances to himself or herself. An agent can be a woman with a child, an old man, blind, deaf or crippled—but all this can be turned in one's favour and against the enemy. Everything depends on the individual and on what additional difficulties that person is willing to undertake for the sake of the job in hand. I know of one case," added Shmelev after a pause, "when an agent had to break his own leg because he was suspected of pretending to be a cripple."

Masha involuntarily glanced at Shmelev's crutches.

"That was a long time ago and it wasn't me," he said, intercepting her glance. "To sum up, as head of the school, I attribute no significance to your query, but if you wish, you can consult our doctor. After all, she's a woman." And for the second time there was the ghost of a smile on Shmelev's face. "She's genuine," he thought, looking at Masha. "I can send her—she won't sell out and she won't crack."

He regarded the conversation as over and, telling Masha that he would be sending for her again on service matters, was about to dismiss her. But for Masha, the conversation had only just begun. Instead of going out, she announced that she had not yet told him the most important item.

Shmelev glanced covertly at his watch—time was precious, but something in this trainee's voice discouraged interruption. Masha moved her chair up a little closer, clasped her hands, and began.

Shmelev was a good listener and was not used to showing surprise. He was such a good listener that he even suppressed his nervous tic when he felt it might disturb the narrative. And, of course, Masha could not surprise him with her story of a husband who had first looked for his own unit, then fought in another, then broken out of encirclement, then landed up in encirclement again, then been a prisoner, escaped, and finally reached his wife.

The in no way surprising thread of this story was only too familiar to Shmelev from other stories like it and from his own personal experience as a man who had already crossed and recrossed the front line twice in the course of duty.

But the tragic significance of what this young woman was telling him stirred a response in him, because he had seen things behind the enemy lines far worse than anything described to her by her husband, and he remembered certain agonising moments of his own when only stamina and experience had prevented him from making the wrong decision.

In Shmelev's opinion, this woman's husband had been in such a predicament that he had not taken the wisest course of action; but under the circumstances he could hardly be held solely responsible.

But when Masha described how Sintsov had ended up in Moscow, and when she looked expectantly at Shmelev, as if seeking reassurance that everything was going to be alright in the end, he had to admit to himself that this he could not give. Yes, if her husband should come across real people, and not just cyphers, then they would simply send him to the front without any more fuss, and he would see action again. But if he should find himself up against some quibbler, then anything could happen! There was no knowing which way things might turn out with such people!

Masha went on talking and looking at Shmelev, and she noticed a curious discrepancy between the reassuring "yes, yes" and "just so" with which he very occasionally punctuated what she was saying, and the displeased expression on his face at the time.

After she had told him everything she had to say, and after he had asked her if that was all, and she had told him, yes, and he had said curtly: "Very well, you may go. That's fine"—she felt that it wasn't anything of the kind. Like her, he wanted everything to be fine, but didn't really know whether it would be, in spite of the occasional "yes, yes" and "quite so".

Shmelev stopped Masha as she was almost at the door.

"Now here's what," he said, his mind finally made up about something he had been debating with himself all through Masha's story. "You needn't tell anyone else what you've told me about your husband. I'm saying this officially. I know what you've told me, and I'm bearing it in mind; but apart from myself, there's no need for anyone else to know. You understand?"

Masha did not, in fact, quite understand, but she felt relieved that she wouldn't have to go through her story all over again.

"I understand," she said.

"Report to me at seventeen hundred hours with your group instructor. You may go!" said Shmelev.

Masha went out and he was left alone. The adjutant looked in at the door.

"Wait a moment," said Shmelev. He was feeling disturbed and wanted to be on his own for a few minutes.

A man who hardly knew the meaning of fear when it came to shouldering a personal responsibility, Shmelev was not overfond of answering for others. During the few seconds between non-committally dismissing Masha and then detaining her with the request not to tell anyone else about her husband, he had done something very rare for him: while fully in a position not to take on the responsibility, he had taken it on nevertheless. During those few seconds, a whole series of possible decisions had run through his mind. He had been wondering whether or not to cancel his pupil's assignment after what he had just heard. He personally had faith in her and saw no reason to cancel her flight, but it could still be cancelled nevertheless, since other people in the school might have a different view of the case.

"But we have to consider her too," he thought. "She could find out or guess that we were intending to send her and had then changed their minds; and that could be a real tragedy for her. Even if she doesn't find out that we were to send her today, she'll be expecting to go soon, and yet nothing will happen, and she'll come to the conclusion that we don't trust her. And that's the worst thing possible for an agent—it can make him or her professionally useless at a stroke."

But if he were to pass on trainee Artemyeva's story to the school commissar (the one whom Masha would have seen rather than Shmelev), then, although not a bad fellow but strictly punctilious in such matters, the commissar would inevitably suggest postponing Artemyeva's flight for a time. And he would do it in such a way as to make it awkward for Shmelev to insist otherwise. But if nothing was said about it to the school commissar, and then Artemyeva talked, he, Shemelev, would find himself in a very awkward position indeed, because not only would he have attached no importance to his talk with Artemyeva, he wouldn't even have mentioned it to anyone.

And yet it was still necessary for her to be sent: it was necessary for the cause, for Artemyeva herself, and there was no justification for not sending her!

"I'm going to do it!" thought Shmelev, furious with himself all of a sudden. "I'll take the full responsibility and send her, only without any preliminary argufying."

The result of all these thoughts had been the exclamation with which he had stopped Masha in the doorway. Now that he had acted on his decision and she had gone out, he smiled with self-satisfaction, and then jeered ironically at himself: "You're a brave one, you are! You're the head of the school, and you've taken a great step. You've decided to send an agent, in whom you have faith, where you think she ought to be sent."

"Oh, Shmelev, Shmelev!" He remembered how his immediate superior had once reproached him at Khalkhin-

Gol. "A medal on your chest, and your chest riddled, and yet you a military man, haven't a scrap of civic courage!"

"The 'haven't a scrap' might have been unfair at the time, but now, when he already had two Orders of the Red Banner on his chest and a new string of dangers behind him, and, moreover, when the Germans were outside Moscow, it was time for him to show all the civic courage he could muster. When, if not now?"

"It's time to look the facts in the face," thought Shmelev, "before it's too late. If they'd faced up to the facts honestly after the Finnish War, and above all if they'd drawn the right conclusions, things might have been working out very differently now. But it wasn't too late, and it was needful and necessary to look the facts in the face, whatever the circumstances!"

He thought with exasperation of himself, and how they were still not telling the harsh facts about the latest developments to people who were to be dropped behind the German lines the very next day and who would come into direct contact not only with the real state of affairs over there, but with exaggerated rumours about it, with slander. And the truth would hit people far more than it had hit the woman who had just left his office. Things must be changed, the agents must be briefed more fully, more honestly, and more courageously. Shmelev frowned as he thought how many obstacles, big and small, would have to be overcome first. For him personally it would be so much easier to recover the use of his leg and fly across the front again on one of those dangerous missions at which he was so experienced and of which he was not in the least afraid!

The aircraft had long since crossed the front line and, according to flight calculations, was approaching Smolensk. The night was windy and the passage bumpy; the plane was continually flying in and out of cloud. Below lay a monotonous darkness: everything over which the aircraft flew—towns and villages—was blacked out, and only occasionally did Masha see winking points of light when she looked out of the porthole. Once there was a whole string of them. At first Masha thought it was a village, and then she realised that it was German traffic moving along a road. The Smolensk countryside was deep behind the German lines and they were not bothering to mask their lights.

During the first hour of the flight towards and across the front, Masha and her two fellow travellers, a boy and a girl who were to be dropped further on, exchanged a few desultory remarks but then fell silent. They didn't want to let their nervousness show, so they ended up sitting separately among the boxes of explosive and sacks of medical supplies with which the aircraft was loaded to capacity. The boy and the girl were flying together and were to be dropped as a pair. Masha lay on one of the sacks and envied them: two were company, after all.

It was midnight. Only twenty-four hours had passed since she had entered her flat and seen Sintsov. She had been through so much since then! She frowned in an effort to recall everything that had happened, everything that she had said and that had been said to her during those interminable twenty-four hours. She tried, but failed. Everything was confused and disjointed. She remembered the fury on Sintsov's face as he talked about the Germans. Then she remembered how she had memorised, at her instructor's dictation, the final details: street, house, password. Then in her mind's eye she saw the pensive expression on the colonel's face as he said "yes, yes", and "quite so"; and then she remembered the road barricade which had not been there in the morning, but which had appeared by the time they drove from the school to the airfield. She remembered, too, the torch shining in her face.

Then she remembered the colonel again, and how that evening, before departure, he had suddenly asked after her brother who had served under him at Khalkhin-Gol. She had said that he was in Chita, and the colonel had tucked both crutches under one arm and, laying his free hand on her shoulder, had said quietly, so that only she could hear: "Don't worry about your husband. Everything will be all right. You hear?" Was he just reassuring her, or had he made enquiries and learnt something?

The school commissar had also shaken hands with her as she left and had said in his deep, morose bass voice: "Remember, Artemyeva, that everyone staying behind here is envious of you. That's the way the young people are here! They don't care about their own lives, they can't wait to see action!" And although she usually liked the commissar and anything he said, at that moment she had liked neither him nor his little speech. It had been so incongruous compared with what had been going on in her mind, although she certainly wanted to see action and had been willing to fly, and she didn't care about her own life. But what he had said had somehow jarred on her.

And now, when she felt that she was spending her last few minutes aboard the aircraft, she was simply terrified. So terrified! Until now, she had considered herself brave by nature and had never imagined that she could feel so frightened at the thought of the black, unknown space rushing past below into which she must jump from the exit hatch in a few minutes' time.

The pilot handed over to the second pilot, came out of the cabin, and told Masha that they would be over her dropping point in three minutes. Masha stood up. The pilot checked her parachute harness and shouted in Masha's ear: "What's your name?" as if it was vital to know at this last moment.

"Veronika," thought Masha, remembering her new name; but, as if saying good-bye to the past, she actually said: "Masha", and looked at the pilot's face, hardly visible in the darkness.

The pilot went up to the hatch and tugged the handle. The door opened, and a blast of cold air burst into the aircraft.

Masha stepped nearer the door, but the pilot held her back and stood for several seconds, his hand resting on her shoulder. The bell jangled somewhere in the plane: the navigator was giving the signal from the cabin; but the pilot still kept his hand on Masha's shoulder. The bell jangled a second time. The pilot took his hand away and said:

"Off you go!"

Masha went up to the door, nearly falling back under the blast of air, bent down, and stepped out into space. The last thing she heard in the aircraft was the faint sound of the third bell, cut off from her hearing as soon as it had begun.

CHAPTER THIRTEEN

As Sintsov went towards the District Party Committee building, the street was cold and deserted. A thin column of smoke was rising somewhere in the direction of the Novo-Devichi Convent. Something was still burning after last night's air-raid.

At the corner of the Sadovaya, Sintsov tripped over a telephone directory. It was lying on the road, half burnt and open at the letter M. "Meyerovich, A. V., Meyerovich, E. F., Meyerovich, I. A. ..." he read as he bent down. Then he kicked the book aside and looked up. The windows had been blown out of a telephone kiosk nearby and the handset had been torn off: all that remained was a piece of protruding flex.

Scraps of dog-eared paper were flying across the street in the cold wind. A militiaman and two belted civilians with rifles were on duty at a grocery stores, of which one window was cracked down the middle and the other blown clean out of its frame. Sintsov wanted to go up to them, but then remembered that he had no documents and might be detained, so he quickly went on his way.

Five minutes later, he stopped at an ancient two-storey house which, in past times, had been yellow with white columns, but was now completely covered with a layer of grey-green camouflage paint.

Sintsov tugged at the cold copper handle and went in, noticing as he did so that there was a lorry parked outside and two men were loading it with sealed bags.

A militiamen with a rifle on his shoulder was standing at a wooden barrier in the vestibule.

"What d'you want, citizen?" he asked.

"The District Party Committee."

"Who did you want to see?"

"Golubev," said Sintsov, naming the committee secretary who had once issued him with his Party card, and wondering with some alarm if the Golubev mightn't have been replaced.

"Comrade Golubev isn't here," said the militiaman. "He's gone to a local organisation."

"Someone else, then," said Sintsov. "It doesn't matter who. I want to talk to...."

"Have you a Party document?"

"No..." said Sintsov after a painful pause. "But I absolutely must talk to someone, so please call somebody."

"I can't, citizen," said the militiaman. "I'm on duty. State your business and I'll phone up on the house line."

At that moment, the entrance door slammed behind Sintsov and a jaunty, fair-haired young man bounded up the steps. He was wearing riding breeches and a close-fitting tunic with the broad belt of a commander round his waist. His tunic was tucked up at one side, and the end of a holster was visible underneath.

"There you are, Yevstigneyev, that's the archives loaded up. And you said we wouldn't be finished before tomorrow," he shouted cheerfully as he ran past the militiaman, taking no notice of Sintsov.

"That's Comrade Yelkin," said the militiaman to Sintsov as the athletic young blond ran past. "He's manager of the Party Records Department. Ask him."

The fair-haired young man stopped on hearing his name, turned round, and called briskly:

"I'm Yelkin. What is it?"

"Comrade Yelkin," said Sintsov in a laboured, husky voice, and he stepped towards him. "I have no documents on me at all, but I was issued with my candidate's card and my Party card here in the District Committee. I must have a word with you—it's absolutely essential," he added hastily, as if this fast-moving young man might suddenly bounce up on his springy legs and shoot off down the corridor.

But Yelkin didn't shoot off anywhere and instead took a step towards Sintsov. At first glance, he thought he had seen this gaunt individual somewhere before, then he decided that he hadn't, and anyway it didn't matter. Hardly anyone came to the District Committee these days except on serious business.

"Come through with me, Comrade," said Yelkin. "You can let him pass, Yevstigneyev!"

The militiaman stepped aside without comment, and Sintsov followed Yelkin, his dilapidated boots scraping over the floor of the District Committee corridor.

The room they entered was small, with a grating over the window and a wall filing cabinet, nearly all its drawers lying open and empty. There were two office desks, a folding bed, and a wooden cot with a palliasse. Someone was asleep on the bed, covered from head to foot in a black civilian overcoat. A rifle stood propped up against the wall at the head of the bed.

Yelkin sat down on the cot and pointed to a chair:

"Take a seat!"

On closer inspection, the blond young man proved to be not so young after all, and his face, though animated, looked tired. As soon as he sat down, he fished out a cigarette, put it into his mouth, and then on second thoughts offered the packet to Sintsov. But Sintsov shook his head. He had been feeling desperately hungry since morning, and he was afraid that smoking on an empty stomach might make him feel sick.

"What can I do for you, Comrade?"

Yelkin worked his shoulders and opened and shut his eyes quickly several times in succession like a man who has long been struggling with a permanent desire to go to sleep.

"My name is Sintsov. I studied at the Communist Institute of Journalism, and was accepted as candidate and Party member here, at the District Committee...."

"I realise that," said Yelkin impatiently. "But what have you come for this time?"

But if Sintsov was going to explain that, then it meant he would have to tell the whole long story.

"I know you haven't the time," he said, looking Yelkin straight in the face, "but give me ten minutes—if you can spare them, of course."

"Why not?" said Yelkin. "Go ahead. You've come to the District Committee. There's no hurry...."

Sintsov thought he would be able to relate the essentials in ten minutes, but he talked for twice as long. Had he come to the District Committee yesterday evening or night, and not at this early hour, it is doubtful whether, with the best will in the world, Yelkin would have been physically capable of hearing him out.

Sintsov finished, fell silent and, reaching for the packet of cigarettes on the cot, lit up eagerly. Yelkin watched him without saying anything, torn by conflicting emotions. Although this man, if he was to believe, had been unarmed and wounded, he had nevertheless surrendered to the Germans, and although he had subsequently escaped, he had not stayed at the front after crossing it, but had gone to his home in Moscow—that is to say, he had committed an act of desertion. But Yelkin still wanted to help him.

Why? Perhaps mainly because of the frank way he had told his story, in which there were things to his disadvantage as well as to his advantage.

"I have no documents at all, and no one to confirm what I'm telling you," said Sintsov, ending as he had begun. "I was with Brigade Commander Serpilin until October the first and he could confirm. He was then sent to hospital in Moscow. But I don't know whether he's here or not. After the first of October, there's no one I can give as referee."

As he described how he came to Moscow, Sintsov mentioned Lyusin, but to use his name a second time, even as proof of his own integrity, to clutch at that scoundrel like a drowning man clutching at a straw, was more than Sintsov could bring himself to do.

"No one," he repeated firmly, standing up and stubbing his cigarette-end out in a tin can on the table.

"How's your wound now?" asked Yelkin suddenly, reminded of it by the reference to hospital; and he looked at Sintsov's bandaged head.

"It's nothing, just an occasional twinge. It's probably almost healed."

Yelkin jumped up off the cot and began pacing up and down the room on his springy legs.

"Of course," he began, "it's a good thing you came to the District Committee. But what's all this business about the

Party card?..." Yelkin shrugged his shoulders in angry amazement and took another two turns up and down the room. "They won't reinstate you," he said decisively, and he stopped, facing Sintsov.

"That's not what I'm thinking about just now, Comrade Yelkin," said Sintsov. "I know what it means to be without a Party card. You tell me one more thing. Where must I go now to report everything that's happened to me? Where can I ask them simply to send me straight to the front as a fighting soldier? I've told you everything, so now you tell me: where am I to get it done? Can they help me here in the Party Committee, or can't they?"

Yelkin shrugged his shoulders. He personally didn't know how to help this man who, whichever way you looked at it, had lost his Party card and had been taken prisoner by the Germans. But he hadn't gone just anywhere, he had come to the District Committee and was standing before none other than himself, Yelkin.

"Perhaps Comrade Golubev could help me when he comes back?" suggested Sintsov, depressed by Yelkin's silence.

Yelkin merely gestured helplessly.

"Golubev.... I haven't seen him for days myself. Have you any idea how much Golubev has to cope with? I haven't been to bed for five nights, and as for Golubev...." Yelkin again waved his hand helplessly and then said with a frown that perhaps the most correct thing to do would be to go to the District Military Commissar. "Who else can send a man to the front? The Regional Military Commissar!" he continued, reaching for the telephone. "Get me Yuferev. Yelkin from the District Party Committee here. Where is he now, then? Can you be more precise? Alright, I'll ring back. The District Military Commissar's not there," he said, replacing the receiver. "They said he's at the barricades near the Crimea Bridge. He's a major, and his surname's Yuferev. Go and find him and tell him your story. You can mention my name and say that Yelkin at the District Party Committee sent you. He knows me."

Yelkin was quite taken with this idea, as if it had solved the whole complicated problem at one stroke.

"If you don't find him or something, come back and get the militiaman to send for me. And I'll give Yuferev another ring in the meantime, just to be sure. Let's try that, shall we?" he concluded amiably.

Sintsov sighed and put on his hat. For some reason, he didn't expect any good to come of this Yuferev, whom he didn't know, and so he didn't want to leave the District Committee.

"Look for him there, by the Crimea Bridge," Yelkin was saying in the meantime. "They're building barricades on both sides—on the Metrostroyevskaya and on the Sadovaya...."

And then, in the middle of all these directions, a thought suddenly occurred to him. "What if he leaves the District Committee and doesn't go to Yuferev but just vanishes? He was taken prisoner after all, and he could do a lot of damage with things in Moscow as they are just now!" And although this idea was at variance with what he had been thinking so far, Yelkin hesitated. He now wanted someone to reassure him that he was doing right to trust this man.

"Or I'll tell you what, just wait a moment," he said. "Wait a moment—take a seat."

Sintsov obediently sat down.

"I say, Malinin!" called Yelkin.

"What?" said a muffled voice.

The figure on the bed stirred and the overcoat fell aside to reveal a man lying with his eyes open and his hands behind his head.

"Listen, Malinin, I've got a problem here. I need your advice," said Yelkin, and he sat down on his cot. "Tell him your story briefly," he said, turning to Sintsov.

"Why repeat it?" said the man addressed as Malinin. "I heard it all. I wasn't asleep."

"How long have you been awake, then?" asked Yelkin quickly.

"I haven't slept at all," replied Malinin. "I covered my head with my coat, but I still couldn't get to sleep."

Malinin spoke morosely and haltingly, as though annoyed at having to open his mouth at all. His was a big, heavy face, grey and tired-looking, with coarse features which were handsome in a saturnine kind of way. His hair, receding slightly at the temples, was ash-grey. The big, powerful mouth was clamped shut as if in anger. Malinin glared inimically at Sintsov without saying anything.

"Well, if you've heard everything, what would you advise?" asked Yelkin.

"Feed the man," said Malinin, gloomy as ever. "There's some bread on the window-sill, and a can of fish. As for the can-opener...." He bestirred himself at last, drew out from behind his head a massive, powerful fist and, taking a jack-knife out of his breeches pocket, offered it to Sintsov. "Here!..." And he thrust his hand back under his head again.

"Oh, yes, you must be hungry!" said Yelkin as an afterthought.

He hurried over to the window-sill, picked up a half loaf and a tin of fish, and put them on the desk before Sintsov. Sintsov unfolded the knife-blade and was going to open the can, but refrained, merely cut off a large slice of bread, and began chewing it as slowly as he could.

Malinin watched him for a moment, then reached out to the table, took the knife, folded back the blade, unfolded the can-opener at the other end, opened the tin, bent back the lid, put it on the table, closed the can-opener again, pulled out the big blade that Sintsov had used to slice the bread and, putting his hands behind his head, returned to his former position on the bed.

"Listen, Yelkin," he said, after watching out of the corner of his eye for a minute or so as Sintsov ate, "you could give him some tea."

"What tea, then?" asked Yelkin.

"Some hot water, anyway. Aunt Tanya's probably got some in the urn. Or shall I get up, if you can't be bothered?"

"All right, stay where you are," said Yelkin, and he went out, taking an aluminium mug from the window-sill.

"Killed a few Germans yourself, have you?" asked Malinin after Yelkin had gone out, indicating by this question that he really had heard everything that had been going on. "Did you actually see them fall, or d'you only think you did?"

"I saw them."

"Eat, don't let me put you off," said Malinin, noticing that Sintsov had pushed away the bread, and he closed his eyes to indicate that he would not be asking any more questions.

Yelkin returned and put down a mug of hot water in front of Sintsov. Sintsov ate three pieces of bread, then tried not to eat up all the tinned fish but couldn't resist it, finished it off, and washed it down with a scalding mouthful of hot water.

"Thanks. I'll go now," he said, getting to his feet.

"So what do you advise, Malinin?" asked Yelkin.

"What is there to advise?" responded Malinin without opening his eyes. "You've done all the advising yourself. Now he must get on with it!"

"See you!" said Sintsov.

"All the best!" replied Malinin, half opening his eyes for a second and closing them again.

Yelkin went out with Sintsov.

"If this comrade comes in again," he said solicitously to the militiaman, "send for me! So it's Yuferev for you next!" he concluded, and Sintsov went outside into the street.

It was no longer the first hour after dawn when it is normal for a city to look deserted. The emptiness was now conspicuous, especially compared to the crush through which Sintsov had battled the day before. There were people about, but not many. There was a queue outside the dairy waiting for it to open. The militiaman was still on duty outside the smashed shop-window on the corner of Zubovsky Square, but the two civilians with rifles were not there any more. Lorries were driving along the Sadovaya. One of them screeched alongside the pavement on which Sintsov happened to be walking. It was loaded with rails and with barbed wire which was dangling out of the back and trailing over the asphalt. There was a small queue of people with suitcases at the bus stop. They looked as though they had long despaired of a bus ever arriving. Other people with suitcases and bundles were trudging along the Sadovaya but there were not many of them this time. There was no comparison with yesterday. Moscow today seemed less alarmed and more ready to resist. "Yes, if they have to, they'll fight here too, inside the city limits," thought Sintsov. "That's why they're putting up these barricades. Surely they'll give me a rifle? Am I really such a bad egg that they won't give me a rifle and let me fight at these barricades? I don't believe it!"

They had treated him straightforwardly at the District Party Committee, without particular sympathy, but without mistrust too, and their attitude had reassured him. And he felt even more reassured because there had been a District Party Committee, and Golubev was still secretary and the militiaman had been standing at the barrier, and the archives were on their way to a safer place, and the telephone had rung and made the connection, and Aunt Tanya, as it turned out, had had hot water in the urn after all.

Behind the turbulent Moscow he had seen yesterday, there was another Moscow, the Moscow of the District Party Committees, calm as always, businesslike, unintimidated. That house supervisor who had thrown the key-ring to him yesterday had been the exception, not the rule, and he was a fool to have thought otherwise yesterday, even if only for a second!

Twenty minutes later, he came to the Crimea Bridge near which they were indeed barricading the Metrostroyevskaya on one side and the Sadovaya on the other. Barbed wire and rails were now being unloaded from the lorry which had recently grated along the pavement past Sintsov. Sandbags were being thrown down from other lorries. Several dozen people were busy tearing out the cobblestones from the surface of the side-street running behind the Metro station. They had evidently started work the previous night: large heaps of cobblestones had already accumulated. Part of the Metrostroyevskaya had already been barricaded: sandbags had been stuffed between two rows of beams driven into the ground, and in front of them, rails and I-beams had been driven in at an angle, like tusks. More girders and rails were being unloaded from several other lorries and were being cut up into lengths on the spot—a welding apparatus could be heard splashing intermittently somewhere nearby.

An elderly lieutenant of the reserve with an engineer's crossed axes on his tabs was standing by the barricade in charge of operations.

"Comrade Lieutenant," asked Sintsov, going up to him. "You haven't seen Major Yuferev, have you?"

"He was here. He brought me some people and drove off. He promised he'd be back," replied the lieutenant without looking at Sintsov. Then he raised his head and asked: "What d'you want? Where are you from?"

"I've been sent by the District Party Committee," said Sintsov.

"What about you?" And the engineer turned away from Sintsov to some other people who had approached him almost at the same time.

There were two women, a skinny, long-necked, bespectacled youth, and two rather scrawny elderly males, almost identical in appearance and both wearing ancient, floppy-brimmed hats.

"We've been sent by the District Party Committee too," said one of the women. "Who else?"

"Very well, you can start carrying the rails and the beams to the welder. Take the sections after they've been cut and space them out on that side where they're going to be dug in."

The engineer walked quickly across the road, showing them exactly where to put the beams and rails after they had been cut into lengths.

"Let's go," said the long-necked youth in the spectacles, turning to Sintsov. "Let's do some heaving."

Sintsov bent down, took hold of a rail and, as he straightened up with the others, realised with pleasure that in spite of fatigue his arms were almost as strong as before. At first, they carried the rails on their shoulders, but then they bent some wire into hooks and began carrying the rails with the hooks inserted into the bolt-holes, in the manner usually practised by road-workers.

More and more people were gathering round. While some carried sleepers or cut and uncut rails back and forth, others were breaking up the road surface with iron wedges. There was a pneumatic drill hammering away on the opposite side of the Sadovaya. The rails and girders were being cut up with the welding apparatus by a broad-shouldered lad in overalls and a quilted jacket, and only an hour later, when he took off his welding mask, did Sintsov realise that the operator was a lively woman with a tip-tilted nose and curly hair.

"Come on, come on, let's have more of those, you old dodderers, or you'll hold everything up!" she shouted to Sintsov and the almost identical pair who were helping him with a girder. These two had in the meantime told him that they were both bibliographers from the Book Centre. An old building not far away on the Sadovaya, it had been destroyed by a bomb, and, as they worked, they had mentioned this several times and simply couldn't seem to get over it.

"I feel embarrassed," said the long-necked, bespectacled youth to Sintsov in a quiet, shy voice. "I'd be at the front, of course, and I shall be; but I've only been out of hospital a week. They removed an inflamed appendix. Stupid, appendicitis at a time like this, eh? What do you think?" And as he walked along with the beam, he fixed his near-sighted, embarrassed gaze on Sintsov.

Sintsov assured him that appendicitis is the sort of thing that happens whether you like it or not.

"You'd be better off not carrying heavy weights, otherwise you might open the stitches...."

"Nuts to them!" said the sick youth angrily, as if his stitches had no right to behave like that at such a time.

They carried girders and rails for an hour and a half or so, and then joined the people digging pits on the roadway.

"This Moscow ground's hard!" joked someone.

"But they're certainly digging plenty of it up," retorted someone else. "Dig, dig, dig!... Wherever you look, they're digging!"

"It's a pity Fritz doesn't know how much we've dug ready for him, because if he found out, he'd retreat like a shot...."

But if they didn't disapprove of this last joke, they didn't encourage it either. People were taking their work seriously. How could they do otherwise? Although no one actually mentioned it, all realised that one way or another they were still putting up anti-tank obstacles in readiness for the German armoured divisions, and not just anywhere, but on the Sadovaya opposite the Crimea Bridge

Then a whole convoy of lorries arrived loaded with anti-tank obstacles which had been hastily welded together out of girders and swathed with barbed wire.

"They're welding them at the Hammer and Sickle Factory," said one of the women working with Sintsov. "My husband was telling me yesterday: they're working day and night and welding thousands and thousands of those things...."

Sintsov toiled away with enthusiasm, thereby stifling any thoughts of what was going to happen to him in the future. "What will be, will be," he thought, lifting the next girder almost with a feeling of pleasure. He no longer felt like giving up this work and going off to look for some Yuferev whom he didn't know, the more so that, according to the lieutenant, the District Military Commissar had promised to be back.

At midday, a woman in a quilted jacket and a grey headscarf came up to the workers and called them out:

"The first batch—those who've been working since night-time—go to the children's home for dinner! Only the ones who've been here since night-time. Those of you who started later, please be good enough to wait a bit. First party, come to the children's home. Follow me!"

Sintsov didn't go with the first party, but found himself with the second one in a single-storey detached house hidden in the inner courtyard of a big block. The children's home had long since been evacuated, and a canteen and drying room had been set up in the house for those working on the defences.

There were no chairs, since there was only children's furniture and the tables were too low, so that they either had to squat down at them, or sit on them, or sup their soup from mess-tins while leaning against the wall. There was nothing else to eat apart from the soup. The better supplied shared their bread with those who hadn't brought any from home; but the soup was good and rich, made with canned meat and pearl-barley.

Sintsov remembered the halt back there in captivity on the road, in the hospital, and, shuddering at the recollection, thought with hatred of the Germans and how Moscow must never surrender, whatever happened. They mustn't even consider the thought!

"Who wants more, who wants more?" shouted the woman in the quilted jacket and headscarf, banging her ladle on the oilcloth-covered serving table. She was dressed exactly as when she had come out into the street, but was wearing a big, dirty apron over her quilted jacket. "Who wants more, workers, before the third batch comes in and eats the lot up!"

Sintsov asked for another helping of soup, and the more he ate, the hungrier he felt. He was evidently returning to normal.

After dinner, they worked until dark. Nightfall coincided with an air-raid. The Metro station was close by, and Sintsov went down with all the rest.

The air inside was warm and humid. Women and children who had gone down earlier had already made themselves comfortably at home with mattresses, blankets, pillows, and bottles of milk. The children, already habituated to these conditions, soon dozed off on their mattresses and blankets.

Sintsov found a vacant place against the wall, hugged his long legs with his arms and lowered his face on to his knees. The warmth and the humidity made him sleepy, and he made no attempt to resist. He had spent the day as he was accustomed—in communal work with other people. Those barricades might never be needed, but he had been helping to build them today and he felt easier in his mind as a result.

"When the all-clear sounds, I'll go outside and find that Yuferev..." he thought, even as he succumbed to sleep.

"Move up a bit," said a woman's voice, "so that I can put my baby down!"

He shifted over without opening his eyes as the child was put down. He could hear it sucking blissfully beside him.

"That was the ninth German rammed over Moscow yesterday," said a man's voice.

"Fancy smashing into another plane like that!"

But a woman's voice, young and agitated, interrupted:

"I don't know, but I think I'd give everything for such people...."

"You can do that, but they haven't time to accept it," responded someone else.

Everybody nearby began discussing the rammings. It was a subject they all found exciting.

"The German air force isn't being as bold as it used to," said someone in a loud bass voice, and several others agreed with him at once:

"True, true, they're not the same.... It's the rammings that have done it. They're scared of being rammed...."

Sintsov's thoughts, already half bemused, became completely mixed up. He thought he was flying somewhere. He dropped off to sleep with this sensation of flight, lifting his head off his knees in a final effort and resting it against the wall.

He was woken up by someone gently prodding him in the shoulder.

"Comrade, I say, Comrade...."

He opened his eyes. The Metro station was almost deserted, except for a few solitary figures here and there. A young woman was tying up a folded mattress with a length of twine. Beside her stood a five-year-old boy in a fur hat.

"It was me prodding you, if you'll excuse me," said the woman, "but you've been fast asleep ever since yesterday. I thought you might oversleep and be late for work...."

"Yes, yes," said Sintsov, bouncing to his feet. "But what ... what time is it?"

"It's seven already," said the woman.

"Seven?!"

He stared at her in amazement, only just realising that he had slept like a log all through the night.

Exactly twenty-four hours had passed, and Sintsov was again standing outside the District Party Committee building. True, it was not looking quite the same as before. Half the window-panes had been blown out, and the windows had been boarded up with plywood painted to match the walls. Diagonally across from the Party Committee, a whole four-storey block had been razed to the ground.

Sintsov had come straight from the Metro because he had felt an impulse to do so and because he had good reason: Yelkin himself had told him to look in again if he failed to find Yuferev. He hadn't found Yuferev yesterday, so he had come back. He opened the door into the vestibule. The militiaman was sitting in his former place, but his cheek and eye were bandaged. "Evidently cut by glass," thought Sintsov.

"Could you call Comrade Yelkin, please?" he asked, going up to the militiaman. "He said I could ask for him."

"Not any more you can't!" said the militiaman. "He's not here! He was hurt. He's in hospital now, getting treatment."

"When will he be back?"

The militiaman shrugged his shoulders.

Sintsov stood in front of him and didn't know what to do. He had arrived confident of success, for some reason.

He would see Yelkin who, as promised, would have rung Yuferev in the meantime. From here he would go straight to the District Military Commissar, and his fate would be decided one way or the other. And now everything had suddenly gone wrong.

What was he to do? Wait for Yelkin here, go and try to find Yuferev, or return to work at Crimea Square? He stood hesitating for about a minute, staring at the floor which was covered with a fine carpet of powdered glass. When he looked up again, he saw Malinin, Yelkin's room-mate, walking past along the corridor—tall, gloomy, staring fixedly in front of him, and carrying an aluminium mug with a handkerchief wrapped round the handle. He seemed not to be taking any notice of anyone, but as he passed Sintsov, he suddenly turned as if he had been looking his way all the time.

"What have you come back for?" he demanded in his morose, rasping bass. "Didn't you find Yuferev?"

Sintsov shook his head.

"Have you come to see Yelkin? He's not here," continued Malinin, looking as if he enjoyed telling this to Sintsov.

"You don't happen to know," said Sintsov, "whether he spoke about me to the military commissar, do you?"

"He never phoned him; he forgot..." said Malinin, as if this were self-evident. Then, quite unexpectedly for Sintsov, he nodded at the militiaman. "Let him through. Let's go," he grunted to Sintsov.

They went into the same room as before — Malinin leading with the mug of hot water and Sintsov behind him, wondering why this gloomy individual should have wanted to see him.

"Take a seat!" said Malinin with a nod at the cot and, putting the mug on the window-sill, he sat down on the chair.

His own bed had been made up in true army style without a single crease in the bedding, and he had avoided sitting on it for that reason.

"Has he been badly hurt, then?" asked Sintsov, nodding towards the head of the cot to indicate that he meant Yelkin.

"A gash on the neck.... He'll survive!" replied Malinin.

"Shrapnel or glass?"

"A sheath-knife," retorted Malinin and, seeing the look on Sintsov's face, he added reluctantly: "What's so surprising about that? D'you think knives aren't being pulled in Moscow these days? Our Moscow crooks aren't letting the grass grow under their feet either. They're getting on with the job. But Yelkin, of course, had to go and stick his nose in," said Malinin, in a tone of voice that might equally have meant censure or praise. "He was driving past at night and saw a shop being looted. Snatched out his revolver and—'Hands up!'.... They promptly slashed him with a knife. Good thing he wasn't on his own—they gave those thieves what for."

It was now clear that Malinin approved of Yelkin's action and only sounded displeased out of habit.

"What are you looking so surprised about?" he asked Sintsov again. "It's a law of nature: at a time like this, all the filth floats to the surface. You look sometimes and wonder if it's all really a bucket full of filth. But it isn't!"

He was evidently extremely upset at some recollection and couldn't stop himself.

"And the beetles of the old regime are getting ready to crawl out of the woodwork at the first chance, too. I gave one fellow a belt on the chops yesterday...." He raised his massive fist and looked at it as if astonished at himself. "Where's my self-control? You might well ask!... I used to have some, but times have changed and I haven't enough to spare any more.... So you didn't find the Military Commissar?" he said, suddenly changing the subject.

"No," said Sintsov, and he explained that he had been helping to put up the barricades by the Crimea Bridge and had spent the night in the Metro.

"And Yelkin had doubts yesterday whether you'd show up..." grinned Malinin. "He was afraid you'd run away!"

"Where to? What for?" asked Sintsov.

"Quite! Where to and what for? But I remember you," said Malinin, changing the subject again. It was his way of talking. "I had Yelkin's job and I made out your papers when you were being accepted into the Party. I've got that sort of memory: something like three thousand acceptances. I've seen people expelled too; and if I put my mind to it, I can remember one in every two."

Sintsov was glad that this gloomy man should have remembered him joining the Party, and in his turn he tried to recall Malinin, but couldn't.

"Don't try," said Malinin, divining his thoughts. "Remembering me doesn't matter. But if I remember you, that does. How did you manage to get yourself into such a mess, my dear comrade?" And Malinin shook his head sadly. In spite of his recollections, he was disinclined to underestimate the extent of the calamity that had befallen Sintsov. "Did you tell the whole truth yesterday, and nothing but the truth?"

"The whole truth," said Sintsov. What else could he say to lend conviction to his case?

Malinin looked at him long and hard.

In contrast to the cheerful Yelkin, this gloomy man who had aged during his years in the Party Records Department, had no second or reserve opinion to draw on in case of emergency. His opinion of people was black-and-white — he thought they were good or bad, and he either trusted them completely or not at all. If he trusted them, then it was all the way; and if he didn't trust them in one small thing, then he distrusted them entirely.

If he had had the least shade of doubt whether Sintsov was telling the whole truth and nothing but the truth, he would not even have considered arriving at the decision which he was about to make. His only remaining doubts were whether he, Malinin, was fully entitled to do so.

"I am entitled!" he thought in the end. "I'll go myself, and I'll be there.... And I'll prove it to Guber.... And if I don't succeed — well, we'll see."

"Now," said Malinin after a pause, "the Communist Battalion has already been formed in the District, but there's a non-Party draft in it as well as Communists and Komsomols. I'm going over there to join them. I talked them into releasing me from my duties last night.... They've made up several more platoons during the night. There are no commanders yet, and I'm acting as senior in my platoon. So I'll sign you on along with myself. We'll be going to the battalion headquarters on Plyushchikha Street in an hour's time. Well, can I put your name down?" asked Malinin, taking out of his breeches pocket a school exercise book folded in half.

"You bet you can!" said Sintsov.

Malinin moved closer to the desk, his chair creaking as he did so, took out of his tunic pocket a pair of spectacles which didn't suit his heavy, strong face at all, opened the exercise book, and ran his finger down the list. It consisted of twenty-six names in numerical order. He moistened the tip of his pen, added the number twenty-seven, and wrote out in copper-plate handwriting: "Sintsov...."

"Name and patronymic?"

"Ivan Petrovich," said Sintsov.

"I. P." wrote Malinin. He blotted the page, put the exercise book back in his breeches pocket, and then said: "We'll go there, and I'll report to the battalion commissar. It's up to him to decide.... Anyway, I'll state my own view."

He didn't stress this last sentence, although it signified a great deal. He had been sitting at the Records desk for sixteen years, and only two years ago, with his eyesight ruined, had become an instructor. His opinion had some weight here in the district, especially in the vetting of personnel for reliability. All the greater, of course, for that reason, was his responsibility for the man sitting before him, and Malinin was fully aware of it, although he didn't stress it too hard.

Sintsov missed Malinin's remark that the final decision would rest with the commissar. He was too happy at his newly-won chance of joining the Communist Battalion—today, what was more, with Malinin—and of perhaps going into action tomorrow.

"I shall never forget this as long as I live," he said.

"Why bother to remember?" replied Malinin in his usual gloomy manner. "If I fixed for you to go with your goods and chattels to Kazan, that would be something to remember," he grinned. "Yesterday, twenty men promised to remember me for the rest of their lives. But what sort of a favour am I doing you? I'm helping you get into action again! You'll end up there anyway, so I'm just cutting all the red tape."

"Alright, I'll say nothing," said Sintsov. "I'm just glad that you believed me. You didn't have to, but you did, that's all."

"Mustn't believe everybody," retorted Malinin angrily, taking it personally as a reflection on his vigilance. "Believe everybody, and you're up the creek in no time. It doesn't matter so much that you go up the creek yourself, but you'll take Soviet power with you. I wanted to have a shave, and changed my mind," he said, switching subjects again. "Have a shave, if you want. My razor and brush are over there on the window-sill. You've still got time...."

Sintsov quickly lathered his face and began scraping off his intractable three-day beard.

"You'll find the alum over there. You look as if you'd been slaughtering a pig," said Malinin, looking over his shoulder at Sintsov's gashed face.

But he didn't have the chance to explain where the alum was. Someone knocked on the door, Malinin called out "Well?..." in an unfriendly voice, and the door creaked open. Sintsov stopped hunting for the alum and turned round. A tall, thin woman was standing in the doorway with a rucksack.

"Hullo, I've brought you your things," she said. Malinin went to meet her.

Sintsov realised that this was Malinin's wife and, trying not to eavesdrop on them, he proceeded to tidy up after his shave, but couldn't help hearing the odd few words.

"That's fine," said Malinin, "but this I don't need. When I said I didn't need it, I meant I didn't need it. Two changes are enough."

"Take them, why leave them behind?" said his wife.

But Malinin growled that he wasn't a camel, and there wouldn't be any porters where he was going.... The next few sentences were inaudible, and then Malinin said:

"Here, that's four hundred."

"Why all that? What about yourself?" said his wife.

"What would I want with money now?" he retorted, and this must have frightened her, for she stifled a sob.

Sintsov finished tidying up and then, not knowing what to do next, stayed sitting with his back to Malinin and his wife. "They're probably whispering their last good-byes," he thought.

"Here, have a set of underwear," said Malinin's voice loudly behind him, and a set of old, worn, but clean linen landed on Sintsov's knees. "You've got none at all, and my wife's lumbered me with more than I need."

Sintsov turned round and saw that Malinin's wife was no longer in the room. They had said good-bye so quietly and inconspicuously that he had not even heard her go out.

Malinin stuffed his razor into the rucksack, put on a heavy old black overcoat on top of his blue, semi-military suit, and a peaked cap of the same heavy material as the coat, picked up the rifle standing in the corner, and slung it over his shoulder.

"Let's go!"

When they went outside, Malinin stopped on the pavement and threw back his head to survey the District Party Committee building, as if trying to imprint it in his memory before leaving.

"How long have you been working there?" asked Sintsov.

"Since nineteen twenty-three in the District Committee, and since nineteen twenty-six here, when we transferred to this building," said Malinin. "Plate-glass windows," he added unexpectedly, "ever since tsarist times, and now the whole lot blown out by one bomb. They've had to board it up with plywood like a sales kiosk."

Yesterday and the day before, Malinin had seen what Sintsov had also seen in Moscow, but, in his position as a District Party official, he knew a great deal more. Yesterday and the day before, the foam had, of course, been seething on the surface; but even under the surface, the true situation was very grave indeed.

Golubev, the Regional Committee secretary, on whom Malinin had managed to pay a farewell call at five in the morning, had looked him straight in the face and had said:

"Yesterday, I gave you permission to leave for the battalion and now I'm regretting it. I could have done with you here...."

"And out there?" asked Malinin, ready to do as he was told, but secretly not wanting the secretary to change his mind.

"You're needed out there too," said Golubev. "You'll probably be thrown into battle almost straightaway."

They were alone in the office, these two who had worked together for eight years.

"What's the outlook for Moscow?" asked Malinin. "Only let's have it straight." He sliced the air with the edge of his burly hand, indicating that he wanted to be told nothing at all or the plain truth. And Golubev told him the plain truth.

"As far as I can see, the situation wasn't quite clear the day before yesterday," he said. "But it's levelling out a bit now. We're evidently not going to surrender Moscow under any circumstances, but it may mean fighting on the outskirts. Maybe on the streets too, at a pinch. We can't rule that out."

Such was the District Committee secretary's attitude, and Malinin had no grounds for disbelieving him. He knew Golubev well as a man who weighed his words before speaking and was not given to idle talk.

"Maybe we really will have to fight in the streets," thought Malinin as he walked beside Sintsov along Plyushchikha Street. "But what does 'on the streets' mean? It means right here, on the Plyushchikha! Germans in this house, and us in that one. Or Germans at the far end of the Crimea Bridge, and us on this side keeping them from the city centre. It means it's going to be like the street fighting with the Cadets in Nineteen Seventeen, only multiplied a hundred times over!"

He tried to get used to the idea as he walked along, but his mind refused to accept it.

"Maybe we'll be sent straight to the front tomorrow," he said to Sintsov after a long silence.

Sintsov nodded. He was wondering whether a rifle would be found for him in the battalion or whether they would be armed at the front itself.

The factory school, now being used as a barracks for the Communist Battalion, was at the back of a courtyard behind a high brick wall near which about twenty men in civilian clothes were milling around.

"Ah, that's the rest of the platoon," said Malinin. "They wanted to assemble at the Regional Committee building, then they decided to form up here. Nearer to the job."

He hitched his rifle higher up on his shoulder with surprising swagger and went up to the men assembled by the wall. They were nearly all getting on in years: many were wearing spectacles, some had rucksacks, others were carrying kitbags, two had small suitcases, and one even had a neatly tied laundry basket.... Three or four had sporting guns, two had rifles, and one had a revolver strapped over his coat. All were wearing belts, and although each was dressed in anything even remotely suitable, they were trying to arrange their clothes so that they would be as comfortable as possible on the march.

As Malinin and Sintsov went up to them, the assembled platoon was making fun of the little grey-haired man with the laundry basket.

"Trofimov's off fishing again. You can tell his wife's packed his things for him! He's got grub for two days, a bottle of vodka and a camping cushion. Everything by the book!"

"Where are your fishing rods, Trofimov? Forgotten them, or something?"

"Ah, Malinin! Malinin's here!" said several voices in greeting.

Clearly, they nearly all knew him.

"The senior in command's arrived. That means it's time to fall in," said someone.

"Where's Ikonnikov?" demanded Malinin, after counting them over with his eyes.

"Ikonnikov won't be coming," replied Trofimov. "I called to fetch him and found a team digging out the cellar... He's trapped down there."

"Are they making themselves heard?" asked Malinin.

"So far they've been knocking to show they're still alive."

Someone mirthlessly joked that there was nothing worse than those cellars, and it was better to wait for death at home in one's flat.

"If Ikonnikov isn't coming, then we're all present!" said Malinin.

They formed up in two ranks. Malinin took his place at the head, and Sintsov found himself alone in the rear rank. And so they marched in column into the spacious courtyard of the factory school past a sentry in civilian clothes. He let them through, greeting Malinin informally:

"How d'you do, Alexei Denisych!"

"How d'you do!" replied Malinin, displeased at this civilian greeting and, leaving the new arrivals in the courtyard, he went into the building to report their arrival to the battalion commissar.

He was a long time inside—about twenty minutes. He finally came out again, looking even more glum than usual.

"Trofimov," he said to the man with the basket, "I'm appointing you senior in command during my absence. Instructions are: today you're all on training. The company commanders are to arrive sometime during the day, and the platoon is to be issued with fifteen rifles. As for the rest, we'll see when we reach the front. General training to commence at ten o'clock. In the meantime, you can warm yourselves up in the barracks. We've been allocated Room Number Nineteen, second on the left. As for you, Sintsov—" Malinin looked at him as if he had toothache and every word cost him a stab of pain—"stay behind. We're going to see the commissar."

"Here we go again," thought Sintsov with sinking heart.

"This is the man. Ask him," said Malinin just as glumly when they went in to the battalion commissar.

It was a classroom, and the battalion commissar was sitting at the teacher's desk. Behind him was a blackboard, half covered with writing. Malinin sat down sideways at a pupil's desk. Sintsov remained standing.

The battalion commissar was a well-dressed man of about fifty. He was wearing a heavy knitted sweater and a dark-blue suit with an old Order of the Red Banner on his lapel. A leather coat and a reindeer-skin hat had been thrown onto the chair beside him. On the table in front of the commissar lay a Mauser with a silver name-plate on the holster.

"You may sit down," he said to Sintsov instead of greeting him. "We shall have to think about what we're going to do with you. I said we didn't want the likes of you, but Comrade Malinin's dissatisfied."

"Your job is to give the orders, and my being dissatisfied doesn't matter!" said Malinin.

"I've forgotten how to give orders!" joked the commissar. "Let me just get into uniform, and then I'll remember. Meanwhile, let's discuss what's to be done. Comrade Malinin has given me a rough outline of your story," he said, turning back to Sintsov, "but perhaps you would like to add a few details yourself?"

The commissar had steely blue hair combed slantwise, a narrow, intelligent face, tight, mocking lips, and no less mocking eyes behind the expensive-looking gold-framed spectacles.

"What the hell can I add?" said Sintsov, looking into those mocking eyes.

Desperation made his remark sound rude, but for some reason this made a favourable impression on the commissar.

"This is what I'm doubtful about, and if you can clear it up for me, state your objections! If you were a civilian, it would merely be a matter of trust. Comrade Malinin believes you, and I believe him. But you're a regular, so won't it mean that we're harbouring a deserter?"

"Honestly, Nikolai Leonidovich, what's harbouring got to do with it!" This was too much for Malinin.

The commissar's spectacles gleamed as he looked at Malinin; then he carried on regardless.

"You are a regular. To explain your past behaviour and to receive a new posting to the front, you should report to the appropriate organisation. In my opinion, these matters are the concern of the Special Department, but I'm willing to let you report to the District Prosecutor, since you are in its zone. It's on the Molchanovka, not far from here—as a matter of fact, I live next door to it. That's where I recommend you to report. But please don't repeat your story to me, because it won't affect my decision in any way. So there you are, that's all," he concluded quietly, but implacably; and Sintsov realised that this polite, smooth manner was habitual with him and did not mean anything.

"At least write him a covering note, Comrade Guber," said Malinin. "After all, the man hasn't any documents at all. He was lucky to find me at the District Party Committee. I remember his face."

"Very well," said Guber curtly, but without any sign of annoyance. He opened a notepad lying on the desk, took a gold-nibbed fountain pen out of his pocket, unscrewed the top, and began writing.

"Your surname is Sinev?" he asked after he had written the first two lines.

"Sintsov, I. P."

"Sintsov, I. P." repeated Guber. He wrote a few more lines, signed his name at the bottom, tore the sheet off the notepad, folded it in half, and handed it to Sintsov. "We haven't got an office stamp—so they'll have to take this on trust! If they take it on trust, well and good. If they don't..." he shrugged his shoulders.

"May I go now?" asked Sintsov, who had gone white in the face.

"By all means."

Angrily, but punctiliously, in correct army fashion, Sintsov executed an about turn and marched out, his tattered boots clumping over the floor.

Guber and Malinin were left together. They exchanged glances in silence. Malinin sighed heavily: he was speechless with fury.

"Say something, Malinin, or you'll choke to death. You can speak unofficially, there's no order in force yet, and I'm only commissar for the time being by grace of the District Party Committee. And anyway we're old acquaintances...."

"You're a charming formalist, you are," growled Malinin. "I'll never understand how you became commissar of a brigade!"

"In the First Cavalry,* I'll have you know!" said Guber jokingly. "But that was a long time ago! Since then, I've worn out nine pairs of breeches in an office. I've been dealing with foreigners for fifteen years and it's wrecked me.... You see how I handle things...."

"I can see that all right," said Malinin. "Left your heart in your brief-case and left your brief-case behind at home."

"Interesting to hear that from you, Malinin. D'you know what they call you—behind your back, of course?"

"Yes," said Malinin. "Malinin and Burenin...." **

"Exactly," said Guber, smiling again. "That's because you've been stuffing your head with District Committee figures for twenty years, and all the questions and answers tally, just as in a textbook! And now you've suddenly decided to spread your wings! The war's going to cancel everything out, is that it? To blazes with routine? That's something I'd never have expected of you!"

"Alright," said Malinin. "So you were afraid to let him—"

* *First Cavalry*—the biggest operational cavalry formation in the Red Army. Founded in 1919 at the time of the foreign intervention and the Civil War.—*Ed.*

** *Malinin and Burenin*—authors of an arithmetic textbook.—*Ed.*

and he jerked his thumb at the door as if Sintsov was still standing there, "—tell you the whole story. You were afraid that you'd decide differently if he did. Please shut up! Shut up if you're ashamed of yourself, and don't pester me...."

"What have I to be ashamed of?" said Guber, flushing; and the mask of defensive mockery was suddenly there no more. "I acted correctly. He's a serviceman. He can go to the Prosecutor's Department and they can sort it out there properly."

"Is everything being sorted out the way it should be everywhere?" interrupted Malinin.

"Whether it is or not," said Guber, "they can cope in the Military Prosecutor's Department, I think, and he'll land back at the front in fine style without any help from us."

"Very well, then, just shut up. You've done it now, so shut up, don't bother explaining any more," said Malinin with a gesture of despair. He stood up, brought his hand up to his black peaked cap, and asked: "Permission to rejoin the platoon?"

Meanwhile, Sintsov was approaching the building of the Military Prosecutor's Department on Molchanovka Street. Twice on the way he had unfolded and read Guber's note. The handwriting was so beautiful and firm and the signature was so authoritative that the paper actually had the look of an official document, although it bore no stamp. It was headed: "To the Prosecutor's Department of the Moscow Military District", and underneath was written: "Direction Order. Comrade Sintsov, I. P., is directed to report to you for the purpose of making a personal statement. Commissar of the Frunze District Communist Battalion, Brigade Commissar of the Reserve N. Guber."

Outside the Prosecutor's Department building an old staff car was parked with an army driver dozing at the wheel. The windows had been criss-crossed with strips of paper, but these had not been much use. Half the glass panes had been blown out. Sintsov pushed the door open and entered. Two doors led inside from the vestibule: there was a sentry standing on duty at one; the other was half-open and there was no one there. Sintsov went through the second door into a room with two round tables and some chairs for those waiting. There were two wooden hatches in the wall. Over one was written: "Permits issued here", and over the other "Mail Reception"; but both hatches were closed. Sintsov knocked, and then knocked more loudly. Still no reply. The door half opened and the sentry looked in.

"What's all the noise about?" he demanded. "There's no one here, so you needn't bother knocking."

"I've got to get through to the Prosecutor's Department," said Sintsov.

"So what? There's no one there, so you needn't knock."

"Then I'll apply to you," said Sintsov.

"No use applying to me," snapped the sentry. "Get out of the building. Have you a permit?"

"No," said Sintsov.

"Then you've got no business in here and I can't let you in.... Now get out!" shouted the sentry threateningly, and he propelled Sintsov out into the street.

The car with the driver in it had gone, and the street was completely deserted. Realising that it was useless trying to approach the sentry again, Sintsov decided to wait outside. Surely one of the departmental staff was bound to drive or walk up sooner or later?

For a whole hour, Sintsov walked up and down the pavement outside the building, shivering in the cold wind and wondering why no one entered or left the building. In the end, it proved too much for him and he went back into the vestibule. The sentry glared at him, darkly suspicious, and, as if seeing him for the first time, asked unpleasantly:

"What d'you want?"

"Perhaps you could ask the duty officer to come down and see me?"

"I'm not calling anyone to come down and see you. No one's allowed to wander about in here. Get out, or I'll arrest you!"

"Arrest me, then," said Sintsov, perfectly willing.

But arresting Sintsov was not part of the sentry's plan.

"There's no point in arresting you," he snarled. "Get out, or I'll use arms! And stop wandering about in front of the building! It's not allowed!"

As he said this, he even tipped his rifle forward. Sintsov calmly eyed the rifle and bayonet, turned his back on the sentry and, without saying a word, went out. All he could do was wait. Perhaps someone would come in or go out anyway.... He avoided walking past the door this time and paced up and down the pavement opposite the Prosecutor's Department.

The street seemed dead. Sintsov lost all count of time and went into the vestibule again. "I'll get them to arrest me! I'll make a scene and refuse to leave. What else can I do?"

With this idea in mind, he went in expecting a third clash with the truculent sentry; but there was a new man on duty—a small Red Armyman with a girlish face and dark eyebrows.

"Comrade soldier," said Sintsov determinedly, taking the paper out of his pocket and going straight up to the sentry. "Here is my direction order. Call the duty officer or report to him. It's urgent."

The Red Armyman took hold of the paper; Sintsov let it go, and stepped one pace back. The sentry appreciated this move and, covertly estimating the distance between himself and Sintsov, began reading the note. For several seconds, respect for the signature "Brigade Commissar of the Reserve" struggled in him with his suspicions of a paper without a stamp. Finally, with another covert glance at Sintsov, he lifted the handset of a telephone.

"Comrade Duty Officer, this is the sentry reporting. There's a citizen here with instructions to report to the Prosecutor's Department from Brigade Commissar—I can't make out the surname. He wants you to come down for a moment. Right you are! I understand.... He's coming right away," he said to Sintsov, and he returned the paper.

About five minutes later, an Army lawyer came out of the door. He was young and lean, and his hastily combed hair was still glistening wet. There was a purple blotch on his right cheek. Before being called, he had evidently been sleeping at his desk with his cheek resting on his hand. He read the paper, returned it, and looked at Sintsov.

"Why no stamp?" he asked.

Sintsov replied that there was no stamp in the Communist Battalion. The duty officer nodded. At a time like this, so simple an explanation could hardly surprise him.

"Well, and just exactly what do you want in the Prosecutor's Department? Why were you sent here?"

"I was sent in connection with my own personal case," said Sintsov, and he looked round. What was he to do, then? Tell everything that had to be told, while standing like this in the vestibule? "I would like you, or anyone you instruct, to grant me half an hour."

The duty officer looked at Sintsov again. This man's face was confidence-inspiring—open, tired, and honest. His uniform, true, was makeshift, didn't fit him, and was dirty; and his boots were in a dreadful state. But the duty officer remembered that he had come with a paper from the Communist Battalion and that, while waiting to be issued with uniform, many put on anything that came to hand. An honest man, no doubt of that. The dishonest ones keep as far away as possible from the Military Prosecutor's offices at a time like this. But the duty officer was unable to listen to what this man had to tell him, he was unable to send him to anyone else, and he was unable to explain the reason why he couldn't take either of these steps.

And the reason was that apart from the two sentries — one relieved of duty and now asleep, the other at his post — he, Army Lawyer Polovinkin, was the only man at present in the building of the District Military Prosecutor's Department. The day before yesterday, after receiving the appropriate instructions, the Department had been transferred somewhere else, to one of the railway stations outside Moscow. The records had been evacuated, and the current files had been taken to the new location. For the last twenty-four hours, there had been nothing in the Prosecutor's Department except empty book-cases, telephones, two sentries, and himself, as duty officer, with instructions to send to the new address anyone who reported to him, or rang up, provided they were authorised personnel only. He couldn't talk to Sintsov down here, because he was supposed to be on duty upstairs, at his telephone. He couldn't take Sintsov up with him, because anyone who went up to the second floor of the building would realise that the Department had left. And this was something that chance callers were not on any account permitted to know!

"Look here," said the duty officer, after thinking over all the possibilities. "You wait here, in that room there, in the permits office. I'm on duty, and I can't absent myself to hear your case, but I'll tell those who can as soon as they're free. We'll either send for you or come down and talk to you. Let him wait in there —" for the sentry's benefit he indicated the room with the two hatches, "— on my authority...."

"Good. Thank you," said Sintsov. "Only I must have been waiting for three hours already."

The duty officer did not know how long Sintsov would have to wait, but the suggestion that he should do so was not hypocritical. To his delight, one of his superiors had phoned an hour ago from the new place and had told him that he would soon be back with a group of staff workers. It had been with this group in mind that the duty officer had asked Sintsov to wait. He went upstairs to his office, and Sintsov waited. At first he was impatient, counting the minutes. Then, losing count of the time, he dozed off, woke up again and, dashing into the vestibule with the urgency of a man who has just woken up, said to the sentry:

"Get me the duty officer."

His determined manner worked on the sentry, who dialled a number, asked for the duty officer, and said:

"The man you left waiting here wants a word with you. Shall I give him the phone?"

The reply was evidently in the affirmative, because he handed the phone to Sintsov.

"What is it now?" said an irritable voice.

"Comrade Army Lawyer," said Sintsov, "no one's sent for me after all!"

"Wait, and you'll be sent for," replied the duty officer.

"But I've got to get back to my unit," said Sintsov, lying over the telephone in desperation. "Otherwise I'll be absent without official leave."

The line was silent for several seconds.

"All right. If you're in such a frantic hurry, write out everything you were going to tell the Prosecutor's Department. When you've finished, tell the sentry, he'll phone, and I'll come down and pick it up."

Sintsov stood there for several more seconds holding the handset to his ear. He could only do as the duty officer had told him. There was no alternative.... Put it all down on paper, leave it here, and he'd see.

"Then I'll return to the battalion," said he with sudden determination and relief.

He felt in his jacket pocket and found some sheets of paper folded in four that he had taken from Malinin at the District Party Commitee to write to Masha, went back into the permits office and, fortunately, found a pen there with a bent but still serviceable nib. After trying the pen and emptying the dregs of two ink-wells into one, he smoothed out the sheets of paper, leaned his chest on the table and, almost without stopping, began writing page after page, only pausing occasionally to straighten the nib when it spluttered more badly than usual and tore the paper.

When he had covered eight sheets and had explained all the circumstances, it was already beginning to get dark outside. He wanted to read straight through what he had written, but he glanced out of the window and, with a gesture of resignation, wrote the concluding sentence at the bottom of the sheet:

"Of all my actions, I consider the following two incorrect: I did not report to the Special Department of the unit stationed near my point of escape from encirclement, but instead travelled by road away from it, as described above; and, on nearing Moscow, I did not go to the checkpoint, but by-passed it. I accept full disciplinary responsibility for the authenticity of the facts as stated by me."

He signed his name, put the date, then read through the closing lines and, after the word "disciplinary", firmly inserted "and Party".

The former procedure was repeated in the vestibule. Sintsov asked the sentry to call the duty officer, the sentry rang him up, and in a few minutes the duty officer appeared in the doorway.

"Have you written it?" he asked and, taking the sheets from Sintsov as by habit, glanced at the heading first to make sure that the statement was properly addressed and then turned it over and glanced quickly at the end.

"Where can we find you when this has been examined? Have you written down the address?"

"Yes, at the beginning," replied Sintsov, and he showed the duty officer the place where he had written: "Communist Battalion of Frunze District: present address—2, Plyushchikha Street."

He showed this to the duty officer, then, as an afterthought, pulled Guber's note out of his pocket.

"Comrade Army Lawyer! Please write on my direction order that you detained me here till evening, otherwise it'll count as absence...."

He had told a white lie. What mattered was not when he returned, but that Guber should see that he really had been to the Prosecutor's Department.

"Very well, I'll write that you were here until eighteen hundred hours," said the duty officer.

"And a stamp if possible, please!"

The duty officer frowned at the thought of having to go up to the second floor, come down, and then go back up again. He grunted, intending to refuse, but then had second thoughts—after all, it was only human!—took Sintsov's paper, went out, and returned two minutes later.

"Here!" he said with the irritation of a decent man who is annoyed with himself at his own decency.

As he went out into the streets, which were now almost in darkness, Sintsov unfolded the paper. There was a small stamp on it: "Moscow District Military Prosecutor's Department". Beneath the stamp was written: "Was in the Prosecutor's Department until eighteen hundred hours.

18.10.41." Then there was a big, beautifully written letter "P" and the down-sloping signature of a man whose name Sintsov would never know.

The all-clear had just sounded after the first air-raid that evening, when the guard commander came to Guber and said that a man named Sintsov was at the gates and was claiming that he had left the barracks with a pass issued by him, Guber, and must now report back to the commissar. Guber smiled wryly, angrily adjusted his spectacles, and said that the man should be brought in; at the same time, he asked for Malinin to be sent to him.

Sintsov walked into Guber's office first. Malinin had not yet arrived.

"Well, now, Comrade Sintsov," said Guber mockingly. "Is the Military Prosecutor's Department closed for repairs, or couldn't you find the Molchanovka, or was it something else?"

Sintsov took out Guber's note and laid it down in front of him.

Guber read the note carefully, as if it had been written by someone else, then turned the sheet of paper sideways and read aloud the entry by the duty officer at the Prosecutor's Department: "Was in the Prosecutor's Department until eighteen hundred hours."

"Does this mean that they dealt with your case and sent you back to us?" said Guber, looking up from the note.

"No," said Sintsov, "it doesn't."

"To be more precise?"

Sintsov told him about the futile spells of waiting and about the written statement he had left in the Prosecutor's Department.

"And did you put down everything Malinin told me about you?"

"Everything," said Sintsov.

"Without concealment?"

Sintsov shrugged his shoulders, and Guber himself had the decency to realise that his question had been foolish. What concealment could there be when, if he was a coward, he could easily have deserted yesterday and headed deep into the rear. And if he was a wangler, he could probably have cooked up some story about himself and latched on to some unit. There were enough people between Vyazma and Moscow who had lost their units and mislaid their documents!

He even whistled at the thought of how many there were, and suddenly smiled at Sintsov, not mockingly, as he had smiled hitherto, but genuinely this time—he could smile like that too—and said:

"Take a seat. Malinin will be here soon, and we can talk it over...."

Guber was in a good mood. Another five hundred rifles had been added to the hundred and sixty that had been in the battalion in the morning. The battalion was now at least armed with rifles, and, most important of all, it was to be transported by road nearer to the front tomorrow. What would happen after that, Guber didn't yet know: either the battalions would all be formed into a division, or they would be used to provide replacements for other units; but at least it was now more like the job to do which he, Guber, as an old cavalryman, had talked his superiors into letting him stay behind in Moscow, after having evacuated his department under command of a deputy.

Malinin entered, saw Sintsov and, as always, scowled at him and nodded glumly.

"So he's shown up," he growled, going over to Guber's desk.

"Take a look at that, please...." Guber slid the note across the table-top, hiding with an effort the mockery in his eyes. "One bureaucrat writes a bureaucratic memorandum, another bureaucrat puts a resolution on it, and a living human being—" he nodded towards Sintsov, "— goes round and round in ever decreasing circles and can't get to the front because of these bureaucrats. What do you think?" he suddenly asked cheerfully. "Can we have done with all this red tape, sign on volunteer Sintsov for your platoon, and say good-bye to official procedure and long live anarchy, eh?"

But Malinin did not take it as a joke.

"What have you decided, in fact?" he asked gloomily.

"What have I decided?" asked Guber in his turn, as cheerful as before. "This paper will stay with me, and he—" Guber nodded at Sintsov, "—will stay with you. If anything happens, I shall justify myself with this document and you will justify yourself with Comrade Sintsov's conduct in battle!"

Guber spoke the last words in an earnest tone and, in contrast to his usual manner, he sounded almost moved.

"I shall justify your faith in me," said Sintsov, rising. "You may rest assured of that!"

"I'm not in the habit of getting emotional," said Guber in his previous mocking tone as he rose from the desk. He was a man with a romantic streak in him, but he always scrupulously suppressed it. He was suppressing it now.

"May we go?" said Malinin gloomily.

"You may go, if you don't wish to state your opinion."

"Why should I? If you'd decided otherwise, I'd have gone to the District Party Committee and lodged a complaint against you."

"Would have availed yourself of the last opportunity?" said Guber stingingly.

"Precisely," said Malinin, and he turned to Sintsov. "Let's go!"

CHAPTER FOURTEEN

The snow had fallen forty-eight hours ago. It was a clear, frosty, sunny day. Malinin had just left the company and was on his way to the platoon. At first, keeping his head down, he had dashed across some open ground along a snow-bleached communication trench, and had then climbed straight up a small rise on the crest of which stood the ruins of the brickworks where the platoon was positioned. Although it was freezing, the sun, especially as he climbed uphill, warmed him even through his fur hat. Malinin stopped to recover his breath, turned round, and looked back.

The view was typical of the countryside outside Moscow: a gently undulating landscape with the black patches of copses and with strips of forest on the horizon. Somewhat nearer lay the black, rectangular, fire-gutted premises of a machine and tractor station, now being used as Battalion HQ. A little further off could be seen the rooftops of a village where the regimental staff were stationed. Every freshly-trodden path and every trench stood out distinctly in the snow. No matter how well they were camouflaged, they were clearly visible from that little patch of high ground. The snow showed everything up.

On the day that the men of the Communist Battalion had arrived as replacements for the 31st Rifle Division, Malinin had been given a rank and had been sent as political instructor of a company. He was still in the same appointment after ten days of fighting.

The fighting had been continuous and bloody. More replacements had been sent to the division after those with which Malinin had arrived. True, the replacements had been quite thin this time, and the impression was that the full complement had not been sent: they were being reserved for future needs. As before, the Germans had been advancing, and today the division was fighting with its back to Moscow, another twenty kilometres to the east of the line on which Malinin had first found it.

During this period, it had fallen back three times from occupied positions: twice when levelling off the front with its neighbours to avoid encirclement, and the third time because one of its regiments had been almost completely annihilated and the other two could not hold out. Only by the morning of the following day, deep in the rear at the reserve positions, did they manage to stop the Germans and pin them down in front with their own fire and with a dense barrage from the heavy artillery far behind them. The division had stuck to these positions, along whose front line Malinin was now walking, and had not retreated any further, although the last three days and nights had been spent in beating off a series of extremely savage attacks.

Such was the situation on the division's own sector, and the fighting outside Moscow had become a vast and prolonged defensive operation which, it seemed, might completely exhaust attackers and defenders alike any moment now. But so far neither side had shown any sign of weakening. The battles had continued with their former ferocity and with the odds in favour of the Germans who, although they had the upper hand, were having to pay more and more dearly with each passing day for every kilometre of terrain captured.

Malinin's feelings were those of many who were then fighting outside Moscow. This time, the German tanks had not sliced through our front like a knife through butter, as had been the case in summer and as had nearly happened again in the first days of the breakthrough at Vyazma and Bryansk. People were gradually beginning to feel differently about things. They were in the state of a spring which has been compressed with gigantic force until it won't give any more; but although it may have been compressed to the absolute limit, it still preserves the ability to uncoil again. And this sensation, both physical and mental, this inner ability to uncoil and lash out, was being experienced by all who had been slowly and viciously driven back by the Germans from one line of defence to another, each one nearer to Moscow.

The men were driving themselves to the absolute limit: they knew Moscow was behind them—there was no need to explain that. But in addition to this, they felt—from the replacements arriving at the most critical moments, from the artillery which was becoming more and more in evidence at the front, and from many other signs, beginning with presents and mail and ending with the tone of the newspapers—that the whole country behind them was straining itself to the utmost not to surrender Moscow.

If there had, indeed, been a moment when Moscow might have suddenly fallen into the hands of the Germans, that moment was long since past. Victory was not expected yet, but no one believed in the possibility of defeat any more. Geography seemed to favour the Germans: they had come nearer than a hundred kilometres to Moscow along several roads; but the dread arithmetic of war, whereby tanks which had penetrated the front could cover such distances in a matter of twenty-four hours, was no longer effective. The tanks could still break through the front, and they did so here and there; but they were stopped somehow or other after only three, five, or seven kilometres. And without that former terrifying arithmetic, geography alone could no longer break the human spirit.

That day, taking advantage of a lull, they had brought the mail from the field post-office. Malinin had received a letter from his wife. After twenty years with him, his own reluctance to betray his emotions had become second nature with her too, and so she had written to him with restraint to say that she was thinking about him constantly and was worried in case he hadn't been issued with his winter uniform in time. They were saying that early frosts were due soon. She also sent him two news items.

The first was about their son. The head of his school, which had been evacuated to somewhere near Kazan that summer, had written that their son, Victor Malinin, ninth former, had disappeared, leaving a note to say that he was off to defend Moscow. In spite of all efforts to trace him, he had not yet been picked up.

"As if they'll ever pick him up, the scamp!" thought Malinin affectionately.

His wife wrote of their son with much grief, which at first evoked no response in Malinin's heart. "So what, the lad's sixteen already," he thought proudly; but then he suddenly remembered the previous evening and the open common grave with the bodies of seven men from the company, all killed on the same day. And on recalling this, he was saddened, although pride for his son's behaviour was still uppermost in his mind.

The second news item was about his wife. The District Housing Department, where she was an inspector, was resuming work again, and she had been appointed manager because their chief, Kukushkin, whom Malinin knew personally, had been called back from Gorky, to which he had absconded without permission, had been fired from his job, expelled from the Party, de-reserved, and sent to the front as a private soldier. Malinin was delighted at this. That they should have restored order in Moscow where people like Kukushkin was concerned did even more to strengthen his conviction that everything was going to be all right in the end. Not only were we not going to give up Moscow, we were damn well not even going to retreat that far.

As for Kukushkin, who in his opinion was an absolute blackguard, Malinin thought bitterly that he would certainly wriggle out of it somehow. Shove him right into the front line and he'd still bob up like a cork somewhere in the rear.

After a rest, Malinin climbed to the top of the hill where his platoon was positioned. Yesterday's fighting had prevented him from visiting it in the daytime or during the night, and he felt himself to blame. He had made it a rule to see each of his men at least once in the course of the day. There were not so many left in the company. Life was like that these days: if you hadn't seen a man yesterday, you might not get the chance today. The platoon had sustained more losses yesterday and, according to the morning figures, there were only eleven men left, including Sergeant Sirota, the platoon commander. This sergeant had been in command of the platoon for a week now, ever since the death on the same day of two lieutenants: one had fought since the beginning of the war, and the other had been posted direct to duty from training school only that morning.

The ruins of the brickworks were not really ruins, since there had been nothing to knock down. Work on building the factory had only just commenced and it had been left unfinished. The foundations of the structure and the kilns had been laid, and the walls had been going up and had reached different levels, but nowhere more than half a window high. Only a short distance away were the foundations of the future factory chimney. The solid round brickwork rose a metre above ground level and the base had been deepened inside for the underground flue. It was a natural reinforced emplacement and needed very little adaptation to make an excellent machine-gun nest.

Three days ago, when they had been taking possession of this position, Malinin, an old machine-gunner, had advised them to make better use of the chimney and yesterday he had seen Sintsov settling in there with his mounted machine-gun. Since the fighting had begun, Sintsov had been in Malinin's company, partly by a stroke of luck, since he might easily have found himself in another regiment and battalion, and partly at the wish of Malinin himself, who had put a word in for Sintsov in the battalion, so that when they had been listing the replacements, Sintsov had been put down for his company.

Sintsov had soon proved to be an experienced soldier who knew how to handle firearms. As always happens during major battles, his duties had soon been upgraded. On the first morning, he had carried the ammunition. By that evening, he had become Number Two at the machine-gun. On the next day, he had replaced Number One when the latter had been killed. Four days ago,when falling back from their former positions to these new ones, Sintsov and his Number Two had covered the company's retreat with machine-gun fire until nightfall and, in the opinion of Lieutenant Ionov, the company commander, had displayed courage and coolheadedness in doing so.

In the excitement of the moment, Lieutenant Ionov had even suggested recommending Number One for a medal "For Valour"; but Malinin, remembering Sintsov's past, had decided to wait, restrained by his own rigorousness and a personal sense of responsibility for Sintsov. He had restricted himself to mentioning the names of those concerned and the conduct of the machine-gun crew in his routine political report, but had kept quiet about the proposal to fill in an awards sheet. The company commander had again spoken of his intention, but had again came up against a wall of silence on Malinin's part and, since he had been thinking of other matters, had simply forgotten about Sintsov.

Malinin now wanted to see Sintsov, but before going to the machine-gun nest, he decided to visit the brickworks where Sergeant Sirota was positioned.

Sergeant Sirota was an old-timer and a section commander, but owing to the heavy losses he had been platoon commander for the last two weeks. He was both pleased and permanently worried concerning how to hold his own in comparison with the neighbouring platoons, which were under the command of lieutenants. Like all the rest, he was not free from a sense of danger; but this did not feature very prominently in his professional attitude. He was just as likely to be killed as anyone else, and that would mean the end of everything, including army service; but the thought of death could not affect his strict devotion to duty.

When Sirota saw the company political instructor in the distance, he tightened the belt round his quilted jacket, made sure that the star on his fur hat was directly over the middle of his forehead, and shouldered his brand-new, freshly oiled submachine-gun. Deliveries of these firearms to the division had begun the week before. Sirota had been the first in his platoon to be issued with one, and he had already tried it out in battle. Although it hadn't the accuracy of a rifle, the fire density was good, and in the early stages Sirota was being almost excessively careful with it.

With the submachine-gun slung over his shoulder, he ran out through a gap in the wall to meet the political instructor. In response to Sirota's strictly formal greeting, Malinin saluted and then put out his hand.

"Well, how are you getting on, Sirota?" he asked, firmly gripping Sirota's burly hand in his own no less burly fist.

"Not so good with the rations, Comrade Political Instructor," complained Sirota at once. As an experienced soldier, he knew that there was a right time and a wrong time to complain to one's superiors, and he always knew the right moment.

"In what way not so good?" asked Malinin, well aware of what was wrong, but pretending that he hadn't already guessed.

"Well, Comràde Political Instructor, the rations detail went off with hot-food containers at dawn, but they might as well have taken the mess-tins."

"They gave you your entitlement for the unit," said Malinin. "What are you griping about?"

"I'm not griping," said Sirota, although he was annoyed about just that. He hadn't reported the losses and had been hoping to collect the rations for yesterday's strength.

"Anything else wrong?" asked Malinin.

"I don't have to tell you." Sirota shrugged his shoulders as if to say: "What's the use?" "They didn't bring any, so what can we do about it?"

"D'you mean smokes, by any chance?"

"What else, Comrade Political Instructor? The ammunition supplies are normal, we're not complaining about them."

Malinin grinned, opened his field-bag and took out four packets of *makhorka*.

"Here, dish that lot out. We had some gift parcels from our well-wishers in Moscow today, and I picked up the *makhorka* while I was about it. There are some cigarettes for us too, but they'll be sent later this evening...."

Sirota took the *makhorka* from Malinin and breathed a sigh of bliss. It was clear from his expression that he hadn't had a smoke for a long time.

"Have one now," said Malinin, seeing the expression on Sirota's face. "I'll have one too." He produced an already opened packet of *makhorka* from his pocket, sprinkled some out for Sirota and himself, and began rolling a cigarette.

"Perhaps we could go inside," suggested Sirota. "We've huddled up against one of the walls and hung a groundsheet up for cover."

"But it's all right out here in the breeze," said Malinin. "The weather's bloody marvellous."

"I won't be a moment, then, Comrade Political Instructor! I'll share out the *makhorka* among the men, if you don't mind."

"Go ahead."

Sirota had been called up for the army under the old regulations—not at nineteen, but at twenty two. He was now twenty-eight, but he looked older. His face was round and healthy-looking. His cheeks were blue with stubble and his forehead was creased with a permanent frown of worry. But now, as he rolled himself a cigarette, the worried expression had melted into a smile. Malinin noticed this and asked:

"What are you so happy about?"

"The weather, Comrade Political Instructor," said Sirota, and he lit up, skilfully shielding the flame with his cupped hand. "It would be a good thing if it froze a bit harder."

"Why?" asked Malinin. "It's no joke being out in a heavy frost."

"I look at it this way: it might be no joke for us, but it'd be even worse for the Germans," said Sirota, grinning as if he personally had it in his power to arrange such a trap for the enemy. "I've got a chemistry student in my platoon—from the fourth course—and he says that their aviation oil can't take it and freezes up. Just look up there." Sirota nodded at the sky. "It's the second day we've been having our kind of winter, and it's the second day that Fritz has had less planes in the air. If the frost hits harder, d'you think their tank oil will let them down too?"

"Don't you be scared of the tanks," said Malinin.

"I'm not scared of them. We've already destroyed two...."

"Two—that's not all by long chalk," said Malinin.

"Not bad for a platoon!" protested Sirota. "Just work it out from the rifle platoons alone. Two per platoon, six per company, eighteen per battalion. Fifty-four per regiment," he continued, counting them off on his fingers. "A hundred and sixty-two per division, and one thousand six hundred per ten divisions. Before you knew where you were, the Germans wouldn't have any tanks outside Moscow. That's what it would be like, if all the platoons did the same! But can you say that every platoon has knocked out two tanks? Just take our battalion. I don't know of any platoon in it that's destroyed two, apart from ours," he concluded proudly.

"So you've worked it out for the whole front," said Malinin with a smile. "You've done your bit, you've knocked out your two tanks, and now you can go and twiddle your thumbs. Let the others have a go; it's their turn, eh?"

"Oh, no I'm not in the habit of reasoning like that. I'm just for the facts. Two tanks per platoon is a lot."

"I'm not saying it isn't," said Malinin. "What I am saying is that you mustn't rely on the oil. The cold'll clamp down, the enemy'll have their oil ruined, the artillery'll stop firing, the sub-machine-guns'll jam, and there'll be nothing left to do but sweep the Germans off the road and stack them up on the verge. That's the wrong attitude; you mustn't get complacent."

"Who says we're getting complacent?" demanded Sirota, who wasn't used to mincing his words when he was "at ease". He shrugged his shoulders, then bent his head back and looked at the sun. "It's all an illusion," he said, frowning into the sun. "As soon as Fritz feels up to it, there'll be nothing left of this fine weather but smoke."

"Anyway, let's have a look at your position," said Malinin. He threw down his cigarette butt, stamped on it, and climbed through the gap first.

Ten minutes later, as always with him during a lull, he was already sitting and chatting with the soldiers. About six men were gathered round him. The rest, including Sintsov, were at their posts; but Malinin was used to the men not all being able to be present at once, and he was satisfied with the audience he had.

"Now then, Mikhnetsov," he said to a slim, swarthy young soldier who was pulling avidly and nervously at a hand-rolled cigarette. "You're a chemist, of course, and I'm not, so you know what it's all about. Now you've been saying that the German aviation fuel is no use in the frosts, and the oil will freeze in their tanks over there; and maybe, according to you, their artillery systems will seize up, and their submachine-guns will start jamming." This idea had been worrying Malinin ever since he had heard about the oil from Sirota, and he was now stubbornly twisting it this way and that, determined to turn it to his own advantage in the end and use it as he thought fit. "Maybe, I repeat, maybe that's so. You're a chemist and it's more obvious to you. But personally, I prefer not to rely on all that. You may have hopes, but I haven't. And I'll go further than that. You're hoping that the German technical equipment will seize up in the frosts; but I'm not relying on it at all. I'm relying on you, Mikhnetsov, and no one else. I expect it of you that no matter what the weather is like, you won't lose your nerve, and that your rifle, and your grenade, and anything else you happen to have, will hit the target and nothing will break down, because if you don't lose your nerve, the Germans will never make it to Moscow, even if their technical equipment runs like clockwork in thirty degree of frost. But if you lose your nerve, then whatever the circumstances, they'll be in Moscow, with equipment or without it and whether there's a frost or not. It won't make any difference! Now then, what have you to say that, chemist?"

Mikhnetsov was clearly no fool. He fully realised what the political instructor was driving at, and he could sense the warmth as well as firmness behind his words. But he passionately wanted the Germans to suffer every conceivable misfortune as they advanced on Moscow, and he heatedly began bringing up a variety of new theories about the Russian winter and the German technical equipment.

"Well, let's assume you're right," said Malinin in a conciliatory tone, feeling that he had already dealt with the hint of complacency that had alarmed him so much. "Let's assume the Germans get into a mess. D'you still realise that what matters isn't them, but you? Not whether their oil seizes up, but whether you hold your ground?" Malinin was still doggedly hammering his point home.

"That's sense, Comrade Political Instructor," chorused several voices.

"Listen, Sirota," said Malinin after a pause. "What day is it? Thursday?"

"Yes, Thursday."

"There's to be a session of the Regimental Party Bureau. Your application is being dealt with and they'll be considering you for the Party."

"I'm scared of questions," said Sirota, suddenly serious. "It's always been like that with me: as long as they don't ask questions, I know it all. As soon as they start asking—I forget the lot. It's as if I was jinxed!"

"He's been mugging up the Charter and the Party History ever since morning, so he's preparing all right," said a middle-aged soldier in a fatherly voice. It was the Trofimov who, while the Communist Battalion had been waiting to move off to the barracks, had been teased by his comrades about having kitted himself up for a fishing trip. In a fur hat and a quilted jacket with a greatcoat over it, he now looked a seasoned soldier, and only his greying moustache showed that he was no longer young. He had joined the company with the same draft as Sintsov was the only Communist left in the platoon after all the losses.

"If we don't count Sintsov," thought Malinin; and then, as an afterthought: "No, Sintsov can't be counted in. With his Party card lost in doubtful and unverified circumstances, he might not be reinstated in the Party—not even with gallantry in action to his credit."

"Trofimov," said Malinin, "you can help Sirota prepare. Never mind him being platoon commander. You're veteran Communist, so in that respect you're his senior."

"He's helping me as it is," said Sirota. "The Party History belongs to him. I only had the Charter with me."

"You brought it with you from Moscow?" said Malinin, looking hard at Trofimov.

Trofimov nodded.

"The lads have been pestering the life out of me about Moscow," he said. " 'How's Moscow? They say there's been a panic.... Tell us what was like.' And I answer: 'If anything happened, it's slipped my mind. All I remember is what Lermontov said: "Now, lads, is Moscow not behind us? Then before Moscow we shall die!" Donkey's years ago, at the dawn of the century, before the Japanese War, I learned those lines in the parish school, and I haven't forgotten them, as you see!' " And he laughed.

"Well," said Malinin, "if its news from Moscow you're interested in, I can give you the latest. I've had a letter from my wife...."

And he told them how his son had run away to the front, and how his wife had gone back to work at the District Housing Department, and how Kukushkin had been de-reserved and sent to the front. The men listened sympathetically. They were all delighted that Kukushkin had been de-reserved. Serve him right, the louse!

"So they're putting Moscow in order," said Trofimov. "That's good. And if your son's run away, well, you'll just have to face up to it, Alexei Denisych. He's still the scamp he always was. I live two streets away from you, and I know his pranks...."

"It's all right," said Malinin, slightly stung by this. "I was a right scamp myself when I was younger."

Trofimov wanted to make a joke of it: "And where did it get you?" Then he remembered that Malinin was political instructor and refrained.

"Tell us," said a pale young soldier who had been silent so far and had been sitting with his cheek resting on his hand, "what's Moscow looking like after the air-raids? I'm a Muscovite myself; I used to live on the Korovi Val, but it's two years since I was called up."

"Your Korovi Val's in one piece," said Malinin. "Anyway, Trofimov must have told you ten times over. You can believe him; he's serious-minded, doesn't drink, and doesn't tell lies, even though he is a fisherman!"

Everybody laughed.

"Even so," said the Muscovite, still harping on his Korovi Val, "is there really as little damage in Moscow as they tell us in the papers?... I mean, they're on the way over every night, droning and droning away...."

"They may be on the way, but they don't get there," said Malinin. "Not every bullet's coming at you, is it? Well, it's the same with Moscow. From here, you get the idea that the bombing's terrible there. Me, when I was on the way to the front, my knees were knocking; but when I arrived, it wasn't so bad."

"Your knees were knocking indeed! A likely story, Comrade Political Instructor!" said Sirota in polite disbelief.

Malinin glanced at him mockingly.

"But that's exactly what they did do! Why, d'you think nothing can put the fear of God into me? It can, and how!" said Malinin. He bent down as a shell whistled low overhead, and still managed to make a joke of it. "You see, I even bow down to shells...."

Two or three smiled, but the others looked grave. The shell had burst too close at hand for it to be treated as a joke. Another shell, also a ranging shot, burst in front. All the men dashed for cover under the walls. The German artillery began frenziedly pounding the whole hill-top and the brickworks. There was an acrid reek of smoke in the air.

"They were trying to range in on us yesterday, the bastards, when we were beating off their attack," shouted Sirota in Malinin's ear. "They hammered us non-stop. And today it's even heavier.... They've started with us."

There was no time to consider whether or not the Germans had really got the range in yesterday or whether they had succeeded today. After putting down a dozen shells around them so close that their heavy breathing rocked the ground several times in succession, the Germans landed one straight inside the unfinished building.

Like all the others, Malinin had been lying under the wall and using it as cover from the shell-bursts outside. He suddenly became aware of a violent impact, thunder, weight, and lack of air. He was showered with pieces of the wall as it collapsed and with frozen chunks of earth ripped out of the ground by the explosion. Gasping for breath and straining with all his might, Malinin began extricating himself from the pile of bricks and earth. He was able to do so because he had clasped his hands round his head before the shell-burst and his arms had been uppermost.

After he had freed his arms and felt his bleeding face, he began frantically pushing aside everything that prevented him from getting up. Finally, deafened but alive, he crawled out of his tomb of bricks and rose unsteadily to his feet. There was no sign of life anywhere. The heavy shell had torn up every centimetre of ground. The snow, mixed with churned-up topsoil and smashed bricks, was black with blood and littered with scraps of uniform and mangled pieces of human bodies. Someone's leg, still booted, had been severed above the knee.

Malinin took a few aimless steps, shuddered, and halted. Something crunched underfoot. He looked down and recognised Trofimov's spectacles in the familiar frame bound with cotton thread.

He went back to the corner where he had been buried and realised that he had come out of it alive precisely because he had been buried. The bricks had tumbled down owing to a shell-blast outside, and the one which had landed inside had exploded when Malinin was already shielded by pieces of fallen masonry.

"Hey, anyone alive? Anyone alive?" shouted Malinin, beginning to remember who had been with him at the last moment.

Sirota had been with him, and that chemist, Mikhnetsov.... But where were they now? On this side of the ruins there was no sign of their bodies, or even of what is usually left of the human body after a direct hit.

"Perhaps they were thrown clear by the blast," thought Malinin; but just at that moment he heard a faint groan from under a pile of fallen bricks in the corner. He began flinging them aside, tearing his finger-nails in the process, putting his ear to the pile, and then throwing more bricks out of the way. He finally dragged Sirota from underneath. He was alive and was even making movements that suggested an effort to stand up, but the lower half of his face was a bloody mess. He was trying to speak, not with his mangled mouth but with his throat, or perhaps not even with his throat, but with his living gullet.

Malinin took a handful of snow and soaked up the blood on the horror that was Sirota's face. Then he pulled a field-dressing out of his bag and, cradling Sirota's head, began bandaging the lower half of his face. At first, he forgot that the wounded man had to breath and he wound the bandage so firmly that Sirota began gurgling. He had to undo the bandage and start all over again, binding the sergeant's face with a now blood-soaked dressing. After he had finished, Malinin dragged Sirota over to the wall and left him with his head up so that he wouldn't choke on his own blood. Only then did he notice a leg protruding from under the bricks where he had found Sirota.

When he had arrived an hour ago, he had noticed Mikhnetsov wearing a pair of old winter boots patched with double felt. Mikhnetsov had said that he had found them recently in an abandoned cabin, and Malinin had wanted to joke that the chemist, who had been claiming that the Germans were in no way prepared for the winter, was himself the best prepared in the whole platoon. He had meant to make a joke of this, but had forgotten. Now, as he saw the patched felt boot protruding from the bricks, he realised that it was Mikhnetsov under there. Without losing any more time, he hastily began digging out Mikhnetsov. He started at the feet, then swore at himself aloud and, judging where the man's head might be under the bricks, crawled over and began digging there. He should start at the head so that the victim wouldn't be asphyxiated, if he was still alive.

Still cursing himself for not having realised something so elementary, Malinin frantically threw brick after brick out of the way. Finally, Mikhnetsov's shoulders appeared. Malinin touched them—the body under the quilted jacket was still warm. He was alive. Malinin began uncovering the neck and head more quickly, but with greater caution. Suddenly, he stopped, holding in both hands a chunk of brick which he had just lifted off the back of Mikhnetsov's head. His body was still warm, but he was dead. The whole upper part of his skull had been sheared clean off by that same piece of brick.

Malinin stood up and bitterly hurled the brick to the ground. As he did so, he heard the intermittent chattering of a machine gun close by. Forty paces away, in the foundations of the factory chimney, men were still alive and firing at the Germans. Malinin knew the rare, overwhelming joy familiar to all, even the bravest, who imagine themselves alone on the battlefield and then discover that they are not by themselves after all.

Malinin went up to Sirota and once again lifted his heavy body with an effort, moving it so that it would be better protected from fragments in the event of more shelling. As it happened, the German artillery barrage had long since travelled deep into the rear. While Malinin was shifting him, Sirota made several feeble movements under the blood-soaked dressing as if he wanted to shout something; then he unclenched both fists, as if amazed at his own helplessness, clenched them again, and was silent. Only his chest rose and fell, wheezing painfully. Malinin took one last look at him, climbed over the wall, and followed a small, waist-high communication trench which had been dug to the chimney, whence came the brisk chatter of the machine gun.

When the shelling had begun, Sintsov and his Number Two, a young soldier named Kolya Bayukov with one year's service behind him, had been sitting at the machine gun in one of two embrasures knocked into the chimney. Without actually firing, they had been sighting the machine gun on some landmarks which had already been ranged. Each had also been rehearsing the other's role—Sintsov acting as Number Two and Bayukov as Number One.

There was a steep downward slope just beyond the embrasure; part of it, being invisible, was dead ground. Then the slope levelled out and became a snowy gully. It ran at an angle to our positions, and after it came an upward incline on which the other platoons of their company were positioned, near three cottages. There were no trenches in the gully itself, as it had been well ranged in from both sides and was covered by two machine guns. Yesterday afternoon, the Germans had tried to launch an attack directly along the gully, but had failed to break through because of the enfilading fire and had not even been able to take their dead away, although they usually risked their lives to do so. It had been said yesterday that there were up to thirty bodies in the hollow; but all that could be seen from the embrasure were a few black corpses lying on the snow. Carrying out aiming and range-finding drill, Sintsov was taking as markers a cart shaft sticking up in the snow and the two end bodies, one at the entrance to and one at the exit from the hollow.

Bayukov, with whom he had been for a week now, in some way reminded Sintsov of the soldier in the Prosecutor's Department who, back in Moscow, had agreed to call the duty officer. Bayukov had the same girlishly smooth, rosy complexion and the same black eyebrows. When he took off his fur hat, the fuzz of close-cropped hair underneath proved flaxen yellow.

"Did you have a kiss-curl when you were in civvies?" Sintsov had asked him on the first day, and Bayukov had smiled and said: "Aha!" Sintsov had thought that Bayukov with his black eyebrows and fair hair was undoubtedly very handsome indeed. His hair was close-cropped now. He was wearing a fur hat that wasn't his own and was too big for him, and his greatcoat bulged over the quilted jacket—but then they had been lying out in the open, first in the rain and then in the frost, and it was no time to be thinking of one's appearance.

They had hit it off from the start or, to be more precise, from the moment when Sintsov had said that each crew member should be able to stand in for the other, and had promptly suited actions to words by practising angle calculations and range corrections with Bayukov in the first hour of the lull....

Bayukov was a collective farmer from near Ryazan, from the forest village of Solotcha on the far side of the Oka. Solotcha was famous for the choice, sand-grown potatoes that bore its name and the fishing grounds on the Staritsa, an old course of the Oka.

However tough the fighting, men don't fight all the time. Bayukov, who could be silent or talkative according to whether or not he liked the company, had found time during that week to tell Sintsov that he hadn't quite finished his seven years at school for family reasons: his father had died, his mother had fallen ill, and for a year he had been a team-leader in the Komsomol potato-farming team, which is how Sintsov had come to learn about the Solotcha potatoes, and after demobilisation from the Army he wanted to study to be an agronomist.

"All I needed was an exam to cover those seven years, and I was thinking of taking it in the Army," said Bayukov. "Then came this business...."

"This business" had been the war.

Bayukov was a trusting, affectionate and inquisitive lad. He kept in his pack a list of all the books he had read over and beyond the school curriculum. There were quite a few of them for one of his age—a hundred and four, and mostly good ones. In the evenings, if circumstances allowed, he used to recall these books and outline their contents in his Ryazan accent in such detail, that Sintsov could only marvel at his memory. Incidentally, Sintsov himself had never read some of the books mentioned by Bayukov.

In action, when he and Sintsov had been fighting side by side, Bayukov had proved brave with the calm, matter-of-fact bravery of a man completely absorbed in his work. In this, he and Sintsov were alike, and so they had understood one another. Sintsov's mind was also wholly given over to battle. He allowed himself no indulgence whatever and made no plans. He saw his whole future life in the war—until death or victory—as that of a soldier, and he was wholly taken up with that life and with carrying out his service duties as well as possible. That Bayukov should have proved to be a good partner during several battles was the most important thing of all as far as he was concerned—so important, that he not only valued Bayukov for this, but sincerely loved him and was ready to do more for him than for many other people whom he had known over the years.

When the artillery bombardment began, Sintsov and Bayukov drew the machine gun a little way back from the embrasure so that the muzzle might not be struck by a stray shell fragment, and then settled themselves down a little lower on the chimney base, which had been laid with heavy fire-bricks. They realised at once that the bombardment was intensive and accurate. The air all round them shuddered under the impact of the dangerously close shell-bursts, but even during this bombardment they felt almost safe in the chimney. The many courses of fire-brick could only be penetrated by a heavy shell aimed at point-blank range, and even then only if the shell struck the surface at right angles. There was little likelihood of fragments flying into the chimney. The day before yesterday, Sintsov and Bayukov had covered it with sheets of boiler iron at platoon commander Sirota's suggestion. Ten millimetres thick, it had probably been intended for the leaves of the kiln doors, and two sheets had almost entirely covered the chimney, leaving only a small gap. The flue ran across the foundations, and it was along this that they now used to crawl into the chimney from below.

"You've got a real pill-box here," Sirota had said yesterday; and that is just how Sintsov and Bayukov thought of their chimney. Only one thing could have wiped them out—a direct hit from above on the sheet iron covering the chimney. In that case, of course, there was nothing they could do, and nothing would be left of them but two wet blobs. But even now, under bombardment, they gave no more thought to such a stroke of bad luck than to any other likelihood of death, always present one way or another in wartime.

The German artillery fire was growing steadily worse. Bayukov began turning out his pockets one after the other and tipping out into his cupped hand, a grain at a time, any *makhorka* that had lodged in the seams. There had been no *makhorka* yesterday either. He had already performed this operation once, but today was patiently going through the whole procedure again. The bombardment was so heavy that he was feeling nervous and consequently wanted a smoke.

"Trying to get a second harvest from one sowing?" joked Sintsov, observing Bayukov's futile efforts. He stood up, went to the embrasure, and looked at the snowy gully beneath.

The shells were also bursting down there, only not so frequently; but there was a heavy pall of smoke hanging over the positions of the three neighbouring platoons on the hill with the three cottages. There was a solid wall of bursting shells, and one of the cottages was missing, as though it had never been there in the first place. All that remained was an empty piece of ground under a pall of smoke. Sintsov's heart sank, not because he was frightened by the continuing bombardment, but because he couldn't avoid thinking: "As soon as the barrage lifts, the attack will begin." He sat by the wall beside Bayukov and waited for the shelling to end. His head suddenly started itching. He took off his fur hat for a moment and tenderly stroked the scar above his temple. Two weeks ago, Zolotarev had thought the wound fatal, and now all that was left of it was this narrow scar with the skin smooth and slippery to the touch and with the bristle of the new-grown hair on either side.

What people think about at such moments varies a great deal. Sometimes they think of important things, sometimes of trifles. Sometimes they let their thoughts wander at will, sometimes they force themselves to think about what, as they imagine, can distract them from the terror of death.

Sintsov didn't force himself. He thought about whatever entered his head; but the thoughts kept barging in and pushing each other out of the way, as if afraid that he wouldn't have the time to think about everything he wanted to think about.

At first he remembered Masha. Several times during the last few days he had felt an impulse to sit down and write to her about what he was doing and where he was. He wanted her to know; but the more urgently he desired this, the more cruelly he asked himself: to what address am I to write? Where is she? True, he had the school's post box number, but Masha wasn't there any more. He hadn't the slightest doubt that she had long been on the other side of the lines, and he now felt that to write to her in an effort to breach the mutual ignorance in which they found themselves would be as silly as to try and poke a triangular soldier's letter through the brick wall of the chimney.

And yet he longed to write to her! As he thought of Masha, he remembered how she had squatted down on her heels that night in Moscow and had washed his feet in the basin, wiping off the scales of grime and how, touching him so very gently, she had cleaned his bruises; and, in spite of himself, he felt such a sudden, tender yearning for her gentle hands that he took fright at the vividness of his memories, stifled his feelings at once, and swore under his breath.

"What wrong with you?" asked Bayukov, who had finally turned out several crumbs of *makhorka* and had rolled a minuscule cigarette.

"It's nothing," said Sintsov with a deprecatory wave of the hand.

"I thought you'd remembered your mother-in-law," joked Bayukov. But the joke misfired.

With the old, dull, familiar pain, Sintsov remembered Grodno and everything connected with that word in his memory, now so scarred and benumbed. Without realising it, he tossed his head like a horse tormented by gadflies. Then he thought of Malinin, whom he had seen in the distance when the latter was climbing the hill, and he remembered their talk on the first day, when Malinin had been appointed company political instructor. Malinin had been going round what remained of the cabins in the village of Klintsy—long left in the German rear—where the company had spent that night. After talking to the men, Malinin had beckoned Sintsov out of the cabin and, his legs planted wide apart and his hands thrust into his pockets—a favourite stance with him—had said gloomily:

"Listen here, Sintsov, write and explain what's happened, and how you're with a regular unit now, and everything is all right here."

"Who else am I to write to now? I've already written..." Sintsov had said unhappily.

Malinin had given him another morose look and had said in the same dissatisfied tone of voice:

"Write it for me. I'll hand it in personally to the commissar or the Divisional Political Department. Then they can decide for themselves where to send it. Just indicate who can confirm what facts—name the people concerned. If they want to check, let them. Write it today while you've got a roof over your head. Goodness knows where we might be spending the night tomorrow! Well, so long." Malinin had nodded glumly and walked off down the street to the next house, but had suddenly stopped and called: "Sintsov!"

Sintsov had come up to him.

"You might mention," Malinin had said, "that I know the whole story from the beginning. So start like this: 'As you already know about me...' and then write: '...but I wish to declare in writing, so that the Political Department and the Unit Command...' Follow me?"

"Yes," Sintsov had replied.

That night he had sat down once again to write his explanation—briefly, and with references to persons, as Malinin had told him.

But no matter how brief he had tried to make it, to write it down all over again after he had already told it to Masha, to Yelkin, and to Malinin; after he had already written it all out in the Military Prosecutor's Department, after he had remembered all this so many times whenever he had found himself on his own, to write it out all over again had proved particularly soul-destroying. But he had done so nevertheless and had handed it to Malinin: this had been on the next day while they were on the march. Skirting its exposed flank, the division had been hastily falling back to the reserve positions. Malinin, squelching through the thick mud and even more morose than usual, had come up beside Sintsov, silently taken the statement from him, and thrust it into the greatcoat pocket. And although Sintsov had seen Malinin many times since, they had never discussed the matter again.

Now, as he listened to the heavy blows shaking the ground, Sintsov tried to imagine how and to whom Malinin had submitted his statement, what he had said as he had done so, when he might expect to be summoned, and by whom: the Political or the Special Department. And although, after ten days of fighting, it no longer looked as though he was going to be recalled from the front line, the knowledge that his fate had not yet been decided was getting him down. There was also the unconsoling thought that he might be wounded and taken back to the rear, in which case good-bye Malinin and that written statement! He would be discharged from hospital, would end up in another unit, and would have to write it all out again from the beginning....

"Listen!" yelled Bayukov in Sintsov's ear, trying to make himself heard over the thunder of the barrage. "I think they've hit our chaps over there!"

Sintsov went to the reserve embrasure and saw through the dispersing smoke that one of the uncompleted factory walls was lower than it had been before.

"Yes, it looks as if they have!" he said, alarmed.

This was approximately ten minutes after the commencement of the German barrage. The shells continued falling for another half hour and then crept back to the rear of the Soviet lines. Instead of explosions, there was only the noise of shells whistling overhead.

"Kolya, keep a look-out over there. Let me know if anyone shows up." Nodding towards the reserve slit from which the brickworks were visible, he returned to the machine gun.

The embrasure commanded an excellent view of the terrain. There was a wall of bursting shells in the background, and German tanks were moving up along the snowy gully between the hill surmounted by the brickworks and the one with the three cottages. From where Sintsov was watching, the tanks didn't seem to be in any hurry, but the foremost ones were already climbing the slope towards the place where there had previously been three cottages, but where only one remained, leaning over at a crazy angle. Somewhere in the cellars under the cottages and in the trenches round them, as Sintsov knew, were two of our platoons.

The leading tank stopped, fired a round from its cannon, and the already lop-sided building fell over like a house of cards. Flames shot out from under the tank and it slewed round on the spot. Then more flames sprang up, and dense black smoke began pouring out of the machine. Tiny black figures jumped out through the upper hatch onto the snow. A few desultory rifle shots were fired at them. Hardly anyone was shooting from where there had been two of our platoons. Another tank rode past the burning one and, crossing over the hill, disappeared behind the crest. The tanks moving along the gully were also advancing unopposed.

A minute passed, and in Sintsov's field of vision there appeared the dark figures of German infantrymen following up in line behind their tanks.

"Bayukov, come here!" yelled Sintsov, and he set his sights on the pre-ranged pole which the German infantrymen would reach in another forty metres.

Bayukov dashed up, straightened the ammunition belt, looked through the embrasure, and then glanced tensely up at Sintsov. "Why don't you start now?" he seemed to be saying. But Sintsov hung on for another half minute. Their aiming point had been worked out exactly and he wanted to make good use of it. The line of Germans drew level with the pole. Sintsov fired a short burst, then a long one, and then a short one as soon as the Germans who had lain down by the marker got up again. The last burst was evidently the most effective. Five of the Germans who had jumped up fell down and made no further attempt to rise or crawl over the snow.

"Well?" Sintsov looked away for a second and hurriedly thrust his face close to Bayukov's. "What about our chaps in the brickworks?"

"No one in sight," said Bayukov. "I'm afraid they've had it." On hearing this, Sintsov fired a shorter burst than he had originally intended, economising on ammunition as men do when they are left on their own.

He and Bayukov kept up their fire for about five minutes, pinning the Germans down on the snow from time to time and retarding their advance. Then the Germans began reforming and running along the far side of the hollow. They were still in range of the machine gun, but its fire was less effective at that distance. The black line of Germans moved over the hill with the three cottages. No one fired at them over there, which meant that our people had been wiped out.

One German machine gunner, together with his Number Two, took up position out there on the snow, his legs flung wide apart—Sintsov and Bayukov could see it all quite clearly from where they were—and began firing back at them. The bullets began chipping the brickwork: one of them clanged on the sheet-iron roof over the chimney. The German was shooting accurately but was badly placed, and after three unsuccessful bursts Sintsov scored a hit. They saw the machine gun tip over into the snow: either it had been knocked over by the fourth burst, or the German had dragged it with him in his death throes. Number Two also lay on the snow, apparently dead but after a few minutes, during which Sintsov and Bayukov fired at other targets, Bayukov tugged Sintsov by the arm and said:

"Look at the Number Two...."

Sintsov looked and saw only one figure lying next to the machine gun in the snow.

"Crawled away..." said Bayukov. "Didn't get behind his gun...." And there was not only condemnation in his words, but the conviction that had he himself been in the German's place, he would not have sneaked away but would have returned to the machine gun and carried on firing.

Finally, the Germans, who in the general fever of attack had not paid any particular attention to this machine gun which was giving them so much trouble, decided to deal with it and contacted their tank crews. The tanks had already begun to move to the right out of Sintsov's field of vision, but one of them suddenly returned. Sintsov at first thought that he had been damaged, but the tank was heading rapidly straight for their hill. When it reached the foot, it slowed down and stopped.

"He's going to open up on us now," said Bayukov.

Sintsov nodded.

"Go and see how our people are getting on."

The turret hatch opened and a tank crewman bobbed up. No doubt he wanted to take a closer look at the lay of the land.

Sintsov fired a burst. The tankman disappeared, the hatch slammed shut, and a moment later a shell struck the bricks near the embrasure. As if to show that he was still alive, Sintsov's machine gun delivered a long and vicious burst at the Germans still running across the hollow.

"They're coming thick and fast, in several waves," thought Sintsov. From where he was, everything was clearly visible. It was the first time in his life that he had been able to see a whole battle as it developed on the field.

"I listened and heard nothing—not a single shot—nothing.... Perhaps I should go to them?" said Bayukov, returning to Sintsov.

"It might be a good idea," said Sintsov, "except that I'm afraid I won't manage here on my own...."

Again the tank placed a shell not far from the embrasure, and again Sintsov fired a burst at the infantry. "You see, I'm still alive!" he seemed to be saying.

"He might want to come closer," said Sintsov, hoarse with excitement. "Prepare grenades!"

"They're all ready," said Bayukov, picking up off the ground a cluster of grenades and showing them to Sintsov.

The tank fired a few more rounds and, as Sintsov had foreseen, decided to come up to within point-blank range. With a muffled rumbling in the first gear—this rumbling sounded terrifyingly close—the tank moved off, slowly climbed up the incline at an angle, then changed direction, zigzagged still higher, and then disappeared from view in the dead ground. Sintsov and Bayukov could still hear it grinding and straining below.

"If he makes it, he'll fire into the embrasure," said Sintsov.

"Aim for the viewing slit," said Bayukov, "and I'll crawl round and get him with a grenade! Right?"

But Sintsov didn't answer and began firing at a fresh group of Germans running across the hollow. The Germans went down and ran on again. Sintsov and Bayukov fired burst after burst at them, each time pinning them down to the ground and almost forgetting about the tank. Part of the new group ran across and bolted ahead out of the zone of fire, but several black blobs were left behind on the snow.

The invisible tank was still rumbling somewhere outside and Sintsov had the impression that it was stationary, neither approaching nor retreating. Finally, it showed up again, only not in the front of the chimney embrasure, as they had feared, but down below at its original starting point.

"He couldn't get up the hill because of the ice!" said Sintsov joyfully, and he wiped away the sweat with his sleeve.

The tank's hatch opened again, the head of the crewman appeared for a second, then the hatch closed and the tank changed position, moving up a little way. The cannon pointed like an index finger as it took aim at the embrasure. Sintsov's heart sank. A shell landed right beside the embrasure, splintering the bricks. Another hit, and another cloud of brick-dust. Then there was another deafening explosion, only not outside this time, but inside. The iron sheets bounded and clanged, and Sintsov was momentarily deafened as his head struck the wall. He thought that the shell had come through the embrasure and exploded inside, although had it done so, there would have been nothing left of him and Bayukov. In fact, the shell had only struck the edge of the embrasure and had burst outside. Only a few fragments had flown into the chimney with the shock wave, but enough to give the impression of a shell exploding inside. Conscious of a dull pain in the back of his neck, Sintsov hurled himself on to the machine gun and immediately spotted a German tankman calmly standing upright in the turret hatch, shielding his eyes against the sunlight with his hand, and trying to gauge the effect of the shots.

Sintsov traversed the muzzle of the machine gun a fraction, caught the upper section of the turret and the tankman's shoulders in his sights, and pressed the firing button, giving this slight movement the full force of his hatred for the Germans. The tankman doubled up and nearly fell out of the turret, but someone inside seized the dead man by the legs—Sintsov was convinced that he was dead—pulled him down into the tank, and slammed the hatch shut. The tank fired three more rounds—but wildly this time, since only one of them hit the chimney—turned round, and went back down again....

Only then did Sintsov leave the machine gun to bend over Bayukov's motionless body. He was lying on the ground and moaning feebly.

"What's the matter, Kolya, what's the matter, my dear fellow?" asked Sintsov, feeling horribly alone.

"They got me in the back," said Bayukov quietly. He half-raised himself on his hands, but his legs refused to obey him.

Sintsov rolled back his greatcoat, then his quilted jacket, and saw a small bloodstain on Bayukov's back. The splinter had been tiny but it had hit the backbone, and Bayukov was unable to move.

"My hands are alright," said Bayukov, flexing his fingers as Sintsov bandaged him. "Move me up and I'll be able to feed in the belt for you."

Sintsov turned him round and moved him nearer the gun. Bayukov groaned briefly, but nevertheless picked up the belt and fed it into the machine gun.

"I can still cope," he said. "But what's wrong with my legs?"

"Just shock," said Sintsov. He wanted to reassure his comrade. "It'll pass off; these things happen...."

He peered through the embrasure in alarm. He didn't want to let any of the Germans through alive if they penetrated into the zone of fire again, although he felt that the more they harrassed the Germans, the sooner it would mean the end of himself, Bayukov, and the machine gun.

For the first time, he realised that the Germans could come up the other slope, and in that case he and Bayukov would not be able to man both embrasures simultaneously. He tore himself away from the machine gun and ran to the other embrasure. The smoke over the brickworks had long since dispersed and everything was quiet over there. They must be all dead. What other explanation could there be? He ran back and again looked out of the machine-gun embrasure.

"Look, look!" he exclaimed delightedly, although Bayukov was right beside him and there was no point in snouting.

Along the eastern edge of the gully and beyond, by the machine and tractor station into which the Germans already penetrated, and to the right, on the neighbouring hill where the two platoons had perished, columns of flame and dense black smoke were shooting skywards one after another with a terrifying roar. The earth itself seemed to be blowing up under the very feet of the Germans. In among the explosions. figures could be seen dashing about, falling in the snow. getting up and running again.... And the explosions went on and on, a whole belt of them chewing up one fresh piece of ground after another.

Bayukov knew what it was. Sintsov didn't, but guessed.

"Katyushas," he said, the first to speak. "Katyushas...."

"Yes. I saw them near Yelnia," said Bayukov.

Both of them, one unharmed, the other wounded, stared as if entranced at this terrifying spectacle which had thrown the Germans into confusion just when the operation had been working out in their favour. Their infantry stayed put and then began ebbing back again. Meanwhile, the Katyusha rockets gave way to ordinary artillery shells which began bursting and flinging black fountains into the air all over the terrain occupied by the Germans only a few minutes ago.

The German tanks turned back, climbed to the top of the hill with the three now obliterated cottages, and began firing from there. But seven of our own tanks crawled to the outskirts of a small patch of forest to the right of the machine and tractor station and returned the German fire. One enemy tank burst into flames. Then another.... And now one of our own caught fire, and yet another.... Sintsov clenched his fists until it hurt as he watched this duel; but our artillery was still hammering and hammering away all over the field in front of the machine and tractor station, and along the hollow, and at the hill with the three cottages, and still further on, behind the hill.... The shells were bursting incessantly, and the Germans were plainly in retreat. They were falling back under fire from the open ground to the hill with the three cottages and, judging by the activity over there, were hastily digging in.

Then Sintsov suddenly noticed that a group of about sixty Germans with a heavy machine gun in tow who had been retreating from the machine and tractor station, without going down into the gully which was under shell-fire, had now swung left and in a long, extended line were beginning to ascend the hill where he was positioned. He delivered a burst at them, and then another. They went down, ran to the left, then further and further to the left, and finally moved beyond his field of vision.

Bayukov helped him several times, feeding in the ammunition belt with unsteady hands. Sintsov stopped firing. It was now time to get the machine gun over to the other embrasure as quickly as possible.

"Kolya, we've got to get the machine gun..." he began, and then saw that Bayukov's head was slumped lifelessly on the bricks. His hand was still on the ammunition belt, but he was unconscious.

Sintsov moved him back and took hold of the machine gun, feverishly wondering how he would be able to maintain uninterrupted fire without a Number Two. Just at that moment, when he was on the verge of howling with frustration, Malinin crawled up out of the flue hole, his grimy face covered with blood, clutching a rifle in hands from which the torn skin was hanging in bloody rags.

"Have you been firing for long?" asked Malinin.

"Over an hour," said Sintsov.

"How d'you mean, over an hour?" demanded Malinin.

He thought he had lost consciousness momentarily, but he had lain senseless for half an hour. He thought he had only spent a few minutes digging out Sirota and Mikhnetsov, but he had been doing so for nearly an hour. And when he had heard the bursts of fire from Sintsov's machine gun, these had not been the first, but the last ones, which Sintsov only just now had been delivering at the Germans as they came up the hill.

Sintsov looked at Malinin's face. He was in no mood to explain how long and in what way he had been firing.

"Get hold of the machine gun," he said to Malinin instead, as if he, not Malinin, were senior at that moment. "Over to the other embrasure! The Germans are closing in on that side!"

They dragged the machine gun across. Malinin, without saying a word, lay down in Number Two's position, and a minute later the Germans came into view, stumbling hastily up the hill.

"Get on with it!" said Malinin quietly.

But Sintsov knew what he was doing and stayed Malinin with a gesture. The Germans were in a hurry, not bothering to take cover and—so he felt—hoped that by coming in from the rear they were in no danger of being fired on. But just in case, their machine gunners had taken up position behind them and were ready to give covering fire to the advancing troops at the least sign of movement above.

"They've set up a machine gun for cover," said Malinin quietly.

Sintsov nodded without saying anything. He had already noticed.

The Germans were still coming uphill, moving deeper and deeper into the most deadly zone of fire; but with each step they were also approaching an area of dead ground inaccessible to Sintsov and his machine gun. Meanwhile, the artillery was still thundering behind them.

"Ours?" asked Malinin, his lips barely moving.

Sintsov nodded, although at that moment he only had eyes for the Germans climbing up the hill and the patch of snowy field behind them. The Germans had only another twenty metres to go before they reached the dead ground, when Sintsov pressed the button and, with a firm, steady movement, swung the machine gun from right to left and then back again, traversing the Germans with a deadly arc of lead before they had time to go down. It was one of those rare occasions in war when an unexpected and cold-blooded burst delivered point-blank at a range of less than a hundred metres mows down a whole line like a scythe. Several men got up again, and made a last dash for the dead ground. One burst!... Then another!... The first of the running Germans nearly made it to the dead ground. To cut him down too, Sintsov had to flog the machine gun until it nearly seized up. The German machine gun raked the embrasure; but it was only a narrow slit on this side and the bullets merely pulverised the masonry round it.

"There'll be more soon," said Sintsov.

Sure enough, another line of Germans got up behind the machine gun and began advancing. Sintsov didn't fire at them, but concentrated on the German machine gun. An answering burst from the Germans sent fine splinters of brick flying into his closed left eye. Shutting his eye still more tightly because of the pain, he gave a last burst at the German machine gun and hit both the Germans lying behind it. One of them rolled over on his side; the other leapt to his feet, tumbled over backwards, and rolled down the slope. The silence behind them was too much for the line of infantrymen. They faltered and then ran back down again.

Sintsov felt momentarily at a loss. He had expected the Germans to advance line by line until he and Malinin lay dead at their machine gun. And now the Germans had suddenly turned tail and run, and he was already shooting high over their heads. He re-set his sights, but it was much too late by now. He released the grip of the machine gun and turned a perspiring face to Malinin.

"Take a look at my eye, Comrade Malinin.... What's happened to it?"

"What are you screwing it up for? Open it!"

"I can't, it hurts...."

Malinin brought his face nearer to Sintsov's and said that it was nothing special, just a graze under the eyebrow. No worse than that.

Sintsov forced his eye open by parting the lids with his fingers. It hurt him, but he could still see.

"Looks as though we've beaten them off," said Malinin.

Sintsov didn't reply, but was thinking the same.

What was going to happen next was a mystery, but for the time being, the enemy had been repulsed. The Germans had wanted to capture this height on their way back, but the general atmosphere of failure had evidently disheartened them, and as soon as they had come up against resistance, they had left the job unfinished.

"Is your Number Two dead?" asked Malinin. "Bayukov?"

"No," said Sintsov. "He's unconscious. It's a good thing you came in time, otherwise I couldn't have coped on my own. The Germans would have taken the whole position."

Malinin made no comment. He kneeled down beside Bayukov and, before touching him, asked Sintsov.

"Where's he hit?"

"The small of the back," said Sintsov.

Like Sintsov before him, Malinin rolled back Bayukov's greatcoat and quilted jacket, pulled up his tunic, and looked for some time at the bandages and the big dark stain showing over the sacrum....

"He's in a bad way," he said. "Have you a spare bandage?"

Without leaving the machine gun, Sintsov pulled a field dressing out of his greatcoat pocket and threw it to Malinin. Malinin tugged the thread, tore open the packet with his teeth and, carefully raising Bayukov's limp body, began to wind a bandage, though not tightly, over the old dressing.

"His legs are paralysed," said Sintsov. "But he went on feeding in the ammunition belt while he was still conscious."

While Malinin bandaged Bayukov, the latter began to moan, though he was still unconscious.

"He's groaning," said Malinin. "Maybe he'll pull through yet.... What about the Germans over there?"

"Not a sign," said Sintsov.

"I think we've got them on the run."

"Take a look out of the other embrasure."

Malinin did so, and rushed back to the machine gun. "Come on, come on!" he shouted hoarsely.

They dragged the machine gun to the big embrasure; but while they were setting the sights, the small group of Germans retreating down the hollow was already beyond the zone of effective fire. The battle was dying down, and the Germans had been driven out everywhere, except from the hill with the three cottages. Our artillery was now shelling the hill, but the Germans had managed to drag some mortars up it and were putting up a heavy answering fire.

In the last two hours, Sintsov had become used to the idea that all our own men positioned up there had been wiped out and that the hill was now in German hands. But Malinin had just realised this for the first time and he ground his teeth in despair. Most of those with whom he had been serving were now dead, either on that German-occupied hill over there, or here, in the ruins of the brickworks.

"The company's done for," he said and, shaking his head, added with unjustified self-contempt: "I've destroyed the company, yet I'm still alive!..."

"What on earth are you talking about, Alexei Denisych!" said Sintsov.

"Shut up, don't say anything! I should know...." Deeply upset, Malinin frantically shook his head. "Look through the other embrasure," he said to Sintsov. "Are there any Germans coming?"

Sintsov suddenly realised that his legs were shaking with fatigue.

"No, there aren't," he said, sitting down by the wall.

At that moment, both of them heard a scraping noise. Malinin reached at his belt for a grenade, but immediately let his hand fall by his side.

The head and shoulders of Sergeant Sirota appeared below in the manhole. The platoon commander had recovered consciousness and had crawled towards the sound of shooting; had crawled on his hands and knees, dragging his rifle with him; had crawled, summoning the strength from goodness knows where, because, as soon as he had climbed out of the manhole with Malinin's assistance, he could not only stand, he was unable to sit down either, and he had to slump against the wall like a sack. The bandaged lower half of his face was black and red, and his forehead and the skin under his eyes were completely bloodless and white as a sheet. He sat without turning his head, only rolling his eyes now at Malinin, now at Sintsov, and struggling to say something. He probably even believed that he was speaking;

but only incoherent barking noises came from under the bandages.

"I understand, Platoon Commander, I understand," said Malinin, bending over him and nodding soothingly. "You've made yourself clear. Everything's under control and we've beaten off the Germans. Our people will be here soon. I expect they'll send us reinforcements...."

But Sirota was still struggling to say something, and again it was impossible to understand a word. Malinin couldn't stand it any more in the end and put a stop to the mutual torture:

"Don't try, Sirota. I can't understand you, anyway: your mouth's all smashed up.... You're just making noises, not words. You'll be taken to hospital and you'll get your voice back again; but don't try now, don't torture yourself...."

Sirota looked at him with wide-open eyes as if in disbelief, but Malinin nodded his head again, and Sirota, reaching for his rifle and laying it with an effort on his knees, slumped back against the wall and closed his eyes.

"How about your side—is there nothing to be seen?" said Malinin after a short silence to Sintsov, who had gone back to the embrasure.

"Nothing to be seen," echoed Sintsov.

"If our people don't come before dark, I'll stay here with them," said Malinin, nodding towards the two wounded men, "and you can go and report. We mustn't give up a position like this. We can still knock them off the top up there, if we don't bungle things," he said, peering through the embrasure at the neighbouring hill. "I wonder what happened to Ionov," he added after a pause, remembering the company commander. "He probably died up there. Not the sort of man to run away from his company.... Why don't you say something, Sintsov?" he asked after several moments' silence.

"I was just thinking," said Sintsov.

"What about?... If it's not a secret...."

"About something I'm missing...."

"To be more precise?...."

"My wife," said Sintsov.

"None of us is allowed a wife here," said Malinin in a gloomy attempt at a joke. "So it's no use thinking about her. But you should write to her after a day like this! Tell her you're alive and well thanks to her Komsomol prayers. She is a Komsomol, isn't she?"

Sintsov nodded.

"You should write after such a battle," said Malinin. "If you don't want to write yourself, give me her address and I'll drop her a line...."

"She has no address," said Sintsov.

Only an hour later, just before dusk, help arrived. The first were three scouts who had been told that, judging by course of the battle, our side had held out on the hill, but the position was uncertain and there was no knowing what they might find. They crawled up to the chimney from several directions—so carefully that Sintsov noticed one of them only at the very last moment.

"We're friends! You needn't hide!" he shouted with relief; and there was such joy in his voice that the scout, reassured that these were indeed friends, stood up in full view.

After the scouts, a platoon arrived at the brickworks, and then, when it was already dark, the battalion commander, Senior Lieutenant Ryabchenko, with some signalmen laying a telephone cable. He had been given the job of knocking the Germans off the adjacent hill during the hours of darkness. It was now as smooth as a billiard ball, but was still being referred to as the hill with the three cottages. Ryabchenko was bringing his command point up to the brickworks before the night's battle, this being the most suitable starting-point for a night attack.

Everything took its course. Malinin reported how the battle had gone here at the brickworks and said that machine gunners Sintsov and Bayukov, with all the odds against them, had acquitted themselves worthily. Malinin could not bring himself to say more than that, but the battalion commander knew in any case that the machine gunners had indeed acquitted themselves worthily. Watching from his command post, he had seen the Germans falling as they moved along the hollow; he had seen the tank try to climb up the slope and drive in; and, later, he had seen the German infantry, when in retreat, unsuccessfully trying to reach the top. In any case, the German losses spoke for themselves. In the regiment and in the division, today's attack was interpreted as an attempt by the Germans to feel for a weak spot and, if successful, to stage a breakthrough; but they had not been successful and there had been no breakthrough. Although losses in the battalion had been heavy—almost the entire Ninth Company had been wiped out—and although the Germans had captured the hill with the three cottages, Battalion Commander Ryabchenko was not downhearted in the general atmosphere of the day's victory, and was preparing for the forthcoming night battle still in an exalted mood, though naturally nervous.

By order of Lieutenant-Colonel Baglyuk, the regimental commander, a battery of heavy regimental mortars was being brought up to the brickworks to support the attack at the closest possible range.

Malinin inquired after Ionov, the company commander. It transpired that he had been wounded during the first few minutes of the barrage, taken away, and sent to the field hospital. Ryabchenko attributed the swift success of the German attack on the hill with the three cottages partly to their fire-power, which had blown everything up there to smithereens, and partly to the fact that neither the company commander nor the political instructor had been there at the commencement of the attack. Although it would have been strange to reprimand Malinin for this when he had been at the brickworks during the attack, and although the battalion commander had no intention of doing so, Malinin nevertheless took the remark as a reproach against him personally and asked Ryabchenko's permission to take part in the counter-attack "on our former hill". Those were his exact words, and they were meant to stress his personal responsibility for the loss.

The battalion commander looked at Malinin's blood-caked face and wondered, with a young man's astonishment, where this officer, nearly old enough to be his father, could find so much strength.

"You should at least have your wounds dressed first, Comrade Malinin," he remarked; but he did not refuse the request.

Malinin turned himself over to the nurse who spent a long time bandaging his battered face and his brick-torn hands. While she was busy doing this, Malinin went on thinking about his annihilated company: would it be re-formed, or, if not, would he be transferred somewhere else where there was a shortage of political staff?

Malinin was bandaged up, and the battalion commander sent for Sintsov and asked him a number of questions. He asked if the Germans hadn't tried to make their way up the hill from the very start. Sintsov said that they hadn't; he and Bayukov had merely kept up an enfilading fire on the gully. Then the battalion commander asked why the tank had turned back before reaching the chimney. Sintsov said that it had evidently kept skidding, and he mentioned the crewman who had stood up in his turret and whom he had shot dead.

"Evidently an officer," said the battalion commander, nodding. "They didn't dare poke their noses in again after you finished him off!"

The battalion commander was then called by the regimental and divisional commanders to the telephone and—succinctly and smoothly—far more succinctly than Malinin and Sintsov, began reporting first to the regimental commander and then to the divisional commander about the battle for the hill with the brickworks. The battle had been conducted by Political Instructor Malinin and by machine gunners Sintsov and Bayukov, who had beaten off an attack by the German infantry and tanks and had held out on the hill until the arrival of our reinforcements. As he reported it, Sintsov and Bayukov had not simply fired on the Germans, but had engaged battle; had not simply fought, but had held the hill. And Sintsov, as he sat wearily on the bricks with the tiny snowflakes falling and melting on his face, found it strange to hear how he had engaged battle and held the hill, as if it had not been him, but someone else.

Both the wounded men, Bayukov and Sirota, had long since been taken to the rear. Only the dead were left behind. For these they dug a grave in the soil, which was not yet frozen solid, right outside the wall of the brickworks; but they decided to bury them at daybreak, because they could not, in the dark, collect up everything that remained of the victims after the direct hit.

Sintsov sat wondering who would be his Number Two at the machine gun now, and whether or not Bayukov would return to his unit, should he recover from his wound. Then he must have dozed off for a moment, because when he heard Malinin's voice in his ear, he jumped with surprise.

"Come on," said Malinin. "They've just rung through from the division. We've both been sent for by the divisional commander."

Malinin was displeased, because he wanted to take part in the night attack on the hill with the three cottages, but only his tone of voice betrayed his real feelings. Orders are orders. Three white blobs were visible against the black background of the ruins; Malinin's bandaged face and his two bulky white hands.

"I thought you were a ghost, Comrade Political Instructor," said Sintsov.

"They've swaddled me up like a babe," replied Malinin irritably. "Let's go, we haven't time to waste!..."

"What do they want to see us for?" asked Sintsov, following him down the slope.

"We'll find out when we get there," said Malinin. "We'll walk to Regimental HQ, and then we'll get a lift in a lorry to the division, I'm told. So you see how urgent it is. They need us badly...."

"I know why," said Sintsov after a long silence. By now they had already descended the hill as far as the ruins in front of the machine and tractor station premises and were cutting across them over the shallow snow.

"Why?" demanded Malinin.

"Because of my statement," said Sintsov.

He had thought of this immediately Malinin had told him they were wanted. And a mood of strained expectancy suddenly replaced the state of physical exhaustion and overexcitement which had dogged him ever since the battle.

"Oh, come on!" said Malinin. "Not much chance! I can see them dragging us straight from battle just for that!"

"What's battle got to do with it? It's just a coincidence. They read it and showed it to the right people. 'What's this? A man like him, and suddenly he's out on the front line? Get him straight back here for vetting!'"

He was not convinced of this deep down, but it was in his nature to be ready for the worst.

"Why send for me, then?" asked Malinin.

"I've used you as referee dozens of times!"

"Nonsense!" said Malinin firmly.

He knew that it was nonsense for the simple reason that he hadn't yet found a convenient occasion to hand Sintsov's statement in to the Divisional Political Department, and he had been waiting over a week for the chance, meanwhile keeping the letter in his greatcoat pocket. But he didn't want to tell Sintsov this at present: the summons to the division would give him the opportunity to hand over the statement and talk to the commissar in the circumstances most favourable for Sintsov—after that day's battle.

"Nonsense," repeated Malinin, looking across at Sintsov without stopping. "I think the reason's quite different: they want to give you a medal for the battle."

Sintsov said nothing. He didn't believe it.

In fact, although Malinin was nearer to the truth than Sintsov, neither of the two suppositions was correct. The real reason for their recall from the front line was quite different and still unknown to them. During the battle that day, Divisional HQ had been visited by an elderly and distinguished writer from one of the Moscow newspapers. He had been allowed as far as Divisional HQ, though with some humming and hawing. If he were killed, they would have something to answer for! But when he learned that evening from the divisional commander that a political instructor and a machine gunner in a front-line battalion had beaten off several German attacks and put paid to some fifty German soldiers, he firmly decided to visit the battalion in person and talk to those concerned. His request was refused no less firmly and he was told, not altogether consistently—which, in the heat of the moment, he failed to notice—that he couldn't proceed to the battalion at present, but that the men he wished to interview could be recalled. He tried to object: why make such a special case of it? But he was told what is usually said under such circumstances: the men would have to be sent for anyway, so now was as good a time as any, since it made no difference to them.

The commissar cut short any further argument by picking up the telephone. Although he was against letting the writer visit the battalion, he very much wanted something written about the men in his division.

And so there were Malinin and Sintsov after the battle, tired out and trudging through the snow from the hill-top down towards the machine and tractor station premises. It had been snowing lightly earlier that evening, but had now stopped. The moon had come out, the snow was shining like silver, and things were somehow beginning to look more cheerful.

"Nice weather!" said Sintsov.

"Look, that's a German over there," replied Malinin, nodding towards the black shape of a corpse, its arms flung wide apart, lying close to the track.

As they drew level with the dead German, they stopped for a moment, looked at it, and continued on their way.

"I can see you were a good Communist!" said Malinin without preamble, pausing almost imperceptibly before the word "were".

They covered another thirty paces or so in silence.

"If you were applying to join the Party again, I'd recommend you without a moment's hesitation," said Malinin, again out of the blue; and he fell silent once more.

"Thanks," said Sintsov.

They walked on for another fifty paces or so in silence.

"But they could still reinstate you ... give you a severe reprimand and issue a new Card..." said Malinin, just as abruptly as on the two previous occasions.

He had, no doubt, raised the subject prematurely; but Malinin had never been able to curb his own stubbornness.

"We'll soon be there," said Sintsov pointlessly in an effort not to betray his agitation.

He had only just finished speaking, when a mortar bomb exploded behind them, and then another....

Sintsov and Malinin threw themselves down together on the sparkling white snow. They felt conspicuous for a whole mile in their greatcoats. The mortar bombs were exploding successively in chessboard pattern all over the snow-covered field. As they burst, they threw up black fountains and filled the air around them with the reek of burning.

"It's not us they're after," said Malinin. "They're just lobbing a few over to shake things up a bit."

Sintsov growled something through his clenched teeth.

Whether the Germans were trying to get them or not, they had lain there for at least ten minutes and the mortar bombs were still falling on the field one after another, now to the right, now to the left, now in front, now behind. Malinin and Sintsov were both overcome by a sense of danger which, so far from being dulled after their heavy day's fighting, was more intense than ever before. They both lay in silence, reluctant to talk, or think, or reassure one another. They only wanted one thing—for this to end as soon as possible so that they wouldn't be killed and could carry on further.

The barrage ended as unexpectedly as it had begun. The white field, on which the evening's snow had only just covered the traces of the day's battle, had again been churned up by the effects of the mortar barrage. It was war again, and it reeked of war.

Malinin and Sintsov stood up and continued on their way. They were not fated to be killed on that snowy nocturnal field. The writer was waiting for them at the divisional commissar's office with his notebook, fountain-pen, and the helplessly apologetic questions that the civilian asks of the fighting soldier. Sintsov's statement was in Malinin's great coat pocket, and the awards sheet for Sintsov for his showing in the day's battle was already being made out in Regimental HQ: it only remained for these two lines to intersect.

The war took its course. Another day was over. And what really mattered most wasn't the written statement in Malinin's greatcoat pocket, or the awards sheet being made out in Regimental HQ, or the hurried jottings in the writer's notebook, but the simple and telling fact that once more, and on yet another sector of the Moscow front, the Germans had accomplished by evening only one-tenth of what they had hoped for that morning.

CHAPTER FIFTEEN

On the night of 6th November, the troop train in which Klimovich's tank brigade had been transferred from Gorky to Moscow was unloading at Kursk Goods Station.

Since he had received no further itinerary, Klimovich was wondering what was going to happen next. Would they be left in Moscow, or would they be sent to the front under their own steam?

Between one and two in the morning, a general from the Moscow Commandant's Office arrived at the detrainment point.

He called Klimovich aside and said that the brigade was to proceed to Podolsk, but first it might possibly take part in the parade on Red Square.

The situation outside Moscow was still ominous, and the idea of a parade had never even entered Klimovich's head. However, he accepted his instructions without the slightest sign of excitement and, applying his hand to his helmet, requested permission to ask a question.

"For the time being, no final orders have been given," said the general with the intention of forestalling the brigade commander's query. "At six hundred hours, you will proceed at the head of your column to the Central Telegraph Office, where you will await orders for the drive-past. The final decision depends on the weather, insofar as it is suitable or unsuitable for flying," added the general, and he pointed his glove at the clear, frosty sky.

He said all this in an undertone, although he could easily have shouted: the last tanks were driving down from their flats.

But Klimovich had meant to ask a quite different question. And he proceeded to do so, his hand still at his helmet in salute.

"Mightn't it be possible to have a preliminary look at Red Square and get an on-the-spot view of the up gradient, and of the down gradient to the Moskva River? I've never been across Red Square," he added, meaning his tanks, not himself personally.

The general granted this request and drove off, leaving a captain from his office with Klimovich.

Klimovich and the captain sat on the ice-cold cushions of a staff-car which had just been unloaded from its flat, drove along the Sadovaya, and turned off down Gorky Street. Moscow was completely deserted. The shop windows had been boarded up with planks and plywood and shielded with piles of sandbags. The troops which were to take part in the parade were not yet moving towards the city centre and there were no pedestrians. Only occasionally did a solitary vehicle roar through with a permit from the Moscow Commandant's Office.

Klimovich and the captain were halted several times and then let through, but they were finally stopped at the Okhotny Ryad. Gorky Street had been cordoned off with a chain at this point, and they would have to go the rest of the way on foot.

Almost the whole of Red Square was covered with a smooth layer of new-fallen snow.

Klimovich walked across the square and went down past the Spassky Tower to the Moskva River. There was no ice under the snow, and the tanks could cross the square at any speed without complications, especially if they kept at slightly longer intervals than usual.

He explained this to the captain from the Commandant's Office as they turned back uphill. The captain shrugged his shoulders and said that it would be no tragedy to extend the intervals. No one would be treading on their heels. He had heard that there wouldn't be much heavy stuff. Then, cutting himself short in mid-phrase, he looked up and halted in his tracks. The sky, which had been perfectly clear half an hour ago, had darkened noticeably.

"Now there's going to be a parade," said the captain.

They walked back across Red Square past the GUM building, painted with multicoloured camouflage squares, past the Lenin Mausoleum with its protective timber casing and the sentries dimly discernible in the depths.... But Klimovich was not as disturbed by the silence and emptiness of Red Square as when, with his feelings well in check, he had crossed it on the way down to the river. The sky was gradually clouding over. A few more hours, and these snow-covered stones would come to life: the troops would march on in their squares, and Stalin would ascend the Mausoleum, for what sort of parade would it be without him?

On the morning of 17th October, when all the brigade personnel who had survived encirclement and the three days' fighting outside Moscow had been recalled from the front and sent through Moscow to Gorky in order to pick up their tanks, Klimovich had alighted from his leading machine on a corner of the Sadovaya near a baker's shop with a smashed window so as to place a signaller. He had only just climbed down, when two women had immediately come up to him, one old, the other young with a beautiful but drawn face. They had stopped in front of him, and the young one, bitterly looking him straight in the eye, had asked him in a voice that had made itself heard all over the street:

"What's this then, tankmen? Had enough of the fighting?"

Looking at the merciless—at that moment—faces of the two women, Klimovich had re-lived everything he had been through—the whole of the agonising road he had travelled, beginning with the loss of his family. All the bitterness accumulated since the first day of the war, all the bloody fighting, all the losses, all the tanks destroyed by the Germans or burnt out by their own side—all this had balled itself up into a fist, and that fist had hit him straight in the heart: "What's this then, tankmen? Had enough of the fighting?"

He had not answered.

Then there had been Enthusiasts' Highway. For the first few hours, Klimovich's column had moved through a dense stream of people. By the end of the first hour, they had already taken into the backs and drivers' cabs of their lorries as many women and children as the vehicles could hold. And yet there had still been more and more of them, and wherever the pace had slowed down, the sides of the lorries had grazed the shoulders of the people swarming alongside.

He and his crews had been particularly distressed because, although armed military personnel, they had found themselves in their lorries in the middle of this defenceless stream and had been heading in the same direction—east, towards the Volga. And they had been stared at with every conceivable emotion: suspicion, indignation, bewilderment, or with the unspoken question: where are you going, and why? And however justified Klimovich and his men may have felt themselves to be, and however many battles and losses to the Germans they may have had to their credit, they nevertheless found it intolerable having to ride along this crowded, teeming road without explaining why they were heading east, because they had no right to offer any explanations.

That had been the situation on 17th October. But now, twenty days later, he and his eighty tanks were to drive across Red Square: sixty Thirty-Fours—machines about which a tankman could only dream—and twenty KVs, heavy and less manoeuvrable, but virtually invulnerable to small-calibre artillery.

If only he had had these in the brigade on the first day of the war!

Eighty tanks.... On the day he had broken out of his second encirclement, near Vyazma, he had, in desperation, cut along the highway straight through between two German divisions and had arrived independently by lorry at the command post of one of our divisions. A young, fair-haired, unshaven general had risen from his map to greet him. He had been in the unenviable position of commanding a group of forces hastily scratched together on the spot.

"Comrade General, Commander of the Seventeenth Tank Brigade Lieutenant-Colonel Klimovich reporting!"

Although Klimovich had been breaking out of encirclement for the last twelve days, he had shaved the day before, his leather coat was fully buttoned, and his shoulder tabs and insignia of rank were in place. This is probably why the general had staggered him with the greeting:

"So the tanks have arrived at last! You haven't come a moment too soon! How many have you brought?"

The happy general had imagined that the tank brigade had been sent up from the rear to build up his own sector, which was drenched in blood and ripping apart hour by hour like a broken sieve, and this colonel with the prominent cheekbones and the tightly buttoned leather coat had come to him like a veritable angel of deliverance.

The blood had drained from Klimovich's face. At first, he had thought he was being made fun of, but he had grasped the true situation in the next second and had bitterly announced that the general was in error: he had just broken through encirclement and had only brought out ten lorries and one damaged tank.

"Oh, hell and damnation! And I thought...." The general had cut himself off, stopped, gone up to Klimovich, and embraced him. "Forgive me, my dear fellow, please don't take offence! I thought reinforcements had arrived."

And, returning immediately to the harsh and urgent business of war, he had asked:

"How many men have you brought out?"

"About five hundred," Klimovich had said. "I'll establish exactly how many in an hour's time."

"Are they fit for action?"

"Yes. But our ammunition's running low."

"I'll give you some. And one tank, did you say?"

"One."

"Still, you brought it out. Matter of principle, or what?"

"Matter of principle," Klimovich had said.

That evening, the last tank had been destroyed by the Germans on the street of the very village and near the very house where Klimovich had met the general. And that had been that....

But today he was to cross Red Square with eighty tanks and drive out on to the Podolsk motorway, heading almost for the very same place.

"The Germans haven't made such marvellous progress since then. Yes, she's snapping back, is Moscow!..."

As he walked back past the Mausoleum, Klimovich stopped. There were sentries at the entrance as before, and in there, behind them, a few steps down, in the depths, lay Lenin. And if Klimovich, even earlier, in his worst moments, had never so much as considered the thought that Moscow might be taken by the Germans, this seemed utterly unthinkable now. To imagine the nazis here, on Red Square, at the Mausoleum, in their uniforms and their caps, with swastikas on their arms.... No, it was impossible. It couldn't happen!

That morning, Serpilin was woken by Regimental Commissar Maximov, his neighbour in the hospital ward.

"Fyodor Fyodorovich, get up! We're going to the parade!" he said, shaking Serpilin by the shoulder.

Finally, Serpilin, as was his habit, pushed himself up on his hands all of a sudden and demanded hurriedly:

"What?... Which parade?... When? Where are we going?..."

He was not yet fully awake, but he pretended to be and, looking the regimental commissar straight in the face, sleepily tried to figure out what had happened. Why was Maximov, who had been allowed into Moscow yesterday afternoon—true, without his final discharge—standing before him still in full uniform and laughing.

"Get up, get up!" repeated Maximov in the meantime, sitting next to him on the bed and gaily slapping a new and brilliantly polished boot with his hand. "Today's the Seventh of November. There's going to be a parade. I'm offering you a lift!"

"What parade?" demanded Serpilin, still afraid to believe that Maximov was in earnest. "The Germans are outside Moscow! What parade?"

"The parade!" repeated Maximov, and a dazzling smile spread all over his youthful face. "Comrade Stalin's instructions. He made a speech in Mayakovsky Metro station yesterday. I was there, only I came back late and hadn't the heart to wake you.... He made a speech yesterday, and now he's announced there's to be a parade!"

"Really? You're not joking, are you?" asked Serpilin, and he carefully put down his legs which were already healed, but were still disobedient and had to be treated as if they were fragile as glass.

"Joking indeed!" said Maximov, smiling again. "And with the weather unfit for flying into the bargain! I've already been out and had a look. The sky's completely overcast, and all for our benefit."

"If you're joking, I'll never forgive you," said Serpilin, looking up at Maximov's smiling face.

"What are you being so grim about?" retorted the other. I've already applied for a car."

"Will they let me go, d'you think?"

"They did the day before yesterday!"

And, indeed, Serpilin, who had already begun walking with the aid of a stick round the hospital garden, had been granted permission to be driven down to the Army Political Directorate and the People's Commissariat to pick up his Party card, military decorations, and general's papers. This was the trip that Maximov had been talking about.

"The People's Commissariat's one thing," said Serpilin, "but...."

"But the parade's another," said Maximov, still smiling, "especially since you're a walking general now, not a bedridden one."

"I'll just have to wear felt boots. I'll never get into my leather ones," said Serpilin, rising somewhat shakily to his feet.

Although he knew that he could only wear felt boots for the time being, habit dies hard, and the very idea of such footwear seemed incongruous in connection with a parade.

"But we're not going to march past: we've been invited to watch from the stands."

"Did you say invited?" asked Serpilin incredulously.

"Yes, invited!" Maximov roared with laughter and slapped his tunic pocket. "I've got the tickets here! I'm friendly with half Moscow—and with half the APD, which is what matters most!"

"In that case, I'd better get dressed," said Serpilin, also smiling in spite of himself and looking delightedly at Maximov.

Tall, broad-shouldered, with a face that was attractive for its strength as well as its handsomeness, Regimental Commissar Maximov was the kind of person whom men find likeable as well as women. And he really was friendly with half Moscow. Serpilin had already become convinced of this, although he had not yet quite decided what to make of his neighbour. Was he simply born lucky, or a man of a seldom encountered gay courage who merely gave the impression of being unusually fortunate? Perhaps it would be truer to say that Regimental Commissar Maximov was both. He had already won three battle decorations by the time he was thirty. These were not so easily won, especially by a political worker; but Regimental Commissar Maximov had three, and behind each of them lay that special concatenation of circumstances about which it is said, if the man survives, that he has been extremely lucky. Twice—at Khalkhin-Gol and in the Finnish War—he had begun by going to the front as APD inspector and had ended up by fighting as commissar of a regiment. After each of these two wars, however, he had been recalled to the APD, and June 1941 had again found him touring the Special Western District as inspector. This time, on the very first day of the war, he had stepped in for the divisional commissar when the latter had been killed, had spent a month fighting his way out of encirclement and, like Serpilin, had been badly wounded while doing so. Since then, as he jokingly put it, he had had nine tenths of his stomach carved up. He had been living on a ghastly diet about which he also joked, and had been occupying the next bed in hospital to Serpilin—not as a patient, but as a kind of one-man variety show, never losing heart himself and not letting anyone else to do so either.

He had been promised conditional discharge within a week, but he had made a joke of that too, as of everything else and, chuckling, had told Serpilin repeatedly that he would not only be going to the front, but, what was more, would wangle some way of being sent back to his own division.

Only at nights—and no one knew about this except Serpilin—when no one could see him or, as he thought, hear him either, the irrepressible Regimental Commissar Maximov would sit writhing in agony on his cot, unable to sleep for hours.

Serpilin's uniform, since he was convalescent, was hanging in a wardrobe in the ward. After donning his breeches and the new tunic with the general's tabs and the two Orders of the Red Banner—the old one, and the one he had been awarded the day before yesterday—he went up to the mirror and smoothed down his thin, yellow-grey hair. Then, sitting on a chair, he carefully inserted his feet into his felt boots, looked at them with wry disapproval, and said to Maximov:

"Well then, if you mean it, I'm ready!"

At half past eight, they drove up to the Central Telegraph Office. The street was cordoned off and no vehicles were being allowed through.

A double column of tanks was standing all the way down Gorky Street from Mayakovsky Square to the Telegraph Office. It was only a brigade, but the sight gladdened Serpilin's heart. They were all machines that meant business—Thirty-Fours and KVs, and not the T-26s that the Germans had made mincemeat of at the beginning of the war.

"We're not allowed to drive any further. My sphere of influence ends here," said Maximov apologetically as they climbed out of the car. "What shall we do—hoof it?"

"We might as well, since we're here," said Serpilin, and he looked at the tanks.

Near the leading machine, from whose turret hatch protruded a sheathed banner, stood a diminutive tank commander in a black belted sheepskin jacket. He seemed familiar to Serpilin, who had such a memory for faces that he remembered even those he would rather have forgotten. But he was pleased to be reminded of this one. Still looking keenly at him, although he had already recognised him, he went up to the tank commander, who had already brought his hand smartly up to his helmet when he saw Serpilin approaching in his general's *papakha*.

"How d'you do, Lieutenant-Colonel," said Serpilin, returning the salute. "I joined you on breaking out of encirclement on the night of October the first, if I'm not mistaken?"

"You certainly aren't, Comrade General," replied Klimovich, although at first, when saluting, he had not connected this tall general limping on a stick with the wounded brigade commander about whom the Army CO had enquired over the telephone: "What does he look like, this Serpilin?" At the time, Klimovich had felt that he would remember this brigade commander for the rest of his life. And now hardly two months had passed, and he had forgotten! Much water had flowed under the bridge since then.

"So he's gone up in the world," thought Klimovich, his eyes still on the general. "And quickly, too. Yet he seemed nearly dead at the time...."

Then he remembered Red Armyman Zolotarev handing him documents belonging to Political Instructor Sintsov, who had been posted missing or, to put it more simply, had been killed. Sintsov had been worried at the time near Yelnia: would his brigade commander pull through? And here he was alive and well, standing before him, Klimovich, in a general's hat, and Sintsov's bones were mouldering somewhere in the forests beyond Vereya....

All these thoughts flashed through Klimovich's mind, but he said nothing, as he was not in the habit of opening the conversation with a senior officer.

"Thank you, Lieutenant-Colonel. Not Colonel yet, then?"

"No," replied Klimovich.

"Thank you for saving us. Glad to have met you! I wanted to write and thank you, but it's a big front...."

He gripped Klimovich's hand, and Klimovich was astonished at the strength in those big, bony fingers.

"They wrote to me afterwards," said Serpilin, gloomy at the recollection, "and told me that not all my men left you safely. They ran into some tanks on the way!"

"Some of them came back to my brigade, Comrade General."

"Were there many?"

"About twenty."

"Where are they now?"

"Some were killed in action, others I sent to the infantry after getting out of encirclement, and one is still with me."

"Who?"

"Zolotarev, a transport driver. He's now driving a Thirty-Four."

"I know him," said Serpilin. He could, incidentally, say this quite truthfully of every single man. "Could I possibly see him?"

"He's a long way off. At the tail end of the column, up near Mayakovsky Square."

"Give him thanks for loyal service from his old divisional commander." Serpilin was still sticking to his guns and referring to the group he had brought up out of encirclement as the division and to himself as its commander. "Did any of the officers join you?"

"One lieutenant—Khoryshev," said Klimovich.

"Is he still alive?"

"He was. I don't know now. I sent him to the infantry."

Serpilin noticed out of the corner of his eye that a captain of the tanks had come up to Klimovich and was waiting for the conversation to end, evidently anxious to discuss some service matter.

But Klimovich, after mentioning Zolotarev and Khoryshev, remembered Sintsov again.

"But your adjutant was apparently killed, Comrade General."

"Sintsov? Is that true?" asked Serpilin, distressed.

"It looks like it," said Klimovich. "He was lying unconscious in the forest, and Zolotarev took his documents and brought them to me. He wanted to get Sintsov out of there, but circumstances didn't permit."

"Yes," said Serpilin. "I ought to write to his family. But how, and where to?..." He glanced at the captain again and offered Klimovich his hand. "Till we meet again, Lieutenant-Colonel. It would be nice if you and I could be fighting together once more; but today we'll just watch your drive-past." He brought his hand up to his *papakha*, turned round and, stepping carefully in his felt boots, limped off down Gorky Street.

Klimovich watched him go and then turned irritably to the captain.

"Well, Ivanov, what's bothering you this time? You kept your head in battle, and now you have a question at every crossroads in Moscow!"

When Serpilin, leaning on his stick, limped up to the stands, they were already nearly full. More than once he had marched past them across Red Square in formation with the Frunze Academy. But in those days they had had a gay, peacetime appearance, with children hoisted up onto the shoulders of the grown-ups, coloured balloons floating overhead, and placards, handkerchiefs and headscarfs waving a welcome.

This time there were two or three military personnel to every civilian. Many, judging by their appearance, had arrived straight from the front line as the representatives of regiments, brigades and divisions currently fighting on the various sectors outside Moscow. They were wearing bedraggled, frayed fur hats, canvas mittens, and greatcoats or sheepskin jackets criss-crossed with revolver and field-bag straps.

Several infantry regiments were already drawn up in squares. But, military and civilians alike, Moscow on the defensive against the Germans was also represented. In the grim yet down-to-earth atmosphere of the stands that morning, there was something that welded armed forces and non-military together. There was also a feeling of inner strength and a tacit challenge in the fact that, with Hitler only a few dozen kilometres away, there was going to be a parade as usual, and all those present were aware of the force of that challenge.

Serpilin was aware of it too. In previous years, as he had marched past the Mausoleum with the Academy, he had known the happy excitement familiar to all who took part in the parades. This time his emotions were more profound and more powerful. He felt happy as he stood there on the stands, although this feeling was countered by the thoughts running through his mind at the time. With particular pain he remembered Sintsov, who had met with the fate that Serpilin had most of all feared might overtake him personally. Sintsov was missing, had died of his wounds alone somewhere in a forest. And yet it had looked as though he had been well out of it. Well out of it indeed!... He remembered with anger Shmakov's letter from the front in which he had written to say that he knew nothing about the men in the last eight vehicles in the column. They had been held up at the bridge and had then evidently been cut off by the Germans.

"'Evidently'!" muttered Serpilin angrily; and he mentally cursed Shmakov. "He seemed a real man, and then at the last moment he turned out to be a slouch.... 'Evidently'!..."

He had been so infuriated by Shmakov's "evidently" that he had not even answered the letter.

His thoughts about himself were heavy too. There had been his conversation two days previously with the Deputy Chief of the General Staff, an old comrade, and one of those who had got him out of trouble. He was hardly the kind of man to be suspected of being ill-disposed towards Serpilin or suspicious of him, and this had made the outcome of their conversation even more painful.

"I asked for a medical report on you," his old comrade had told him after congratulating him on his promotion and on everything else that merited congratulation. "On the one hand, they've amended your records for you, and on the other hand, they've spoilt them—the doctors this time. Strictly speaking, it's too early for you to be thinking about the front. Your health isn't too good; in general, you've had a rough time of it, and being in encirclement didn't do your health any good...."

"About that 'in general', I've forgotten it, and I don't want to be reminded of it by you, let alone anyone else," said Serpilin in a sudden burst of fury. "As for encirclement, dozens of generals have fought their way out and gained battle experience at the risk of their lives, and not just so as to sit wasting it in the rear! As soon as I'm fit for active service, either send me to the front, or I'll go to Stalin!"

"So that's your attitude, then!" said Serpilin's old comrade, even frowning at his tone of voice.

"Yes, that's my attitude!" snapped Serpilin.

He had remembered this conversation several times as he had limped in his felt boots from the Central Telegraph Office to the stands. And the harder it had been for him to walk, the more painful that conversation had seemed in retrospect.

"Perhaps it really would be best for all concerned if you were sent somewhere beyond the Volga to form units? That's a necessary job too..." he thought self-mockingly.

There were other dismal thoughts passing through his mind. And yet, in spite of them all, Serpilin was feeling happy on the stand in Red Square. Clearly, the snowy morning, the squares of troops drawn up and waiting, and the almost shattering news that there was to be a parade today, all contributed to produce a feeling of happiness in the assembled spectators. It was the first perceptible intimation since the beginning of the war of a still incredibly remote victory, and it was being felt that morning in Red Square simultaneously by several thousand people.

"Of all the rotten luck!" The agitated voice in his ear was Maximov's: he had temporarily disappeared and returned. "One regiment from my division is here.... Over there, by GUM." Maximov pointed to the unit, a dark rectangular mass in the far right-hand corner of the square. "They've been telling me that the division is in action; but now it turns out that they recalled it five days ago, made up the strength, and sent it through Moscow to a new sector. And that regiment over there's going to be sent straight from the square as well. And I never even knew! What a business!"

Maximov was simultaneously elated and depressed.

"You can't be lucky all the time, then," joked Serpilin. "You've missed your chance this time, for once. Perhaps after the parade...."

"What about after the parade?" interrupted Maximov. "Ask to be a supernumerary commissar? Better I'd never known about it!" He made a gesture of exasperation, but couldn't help staring across at the columns of his regiment outside GUM.

Serpilin also looked that way and thought enviously that although Maximov would end up with some other division and not his own, his request would probably be granted and he would soon be at the front.

If, as he stared in the direction of that regiment, Serpilin had been able to distinguish the faces of the soldiers at that distance, he would have seen standing in the first rank of the right-flank battalion the familiar tall figure of his former adjutant in an old, soiled hat and a new sheepskin jacket that was a little too short for him, with a submachine-gun slung across his chest.

On the day after the fighting round the brickworks, the division in which Maximov had been commissar at the beginning of the war and in which Sintsov was now serving, had benefited by a stroke of luck that rarely befell any unit outside Moscow during those months. Instead of being sent replacements out on the front line, as was customary, a substitute had been found and it had been withdrawn to the immediate rear. True, in spite of heavy losses amounting to two-thirds of its full strength, they had not been allowed long for replacements—five days in the rear in all—and on the sixth day there had been an emergency recall. Divisional HQ, an artillery regiment and two rifle regiments had been sent that very night through Moscow to beyond Podolsk, where the Germans, who had quietened down a little, were beginning to show dangerous signs of activity. Only one regiment had been retained for the day in Moscow to take part in the parade.

The command to bring the troops to attention had not yet been given. The commanders and political instructors were pacing up and down the front of the lines. The men in the ranks were discussing whether they would be sent to the front after the parade on foot, in lorries, or by train. The second and main topic of conversation was the parade and whether Stalin would be there. Most considered that he would, but some had their doubts.

"He won't be there, Sergeant—you'll see," said a diminutive submachine gunner to Sintsov—a new arrival who had joined the division on being discharged from hospital.

"Why not?"

"Because I'd certainly never allow him to come here to the Square and appear in public. Too dangerous!" The submachine gunner nodded towards the low, grey-white, misty blanket of cloud in the sky. "I'd be afraid for him!"

"Aren't you afraid for yourself, then?" asked Sintsov, also looking up at the sky.

"No, I'm not. The Germans aren't going to put themselves out for me. But they will for him. Maybe the sky is clouded over; but suppose they came diving out from behind? What could you do about it then?..." And the submachine gunner firmly reasserted that if he had any say in the matter, he would never allow Comrade Stalin to appear at the parade.

At that moment, Sintsov was approached by Battalion Commander Ryabchenko with Malinin, who had been given a bar to replace his three pips and had been appointed battalion commissar.

"How d'you do," said Malinin to Sintsov in his usual morose voice and, as always, glared at him darkly as if Sintsov had wronged him in some way. "The regimental CO has told the battalion commander that the order has come through Divisional HQ. Bayukov and yourself have been awarded the Red Star for the brickworks—so let me congratulate you!"

It was an odd habit of Malinin's that the more feeling he put into what he was saying, the more gloomy and unfriendly was his manner of saying it. From the sound of his voice alone, any outsider might well have thought that he was admonishing Sintsov, not congratulating him.

"Yes, indeed!" confirmed Ryabchenko gaily, "I heard it myself! Congratulations, Comrade Sintsov!"

Sintsov said: "I serve the Soviet Union"; but, to his own astonishment, he did not feel happy. Doubtless the happiness would come later, but for the moment he felt nothing. He remembered the brickworks; he remembered the mangled Sirota and the badly wounded Kolya Bayukov; he remembered how they had buried the remains of all the others the next morning; and his joy stuck halfway, like dry biscuit in the throat.

"May I congratulate you too, Comrade Senior Political Instructor?" he asked, observing that Malinin and Ryabchenko were showing no intention of leaving.

"I haven't done anything to speak of," said Malinin in the same lugubrious voice; and Sintsov simply couldn't make out whether he had been decorated or not.

Malinin had not, in fact, been decorated, because it had been decided to recommend him for the Order of the Red Banner, not the Red Star; but the Red Banner was awarded by the Front, and someone there, in order to cut down on the awards and without going into details, had struck out Malinin's name along with a number of others. But Malinin was unusually indifferent to not receiving an award, even for a man who was anything but vain. The reason was that he really believed that he hadn't done anything to speak of, and that it was the men who mattered, not himself. He was entirely satisfied now that Sintsov, who had been retained with the unit, and Bayukov, who was recovering in hospital, had both been awarded the decorations for which he had recommended them. Whenever he spoke up for someone, he always did so grudgingly; but he always stuck to his guns afterwards and took a refusal badly.

"Listen, Sintsov!" he said after a pause. "You've been promoted to Senior Sergeant and decorated. The divisional newspaper's given you a write-up. Before we go into action again, I think you should apply for reinstatement to the Party. What's your view?"

What was Sintsov's view? Malinin knew that better than anyone.

"I should have thought today would be a suitable time to write out your application," said Malinin, glancing up at the sky, from which a few snowflakes were just beginning to fall.

There was an unusually solemn note in his voice. Like everybody else, he was excited about what was going to take place on Red Square.

"I'll write an application, if you don't think it's too early, Compade Senior Political Instructor," said Sintsov; and he looked straight at Malinin, as if to say: "Haven't you perhaps brought this up prematurely? If so, why didn't you think first? And if it isn't too early, then back me all the way, because if you don't give me your backing, who will?"

Malinin caught Sintsov's eye and held it for several seconds. During the last few days, while the division had been receiving replacements outside Moscow, Malinin, without saying anything to Sintsov, had made the requisite formal enquiry through the Divisional Political Department and had received a reply. Yes, the registration card on Communist Sintsov, I.P., was in the files where it ought to be. His Party membership was being confirmed by documents, without which the question of his reinstatement could not even be considered. This had been the first important move, and it was what Malinin was thinking about now. But from his eyes it would have been difficult to guess what he was actually thinking at that moment. He looked as though he was not thinking about anything in particular and had merely decided to look intently at Sintsov as if to say: "So that's the sort of person you are, Ivan Sintsov. Well, well!"

Suddenly, the command came reverberating their way from somewhere on the right:

"Atten—shun!"

Ryabchenko leaped forward as if on springs. Malinin stepped after him awkwardly, and the lines began to level off.

"Look, look ... just look!" It was the submachine-gunner whispering in Sintsov's ear as they dressed from the right—the one who had been saying that he would never allow Stalin to be present at the parade. "Just look!"

Sintsov looked in front of him. And, like the thousands of men standing with him on the square, he saw, through the white veil of snow as it began to fall more and more thickly, Stalin, in greatcoat and fur hat, standing in his usual place on the wing of the Mausoleum.

"Yes," said Serpilin after the parade, as he and Maximov drove to the Timiryazev Academy, now converted into a hospital, "if you make a sober estimate of the situation on the various fronts, it's still hard to believe that we'll ever be back where we started: fighting on the state frontier. But there's one thought that consoles me."

"What's that?"

"When I was crossing the Dnieper at Mogilev with what was left of my regiment, it would have been hard to imagine that there would be a parade in Red Square on the 7th of November and that I would be there. My mind just wouldn't take it. Although I tried to keep myself in hand, deep down my thoughts were too black for such a notion. When you think about it all, it's as if there were two different people in you. One says: 'It's too early to celebrate—too early!' But the other says: 'Too early? But you must!' How can I put it to you? In spite of all their successes, I sense a difference between us and the Germans to our advantage, and not only in general, but even in purely military terms. I don't believe that they'd have held a parade in Berlin if we'd been sixty kilometres away. I don't believe it, and that's flat! Anyway, enough of that. Generally speaking, things are settled at the front, not on the parade ground.... Did they promise to discharge you next Friday?"

Maximov didn't reply. He was sitting next to Serpilin and staring fixedly ahead of him. When the car stopped and Serpilin carefully climbed out, Maximov, without moving from his seat, held out his hand:

"All the best, Fyodor Fyodorovich! I hope they discharge you soon!"

"And you?"

"Me? We'll assume I've skipped off. I'll ask them to send me to the front. Between you and me, I'll never be really fit again; but a week isn't going to settle it one way or the other. Either they'll order me back in disgrace, or they'll send me straight off somewhere tomorrow."

"So what's it going to be? Am I to wait for you to come back or not?"

"Don't wait. I'll get my way. Whatever happens, I'm still born lucky!"

Maximov smiled and even winked at Serpilin. And Serpilin, as he looked at him, suddenly thought: "What was *I* like at thirty? And how long ago was that?" Then, in answer to his own question: "Nineteen twenty-five, the first year after Lenin died. Frunze was still the People's Commissar for the Navy.... I was commander of a regiment at Takhta-Bazar and was studying for the academy.... Dear me, that was a long time ago indeed!" And with these memories at the back of his mind, he said good-bye to Maximov and glanced once more with pleasure at his cheerful, good-natured face. "Well, he was born lucky. I hope no bullet ever gets him, and his wife doesn't stop loving him, and he never has a single stroke of bad luck! Why should everybody have a hard life?" thought Serpilin without envy.

When he returned to the hospital ward, he found his wife waiting for him.

In honour of the holiday, Valentina Yegorovna had put on an ancient black silk dress that Serpilin knew of old. As soon as she rose to meet him, her lips compressed, Serpilin realised at once that she had been there for some time and had been angry with him for several hours.

"It's all your Maximov, I know," said his wife as she came forward to meet him. "Conspicuous by his absence, I notice! Where is he? Scared of showing his face to me?" She had already realised that she would have to forgive her husband anyway on account of the holiday, and only for that reason had she spoken first.

"Whistle for him!" said Serpilin. "He reversed his car in the yard and drove off to the front."

"With whose permission? He's not supposed to be discharged until next Friday!"

"He says they'll let him go."

"I suppose you're thinking of doing the same."

"Well, we'll see!..."

"I was listening to a broadcast," said Valentina Yegorovna, "only at first I didn't realise it was Stalin speaking. I don't know why—the radio was on all the time, and yet the speech only began halfway through...."

Serpilin shrugged his shoulders in surprise. Neither of them knew or could have known that, owing to the risk of a

German air-raid, it had been decided not to broadcast anything until after the parade was over. It was only at the very last moment that Stalin, when already at the microphone, looked up at the sky, saw that it had begun snowing heavily, and gave the order for all radio stations to be switched on. But it had taken several minutes for his instructions to be passed on and carried out....

"When I realised who it was, I actually cried...."

"Why?"

"I don't know. I just went and cried.... Are you going to lie down?"

"No," said Serpilin. He was overexcited and didn't want to lie down. His wife understood and didn't insist.

"Very well. Only do take off your boots."

"There's plenty of room in them."

"What's that to do with it? Aren't your legs hurting you?"

"Just a bit."

Serpilin took off his boots, stood them near the wardrobe, crossed the ward in the stockinged feet, and sat in an armchair half-facing his wife.

Valentina Yegorovna had not left Moscow at all. Since the outbreak of war, she had worked as a nurse in the hospital next to her home on the Pirogovskaya, and when Serpilin had been brought to the "Timiryazev", she had made the journey every day for the last five weeks as her duties allowed, sometimes in the morning, sometimes in the evening.

After five years of separation, when Valentina Yegorovna had finally seen her husband again, she had improved and blossomed out in the space of five weeks and, from the anxiety-ridden old woman he had been so shocked to meet a few days before the outbreak of war, had changed into a woman as beautiful, if no longer as young, as she had been a few years ago. During the years of his absence, her hair had begun to go grey, especially at the temples; but she had plucked up her courage one day, dyed her hair, and had come to the hospital grey-headed no longer. When Serpilin had begun teasing her, she had not been hurt, but had said in a reproachful voice that had touched him to the heart:

"Well? You want to tell me I'm wasting my time and you love me anyway? I know. I dare you not to!" And, after a pause, she added: "Have you wiped out those years?... Or are you only pretending?"

"I've wiped them out," said Serpilin. And he was telling the truth.

"So have I," she said, and she smiled, though not very gaily. "This is not natural,"—and she touched her hair—"but if it was, I wouldn't darken it again...."

"What was it like at the parade?" asked Valentina Yegorovna when Serpilin had settled himself in the armchair.

He told her about the parade, and then about his conversation at the People's Commissariat two days ago. He had seen his wife that evening; but she had been terribly angry with him for getting up before he was supposed to, and she simply refused to listen. She had imagined that his premature departure from the hospital had left him feeling worse, and no argument could prevail on her under the circumstances.

"Never mind, you could have picked up your documents and medals a week later. Nothing would have happened to them, or you!" she had insisted implacably, unwilling to listen to his protestations. And the day before, as a mark of protest, she had even missed a day and hadn't come to visit him.

But now, after the parade, she hadn't the heart to upbraid him for today or the day before. She already regretted having refused to listen to him.

Once he had begun his story, Serpilin didn't hold back what anyone else in his position, talking to anyone other than Valentina Yegorovna, would probably have omitted. He told her about the rotten medical report, and how Ivan Alexeyevich (as his old comrade was called) had threatened to send him to the rear on the formation of units instead of to the front.

He described all this without a qualm, knowing that, despite her anxiety for his health, his wife understood: not to go to the front after hospital would be a disaster for him, and she did not want that. On the contrary, she wanted things to work out as he wished, even if this might mean more anxiety for her. And for this he loved her with that great, unageing love which fate does not bestow on people every day or under every roof.

He also gave her the full details of another part of the conversation with Ivan Alexeyevich which had annoyed him, though for a different reason.

It was about the 176th Division, the remnants of which he had commanded after Zaichikov, its number, and its colours, which had been delivered by Shmakov to Front HQ.

Now, after a long time at hospital, after all that had happened since that time near Vyazma and Moscow, Serpilin had, of course, not raised the matter on which he had once intended to insist: that the division should be retained as such. He knew that this was impossible; but the very impossibility of it had left him feeling bitter and, partly even in defiance of common sense, he had begun questioning Ivan Alexeyevich concerning the whereabouts of the divisional colours and saying that it would be a good idea if, although the same personnel couldn't be remustered, the division could be reformed with the same colours and number.

"Well, some such division will no doubt be formed with that number," Ivan Alexeyevich had replied casually, not concealing that the matter meant little to him.

"It's important that the unit should have a tradition."

"Maybe so, but who's going to worry about that now? If you get the appointment, you won't want to form a new division, you'll want to be given one that's ready and to take over from someone who's left or been found unsatisfactory, so that you can go straight into action! And I suspect that if you are appointed, you're hardly likely to ask what it's done and how things have been; you'll ask how many there are on the strength, and how many weapons, and where the division is, and you'll go and take over command. Or do you measure yourself by one yardstick and others by a different one?"

"Perhaps. But d'you think the units are going to have their history put on record, or aren't they?"

"They are," said Ivan Alexeyevich. "But to tell the truth, no one at present wants to go back to Adam and Eve and how they ran for it...."

"They didn't run for it!" snapped Serpilin, raising his voice.

"I appreciate what you've been through," said Ivan Alexeyevich, "and not only you.... But a fact is still a fact: not a single division has a history of an advance to Königsberg or, at the worst, to Warsaw. The only history is of the retreat to Moscow. We have to face up to the truth. And while there's a war on," he said stiffly—and Serpilin knew that he was right—"and while there's a war on," repeated Ivan Alexeyevich, "we'll start writing history from the moment when we start winning! From the first advance operations. We must remember that—while there's war on. And we must hammer the same point home to everybody else. After the war we can begin all our reminiscences, in chronological order, from the beginning. All the more so, since there's a great deal it would be better not to remember."

"Listen," said Serpilin, leaning over the table and looking him straight in the eye. "You were sitting right here in the same place just before war broke out. Tell me: how did it come about that we didn't know? And if you knew, why didn't you report it? And if he didn't listen, why didn't you insist? Tell me that! I haven't had a moment's peace of mind through thinking about it ever since the first day at the tront. I haven't asked anyone yet, but I'm asking you now...."

"Ask something easier!" said Ivan Alexeyevich, suddenly banging the desk with his fist; and for a moment his eyes were bitter and unhappy.

Serpilin was not intimidated by that look: he wanted to ask more; but Ivan Alexeyevich stopped him, flattened his hand on the desk, and said firmly, almost menacingly:

"Shut up! I don't want to tell lies, and I can't give you any answers!" Then, swallowing as if in need of air, he asked in a quite different tone of voice: "How's your Valentina Yegorovna? How's her health? How's she looking? She came to see me when you were in encirclement. She was in a bit of a state...."

Serpilin repeated the entire conversation to his wife, and with all the details, which made him turn pale as he told her, and which made her go white in the face too as she listened.

"I don't understand," said Serpilin, leaning forward and looking intently into his wife's sad eyes. "I don't understand—I don't understand how a man like Stalin couldn't have foreseen what was brewing! I don't believe he wasn't warned about it."

"How is Stalin looking, by the way?" asked Valentina Yegorovna, perhaps anxious to lead this painful conversation in another direction, perhaps following her own private train of thought.

Serpilin considered for a moment.

"How is he looking? The same as usual, in my opinion."

And he remembered that for some reason he had not listened too closely to Stalin's tired, hollow-sounding voice, but had simply watched him.

Stalin had stood there and made a speech. The Germans were outside Moscow, and he had stood on the Mausoleum and spoken. And the troops had been drawn up in front of the Mausoleum, and this had been the November parade in Moscow, and in this lay the most important thing that Serpilin had felt during these minutes. "Yes, and all the others too probably," he thought.

"He must be finding it all very hard," said Valentina Yegorovna.

Serpilin looked at her and thought of the old quarrel between them. Each refused to give way to the other and, more often than not without saying a word to one another, they had quarrelled about it silently, physically together and yet apart—and for many years now.

His wife, as Serpilin knew, was passionately convinced that everything bad, past and present, happened independently of Stalin simply because he was unaware of it or because they had given him a false account of it; and this had affected his judgement. She had thought this even during the years when she had been deprived of her husband.

Serpilin himself thought otherwise. He had known Stalin of old. As far back as Tsaritsin in 1918, he had seen him a number of times at Headquarters and in the trenches, had talked to him, and since then had remained once and for all under the spell of his personality: tough, strong, and unique. For just that reason, he had to force himself to imagine how such a man could have been deceived, twisted round someone's finger, compelled against his will to do what he did not want to do. Serpilin felt that he understood what sort of a person Stalin was and that he knew the full value which Stalin put on the army and everything he did for it; and so he could not reconcile himself with what had happened to the army in 1937 and 1938. Who had stood to gain by it? And how could Stalin have allowed it?

And the outbreak of war? And that after Stalin had foreseen Munich, after he had signed a pact with the Germans in 1939, thereby preventing the English and the French from making cannon fodder of us once again!

And then, after all that, to let war catch us napping! How could this have happened?

"Yes," said Serpilin after a pause. "He's all right. He looks fine," he continued. "He's aged a little, that's all...." And then he thought to himself how he had never felt, and probably never would feel, such agonisingly conflicting emotions as those he felt for Stalin, who had today done something that few others would have dared in his place: he had held that parade with eighty German divisions outside Moscow....

Exactly twelve hours after the parade was over and Red Square was empty, the 93rd Regiment of the 31st Rifle

Division, with Senior Sergeant Sintsov on its strength, had already sent one battalion into a night battle for the village of Kuzkovo exactly eighty kilometres south-west of Red Square as of the crow flies. According to the preliminary plans, Regimental HQ should have been stationed in Kuzkovo, in the second echelon; but things had worked out otherwise.

In the morning, when the parade had been taking place on Red Square, the Germans had launched several simultaneous attacks on the thin line of the division which was covering that sector and which had been bled white in a long series of battles. At first, the Germans had made no headway. They had been stopped by our fire; but they had thrown in fresh forces, probed further, finally broken through the front and, after covering five kilometres during the day, had taken three villages, Kuzkovo included. The regiment, which had been brought up from Moscow by nightfall and had supported the retreating units from behind, had been ordered to restore the situation during the night. The two other villages, despite orders to take them, had not been recaptured, and the line of the front up to 15th November—that is, until the new big German advance—had run along their eastern outskirts; but Kuzkovo had been recaptured from the Germans towards midnight by one battalion of the 93rd Rifle Regiment and by a company of Lieutenant-Colonel Klimovich's 17th Tank Brigade.

Kuzkovo had been at the tip of the Germans' daytime spearhead. The enemy had not captured it until towards evening and had not been able to dig in properly. Although the order of the German command not to retreat one step had been as categorical as our command's order to take Kuzkovo at all costs, one order had been carried out and the other had not, as always happens when two such orders are given simultaneously and are concentrated at one point on the front.

The tanks had been mainly responsible for Kuzkovo being retaken without heavy losses. The Germans had thought that there weren't any on that sector of the front, and, indeed, there hadn't been in the morning, so their surprise attack had been doubly effective.

After replacements had been sent to the division, a platoon of submachine gunners had been formed in each battalion, the men having been handpicked from those who had already been in action. Sintsov had been selected as section commander in one such platoon and, along with other submachine gunners, he had followed the tanks into Kuzkovo.

The tanks had burst straight into the village. It had been a moonlit night, the street had been white under a carpet of snow, and when the Germans had begun dashing out of the houses and running across, most of them had been mown down on the spot—some by the tanks, others by submachine gun fire.

Estimates for the report to the division had been postponed till morning; but even now, at night, the command believed that something like a company of Germans had been wiped out in the night battle. Our own losses had been small—only one killed and three wounded in the submachine gunners' platoon. This relatively easy success, especially just short of twenty-four hours since those same men had paraded in Red Square, had kept many of them awake afterwards in spite of fatigue.

The battalion was hastily digging in on the approaches to Kuzkovo, HQ was set up in the village, and the submachine gunners were allotted two houses near the command post. They had done a good day's work, and, together with the tank crews, considered themselves the heroes of the hour; and being given a rest and not being made to dig trenches in the snow like the others had helped to keep them in a good mood.

The house next to the two in which the submachine gunners had been quartered for the night had been burnt down when the Germans had taken the village. Several corpses had been lying under the debris and charred timbers. At first, when the submachine gunners had come upon the ashes, they had thought that the Germans had burned our own POWs alive. But afterwards they dragged out from under the beams a number of rifles and a submachine gun with a warped butt.

There were no inhabitants in the village. One could only guess what had happened in that house during the day.

"They obviously put up a fight, didn't want to surrender, and then the Germans set fire to the house," said someone.

"They won't have been prisoners if they were armed."

One of the platoon spent a long time cleaning the submachine gun salvaged from the ashes. He cleaned and cleaned away, finally spat, and put it aside.

"What's the matter?" he was asked.

"D'you expect me to clean it in one go? Must have been a hell of a fire."

"Yes, it was really hot in there!" said someone in an attempt at a joke; but it fell flat. In spite of the easy victory, all the men were appalled at being so close to the ashes and the bodies of men who had been burned alive. In some other battle, they might meet with a similar fate. Nothing would be left but dead bodies and charred weapons, and no one would ever be able to find out how it had happened....

The damp logs, hissing and snapping in the stove, cast a dim light round the house, which did not look lived-in and had probably long been abandoned by its inhabitants. Several of the men were asleep, lying along the wall and huddling close to one another for warmth. The rest, Sintsov included, were sitting at the fire. He was thinking back to the morning, the Red Square, the crowded stands, and Stalin in greatcoat and fur hat speaking from the wing of the Mausoleum.... And although it had all actually happened, it was hard to believe that it had been only that morning....

"Pity we didn't catch a single Fritz," said a little submachine gunner named Komarov who had been next to Sintsov on parade and was now sitting beside him.

"And what would you have done with him if you'd caught him, eh, Komarov?" asked the soldier who had been cleaning the fire-damaged submachine gun.

He was a lean, long-limbed, sinewy man of great physical strength. He looked about thirty. He had a fine-sounding name: Leonidov. When Sintsov had met him five days ago, he had introduced himself by saying: "I have a fine-sounding name: Leonidov." It had been impossible to tell from his grin whether he was joking or in earnest.

"Well, Komarov, why don't you say something? What would you do with a Fritz if you caught one now?"

"I'd tell him about the parade and how we marched past today, and how Stalin made a speech."

"How would you explain that to him? D'you know German?"

"I'd do it through an interpreter."

"All right, then. So they'd give you an interpreter and you'd explain. And then what?"

"I'd let him go."

"You'd *what*? Let him go?"

"Yes, I would. Let him go to his own side and tell them."

"You'd let him go alive, just like that?"

"Well, he couldn't go dead, could he?"

"Say, that was neat, the way you got those two Germans, Senior Sergeant. I'd just emptied my ammunition drum.

'They'll get away behind the hillock,' I thought; and then you cut them down on the spot," said the third submachine gunner, a corporal named Pudalov, interrupting the conversation and turning to Sintsov.

Sintsov had known him for three or perhaps four days, and had already noticed that Pudalov, although a very punctilious soldier, would, at the slightest opportunity, butter up even as humble a superior as his section leader. Sintsov had indeed shot down a fleeing German by the church with a burst, but only one of the enemy, not two. The second had managed to run away. Pudalov knew this, but evidently saw no harm in flattering his section commander.

"The second one got away," said Sintsov. "I was nearly at the end of my ammo."

"Incidentally, those Germans can run like the wind when they see tanks coming. They don't like them at all," said Leonidov. A cruel smile appeared momentarily on his gaunt, narrow face. "If only they could make so many tanks that we could all get into one each and squash them like chickens!"

"Pestrak, hey, Pestrak!" He began nudging a soldier who was sitting fast asleep next to him, his tired head flung back.

The soldier's face was young and handsome. But even in sleep his face had an expression of inhuman exhaustion, and Sintsov felt sorry that he was being disturbed.

"Let him sleep," he said.

"No, let him tell us how he was frightened out of his wits by one of his own tanks. It was going past us, and you should have seen him dive straight into a snowdrift flat on his face and lie there without budging.... Pestrak, hey, Pestrak!"

But Pestrak slept on, and the expression of mortal fatigue on his face was due not to his being more tired than the rest—on the contrary, he was younger and stronger than many—but to the shattering impact of the day's impressions. Although the submachine gunners' platoon had been handpicked from men with battle experience, Pestrak, Sintsov gathered, had been in action for the first time that day, although he had come to the unit after being wounded. And, incidentally, what was so surprising about that? Was it so unusual for a man to be wounded long before he first laid eyes on the enemy and fired at him, even at long range?

Sintsov sat at the stove and looked at the men in his section sleeping, or sitting with him at the fire, and thought how he had known Leonidov longer than all the others—five whole days—and Pestrak for only two. He looked at them, and reflected that in his whole life he had never known so many transitory meetings, inseparable comradeships, and last good-byes to so many people as during these five months of war. There had been the artillery captain in the woods near Borisov; and the battalion commissar from the Frontier Guards who had been killed by a bomb; and the colonel with whom he had tried to find a train for Mogilev; and the bomber pilot, and the captain of the tanks whom he had met again near Yelnia and had lost contact with once more; and Khoryshev, with whose company he had been political instructor; and Zolotarev, with whom he had been heading back to their own side and who, if still alive, was the only living soul who could confirm that he, Sintsov, was telling the plain truth from beginning to end....

And Kolya Bayukov? Was he alive, and was he recovering from his wound or was a cripple for life? And where was he? How would it be possible to write and tell him about his decoration? And what could be done about it anyway? People were disappearing all the time and new ones were arriving—and it couldn't be otherwise at the front. So it had been, and so it would continue to be. Men were being killed and wounded, returning from hospital, arriving with replacements, fighting, going back to the rear with their arms in slings or their heads bandaged, saying good-bye, sometimes exchanging addresses, but more likely not doing so....

"Well, lads, shall we sleep?" said Sintsov, driving all these unwanted and unwelcome thoughts out of his mind. "Let's make the best of it while we can. They haven't promised not to wake us before morning, you know."

The submachine gunners began making themselves comfortable. Sintsov was also getting ready to lie down, when the door opened suddenly and Malinin entered the cabin.

"What's this? All settled down for some shut-eye?" he asked in his gloomy voice.

"Yes."

"What's the food situation?"

Sintsov told him there were still enough dry rations for tomorrow.

"I think we'll be bringing up a field kitchen by morning," said Malinin. "All right, have some rest. You've done well, you can sleep with a clear conscience."

He stopped at the door as if intending to go out, but didn't do so.

"You haven't forgotten this morning's conversation?" he asked Sintsov.

"No, I haven't."

Malinin unfastened the top hook of his sheepskin jacket, thrust his hand into his breast pocket and, taking out a sheet of exercise paper folded in four, offered it to Sintsov.

"Here, I've written that out for you. Attach it to your statement."

"Thanks," said Sintsov.

"I'm not giving it to you for your thanks," said Malinin, "but because I believe in you."

He shook Sintsov firmly by the hand and said something that Sintsov would never have expected of him.

"There's only two of us left out of our company, not counting the ones in hospital. Just you and me. Who would ever have imagined it?"

And at that moment there was a flicker of expression in his eyes that made Sintsov think: "Everybody wants to live. Malinin too."

"Well, anyway, all the best...."

Sintsov wanted to see him out, but Malinin made an irritable gesture and went out.

Sintsov sat down by the stove, unfolded the sheet of exercise paper and, by the weak and fading light, read: "I, Malinin, Alexei Denisovich, member of the All-Union Communist Party (Bolsheviks) since 1919, hereby give as my real and considered opinion...."

Sintsov read it right through as far as a passage which it would no doubt have been hard to expect of Malinin in peacetime—"I can confirm his past history only as from October this year, but I can vouch for him as for myself"—folded the paper in four again, put it in his tunic pocket and, hearing a tank rumbling along the street, went outside.

The street was brilliantly lit by the rays of the moon. A Thirty-Four had stopped near the house. Two of the crew were standing up in the open turret hatch.

"Hey, infantryman! Haven't got a smoke, have you?"

"Yes," said Sintsov. He went up to the tank and pulled out of his sheepskin jacket pocket a half-smoked pack of "Byelomor" cigarettes, all that he left of the Moscow holiday bonus.

"You owe us some. If it weren't for the tanks, you can bet your boots Fritz would be giving you hell. One each, and one more each to spare. Okay?"

"Fair enough," said Sintsov.

The tankman counted out the cigarettes, disappeared down the hatch—probably to give his share to the driver-mechanic—and then bobbed up again and returned the packet to Sintsov.

"Thanks."

"Are you leaving, then?" asked Sintsov.

"We are. You won't surrender the village without us, will you?"

"Not likely," said Sintsov.

"Anyway, if you can't hold out, climb up into the belfry and bang away. We'll hear you and we'll come back." And he shouted down into the interior of the machine: "Hey, Petya, start her up and let's get moving!"

The tank roared into life and, leaving two grooves of chopped snow in its wake, lumbered off down the moonlit street.

Sintsov stood leaning up against the wall of the cabin and watched the tank until it turned a corner and vanished from sight. He did not know that his cruel and capricious wartime luck had only just missed reuniting him with the man he so badly needed to meet—tank driver Zolotarev, who had been told only a minute ago: "Hey, Petya, start her up and let's get moving!"

CHAPTER SIXTEEN

The old manor house stood on a low but conspicuous rise, and the old park sloped down on either side of it: back, towards our rear, and forward, towards the Germans. The village of Dubrovitsi, taken by the enemy several days ago, lay on the far side of the ice-covered brook that wound through the vale.

The hill had been rocked for days in succession by bomb explosions and artillery fire, the trees in the park had been snapped off like matches, and the house had been smashed to smithereens by direct bomb hits. The belfry of the manorial church had been gnawed away by shell-fire up to the first storey. Pock-marked by the black stains of explosions, the snow in the park resembled a chess-board.... But however much the Germans shook and blasted that terrain, the division, after several forced withdrawals, as if furious with itself and its neighbour units, seized hold and hung on with its bare teeth to the hill and the old manor house and, so it seemed, only clamped its jaws tighter.

For the last fifteen days, counting from the morning of November 15, the Germans had been advancing in full force on Moscow, trying to tighten a pincer movement on the capital from north and south and, at various points, thrusting nearer and nearer on the central sectors of the front. In a two weeks' advance they had taken Klin, Istra, Yakhroma, Solnechnogorsk, Venev, Stalinogorsk, Bogoroditsk and Mikhailov. In the north-western area, only twenty-five kilometres lay between them and Moscow....

And here, too, although the division had gone into battle after the parade on the Red Square under direct orders not to retreat a single step, it had nevertheless been compelled to fall back more than once.

True, stories were coming in from the rear that they had the support of second echelon units, and behind them, apparently, there were units of a third echelon. But even if the soldiers' "bush telegraph" was discounted, the men fighting out on the forward positions were themselves beginning to realise that there was some kind of a build-up in progress behind their slender but tough line of defence. They no longer felt the involuntary chill down the spine that occurs when you know that there is no one behind you, and that if you fall down, then the enemy will step over your body and march inexorably onwards....

They were saying—and the recent battles seemed to confirm this—that the advancing Germans were nearing the end of their tether. But who was to know how much more of this "tether" they had left? Yesterday, all had been overjoyed that Rostov had been won back from them on the southern front, although this news had been the first indication that Rostov had actually fallen. Today, in a morning bulletin transcribed from the radio, it had been announced that we had withdrawn from Tikhvin several days ago. We might retake it, like Rostov; but in the meantime we had abandoned it....

It was about Rostov and Tikhvin that an argument was raging in the submachine gunners' dug-out—an old brick hothouse roofed over with two layers of beams—from which it was only a stone's throw to the command post of the battalion in the cellar of the manor house and to the front line, which ran along the edge of the park below.

The argument was between Leonidov and Komarov. The

fiery Leonidov had been attacking the Informburo bulletins and the reasonable Komarov was defending them.

"Give over, Komarov," said Leonidov teasingly, "it's always all right with you. But what's right about it when they tell me that Rostov's been taken from the Fritzes, and I rub my eyes and think: 'Goodness! So we're supposed to have taken it, are we? When did we give it up, then? Have I been asleep all this time and just woken up?' It's the same with Tikhvin. All right, they've abandoned it, worse luck. But you tell me something: they pulled out only 'a few days ago'; but mightn't it actually have been a month back? What's really been happening?"

"You're a fool!" said Komarov. "What would you stand to gain by it if you knew a week earlier?"

"I wouldn't mind standing to lose by it. I just want to know all the facts."

"But perhaps it's not supposed to be published! Perhaps the Germans aren't supposed to know!"

"What?" Leonidov even shot to his feet. "You mean to tell me Fritz doesn't know what he's captured? He's taken Tikhvin and he hasn't realised it? Did we make a secret of it when we took Kuzkovo? You bet we didn't! Our regimental commander damn well nearly rang up the Army direct from Battalion HQ, I heard it with my own ears. But when we were retreating, no one breathed a word, naturally...."

Then the anger on Leonidov's face gave way to sorrow. "I'm sorry about Tikhvin! I'm from Kaivaksa myself—you could say I was a Tikhvin man. They've taken Tikhvin, and I never even knew about it."

"What's this Wax you come from?" said the peaceable Komarov, deliberately teasing the quarrelsome Leonidov. "What's this Wax, then?"

"I didn't say Wax, I said Kaivaksa. There happens to be a place of that name near Tikhvin!" retorted Leonidov angrily.

But Komarov didn't want to miss this chance of putting one over on Leonidov.

"You're a fine one! They can't even write their bulletins without you!"

"Listen, Senior Sergeant," said Leonidov, turning to Sintsov, who was sitting behind a desk improvised out of a door on some bricks and was writing a letter to his wife. "What's your opinion? Is a man given a head for 'yes' or for 'no'?"

"To keep his brains in," interjected Komarov before Sintsov could look up.

"And what does he keep his brains in it for? For 'yes' or for 'no'?" persisted Leonidov.

Sintsov looked up from his letter. It was warm and dry in the dug-out, and it was quiet today as well. For the first time in several days a lull had set in that morning. It was the first day on which they had not seen someone killed or wounded, and death only made its presence known by the noise of gunfire to the right, in the neighbouring division. It was a fierce bombardment: a violent battle was evidently raging over there. But as long as there was no need of immediate support, which could be demanded of them at any moment of the day or night, Sintsov, like all the rest, was glad that the Germans were concentrating on their neighbours instead. Clearly, the men could never survive on the front line without that streak of soldier's selfishness. In half a month's fighting four men, himself included, were left out of the original seven in Sintsov's section. While dragging a wounded man from the field of battle, Corporal Pudalov had been killed—the one who had loved making up to his superiors, but who, in his last moments, had rendered service to a comrade and had paid for it with his life. Two men had been wounded and sent to the field hospital. There was one more wounded man, Pestrak; but he had refused to leave his unit and, pulling through thanks to his own superhuman strength, had stayed in action despite a jagged shoulder wound. He had just gone off to fetch dinner, and, apart from him, the entire complement of the section was now in the dug-out: Sintsov and these two submachine gunners who were permanently at loggerheads, Leonidov and Komarov.

"A fine thing to quarrel about!" said Sintsov. "If your head's got nothing in it but 'yes' or 'no', what kind of a head is that? A quiz, more likely."

He knew what Leonidov meant by his 'yes' or 'no': he meant that a man has a real head on his shoulders if he knows when to say 'no'. Leonidov was brave in battle, but stubborn almost beyond the limit allowable under the rules of army discipline, and he had been infuriated by the complacency of Komarov, who usually considered that the people on top knew what they were doing. In some other dispute, Sintsov might have supported Leonidov; but Leonidov had picked on the bulletin, and this was to no good purpose. It was not in order to doubt the truth of the bulletin at the front, and certainly not before the others.

"What's the point of doubting it privately either?" thought Sintsov. "The bulletin doesn't give everything, and it can't.

What difference does it make whether Tikhvin fell today or three days ago?... Perhaps they were still hoping to retake it and didn't report the loss, just as we never reported to the Army when we were driven out of Kuzkovo, because we all thought we'd get it back again. But we had to report it in the morning whether we wanted to or not...."

"Who are you writing to, Senior Sergeant?" asked Leonidov after a silence.

"My wife."

"So I've noticed. That must be the second time you've written to her, if not the third; but you haven't had any reply."

"No."

"You should put in a complaint!" said Leonidov, half teasing, half sympathetic.

"Complain to whom? I know the field post number, and that's all. I'm writing into the dark and getting no reply," said Sintsov, responding to the sympathy and taking no notice of the mockery.

"I'm in the same boat—no reply," said Leonidov. "Yesterday I thought I knew how things stood. Today it turns out that I don't. I thought the Germans were near Volkhov, and now I hear they've overrun Tikhvin. A real bolt from the blue! I've got a family there. And it suddenly occurred to me: it's not just me that's found out too late that the Germans are in Tikhvin. Have the villagers had a nasty shock too? Our troops there in the morning, and then the Germans by evening? My father's living there—he was crippled in the Civil War. If he didn't know in good time, he can't have got far."

It was only then that Sintsov and Komarov fully grasped the reason for Leonidov's unusually bad temper.

"You go ahead and write, like the senior sergeant," said Komarov.

"Where to?" demanded Leonidov.

"Why, that Wax of yours...."

Komarov hadn't meant to tease him this time, but in making the same joke twice he had forgotten the real name of Leonidov's native village.

"Kai-vak-sa!" corrected Leonidov angrily, enunciating each syllable separately. "And if you twist it round again, I'll give you a thick ear."

"Anyway, you write," repeated Komarov, ignoring the threat. "Who knows what goes on in wartime? They say the Germans've got Tula surrounded, but they haven't actually taken it. Maybe it's the other way round where you come from. Maybe the Germans have taken Tikhvin and our troops have got it surrounded. Sit down and write a letter."

"I'll do no such thing," said Leonidov stubbornly. He wasn't the kind of man to clutch at straws.

Moving up a little to allow more light to fall on his paper, Sintsov returned to his letter. Leonidov had been right. In the last few weeks he had sent two letters to the mysterious post box number he had written down back in Moscow. In his first two letters, he had told her about the battle at the brickworks, about the parade, and about his award. In the third, the one he was writing today, he was telling her about what mattered to him more than anything else—that he had applied for reinstatement to the Party and that his deposition had already been examined by the Regimental Party Bureau and sent to the Divisional Party Commission for confirmation. As soon as the photographer arrived at the front line to take the necessary photographs for his documents, he would be called before the Party Commission in a matter of days.

He described all this briefly, with restraint, and without going further into his feelings. Masha knew better than anybody how much it all meant to him. And, in any case, it's difficult writing long letters when you're not sure that they'll reach their destination and when you haven't even a notion of how they can ever arrive.

He finished the letter, folded it into a triangle, and then, as before, wrote under Masha's surname: "In absence of addressee, please open." He wondered if a miracle might happen, and not only might the letter be opened, but Masha, wherever she was, might be informed of at least one item of news: he was alive. Perhaps even over the radio. In the final analysis, would it be so difficult for them to send a few words if she made radio contact with Moscow: "Your husband is alive and well"? Even if it had to be coded, how much was there to code? Very little! And one person's mind over there behind the German lines would be at peace. "Need it really be so difficult? And even if it is, surely they could take the trouble?" thought Sintsov with a sudden burst of fury against some purely imaginary person who didn't want to bother about Masha.

Pestrak came into the dug-out, his huge shoulders bowed. He was carrying a milk can which had, in the last few days, been doing duty for the thermos, now riddled with shell-splinters. He also had two loaves of bread under his arm.

"Now we can all have a tuck-in," said Leonidov, rubbing his hands.

"Maybe we should wait till the boys come from their duties and the platoon commander gets back? What d'you think?" said Komarov.

"Have you brought any newspapers?" Sintsov asked Pestrak.

"Yes."

He opened his greatcoat and, pulling out a crumpled newspaper from his breeches, began smoothing it out.

"Is it the Army paper?"

"Try one higher," said Pestrak. "*Izvestia*!"

"You're a smart one, I must say," observed Leonidov.

"Got it in the cookhouse," said Pestrak. "There was a correspondent feeding his face in there, and he left a stack of papers."

"They must have fed him well, then," said Leonidov.

Pestrak left this comment unanswered, neatly smoothed out the paper once more and, giving it to Sintsov, said that he had been walking back to the front line with a photographer from the division. He had asked to be shown the battalion command post and had gone to see Malinin.

"So that means you'll soon be buying drinks all round," said Leonidov to Sintsov.

The submachine gunners were well and truly in the picture. They knew that Sintsov was being reinstated to the Party and, like several others in the battalion who had already been before the Party Bureau, was waiting for the photographer to arrive at any moment.

"It looks like it," said Sintsov, smiling. He was pleased about the photographer's arrival and had no reason to hide this from his comrades.

"D'you want to borrow my razor?" asked Leonidov.

He had an excellent cut-throat and didn't begrudge lending it to others.

"I can manage with my own," said Sintsov.

"What sort of a shave will you get with yours? You'd be better off using a scythe."

Sintsov filled a tin with water from a bucket near the stove and put it on to heat up.

"I'll read the interesting bits aloud, shall I?" said Leonidov, taking hold of the newspaper. He loved reading aloud, but only in bits, picking out the ones he considered worthy of attention.

Sintsov took his brush and soap out of his kitbag. The soap

was in a pink celluloid soap-box, and the brush, a good one, was new. He also had a safety razor, but it was useless: there were no blades. Sintsov had found all these items in a gift parcel. Presents had been coming to the division from Altai, where it had been stationed before the war, and instead of arriving by 7th November, they had been two weeks late. Few of the Altai people were left in the battalions and companies, and the only one among the submachine gunners was Karaulov, the platoon commander. That the presents should have come from as far away as Altai had particularly touched the men, and the submachine gunners had written a letter of thanks to Karaulov's fellow countrymen. Sintsov had taken it down to dictation, while Karaulov, standing behind him, had from time to time interpolated some rather choice language about the Germans. That day he had let his feelings get the better of him and had had too much to drink—a rare occurrence with him.

Sintsov remembered this as he got out his soap and brush. He lathered himself with the tepid water and borrowed Leonidov's razor.

Leonidov read from the paper, turning thoughtful and stopping in mid-sentence, then beginning again, also in mid-sentence. To start with, he commented that the *Izvestia* was an old one and, according to the news bulletin in it, Rostov had not yet fallen and Tikhvin had not been abandoned. Then he began reading about the labour achievements of the men and women workers in the Urals, fell thoughtful, probably about his home, read the rest of the article in silence, turned the paper over, and again immersed himself in the bulletin.

"Here we are," he said, tapping the paper with his finger, "here we are! I noticed it in the Army paper the day before yesterday and wanted to read it to you, but someone whipped it from me.... Here we are...." And he began reading slowly in a loud, angry voice: "The German fascist villains are taking their bestial revenge on wounded Red Army soldiers whom they take prisoner. In the village of Nikulino, the fascists hacked to pieces eight wounded Red Army artillerymen; three of them had their heads cut off...." He put his finger on the place as a marker, looked up bitterly, and demanded: "Well?" He put the question as if he was having an argument with someone. Then he looked down again at his finger and repeated: "'Three of them had their heads cut off....' But I killed a German yesterday, and Karaulov gave me a clout on the ear. True?"

"Served you right," said Komarov. "I mean, the men had got him alive for interrogation, and you went and killed him! A right crack shot you are!"

"Well, I took him prisoner, didn't I?"

"You weren't the only one that did."

"All right then, so I get a thump on the ear," said Leonidov. "But if he hadn't been the platoon commander, he'd have bitten the dust, believe me! All right, then," he repeated. "But he threatened me into the bargain. 'If you do that again,' says he, 'I'll have you courtmartialled!' What am I supposed to make of that?"

"Don't kill a prisoner wanted for interrogation—that's what you're supposed to make of it," persisted Komarov.

"And what am I to make of it when the Senior Political Instructor gets at me into the bargain? He didn't talk about interrogation. He says: 'As soon as a man's been taken prisoner,' he says, 'you have no right.... What right have you got?' he says to me. But this here—" Leonidov stabbed the newspaper so hard with his finger that it went right through the page. "Have I the right to read it or haven't I? I can see in the paper with my own two eyes that people are having their heads cut off! So I get a clout on the ear? Yes?"

He fell silent, waiting for an answer. But nobody replied. He lowered his finger and read on further, his voice a shade higher pitched than before.

"In the village of Makeyevo, Company Commander Comrade Mochalov and Company Political Instructor Comrade Gubarev discovered the brutally mangled bodies of Red Armymen F. I. Lapenko, S. D. Sopov, and F. S. Filchenko. The fascists had tortured the wounded men, gouged their eyes out, cut off their noses, and slit their throats...." He looked up from the newspaper again. "What are they telling us all this for, eh, Senior Sergeant?"

"To get your blood up."

"My blood is up as it is."

"You still shouldn't touch a prisoner taken for interrogation," commented Komarov, who didn't like to let go of a thing once he'd got his teeth into it. "Once he's a prisoner, it means he's a prisoner."

"You're much too kind-hearted for my taste," said Leonidov nastily.

Sintsov put aside his razor. Leonidov's last words had angered him.

"You needn't keep shoving blood-lust down our throats! Wait till I've finished!..." He slapped his knee, seeing that Leonidov was about to interrupt him. "You've got it in for the nazis! And how many fascists have you got to your credit? Two, apart from that prisoner, isn't it? But Komarov's good-natured, and he's bagged four!"

"They don't all go on record," replied Leonidov morosely.

"None of us gets them all recorded. Komarov hasn't had all his recorded either. Where did being hard get you? Was it because you hadn't killed enough and decided to add a third one to the list? Killing prisoners is the cheap way of going about it!"

"A lot you know about how I feel!" interrupted Leonidov.

"I do indeed!" snapped Sintsov. Fate had toughened and robbed him of the last traces of his old pre-war softness. "You've a lot to learn, and that's a fact!"

"No more than you!"

"A great deal more! I might point out that your first real taste of action was at Kuzkovo!"

"A hell of a lot you know about me!" said Leonidov, angry, but disconcerted.

"I'm your section leader, and I'm supposed to know everything about you," said Sintsov, controlling himself at the thought that he was, in fact, their section leader. And his own sense of justice reminded him that at Kuzkovo, Leonidov, like Pestrak, had actually taken part in an attack for the first time. But he would never have guessed as much from Leonidov's conduct and only learned about it subsequently. Leonidov had killed two nazis, not four, not because he was less brave than Komarov, but because things had simply worked out that way in battle.

Sintsov picked up his razor again and glanced out of the corner of his eye at Leonidov, who was stubbornly concentrating on his newspaper, and once again decided that he had been right. There's no need to ram your blood-lust down other people's throats. We're all exactly alike in war; the hard are hard, and the good are hard too! And anyone who isn't hard either hasn't seen anything of war, or thinks that the Germans are going to go easy on him for his goodness.

He finished shaving and went outside in his undervest, rubbed some snow on his face, which was burning after his shave, and went back inside to get dressed.

"Well, you know where he...." It was Leonidov speaking as he went back into the dug-out. He was probably arguing with Komarov. "I'm blood-thirsty, and he's a flipping angel.... But you should have seen him break his gun in two over that Fritz's helmet near the dug-out!"

As Sintsov entered, Leonidov stopped short—not because he was afraid to continue, but because he simply didn't want to—this being typical of the man.

"What else have you been reading?" said Sintsov in a conciliatory tone of voice, after putting on his sheepskin jacket and fur hat and slinging his submachine gun with its mended butt across his chest.

"More of the same," replied Leonidov in an unfriendly voice, and he stabbed his finger at the end of the paragraph he had just been reading out: "The body of doctor's assistant Comrade Nikiforov was found in the village of Yekaterinovka. The Hitlerites had beaten up the seriously wounded man with their rifle-butts, stabbed him with their bayonets, and slashed his face with a razor."

"A razor, eh?" thought Sintsov suddenly, almost physically feeling himself wounded and unable to move while a German sat on his chest and carved his face with a razor.

"I'm going to get myself photographed," he said aloud. "If Karaulov comes, tell him."

When he had first left the dug-out to wash his face, he had not particularly noticed it; but now he suddenly became aware of nature in all its beauty on that sunny winter's day: the unusually dark blue sky, the whiteness of the snow that had fallen during the night, the smooth shadows of the tree-trunks, and even the wedge of aircraft flying so high that their thin, distant drone didn't seem in the least dangerous.

They had just been arguing in the dug-out about war and death, and how to kill people, and whether in doing so one could be good and bad at the same time.... But now, as he stepped over the bomb-shattered tree-trunks and made his way towards the ruins of the manor house along a pine-tree avenue flooded with sunshine and dappled with shadows, he considered how ill-fitted was man for the way of life known as war. He tried to adapt himself to it, and others were compelling him to do so; and yet absolutely nothing came out of it if you bore in mind not the behaviour of a man, on whom the time spent in war gradually begins to tell, but his feelings and thoughts at moments of relaxation and peace when, simply by closing his eyes, he can, as if from non-being, mentally return to the normal human environment.... No, you can learn to make war, but you can never become habituated to it. You can only pretend that you've become used to it, and some pretend very well indeed, while others are unable to do so and, no doubt, never will be. He was himself apparently able to put up this pretence, but what good was it doing him? It only needed the sun to warm him a little, the sky to be blue, some aircraft to be flying somewhere else, and the artillery to be shelling some other target, for him to walk along and yearn so much to live that it was all he could do not to throw himself down on the ground there and then and burst into tears, and ask desperately for one more day, or two more, or a week of this innocent peace merely for the sake of knowing that while it lasted you wouldn't be killed.

At the ruins of the manor house, still deep in thought, Sintsov bumped into Sergeant-Major Vasyukov of the machine-gun company, who was also to be photographed for his Party card.

"What's this, having your photo taken?" asked Sintsov cheerfully.

"I already have," said Vasyukov, stroking his moustache. He smelt of eau de cologne.

"Where's he taking them?" asked Sintsov.

"Here, behind the house. He stands you up against the wall as if you were going to be shot," joked Vasyukov.

"Are the others still there?" asked Sintsov.

"They've already been done. I thought you'd had yours taken before me. Better get moving and catch him up; he's only just this minute gone to the regiment!"

Sintsov was going to hurry off, thinking how it was his own fault for bothering to shave. Then he remembered Malinin's punctiliousness in such matters and realised that they couldn't have managed to collect, photograph, and dismiss Vasyukov and the others in such a short time. This meant that Malinin had already known the photographer was coming and had told them to get ready and show up. There was no point in chasing after the photographer. Those who were supposed to be photographed for party documents had already been photographed—all except himself, that is, because the Divisional Party Commission had decided not to issue him with a new Party card. What other explanations could there be? It was the only one possible!

He stopped, at a loss.

Up till now, during the last month and a half at the front, he had been encouraged in difficult moments by the thought that sooner or later everything in his life would be restored to what it had been before, that he was bound to achieve this himself with the assistance of others! There had been days of particularly fierce fighting, like the one at the brickworks, when war had obliterated everything else from his mind and when nothing had seemed to exist any more except the machine-gun juddering viciously in his grip and the tiny black figures of the Germans on the white snow caught in the sights. And yet, even at times like that, this hope of trust and justice had been alive somewhere at the back of his mind—had not only been alive, but had helped him to fight as he had done.

The day when he had been called before the Regimental Party Bureau to give an oral account of the loss of his Party card had remained in his memory as his last day of trial—or so he had thought at the time.

The Party Bureau had believed him over what mattered most—that he was telling the truth about that morning near Vereya when he had recovered consciousness alone, without Zolotarev. And although at first glance this had seemed unlikely to them too, they had eventually realised that he was telling the truth precisely because he was a Communist and refused to lie, even if a lie might prove his salvation. "Comrades!" he had said to the Party Bureau. "What else can I say to you? I don't know what happened to it. If you'd been in my place, and if you'd known that you hadn't torn up and buried your Party card, how would you have brought yourself to say that you'd buried it? I never tore it up and I never buried it! I don't know, maybe I would have buried it if there had been nothing else left. But I didn't bury it, do you understand? Decide as you know best, but I'm not going to lie to you!"

They believed what others had doubted, and they believed not because they were gullible, but because they now knew him better than those others had done. They knew him from his service, his battle record, and so they decided to take him at his word.

He was given a severe reprimand for losing his Party card and it was decided to request the Divisional Party Commission to issue him a new one. "Don't think that because they believed you, the reprimand loses force," Malinin had told him that evening on the way back to the battalion. "It's still valid! Not for losing your card, but because after that you drifted all the way to Moscow and nearly got yourself signed on as a deserter! Communists don't act like that."

And although he was talking about a severe reprimand, Sintsov had agreed with Malinin, smiling happily. He had been happy that day and, it had seemed at the time, no one could take it away from him!

And now they had done just that! The happy self-confidence with which he had been living for the last few days and with which he had come here after getting ready so carefully—all that had collapsed.... This meant that in the division or somewhere else he had been disbelieved again. They had disbelieved his past, although his present was an open book to them all!

He stood there for a whole minute, torn by all these thoughts, and was even about to turn round and go back to the dug-out; but he thought better of it and went to see Malinin.

Malinin was sitting at a table with a sheepskin jacket over his shoulders and listening with a displeased expression on his face to an old woman sitting opposite him in felt boots, a warm scarf, and a black railway greatcoat. Judging by her voice, she was complaining about something.

When Sintsov entered, the woman stopped talking, and Malinin, with the same expression of displeasure, half turned to him.

"Well, what is it?"

"Permission to have a word with you, Comrade Senior Political Instructor."

"In a moment. Sit down and wait," said Malinin gloomily.

Sintsov sat on the rickety bench by the doorway and, with nothing better to do, took yet another look round the cellar which was now serving as command post and quarters for Malinin and Battalion Commander Ryabchenko. The cellar was low and long; half of it was piled to the ceiling with lumber—all that remained of an evacuated hospital. At first, Ryabchenko hadn't wanted to use the place for this reason; but the cellar was warm, and since Malinin loved warmth and didn't fear infection, he had stuck to his guns. The hospital lumber had been sprayed with disinfectant, and the remains of stools and corrugated cardboard packing boxes for drugs were being used to feed the stove.

The woman was from Podolsk and was complaining that she had volunteered as medical orderly for the division; but now, when all had been allocated to their battalions, it transpired that she was not being taken on.

"You weren't here in the morning," complained the woman, "so I saw your second-in-command, the little red-haired fellow...."

"Not my second-in-command," said Malinin reprovingly, "but the battalion commander. That was the battalion commander himself."

"Well, I don't care anyway," said the woman. "He took two young girl nurses. As for me, I'm superfluous, he says. Mind you, he's still just a boy, so I can understand...."

"You cut that out," said Malinin angrily. "Cut out the innuendos, d'you understand?"

"So what am I to do now? Go back to Podolsk?"

"It could be."

"I shan't go! You're an adult, you've got to understand! I've spent thirty years working in hospitals—twenty of them in our railway hospital alone. What do I want out of it? Nothing. It just rattles me that you've got such inexperienced orderlies working for you. There's little enough they can do. They're just lucky enough to be young. But I could bandage up three cases while they're doing one. That's what annoys me!"

"The wounded don't just have to be bandaged, they have to be carried off the battlefield," said Malinin. "And on the battlefield, you need strength and youth."

"You're not all that young yourself," said the woman.

"That's true," he agreed.

"But you found yourself a place in the war: you didn't worry about your age."

"Well, what of it?"

"Everything! Let the young ones carry out that red-headed boy of yours if he thinks he can rely on them more, and I'll hoist you up on my shoulders, seeing you're an old man!"

"Ah! Division of labour!" said Malinin, smiling for the first time during the whole of the conversation at this unexpected turn of thought.

"I've got my own felt boots," said the woman. "Just let me have a greatcoat. Mine's black, it shows up on the snow." She considered the matter settled, as, indeed, it was. "Here!" She rummaged in her greatcoat pocket, pulled out a piece of paper, and laid it on the table before Malinin.

"What's that?" he asked, without looking at it.

"Why, it's my assignment paper from Podolsk," she said. "What did you think it was? I didn't come to you on charity work; I was selected for the Army by the District Party Committee."

Malinin didn't answer, took the paper, wrote something on it in pencil, then paused, looked at the woman, and asked:

"D'you want an indent for a fur hat?"

"It depends on what you are going to call me!" she answered happily, and her voice had the familiar ring of the cheery hospital matron. "If it's 'Auntie Pasha', I'll wear a headscarf; but if its 'Private Kulikova', then write me a note for a fur hat!"

"Right, I will," said Malinin. He scribbled another line and handed the paper back to her. "Go and enter your name for rations and kit. As for the other formalities—the battalion commander'll be back and we'll sort that out with him. You'll have to come back again." He nodded, without rising, and, paper in hand, the woman walked past Sintsov on her way out.

He clearly saw her face with its deep wrinkles—the face of a woman already old, but still tough after many years of continued and unrewarding drudgery. As she passed Sintsov, she glanced at him briefly, the light of victory still shining in her eyes.

"But what victory?" thought Sintsov, going up to the table in response to Malinin's gloomy gesture of invitation. "To go as medical orderly with a battalion or company into that hell! Anyone else might run a thousand miles sooner than win that kind of victory...."

"Well, what have you come here for? To air your grievances?" asked Malinin, coming straight to the point and motioning Sintsov to the seat.

Sintsov sat down on the still warm stool.

Malinin looked at him, and the more he realised how crushed Sintsov was, the more gloomy he looked himself. In taking on the responsibility for another person, Malinin was in the habit of thinking about him more than about himself.

Sintsov was unaware that the question of issuing him with a new Party card had not gone through the Regimental Bureau as smoothly as he had thought.

Malinin had talked to the secretary for a whole hour before his session of the Bureau.

"You've written a good report on him, and you haven't minced your words," the secretary had said. "Basically, there are no objections. But just think about it: you've had more experience of these things than I have. Isn't it a little premature to bring up the matter of a man who lost his Party card only a month and a half ago?"

Malinin had angrily retorted that this might be so, but perhaps it was also too early to send him to the front? They hadn't had any qualms about sending him up to the line, or leaving him behind a machine gun at the brickworks to face a

German attack, or awarding him an Order for this; yet they were scared of issuing him with a Party card.

"Personally, I'm not worried," he had said. "As for your 'premature', there were only two of us left in action out of that company after the brickworks—him and me. So perhaps if you wait long enough...."

After this expostulation, the objection was struck off; but another one came up.

It concerned what the secretary described as Sintsov's confused explanation of how he had lost his Party card and other documents.

"It may be true, it may be false, it may be his memory's at fault.... It's hard to believe!"

"What does he stand to gain by lying? He could say he buried them and leave it at that."

"Perhaps he thought this one up in the heat of the moment and decided it was for the best, and then when he realised it wasn't, it was too late to go back. It can happen, can't it?"

"Anything can happen!" said Malinin. "But personally, I believe him. Go on, put it up to the Bureau and see whether they believe him or not...."

They had believed him. But later, after the session of the Bureau, the secretary had sat with Malinin, who had stayed behind to help him draw up the protocol, and had said with a sigh:

"You should know better, of course, being an old personnel officer; but I'm afraid the Divisional Party Commission won't approve our resolution on the strength of such an explanation of the loss of his Party card."

"We can only wait and see," Malinin had answered, convinced that he was in the right.

Well, they had waited, and they had seen!

Malinin had heard about it two hours earlier, when the secretary of the Regimental Bureau had phoned to say that a protographer would be coming from the division and all those accepted would have to stand by, except Sintsov.

Malinin had not said anything at the time, but he had privately decided that he would get through to the divisional commissar over this business. True, the division had been unlucky. It had had three commissars in succession since the beginning of the war. The commissar to whom Malinin had personally handed Sintsov's statement after the battle at the brickworks and through whom he had subsequently enquired about the record card, was now in hospital. He had said of Sintsov that the matter was clear: let him go on fighting; the question of his reinstatement to the Party could be raised if he acquitted himself in action. That commissar had gone, there was a new one now, and the whole case had to be examined again from the beginning with him.

"All right then, so I'll begin all over again," thought Malinin doggedly, "and if I have to, I'll write to higher authority." He had been expecting Sintsov, and would even have been surprised if he had not shown up, for this would have meant that he did not consider himself in the right.

"Well, that's how it is, Sintsov!" said Malinin, the first to break the long silence.

"Haven't they confirmed it, then?" asked Sintsov.

"They've shelved it for the time being."

"Why?"

"I don't know yet."

"What d'you think?"

"I think it's for the same reason...."

"Alexei Denisovich, can I be perfectly frank with you?" asked Sintsov in a voice that boded little good.

"Fire away," said Malinin.

He realised that Sintsov had been stunned by the shock and had to speak his mind.

"Well, let him," he thought. "If it's boiling up inside him, he won't be able to hold it back anyway. He'll spill it all out. Better to me than to someone else."

"So I can be perfectly frank, can I?" said Sintsov, as if hesitating whether to speak or not.

"You can't scare me," said Malinin. "I'm not afraid of the truth—or of lies, either."

"Then tell me," said Sintsov—and his face was white—"What matters more? A man or a piece of paper?"

"What do you think?" asked Malinin, and there was a steely ring to his voice.

But Sintsov ignored it.

"I now think that the paper matters more. It's lying and rotting somewhere, and it's thinking: 'It's no use, Sintsov! You consider yourself a man without me? No, you're nothing of the kind! You're not to blame, you didn't throw me away, but I'm not going to let you live without me!'"

"That's what it's saying to you. But what are you saying to it?" asked Malinin with the same subdued steeliness in his voice.

"I'm not saying anything, Alexei Denisovich! I write out applications and statements.... I wait to see which of us is going to win—the paper or me," said Sintsov bitterly.

"If it's only a piece of paper lying there and rotting in the forest, why all the fuss? But if it's your Party card, well, no one forced you to join the Party; you came of your own free will and you knew what a Party card stands for! But if you stick to your guns and insist that you didn't bury it, so help you—if you stick to your guns, then it's not a matter of indifference whether you buried it, or tore it up or something.... If you buried it, you're one kind of person, if you tore it up, you're another, and if you lied, then you're another still."

"And if I told the truth? Are we ever going to learn to trust people all the way, or is it just not worth bothering?" interrupted Sintsov.

"Who are you getting at?" interrupted Malinin in his turn. "Me? Because I personally advised you to apply and now haven't succeeded in getting my way?... Correct, but premature. I haven't gone back on my word yet.... Or are you getting at the Party Bureau? It's still too early, and it hasn't had its final say.... Are you mad at the Divisional Party Commission? Have you actually met anyone from there personally?" demanded Malinin, interrupting himself this time.

"Not yet. Why?"

"And they haven't seen you! And they don't believe our pieces of paper!" grinned Malinin. "Maybe for them, as for you, a man is worth more than a piece of paper! Maybe they want to have a look at you first before they make up their minds! Or don't you allow them that right? Well, I do. On the other hand, I also grant that some stickler for routine may be sitting up there and he won't be softened from below, he'll have to be handled from above. The Party's big, and there are all kinds of people in it. Since it's complete frankness you want, I'm telling you this! But don't you dare get at the Party!" He suddenly raised his voice and rose to his feet. "'When are we going to learn to trust people?'" he said, mimicking Sintsov. "You're quick off the mark, aren't you! You've made a whole slogan out of one little sore spot."

"That sore spot hurts just the same," said Sintsov, also rising to his feet.

He was not offended by Malinin's outburst. He felt that Malinin had been as badly disturbed by what had happened as himself, and this feeling more than anything else helped him to realise how right Malinin was at this moment.

"Here, shake," said Malinin, offering his hand over the table in his habitual gesture of greeting or farewell, and he he said good-bye, frowning and not looking directly at Sintsov.

"Alexei Denisovich," blurted Sintsov, unable to restrain himself as he shook Malinin's hand. "Tell me, they're not holding back my Order for the same reason, are they? They're taking a long time to give it to me."

Malinin merely smiled at the foolishness of this supposition. Sintsov's frankness even pleased him, for there was trust behind it.

"I can see you've really gone mental. They say the general's been carrying the Orders around for three days now. He decorated the artillerymen the day before yesterday. Yesterday he was with the Ninety Second. He might be with us today."

Sintsov asked permission to dismiss, but turned round in the doorway and repeated what he had once said to Malinin back in Moscow in the District Party Committee.

"Whatever happens to me, I shall never forget this as long as I live."

"Pooh!" said Malinin with a deprecatory gesture of the hand. "You'll see me on the street in Moscow after the war and say: 'How do you do, Malinin!' and that'll be that!" He repeated the gesture, moved along the table, and then abruptly turned his back. He was not in the habit of listening to protestations of gratitude.

After pacing up and down the cellar and glancing out of the corner of his eye at the door as it closed behind Sintsov, Malinin sighed heavily, sat down at the table, took a letter out of his tunic pocket, put on his spectacles and slowly, as if checking to make sure that what he was reading really had been written there, read it for the third time that day. The letter was from hospital and it contained the news that his son Victor was there with an amputated right arm. He was recovering successfully after his wound, but requested that his mother should not be informed. As he read the letter through, Malinin stopped at the word "successfully". He took off his spectacles, put them down on the table in front of him, and stared fixedly at the wall.

His wife had to be informed nevertheless; if she received no letters for some time, she would decide that he had been killed. She must be comforted; but he himself had no one to turn to for sympathy. Asking for sympathy wasn't part of his job. He would simply have to get used to the idea that his son had lost his right arm at the age of seventeen. And it was going to be hard to get used to.

The door was flung wide open, and Senior Lieutenant Ryabchenko, the battalion commander, burst into the cellar. He ran quickly down the stairs, his non-regulation cavalry spurs jingling on the stone steps. The long greatcoat hanging jauntily from his broad young shoulders swirled round his highly polished boots, and there was an expression of mingled happiness and concern on his ruddy, birdlike face.

"Had a letter?" he asked gaily.

"Yes," said Malinin, and he pocketed it without saying anything further.

"The general will be here in an hour to present the decorations," said Ryabchenko, still in the same cheerful tone of voice. "Mine's there too, the one I was awarded in July. I thought they'd gone and lost it while I was kicking around the hospitals. But it's turned up just the same!"

He sat down on the stool, cheerfully slapping his boot with his gloves and throwing open the skirts of his greatcoat.

"He promised to come, and then he gave everyone who happened to be in Regimental HQ a ticking-off: 'Why,' says he, 'haven't you been able to get me a prisoner for interrogation on your battle sector for two days?' That's to the regimental commander. And then to me: 'I happen to know your men got one yesterday and failed to bring him in, the fools....' Who spilled the beans?"

"I mentioned it in yesterday's political report," said Malinin calmly.

"That was quite unnecessary!" said Ryabchenko.

"An old argument, and a waste of time," creaked Malinin like a rusty door-hinge.

Ryabchenko waved the matter aside exasperatedly and refrained from entering into an argument.

"Tell me," he exclaimed after a pause, "why are our men so untrained? We train and train them, and they seem to understand, and then the moment they set eyes on a prisoner, they promptly let him have a bullet through the head!"

"We're not the only ones doing the training," said Malinin. "We're training them our way, but the Germans have other ideas. We say to our soldier: don't touch them! But he's seen with his own eyes how the Germans burned our people alive in a house in Kuzkovo. After that, he's ready to start tearing Hitler or Goebbels limb from limb; but he doesn't know whether he'll live to get the chance. He won't, most likely. In the meantime, while he's itching to lay his hands on Hitler, along comes an ordinary corporal and gets it instead!"

"So you're justifying his conduct?"

"I'm not justifying it, I'm explaining it to myself for my own benifit. How is that our men aren't beasts, and yet they sometimes behave as if they were? The Germans must have put in a lot of effort to drive them to such extremes."

"What are you getting at?"

"What I'm getting at is, we've got to work so that there should be no repetition of such incidents. I recorded this particular case in writing as due to my own negligence and included it in my political report for that reason. I know you're against washing dirty linen in public; and washing dirty linen in public is bad; but washing dirty linen in private is even worse."

"Anyway, Dad, how have things been without me?" asked Ryabchenko, looking at Malinin's gloomy face after a pause.

"As clear as mud. They sent a photographer to do the men for the Party documents, but Sintsov's been turned down flat."

"What the hell do they think they're playing at?" shouted Ryabchenko. "We both wrote, we both backed him up.... What more do they want?..."

"Oh yes, you and I together are a force," said Malinin, amused at Ryabchenko's youthful fervour, and he glanced across at him good-naturedly and almost affectionately from under his knitted brows. "A great force!" And, after a silence, he added: "But we evidently don't count everywhere."

The general arrived exactly an hour later on the sleigh belonging to Regimental Commander Baglyuk. The adjutant sat behind the general and Baglyuk, while Baglyuk himself drove the horse.

Ryabchenko and Malinin went out to meet the general. Four men to be decorated, not counting Ryabchenko himself—Sintsov, his platoon commander, Karaulov, and two men from the rifle companies—had been summoned to Battalion HQ in good time and, standing a little way off, were waiting for the general to arrive.

The first to jump down from the sleigh was Baglyuk. He handed the reins to the adjutant and said:

"Drive round the back of the house."

The general also jumped lightly down from the sleigh. He was of medium height, but seemed short beside the extremely tall Baglyuk. He was wearing an ordinary fur hat instead of a *papakha*, a sheepskin coat with crossed straps, and felt boots. The unfastened collar of his coat revealed the edges of the red general's tabs on his jacket. General Orlov's moustaches were like two black toothbrushes. He had the yellowish skin of a Tatar, and his narrow eyes, as black as his moustaches, were cheerful and still youthful.

Ryabchenko gave the command "Attention!" The general received the report, gave the command "At ease!", then glanced happily at the sun which was going down behind the forest, and asked for some kind of table to be brought out.

"We'll present them out here in the sun instead of crawling down into those catacombs of yours. Besides, they stink of carbolic."

He was in a splendid mood for a number of reasons.

Yesterday evening they had been assembled at Army HQ and briefed about a plan for an advance operation by the whole Army. All divisional commanders had been asked for the latest information on the strength of the enemy in front of them, and each had been ordered, on the basis of the Army directive, to plan a battle in his sector of advance.

Judging by the Army directive, the main push was not going to be made on their own particular Army sector; but it was clear by all indications that the proposed offensive was going to be a big one, and even though theirs might be a second-degree sector, at least they were going to take part in it! Thank goodness for that!

Throughout the past few weeks, the general had felt with his whole being that the Germans had been pushing and pushing at us, and although we had been falling back, we had retreated very little—almost imperceptibly, despite the force of that pressure. He had felt this with his whole body and with that of his division, bled almost white with incessant battles. He knew that second echelons had come up from the rear, but he had not been given any replacements for a long time, and he had realised that this was not the callous parsimoniousness it seemed. In a word, the intimation of a change for the better had been in the air for nearly a week; but yesterday's summons to Army HQ had not been an intimation, it had been the prelude to the real thing!

At the council, in answer to the question: what did he need, the general, knowing the Army Commander of old, had naturally asked for more than he actually needed and had met with a rebuff. The Army Commander had smiled and said to him: "I may have served under your command once, Mikhail Nikolayevich, but you needn't expect more of me than is allowed by divine law!" But even this rebuff had not disheartened him. What really mattered was that there was going to be an offensive! And this was making him extremely happy.

On his return, the general had spent the rest of that evening and all the night sitting with his Chief-of-Staff over a first draft of the plan, had left him in the morning to work on it further, and had himself gone to Baglyuk's regiment, having decided to do three jobs at once: to present the awards; to put on pressure about the capture of prisoners for interrogation in order to clarify the situation before the division's front; and, finally, to pay a personal visit to all three battalion observation posts, because it was here, with Baglyuk, that it would be most convenient to launch the attack, and he wanted to check the terrain on the spot with his own eyes.

He had already visited two battalions. They had promised to get him a prisoner, and had even pledged their word of honour. What he had seen from both battalion OPs had only confirmed his preliminary plans. To cap it all, the sun was shining for all it was worth and the Germans were not firing....

"See what a good mood he's in, he's laughing!" said a voice beside Sintsov. It was Junior Lieutenant Karaulov, the platoon commander, who had been with the regiment for three years' regular and nine years' extended service.

"Perhaps he's had a few for dinner," said Sintsov.

But Karaulov emphatically shook his head.

"He doesn't drink. He's one of our people—the Altai Old Believers. Doesn't even touch beer."

"Perhaps he's an Old Believer too," joked Sintsov.

"He's a Party member," said Karaulov, refusing even to notice the wisecrack. "But his family were Old Believers."

He didn't like jokes as a rule, particularly about his superiors, and, as he answered, he glanced sharply at Sintsov. Was he going to try and be funny again? But Sintsov wasn't. He knew that Karaulov's heart was in the right place, but that he was inclined to be hypersensitive. He had been promoted to Lieutenant for outstanding courage in battle without graduating from a proper military school, was extremely touchy about his lack of education and suspecting not without reason that his subordinates sometimes laughed at his expense, cut short any jokes at the slightest opportunity.

When he realised that Sintsov wasn't smiling, Karaulov relaxed. He respected Sintsov and knew that he had begun the war as a political instructor, and if Sintsov were to become one again, Karaulov would have considered it perfectly in order to serve under him. But since Sintsov was for the time being a section commander in his platoon, Karaulov, being the kind of person he was, was less inclined to tolerate disrespect from Sintsov than from anyone else.

"He may be laughing now but it doesn't mean a thing," he told Sintsov, looking at the general almost with rapture. "He's just as likely to clamp down the next minute." Karaulov even brandished his fist in the air with pleasure to show how tough the divisional commander could be if anything happened to rub him up the wrong way.

A table had been fetched from the cellar in the meantime. The general took his field bag off and handed it to his adjutant. The adjutant took out five little red boxes and five certificates, glanced at the certificates, looked inside the boxes, then put one certificate under each box and, going up to the general, spoke to him.

The general turned round, the smile vanished from his face, and suddenly he looked stern and handsome.

Ryabchenko himself was to be decorated, and so the command was given by Baglyuk.

As he drew himself up to attention, Sintsov thought of Malinin. "Why I am getting one, and not Malinin? But if you even mentioned it to him—he'd snap your head off!" he thought respectfully of Malinin.

"Senior Lieutenant Ryabchenko! March forward to receive your decoration!" commanded the general's voice.

And Ryabchenko, the skirts of his greatcoat swirling, took three smart steps forward and halted before the general, his white face flung back and his red sidebeards showing under his fur hat, which was slightly askew.

Karaulov was the one before the last to receive his award, and Sintsov himself was the last. When the general called Karaulov, read the Order of the Military Council, congratulated him, and began fastening the Order of the Red Banner to his tunic, Karaulov's forehead perspired with excitement.

"I'm very happy for you, Karaulov!" said the general, tucking his hand under Karaulov's tunic in order to affix the Order. "And I'm happy that I should be giving you this Order personally. Six years—that's half of your army service—we served together and we expected war any time.... And now you're already an officer and you have a battle decoration to your credit. It's a fine thing for our division!"

Karaulov's lips actually trembled as he listened, and Sintsov, called in his turn and marching forward, could still hear Karaulov breathing heavily behind him.

The general read out the order while Sintsov stood at ease, and the adjutant, as if Sintsov couldn't have done it himself, unfastened the hooks on his sheepskin jacket and poked a hole in his tunic with a small knife. The general held the Red Star in the palm of his hand, slowly unscrewed the nut and, putting his cold hand under Sintsov's tunic, began fastening on the Star.

At that moment, his face was very close to Sintsov and he remembered how he had first seen the general in a helmet with a wet cape over his shoulders at Dorokhovo in October when he had come to the Communist Battalion to pick out replacements for the division. When the general had asked who was coming with him, the whole battalion had stepped forward as one man.

After he had affixed the Order, the general stepped back half a pace and offered Sintsov his small, strong hand.

"Congratulations!" he said, looking up at Sintsov. "How long have you been with the division?"

"Since the nineteenth of October. I came with the Moscow replacements."

"From the Frunze Communist Battalion!" Malinin reminded him with a note of pride in his voice.

"Good replacements," said the general and, looking up at Sintsov again, asked: "Are you a Communist?"

"Yes!" said Sintsov, catching Malinin's eye.

No, it wasn't any use Malinin looking at him like that. Sintsov wasn't going to say any more or make any requests. This wasn't the time, the place, or the occasion. As for his answer, well, what else was he if not a Communist? Let the battalion commisar correct him if it wasn't so.

But Malinin didn't correct him, and Sintsov took three paces back and rejoined the line of decorated men.

The general looked them over, put his hands behind his back, transferred his gaze to Baglyuk, then looked at the newly decorated soldiers again. After a moment's pause, he said that the division had so far honourably carried out all the command's orders, but there were even more difficult and more responsible tasks to be faced soon, and he was sure that the comrades who had been decorated today like all the other soldiers and commanders in the division, would carry them out honourably and successfully.

"Meanwhile, for today," and there was a twinkle in the general's narrow eyes, "there's just one little job to be done...."

Baglyuk, who had already visited two battalions for the presentation of awards and knew what was coming, shifted awkwardly from one foot to the other and lowered his high-domed, bull-like head.

"I see that your regimental commander Lieutenant-Colonel Baglyuk," said the general, who had noticed Baglyuk's movement and had glanced in his direction, "is already cringing, because I'm going to tell him in front of you all that this job should have been done yesterday. But better late than never, and we must have a prisoner for interrogation by morning. Alive, not dead! Who feels up to it?"

Sintsov thought that the general was looking expectantly at him, although in fact his eyes were on Karaulov beside him.

"We'll get one, Comrade General!" said Sintsov, accepting the challenge. As he stepped forward, he felt Karaulov's shoulder touch his. Karaulov had moved at the same time, but without saying anything.

"Fine, that's a deal, then," said the general, not in parade-ground style, but in an unexpectedly informal and comradely kind of way. "Do you know the enemy positions and approaches well?"

"Yes, we do!" It was Karaulov this time.

"So you could show me where you're thinking of getting across?" asked the general, and his eyes twinkled again.

He wanted to carry out the last part of his plan and look in on the battalion OP, but to avoid the over-solicitous Baglyuk's customary: "Don't go, you're not supposed to," he had decided to take Karaulov and this sergeant instead.

"Perhaps we'd do better to take a look from the regimental OP," said Baglyuk, making what he knew to be a hopeless attempt to dissuade the divisional commander.

"I can always get your OP: but if I want to see the gap the lads are going to crawl through for their prisoner, I've got to look from the battalion OP. I don't come here every day of the week," said the general. "You stay here, Comrade Baglyuk, and carry on with your duties. These two—" he nodded towards Karaulov and Sintsov—"and the battalion commander can come with me."

"At least let me have your supper ready for you when you come back," said Baglyuk.

"Thank goodness you've got the idea!" replied the general gaily; but, not fully convinced that Baglyuk had really done so, he added: "I shall consider it an honour to have supper with you and the decorated men". He turned to Karaulov.

"Well, Karaulov? One glass won't do any harm before reconnaissance, will it?"

"It won't do me any harm, Comrade General!" said Karaulov. "But I'm afraid you won't drink yours."

"You're out of date, Karaulov! I didn't use to, that's true! But ever since the People's Commissar fixed the ration, I've been drinking in obedience to orders. And you—" the general turned to his adjutant, who was looking on in bewilderment—"nip over to the mortar crews."

"They could be telephoned," interposed Baglyuk.

"Go to the mortar crews," said the general, ignoring the remark, "and tell Firsov that I apologise. Although I did give him my word, I won't be coming to present the awards today I won't be able to make it. I'll be there tomorrow."

Displeased but punctilious, the adjutant saluted and hurried off to carry out his orders. The general turned and, without looking back, quickly walked round to the other side of the ruined manor. He had already been to the battalion OP and he knew his way. Ryabchenko, the skirts of his greatcoat brushing the snow, hurried after him with Karaulov and Sintsov behind. At first they proceeded along the reverse slope of the hill where they could not be seen by the Germans, then along a gully with a path worn along the bottom; then they climbed into a communication trench and went along it to a barely noticeable prominence directly over the gully. A stone summer-house had stood there once. It was now in ruins; but Ryabchenko's observation post, with its periscope looking directly across at the enemy, had been dug out and effectively camouflaged immediately under the solid brick foundations.

Ryabchenko was now leading the way, followed by Karaulov and then the general, with Sintsov bringing up the rear.

Karaulov was noticeably holding back, as if he wanted to shield the general from the Germans with his big, rectangular frame. Perhaps he was doing just that.

"Hey!" said the general, and playfully, but vigorously, he poked Karaulov in the back. "Get a move on, or I'll be treading on your heels." Karaulov quickened his pace, and the general, falling slightly behind, called out to Ryabchenko: "Well, Senior Lieutenant, are you sure you won't freeze in that cavalry coat of yours? You certainly have a fine...." It was as far as he got.

The mortar bomb burst beside the communication trench. Sintsov flung himself face down, instinctively clasping his hands behind his head. When he got up again, he saw the general lying supine on the bottom of the trench with his head near Sintsov's feet, his wide-open eyes rolling and his lips moving soundlessly.

Sintsov went down on his knees and, for some reason, first of all replaced the general's fur hat, which was lying on the ground beside him. He then began to lift him up from behind, having already noticed that the general's whole chest had been ripped apart under the open sheepskin jacket: pieces of cloth were sticking up and a patch of bare, bloodstained skin was visible. He lifted the general higher and higher by the shoulders, then suddenly heard a bubbling noise which sounded like a voice, but was actually the blood spurting from the general's throat.

At that moment, his eyes met those of Karaulov, who was twisting round in the narrow trench so as to take the general in his arms more easily.

"Let him go!" said Karaulov. "He's dead!..." He took off his fur hat and burst into tears.

A cluster of mortar bombs burst behind them in the park by Battalion HQ, and everything became quiet once more.

The Germans had simply been making their presence known towards evening, and, as usual, had been aiming for the ruins of the manor house. The bomb that killed the general had been a chance undershoot.

"We'll carry him on my greatcoat," said Ryabchenko, and he began taking it off, but somehow oddly and awkwardly. "Help me," he said to Karaulov with a groan. "I've got a splinter in my wrist." Then Sintsov noticed that his left wrist was covered in blood.

"Why mess up your greatcoat?" said Karaulov through his tears. "I'll carry him back."

His own sheepskin was gory from top to bottom. All the blood from the general's throat had spurted straight on to Karaulov: even his face was splashed with blood, which he had rubbed over his cheeks with his tears.

He took the dead man in his arms as he had intended to when he had thought him still alive, rose on to his knees, then stood up, and set off with his burden along the communication trench back towards HQ.

Sintsov walked ahead of him, looking back from time to time.

"Perhaps we could carry him together?" he suggested after they had gone about fifty paces.

But Karaulov merely shook his head.

His face was red with exertion and the tears were still streaming from his eyes.

And so he walked to HQ without surrendering or sharing his burden, and he did not let anyone else carry his divisional commander.

Sintsov ran ahead to HQ two minutes earlier and, as Karaulov came up, Baglyuk and Malinin, shaken by the news, had already dashed outside.

Karaulov went as far as the wall, leaned against it, panting for breath, and asked almost inaudibly:

"Where shall I put him?"

He didn't want to put the general down on the ground. So he asked his question and, unable to stand on his weakened legs any longer, swayed and, his back sliding down the wall, sat on the snow, still cradling the dead general in his arms as if he were a little child.

The sleigh drove up a few minutes later, and Karaulov and Baglyuk laid the general's body on hay covered with sacking. Ryabchenko, who was standing by them, kept bending down to scoop up a handful of snow and apply it to his wounded hand. The snow reddened at once and fell away in rosy-coloured flakes.

Malinin turned up the battalion commander's greatcoat sleeve—it was beginning to soak up the blood—and, since Ryabchenko in the stress of the moment didn't want to leave, he sent for a doctor or nurse.

Then Baglyuk, before taking the general away, went down into the cellar to ring the regiment and the division. Inured to losses as they were, this calamity was the worst yet, all the more so for being totally unexpected. Due forewarning had to be given.

The general was lying on the sleigh. The horse stamped on the snow, pulling gently at the shafts.

Malinin, Ryabchenko, Karaulov and Sintsov stood close by, looking at the dead man and each thinking his own thoughts. Malinin was thinking that the general was almost the same age as himself and also probably had grown-up children who were or would be at the front.

Although Ryabchenko was as shaken as all the others, his shock was mixed up with the thoughts about his own wound. If the bone wasn't broken, then he could stay in action. He kept applying more snow to ease the pain, flexing and unflexing the fingers of his wounded hand. No, it didn't look as though the bone was broken.

Karaulov was remembering how, just before the mortar bomb had landed, the general had poked him in the back and he had gone three paces ahead. He should have disobeyed and held back, and then this would never have happened. By "this would never have happened" he meant that he, and not the general, would have been in the way of that splinter, and all the unselfishness of his soldier's heart lay in the simplicity of this idea and in the force of his anger with himself.

Sintsov was thinking that when the four of them had been walking along the communication trench, he had suddenly felt afraid, and he had regretted accepting the challenge to take a prisoner. But now, after that violent death, everything in war seemed equally terrifying and equally unterrifying, and he no longer regretted volunteering.

Only the general was not thinking anything at all.

How cheerful he had been that day! More cheerful than he had remembered being for a long time. He had been positively bursting with happiness at the thought of the forthcoming offensive. Usually far from given to merriment, he had been smiling with or without cause all that day.

No, he had not been destined for the offensive. But how he had waited for it! How much agony the retreats had cost him! How many times and in how many ways! With what suffering, what sense of humiliation in his soldier's heart he had fallen back! How many days and nights he had cherished this dream, on the very threshold of which he had met with such fatal bad luck! If the dead could think after death, he would probably be thinking about just this, and if the dead could weep, then his eyes would probably be weeping tears of unbearable disappointment!

The general lay motionless in the sleigh and stared at the four living people with whom only half an hour ago he had been laughing and joking; he stared at them with wide-open, dead eyes that were already beginning to glaze.

Baglyuk returned. The general's body was covered so that anyone they chanced to meet on the way should not know prematurely that the divisional commander had been killed, and the sleigh with Baglyuk and the general's body set off on the return journey.

"It's going to be a nasty shock for the division," said Malinin, watching the sleigh as it disappeared round a corner.

The Army doctor, out of breath after walking through the snow, arrived with the nurse and an orderly (not a single wounded man in the battalion today) and took Ryabchenko down into the cellar to dress his wound.

"I've got a good constitution, it'll heal quickly!" said Ryabchenko as he went away, reassuring himself more than Malinin.

He was a brave man, but he already knew from his first experience of being wounded that he was afraid of pain, and so he was now nervous at the thought of having his injury dressed.

"What about getting that prisoner, Karaulov?" asked Malinin, after Ryabchenko had left.

"What about it? We'll get one, Comrade Senior Political Instructor!" said Karaulov, looking up with tear-swollen eyes in some amazement at Malinin. The question had shocked him. After the general's death, his last order was, for Karaulov, the holiest of holies.

"This is what I think," said Malinin. "Let Sintsov get himself a partner and start right away."

"What about me?" demanded Karaulov in a voice hoarse with agitation. "I gave the general my word! Don't you try and make me go back on it!"

"You certainly did," said Malinin, "so you must see that the mission is successful whatever happens. Cover their passage through the positions," he nodded at Sintsov, "and if things don't run too smoothly for them, then I authorise you to go in and make a second attempt yourself...."

"'If things don't run too smoothly'! How cautious can you get!" thought Sintsov; and a chill ran down his spine.

"So that's that, Comrade Karaulov," said Malinin, noticing that the platoon commander was about to object. "Now get on with it!"

Malinin eschewed the professional military manner and, when giving orders, often used non-regulation language; but he had character enough not to have to give his instructions twice.

Karaulov and Sintsov left. Malinin stayed behind, but didn't go down into the cellar.

"Who knows?" he thought. "Having a wound dressed is no joke. Ryabchenko's young and vain. If he groans in front of me, he'll feel ashamed of himself afterwards."

When he knew there was no way of avoiding it, Malinin had no qualms about causing unpleasantness; but he didn't like touching people on the raw unnecessarily. So it was with Karaulov. He had withdrawn him from the mission on a reasonable pretext, trying not to cause offence. In fact, he simply didn't want Karaulov to go to the Germans, because on this particular day he could easily overdo it and get himself killed. That, at least, was how it had seemed to Malinin after he had seen the full extent of the shock to Karaulov. True, Karaulov was the type of whom people love to say that they have the hide of a rhinoceros. But Malinin didn't believe in the protective powers of rhinoceros hide where human beings were concerned. They had used the same expression of him more than on one occasion when, in fact, he merely had self-control. And that's all there was to it.

The general's adjutant appeared on the track that skirted the ruins of the manor house. He had been to the mortar crews and was in a great hurry. From a distance, he couldn't see anyone but Malinin and thought that he was late.

"Where's the divisional commander? Has he left?" he asked as he came up.

Malinin looked the adjutant straight in the eye, sighed, and instead of giving a direct answer, said:

"Go straight down the slope. The sleigh's just left; you'll catch it up before they're round the hill...."

The adjutant hurried off down the path at the double, holding his field bag down with one hand to prevent it from slapping his side, and Malinin once again thought what had already crossed his mind as he watched the sleigh drive off with Baglyuk and the general's body: "This is going to be a nasty shock for the division ... very nasty...."

Before going into the submachine gunners' dug-out, Karaulov removed his sheepskin jacket and tried to rub the blood off with snow, but couldn't.

"At least wipe your face," said Sintsov, who was beside him.

Karaulov scooped up a handful of snow and rubbed it several times over his face.

"How's that?"

"Here, let me!" said Sintsov, and he removed with his nail the last few congealed traces of blood still adhering to the skin by Karaulov's ear. Only then did Karaulov put on his sheepskin again, and both men went into the dug-out.

The rumour of the general's death had already reached the dug-out.When Karaulov began briefing them on the mission and said that the promise to get a prisoner had been given to the divisional commander in person, all felt that this was particularly binding now that the man to whom it had been made was dead.

After briefing them on their mission, Karaulov said that he would personally see the reconnaissance party off and meet it on its return, and asked who would volunteer to go with Senior Sergeant Sintsov.

"I will!" said Leonidov quickly, as if afraid that someone might beat him to it.

Sintsov had secretly been hoping that Komarov would be the one to volunteer. His calm and steadiness were after Sintsov's heart and inspired a particular trust in the man.

But Leonidov volunteered and looked round dangerously, as if someone might snatch the morsel out of his mouth. And at that vicious look, no one else took up the challenge.

That Leonidov should have volunteered instead of Komarov went against the grain with Sintsov, but there was no cause to quarrel. Leonidov himself had been told a few home truths by Sintsov that day, yet he was coming nevertheless. Perhaps he was even doing so in order to show that the insult had been unjustified.

"He's a bit nervous, but that doesn't matter so much..." thought Sintsov, trying to reassure himself and, for the last time regretting that it wasn't Komarov coming with him, he said:

"That's that, then, so let's get ready!"

They dressed lightly, without sheepskins, wearing quilted jackets belted round the waist and taking submachine-guns, knives, two grenades each in case the worst came to the worst and they were spotted, a packet of cotton wool for a gag, and a length of telephone wire to tie up the prisoner.

At the last moment, when Karaulov had given them full instructions and all they had to do was climb out of the trench and crawl down through the thin, snow-covered scrub to the brook in no man's land, Leonidov suddenly whispered something quite unexpected in Sintsov ear:

"If it hadn't been for me yesterday, we'd be sitting in the dug-out and drinking to that medal of yours today...."

And Sintsov realised that it wasn't out of spite that Leonidov had volunteered for the patrol: he just didn't want others to risk their lives because of the prisoner he had killed the day before.

"Wait, we'll drink to it yet," said Sintsov, and he felt the prickly touch of the snow on his cheek as he clambered over the parapet.

Three hours later, when they had already crawled back as far as the gully dragging a prisoner behind them, and had less than a kilometre to go before reaching our own positions, their luck ran out. They came upon some mines and Leonidov's foot was blown off. Sintsov tied his belt round the wounded man's leg below the knee and thought with inexpressible bitterness: "So much for our drink!"

The German, bound hand and foot, lay beside him in the snow. At first they had led him along with his hands tied together, but for the last half kilometre they had been dragging him through the snow. He lay there breathing heavily through his nose. He had been gagged.

The mines had almost certainly been their own. If they had been German and the enemy had known about them, they would have sent some shells over as soon as they had heard the explosion. But everything was quiet on the enemy position, they had not yet noticed the disappearance of a soldier who had fallen asleep in the trench, and they had probably taken the explosion for a mortar bomb from the Russian side.

"What are we going to do?" asked Leonidov quietly as he fought the pain.

Who knows—perhaps he had cried out at the moment of the explosion when his foot had been torn off; but since then he hadn't uttered a sound: neither when Sintsov had cut away with his knife the flaps of skin on which the foot was still hanging, nor when he had bound an emergency field dressing round the stump, nor when he had tightened his belt round the leg below the knee. No two ways about it, Leonidov was tough!

"We'll wait a bit and crawl on further," said Sintsov. "You'll start losing strength, but I'll keep you going."

"What about Fritz?" asked Leonidov.

Sintsov shuddered at the thought that, since he couldn't shoot him, he would have to cut the prisoner's throat before dragging Leonidov back to the lines. It would be too risky to leave the German behind with the intention of returning for him. He might work his way loose or tear out the gag, they might not make it to their own lines, and the thought of being killed while leaving that nazi alive was more than he could bear.

"What else *can* we do?" said Sintsov; and Leonidov realised from his movements just exactly what he had in mind.

"Take him and drag him with you!" said Leonidov. "Orders are orders. Can you cope by yourself?"

"I'll manage, only...."

But Leonidov again interrupted him with a heated, feverish whisper. His strength was clearly failing fast.

"Drag him with you, and I'll crawl on after you...."

"All right," said Sintsov, suddenly agreeing with Leonidov. "But you stay put. I'll get him back and come for you. I'll get some of the boys and I'll be back. Just stay where you are. Don't go anywhere!"

He was afraid that, as his strength failed him, Leonidov might crawl off somewhere.

"Will you come back?" In spite of his self-sacrificing decision, Leonidov very much wanted to live, otherwise he would not have asked such a question.

"I'll be back in person ... I give you my word!"

In order to make it easier for himself, Sintsov discarded his jacket, left his submachine-gun beside Leonidov and, with only a knife and a grenade in his pocket, crawled off, dragging the German behind him.

The German, as it subsequently transpired, was neither big nor heavy; he was actually quite a small man; but just try dragging a sack like that over the snow without raising your head!

Sintsov hardly believed that he had made it when, some fifty metres away from the trenches, he saw Karaulov and the local company commander, who had both crawled out to meet him. He was already done in and, although he had been crawling over the snow, he was soaked from head to foot in sweat.

"Where's Leonidov?" asked Karaulov.

"Back there, wounded ... going to fetch him now," said Sintsov, gasping for breath after every word.

Karaulov asked no more questions until the three of them had dragged the German into the trench.

"Well, what's happened to Leonidov?" asked Karaulov.

"In a moment ... I'll tell.... Take out ... German's ... gag, or else...." Again, Sintsov was unable to finish. He was totally winded.

They removed the gag from the German's mouth and he began coughing convulsively, as if he had consumption. Then he threw up: either out of fright, or because his mouth had been stuffed up for so long.

"Leonidov's foot's been blown off," said Sintsov. "I'm going to fetch him now."

"Where d'you think you're going in that state?" demanded Karaulov. "I'll go myself at once. Just tell me where."

"No," said Sintsov. "I'll come with you. Only let me get my breath."

The company commander offered him a hip-flask.

"No, I mustn't," said Sintsov. "I'm scared it might weaken me. And I'm so hot. I could do with a drink of water though...."

But there was no water available, so he scooped up a handful of snow and began sucking it.

"You stay here," said Karaulov in a voice of authority this time. "I'll find him. I'll take Komarov with me."

Komarov was there too. It turned out that Karaulov had taken him as a partner—"In case things don't run too smoothly," thought Sintsov, remembering Malinin's expression.

"I don't care what you say, I'm coming with you," he said, spitting out a mouthful of snow and feeling that nothing on this earth would make him go back on his decision. Not even an order, because without him Karaulov wouldn't know where Leonidov was, and he had promised to go back for him.

"Let's go, Comrade Junior Lieutenant. You won't find him without me anyway...."

He suddenly remembered all the horror he had experienced in the forest when he had recovered consciousness alone and wounded, had crawled along the ground, had then raised himself to his feet, and had seen a German bearing down on him with a submachine gun. No, that's not going to happen to Leonidov!

"Let's go," he repeated and, without waiting for Karaulov's final decision, he was the first to climb out of the trench.

CHAPTER SEVENTEEN

Serpilin was only given his posting to the front after a second medical commission, and even then not straightaway. The commission met on 25th November, and his posting came through a week later. He was called to the General Staff in the morning, and in the evening he was to take over a division fighting the Germans outside Moscow.

"We sent a report to Comrade Stalin about you," said Ivan Alexeyevich, offering Serpilin a seat opposite him, but with the proviso that their farewell conversation would not be long one. "We also put in a report about your letter, in which you demanded to be sent to the front at all costs, and so forth...." (Serpilin had sent this letter after the second commission.) "I'm not going to hide it, we were against the idea. We wanted to keep you here, with us ... but"—Ivan Alexeyevich shrugged his shoulders—"he made his own decision, and so you're in the right now, not us. He said: 'If he wants to go to the front, let him have a division.' Between you and me and the doorpost, they very nearly shoved you off to the Karelian front. He doesn't like saying the same thing twice. He kept asking: 'Well, has he left?' What could we say? But the day before yesterday there was a crisis outside Moscow. A fine divisional commander was killed by a stray mortar bomb, Major-General Orlov. Did you know him?"

"I've heard of him," said Serpilin. "He was in the Siberian Military District before the war."

"That's right, the Altai Division," said Ivan Alexeyevich, with a nod. "At first, they were thinking of replacing him with the Chief of Staff, and then the Army commander rang up and asked us to find someone more capable. They finally settled on you."

"Well, thank you!" said Serpilin.

"Hold your horses," said Ivan Alexeyevich. "True, it's a regular division, and a good one, but it's been knocked about—pretty badly—cruelly, in fact. Orlov was a capable commander, to give him his due, and they got used to him during the last six years. So you won't be arriving at the division to take over from some youngster; it'll be tricky for you. Well, since you didn't want to work with us here, have a nice journey!" concluded Ivan Alexeyevich.

He sounded aggrieved. Serpilin's old comrades had wanted to do their best for him, but he had stuck to his guns and written to Stalin over their heads. But Serpilin didn't feel guilty. He wanted to be at the front, and in this matter he couldn't consider the feelings even of those to whom he owed so much.

"Take over an Army," he said joking his way out of any possible argument, "and then I'll be serving under you again!"

"Take over an Army, take over an Army!" said Ivan Alexeyevich grumpily. "You think it's all cakes and ale, sitting here? I'd probably be better off between a hammer and an anvil! I'd take an Army if I could, but we don't all have as much luck with our letters as you do. 'I want to go here, but I don't want to go there'—you can get it in the neck for that!"

Serpilin thought how he hadn't always had so much luck with his letters either. He had written to that address before and had received no reply. Oh, well, to hell with them, those letters! But for this latest decision he'd be grateful till his dying day!

"Do you know your future commander?" And as he stood up, Ivan Alexeyevich named the CO of the Army which Serpilin would be joining.

Serpilin said that he remembered him and had been with him at the academy, but two courses ahead.

"So he was two intakes younger than you, and now he is one star senior," joked Ivan Alexeyevich. "But I'd say he's earned his promotion. He had rotten luck at the beginning of the war. He took over a mechanised corps when it was, so to speak, in process of formation: old tanks just about to be written off, and the new ones just about to arrive. But he didn't handle that mechanised corps badly at all, especially compared with certain other commanders. He fought his way out of encirclement. And he's given a good account of himself here too, outside Moscow.... Anyway, you'll see best from below, as the saying goes."

"Why? Can't you see properly from above?"

"How am I to put it to you? It varies. You know how it goes sometimes: top rank, and had it for ages, and yet still playing with one finger on his military piano. Plucks it in memory of old times like a balalaika, and we, the ones in between, we can tell from the way things are going what sort of music he's making. But upstairs"—Ivan Alexeyevich glanced briefly at the ceiling—"they may not have even started listening! Oh, and by the way," said Ivan Alexeyevich, offering his hand to Serpilin, "Baranov's widow came to see me here yesterday. I remembered our conversation and told her she should look you up. You can tell her yourself. I didn't take it on myself to do so."

Serpilin frowned.

"When are you leaving to take over the division? Today or tomorrow?"

"I'm going straight to Front HQ, if you let me have transport," said Serpilin. "From there I'll go home for an hour or so to pack, then to the new place at night. Or so I was intending."

He didn't want to talk to Baranov's widow, and he thought with relief that since he was leaving for the front that day, he would miss that particular treat.

But things worked out otherwise. He returned from his visit to Front HQ at Perkhushkovo sooner than expected, and when he called at home to have dinner and pick up his things, his wife, whom he had rung about his posting while he was still at GHQ, said with some annoyance as she stood over an empty suitcase:

"Some Baranova has rung twice, and she's been being very persistent. I told her you were leaving for the front today, but she said she'd ring again anyway. Who is she?"

"Baranov's wife. Who else?"

Husband and wife looked at one another. Valentina Yegorovna knew that he had grounds to consider Baranov one of those responsible for what had happened to him in thirty-seven. She knew that fate, as if out of malice, had brought her husband and Baranov together again in encirclement. And now—this was the last straw—that he would have to talk to Baranov's widow just before leaving for the front.

She could see it on her husband's face. If Baranova rang up, he would be bound to invite her over. She could only hope that the woman wouldn't phone after all. Both were hoping for this as they had dinner.

Serpilin was animated and chatty at table, but Valentina Yegorovna had little to say. She had long known that he wanted to take over a division and she knew that he had written to Stalin about it. She had believed that his request would be granted. They had long known and understood one another fully and all the way. Mutual understanding is not, of course, all there is to love, but is such an important part of it, growing even more important over the years, that without it love is hardly worthy of the name. A deep and total understanding of everything that troubled or gladdened Serpilin had long been the main part of Valentina Yegorovna's love for her husband. She was glad for his sake that he was leaving to take over a division, although she was secretly in revolt against the idea: another spell of separation, another spell at the front, and once more the tense, sleepless life, with his health even less than half recovered.

She refrained from mentioning this openly, not wanting to upset him before the journey; yet she was in no state to talk about anything else. She sat without saying a word all through dinner, and her awkward silence was not the consequence of a quarrel, as a casual visitor might have thought, but the result of love and self-restraint.

There was one more feeling—alarm. Sitting at the farewell dinner opposite her husband, Valentina Yegorovna remembered that he was leaving to take over from a man who had been killed. His new appointment could mean death for him too; but it was not done to talk about this in their family.

"Listen, Valya," said Serpilin, about to take some tea, then pushing his glass away. "D'you know what I meant to say to you?..." He wanted to tell her that after he had left she should immediately go back to nursing, which she had temporarily given up when he was discharged from hospital and allowed home. He knew that she would go back to work tomorrow anyway, but he wanted to make it clear that it was important to him as well as to her.

He only had the chance to say this later, however, at the last moment of farewell. The telephone rang, and an unhappy, peremptory woman's voice said that it was Baranova calling: she knew already that Serpilin was leaving for the front, but she was ringing for the third time, from a phone booth on the street corner this time, and he had no right to refuse to talk to her for ten minutes.

Serpilin disliked being reminded what rights he had and didn't have; but since Baranova had rang, he did not refuse her request.

"Come round, I'll be expecting you."

He hung up and asked his wife if she happened to remember Baranova's first name.

"I don't remember her at all," said Valentina Yegorovna, not hiding her dislike.

Baranov's death had not reconciled her to him. She was still fuming at the thought that the last half hour before parting with her husband was to be sacrificed to the wife of the man who had gone to some trouble to deprive her of her husband for the four longest and most terrible years in her life.

"She's got a nerve all the same!" she said determinedly, and most probably, unfairly and then, unashamed of her unfairness, she snatched up the suitcase and went away to the kitchen to pack her husband's things, since she didn't even want to set eyes on the woman.

Serpilin finished his tea alone, trying to remember Baranova's name and patronymic and what she looked like. Younger, he thought, than Baranov himself had been. He remembered meeting her in 1936 at the railway station when they were leaving by train for the autumn manoeuvres in Byelorussia. She had been seeing her husband off. It was then, apparently, that Baranov had introduced them.

The woman to whom he opened the door a few minutes later was certainly not old and was wearing Army doctor's uniform. If Serpilin's mind had been running in that direction, he would no doubt have mentally noted that she was attractive.

He helped her off with her coat, gave her a seat at the

table, and offered her a glass of tea. But she refused hastily, glanced at her big, man-sized wrist-watch, and said that she would take up exactly ten minutes of his time, as she had already informed him over the telephone.

She had known for a month that her husband had been killed, and her elder son, aged eighteen, had left for the front as a volunteer on learning of his father's death. She had approved of this. She had been officially informed of the date when her husband had been killed—4th September—and they had told her that she could raise the matter of a pension. But she had not yet completed the formalities.

"Anyway, all this pension business isn't so very important," she added hurriedly. "As you see, I'm in the army. I'm chief surgeon of a hospital, my elder son's at the front, my youngest's with my husband's parents and he's quite settled there, so our family's not in need of anything." She spoke as if she wanted to shield herself in advance against a suspicion which Serpilin did not harbour. "But only yesterday, after a lot of telephoning, I got through to..."—she mentioned Ivan Alexeyevich by his surname—"in the hope that a man in his position might know more than anyone else. He did, in fact, tell me straightaway that my husband was on the way out of encirclement with you and he advised me to approach you."

"Damn him for it! He's hung a millstone round my neck, and hers too," thought Serpilin with a sneaking sympathy for this woman who was showing so much character.

Serpilin was not easily moved: he trusted emotional restraint more; and now, in the tense voice of this woman and in her eyes he read more grief than if she had dissolved into floods of tears in his presence.

"Yes," he said aloud. "We were indeed in encirclement together."

He spoke slowly, thinking over the questions that he had mentally asked himself: What was he to tell her, and what had she been told already? Information about Baranov's death could only have come from Shmakov and from the personnel lists that he had handed in on coming out of encirclement. But had Shmakov included some form of explanatory note, and what had they told this woman? Had they taken pity on her, and did she, in fact, not know? Or did she know more than she admitted, and was she trying to check with Serpilin? All these possibilities were equally likely and were not at variance with the sincerity and depth of the grief he could hear in her voice.

"Yes, we were indeed in encirclement together, and he was killed on the fourth of September," said Serpilin. He had not yet quite made up his mind to talk to her, but she noticed the slight hesitation in his voice and said:

"Please tell me the whole truth. What happened, exactly? It's important to me, because my sons want to know, especially the elder. I promised to write to him at the front."

But now that she had asked for "the whole truth" and had mentioned her son again, Serpilin decided not to tell her the whole truth, nor half, nor even a quarter.

He told her that he had met her husband at the end of July when he was on the way with his unit through the forests from Mogilev towards Chausy; that her husband, in the conditions of encirclement, like certain other commanders—Serpilin got this phrase out with some difficulty, although it was only a white lie—had fought as a private soldier and had died on the fourth of September at the very beginning of a battle which had broken out that night as they were crossing a highway. He had not himself seen what happened, but he had been informed that Baranov had died bravely.... Again with an effort, he said this not so much for her sake as for her son's, to whom she would be writing at the front.

"So, as you see, unfortunately, there's little I can add. I had half a thousand men under my command at the time and I can't remember all the details about each one. It was hard going, with many battles and losses, and in the last battle, when we'd nearly joined up with our own side, we lost half our strength. This doesn't make it any easier for you, I know; but only a few of us made it...."

"Perhaps there's something else mentioned?" And she scrutinised Serpilin's face intently.

At first, he thought that his tone of voice as he spoke about Baranov had given him away—but no, he had evidently managed that all right. Then it occurred to him that she might have wondered why her husband, a colonel, should have been serving under him as a private soldier.

But, as he looked into her eyes, he realised that neither supposition was correct. She had simply known or guessed something about her husband that had made her fear for him. She had obviously loved him, but had feared for him at the same time: what would he turn out to be like in war?

She was hoping to learn something good about her husband. That was why she had come, and yet, at the same time, deep down she was afraid of hearing something bad. So now, when Serpilin fell silent, she suspected that there was something bad after all that had merely been left unsaid.

"Perhaps there's something else?" she repeated.

"Perhaps ... perhaps..." he thought. But aloud he said: no, he had told her everything as it had happened, and she could write and tell her son.

"What matters most is the son, not her," he thought again.

This time she appeared to believe him.

"I shall write to my son and mention your name," she said.

"Do so by all means," he said. But inwardly he was thinking: the devil only knew, but that Baranov, whom he hated so much, must have had something about him to deserve the love of such a fine woman.

He saw her into the passage and helped her on with her coat. She thanked him and left.

When he went back into the room and glanced at the clock, he saw that she had only taken four minutes more of his time than she had promised. For a woman who had come on such a mission, this was an achievement.

"Yes, she has character. But what was it that she loved Baranov for? Or was it, as they say, for no particular reason? Just like that?... It can happen too, evidently..." he thought; but he was unable to make head or tail of it himself.

"Has she gone already?" asked Valentina Yegorovna as she entered the room.

Even Baranova's hurried departure hadn't mollified her. She had simply decided that Serpilin had told the woman the whole story and she had left early for that reason.

"Well, did you tell her all?" she asked, unable to contain herself.

"I didn't tell her anything!" replied Serpilin with dissatisfaction. He didn't want to discuss the matter any further. "I told her that he died bravely."

"I didn't know you were in the habit of lying," said Valentina Yegorovna grimly.

"S-bends—drive slowly!" said Serpilin angrily. "Her son went to the front as a volunteer to avenge his father. Who d'you want him to avenge? A coward?"

"Is there no one to avenge for except his good father, then? If his father was alive, does that mean the son could go to the Urals instead of to the front? Sorry, I don't agree with you!"

"You'd agree if you were in my place...." Serpilin had it in mind to say that it was one thing to argue about the rights and wrongs of a case, and another thing to look a widow in the eye....

But Valentina Yegorovna interrupted him:

"There's no need for me to be in your place. I've seen enough in my own!"

If they had carried on with this conversation much longer, it would have flared up into a quarrel; but both of them realised it in time, stopped, and changed the subject. Serpilin reminded her that she should go straight back to her work at the hospital, and she told him that he should wear leather boots less often—at least, as long as his legs were hurting him.

"You could perfectly well travel in felt boots today, for instance...."

And with this reasonable suggestion, the normal farewell conversation began.

Half an hour later, Serpilin had crossed Moscow city limits and, after presenting his documents on the way out, was already travelling along the road to the front.

Serpilin arrived at Army HQ and, after finding the log house where the Army Commander was quartered, went inside and was greeted by the adjutant, who invited him to make himself comfortable and wait.

"The commander's resting," he said, "but he asked to be woken at twenty-two hundred hours, or on your arrival, if earlier."

So saying, the adjutant went out. Serpilin glanced at his watch (it said 21:50) and looked round the room.

Even the temporary quarters of a military man give a certain impression of its owner. It was cold, clean and bare in the Army commander's room, and everything superfluous had been removed, leaving a table, chairs, and a bookstand with a bundle of books on the shelf, copies of *The Red Star* clipped together on another, and a pile of maps on the third. Spotless sheets of paper had been secured to the table-top with drawing pins: evidently, they had to be changed daily.

The man who worked in this room was clearly a pedant. Serpilin involuntarily remembered Ivan Alexeyevich's casual remark that the Army commander was a tough egg.

"I thought you'd arrive later. My apologies!" Serpilin was snapped out of these reflections by the sound of a polite but sharp voice behind him.

Serpilin rose to his feet, but the man who had just spoken was not in the room any more. He had quickly crossed from one door to the other, and Serpilin had glimpsed the towel round his neck gleaming in the half-light.

Two minutes later he shot back again, every bit as quickly, but without speaking, and two minutes later he came into the room, thrusting his fingers down under his belt and straightening the folds in his tunic with a last precise movement.

Serpilin introduced himself in the formal manner expected of a new divisional commander on arrival at Army HQ.

The commander listened to him standing, briefly shook his hand, nodded abruptly, and invited Serpilin to sit at the table.

"So that's what you're like!" he said, looking at Serpilin. "When the Lieutenant-General—" he mentioned Ivan Alexeyevich's surname—— "was putting you up to me for the division, he gave such a glowing picture of you that I imagined someone out of Lermontov: 'You shall be a giant in stature with a Cossack's heart....' I even hesitated. I'm nervous of friendly recommendations, I must confess. Did you and he serve together?" he asked, meaning Ivan Alexeyevich.

"Yes, we did," said Serpilin, without going into details.

This pleased the commander.

"So that's what *you*'re like," thought Serpilin, looking at him.

Before him sat a man, small in stature and ordinary in appearance; a round head on the short, burly neck; hair close-cropped, with a small white tuft in front. A very young, smooth, almost unwrinkled face with a single sharp line etched on the chin. A field tunic without medals and with khaki-coloured tabs. The commander looked as though he went to deliberate trouble to avoid anything superfluous in his work-room and in his outward appearance. Serpilin knew that he was forty, but the boyish crew-cut made him look a good five years younger, and his voice also was young, being clear, and resonant.

Serpilin was expecting to be questioned about his service history. This would have been perfectly natural on meeting a new divisional commander. But the Army commander immediately began by saying that he had already familiarised himself with Serpilin's service record.

"We will consider that our acquaintance has already commenced. We shall complete it in battle. But I shall now put you briefly in the picture."

He reached out to the bookstand and, without looking, unerringly selected the map he wanted from its place on the shelf.

"This is where we are now." The tip of his finely sharpened pencil unhesitatingly found the precise spot on the map.

He indeed summed up the situation very briefly, as if mentally numbering off the words; but thanks to this very succinctness, the picture he gave, shorn of all irrelevant detail, was remarkably clear.

The five Army divisions occupied seventy kilometres of the front and were all in the first echelon. During the last few days, there had been virtually no Army reserves in hand. But, in the commander's opinion, the Germans had none left either. Although they had been advancing on various sectors over the last few days and had scored a few local successes, their attacks had had, as he put it, "an ungrounded character", and one had the feeling that here, at least, on the Army's sector, they had no substantial reserves to follow up any success that they might have achieved.

"I say 'substantial' to be on the safe side, although I personally think that there are no reserves opposite us at all."

He next went on to explain the position concerning the forthcoming advance on the Army's sector, which was due to begin in a matter of days and of which the divisional commanders had already been informed, Serpilin's predecessor included.

"We ourselves are not going to be the star performers in this advance," said the commander. "A fresh Army is to be introduced to the left, between us and our former neighbour"—he mentioned the Army's number—"and it will occupy part of our neighbour's sector and part of our own. We are withdrawing our left-flank division to the reserve, and so you, as it happens, will be adjacent to our new neighbour, the star performer. But during the first week, it is proposed that we should move out to this point here!—" The distance he indicated with his pencil on the large-scale map was impressive—something like a third of the length of the table. "Needless to say, in the snow and under enemy fire it won't be as easy as running a pencil over a map," he added, putting the pencil down. "So we shall have to exert ourselves. In the meantime, I'm not very well off. I have at my disposal as of today..." he mentioned such a meagre number of available troops that even the hardened Serpilin was shaken.

The commander noticed the expression that flashed across Serpilin's face, but said nothing. In his opinion, Serpilin shouldn't have to be told that keeping the Germans out of Moscow was no easy matter and was costing them dear.

"Yes, we're not very well off," he repeated, but using the plural this time. "We'll probably manage to scrape up a few replacements in our rear units—we've been scraping the barrel there for the last five days. But we mustn't count on a big haul. We've been promised replacements by tomorrow evening, but nothing sensational, since, I repeat, we are not the star performers. The situation in your division is a little brighter than in the others: before they transferred it to us, they withdrew it from the front and gave it replacements."

"I saw one of the regiments on parade on November the Seventh," said Serpilin, availing himself of the commander's pause.

"I was waiting for it that day like manna from heaven," said the commander, and he went on to divisional matters.

The plan of battle for the division's sector, as drawn up by its former commander and Chief of Staff on the basis of the general Army directive, was acceptable, in his opinion, but required further elaboration.

"General Orlov was killed while he was working on the final details," said the commander. "He went to a battalion OP to settle them in the afternoon and never came back. I understand it was a stray mortar bomb. Not that they carry an inscription stating whether they're stray or otherwise. Tomorrow evening I'm sending for all the divisional commanders. This leaves you less than twenty-four hours to work out all the final details. Time is short, and your position, as new divisional CO, is a difficult one. But I preferred to appoint a divisional commander on the eve of the offensive rather than swap horses in mid-stream later. I used to think battle experience and knowledge gave the Chief of Staff first claim to the command of the division; unfortunately in my position we have to think ahead about whom to replace with whom...."

Serpilin nodded agreement. How could it be otherwise!

"But when I arrived at the division, I found a man shattered with grief. True, he'd served for twenty years with the divisional commander and his grief was understandable. But at the same time I didn't notice a scrap of independence and self-confidence in him—nothing to suggest that whatever may have happened, the division was his now and he would command it as his judgement prompted. And without that feeling, it's impossible to command, especially after a CO like Orlov. I knew him too in his green and salad days. I served in his company. No, it hasn't worked out with Rtishchev.... If a man is purely concerned that things shouldn't turn out worse than they were and to do exactly what's been done before, the outcome is a foregone conclusion: the same thing, only worse. In short, I didn't feel that he was a divisional commander," said the Army Commander grimly, and Serpilin realised that his first impression had not been mistaken: this man was outwardly good-mannered, but he was a tough egg. "Go and sum up the position for yourself. If he is going to carry on in the Orlov tradition—and Orlov set a fine precedent—I think you will support him in this; but if he doesn't snap out of it and stop grieving and living in the past—in a word, if he's a drag—you will report to me. We'll transfer him to another division and send you someone else instead.... As for the commissar, well, he's a decent fellow, he's brave, and he loves the front line. I won't say any more; I don't know enough yet. The commissar before him was good—excellent, I would say; but the division has had some bad luck: he was wounded a week before Orlov was killed. If you want further details about this, call on the chief of the Political Department. He's asked for you to visit him. How about a glass of tea before you leave?"

Serpilin thanked him. He had been frozen stiff during the journey and wouldn't have said no to a glass of vodka. But the tea, as it turned out, really was just that. Two steaming glasses of strong tea and a plate of biscuits covered with a serviette were already laid out waiting for them in the next room on a table near the bed, which was covered with a carpet brought, no doubt, by the Army Commander to the front.

"You know, I don't seem to remember you at the academy," said the Army Commander, as if drawing a demarcation line between official discussion and informal chat.

"I don't remember you either," said Serpilin.

Now that they were discussing the past, he felt on equal terms with the commander.

"Afterwards, according to your service records,"—the commander didn't intend to hide his source of information—"you came back and held the chair of tactics, did you not?"

"Yes," said Serpilin, "until thirty-seven."

"So we just missed meeting again, then. In thirty-six, they were fixing me up with a teaching post in the academy too and then at twenty-four hours' notice I packed and left for Spain—you never can tell what's just round the corner, as they say...."

"And after Spain?" inquired Serpilin.

"I was in the General Staff. Then, just before war broke out, the gods deemed me worthy of a mechanised corps." Mentioning the mechanised corps evidently reminded the commander of encirclement, because he immediately asked Serpilin how he had broken out near Yelnia and whether he had sustained heavy losses.

"Yes," said Serpilin. "Over half."

"The same here..." said the commander thoughtfully, for the first time looking to one side instead of straight in front of him. "Nasty business, encirclement. A painful memory; I don't ever want to go through it again. Great contradictions: a man joins you voluntarily the day before and goes with you through every danger, right back towards your own side; and yet on the next day you shoot him in front of the assembled troops for disobeying an order. And you can't act otherwise, you have no right to, because two or three orders disobeyed in encirclement can mean that everything goes to pieces. It will go to pieces too, although most of the men joined voluntarily. They could have gone wandering off any old where, yet they've come to you. But once they've done so, then from that moment on, orders are in full force. Isn't that so?"

"It certainly is!" said Serpilin.

"One comrade who came out of it with me,"—the commander paused fractionally before the word, "comrade"—"accused me of exceeding my powers. I won't dispute it, maybe it was ruthless of me to insist on the unquestioned execution of my orders. But let's just ask ourselves: why does a man refuse to obey an order? More often than not because he's afraid of being killed while he's carrying it out. So now let's ask: how can he overcome that fear? With something stronger. And what's that? It varies according to the circumstances: a newly awakened belief in victory; a recovered sense of dignity; a fear of showing oneself up as a coward before one's comrades; but sometimes just the fear of execution. That, unfortunately, is the case. And the man who reported me afterwards and accused me of ruthlessness, exceeding my powers, and so forth, came out of it with a clear conscience: there was nothing to write about him, good or bad. But he didn't lead those men out of encirclement—I did. No doubt you've come up against this problem too?" The commander looked searchingly at Serpilin.

And Serpilin, silently nodding his agreement, thought that the man sitting before him had nevertheless probably been no more ruthless than the circumstances had demanded, otherwise he would not have been looking back on the affair just now and insisting, with all the strength of his character, that he was in the right. People with a guilty conscience try not to remember, least of all openly in front of others. But that this man's character was clearly not made of sugar didn't matter. To hell with character! Character can be tolerated when there's a soul behind it.

"Well..." the commander swallowed his last mouthful of tea and rose to his feet. "I wish you success in the forthcoming offensive! Perhaps at long last, we can live down the encirclement by smashing the enemy and booting him all the way back. I can't tell you how desperately I want to do this! For everything and for everybody—even for those that one had to shoot with one's own gun owing to circumstances...."

He banged the chair violently as he pushed it back under the table, and this movement, too, betrayed the real temperament seething under the restrained and humdrum exterior.

"Call at the Political Department, then you can go by car. There's one ready. My adjutant will drive you to your destination."

When Serpilin looked at his watch after shaking hands with the commander and going outside, he saw that it was twenty-three hundred hours. The conversation had lasted exactly sixty minutes. At the precise moment when Serpilin went outside, a car drove up to the house. Yes, even when indulging in a heart-to-heart talk, the commander was able to time it to a second.

The head of the Political Department had his quarters four buildings away. Serpilin opened the door, asked permission to enter and was astonished and overjoyed to see that the man getting up behind the table to meet him was Maximov.

"How d'you do, Maximov, you lucky fellow!" exclaimed Serpilin in spite of himself, standing in the middle of the room and shaking hands with a smiling Maximov. Only afterwards did he withdraw his hand, apply it to his general's hat, and announce strictly according to form, although smiling inwardly, that Major-General Serpilin, Commander of the Thirty-First Rifle Division, was at the disposal of the Head of the Army Political Department.

"Well, since you've reported," said Maximov, taking Serpilin by the sleeve, "you can stay with us for five minutes. I'll introduce you straightaway!"

"Very well, but be sure it's only five minutes," said Serpilin, tapping his wrist-watch. "Someone higher up than you has ordered me to proceed directly to the division!"

"Is he chasing you, or are you in a hurry anyway?"

"In a hurry, to tell the truth."

Serpilin was introduced to four men who had been sitting with Maximov and had risen to their feet when he entered the room. He sat down at the table without removing his greatcoat, thereby indicating that, however delighted he might be at meeting Maximov, he would nevertheless be leaving in five minutes.

Of the four to whom Serpilin was introduced by Maximov, one was an army man—a colonel—and the other three were civilians, also dressed, incidentally, in military uniform—boots, tunics and officers' belts, but with no tabs or insignia of rank.

Two of the civilians were the Secretary of the Party Committee and the chairman of the municipal Executive Committee of a small town outside Moscow just in the Army's rear. Serpilin had driven through it an hour ago. The third civilian, an old man with a badly scarred cheek, was the director of a furniture factory.

"By order of the Military Council, the Head of the Rear Services and I are commandeering a few extra odds and ends from the comrades here."

"What's this 'commandeering' of yours?" said the secretary. "You've no need to commandeer from us: we're offering of our own free will."

"Well, you're a tightwad, you are," said the Head of the Rear Services.

"We're collecting tribute from his industrial mammoths," said Maximov, laughing. "From the garment factory and what used to be a furniture factory but now makes skis. They're turning out camouflage cloaks for us and making skis and machine-gun sledges on ski-runners. We asked them for more today, and we've brought them here to talk them into letting us have it."

"Oh, give over," said the town Party Committee Secretary with a deprecatory gesture. "You should be ashamed of yourself, talking like that! D'you think we need you to convince our women to go on working night after night non-stop? Why don't you just admit you miscalculated in the beginning and now you want another three hundred pairs of skis?"

"I'm not disputing it," said Maximov, and he nodded towards the old man with the disfigured cheek. "But you'll talk till you're blue in the face before you'll get anything out of him! And if only the skis were at all decent! You only have to stand on them, and believe me, as an experienced skier, you feel like bursting into tears!"

"You can't get good skis out of unseasoned wood, much less if it's damp right through," said the old man calmly. "But we'll let you have the quantity you want." He turned and nodded to the town Party Secretary. "I've made my estimate. We'll make them."

Serpilin was pleased that the subject hadn't been changed on his arrival and that he had plunged straight into the world of army supplies, especially since this particular aspect of it reminded him that the offensive was imminent. He would have been delighted to sit there a little longer, but time was pressing.

"All the best, comrades!"

"I'll see you to your car," said Maximov, also getting to his feet.

Serpilin shook hands with each in turn, ending with the director of the ski factory.

"I served under you once, Comrade General," he said, holding on to Serpilin's hand.

"When?"

"When you and I were beating hell out of the generals," said the director with a smile that twisted the scar on his cheek into a comma. "I joined you with the replacements from the Moscow workers to fight Denikin! You were positioned just south of Navlya in the Bryansk gubernia at that time."

"I was there all right," said Serpilin. "So I needn't worry about skis for my division, then?"

"Consider yourself in the bosom of Christ!"

"I'm so glad we've met again, Fyodor Fyodorovich. I'm very glad..." said Maximov as he went out with Serpilin on to the moonlight-flooded village street, which would have looked more peaceful had it not been for the fresh, snow-sprinkled bomb crater.

"So am I," said Serpilin.

"I'm so glad," repeated Maximov, "that I feel like asking to come back to your division as a commissar. Especially since I fought with it, was wounded in it, knew the old commander and loved him, and buried him yesterday with my own hands. I could weep when I think about Orlov! But since it had to turn out that way, at least I'm glad you've come to take over. Seriously, if I had any say, I'd join you as commissar. There's just one snag: now that they've promoted me, they won't demote me unless I do something awful."

"Do something awful, then," said Serpilin.

"Very well, we'll see!" said Maximov so earnestly that Serpilin smiled.

"I shall be waiting. Meanwhile, tell me about the present commissar."

"His name...."

"His name I know at least. Permyakov. But what about the rest?"

"He arrived less than a week ago. He was commissar of a corps in the Crimea. The corps didn't show itself to advantage at Perekop, as they say, and the commissar, poor wretch, was demoted. I don't know who was to blame: him or someone else. Judging by his conduct in action here, it looks as though someone else was. Any more questions?" added Maximov, half in jest and half in earnest.

"A great many, but we haven't much time...."

They were both standing beside the car and were reluctant to take leave of one another.

"We're now getting ski battalions ready," said Maximov. "D'you know who he was—the third civilian sitting in my office—the glum one who never spoke a word?"

"The chairman of the municipal Executive Committee. You did introduce us," said Serpilin.

"That's his temporary post; he's really secretary of the occupied region over there, ahead of us." Maximov nodded towards the front line. "I didn't send for him; he came of his own accord. He's sensed there's going to be an offensive, and he's sniffing around to find the best place so that he can re-enter his own town with the first units."

"We all have our worries," said Serpilin. "I'd like to retake Mogilev...." And with heart-rending anguish, as in a waking dream, he saw before him the shell-riddled Mogilev grain elevator from which Shmakov had looked out for the last time that evening as the Germans were herding a column of prisoners through the dust....

"Fyodor Fyodorovich, I hope you're going to take off that *papakha* of yours, and that greatcoat too. They have snipers, you know, and you're much too conspicuous. You're a man-and-a-half tall. Anyway, you'll be warmer in sheepskins and a fur hat," added Maximov solicitously.

"I'll take them off," said Serpilin. "I've got everything I need in the car—fur hat, sheepskin, felt boots, even. Don't worry, I won't be caught by any snipers, and generally speaking, I've no intention of dying. It doesn't happen to be one of the things I have in mind just now."

"Was it ever?" asked Maximov.

"How can I put it.... During the last few days in hospital, I must admit, I felt low and re-read Dostoyevsky...."

"What was getting you down?" joked Maximov. "Hospital, or Dostoyevsky?"

"Both," said Serpilin. "Perhaps you remember the bit where Raskolnikov's arguing about the man who is ready for anything just so long as he's allowed to live—even if it means spending his whole life on a square yard of ground, alone, without people, in the dark, standing in silence, but at least living and not dying! Well, I don't agree with that; I only agree to live on certain conditions."

"Such as?"

"That we beat the Germans! What sort of a life would it be otherwise? In the dark, in terror, saying nothing, on a square yard of ground? I don't hold with that kind of life. I don't suppose you do either."

He shook Maximov's hand firmly again and drove off.

To reach Divisional HQ meant driving back to the main road from the village, proceeding along it for about seven kilometres, and then turning off to another village. Serpilin reached the main road fairly quickly, but his car got stuck there almost immediately. Infantry were moving up to the front on either side of the road, and in the middle, stretching away into the far distance a howitzer regiment with mechanised traction was at a complete standstill. The road ahead climbed upwards, and it was doubtless somewhere up there that the lorries were skidding and the bottleneck had occurred.

The driver skirted round several lorries, went on to the verge, got stuck, jumped out into the snow with a shovel, drove back onto the road, skidding slightly in the process, drove round another lorry, and then stopped rather than risk being stuck in the snow again.

The Army Commander's adjutant jumped out of the car and ran forward to the head of the stationary column.

"He'll clear it all right!" said the driver confidently.

His prophecy was not fulfilled. Twenty minutes passed, the infantry continued marching past, stringing out as they went round the vehicles, along the verges and over the snow; but the vehicles still didn't move.

Serpilin climbed out of the car and paced up and down without particular impatience, squeaking over the snow in his felt boots which, after his visit to his superiors, he had put on instead of his leather ones. They would, after all, reach the division at night. He intended to tour the regiments there and then, he had no intention of sleeping, and he wasn't much worried by the minor hold-up, whereas the sight of troops and equipment moving up to the front was yet one more joyful reminder of the offensive.

Serpilin was feeling simultaneously happy and worried. Strictly speaking, he had not commanded a division since peacetime. The breakthrough out of encirclement with a few hundred men had been a severe, but nevertheless one-sided, test, and he was thinking with some anxiety about the forthcoming advance. He was worried about the general success of the operation, like all who knew that preparations were under way, and he was worried about himself; would he be able to master, completely and down to the last detail, all the parts of as complex a piece of machinery as a division in the few days that remained? He considered that he would be able to cope, otherwise he would not have applied for a division in the first place. But merely to "cope" would not be enough. He was going to have to command it in our first big push, and to command it well, in an exemplary manner.

"And this lot are fresh, by the look of them," he thought, watching the infantrymen as they crossed the gaps between the vehicles and howitzers on the other side of the road. "They haven't seen action. And their commanders, for the most part, probably haven't seen action either. And in war, whatever you say, the first day's the worst...."

Preoccupied with these thoughts, Serpilin continued pacing up and down until the figure of the adjutant, breathless with running, suddenly loomed up in front of him.

"The major here,"—he indicated a tall officer with him—"is responsible for the movement of the column on this sector. I've been explaining to him that you're waiting, and he doesn't do anything about it! I had to ask him to come and speak to you!"

Serpilin drew himself up to his full height (he had been walking up and down with his hands behind his back, engrossed in thought) and eyed the insubordinate major.

The major brought his hand up to his fur hat and reported in a chesty but cheery voice that he was Major Artemyev, commander of a regiment in the division at present on the march.

In spite of his hoarse voice and the bandage swathing his neck up to the chin, the major was the picture of health: big, red-haired, with broad, square shoulders and with a strong, weather-beaten face that was ruddy even in the moonlight.

The adjutant had evidently been hoping that Serpilin would admonish the major there and then, but Serpilin began on a different tack.

"What's the matter with you? Sore throat, or something?"

"Exactly! A sore throat!" articulated the major in the same hoarse and cheery voice.

"Do you intend to keep this traffic-jam going for long?"

"The infantry's just moved up, Comrade Major-General. We'll have five or six more lorries up the slope by hand and set the intervals. The rest will go under their own steam. In ten minutes we'll have the whole thing dealt with. I've been explaining all this to the senior lieutenant," and he nodded towards the adjutant as if annoyed at being called away from his work for nothing.

"Good, I'll give you ten minutes," said Serpilin with a glance at his watch. "But no longer! Have you been in action yet?"

"What did you have in mind, Comrade Major-General?"

"Your regiment, since you're in command of one, and your division...."

"Most of the men in the ranks have not been in action, but their commanders fought at Khalkhin-Gol. Of course, the fighting there...." He evidently wanted to explain that the battles at Khalkhin-Gol had not been like these in the present war....

But Serpilin cut him short:

"I mustn't keep you. I hope you bring more battle honours to your division."

"Thank you, Comrade General! I'll go and clear that bottle-neck now." The major glanced at his watch, and hurried off at the double along the column of vehicles.

Serpilin reached Divisional HQ at one o'clock at night. The divisional commissar was not there: he had left for one of the regiments at midday, but the Chief of Staff had not gone to bed and was waiting up for a new commander.

At Serpilin's suggestion, they began by examining the already prepared plan of battle which, at first glance and without on-the-spot estimates, seemed reasonable to Serpilin.

The Chief of Staff—a small, tired, sad-looking colonel—had evidently decided beforehand that he would not, and could not, get on with new commander. With the deliberateness of a man who had no intention of considering whether what he says will please or displease, he mentioned the dead divisional commander at almost every tenth word in his quiet, level voice: "As was suggested by General Orlov"; "As was indicated by General Orlov"; "As was planned by General Orlov"; "As was estimated by General Orlov".... Finally, Serpilin became fed up with this.

"Listen, Colonel Rtishchev," he said. "Did you personally take part in planning the battle? Who worked it out? Was it you or wasn't it? It's important that I should know for future reference which of us in this division will be keeping the records of the action, you or I? I am accustomed to it being the responsibility of the Chief of Staff. I imagine you and I were at the same school. If this is not so, let's have the situation clarified once and for all!"

Slowly and reluctantly, Rtishchev looked up at Serpilin and said that he had, of course, made all the detailed calculations himself.

"I never doubted that in the slightest. So why do you keep pushing General Orlov under my nose all the time whether it's to the point or not?" said Serpilin, who was determined to go through with it. "I've already heard that you had a superb divisional commander before me. I've heard it at Front HQ and I've heard it in Army HQ. So there is no need to force it on my attention. I'm delighted at having come to a division with traditions of its own. But I will not have its former commander pushed down my throat. I am the divisional commander now, and this is not open to further discussion directly or indirectly by yourself or anyone else! Take note of this in future: don't trouble to remind me what an excellent divisional commander General Orlov was. I will myself find the appropriate form and occasions to mention in what way I, as a divisional commander, am indebted to my predecessor, and to you as Chief of Staff, although it is not customary with us to praise the living. So now tell me, how do you feel about the matter?" asked Serpilin after a short pause and quite unexpectedly for the other.

He had wanted to hit off with this man from the start and, having first stated his feelings now wanted to give him the chance to speak his mind if he cared to. If he did, then that meant they would get on; but if he crawled back into his shell, that wouldn't be so good.

"What can I say, Comrade General?" said Rtishchev after a pause, looking at Serpilin with his deep, sad eyes. "Misha Orlov—don't take it out of me for saying this, but he's dead, and in service terms nothing ties me down any more—after twenty years in the Army I shall never forget him anyway, and I don't want to. And, frankly speaking...."

"Only frankly!" said Serpilin.

"...And, frankly speaking, since you want me to be perfectly frank, you'll never replace him as far as I'm concerned."

"We'll hit it off," thought Serpilin.

"I can see you loved the divisional commander," he said aloud. "But what about the division?"

"I was just going to talk about that. I love the division, and from you—if I have the right to expect anything—I only want one thing: that you should be a worthy successor to its former commander. My own self matters little here...."

"Not at all! You are the Chief of Staff," interrupted Serpilin in spite of himself.

"...Matters little here," rejected Rtishchev stubbornly. "But I want to tell you that even now, after all our losses, we have over thirty commanders in the division who graduated from the Omsk Infantry School, where Orlov served for ten years before he came to the division—and they're all pupils of his. And this, you know, is a fact worth reckoning with, and such traditions have to be taken seriously. Perhaps it wasn't very clever of me to keep on harping about Orlov. I'll admit I wanted to drive it home. Forget it! But the interests of the division are at the back of it all."

"Agreed," said Serpilin.

"That's the essence of it," said Rtishchev, and he looked at Serpilin again with his sad eyes which, without their original hostility, had become even sadder. "As far as I personally am concerned, well, I just can't get over his death, and that's all there is to it. I'm taking it badly."

"Assuming that to be so," said Serpilin, "how are we going to carry on fighting in future?"

"We'll carry on fighting. It hasn't driven everything I ever learned about war out of my head, and I'm no more afraid of death than anyone else."

"Let's go and visit the regiments," said Serpilin.

"Is it worth it?" asked Rtishchev. "In the morning, perhaps?"

"It's a long time till dawn—five hours," said Serpilin. "While it's dark, we'll take a look at the front line, especially where you can't get through in the daytime. We'll visit the observation posts in the morning. I understand General Orlov was killed at an OP? In whose regiment?"

"Baglyuk's," said Rtishchev.

"Which regiment is the commissar visiting?"

"The same one—Baglyuk's."

"Right, we'll start with Baglyuk too," said Serpilin.

CHAPTER EIGHTEEN

Klimovich sat in the operating room and waited while the plaster was being prepared. Twenty-four hours ago, he had received what he had called a minor bullet wound just above the wrist, but his arm had begun to hurt him badly during the night, and he had gone to the neighbouring rifle division's field hospital. The wound had proved worse than he had thought: the bone was fractured, and although he had no intention of letting such an injury keep him out of action, he had been forced to agree to a plaster cast. He sat in his tunic with his sleeve rolled up to his shoulder and, conscious of the goose-pimples rising on his skin in the cold draught, stared outside through a broken window. He could see a house opposite, also with smashed windows, and the top of a black German staff bus parked before the hospital entrance.

Our counter-offensive outside Moscow had already been in progress for some forty-eight hours along the whole front.

The field hospital had been set up in the hospital building of a district town only captured that day at dawn.

"They certainly moved in fast," thought Klimovich approvingly of the field hospital.

His own Medical Company had got stuck in the snow somewhere during the night, and he had been obliged to go to his neighbours to have his wound dressed.

The town was small and insignificant, and anyone hearing it mentioned in peacetime would have probably asked its name again and tried to remember where it was. Near Moscow, or perhaps on the Volga?... But now, at the beginning of December 1941, its name was like music to everyone's ears. A town recaptured from the Germans! They still weren't used to the idea.

It had been taken, after a brief night engagement, by two regiments of the 31st Rifle Division. For this success they were mainly indebted to their neighbours—a Far Eastern division and Klimovich's tanks, which had broken through some fifteen kilometres to their left. The tanks had cut off the Germans' retreat in the evening, compelling them either to fight in encirclement or to fall back immediately, abandoning everything that they couldn't take with them. The town and its environs were choked with abandoned German vehicles—the rear equipment of an entire motorised division.

While waiting for his cast to be prepared, Klimovich closed his eyes. At first, he seemed about to doze off there and then, sitting on a stool with his wounded arm resting on the edge of the table. And there would have been nothing surprising about that. For a whole month, while his brigade was thrown from one place to another in order to plug this or that gap, he had been sleeping in snatches—two or three hours at a time and, in the last few days, never more than an hour. Yes, he might well have expected to doze off there and then, but he didn't. He was far too wound up after the recent events and no matter what externally impenetrable armour of calm and habituation to military duty he might have donned, once the offensive had begun, it had turned out that grief was not the only thing a man could find hard to endure. Great happiness is also hard to bear! It, too, can drain you of all your strength.

Of course, those boys from the Far East, who had gone into battle yesterday for the first time and had pushed the Germans back non-stop for fifteen kilometres, had straightaway known the kind of happiness that is the envy of every military man; yet they could not have understood what Klimovich was going through. Only a man humiliated and outraged by retreats and encirclements, only a man who had poured the last few drops of petrol over his last tank and left behind him a heartrending farewell black column of smoke, and who, with a submachine gun slung round his neck, had marched for weeks through the forests or along routes down which German tanks were thundering on their way east—only such a man could really have understood Klimovich and the full degree of savage pleasure he had felt during those thirty-six hours, from the time when yesterday at dawn he had penetrated the German defences and proceeded to smash their rear units up to the moment when, on his way to the field hospital, he had raced through a town choked with abandoned German transport and littered with German staff papers blowing in the wind.

Yesterday at dawn, after the breakthrough, when the outcome of the battle had already been decided and its iron clangour had begun to quieten down, a last shell had lodged in the turret of the deafened Klimovich's KV. He had climbed out to find his tank black all over, with everything blown off that is usually attached before battle: tools, spare tracks, chains. All that was to be seen was smoke-blackened iron. While inspecting his tank, he was hit by a German submachine-gunner up on a roof-top. The German was shot dead. Klimovich's arm was bandaged up and he transferred from his KV to a Thirty-Four and rode on further.

In the afternoon, he and several other tanks had burst in on a retreating artillery column, and with their first successful shots, had blocked it at both ends. At first, the Germans had scattered; but, to render them their due, they had soon rallied, had deployed several guns and, under cover of their fire, had even tried to make their way to the tanks. The tank crews had been forced to do everything at once: finish smashing the column, shell the still active guns, and defend themselves. The enemy might sneak up to a tank and set it on fire before anyone even noticed what was happening. Klimovich had ordered the radio-operators out of their tanks and had placed them with the machine-guns in a ring round the tanks. Finally, they had shot down the attacking Germans, knocked out the guns, and set the lorries on fire. After a hasty count, it turned out that they had wiped out a whole artillery regiment. Klimovich had been unable to remember anything like it since the beginning of the war.

At night he had burst upon a German motorised column crawling, with headlamps blazing, through a blizzard. The drivers had scattered through the forest, abandoning their vehicles with the lights still on and the engines running, and the soldiers of an SS division had poured out of the backs of the lorries into the snow and put up their hands. Back in June, the Germans had thought it could never happen; but they had been forced to learn how to do it in December notwithstanding!

This morning he had taken a fortified point deep in the rear of the enemy defences and, with his own eyes, he had seen the infantry scrambling out of their trenches and running—running for dear life before our tanks. He had himself taken part in that attack and had seen the nazis running for it as much as two hundred and as little as twenty metres in front of him. He had fired his machine gun at their retreating backs and had seen their faces turned round as they fled....

His mind had become burdened with such appalling memories during the war that for any other man who had not been through so much, one would doubtless have sufficed for a lifetime. Some of them made even him shudder. As if anyone could remember, without a shudder, burying the tank crews, when you have to drag out of the machine all that remains of those inside after battle and when words can never describe what it's like in there!... And if the tank is still serviceable, then you have to clean and scrape out the interior before the next crew mans it and goes into action.

They say that such experiences toughen the spirit. This is true. But they also lacerate it; and so a man lives to fight on with his spirit both toughened and lacerated. These are two sides of the coin, whatever may be said about it, there can be no escaping this fact. Klimovich's spirit had been lacerated as well as toughened, even by the thought of that morning when the Germans had been fleeing from the tanks and looking round to see whether death was upon them. He could not forget the human face that had gleamed briefly in front of his tank and had vanished just as suddenly with its unvoiced scream: "Don't!... I'm frightened!..." It haunted his memory and would not go away; yet it was also part of the feeling of victory with which Klimovich had been living for the last two days. A man will sometimes imagine that war is leaving no ineradicable scars; but if he is truly human, then he only imagines it....

That was probably why the young, plain-looking but kindly woman doctor, as she looked at Klimovich's face and bound up his arm with great care so as not to hurt him, suddenly asked with solicitude and quite irrelevantly:

"Where's your family, Comrade Colonel? Is it far from here?"

"Yes," said Klimovich, starting in his surprise and, with the first word that occurred to him, defending himself against this unasked-for reminder of his personal tragedy.

Rather than think about what he preferred to forget, he wondered how his new driver-mechanic from the Thirty-Four was getting on. Klimovich had brought him to the field hospital to have his head treated for burns which had turned septic.

"There's no telling whether it's snow crunching or glass," said Klimovich as he left the hospital, frowning in the daylight.

He was wearing his sheepskin jacket buttoned over his bandaged arm with one sleeve dangling empty. Captain Ivanov, who had become his rear assistant again after the reorganisation of the brigade, was waiting for him. It was he who had persuaded Klimovich to have his wound dressed and had driven him in his car from the front line with the idea of having a look round the town while he was about it.

"You can't get into a tank in that state, Comrade Colonel!"

"Never mind, I'll manage. And how are things with you?" Klimovich turned to Zolotarev, to whose Thirty-Four he had transferred after being wounded.

"Everything under control, Comrade Colonel, except that they've shaved half my head."

Zolotarev's burns were so heavily bandaged that his tank helmet was perched precariously right on top of his head.

"Let's go home," said Klimovich, meaning the brigade.

"Only let's visit the divisional commander on the way!" requested Ivanov.

"Whatever for?"

Ivanov expressively swept his hand round, indicating the German vehicles choking up the street. "I wanted to organise us a few odds and ends! I'm worried the infantry'll get their hands on the stuff. Let's look in for a moment."

"We've no sooner captured our first war matériel than you start setting up in trade!" said Klimovich with a frown; but since he realised that Ivanov was acting in the brigade's interests, he left it at that.

Ivanov directed the driver from the back of the car, not forgetting to draw his brigade commander's attention to the captured transport.

"Look over there—that's a tank regiment's mobile transmitter. That's their repair van." He pointed to a vehicle with two tankmen poking about inside the engine.

"Are they your men?" asked Klimovich.

"Of course they're mine! And whose trophies are those, in all conscience, if not ours?"

The German vehicles were mostly big transport lorries and staff cars, but there were also armoured cars and tanks, likewise abandoned in the general panic.

"Honestly," grated Klimovich in annoyance as they drove up to divisional HQ, "if we'd only started the war like that."

The driver pulled up outside a small house on the outskirts. Communications had been laid on, and a white-painted staff-car was parked at the gate.

When Klimovich and Ivanov went into a low room cluttered with furniture and pot plants, Serpilin, who had arrived five minutes earlier, was pacing up and down, the skirts of his sheepskin jacket flying. He was talking excitedly to Rtishchev, who was seated at a table, about the great improvement in the morale of the troops: their spirits had risen yesterday, but it had been particularly noticeable today after the capture of the town.

"As soon as they went through the town and saw everything, they cheered up! They've a battle ahead of them, and they know that some of them won't be alive tomorrow; but just look at the way they march! Frankly speaking, I was afraid this morning that the regiments would be satisfied with what they'd done and I'd have to boot them out of the town. Nothing of the kind! They took it and pressed on! D'you know how far Dobrodyedov's gone?"

"He was in Zarubino by fourteen hundred hours," said Rtishchev. "No communications as yet! We're laying them on!"

"You won't catch up with him in a hurry: he's here already!" Serpilin stabbed the map with his finger at a point some four kilometres beyond Zarubino. "I've only just got back from there!"

He had visited the two regiments that had taken the town during the night, had looked in briefly on HQ, and now wanted to see Baglyuk, who was by-passing the town on the right.

Serpilin was aware of the general situation and realised that he was much indebted for the quick capture of the town to the tanks and his neighbours on the left, who had thrown the Germans into headlong retreat. But the town had actually been taken by Serpilin's own regiments, and to have expected him, in the first flush of attack, to think more of his neighbours' help than of the success of his own division, would have been to demand too much. He had worked feverishly on the eve of the advance. He was now tasting the first fruits of victory and was delighted that his division had liberated one of the first towns outside Moscow. To his great joy, losses during the first twenty-four hours had proved less than expected.

"Comrade General, request permission to introduce myself: Commander of the 17th Tank Brigade, Colonel Klimovich!"

Serpilin turned round and, his steel teeth gleaming, shook Klimovich by the hand.

"Have you been a colonel long?"

"A month. When you asked me by the Central Telegraph Office, the order had already come through, but I didn't know about it."

"I've already heard," said Serpilin cheerfully, "that Colonel Klimovich's tanks have been co-operating with my neighbour. The same Klimovich, I asked myself, or not? Then I decided it must be! We're still not so well off for tanks, unfortunately, and I thought there could hardly be two Klimoviches in two brigades outside Moscow at the same time!"

"To be frank, I wasn't expecting to meet you, Comrade General," said Klimovich. "I thought I'd be seeing Orlov again. We were in action together early in November...."

"Yes," said Serpilin, his smile suddenly fading. "General Orlov dreamed more about leading his division in an offensive than about going to Heaven; but he didn't live to see the day—so Serpilin is advancing now instead of Orlov. War plays such rotten tricks, and none of us is immune."

He sighed, not thinking of himself, but of Orlov. He really must find time in the next day or two to write to the widow in the evening and tell her that the division, following the tradition set by her husband and avenging his death, was advancing and pursuing the nazis.

Such were his thoughts; but aloud he asked Klimovich if he had been transferred to co-operate with his 31st Division.

Klimovich said that this was not so; he was still subordinate to Serpilin's neighbour on the left. He had come to visit the field hospital and have a look at the town.

"I've been in the war a long time now, but apart from Yelnia, I haven't seen a town recaptured from the Germans!"

"Yes," said Serpilin. "The first town! The first town—just

think of it!... The devil knows, you were lucky at Yelnia; but I'm taking my first town in the sixth month of the war! And even that with yours and God's help."

So saying, he looked at Klimovich and added, with a grin, that their Far Eastern neighbours probably had a bone to pick with them. They had delivered the main blow, but we were collecting the kudos. Anyway, what was the point of totting up the balance? Things didn't always work out just so in wartime!

Although this was magnanimously put, he couldn't hide a note of delighted self-satisfaction. Whatever the full picture might have been, his division had taken the town nevertheless.

"Perhaps we could have a friendly glass of tea? Or don't you tank people drink tea?"

But Klimovich declined. He was already worried about his brigade. True, the commissar and the Chief of Staff were there, all the necessary instructions had been given, and refuelling was now in progress before the night operation; but he was still not easy in his mind.

"No, thank you, Comrade General," he said. "I must go. But I have one request. Since you admit our part in the success, my rear assistant is staying behind—he wants to get hold of some captured war matériel, especially the transport.... In other words, pity a poor orphan!..." So saying, he nodded at the red-headed Ivanov who was standing at attention. Serpilin smiled at the incongruity of the remark and at the self-confident look of the rear assistant.

"Not much hope of refusing him.... What do you think?" he continued. "Were the Germans expecting our advance or not? It's clearer to you, since you caught up with the German rear units. Some of my prisoners indicate they weren't expecting it, and others say they'd heard of an imminent withdrawal. What's your opinion?"

Klimovich thought it over for a moment and said his own impression was that some German units had already been given instructions to fall back, but others had received no such order. This had resulted in much confusion....

"That's probably so," agreed Serpilin. "But I personally suspect that if we had put it off for a week and hadn't timed it right, we'd have been dealing with an organised retreat. I have a feeling we smelt the right moment!" he exclaimed delightedly, and he even sniffed at the air.

Although overjoyed at what had happened, both simultaneously thought of the same thing: in the last two days, the

German resistance had been partly broken; but how much was left for tomorrow they didn't know. As they took their leave of one another, they could read this disturbing thought in each other's eyes.

"I ran straight into his brigade when I broke out of encirclement," said Serpilin, after Klimovich had left, to Rtishchev, who had been quietly getting on with his work during the conversation.

Rtishchev nodded. In general, he worked hard and said little, as if to imply with his silence: "It's no concern of yours what sort of a person I am, or what I was like under the former divisional commander. You've heard me out on this subject once, and I'm not going to raise it again. As for the rest, judge for yourself. I'm here for you to see."

Although Serpilin was hardly gladdened by this attitude, it suited him well enough, and in any case he had no time to think about the matter.

He asked Rtishchev a few of the questions usually put by a divisional commander who has been out visiting his regiments at the front for half a day to a Chief of Staff who has been left behind at the command post: What news from our neighbours on the right and left? What's the situation as regards ammunition? Are the rear units keeping up alright? Has the Army command rung through?

To their left, in the neighbouring Army, things were going well, but their neighbour on the right was lagging behind: the consequent bulge threatened to become a breach. The Chief of Staff rang through the Army and inquired about the situation. Since he refrained from criticism and did not hold anyone else up as an example, it could be deduced that no one else in the Army was doing any better. Today, also, they could claim the greatest credit for the success.

On hearing all this news, Serpilin, without even bothering to take off his sheepskin jacket, sat down for a glass of tea.

"I like that!" came a sharp, mocking voice from the doorway. "Half Russia still to be taken back from the Germans, and the divisional commander has occupied one point on the map and decides to throw a tea-party."

Serpilin, who was sitting with his back to the door, turned round and rose to his feet a second after his Chief of Staff, who had already sprung to attention. It was the Army Commander on the threshold. In spite of the bitter cold, he was in full dress uniform—leather boots, greatcoat, and *papakha*. His face was ruddy from the cold and, it seemed to Serpilin, he had an ugly look.

"Report the situation!" said the Army Commander and, handing his greatcoat and *papakha* to the adjutant, he went up to the table.

Bending over the map with him, Serpilin reported the situation and marked in pencil the progress made by his two left-flank regiments. The pedantic Rtishchev, before receiving the written reports from the regimental commanders, had marked their progress with dotted lines only.

"What? You've advanced up to *there*?" asked the Army Commander incredulously, watching as Serpilin drew thick red lines over the dotted ones. He had a feeling that the divisional commander was allowing himself a little wishful thinking in his presence. "Have you advanced, or are you just assuming you've advanced?" he asked bluntly.

"We've advanced," said Serpilin.

"I can't believe it somehow," said the Army Commander.

"And I'm accustomed to believing the evidence of my own eyes!" said Serpilin firmly, aware of the full importance of this moment in his relations with the Commander. "I'm assuming," he added, looking down at the map again, "that we've already progressed as far as here, and here...." He drew two dotted lines. "And here—" he rested the pencil on the thick red lines, "I have been in person." He glanced at his watch and stated to the minute when he had been at each of the two points.

The Army Commander often—perhaps more often than was needful—spoke to his subordinates in the cold, sharp manner with which he had first addressed Serpilin. He was no respector of vanities, could touch people on the raw when he was annoyed with them, and allowed them no right to take offence, much less to contradict him if, stung by his manner, they were nevertheless in the wrong. But he had one saving grace that kept him on the right side of the mark between authoritativeness and wilfulness. He would tolerate a rebuff, if it was justified, and he had met with one just now.

"So," he said, speaking with as much asperity as ever. "The situation here is clear. How is it on the right, under Baglyuk?"

"I'm just going out to see him," said Serpilin; and he turned to Rtishchev. "Report on Baglyuk's progress."

"Will you offer me some tea?" asked the Army Commander, sitting down after he had heard what Rtishchev had tosay. "Then you won't be ashamed to sit here drinking tea on your own."

And he smiled faintly to indicate that he was joking.

"May I ask, Comrade Commander, how things are with the other divisions?" asked Serpilin when the Commander had swallowed his first mouthful of tea.

The Commander looked at him, frowning. Had things been going badly for Serpilin, he would have answered differently. But Serpilin was doing all right just now, and so the Commander's tone was friendly.

"So-so, Fyodor Fyodorovich. The situation leaves much to be desired. We're not accustomed to major offensives, and it tells. The ability of the commanders is not up to the fighting spirit of the troops. They're not used to advancing. They've lost the knack, they've forgotten how!" he repeated angrily. "Some have to be pushed—pushed so hard that one's arms ache."

He raised both arms up from the table and vividly demonstrated how he had to push those who were not moving fast enough. He had, in fact, spent the greater part of his time during the last two days doing just that—pushing everybody on. On and on—everybody, from divisional to batallion commanders! The Army was carrying out its task on the whole, but he was still concerned, since they could be doing even better. Whenever they forged ahead and came up against weak opposition, they would suddenly stop, fearing for their flanks. Whenever they found strong pockets of resistance, they attacked desperately and repeatedly, but did not dare risk pincers movements in depth, again fearing for their flanks.

Serpilin's division was moving faster than the others and the Army Commander was less worried about him than about the others. At first, he had intended to go straight to the neighbouring division, whose dilatoriness was creating a dangerous breach between itself and Serpilin. The Army Commander had ordered the divisional and regimental commanders not to worry about their flanks; but without realising it himself, he had been needlessly worrying about the Army's flanks, and he lacked the necessary experience to understand this fully. But however anxious he might have been to visit the neighbouring division, he was only human and hadn't been able to resist taking a quick look at the first town taken by his Army. He could have postponed calling on Serpilin until evening, but had called on him during the afternoon instead.

"I've pushed and I've pushed," he said, suddenly speaking his mind, and speaking it with the frankness of which only the most self-confident are capable. "Then I decided to have a look at your trophies to ease my mind! A decent haul, I might say, and something to write home about."

He finished his tea, stood up, and asked Serpilin:

"Baglyuk next?"

"Yes."

"Just one thing before I go, then. I'll push that neighbour of yours, Davydov, if I have to cover his back with bruises. But don't you use his slowness as a pretext! Give Baglyuk the job of forging ahead to this point here!" The Army Commander indicated a railway station on the map within twelve kilometres of their present position. "He's to be there by dusk, take it during the night, and proceed further! Move your command post up there by morning or, even better, take your whole HQ with you!"

With a brief glance at Rtishchev, the Commander nodded slightly, and the adjutant came up with his coat before he even had time to turn round.

The telephone jangled. Rtishchev picked up the receiver and said that Army HQ was on the line.

"Tell them I've gone to see Davydov. They can ring me there in an hour," said the Commander, and he hurried out, accompanied by Serpilin.

The cold hit him the minute he was out on the porch, and Serpilin couldn't resist observing that a sheepskin jacket was more reliable than a greatcoat.

"I'm not accustomed to anything else," said the Commander. "You needn't take that personally," he added with a glance at Serpilin's felt boots and sheepskins. "Get to that railway station in your felt boots and I'll be duly grateful. But if you mark time, even leather ones won't save your bacon." He grinned, thinking of one man whose leather boots certainly weren't going to save his bacon—the dandified Colonel Davydov, commander of the neighbouring division. And, repeating that Voskresenskoye station must be taken overnight, he left a minute before Serpilin.

"I'm afraid we'll all be footslogging it by nightfall, irrespective of rank," said Serpilin as he took his place beside the driver and looked at the snowflakes whirling through the air.

Baglyuk's regiment, which Serpilin was on his way to visit, was bypassing on the right the town that had been taken during the hours of darkness.

The regiment had grumbled about this and had envied its neighbours, but on the whole there had been no time for complaints or envy. During the first twenty-four hours, the regiment had liberated six villages and, since that morning, another five. But if the word "liberated" may have had some semblance of the truth yesterday, all the villages taken today had been burnt almost to ashes by the Germans. They had begun setting fire to them the previous evening, and all night, as the regiment advanced, several fires could be seen flickering ahead on the horizon.

During the first twenty-four hours, Ryabchenko's battalion had been advancing at the spearhead of the breakthrough; but since morning it had been stuck at the crossroads on the approaches to the little hamlet of Machekha, which the Germans were determined to hang on to at all costs. Forty men had been killed or wounded in the five hours' fighting it took the battalion to gain possession of the last few smouldering timbers—all that was left of the hamlet.

Ryabchenko, with one company, was now trying to catch up the leading battalions, and Malinin was closing up the gaps between the other companies, which were struggling down the snow swept road across the fields. Yet another village had been taken ahead of them, but had also been burnt down first, they had heard. The smoke of the fire hung over the snow as a reminder that they must get a move on.

"Smoke all round us," said Sintsov, drawing level with Karaulov.

His feet were sticking in the snow, the wind was blowing straight in his face, and he had to make an extra effort merely to overtake Karaulov.

"What?" asked Karaulov, who hadn't heard him.

"I said there's smoke all round us."

Karaulov nodded and wiped the snow off his eyebrows and moustache with his sleeve.

"I've been counting them up as I go," he said, without turning his head. "There were five lots of smoke in the morning, and now there's eight. They're burning more and more. Eight! And then there's the one we just took—what was its name?..."

"Machekha," said Sintsov.

"That's it, Machekha! That makes nine! There used to be a Machekha, and now isn't one any more. And there were people living there too.... I don't know what the nazis are up to. Are they determined to leave us without a roof over our heads? All right, so we'll sleep out in the snow and we'll catch them up just the same! And since they're such bastards, I'd issue an order to the Army: no prisoners to be taken as long as they're burning everything down. Anyone who sets a house on fire pays for it with a bullet through the head! What d'you think?"

Sintsov thought the same as Karaulov; and, indeed, Karaulov himself had dealt accordingly with some incendiaries they had caught in Machekha. But he believed in law and order, and wanted what he had already done, and intended to do in future, to be carried out under instructions, not in a fit of personal fury.

"Who got that German officer by the stables?" asked Karaulov.

"Komarov."

"I saw you and your section go behind the blaze, and then I couldn't hear anything but their submachine guns. Have they mowed you down, I thought? Then a grenade—and they weren't firing any more!"

"It was Komarov who lobbed the grenade," said Sintsov.

"Yes," said Karaulov. "But I thought they'd wiped your whole section out!"

Sintsov's section now consisted of only two men: himself and Komarov; but to Karaulov, a section was still a section, whatever its latest strength might be....

"Here's another dead'un," said Karaulov, and he stopped by the corpse of a German lying at the roadside and already half covered by the blizzard.

The German was lying on his back with both hands clutching his head and one leg drawn up under his body while the other, long and thin, projected straight out over the road.

Karaulov nudged the leg with the toe of his felt boot, but it only moved away and then swung back to its former position.

"The dead don't look the same in winter as in summer," said Karaulov. "Some of them look like dolls, not like human beings at all!"

He gave the dead man's leg another push, but it only moved back again. Then he stepped over it and carried on. As he looked back over his shoulder, Sintsov thought that the dead indeed look more horrible in summer. However strange it may seem to put it like this, they seem more alive and have more of the human being about them, and this can give a man the shudders, suddenly reminding him of himself and of the fact that these dead too were alive not long ago. But in the winter frosts they look as though they had never been alive in the first place.

Karaulov was in front again; Sintsov could see his broad back ahead and hear Komarov's laboured breathing behind. He had fallen ill on the eve of the advance. His chest had been sore and he had coughed continuously. He had probably caught a chill when they had dragged Leonidov back together. And now Komarov was marching along with a cold and without rest or sleep for the last forty-eight hours. But he never complained and only coughed painfully from time to time.

"And now Leonidov's in hospital in Podolsk, or maybe Moscow, or perhaps even further away than that, and he's in between sheets and under a blanket," thought Sintsov enviously of Leonidov, lying between sheets minus a foot.

He would like to have been wounded himself, only not as seriously as Leonidov, but like Bayukov, whom Malinin, true to his word, had finally managed to trace. Bayukov had written to thank them for telling him about his medal and had said that he was beginning to recover.... Sintsov wouldn't have minded recovering in between hospital sheets like Bayukov.

It cost him considerable effort to banish this thought from his mind, a thought which occurs to soldiers in wartime far more often than they would care to admit. What helped him wasn't the awareness that it was disgraceful and cowardly, but the recollection, which had suddenly stabbed him like a knife, of the four bodies taken down from the gallows by them in that same hamlet of Machekha just after they had captured it. Three of the victims had been men, and the fourth had been a woman.

Sintsov had cut through the four twisted strands of coloured German telephone wire on which they had hanged this woman, or rather girl, to judge by the young marble-white face.

He had severed the wire with his knife, taken the body in his arms, and laid it down on the snow. He would surely remember that moment for the rest of his life. The girl had been wearing a black, coarse wollen coat unbuttoned over the chest, and there was a knitted jacket visible underneath. One leg was shod in a worn felt boot, newly soled and roughly trimmed round the top; the other was clad only in a stocking with a big hole in the knee revealing the white, lifeless skin. The telephone wire had cut deep into her long white neck, her head was twisted to one side, and her expression seemed to be saying: "What d'you want of me? Why don't you leave me alone?"

The victims had been hanging there for some time and, when they were taken down, were so lifeless, icy, and marble-white, that it seemed that if they were put down carelessly or bumped against something, a piece of face or hand might easily come off. But now that these dead people, these partisans—as was written on the board nailed above their heads—had been left behind under the ground in a hastily dug grave, their lifelessness and marble coldness had already faded from memory. What one remembered was that they had once been alive, and Sintsov, recalling how he had taken the girl down from the gallows, thought of Masha with an emotion akin to horror. Once—probably because the hanged girl had been wearing one boot and a torn stocking—he suddenly recollected how he had carried the little doctor on his back and, remembering the doctor, he thought with horror of Masha again. This unbearable and terrifying recollection drove out of his head any thought of how nice it would be to be lying and recovering from some wound in a clean room between sheets and under blankets.

Where was she? And was she alive? Now, after all that he had gone through, he was struck by the absurdity of all he had said to her in their last moments together when, stammering with concern for her, he had asked her to be careful. Had those been their last moments together? He didn't know, like millions of people who had said good-bye to millions of others.

"Well?" His dismal train of thought was interrupted by Malinin, who was marching along the road with the battalion. He had chased up the rear and had moved up towards the head of the column. "How's the war going?"

"Not badly at all, Comrade Senior Political Instructor," said Sintsov, turning round to answer him. "Only one snag: we can't get there quick enough." He nodded at the smoke ahead of them.

Other columns of smoke, which had recently been climbing skywards all over the horizon, had already been shrouded by the blizzard; but this one, quite near, was still billowing blackly in front of them.

"Is it going to go on like this?" asked Sintsov after he and Malinin had walked together a little way without speaking.

"It depends on us," said Malinin.

He was no lover of platitudes, but what could he answer to such a question? Yes, it depended on them. Who else, after all? And, in the final analysis, that was how it was, although it seemed not to depend on Karaulov any more, or Sintsov, or the other soldiers marching along behind them, or Malinin or Ryabchenko, all of whom had in the last two days done everything of which they had been capable and who were continuing to push on ahead as fast as they possibly could.

"Still, I found two villagers here," said Malinin. "They tell me the Germans had a big shooting-match amongst themselves on the highway near the two abandoned tanks. Did you see them?"

"I did," said Sintsov.

"Their motorised column was retreating and the petrol ran out. So it came to a real shooting-match with their own tank crews! A shooting-match! Anyway they managed to drain the petrol out of the tanks into the transports and drive off. A nice business, eh?"

He was consulting Sintsov as a former political instructor: mightn't that be a useful item with which to boost the men's morale?

Sintsov remembered the two abandoned tanks near the road and vividly pictured in his mind's eye the German tanks and infantry fighting for petrol in the snow during the night....

"A nice business," he said, "only...."

"What?" demanded Malinin quickly.

"Only it would be better if we had a little more heavy transport ourselves!"

"It's feet that count in such a winter," said Malinin.

"That's true, it's feet that count!" said Sintsov, moving those same feet through the snow with an effort, as if each one weighed a ton.

Then he stopped talking. He was so tired that he had no wish to make conversation. But Malinin interpreted this in his own way: "He must be feeling it badly!"

On the very eve of the offensive, five Party cards had been delivered to the battalion and issued, but Sintsov had not been included. Malinin, who had not had the opportunity to discuss this with the divisional commissar and had thought of himself that all men are mortal, had, with enormous difficulty, snatched five minutes there and then on the night before the offensive and had written a short letter about Sintsov straight to the Army Political Directorate. With the bluntness and asperity of which he was capable when he considered himself in the right, he had written that the Divisional Party Commission had unwarrantedly blocked a decision by the Regimental Bureau and had not settled, even before the offensive, the question of the Party membership of a man who, any day and at any time, might lose his life without ever having lived to see his name cleared.

He didn't want to tell Sintsov prematurely about this letter, which had probably not yet reached its destination; but he felt a need to encourage him in some way.

"Don't think I've forgotten," said Malinin. "In fact, don't think about it so much. I'll do the thinking for you now."

Malinin spoke these clumsy words in all the sincerity of his heart; but Sintsov smiled in spite of himself. He trusted Malinin, but he couldn't help thinking about it. And in this, Malinin was powerless to help him. Sintsov had thought about it time and time again during the last two days, although just now, while walking beside Malinin, his mind had been on something else until Malinin had raised the subject.

"Of course, while we're on the march..." said Malinin, not finishing a sentence of which the end was already a foregone conclusion. "But as soon as we stop, we'll sort out this business of your Party card at once."

"Alexei Denisovich!" said Sintsov, raising his head and looking sadly and bitterly at the smoke ahead. "I'm agreeable to anything just as long as we don't stop for long!"

"Even a lorry can't keep going without a break, so save your breath," said Malinin gloomily. "Or d'you think we'll get to Berlin without stopping?"

"If we make it to Vyazma at least," said Sintsov.

Malinin grunted vaguely, neither encouraging nor denying. Vyazma, of course, was not such a long way off, but they would hardly get as far as Vyazma without a break and replacements.

"Mind your backs!" shouted Komarov behind them.

A sleigh drove past. Malinin stepped back onto the road and, under the impression that Sintsov was still beside him, said that it was the new divisional commander. He had seen him once at Regimental HQ before the advance.

But Sintsov was not walking beside Malinin; he was standing at the side of the road where he had stopped to give way, knee-deep in snow and looking at the departing sleigh in which, sitting beside Baglyuk—no, he couldn't have mistaken him!—Serpilin in person had just swept past.

"Why have you dropped back?" shouted Malinin; and Sintsov, heaving his legs out of the snowdrift, struggled onto the firm road surface, caught up with Malinin, and carried on beside him.

"D'you know who just drove past?" said Sintsov after a pause.

"Yes. That was the new divisional commander," said Malinin.

"What's his name?"

Malinin frowned, trying to remember. The divisional commander's name was on the tip of his tongue. He had jotted it down in an exercise book, and the exercise book was in his bag; but he didn't want to take off his mitten in this cold.

"I recognised it when I heard it—it seemed damned familiar somehow, but I've forgotten it."

"Serpilin," said Sintsov.

"Yes," confirmed Malinin, and he looked intently at Sintsov. Now that Sintsov had come out with the name himself, he remembered why it had seemed so familiar.

"The same one?" he asked.

"The same one."

"For goodness sake! I feel like running after that sleigh!" said Malinin, overjoyed for Sintsov's sake. He realised that the presence in the division—as its CO, what was more—of the very man under whose command Sintsov had broken out of encirclement, could very much simplify the progress of his Party case.

"No, I won't run after it!" thought Sintsov, in complete contradiction to the thoughts which had occurred to him every time he had imagined meeting Serpilin, even though the possibility had seemed beyond his wildest dreams. Without realising it, he had gradually and imperceptibly become used to the difficult but proud conclusion that everything affecting his future must be decided properly, even without such an encounter, not because a witness to his past had been found, but because there were people who knew how he was fighting now: Malinin, and the battalion commander, and Karaulov, and Komarov, who was coughing away behind him at that very moment....

There had been a time when he had hoped for a miracle. The encounter with Lyusin had seemed just that, but it had subsequently turned out to be a smack in the face. Even then he had still dreamed of a miracle and of how everything would suddenly be cleared up; and at such moments he had usually thought of Serpilin.

But he now wanted everything to take its course and continue that way. When they decided on his case, they should not be believing General Serpilin, who had known

Political Instructor Sintsov when he was carrying a Party card in his tunic pocket; they should be believing—implicitly and without reservation—former Red Armyman and now Senior Sergeant Sintsov who, with many thousands of others like himself, had not surrendered Moscow to the Germans and was now driving them back again.

He felt he deserved this, and even another hold-up or refusal could no longer shake his sense of personal strength and rightness. Yes, he had mentioned Serpilin's name in his statement. If they noticed this and showed it to Serpilin, and if Serpilin found it necessary to send for him—well and good; he would be glad.

But he wasn't going to run after that sleigh!

"Alright, then," said Malinin without the slightest notion of what was going on in Sintsov's mind. "As soon as we get a breather, we'll arrange a personal interview. So don't get into a state about it."

Sintsov wanted to tell Malinin frankly what he was thinking. After all, Malinin was entitled to know. But simply to say that he had no desire for a personal interview would only have astonished Malinin, and he didn't feel up to explaining it all in detail just now: the snow was falling so thickly, the wind was blowing so hard, it was so difficult and so cold fighting it, and with each step it was becoming more difficult than ever.

CHAPTER NINETEEN

By night, Ryabchenko's battalion, pressing steadily onwards, took three villages. Two of them had been burned to the ground and one was only three-quarters destroyed. As they approached, it was still intact. Then, as the opening shots were exchanged, the first few houses burst into flames and within an hour half the village was ablaze.

This spectacle goaded the men, in spite of the savage German defensive fire, to burst into the village and prevent it from being completely razed to the ground. It was all happening right in front of their eyes and nearly drove them crazy. While some of the Germans machine-gunned them through slits cut in the walls, others ran about setting fire to the houses. Their figures could be glimpsed sprinting from building to building in the light of the flames. This maddened the men so much that when they finally burst into the village they still had enough strength to tear apart the burning timbers and put out the flames in the houses which had just caught fire.

But after this they were overwhelmed with such indescribable exhaustion that even without Ryabchenko's order to fall out and have a rest, they wouldn't have been in a state to march another step.

After posting the look-outs, Ryabchenko ordered the company commanders to brew tea wherever they could, feed the men and, above all, get them to lie down and go to sleep as soon as possible. But many were so done in that, as soon as they had crowded into the surviving houses, they collapsed as if shot and hadn't even the energy to eat before going to sleep.

Ryabchenko was afraid that Baglyuk might turn up in the middle of the night and send the battalion further on the advance. He prayed for this not to happen, anxious that his men should snatch as much sleep as possible.

To the left, on the horizon, a red glow over Voskresenskoye station could be seen through the blizzard. At two o'clock in the morning, Baglyuk drove up in his sleigh with the divisional commander and ordered Malinin and Ryabchenko to rouse the men at once.

Baglyuk's two other battalions had unsuccessfully been trying to take the station for over three hours. The Germans were putting up a desperate fight and were burning the station before their eyes, exactly as they had burned the village here.

Ryabchenko was told to get his battalion up and, with a last effort—which meant a seven-kilometre forced march—to cut off the road along which the Germans were withdrawing their rear units from the station. If he cut off the road, or at least reached it, the Germans would give up the station and begin pulling out.

That was how Baglyuk put the assignment. But the divisional commander asked how much time Ryabchenko and Malinin needed to get the men on their feet.

Ryabchenko had the honesty to say: "Half an hour." He expected to be shouted at for this, but preferred to risk that rather than falsify the situation. He simply couldn't wake the men and form them up in less than half an hour after all the marching they had done in the last two days.

Baglyuk seemed about to explode. But the divisional commander forestalled him and, glancing at his watch, said calmly:

"Very well, but make sure that your half an hour really is only half an hour!"

Ryabchenko and Malinin saluted and set about their difficult task. Only something exceptional can get men onto their feet when they are in such a state: an avalanche, a flood, a fire, and, of course, war, when a single day's fighting can cover all these words which sound so ominous in peacetime.

Half an hour later, Ryabchenko's battalion, which numbered only just over seventy men towards the end of forty-eight hours' advancing, formed up in two ragged ranks.

The fire in the distance was glowing more redly than before.

Ryabchenko gave the command "Attention!", and Serpilin went up to address the battalion.

He told them briefly what Baglyuk had told the commander and the commissar, and said that two things now depended on them: first, that something should be left of the station other than smoke and ashes, and that the people there—women and children—should have some sort of shelter tomorrow; and, secondly, that their comrades should not have sacrificed their lives in vain for the station over there. They had been attacking for four hours now, and they still hadn't managed to take it; but the Germans would run for it as soon as the battalion showed up in their rear and cut off the road.

As divisional commander, he knew that they had fully carried out their morning assignment and had done everything that they possibly could today, but he must still ask them to go and cut off the fascists' line of retreat.

"This is my request. And it's a big one," he said in conclusion; and although he spoke almost exactly as if he were giving an order, and although he could simply have said: "that is an order", he used the word "request", and this word stirred something in most, if not all, of those tired hearts, although a word is still only a word, and it meant that they had to leave their warm and bloodily earned night's rest, push on again through the blizzard, and engage the Germans in battle over there.

"Comrade General, the battalion will fulfil the task you have given it! We shall carry it out and report before dawn," said Ryabchenko, as if trying to compensate with his jauntiness and ringing voice for the glum silence in which the men of his battalion were standing.

He gave the command, and the column moved off.

Serpilin stood watching his troops march past, and his face, as tired as theirs, showed gratitude and an understanding of the full measure of what they were doing. He would have done the same in their place, but this did not prevent him from appreciating their self-sacrifice. Does the right to give orders exclude the need to feel gratitude towards men whose duty leaves them no alternative but to carry out your orders to the letter? And, as you carry out other orders, however exacting, do you not sometimes hope for gratitude, even if only in the eyes that are watching you?

When nearly all the column had marched past Serpilin, he remembered that one very tall soldier had caught his eye when the men were only just falling in: the soldier had looked vaguely familiar.... As he watched the tail-end of the column go by, he remembered this, then forgot it immediately as soon as Baglyuk asked him whether it would be enough to leave one platoon behind on guard.

"Who is there to guard?" said Serpilin with a sharp look. "Me or you? If you, then take this platoon with you, because you're going with the battalion commander, and don't come back until you've sent me a report that you've cut off the road! But if you mean me, I'm going back to the station immediately and I shall stay there with your battalions until we've taken it."

"But aren't you going to move the divisional command post here?" asked Baglyuk, indicating the village and showing no reaction at the idea of being sent off with the battalion.

"I'll set it up by morning. But as soon as the supply company arrives, I'll send it straight in to attack the station. Leave three of your men here till morning so that the village won't be left empty. But send all the rest ahead! I don't want to see a single extra man here in five minutes' time!"

Baglyuk left three men, his sleigh, and his submachine gunner and, his boots furrowing the snow, went off after the battalion.

Serpilin took a last glance at the receding troops and, before driving back to the station, went into the nearest house.

Some victims of the fire—women and children—were warming themselves inside. Serpilin greeted them, shut the door behind him, took his hat off on the threshold, and wearily passed his hand over the head. He felt an irresistible urge to find himself a corner there, and then in the cosy human warmth of that house to lie down, and go straight to sleep.

An elderly woman, her head bent low, was scraping the table with a knife.

"What's that you're doing?" asked Serpilin.

"Cleaning up after the Germans," she said, without looking up and carrying on with her work. "They're not human—they used to sleep on the table!" Then she straightened up, looked at Serpilin, and told him that the Germans had killed her youngest son the day before. He had wanted to drive the cow into the woods. They had chased after him and shot him. She told the whole story in a rush and seemed to be thinking that as soon as she had finished, Serpilin would put matters right there and then.

"Were many people from your village killed? Were many murdered and tortured?" asked Serpilin, controlling his feelings with an effort.

Interrupting one another in their eagerness, the women began telling him who had been killed and how while the nazis had been in occupation. Serpilin, stooping in the doorway, listened to them and was filled with fresh hatred, although it might have seemed that there was nothing to add to the hatred he already felt for the Germans.

"Comrade General!" It was one of the submachine gunners left behind by Baglyuk: he had just opened the door behind Serpilin. "They've found two Germans in a cellar. They were hiding. What shall we do with them?"

"Till we meet again, good-bye," said Serpilin, bowing to the women. "When we bring up our food supplies, we'll distribute some to the fire victims for children." He put on his hat and went out after the submachine gunner. "Where are they?"

But, even as he spoke, he saw the Germans standing between the two soldiers who had caught them. They were wearing ankle-boots, greatcoats, and forage caps with the flaps pulled down over their ears, and were trembling with cold.

"Aus welchen Division?" demanded Serpilin.

One of the Germans replied that he was from the 114th.

"Und Sie?"

The second said that he was also from the 114th.

"Was machen Sie hier?"

The Germans said nothing, but one of other captors, who had understood the question perfectly, answered for them:

"The way I see it, Comrade General, they're firebugs from the Feuerkommando. They didn't get away in time and hid in the cellar!"

"Zeigen Sie ihre Hände!" said Serpilin grimly.

One of the Germans stepped back, not understanding what was wanted of him. The other stood stock still.

"Show me your hands," repeated Serpilin in German, taking a pace forward.

The German, frightened, held out his hands for Serpilin.

The Russian beside him wanted to push him back. What was he shoving his hands in the General's face for? But Serpilin stopped him.

"Und du?" And Serpilin bent down from his full height to sniff at the hands of the second German.

The hands of both smelt of petrol. Both were silent. One was trembling slightly, the other was petrified with despair at the prospect of inevitable death.

"Shoot the bastards!" said Serpilin to the soldiers and, turning round, he went to his sleigh.

On the road he saw the shapes of men trudging against the wind, shielding their faces with their hands. One of them put on speed and ran up to Serpilin; another followed immediately behind him. They were the division's chief of signals and the commander of the Supply Company.

"So you've arrived at last," said Serpilin to the chief of signals with annoyance. "Better late than never! Lay on communications to this point! Tomorrow, judging by the situation, there'll be a command post here by midday at the latest! as soon as you've made contact, tell Rtishchev that I'll be outside Voskresenskoye until we've taken it. What about Rtishchev—is he on the way?"

"No, Comrade General," stammered the chief of signals.

Headquarters is on the way, but Colonel Rtishchev was blown up by a mine."

"Wounded?" asked Serpilin quickly. "Has he been taken to hospital?"

"He was killed on the spot, Comrade General."

"Hell and demnation!" Serpilin angrily thumped his frozen sheepskin jacket. However much he had tried to drive the thought from his mind, he had suspected ever since their very first meeting that Rtishchev with his sad eyes was not long for this world and was going to be killed. He had read it in the man's eyes, and now it had happened! So he had been killed after all! He had only outlived his divisional commander by a week.

He felt sorry about Rtishchev and was upset at the accuracy of his own prediction But all he said was:

"Who's taken over from him? Shishkin?"

"Yes."

"Then tell him everything I told you. As for you, Rybakov," said Serpilin, turning to the commander of the Supply Company, "make for Voskresenskoye! Are the men frozen?"

"Very much so, Comrade General!"

The men of the Supply Company were already coming up and crowding together behind Rybakov. These were Serpilin's reserves and they had not yet been in action during the last two days.

"Fifteen minutes to get warm, then proceed to Voskresenskoye!"

"Which way?" asked the Supply Company commander who thought they had already arrived at their destination.

"Which way? That way, where the fire is and there's a battle on."

"What road should we take?" asked the company commander still upset and not yet in full possession of himself.

"There isn't any road. You can see the fire over there—that's your bearing! Head for it! And be quick about it. I'll be waiting for you there," said Serpilin. As he went to his sleigh, he heard a rifle shot quite close, and then another.... It was the Germans from the Feuerkommando being executed.

"Must write ... and not just to Orlov's widow now, but Rtishchev's too.... These things all happen so quickly..." thought Serpilin bitterly and, getting into his sleigh with another glance at the glow in the sky, he thought with anxiety of Baglyuk: "Get there quickly or we'll never take Voskresenskoye."

No matter how much they tried, they were still unable to capture Voskresenskoye station. Each time our infantry got up and went into the attack, the Germans forced them to go down in the snow with mortar and machine-gun fire and went on burning house after house. They went about it so callously that, as you looked on, you felt like tearing your hair with frustration.

Serpilin returned just when the latest attack had failed and the men had lain down in the snow immediately before the station. If they'd just had a few guns available, even those few scattered lines of infantry might have been able to break through into the station after knocking out the machine-gun posts. But there was no artillery: it was snow-bound somewhere behind in the blizzard and was not making its presence known for the time being. The divisional commissar, who had stayed on while Serpilin was away with Baglyuk, couldn't stand it any longer and said that he would himself go and drag at least one battery back with him by the scruff of its neck! He couldn't bear to watch men being killed in attack after attack, with the station burning away before their eyes.

Serpilin didn't argue with him. If they could only bring up the guns indeed! It was a matter of life and death.

The commissar mounted a horse and disappeared into the snowstorm. Serpilin ordered the attacks to be called off. There was no telling which would happen first: whether the artillery would be brought up, or whether Baglyuk would turn up behind the station. Until then, it couldn't be taken.

The cold was getting worse, but Serpilin was unaware of it. His temporary command post was in a stone railway hut on the tracks within half a kilometre of the station. But he stayed outside all the time, only taking cover behind the wall from the German mortar bombs which kept coming that way and falling short of their target. Bitter, tense, powerless to take his eyes off the spectacle of Voskresenskoye in flames, he kept thinking about Baglyuk. Within the hour, even in this weather, he should come out onto the main road behind the Germans provided nothing stopped him. But what could stop him? Two or three well-placed machine-guns covering the road! It would take an hour or two of messing about before they could be outflanked and destroyed! Even if Baglyuk showed up in time, it would still mean waiting for another hour and staring helplessly at those fires!

The supply troops were late for some reason, and it was them that Serpilin wanted to throw into the attack as soon as Baglyuk made his presence known in the rear of the Germans. He had given Rybakov fifteen minutes' rest. According to his watch, it was time the company was here. He was so impatient that he even sent a man out to meet Rybakov and make him get a move on.

Maximov found Serpilin in this edgy and ugly frame of mind behind the wall of the railway hut. Sent by Army HQ, he had abandoned his car five kilometres away and had finished the journey on foot. He was covered in snow, and Serpilin failed to recognise him at first. Someone else was visible behind him.

"Well, Fyodor Fyodorovich, how's the war going?" asked Maximov gaily, wiping his face and brushing the snow off his hat. "What d'you think, will you take Voskresenskoye soon? The Army Commander's ordered me to chase you up. He says the calendar date's past!"

"Calendars are always wrong!"* snarled Serpilin.

Their moods were very different Maximov, who had left the Army command post three hours previously, knew that by nightfall the German resistance had begun to crack almost everywhere. Serpilin's neighbours had surged forward, had drawn level with him, and were even outstripping him. Although the Army Commander, as he saw Maximov off, had said that there had been no report from Serpilin for some time ("Have a look—I'm afraid he's got stuck outside Voskresenskoye."), Maximov, in the general flush of success, had assumed that the station would be taken while he was still on the way.

Even now, when he discovered that he had been wrong and Voskresenskoye had not been taken and was in flames, he still imagined that the rest would be plain sailing. One more attack, the station would be ours, and he would merely have to report that the 31st Division, which had begun the advance so well, was still tops.

Serpilin, however, did not know how his neighbours were faring. It would have delighted him if he had, but it wouldn't have made his own position any easier. All he knew was that he had so far failed to carry out his orders, was bogged down outside this damned Voskresenskoye, had tried to outflank it from both sides, had failed, had incurred heavy casualties by sending the men into frontal attacks, and had not thrown the battalion soon enough into the deep outflanking manoeuvre that the situation demanded.

He now had to keep control of himself and wait for Baglyuk, or the guns, or, best of all, both.

Although Serpilin had spent the whole day chasing up Baglyuk and the other regimental commanders, he was in no mood for someone to come and chase him up in his turn. And he didn't hide it, furious with himself and with Maximov for his foolish "Well, will it be soon?"

"Taking built-up areas isn't like boiling eggs, Comrade Chief of the Army Political Directorate," he said to Maximov, "three minutes soft, five minutes hard! If it was

* The phrase is a quotation from a famous play by Griboyedov, *Wit Works Woe.—Ed.*

just ourselves firing, it could be calculated down to the last minute ... but the Germans, blast them, are firing back!"

As if to illustrate his point, a German company mortar bomb crumped ahead of them a hundred metres away from the railway hut.

"Why don't you attack? What are you waiting for?" insisted Maximov, not because Serpilin's reply had rattled him, but because he was dying to see Voskresenskoye taken now that he had arrived, and was ready to do anything, even if it meant getting the men on their feet and leading them into the attack himself!

"I'm outflanking with one battalion," said Serpilin. "But the men are tired, there's a blizzard raging, and they're driving themselves to the absolute limit. I'm waiting for them to come out on the road in the rear of the Germans."

"Where's Permyakov?" asked Maximov, meaning the divisional commissar. "Is he with the other regiments?"

"No, he's here. We're all here..." said Serpilin. "We must take this frigging Voskresenskoye. It's the whole crux of the matter. As soon as we've taken it, it'll be a complete walkover for the other regiments! The commissar's gone to fetch the artillery—our guns have got lost in the blizzard somewhere. If he succeeds, I'll be glad to go down on my bended knees and kiss his feet, I swear it—just so long as they bring me the guns!"

"So you've been hitting it off together?" asked Maximov.

"Each is doing what he can," replied Serpilin and, pointing angrily at the burning station, he added: "Only bastards couldn't hit it off in such conditions; but thank goodness he and I aren't bastards! When the commanders don't get on, men are killed!"

"The railway school's on fire!" unhappily exclaimed the man who had arrived with Maximov. He had been keeping his distance, but had now come forward and, shading his eyes with his hand, was gazing at the fire.

"You be a bit more careful about poking your head out from behind that hut! A mortar bomb could land any moment!" shouted Serpilin.

At first, he thought that Maximov had brought some instructor from the Political Department with him; but he now recognised this incautious man as the secretary of the local District Party Committee. They had met briefly that morning in the newly captured town. The station belonged to his district too, and Serpilin now remembered the secretary asking him when he expected to take Voskresenskoye. This had been in the morning. "Surely it was never today?" thought Serpilin. "Only today? No, it must have been ages ago! So much has happened since then!"

"I didn't recognise you at first," he said. "That's a good sign. Means you'll make a fortune."

"Some hope..." replied the secretary dismally as he watched the fire, and, unable to stand it any longer, he went out into the open to get a better view of a column of flame that had only just shot into the air. "They've set fire to the warehouses at the goods station—Numbers Two and Four!" he shouted miserably.

"He insisted on coming with me," said Maximov. "He thought that by now...." He didn't finish what he was going to say but asked Serpilin quietly, almost in a whisper: "Fyodor Fyodorovich, when d'you think you'll take the station?"

Serpilin glanced at his watch.

"I'm waiting for Baglyuk. He's bound to come out on the main road in half an hour ... bound to," he repeated.

"Well, Baglyuk'll do anything he humanly can, he's that sort," said Maximov.

"Who knows who can do how much?" said Serpilin. "Maybe he will,or maybe someone else in his place might do more and do it sooner! I've been doing my level best today too—or so I thought. Maybe someone else in my place would have already taken that place over there!"

"Never mind, Fyodor Fyodorovich, you'll take it," said Maximov, sensing that this was the right thing to say. "Davydov couldn't make any headway at all this morning, but three hours ago he reported taking Yekaterinovka."

"Really?" said Serpilin. "Good for him!"

"And the Twenty-Third and the Ninety-Second have also pushed ahead...." Maximov named the points to which these divisions had advanced.

"Yes..." said Serpilin, "that's good.... Very good," he added, still unable to tear himself away for a second from the station, which he had yet to take himself.

"They've set fire to the other warehouses," said the district Party secretary, still shading his eyes with his hand. "It'll be the elevator next—it's beside the fire."

"What are you croaking about?" exploded Serpilin. "What are you driving me up the wall for? D'you think I didn't hope to hand your station over to you in one piece?" The full force of his pent-up misery finally showed in his voice.

"It's burning in front of our eyes!" replied the secretary.

"Yes, it's burning in front of our eyes," repeated Serpilin bitterly. "I have eyes too, you know...."

At that moment, Rybakov, commander of the Supply Company, appeared out of the blizzard, the shapes of his men stringing along behind him.

"Comrade General, permission to report...."

"You should have reported half an hour ago," snapped Serpilin.

"The men are terribly tired, Comrade General."

"I know."

Rybakov stood in front of him, knowing that he was to blame. He had failed to carry out an order and had given the men a forty-five minutes' break instead of fifteen; but they had been so tired that even their rest had done them no good and they had not made up for lost time on the way. But Rybakov also knew that he couldn't have done otherwise; he had wanted to act for the best, not the worst. Moreover, he knew that however much the divisional commander might curse him, in twenty or thirty minutes' time he would have to go into the attack with his Supply Company because, however much they might curse him, they would not let him off the attack. Faced with this prospect, Rybakov couldn't feel as guilty as he might have done under other circumstances.

But Serpilin was aware of this too, and, swallowing an outburst provoked by nervousness rather than by anger, he quickly told Rybakov to get his men together and concentrate them for an attack over there. He pointed ahead to the roof of a barn protruding out of the deep snow, where the battalion command post was.

And Rybakov, giving the divisional commander the unintimidated and almost indifferent stare of a man whom no order could compel to do more than he intended to do of his own free will or than his conscience prompted, said "Right!" and went to his men, who were coming up out of the snowstorm in ever-increasing numbers.

"Listen, Fyodor Fyodorovich! Perhaps we could lead it into the attack?" Maximov nodded at the company as it passed by in the blizzard. "Let's go with it...."

"Hold it, Maximov, don't be so impatient... I've been impatient all day, but now ... I'm not in a hurry, even with you breathing down my neck." He nodded towards the district Party secretary. "We're dealing with men here, not logs of wood.... I certainly don't want to throw them into the fire for nothing.... Let's have patience. I know it's difficult, but we must. Baglyuk should show up any moment; I can feel it in my bones... He knows how much the time factor counts just as well as we do. I'm glad you've come, but do me a favour and don't rush me."

"Perhaps we could at least go up to the battalion for the time being until the attack starts?" said Maximov.

"What d'you think this is, then? The rear of the Army? We're only five hundred metres from the Germans.... D'you want to be two hundred nearer?"

"Yes."

"Off you go then ... but I'll stay. I've got two battalions here, and I must be able to handle both...."

Maximov thought that Serpilin would either go with him or would not let him go on his own. But if Serpilin didn't like being held back, he didn't like holding others back either. If Maximov wanted to go to the battalion, let him. If he urgently wanted to join in the battle, let him. A good man, and a brave one. It would be an excellent thing if he went to the battalion—he could talk to the men before the attack! If Serpilin could have divided himself into several parts, he would simultaneously have stayed where he was and gone out to both his battalions.

"Off you go," said Serpilin, "only don't overdo it out there in front," he added, not because the remark had any particular meaning, but simply because he had momentarily remembered the dead Rtishchev, although Rtishchev had been killed ten kilometres away in the rear and on terrain over which Maximov had driven and walked unscathed.

"Are you going to stay here?" Maximov asked the district Party secretary.

"I'll go with you," said the secretary, and he adjusted the rifle on his shoulder. For the first time, Serpilin noticed that he was armed.

"Where is it? At that barn?" asked Maximov.

"You'll be escorted," said Serpilin, and he called for a runner.

"You know what?" said Maximov, as they waited while the runner was being sent for. "Your old commissar, Shmakov, came to Army HQ yesterday. He sends you his greetings."

"Really? Well I'll be damned!... Shmakov!... How come?..." exclaimed Serpilin, quite forgetting how furious he had been with Shmakov while in hospital. "Where from? What's he doing now?"

"He says he was a regimental commissar, but a month ago he was slightly wounded, and after he recovered he was recalled to the Army Political Directorate to join a team of lecturers."

"A lecturer again.... Well, that means water's found its own level and all's going to be well with the Army..." said Serpilin, half in jest and half in earnest.

He wanted to ask Maximov whether Shmakov would be with the Army for long and why he had merely sent his greetings without coming straight to the division. But it was already too late for more questions. The runner arrived, and Serpilin told him to take Maximov to the battalion commander.

Maximov left. Exactly a minute later, the divisional commissar was standing in front of Serpilin, gasping for breath and streaming with perspiration. He was wiping his face clean of the sweat and of the snow stuck to the lock of hair protruding from under his hat, and was asking something in such a hoarse voice that Serpilin failed to understand him at first.

"How are things with you here?" the commissar was saying.

"The same for the time being.... Except that Rybakov's arrived. How about you?" asked Serpilin.

But it was obvious from the commissar's happy face how things were with him. He had brought the guns and, judging by his appearance, had dragged them up in the literal sense of the word. He had evidently been helping the men to haul them out of the snow.

"Three, not four," he said. "The gunners are getting them into position already, over there to the left." He pointed with his hand. "They say they're going to open fire in ten minutes.... Pity we haven't got four, but one went down into a gully, and we just couldn't get it up again.... Knocked ourselves out trying...."

"To hell with it, we'll get it out later. Thanks for those three anyway," said Serpilin, and he embraced the elderly, tired commissar.

War is certainly a strange business! He had only just been thinking about Shmakov, to whom he was bound by so many ties that they might be expected to remember each other for the rest of their lives! And yet Shmakov, although he was with the Army, was a thousand miles away to all intents and purposes; yet Serpilin and this man who was standing before him and whom he had known for only five days in all, already had so many divisional concerns and worries in common that they both thought themselves the two closest people on the face of the earth.

Suddenly, from a long way away, from beyond the station, from behind the glow of the fire, came what Serpilin had been waiting for—the sounds of battle, distant, faint, but none the less audible.

"Baglyuk!" was all Serpilin said, and he sighed as if an enormous mountain had suddenly fallen from his shoulders.

Malinin was lying on the earth floor of a barrack hut. The heap of frozen straw underneath him was just beginning to thaw out. There were several other wounded men lying or sitting near him.

A log was smoking and hissing in the stove. None of the others happened to have an axe, and they had been forced to take a whole beam as it was and push one end into the stove, shoving it in further from time to time.

Malinin was lying and concentrating on what was happening inside him—the knife-sharp stabs of pain in his bullet-wounded stomach—and on the battle raging outside the hut. The fighting was waxing and waning by turns, gradually moving towards the right into the German rear. By all indications, the station had already been captured and the Germans, though snapping back viciously, were steadily retreating. That they should be retreating was due to the battalion under Ryabchenko and Malinin. It had finally come out on the main road by this abandoned, snow-bound barn and had struck at the German units pulling out of Voskresenskoye. It had then straddled the road and was not letting any more Germans through.

But Malinin was no longer taking an active part in all this. He had been wounded at the very start of the battle during the attack on the German column. The Germans had returned fire and Malinin had received a bullet-wound in the stomach. He had always secretly feared this. He believed that a stomach wound meant certain death. He had expected to die as soon as he was hit, and when Karaulov had dashed up to him shouting: "Let me bandage you up!" Malinin, hoarse with despair, had said: "Don't bother, I'm as good as dead!"

Later, however, he had been attended to by Kulikova, the old medical orderly who had once promised to carry him off the battlefield. When she had began dragging him through the snow, he had said: "Wait, I'll get on my feet." He had, indeed, half risen and then stood up, and had thought: "Well, I'm on my feet, so I must be alive!" True, he had only taken three steps and then he had been caught by Kulikova and a soldier who happened to be nearby; but after those miraculous three steps he no longer believed that he was going to die.

He was able to suffer in silence because he didn't believe he was going to die, and also because he was battalion commissar and his wounded men were lying round him. It also helped that he hadn't immediately become indifferent to everything happening round him after his wound, as is often the case with weaker men. He continued taking a keen interest in what was occurring on the other side of the wall, listening to the battle and, in a voice interrupted by bouts of pain, giving his own interpretation of events outside to the other wounded men.

Serpilin's calculations had proved correct. As soon as Ryabchenko's battalion reached the road in the rear of the Germans, they began hastily falling back from the station. But the battalion exceeded its orders. It positioned itself on the road and beat off attacks by the retreating Germans until they were compelled to abandon their transport and go across open ground. Baglyuk appraised the situation and, leaving Ryabchenko with half the men on the road, also went across open ground to the left and, seizing a nameless hamlet of three houses in the snowy fields, occupied them and from there kept up a machine-gun fire which forced the Germans to veer away from their line of retreat and go further out into the fields and the snow. But more than that he was unable to do.

The medical assistant and Kulikova attended to the wounded, and all of them, including the walking cases, were accommodated in the barn, because Ryabchenko was afraid of sending them to the rear just now, at night-time. The walking cases might lose their way in the blizzard, and there was no transport for those like Malinin who had to be carried. They couldn't expect any form of conveyance before morning, but it would soon be dawn. In any case, who knew which way the Germans might blunder as they retreated? The wounded might easily run into them on their way to the rear. One's blood ran cold at the mere thought.

The battle on the road had died down half an hour ago. The right, where Baglyuk had taken the hamlet, was firing to be heard from time to time. There were sporadic shots in front, probably at isolated Germans, or perhaps just because of the blizzard, in which the eyes can play strange tricks.

Although the stove was burning in the barn, it was cold: the doors had been wrenched off their hinges, and the wind, blowing aside the ground-sheet suspended across the doorway, had already swept a mound of snow onto the threshold.

Kulikova had shoved a bucket of snow into the stove to melt it and was taking water round to the wounded in a mess-tin. The water was warm and dirty, with bits of straw floating about in it.

Malinin wanted a drink, but this was out of the question with a stomach wound.

"Listen, Kulikova," he said, beckoning her over. "If you can find the time, go out and take a look for me. If Senior Sergeant Sintsov is nearby and can leave his post, I'd like him to come and see me while things are quiet."

"All right," said Kulikova, none too pleased. "But you should get some sleep. Haven't you had enough of talking to the men?... You can talk your head off in hospital when you're convalescent.... But for the time being, you'd do better to keep quiet."

The wind howled in the doorway. Kulikova went out. Malinin watched her go, closed his eyes, and thought that if they went on losing as many as today, they would need replacements very soon, otherwise they wouldn't get much more fighting done.

"What is this?" he thought. "All those people who won't live to see.... What sort of a damned life is it, when people are dying every day and you can't even keep count?" And, of course, war was indeed a damned life, although he had volunteered for it of his own free will, convinced that there was no alternative.

He thought of his son who had lost his right arm and was in hospital. Then, his eyes still closed, he heard someone gently calling his name: "Alexei Denisovich..."—calling him softly, as if to ascertain whether he was asleep or not. He opened his eyes, thinking that it was Sintsov. But it was battalion commander Ryabchenko. He didn't look himself at all. His young face was covered with a thick red stubble and exhaustion had temporarily aged him. He was standing over Malinin in his cavalry greatcoat, torn and blackened since that afternoon when he had helped the men to extinguish the fires. His left hand, the one wounded before the advance, was swathed in a grimy bandage, and his right hand was resting heavily for support on a broken spade handle. The toes of his right foot were so badly frostbitten that he could only walk on the heel.

Malinin looked at the man standing over him, Senior Lieutenant Ryabchenko, his battalion commander, who had seen everything, had retreated as far as Moscow, and was now in his second day of advance from the city: three times wounded, only once put out of action, frostbitten, and so young that Malinin might have been his father.

"Well, what's brought you here, Battalion Commander?" he asked, unaware that owing to weakness and pain he was scarcely audible which was why Ryabchenko was bending down so low. "What's brought you here?" he repeated.

"I've come to visit the wounded."

"How's the battle going?"

"Normally." Ryabchenko glanced at Malinin, then looked round over the other wounded and, in spite of his exhaustion, smiled his youthful smile. "Just a matter of waiting till morning. I desperately want to see what we've picked up! The lads have been reconnoitering ahead. They say there are German lorries stuck in the snow all over the countryside."

"Never mind, it'll be dawn soon and you can count them," said Malinin.

And because he said "you" instead "we", as he would have done at any other time, Ryabchenko remembered with a sudden pang of regret that dawn would see the arrival of the sleigh which he had sent someone to find at all costs, and Malinin would be driven away from him and the battalion, and they would never meet again. Even if Malinin survived his stomach wound, it was hardly likely that at his age, after anything so serious, he would be sent back to the front, much less to a battalion at the front line. "Not a chance!" thought Ryabchenko; but all he said was:

"Well, how are you?" He couldn't think of any other way of expressing his concern for Malinin.

"I'm alright," said Malinin. "We won't come to a bad end in here. We're lying at the stove and keeping ourselves warm. Go and attend to your duties, don't let us distract you from them." And, remembering what he had said to Kulikova, he asked Ryabchenko to send Sintsov if possible. They had a certain matter to discuss....

Ryabchenko nodded. He knew about it: Malinin had told him.

"Off you go," said Malinin. "A young man, and walking with a staff like an apostle," he added with a smile. But a stab of pain suddenly turned that smile into such a grimace that

Ryabchenko could have wept. "Go, go," repeated Malinin, looking into the other's moist eyes, and he added, not in words, but with all intensity of his feelings: "Go and live, stay alive, please! You're still young, you're only half my age, you must stay alive! If anyone needs that, it's you.... Please stay alive, d'you hear me, Battalion Commander Ryabchenko?"

Ryabchenko turned round and, leaning on his stick, hurried out, because of all the distressing sights which he had to witness during the war, that of the wounded was always the most painful to him. Ryabchenko went out, and Malinin went on staring at the ground-sheet as it billowed in the doorway, letting more and more snow drift in underneath. A young soldier next to him, also wounded in the stomach, was groaning piteously and monotonously. He kept asking for water, although, like Malinin, he was not allowed anything to drink.

Malinin had sent for Sintsov because he realised that he would soon be taken away and there wouldn't be another chance to talk about the letter to the Political Directorate. Meanwhile, as he waited for Sintsov, he was thinking about something else—himself without his battalion and his battalion without him.

He felt like a man thrown from a train going at full speed. One second ago, he had been travelling along with all the other passengers, and now he was suddenly lying on the ground and looking at something enormous rushing past on which he had only just been riding and on which he would never travel again! War is always separating people: sometimes forever, sometimes only briefly, sometimes with death, sometimes with disablement, sometimes with a wound. And yet, however much you may ponder over the meaning of separation, you only really understand it when it catches up with you personally.

He was accustomed to nothing being done in the battalion without him—and yet the battalion was already managing without him and he was no longer needed by people: all they needed to do was load him into a sleigh as soon as possible and drive him back to the rear. The battalion would carry on. But it was not for him to catch up with the battalion any more, or march with the men, or communicate to them with a glance, or words, or anything at all. What more could he do for them now? Nothing. And although, while thinking along these lines, he naturally thought about himself too—how could he have avoided it?—basically he was not thinking about himself, but about others. He was even thinking about others now, although he was wounded, and although in his position many others, not bad people at all and even quite good, begin to think greedily about themselves, as if compensating for all those days and nights in action when they have thought about themselves so little! And the extent to which even now he considered other people more than himself was perhaps the strongest and most important thing about him, a man who was no longer young and had been gravely wounded.

Sintsov had heard two hours ago that Malinin was wounded in the stomach, and seriously at that; but he couldn't go to him, because at first he had been engaged in battle and then, when the fighting had died down, he had been unable to leave his post without orders.

Only now, under instructions from Ryabchenko himself, did he visit the barn and realise in what a bad way Malinin was. His expression betrayed his thoughts, and Malinin understood: Sintsov's acutely distressed face was condemning him to death. He realised this, but he refused to agree.

"What are you looking at me like that for?... You're not a priest, and I haven't sent for the last rites.... I want to talk to you about a certain matter—that's why I've sent for you."

Sintsov laid his submachine gun on the floor and sat down beside Malinin.

Although Malinin was very weak, anger had lent force to his husky whisper, and Sintsov could hear every word.

"Pity I can't leave you in my place," said Malinin, looking into Sintsov's eyes.

Sintsov didn't answer. What could he say in any case? He could hardly thank Malinin for saying that....

"When you're reinstated in the Party, don't go to that editorial office of yours," said Malinin, still looking into Sintsov's eyes.

"But I don't want to go and work for any newspaper! You think that's what I've been making all this fuss about! Why d'you think that about me?" Sintsov wanted to exclaim; but he caught Malinin's eye again and realised that Malinin was not thinking anything of the kind and simply didn't want him to leave the battalion, now or later! He would feel easier in his mind if Sintsov stayed on.

"Listen.... This is why I've sent for you..." began Malinin after a pause while he waited for a bout of pain to pass off. He hadn't broached it at first, but only towards the end of the conversation, because he considered this the most important thing that he had to tell Sintsov. "You should know this.... I wrote the day before yesterday...."

At that moment, there was a violent outburst of German submachine-gun fire near the barn, and our own machine gun stuttered into life. Sintsov had no time to say good-bye to Malinin or even to think about it. He snatched his submachine gun up off the floor, crossed the hut in three bounds, and dashed through the doorway as the shooting outside grew in intensity.

Malinin lay in the barrack hut, helplessly listening to the shots as they rattled outside, at first loud and rapid, then less and less frequent and gradually receding into the distance.... He lay and listened, and thought with relief that the attack had been beaten off and the battle was over, not realising that he was wrong and that he was simply losing consciousness and could no longer hear anything at all....

When Malinin came to, it was light all round. Fine, sparse snowflakes were drifting down from a white sky, and out of the corner of his eye he could see white snows mounting to the horizon to the left and right. He was lying on his back, on a sleigh which rocked smoothly from time to time as it glided softly over the snow. Someone else was lying beside him, crowding him slightly. Behind him, the driver was urging on the horse in a high-pitched voice. Athwart the sleigh at his feet sat Karaulov, one leg stretched out. It was bandaged and in a splint, and had evidently been fractured above the knee. He was smoking, his head turned away from the oncoming wind.

Two more sleign-loads were bringing up the rear. It was impossible to see who was driving the furthermost one, but the nearest was being driven by an unfamiliar soldier sitting on the cross-piece, a bloodstained bandage over one eye. Malinin saw all this as he came to, but he didn't say anything for several minutes, concentrating on the dull, now bearable pain in his stomach. After yesterday, it hardly seemed like pain at all.

"Looks as though I'm alive," he thought and, before calling out to Karaulov, felt gently with his hand to see who was lying next to him. It was a corpse, its back turned to Malinin. As soon as he touched it, Malinin had felt the lifeless hand with the fingers splayed out like twigs.

"Who's this that's gone to meet his maker?" asked Malinin.

Karaulov heard him and turned round joyfully.

"I was hoping you'd come to!" he said and, wincing slightly, he moved up his leg a little way.

"Who's this?" asked Malinin again, rolling his eyes sideways towards the dead man.

"Grishayev," said Karaulov. And, as if apologising, added: "He was alive when they put him there."

Grishayev was the young soldier with the stomach wound who had been groaning back in the barrack hut and complaining because he was not allowed to drink. He now lay there cold and dead, his back pressing heavily against Malinin's shoulder. Malinin remembered how in November, while they were still in retreat, he had lain down to sleep on the floor in an unheated, icy threshing barn. He had been terribly cold at first and, because of this, he hadn't really known whether he was asleep or not. Then he had felt warm and had dozed off. When he had woken up, he had discovered that two soldiers—one of them Grishayev—had lain down close to him on either side and had covered him with the hems of their sheepskin coats so that he could get a proper night's sleep before battle.

"When were you hit, Karaulov?"

"First thing this morning," said Karaulov with a frown. "I went to have a look at the lorries the Germans left in the fields overnight. One swine was hiding in the driver's cab, and he chucked a grenade out."

"Did you get many lorries?"

"Yes. They were scattered all over the fields. I don't know how many. They were still counting them while I was there...."

"Why, have they left you in the second echelon?"

"What d'you mean, the second echelon? Just as they were putting us on the sleigh, Baglyuk came with orders to advance."

"So Baglyuk's alive, then?"

"He is."

"And Ryabchenko?"

"He's alive too. Badly frostbitten, though."

"How many wounded did they take away? Only three sleigh-loads?" asked Malinin with concern, estimating the number of men in the barn and allowing for the ensuing battle....

"Why only three?" said Karaulov. "There's two more in front. We're taking twenty men. The slightly wounded have gone to the warming station in the village—the one the divisional commander went to."

As he thought about the other wounded, Malinin remembered his own pain again, and closed his eyes as if listening to it. They rode on in silence for several minutes.

"Like a smoke?" said Karaulov. "I'll roll you one."

"I don't want to," replied Malinin, the metallic taste of oncoming nausea in his mouth. "I'm scared it'll make me sick. How long have we been moving?"

"About four hours," said Karaulov. "We met the Army Commander on the way, quite a while ago, not long after we started out. He came up and asked us who we were, and from what unit; but you were unconscious. He was in a good mood! Said things were going fine! 'Get well soon,' says he, 'and we'll meet again outside Smolensk!'"

"That would be good!" thought Malinin; but aloud he asked what the Army Commander was travelling in through such snow.

"The cab of a lorry. It got stuck and we passed him on the road. He came up to us while they were heaving it out of the snow."

Karaulov fell silent, and although Karaulov's story of the meeting with the Army Commander had cheered him up, Malinin thought with pain that Smolensk was still a long way off. Easier said than done. And there were still hundreds of kilometres to go beyond Smolensk—all our land, all occupied, and millions of people on it. Getting it back was going to be no joke!

Perhaps his thoughts were to some extent influenced by his own serious wound and by the uncertainty of whether he would ever be able to return to action. But the chief factor was his stern and sober view of things, acquired during a long and hard life: whatever you take on, it's all work and none of it's easy, to say nothing of war!

"Is it true they'll soon be taking Smolensk?" said a voice behind Malinin.

He had guessed from the voice egging on the horse that it must belong to a woman or a boy. He had not been mistaken. The voice that asked the question was piping and thin—very much that of a teenager.

"Who might you be?" asked Malinin. "How old are you?"

"I'm nearly fifteen."

"He's from the hamlet," explained Karaulov. "Offered to come with us and bring his own horse."

"Very sensible," said Malinin with a faint smile. "You know what our men are: you might never get it back."

"That's not the reason," said the unseen driver offendedly. "I could stay on with your unit."

"Then I apologise."

"Give us a smoke, Lieutenant!" The childish voice sounded brave, but not quite convincing.

Karaulov looked stern, but he nevertheless took the unfinished hand-rolled cigarette out of his mouth and nipped off the end. The boy reached his hand, red with cold, over Malinin's head and took the cigarette from Karaulov.

"I know this place," said Malinin, rolling his eyes sideways. The German tanks were standing by the road. They were quite unmistakable. The gun of one was aimed straight at the turret of the other. These were the tanks which they had passed yesterday, and Malinin had said that the Germans had drained them of their petrol. This meant that they had already covered some twenty kilometres on the return journey. Yes, the battalion had certainly moved on since yesterday....

Malinin then asked Karaulov who had been appointed by Ryabchenko in his place as platoon commander, and on hearing the answer he was expecting—"Sintsov!"—he remembered with annoyance that he still hadn't been able to tell Sintsov about the letter to the Political Directorate. As he thought about it again, he didn't know that it had been a waste of time accusing the Divisional Party Commission of obstruction. The Divisional Party Commission had not had anything to do with it.

Sintsov's Party case had been forwarded to the Army Political Directorate on the request of an instructor who had read the surname and had suddenly remembered a document which had passed through his hands. This document had simply been a small sheet of paper covered with the sprawling handwriting of a soldier. Red Armyman Zolotarev, who had come out of encirclement on the Army's sector, had written to the Political Department about the circumstances in which Political Instructor Sintsov, I. P. had been killed. He requested them to inform the next-of-kin if possible. There hadn't been time to take action on this letter, but the instructor hadn't been able to bring himself to tear it up, and it was now lying next to Senior Sergeant Sintsov's application for reinstatement to the Party in a file inscribed "To Be Reported", although there was no one to report it to at the time: the advance had commenced, and Regimental Commissar Maximov, head of the Political Directorate, had been at the front line over two days.

No doubt if Malinin had known all this, his mind would have been more at ease when he thought of Sintsov. Or perhaps not. Perhaps he would still have been angry that the instructor had not had, or made, the time before the offensive to report all this to the appropriate authority, and so somewhere in the snows a man was walking on the brink of death who still didn't know that the last stain of suspicion had been removed from him.

"So Sintsov's taken over from you—that's alright!" said Malinin to Karaulov after a pause. He said it as though he were still in the battalion and his approval was required. "And has the battalion commander refused to be evacuated again?"

"He certainly has!" said Karaulov approvingly.

"Whose are they?" asked Malinin, hearing a sudden drone in the sky and sensing that the boy behind him had started.

"Ours," said Karaulov.

One after another, four squadrons of nine bombers flew over the wounded men, slowly cutting across the white winter sky and heading from east to west. The sleigh stopped for a moment, and the ones behind also pulled up, just in time to avoid a collision.

The boy driver, Karaulov, and Malinin looked with equal relief and gratitude at the aircraft in the sky.

"Have they gone? Can't you see them now?" asked Malinin, unable to hear the droning any more and not in a condition to raise himself on his elbows to watch the planes as they receded into the distance.

"We can still see them; now they're almost invisible.... They've gone," replied Karaulov, watching the tiny black specks until they disappeared over the horizon.

Ten kilometres from the barracks where Malinin had lost consciousness during the night, and thirty kilometres from the place where the sleigh train loaded with seriously wounded was driving back into the rear over the deep snow, Ryabchenko's battalion, relieved that the blizzard had died down, was heading west.

After Voskresenskoye had been taken, those of Serpilin's regiments which had been less badly knocked about in yesterday's fighting had pushed forward, and the battalion had been on the march since morning without firing a shot, only occasionally coming upon German vehicles abandoned in the snow and the bodies of dead and frozen soldiers.

That they were advancing without a shot being fired was, they knew, only temporary, because gusts of wind were wafting the increasingly distinct sounds of artillery fire from both sides, and the smoke of a fire like yesterday's had been visible on the horizon for the last half hour.

Sintsov, Komarov, and two more submachine gunners—all that was left of the platoon—were marching in file behind Ryabchenko, who was on horseback. He should have gone to the field hospital long ago, but he had refused to give in and was riding on, his frostbitten leg held free of the stirrup and yesterday's staff lashed behind him to his saddle in case he should have to dismount.

"Senior Sergeant, d'you think we'll get replacements soon?" asked Komarov, drawing level with Sintsov.

"How should I know?" Sintsov shrugged his shoulders, and thought that there would be no replacements until they stopped and ran into the Germans somewhere: they were hardly likely to be brought up in lorries over such snow, and as long as they marched on without stopping, as today, no one would ever catch them up either.

Komarov was feeling bad because losses in their platoon had been so heavy, and he was seeking moral support from his section leader, now platoon commander; whereas Sintsov was thinking that if Komarov hadn't come to the rescue that night at the barracks by shooting down point-blank a German who had charged him at the last moment, then his number would have been up and there would be nothing more for him to think—not even about whether there would be a battle today and whether he'd come out of it unscathed.

But he was reluctant to put his thoughts into words, and so he merely looked gratefully at Komarov.

"What do you think—will we catch up the Germans today or not?" asked Komarov.

Sintsov looked at him and realised that Komarov was feeling the same way: he wanted to catch up with the Germans, but would regret an end to the respite after yesterday's battle.

"It looks as though we'll catch them up," he replied, trying to suppress these feelings and quickening his pace. "Smoke in sight again!"

In the distance, across the snows, at the point for which they were now heading in such a hurry, they could see the smoke of a burning village.

"Komarov, I say, Komarov!"

"What?"

"Give us a cigarette!"

"Why on the march?"

"I suddenly feel like one...." Sintsov didn't try to explain why. It was because, as he looked at that smoke in the distance, he was trying to inure himself to the painful thought that however much they may have put behind them, there was still a whole war ahead....

1955-1959

The author wishes to express his profound gratitude to all those comrades — veterans of the Patriotic War — who were kind enough to share their personal reminiscences with him, and also those of them who read through the novel while it was still in manuscript and helped with their comments and advice.

K. Simonov